no reason for murder

no reason for murder

Ayako Sono
translated by Edward Putzar

MUSE

ICG Muse, Inc.
New York, Tokyo, Osaka & London

JLPP

This book is published within the Japanese Literature Publishing
Project managed by the Japan Association for Cultural Exchange
on behalf of the Agency for Cultural Affairs.

Published by ICG Muse, Inc.
420 West 42nd Street, #35B, New York, N.Y. 10036

Distributed by Yohan, Inc.
Striped House Building 2F, Roppongi 5, 10-33 Minato-ku,
Tokyo 106-0032

TENJO NO AO by Ayako Sono
Copyright © 1990 by Ayako Sono
Original Japanese edition published by the Mainichi Newspapers Co.
English language edition published by ICG-Muse Inc, 2003.
English translation © 2003 by Edwards Putzar.
All rights reserved. Printed in Japan.

ISBN 4-925080-63-3

Cover design by Takumitz Ohga
Illustration by Hikaru Hatano

Contents

Translator's Preface

No Reason for Murder (Tenjo no Ao) first appeared in serial form in the Asahi Newspaper, Tokyo, in 1990. It was then published in book form by Shinchosha, Tokyo, and was made into a TV serial. It was a great popular success in Japan. The story of the psychology of a Japanese serial murderer and how the Japanese police system operates in dealing with him were topics unique in Japanese literature.

Ayako Sono's long career as one of Japan's prominent novelist and essayists has been characterized by her shrewd intelligence, her social observations and concerns, and her understanding of the Japanese world at ground level, the level where real people live. Through these qualities, her writing offers an informed and critical portrait of modern Japanese society. For the foreign reader, her work offers a vivid and close-up portrait of a broad slice of the Japanese world.

Sono has been producing novels with somewhat sensational and realistic content during the past 20 years. In her recent fiction, she has been focusing on problems in Japanese society. She is a Japanese Catholic, one of several amongst the active, non-establishment intellectuals, including Shusaku Endo, who have been taking a hard look at Japanese society and its faults. The fact that Sono is a Christian gives a special edge to her writing, not because it is in the least bit foreign to her subject-matter—Christianity has been in Japan since the mid-16th century—but because she is able to view Japan against a moral background that sharpens the generally pragmatic social ethics of her world. She is not dogmatic but a humanist whose compassion stems equally from Buddhism and Christianity.

Her career has encompassed decades of profound transformation in Japan, but what consistently unites her vision as an artist is a humanistic concern for the quality of life both in her home country and abroad. She has traveled the globe with a compassionate and well-informed mind. Her revelations of both individuals and society in general bring to both her essays and her novels the ring of experience and truth, whether she is writing on the hellish conditions of laborers building a road in Thailand—where she is often a visitor—or taking her readers though a year in the practice of a gynecologist in Japan (*Watcher from the Shore*). Such is the basis of her great popularity, along with an enduring faith in her as a responsible intellectual.

No Reason for Murder is a thoroughly Japanese novel, not at all colored by the Westernized styles of late 20th century Japanese fiction. The author is critical of the sloppiness in thought and behavior in contemporary Japan, its lack of intellectual and spiritual direction, and its materialism. But so was Yukio Mishima, another significant post-1945 novelist. By giving us a deeply-felt and fully-realized view of their time and place, both authors belong to the intellectual class of Charles Dickens, Leo Tolstoy, John le Carré and the 17th century writer Ihara Saikaku. In the end, there surely is no more vital role for storytellers—or indeed for any artists—than to examine and shape the dialog between the individual and the society of their time.

The complex personality of the novel's central character, Fujio Uno, is more than an individual portrait, just as Yukiko Hata, his opposite in every way, is developed as a positive symbol. Both figures are alive and well and living now in Japan, and the country's future may well be shaped in the evolving dialog between the two extremes.

The action in the novel takes place in Yokohama, the huge port city just south of Tokyo, and the Miura Peninsula at the southern end of Tokyo Bay (see map page 12). The hilly and densely-wooded peninsula is an interesting mixture of farms (cultivating *daikon* giant radishes, cabbages and watermelons in particular), small fishing ports, industrial areas, residential developments for commuters to Yokohama and Tokyo, and weekend houses. It is easily reached from Tokyo in about one hour by car or train. Despite the heavy influx of visitors in summer and the development of golf courses and holiday homes, many of the peninsula's short, steep valleys still feature unspoilt deciduous woodland, much of it largely impenetrable. From the black sand beaches and rocky outcrops of the west coast, there are fine views of Mt. Fuji and Enoshima Island across Sagami Bay. Ayako Sono is very familiar with the area, spending a lot of time at her house on the peninsula.

The private Keihin Kyuko Line—famous for its shaky cars—runs from Tokyo to Yokosuka via Yokohama. It then follows the eastern coastline of the peninsula, passing close to the long sandy beaches of Miura Kaigan. When they go for a drive together, Fujio meets Yukiko at a station at the northern end of Miura Kaigan. The line then heads west to terminate at Misakiguchi near the southwestern end of the peninsula, the area in which Yukiko lives. The nearby port of Miura is the home base for a deep-sea tuna-fishing fleet. Fujio and his family live in the city of Yokosuka. Located on Tokyo Bay, it is a bustling commercial center and home of the US Pacific 7th Fleet and Japanese Self-Defense Force facilities.

Tenjo no Ao, the Japanese title of the novel, refers to a variety of morning glory flower called 'Heavenly Blue' that features strongly in the story. It is written using the characters for 'heaven' and 'blue'. However, it seemed preferable to use an English title which would give foreign readers a better indication of the contents. I chose 'No Reason for Murder' based on Fujio Uno's words in Chapter 25. The title was approved by the author. The chapter titles are close translations of the original Japanese chapter titles.

In this translation, all Japanese names are written in the Western order, with the family name second; that is the convention used by most Japanese today on their bilingual name-cards. One problem facing any translator from Japanese is that Japanese people tend to refer to each far less by their given names than is normal in the West; the subtle use—or non-use—of honorifics can reflect various degrees of politeness, respect or even age difference. Use of titles is more prevalent than in the West. We may often refer to people as 'Doctor', 'Professor' or 'Sir', but we are less likely to address a sister as 'elder sister', a customer in a shop as 'respected customer' or the old lady next door as 'Granny'. I have tried to make use of honorifics and names as natural as possible for an English-speaking reader.

Retention of the Japanese suffixes, such as *-san* and *-chan* tends to clutter an English text. The general policy in this translation has been to substitute *-san* either with the name or with 'Mr.', 'Mrs.', etc, as appropriate. However, there is one point in the novel where Yukiko and a policeman discuss the use of the polite *-san* suffix to refer to Fujio Uno after his arrest, as opposed to the simple surname preferred by a higher-ranking interrogator. There I have used 'Mr. Uno'. This is of some significance because Japanese society tends to work on the principle of 'guilty until proved innocent' rather than the other way round. As a result, the

Japanese media have a habit of referring to any suspect after arrest simply by their name—all honorifics are dropped.

The suffix -*chan* also appears frequently in the Japanese text. It is used for children, young women and close female friends or relatives. For example, the murdered schoolboy in this novel is often referred to as *Ken-chan* by the media. The equivalent would be something like 'Little Ken', but I have avoided that. Some uses of the -*chan* suffix have, however, been retained where the nuance of their use is significant. One is for the nicknames used by Yukiko and her sister: *Yuki-chan* and *Tomo-chan*. Another is when a schoolgirl starts off referring to a pop star as *Jun-chan*, but sometimes changes to simple *Jun* to suggest greater familiarity.

Since this is a novel centering around the psychological state of the two main characters, some of the 'thought bubbles' are rendered in italics. These correspond to passages in the original Japanese where the writing suggests their thought processes. The letters written by Fujio towards the end of the novel contain various mistakes with *kanji* characters. I have attempted to give a similar effect in English by using some mis-spellings and poor punctuation.

Two features of Japanese houses that appear many times in the book perhaps need explanation. One is the *genkan*, which I have decided to translate as 'hallway'. This is the entrance area to a house or apartment just inside the front door where shoes are removed and left. In a large house or hotel, the *genkan* may be the size of a large room, with one or two steps up to the main flooring area of the first floor. In a small apartment, it may only be large enough for three or four pairs of shoes and have only a token step which leads straight into the kitchen or living-room. Slippers for outside use are usually left in the *genkan*; Yukiko slips into a pair when she rushes to her neighbor's house.

The other traditional feature—which is now gradually disappearing from Japanese living-rooms—is the *kotatsu* heated table. This is a low table with an electric heating element fixed on the underside for warming the feet in winter. A large square futon is draped over the table frame to keep the heat inside and the loose table top holds it down. A *kotatsu* is generally used in *tatami* mat rooms; until recently, few Japanese houses had underfloor heating.

I should also perhaps explain that most of the hotels Fujio takes the women to are the so-called 'love hotels' that can be found all over Japan, both in the center of cities and in the countryside. They became a necessity because of the cramped living conditions many people have to live in and the general lack of privacy. Not only do they focus on anonymity, they also provide reasonably-priced rooms of all shapes and sizes equipped with many attractions. Room can be hired for 'rest periods' of two or three hours or for the night. Besides being ideal for illicit relationships, they are also used by many couples in search of a few hours of private fun in interesting surroundings.

Finally, I should like to thank all those who have contributed to this project: the author, Ayako Sono, for her cooperation and hospitality; Yoko Toyozaki and Stuart Varnam-Atkin for their many ideas and meticulous editing and checking, assisted by Yuri Ogura and Sahira Iqbal; Hiroshi Kagawa for his suggestions on an early draft; Oki Murata and Chris Braham of ICG Muse, Inc., for their enthusiasm; designer Takumitz Ohga; the Bunkacho for including this title in their project; and my wife, Yaeko, for constant support as I slaved over a hot computer in the Arizona desert dreaming of the heavenly blues and greens of the Miura Peninsula.

Edward Putzar
May, 2003

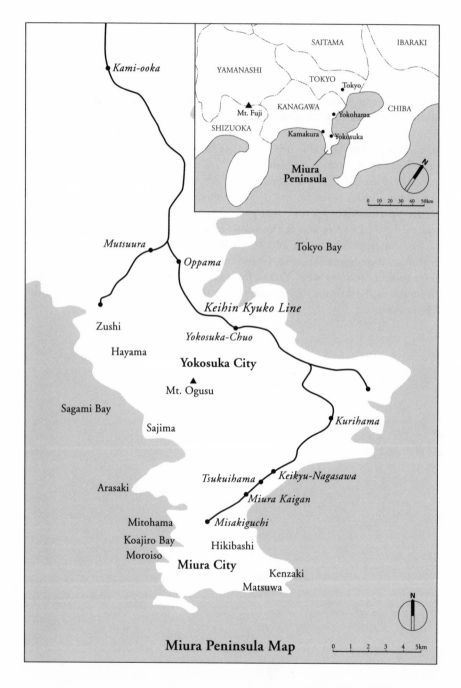

Miura Peninsula Map

Chapter 1

FROM OUT OF THE MORNING SUN

YUKIKO Hata was trimming the morning glories along her garden fence in the dull early-morning light when she noticed the man walking toward her. For a moment, she caught her breath, an odd reaction for her. Perhaps he only wanted to cross the street; she had no reason to suppose that he was aiming at her.

Over there, to the west of her house, the land was still rice paddy. In this mild place by the sea called Shonan, old farm families were now living beside office workers, escapees from the city who had moved there looking for inexpensive residential land. It was a mixed kind of place, no longer as harmonious as it once was.

The man looked a little over thirty, perhaps thirty-five. With his heavy eyebrows and gentle, well-formed face, he rather resembled her father, who had died at the age of sixty. If her younger brother were still alive, Yukiko thought, he might be about the same age.

Whether or not he was aware of her being there, the man stopped barely two steps away and looked at the flowers.

'Beautiful blue color, aren't they?'

The flowers must have attracted his attention because they were rather special. Their vines, growing up some ten feet around a dead tree in the garden, wreathed the tree in blue. But the man's remark clearly acknowledged Yukiko's presence in the shade of the flowers.

'What do you call this kind of morning glory?'

Yukiko stood up slightly embarrassed, not wishing to meet anyone. Her untied hair was in disorder. Even though she usually wore it loose, she had not been out of bed long and had not even combed it.

'Heavenly Blue,' she answered, using the English words.

'Sorry. What's that mean in Japanese?' The man was quite open with his question.

'I heard it means the color of the sky.'

'Ah, of course. Morning glories should have this kind of color and shape. Those recent varieties with rumpled petals or a white pattern, or made to look like peonies—I don't like those.'

'Those with white stripes like a wheel are called *yojiro-zaki*.'

'I've no idea how to write that!' he replied. 'Anyway, I like the color of these.'

Yukiko even told him about the price of seeds.

'They're quite cheap. Other varieties are around 200 yen a packet, but these are only 150 yen.'

It seemed to her that the man was laughing slightly at her, but she didn't feel uncomfortable. 'Do you like plants?' she asked.

'No, not particularly,' he replied. 'It's just that I helped a friend once with some work with plants, that's all.' He seemed to be brooding on the distant past, but his expression suggested pleasure. 'That's a nice idea, growing them up over the dead tree. People usually grow them on a lamp post, or on a fence.'

Yukiko wondered whether he had a job or not; if he did, she was slightly concerned that spending time like this might cause him to be late.

'I was looking at a magazine once that had pictures of some place abroad, like Italy, or maybe Israel,' she explained. 'Anyway, there was a huge palm tree with a bougainvillea growing up the trunk. It looked as though the trunk had a red carpet wrapped around it. I thought that idea was attractive, so I copied it. But because my tree is smaller, this is all I could do with the morning glories...'

'Do you get seeds from them?'

'Yes.'

'Would you mind saving a few for me to plant next year? I could stop by and pick them up.'

'Certainly, if you think these will do.'

Yukiko thought she should politely have told him that, for really nice flowers, it's best to buy fresh seeds from the seed store each year, and that he could buy seeds for ordinary flowers like these anywhere at all. Still, she agreed with his request. A sturdy arm appeared from his light blue polo shirt and waved farewell. He smiled and went on his way.

Yukiko wondered what had brought him along this road. So few people came this way. Her house was not exactly in a lonely spot, only a couple of hundred meters from Isobe Elementary School, but it was summer vacation now and quiet. On school mornings at other times, the children came chattering along the nearby path like a line of ants. And if the wind was in the right direction, it could even be noisy with all the announcements and music that came over the loudspeakers in the schoolyard.

Most of the children came along from the main street where the bus ran. The bus stop was also called 'Isobe', and during the day few people got off there. There was a line of shops amidst a row of decrepit, frail old buildings, including the Shinano Noodle Shop, the Tanaka Pharmacy, and the White Sail Coffee Shop that had long been closed. In truth, there was little reason for a coffee shop to succeed on this unattractive street, no matter how many cars passed by on summer tours of the Miura Peninsula.

Beyond the paddy field to the west of Yukiko's house, it was only a mile or so over the fields to the sea and there was not another house the whole way. The land had been left wide open by a railway company for future development. Rumor had it that something like Disneyland, or maybe a private yacht harbor, might be built there, but no one knew for certain what plans there were. Beyond the land was Sagami Bay. When the wind was just right, you could smell the ocean and catch sight of sea gulls flying.

'Yuki-chan!'

Yukiko's attention returned to the sound of a voice calling from the house.

'I'm coming!' she replied.

It was her sister Tomoko calling; she was two years younger than Yukiko. No one guessed the two were sisters, but when told they were, most people supposed that Tomoko was the elder. The two called one another by the affectionate names 'Tomo-chan' and 'Yuki-chan'; nobody could guess their age relationship.

The two women had lived alone for some years. They were thirty-six and thirty-eight years old. Their younger brother, Hirofumi, had died suddenly of a heart attack five years ago at the age of twenty-five, while climbing Mt. Hotaka in the Japan Alps.

With her strong chin and square face, Tomoko took after her mother. She was somewhat dark-complexioned and had a double fold of the eyelids that made her eyes look large. With her light-toned skin, oval face and single-fold eyelids—which meant that her eyes never appeared very big—Yukiko looked more like her paternal grandmother. But, unlike Tomoko, who used contact lenses to correct her myopia, Yukiko's eyes required no correction.

In this house of theirs, Yukiko earned a living as a seamstress of Japanese-style clothing. Previously, she had worked for ten years in a tax accountant's office. But working with other people was not part of her nature, and since she had always liked working with her hands, she began sewing professionally at home immediately after her brother's death.

Tomoko was quite opposite in nature. She was unable to remain at home for a single day. She had started working in a publishing company right after graduating from a coeducational private university. Working in the mass media environment suited her. For several years, she had kept a one-room apartment in Tokyo where she stayed three nights of the week. From Shinagawa Station on the Keihin Kyuko Line, it was slightly more than an hour to this house by the sea. Tomoko returned there like some office worker who lived mostly away from home. On the nights she worked late, proofreading or the like, she would come home by taxi straight from the printing plant. She might not reach home until 6 or 7 a.m., but, if she had telephoned first, Yukiko would have the bath prepared for her. After a bath and a couple of glasses of whiskey and water, Tomoko would fall soundly asleep. She would get up at about 4 p.m. and take another bath. Then the two sisters would sit at the table face-to-face and have a leisurely dinner together.

The overall housekeeping and management of the house was left up to Yukiko. It had been six years since the two women had left their mother's home in Yokosuka and taken this house together. After their father's death, their mother had remarried and so, rather later than usual, the sisters took the occasion to leave home. The commute to Tokyo was long, but the price of land was still low. Fortunately, the media business didn't start up very early in the morning, so Tomoko didn't have to worry about the rush hour. It was also to her advantage that their railway station was at the end of the line; she could always find a seat on the train and spend her traveling time reading.

Yukiko had provided a down payment on the house out of her small savings, combined with Tomoko's savings. Tomoko was responsible for the loan. At the time they bought the house, neither sister was thinking they would ever settle down in a normal kind of marriage.

The previous evening, Tomoko had returned from work about 9 p.m. Yukiko left the garden, entered the house, washed her hands, and called to her sister, 'Good morning. You're up early.'

Instead of replying, Tomoko turned on the CD player and started listening to a recording of Wagner's *Parsifal*.

Yukiko had no interest in things like opera or Western classical music. She found the sound quality of CDs pleasant, but, in fact, she often felt irritated with anything as heavy as Wagner. But it was basically Tomoko who earned the money to support them. Yukiko was aware that she put up with Tomoko's ways just as though her sister was the man of the house—the breadwinner.

'What would you like for breakfast?' Yukiko asked.

'Oatmeal's fine,' Tomoko replied.

Tomoko tended to have temporary eating fads. She would eat oatmeal every day for two or three weeks running. Oatmeal seemed like a simple thing, but actually it was a difficult food to prepare. If you were not careful to add just the right amount of salt, it immediately turned bad.

Though she was not especially fond of oatmeal, Yukiko placed a bowl for herself on the table.

'Will you be coming back from Tokyo the same time as yesterday?' she asked Tomoko.

'Don't know.'

Yukiko asked nothing more. It was an unwritten rule that she wouldn't pursue the matter. In fact, among the authors who provided manuscripts for Tomoko's company, there were those who asked for someone to come for their work in the middle of the night, and even some who said they would hand over their manuscript and then disappeared somewhere.

Tomoko's life was a model of free existence. There were times when she went drinking after work with friends, and on occasion someone might take her to play mahjongg all night long. She had her own apartment for when she stayed in Tokyo, but there were many nights when she didn't stay there. She knew plenty of congenial men. If she wanted to meet someone, she might go to a friend's home, or jump into a car with a friend after work and go off to a nearby hot spring— like Hakone or Yugawara—to spend the night. Tomoko wasn't lonely, and Yukiko said nothing about her sister's lifestyle. She thought it was agreeable enough.

When she couldn't take time to meet men, Tomoko consoled herself with music. After a busy day absorbed in work, she might feel frazzled and covered with grime. If her hands were dirty, she could wash away the dirt with warm water; but when she was a little tired, she couldn't scrub off the weariness of her jangled mind and nerves with just a bath. Listening to fine music, Tomoko said, made all the bad things disappear.

Yukiko ate her oatmeal. 'The morning glories are at their best now,' she remarked to her sister.

'Uh-huh.'

Yukiko intended to mention that someone had noticed the flowers and praised them, but Tomoko wasn't encouraging conversation just then and Yukiko fell silent. If Tomoko had asked her who she'd been talking to a few minutes ago, she would have told her immediately about the man. But Tomoko had no thought of anything like flowers on her mind.

'Yesterday was awful,' she announced. 'One of the girls in the editorial department was bringing in a manuscript and she left it on the train.'

Yukiko caught her breath, astonished. 'How many pages was it?'

'About 30,' Tomoko said, showing no concern.

'Did you get it back?'

'No way. But it's not as though it's gold or a piece of art—it's worthless to anyone who finds it.'

'So what will you do?'

'No problem. There's a copy in the computer.'

'Oh! I thought it might be handwritten. So all you have to do is explain what happened and get another copy. Right?'

'Of course. But the author isn't the obliging type. He said something like "Don't tell me it's only a copy! Your editorial office shouldn't shrug off things so lightly."'

'Why couldn't he just say "Don't worry, it was only a printout. The original's in the computer."?'

'Because he's an ass. And the more of an ass you are, the more arrogant you become.'

'So did someone go and apologize?'

'Yes. The editor-in-chief, of course.'

'That's too bad for him.'

'No, it's OK. He'd take it like water off a duck's back,' Tomoko said. 'By the way, Yuki-chan, I'm sorry to bother you, but would you mind paying for the opera tickets today? Here's the money. It's for two in Row S, three performances.'

Surprised, Yukiko said she would, but she noticed the set expression on her sister's un-made-up face as she counted out eighteen 10,000 yen notes. She had no idea who her sister was going with, or whether Tomoko was paying for both or only her half, but she felt that even half of that amount was a lot of money for tickets.

'When is it?'

'Three performances, at the end of October and the start of November. They were just about sold out the day the tickets went on sale.'

—*November! Such a long time from this summer heat! Before that, there'll be the end of the summer vacation and the lingering heat. Soon I'll be getting busy again with all the orders for appropriate clothes for the events coming up. First, it'll be the 7-5-3 Children's Festival, then autumn weddings, and after that the end-of-year and New Year events. I wonder if that man who asked for the morning glory seeds will come back for them in the autumn? He sounded as though he liked plants. If he really does come, I could show him around the garden...*

Yukiko thought of that as her precious secret rather than as something that might actually happen.

And of course she thought of him again later, when she collected the seeds. Ever since the first time she looked down the road, she had the feeling that he was there, but of course she never actually saw him. She imagined that he had come from Tokyo to do some fishing, although they said that the sea off the Miura Peninsula was not very good for fishing. Nonetheless, fishermen came there. But somehow that man didn't seem to be the fisherman type.

She divided the seeds into two parts; she would give half to him and plant the rest herself. She thought that if she didn't label them she might throw them out with the waste paper. It was Yukiko's nature to keep things in order, which made Tomoko call her 'a demon for throwing everything away.'

Yukiko was about to write 'Heavenly Blue' on the envelope so as not to forget what type they were, but then she recalled that the man had said he didn't understand English. Surely he must have known some English, but perhaps he was just reluctant to show off what he knew.

She wrote the name in Japanese on the envelope and put it away in a drawer in her sewing room. She wasn't really waiting to meet the man; and yet sometimes, when she happened to look down the road, she half expected him to appear. An objective observer might have said that the very act of gathering the seeds and putting them aside showed a certain concern.

—*Perhaps he had just been passing by and paused for a moment to exchange a few civil words? Asking me to save some seeds might have been no more than a whim. It was probably a good idea not to discuss the matter with Tomoko. She works as an editor and prides herself on getting to the bottom of everything she hears. She tends to regard almost anything that I happen to say as a reflection of my innocence...*

But the man didn't appear, not even at the start of winter when the clear morning sun set the earth glowing. Yukiko half expected him to walk by, but there was no sign of him.

One day in early December, it was cold and there was a thin layer of clouds. The days were usually clear and refreshing at this time of year, but recently the weather had been unpredictable. A cold, westerly wind was blowing, so Yukiko didn't feel like going out into the garden. There were even rough surf warnings on that side of Kanagawa Prefecture. Yukiko sensed the roughness of the surf, even though she couldn't hear its pounding from the house. In bad weather, she left the lamp on in the small sewing room until about 10 a.m., with the clothes she was making spread out all around her. Tomoko hadn't returned home for three days; she would be busy preparing the magazine's New Year edition.

At the sound of the front door sliding open, Yukiko called out to see who was there.

'Did you save some morning glory seeds for me?' came the sound of a voice she recognized.

Promptly smoothing her hair, Yukiko went to the hallway and found the man standing there in a jumper.

'The morning glory seeds...Did you save some for me?' He spoke in a tone that suggested he had come to retrieve something he himself had forgotten.

'Of course, but I thought you might have forgotten about them since you didn't come by,' Yukiko replied.

The man momentarily showed an expression of displeasure, but then said, 'Oh, I remembered, but I've been busy with work, that's all.'

Yukiko might have gone directly to the drawer and brought him the seeds, but it seemed inhospitable to leave him standing there in the cold with the wind seeping in under the door.

'Please come in, won't you? Even for just a cup of tea,' Yukiko said hesitantly.

'Is it all right?'

'Of course. Besides, it's cold here in the hallway.'

'Then I'll come in for just a moment,' he said. Slipping off his shoes, he seemed to be a bit flustered as he faced her. 'My name's Uno,' he said, adding, 'Do you know Jukichi Uno, who's with the New Theatre? Do you go to see plays?'

'No, I don't...Is he related to you?'

'No, no, I've no talent as a actor.'

'The place is not very tidy,' Yukiko said. 'I make Japanese clothes for a business.'

There was really no place in the house for a guest; the small sitting room with Western furnishings was freezing cold and bringing in a heater would hardly make it warm enough.

Yukiko was in the midst of sewing a long-sleeved, black kimono decorated with yellow and orange chrysanthemums and a scattering of tie-dyed white spots. The room was cluttered with her work, but the warmth of the kerosene stove reached everywhere. There was no need to clear a special place for her guest to sit near the heater.

'Ah, you sew,' the man called Uno said, seeming to admire her work.

'Yes, my mother was good at it and I must have picked up my liking for sewing from her. I used to work in a company and take lessons in the evenings.'

'Really? Where did you work?'

'At a tax accountant's office. I was there for years, but actually I don't care much for working with other people.'

'Well, if you can sew kimono it's better to work at home.'

Yukiko put aside the piece she had begun and asked Uno if he would like some *manju* dumplings. She asked first because she wasn't sure it was right to serve a man something sweet all of a sudden without asking.

'That would be fine. I don't drink alcohol.'

'They're just bean dumplings that someone in the neighborhood gave me the day before yesterday, but they're a specialty and delicious. They may be a little hard, so I'll steam them for a moment.'

In the kitchen, Yukiko brought out a steamer-kettle from a set of small utensils that might have been a child's play set and began to warm three dumplings. Then she returned to her workroom and seated herself on a thin cushion opposite Uno.

'You said you were busy. What kind of work do you do?' she asked.

'Oh, various things. I'm not the luckiest of guys, believe me. Whenever any job starts going well, some problem always comes up. Right now, I'm working in the fertilizer business, but that's not been for very long.'

'And do you work around here?'

'Not at present. I used to come this way to the farmers' co-op. But, to tell the truth, I really come out here because I like nature. In sales work you get odd bits of free time, so when I'm free I take walks by myself. I drive, but sometimes I ride a bike or just stroll along...'

Something odd in his words touched a nerve in Yukiko.

'You're fond of nature?'

'Yes, why do you ask?'

'Oh, nothing. Only, the word 'nature' seems like something a high school student would say.'

The man looked slightly offended.

'Oh, I'm sorry,' Yukiko said. 'My sister is an editor and she's always correcting my use of words. I suppose I've picked up the habit.' Uno was silent. 'Well, I understood immediately what you meant by liking nature. You do seem to like flowers. Anyway, before I forget, let me give you the seeds.'

'Yes, right. That's what I came for.' Uno accepted the envelope as if he wanted to retrieve his good mood.

'When should I plant these? Please let me know when it's seeding time.'

'But I don't know your address, so how can I?'

'Oh, sorry. These days I'm staying with my parents.'

Yukiko said nothing.

'I'm divorced, you see,' Uno said, 'I don't like speaking ill of my ex-wife, so I've decided not to talk about her. But my parents were pretty angry about the divorce, and it was hard to keep them soothed.'

'How long were you married?'

'Six years. I married early.'

'Any children?'

'No. We spent the kind of life where we couldn't have children. How about you?' Uno said. 'Where does your husband work?'

'I'm single.'

'Oh?' Uno made a sound in his throat and then said, 'So if we meet now and then, no one would have any reason to complain.'

Checking on the time, Yukiko went to see how the dumplings were doing. She thought they'd become soft enough and put them on a lacquered cake dish.

'Please eat them while they're warm,' she urged.

She also placed a cup of green tea in front of Uno.

'This tea isn't anything special. But if I drink better quality tea, it disagrees with me.' Yukiko said. 'I suppose it's because I work sitting down.'

Uno thanked her. He tasted the dumplings and seemed to enjoy them.

'When I was at elementary school,' he said, 'there was a dumpling shop nearby I often went to. I wonder how the old lady there is doing?'

'Where did you go to school?' Yukiko asked.

'My father worked in various places. It was hard. We moved to Shizuoka and Sendai, three places.'

'There was a kind of Japanese deli near my elementary school, too, and I used to buy croquettes there. They were called 'meat croquettes', but there was hardly any meat in them at all.'

'But I think they're still good without much meat.'

'I used to buy them and take them home for a snack. They were wrapped in newspaper, and so just carrying them would warm my hands. Listen, how about going for a drive in my car sometime? You can take a break from work sometimes, can't you?'

'Yes. I work for myself, though sometimes I have to work till very late at night.'

'Yeah, the same with me. In sales you're working for yourself, too.'

'I hardly ever get a chance to go out,' Yukiko added.

'Why do you live like that?'

'I go out to church on Sunday. Not every week, though. I'm a Christian, you see.'

For a moment, Uno's expression seemed to go intense. Then he said, 'What did you say your name was?'

'I'm sorry. I only heard yours and didn't tell you mine. It's Yukiko—'yuki' as in 'snow.''

'Yukiko Hata.'

'Yes.'

'Let me give you a call. I suppose you wonder why I prefer you not to call my house? Well, there's still a lot of commotion about the divorce and my mother is very sensitive. If a woman calls me, she immediately thinks it's my ex-wife's elder sister telephoning to bully me, however much I explain to her.'

'Of course, I won't call,' Yukiko told him. 'But it would be just fine for you to call here and invite me out.'

Uno acknowledged the idea, and Yukiko wrote her telephone number on a piece of memo paper.

'This has been a nice day,' he said.

'Nice? It's been miserably cold, this weather.'

'No, I didn't mean that. I meant because I could meet you,' Uno remarked as he got up.

The next day, the wind had subsided and the sky was clear. Yukiko had not been outside for two days. The wind had blown some bamboo grass leaves up outside the gate.

Living alone next door was a 79-year-old woman, Hatsu Iwamura. She got around by herself, but was very deaf, and her eyesight was also becoming weak recently because of cataracts. She had to turn up the sound on her television quite loud; it was bit annoying for Yukiko when the doors and windows were open in the summer. Yukiko did nothing inside the Iwamura house, but she often swept up the leaves outside. There was a good place to discard them in a corner of the field across the street—not exactly a compost heap, but a pile of leaves about a meter high.

When Yukiko took the garden sweepings across the street, she noticed a square of paper on top of the pile; curious, she picked it up. It was the seeds she had given to Uno the day before. The words, written with water-based ink, were beginning to blur. She stood there dumbfounded.

—*What does this mean? Did he come all this way to get the seeds and then just throw them away? No, I mustn't assume that. I presume he stopped his car near here. I didn't go out, so I don't know what kind of car he was driving. When he took out his car keys, the envelope of seeds must have come out, too, and fallen. Yes, something like that must have happened. But if that was the case, surely he would have noticed when he got home? Well, men's pockets are like a storeroom! There are some men who don't empty them out for a month or so. He must still think that the seeds are in his pocket. If the seeds get some moisture in the spring, I'm not sure whether they'll begin to sprout or not. But I feel a bit sorry for them. I don't want to leave them here...*

She gathered the moist seeds in a piece of tissue paper, thinking that the sun's rays would dry them nicely during these clear days of winter. If she knew his telephone number, she could call him and find out whether he realized that he'd lost the seeds, but she had no idea where he lived. Along with the other things, Yukiko now felt that there was something not quite right about him.

—*That's all right, though. I don't think you should only associate with good types. He's not really any different from a number of men I've met before. But even so, all things considered, I think it would have caused a big fuss if I'd told Tomoko about him...*

Chapter 2

AN EXCURSION

TOMOKO hated the New Year season. She said it was depressing for a woman without a family to see people spending the New Year with their relatives.

'Really, Tomo-chan,' Yukiko told her. 'It's not that you don't have any family; after all, we two sisters are living together.'

Tomoko only replied with a cool look and silence, as if to say, *You're so insensitive! Do two sisters living alone constitute a family?*

Yukiko understood, but, on the other hand, she didn't object to a bit of leisure at the end of the year. Getting through the rush of work of that season was like the end of a battle, and then the familiar scenery of the Miura Peninsula became for her a bright pleasure.

—*But there's a difference between what appears pleasurable and real happiness. If the reality you endure is filled with pain, then a moment of sunlit pleasure gives you a real sense of ease. Tomoko's life, too, is as narrowly confined as that of any office worker, and there's not much she can do about it...*

Occasionally, during her New Year vacation, Tomoko went abroad on a trip. But Narita Airport was always jammed at that season, and going to Europe for eight days was very hectic.

—*And yet she leaves me here alone. In some ways, it's a bit cold of her to do that. But old Mrs. Iwamura next door, at the age of seventy-nine, is always alone. Thinking about her, I feel grateful that I still have my sister to live with. If I lived all alone, I think I might forget how to speak altogether!*

This year, Tomoko had stayed at home.

—*It could be because she's a bit short of money, or perhaps she just feels tired and doesn't have the energy to go on a trip abroad...*

Of course, Yukiko had arranged an elaborate New Year meal—even though all the items were bought from a shop—and decorated the *tokonoma* alcove in the *tatami* room with a pine branch, chrysanthemums and some sprigs of heavenly bamboo. Tomoko was indifferent to such things and may not even noticed the display. She toasted the New Year with special *sake* and then withdrew to her room to sprawl out on the sofa and listen to another opera on CD.

Yukiko made it a policy not to go into her sister's room. But today she decided to go in to offer Tomoko some *oshiruko* sweet bean soup, a New Year specialty. Tomoko's ashtray was full of cigarette stubs and there was a brandy glass with some liquor still in the bottom on the table next to the sofa.

—*Should I warn her that drinking and smoking at the same time is bad for your health? Maybe not. She's an adult, so she has to take responsibility for her own life...*

Yukiko said nothing.

By the second day of the New Year, Tomoko had pulled out of her fierce, lazy mood and cheerfully prepared to go out. She declared to Yukiko that she had an appointment with friends from her office. These days there were plenty of married couples without children who were keen to include single friends like Tomoko in some activity such as playing mahjongg.

Tomoko would not be returning home that night. Yukiko was relieved. She would miss her sister to some extent, but she could also relax when the troublesome lord of the manor, so to speak, went away. As though it had been awaiting Tomoko's departure, the telephone rang.

'It's me.' The voice was Uno's. 'Happy New Year!'

'Happy New Year,' Yukiko replied in a controlled tone, recalling the matter of the morning glory seeds.

'I thought of telephoning you earlier, but...'

'Have you been ill?'

'No, I'm fine. It was my mother.'

'What happened to her?'

'She had a terrible cold that just wouldn't go away.'

'That's too bad. Colds seem to get to the stomach this year.'

'Anyway, she's better now.'

'Really?'

'Yes. And thanks for the morning glory seeds. I'll plant them carefully in the spring.'

Yukiko said nothing. In spite of what she knew, she felt confused. He had spoken so sincerely that she almost shot back at him, *That's not so at all! Just look if those seeds are in your jacket pocket.* But she couldn't quite bring herself to do that.

'And the dumplings were delicious,' he added.

'Not really...' Yukiko replied.

'Well, as I mentioned before, would you like to go for a ride sometime?'

'Yes. Thank you.'

'So you'll go with me?'

'Well, I'm usually here alone, so it's all right.'

There was a smile in Uno's voice. 'That's good, staying loose!'

'When are you suggesting?'

'Any day that's good for you will be fine for me. Like I said last time, a salesman's schedule is easy, so I can meet you any time.'

'How about Thursday, then, the day after tomorrow...?' Yukiko suggested.

Tomoko didn't usually come home on Thursdays.

'OK. How about meeting at 11 o'clock in front of Keikyu-Nagasawa Station?'

'Yes, all right,' Yukiko said.

'Hey, thanks. What a good omen for this year!'

—*What a tedious comment!*

'That's a phrase to use when your business has gone well,' she replied.

'Perhaps you're right.' He took her comment without question.

'By the way,' Yukiko said, 'I wanted to ask you something. How old are you?'

'Me? I'm thirty-five,' Uno replied.

'You look young. I thought you were younger than that.'

'That's because I'm not very smart!'

'I'm thirty-eight,' said Yukiko.

'No kidding! I thought you were only about thirty-three.'

'You flatter me!'

The following Thursday, while waiting for Uno at the station, Yukiko recalled their telephone conversation. It was already 11:10 and he was nowhere in sight.

—*Since he now knows that I'm thirty-eight, he might have changed his mind about showing up today. I don't think I look any younger than my age; perhaps he thought we were about the same age because I look a bit stupid...*

Coming out here on a date with Uno, Yukiko couldn't help mulling over the business of the morning glory seeds. When she was sewing, her mind was blanks, so she could attend to other things while her fingers kept busy. But that was not really the way she wanted things to be.

—*On the telephone, I ought to have said, 'Tell me truthfully, do you have the seeds any more?' Now it will come down to a heavy accusation. Still, even if he did lie, a handful of morning glory seeds is hardly something to hold against him. We're two different people, and there's no cause to treat this like a crime. The best thing would be just to forget it and see how he acts from now on. Maybe he thinks the seeds are still in his pocket? If he hasn't appeared by 11:30, I'll do some shopping at the supermarket in front of the station and then go home. It's slightly cloudy and not the best day for a drive, anyway...*

But at 11:21 by her watch, a white car came into view, just an ordinary Japanese make and shape. Startled, Yukiko knew it must be him.

'Really sorry,' Uno said from the open window on the driver's side. 'The road was packed all the way.'

—That's a lie! On the phone, you said yourself that it took only 30 minutes to drive here from Yokosuka, probably from your parent's house where you're staying. I can't imagine there's anywhere very crowded between Yokosuka and here at this time of day...

'You must be busy...' Yukiko said in a tone so sweet she surprised herself.

'No, not so much, but that ex-wife of mine was on the phone all morning and...'

'But you're divorced, aren't you?'

'Sure we are, but her family is after money. I've told them, I don't have that kind of money, but they won't let up. They keep saying it's not enough.'

'And why is that?'

'According to them, even her playing around was my fault. They say I changed her fate.'

'And what do you think?'

'I suppose it's fifty-fifty. But one thing is sure, you can't repair someone's fate just with money.'

Uno headed the car toward the west side of the peninsula.

'Where are we going?' Yukiko asked.

'I thought we might go out toward Zushi. Is that OK? So it will feel like a date, you know.'

'There's something I'd like to ask you,' Yukiko said.

'What's that?'

'Your name.'

'Didn't I tell you?' Fujio said, retrieving the childish tone he sometimes used.

'You told me your family name, but not your given name.'

'Oh, that's right. The fact is I don't like my name much, so I try to keep it hidden.'

'Is it that bad?'

'It's Fujio. Like Mount Fuji with an 'o' on the end.'

'Why do you think that's so bad?'

'It's just that I don't like it. It's like something out of a comic book.'

'I don't think so at all,' Yukiko said.

'Maybe I need a pen name. Even if I'm not a writer, I should use a pen name.'

'You know, it's taken us a while to get to know each other,' Yukiko said.

'And we still don't,' Uno laughed. 'I don't know you at all. I'd like to, though.'

Yukiko was at a loss for a reply.

'We've been talking a lot about me up to now' Fujio said. 'May I ask about you?'

'Certainly, but there's nothing interesting about me at all.'

'You're living alone now, but have you ever been married?'

'No, but once I thought that I was going to be married.'

'I guessed so. Why didn't you?'

'He said that he didn't want to marry, that's all.'

'You really give painfully straight answers! And so you just said to him, "That's all right"?'

'But a marriage wouldn't last if you had to strain yourself, would it?' Yukiko said.

'Now that's what I like to hear! There can't be many people who would understand that.'

'I used to walk along the shore around here with him a lot.'

'Perhaps we shouldn't have come here?'

'No, it's all right. Only I haven't been down here much since then. But since we're here, I'm not bothered at all.'

'There's a new tempura place in Hayama called 'Tenko'. Do you know it?'

'Probably not, if it's new. I only know the old places.'

'I see. Then would it be all right if we went there for lunch?'

'Of course. Anywhere is fine.'

Tenko was a modern tempura restaurant with a large parking lot not far from the Hayama Imperial Villa. The elaborate exterior seemed to have convinced customers that the tempura was good since there were already a number of cars in the lot.

'What kind of tempura would you like?' Uno asked Yukiko.

'Well I like tempura on rice, *tendon*, best,' she told him.

'In a box?'

'No, I don't like it served in a lacquered box. I prefer in a bowl.'

'Great. That's the cheapest!'

'And that's fine with me.'

'How about the tempura lunch?'

'Thanks, but it's not good for me to eat that much in the middle of the day.'

'Then I'll have the same.'

'Don't hold back, you're still young,' Yukiko teased. But Uno ordered the same thing as her.

Yukiko explained to the kimonoed waitress that shrimps did not agree with her and that if they came in the tempura she would prefer some kind of substitute. The waitress suggested vegetables and Yukiko agreed.

When the girl was out of earshot, Uno said, in a fierce tone, 'Stingy little...If you don't want shrimps, then she should have offered you some local fish like Japanese whiting.'

'It's perfectly all right. I like vegetables.'

Uno seemed to be enduring his anger in silence.

'There, now,' Yukiko said. 'Let me tell you something more interesting. The scenery round here has changed a lot. You know, I'm really surprised that you've brought me here."

'How come?' asked Uno.

'You see that five-story apartment block over there?'

'The condominium?'

'Mmm. Apartment block, condominium...whatever. Well, I was expecting to get married and live in that block.'

'Things went that far?'

'Yes. He said that if we got engaged we would have a chance of applying for one of the larger apartments for families. So that's what we did and I signed my name as his fiancée. Lucky guy that he is, his name was drawn the first time around.'

Fujio was silent.

'It didn't take long for me to see that it wasn't really *me* that he wanted, but a big and inexpensive apartment. Anyway, when that was all settled, he was ecstatic. He said, "Now I've got a home!". And then he approached another woman.' Actually, Yukiko didn't know that for a fact. 'One day he suddenly declared that somehow he didn't want to get married, and six months later he married another woman. I suppose he's still living over there.'

'And you let him get away with it without saying anything?' Uno asked.

Yukiko nodded ever so slightly in reply. 'Well, I don't really know how to put this, but what was there to say? I was aware that there was nothing you can say to change someone else's mind.'

Again, Uno seemed displeased.

'But I came here one day after they were married and living in the apartment I had expected to live in.'

'Do you know which apartment it is?'

'No. I never went there. I know it's on the third floor, but that's all. It was at night, and from somewhere over here I could clearly see the lights in the apartment block windows. I stood under that big tree across the road staring at that light. It was terrible. It wasn't just my feelings—it hurt me physically, too. I was more than miserable. I hit rock bottom. It was like I was covered with mud and a cold rain was pouring all over me. I didn't cry at all—not then, not a bit. Then I went down to the ocean. There was a bright moon that night. It was winter and so the air was clear. Then I cried and cried. I kept telling myself I mustn't make a sound.'

'Not even when you were crying? That was a funny thing for you to worry about. Was someone with you?'

'No, but I thought it might be impolite if I made any noise.'

'Who would you have been impolite to?'

'I don't know. To the sea or the beach—perhaps to the moon. I was terribly hurt, but it was only a huge tragedy for me—nobody else was concerned about it. I thought to myself that it was painful for me, but nobody else was in pain. It would have been wrong to make a fuss.'

'I think it's better to let it all out when you're hurt,' Uno said.

Yukiko smiled. 'I was aware that we just have to put up with things, no matter what—sickness, death, separations.'

'You're a wonder.'

'No, I'm not. I'm just very subdued about things that have already been decided.'

'Not me. I can't think like that.'

'That's just because you're young.'

'Not that young. There's only six years' difference between us.'

'Three years, if you're thirty-five. I'm still in my thirties, you know.'

The waitress brought their *tendon*.

'So what have you got instead of shrimps?' Fujio asked.

He repeated the question, so Yukiko peeped into his bowl to check the difference.

'Ah, it seems that I've got one extra mushroom.'

'I feel very displeased with this restaurant.'

'Now, don't be angry about it.'

'What happens to you when you eat shrimps?' Uno asked her.

'They're bad for my stomach. Rich food doesn't agree with me.'

While eating his *tendon*, Uno suddenly said, 'After we finish, how about going to a hotel?'

'Not today,' Yukiko said. 'I may feel like it sometime, but going to a hotel and eating are different things.'

'I'd just set my mind on going.'

'Well, things don't always happen as you wish in this world. As I've just told you about myself.'

Uno was silent.

'Are you a strong drinker?' Yukiko asked.

'I can't drink a drop.'

'Really? But you look strong.'

'Its my constitution. If I touch alcohol at all, my heart hurts. I have a weak constitution.'

'That's not a weakness in the least. For example, I don't think it's very masculine to use alcohol as an excuse for your actions. A person ought to clearly acknowledge whether what they do is right or wrong.'

'You think so?' Uno said with interest. What you say is different from what other people say.'

'It's just because I'm alone. I don't have much chance to be influenced by people.'

When they finished eating, Uno had some more tea and said, 'Since we can't go to a hotel, all this is suddenly a bit dull.'

'That's the way it is. Life can't be amusing all the time.'

They went to the cashier and Uno gave the girl a 10,000 yen note.

'I'm sorry sir, but I wonder if you have anything smaller?'

A vein throbbed on Uno's temple. 'No change? And this is a restaurant?'

'I'm terribly sorry,' the cashier said. 'We aren't usually like this, but today there's been one customer after another with large bills.'

'I have some money,' Yukiko said. 'Do you have 400 yen? I've got 2,000 yen here.'

'Yes, I do.'

'Then just give it to me.'

Yukiko paid the money and went outside.

'I'll take you home,' Uno said. 'I really thought we might go to a hotel. I'm feeling a bit bored now.'

'Well, I'm sorry, for your sake, but that's not really for me.'

They walked slightly apart to where the car was parked. The sun was behind a cloud and the wind was cool.

'Aren't you working at all today?' asked Yukiko.

'No. I've got places I can visit if I want to. After I take you home, I'll just go home myself,' Uno said sullenly.

It was not a date that left a pleasant aftertaste. It seemed that, right from the start, Uno had only intended to take Yukiko to a hotel and to bed. The matter of the morning glory seeds was still unclear; and besides, while it was only a small matter, Yukiko had paid all but 400 yen of the lunch bill.

Even when they parted, Yukiko still had not learned either Uno's address or telephone number. That, too, was unfair, she thought.

But Uno called her the next day to mollify her and apologize for asking her to go to a hotel.

'It made me feel so awful thinking you were mad and wouldn't forgive me,' he said.

'It's not all that big a thing,' Yukiko told him.

'I was afraid you would say you wouldn't want to see me any more. I couldn't sleep last night.'

'Then, from the beginning, you shouldn't have suggested it.'

'The truth is that after I left you in front of your house I wanted to say something more appropriate. But I was obstinate because you turned me down.'

'How about growing up a little?'

'Hey, to what extent do you intend to treat me like a child?'

'Oh, just to the extent of our age difference.'

'So you think you can boss me around?'

'That's right. But, since you're a man, I won't try to boss you. However, I won't go along with you when you're wrong.'

'Have you been like this all your life?'

'Oh, I'm not bragging about it. In fact, I don't have anything to brag about.'

'I don't know anyone who says things like you do. If I did, my life would be a lot different.'

'You really ought to stop blaming other people. If you're a decent person, that's an achievement in itself. If you're living a good-for-nothing life, then that's your own responsibility.'

'Will you see me again? Please? I'd like to meet you again, *today*.'

'Well, if that's a good thing, then it will surely happen soon. But today I have some work to get out. So I can't leave here for long.'

'All the women I've been with so far have chased after me. But, this time, *I* have to chase after *you*!'

Yukiko didn't know what to answer to this hackneyed phrase. After some thought, she said, 'Well, you too, good luck with your work.'

'Yeah.'

'Bye, now,' Yukiko said.

'Really, I'd like to meet you.'

'Yes. Goodbye.'

—*I think the degree of relationship we've reached is just about enough. There must be so many examples of that level of impure encounter tucked away in corners of the world...*

Tomoko returned home the day after next.

'Yuki-chan,' she asked, 'did you go out the day before yesterday? You weren't here all afternoon, were you?'

Tomoko was direct in her feelings; there was the echo of a grilling in her voice.

'I was out for a while. Did you call?'

'Yes, there was a telephone number I wanted you to look up in my address book. I called and called, but I couldn't get you.'

'I came home just a little after two o'clock.'

'Well, it was too late then. Who did you go out with?'

'A Mr. Uno, someone who came to get morning glory seeds from me. He said that he was in the fertilizer business.'

'Where does he live? Did you get his card?'

Yukiko could hardly say she didn't know either his address or his telephone number.

'He didn't give me his business card. He came for the seeds, and since he didn't have any work on that day he said he'd treat me to a drive to thank me for the seeds. So I went.'

Of course, Uno had said nothing about returning a favor, and Yukiko knew perfectly well that was not in his nature.

'He's a salesman? Be careful of him.'

'I know.'

'Many guys who are not really salesmen will say that's what they do.'

'Yes, that's true.'

But Yukiko hadn't been deceived. She already sensed that Uno was hardly a saint.

'Listen, Yukiko, the fact is that I met one of our photographers who said he saw you at a tempura place with a man.'

'Is that so?' Yukiko said. She couldn't recall any of the other customers at the restaurant. 'How does he know me?'

'You remember the tall young man, the one with naturally curly hair, named Asakawa, who called to me when you and I were getting off the train once in Shinagawa?'

—*That must have been a couple of years ago. Yes, I remember. Tomo-chan introduced me as her elder sister...*

Asakawa had apparently come to the west side of the Miura Peninsula to take pictures and had spotted Yukiko when he went in for lunch. He'd told Tomoko about it.

'What a news network! I wouldn't be so surprised if the word had passed around in a few days, but the very next day, that's really something. It seems that in the case of rumors, it's true that 'ill news runs apace'!'

'Aha, now you realize—I'm in mass communications!' Tomoko said.

'But I don't think I'll see him again,' Yukiko told her. It was a deliberate white lie. 'The reason I don't even know where he lives is that I'm not intending to associate with him.'

'Just as well,' Tomoko said, looking relieved.

Chapter 3

FUJIO'S CASTLE

THE 'Uno Fruit & Vegetables' store was at the end of a busy street in the city of Yokosuka. It was a two-story steel and concrete building on a corner, with a china shop to the right, and to the left, separated by a narrow alley, a Japanese confectionery shop called 'Wakana.' On the roof of the store, where there had originally been nothing, there was now a small, six-mat prefabricated room, the kind of structure advertised as just the thing for the student preparing for examinations and in need of a quiet place to study. Of course, it was not equipped with water or a toilet.

Fujio Uno had had this small room installed after his divorce, and he spent almost all his idle time there. At first, just the small room was enough, but, naturally, he soon brought in a kerosene stove. And when summer came, he complained and had his parents install an air conditioner, which, because of the rooftop location of the room, did not completely dispel the heat.

Since then, Fujio often went out to hang around on summer afternoons until the sun set. Because he preferred not to be too conspicuous, he went to movie theatres in nearby towns, such as Kurihama and Oppama, and also killed time playing pachinko. Occasionally he helped out at the store; but he soon became bored and would go to his own room to lie down and watch television or read a pornographic magazine. That ensured his parents and his elder sister's husband wouldn't count on his help.

Fujio gave a huge yawn after the end of his telephone call to Yukiko. He always used a phony name when he approached women; only this one time with Yukiko had he used his real name. But he had not told her his real age; he was still only thirty-two, although he had said thirty-five. He had no particular reason for doing that. Some women liked younger men, but he felt that was not quite right for Yukiko Hata. He felt that he was a genius in such matters concerning women.

—*Anyway, she doesn't amount to much. She's not young, first of all. She does have beautiful transparent skin, so I suppose she could be described as 'a beauty with freckles,' but...*

Fujio liked women to be young—twenty-five at most, and preferably in their late teens.

Today, he didn't especially want to meet Yukiko. It would be another matter if she were going to a hotel with him. Saying he'd like to see her right away was simply a figure of speech in that situation, because today he was certainly not in the mood for getting together with her. His big problem was how to get through the day.

His sister Yasuko's husband, Saburo Morita, had worked for a long time helping Fujio's father to run the store. Yasuko and Saburo had bought an apartment five minutes' walk away and they were still paying on the loan. They had two daughters, aged six and ten.

Saburo and Fujio were as different as dogs and monkeys. At first, Saburo had complained to Fujio's parents about giving Fujio a lot of money under the name of a salary, but when they wouldn't hear of such a thing, he just stopped talking to Fujio, even when they came face-to-face in the store. As a result, Fujio spent all the more time shut away in his rooftop castle.

Fujio picked up his jumper from where it lay on the *tatami* mat, threw it over his shoulders, and prepared to go out. He had no idea where he was going, but just the fact that his brother-in-law was downstairs working was enough to make him feel irritable.

Again this morning, the prevailing westerlies were blowing. The cold breeze contrasted with the strong sunlight shining on the Shonan area.

He told no one about going out, but someone must have heard the sound of his footsteps descending the stairs. Fujio heard Saburo's voice echoing after him. He was calling out to Yaeko, his mother-in-law, who was in the living room at the back of the shop, telling her that Fujio had gone out again and she should check his room for fire hazards.

Instantly, anger cut like a knife into Fujio's brain. His white car was parked on the empty land just behind the store. He wanted to go back and slam Saburo to the floor, except that his mother would see all the sniveling; instead, he left, pretending he hadn't noticed anything at all.

—*What was that 'again' business—and Saburo all but ordering Mother to go and check my room?*

Today, as usual, Fujio had gone out without turning off his kerosene stove. Saburo was convinced that a fire was going to start sometime, so he was always nervous about Fujio's actions. And twice in the past, in fact, Fujio had caused a fire by his leaving clothes next to the stove.

He might have walked if the wind had not been so strong, although these days he rather despised walking. He didn't particularly want to meet anyone he knew. When he did meet someone, he would sometimes greet them but sometimes not. He thought people would think, 'There goes that good-for-nothing, lazy son of the Uno family.' He regarded everyone in the neighborhood as his enemy.

On the other hand, when he was riding in his car, a small Japanese-made 'Esperanza', Fujio was completely in his own world. In that space, no one would criticize anything he wanted to think or say and there was no restraint on his actions. He had always hated doing anything in a group. He liked to say 'Human beings are solitary.' At school he could never stand playing games with the other students. When running alone, he ran with all his might. And of course his mother praised that quality in him. 'Fu-chan has an independent spirit and doesn't depend on other people,' she would say. 'It's really marvelous how he likes to do things himself.'

So from the time he'd left high school right up to the present, the various jobs he'd had all lasted only a brief time because they involved being with other people. He was first employed at a small hotel in Yokosuka, which he thought that was better than working at the fruit and vegetables store. He'd quit that job in March the previous year and started working as an apprentice in a sushi shop. After that, he'd worked as an assistant at a funeral parlor, in a lumber yard, as a bartender, and so forth. He'd also worked part-time in a seed shop for six months, watering the plants and looking after seedlings at the nursery. But he quit before the winter cold set in.

As Fujio pulled his car out of its parking place, he noticed the old woman in the confectionery store across the way. He was sure she was always spying on him and putting out nasty gossip about him. For a moment he wanted to cross the street and ram the car into her place. The only thing that kept him on track was the thought of getting away from his house all the sooner.

Fujio pitied himself for lacking a normal home, a place of welcome. To begin with, there was his sister's husband, an outsider who had no reason not to treat Fujio decently in the first place. Saburo had originally worked in the central market, and would have remained a hired man if he hadn't married Yasuko. Every time Fujio came back to live at home, his mother would turn to Saburo, and to Shingo, Fujio's weak-willed father, and say, 'Fujio doesn't have to work outside; he could help with the family business. He will works perfectly well if it's family work.'

Fujio actually believed this himself at first. But soon he came to think that he couldn't even work in his own family's business because his brother-in-law had pushed him out. Fujio was sure that Saburo had no imagination; he was the kind of guy who could be at the same job for one day or ten years. Everything Saburo said was to justify himself, everything bad was done by other people. And every word that Saburo spoke made Fujio angry. Fujio's father had made his son-in-law the one who actually ran the store just to please his daughter.

As he pulled out in his car, Fujio felt something close to pain from the glance of the old woman at the confectionery shop. All that damned muttering from Saburo and his mother seemed to stand in his way. He whipped the car out of the parking area, hardly glancing either way. If he had not then immediately jammed on the brakes, he would have hit a young woman walking down the street pushing a baby carriage. Fujio then slowed down to an innocuous speed, but not because of the near miss. By the time he reached the main street he was driving normally. He was on his way out in search of someone with whom to pass a pleasant afternoon.

One day, Saburo, in a particularly good mood, had talked about a TV program he had seen the previous day called *How Birds See Things*. It had reported that birds see the world in monochrome and that only the things they eat appear to them in color. Saburo had said that things like the fruit of trees were all orange, and Fujio, listening in silence, felt that he and the birds were just alike. For him, most human beings were monochrome and had no meaning. But there were things that stood out clearly in color amidst the colorless throng: young women—or rather, to put it frankly, women who cover their sexual organs with human-like flesh and clothing. For him, young women were walking sexual organs. Like fruit to a bird, Fujio could sense the brightly-colored signals being sent to him by those sexual organs.

Fujio cruised along aimlessly for about thirty minutes. Just when he thought he had seen a target, the woman turned into a side street and he lost her. Soon after that, Fujio felt he had the eyes of a bird even more than ever. The next brightly-colored object he saw was a girl with long hair tied in a pony tail. Fujio slowed his car down next to her and called out, 'Excuse me, please, but can you tell me the way to Kurihama Library?'

He had not the slightest difficulty inventing a lie for the occasion. From place to place, and at a moment's notice, he could always make up a story.

'Well, let's see...' the girl began.

From the rear she looked to be in her teens, but now she seemed a little older, maybe even twenty-three. She had a dark complexion, a high nose and double eyelids that gave her a flashy look.

'It's in that direction,' she said, 'but I'm not sure how to get there. You have to turn after a few stoplights, but I don't know which one.'

'If it's all right, I wonder if you could ride and show me. I'll take you to your house afterward. Do you mind?'

'Not at all.'

—Half way home!

Fujio stretched over to unlock the passenger-side door from the inside. Without any hesitation, the blue-coated girl slid in lightly over the seat cover, her short skirt sliding up to give a glimpse of underwear.

'What a dull place to go, eh? To a library!' the girl giggled.

'Is a library really so dull?' Fujio kept the car stopped and pretended to pay close attention to what the pony-tailed girl said.

'If you want to read a book you ought to buy one, don't you think? They don't cost much.'

'Yes, that's really true,' Fujio replied.

'I guess you have enough money to buy magazines?'

'Maybe just enough. You see, I'm not working.'

'Lose your job?'

'No. I want to work, but I'm not that strong and can't find a real job. My kidney went bad when I was in high school. I'm better now, but sometimes I get tired. So I had to quit college.'

'You look perfectly fit to me,' the woman said.

'If the weather changes even a little bit, it starts up again. My father isn't flush with money, so I have to be careful,' Fujio said. Now, he had set the stage for his reason for going to the library.

'What does your father do?'

'He teaches at a provincial university, so he lives away from home like a business bachelor. That leaves just my mother and me.'

The important elements in this fabrication came from Fujio's experience of working for three months in the hotel and in the seed business for six months, periods when he was in contact with society. At the hotel, Fujio heard his friends talking about the guests, and in that way he became familiar with gossip from every kind of occupation. He had learned then just how vulnerable university professors are with regard to money, poverty and fame, and how many doctors were addicted to drugs.

What he had learned from the seed business was mostly about sickness—not the sicknesses of plants but of the guy he worked with, who had been about the same age as his father. In the past, that man had encountered every kind of illness, and now his greatest principle in life was to avoid being sick. To that end he rejected all ambition, and except for his obligations to the world of pleasure, he just lived. He told Fujio about all kinds of sickness and even lent him books on the subject. The time when he worked at the seed store was a relatively stable period in Fujio's life, and so he had read all the books about illness. He had become such an expert on various illnesses, he could tell a lie about such things with ease.

'Well, I think I'll give up on the library today,' Fujio said.

'So then what are you going to do?' the girl asked.

'Spend some time with you. How would that be?'

'That wouldn't be bad, but...'

'Great. How about a drive somewhere? After all, this kind of chance encounter doesn't happen so often.'

The girl didn't reply, but neither did she reject him. Fujio started the car.

'Where did you go to college?' the girl asked.

'Chuo University. I was going to be a lawyer. But with my illness, they said that I wouldn't be able to stand the hard life of a lawyer.'

While he drove, Fujio glanced at the girl and questioned her.

'What did you say your name was?'

'Why do you need to know my name?'

'Because I have to call you something, don't I?'

'What name would you like?'

'How about 'Yoko'?'

For an instant, the girl looked startled, then she recovered her nonchalance and said, 'Then Yoko it is.'

Through the girl's open coat, Fujio had glimpsed a pendant in the shape of the letter 'Y' and so had tried the name Yoko. He seemed to have hit the mark.

'So, Yoko, let's go for a drive.'

'I haven't heard your name, you know.'

'I'm called Wataru,' Fujio said. It was a name he used a lot in his anonymous life. A false name let him feel at ease.

'Married?' Yoko asked.

'No way. I can't even make it alone.' Fujio put on his pitiful look and then asked, 'And you? Married?'

'No, I'm not.'

'Good.'

'Why "good"?' she asked.

'Because if you were married, you would have to be home at a certain time for your husband, not to mention other annoyances. If you're single, you're just like me.'

'Oh, no,' the girl insisted. 'My father and mother are really strict. I have to be home by dinner time. I don't have a job and I can only go out in the afternoon. That's the way those two think, believe me.'

'Where were you going just now?'

'Just some shopping. I was going to Asano-ya to buy some makeup.'

Asano-ya was a well-known supermarket in the city.

'Then you ought to do your shopping first. I'll wait for you in the parking lot,' Fujio said, and without waiting for an answer he headed for Asano-ya.

'That's sure nice of you,' Yoko said.

'Why do you say that?'

'You know. Most guys aren't like that.'

'Do you know a lot of guys?' Fujio asked with a grin.

She didn't answer. Fujio stole a look at her. Yoko had opened the window a bit and the wind was ruffling her hair. When they reached the Asano-ya parking lot, Yoko asked Fujio to wait, saying that she would be right back. But Fujio replied good-humoredly that he would go with her and got out of the car.

'Would you get in trouble if someone saw you with me?' he asked.

'No, but someone would tell my mother pretty quick.'

'Don't worry, I'll keep my distance.'

Fujio walked a few steps behind her, though not because she asked him to. At that distance, he could take a good look at Yoko's figure. She had been wearing an overcoat up to now and he couldn't see her tight-skirted hips. He thought it would be exciting if she took the coat off. She had nice curves. She had said that she was living with her parents, but Fujio sensed she was as experienced as one of those free-and-easy office girls.

Just like a regular department store, the supermarket had salesgirls stationed in the cosmetics section. Fujio stood next to Yoko as she selected her makeup, listening to the exchange with the salesgirl and yet keeping a certain distance from her so that anyone seeing them would not assume they were together. Apparently, Yoko had come to buy mascara and eye shadow. The salesgirls brought out a variety of colors of shadow makeup, but none of them was quite right, and finally Yoko bought only the mascara.

As Yoko made her purchase, Fujio stared into her purse. He was not interested in learning how much money she had; he simply liked to catch a glimpse of other people's lives.

He could not be certain, of course, but Fujio somehow felt that Yoko wasn't single. Her purse, colorful in blue and green, was not particularly old, but as a purse for an unmarried girl it seemed to be much too full. Fujio often wondered why a married woman's purse was always so stuffed—or such was his impression. Yoko's purse was not filled with money, but rather with all the odd bits of a married life: notes, receipts which hadn't been put away, buttons that had fallen off clothes, coupons from the market to collect in order to claim 2,000 yen's worth of goods, hair pins, and so on. The purse had a certain kind of life-worn look about it.

They left the cosmetics counter and walked toward the parking area exit keeping a certain distance. With his longer stride, Fujio was naturally ahead, and when he glanced back, Yoko wasn't there. He looked all around. For a moment it crossed his mind that she had ducked out. He felt a catch in his chest, and then his eagle eyes caught sight of her light blue overcoat. She had two plastic bottles in hand, the kind used for a certain brand of soy sauce, and she was heading toward a cash register. Fujio stopped.

—*Why is she buying soy sauce?*

As Yoko finished paying, Fujio came up next to her.

'You gave me a surprise, disappearing like that!'

'I'm sorry. This soy sauce was so cheap I decided to buy some.'

Fujio walked in silence, but suddenly his easy manner was gone. He felt as though the scab of an old wound had been torn away. Midori, his former wife who had chucked him, was one of those who was careful to buy things on sale. She had kept a proper record of all her purchases in a household ledger. But the accounts she kept were not accurate. Things like bean paste, soy sauce, bread and butter were all recorded higher than the real cost. She spent the money she skimmed in that way on a man she went out with.

Even now, Fujio vividly remembered the day that he discovered what she was up to. He had secretly followed Midori to the supermarket. From a distance, with his sharp eyes, he had noted the prices of all the things she purchased. He had pretended to be in a better than usual mood for the rest of the day, while Midori didn't set foot out of the house.

In the evening, when he was sure that she had finished with the ledger, Fujio casually asked, 'How are the accounts these days?'

'Almost everything's gone up a lot,' Midori replied.

Pretending interest, Fujio opened the book and had a look. All the items, including eggs, a broom, an earthenware pot, and even a bath mat were entered from ten to several hundred yen higher than the actual price. There were even entries for things she hadn't bought, like cushion covers for 2,800 yen, and three pairs of panties for 1,500 yen.

'Cushion covers?' Fujio said, without letting her see that he was angry. 'What kind did you buy?'

'Oh, I left them at the futon shop to be stuffed.'

That was a lie. The floor cushions they used had foam rubber inside, so they didn't need any stuffing. But of course she would dash out the next day and buy some new covers.

'I see. That's nice. But actually the panties are better. What kind did you buy? Let me see.'

'No, no. I'll show you later tonight,' Midori said with a flirtatious look.

'Come on, show me now!' Fujio pretended to pout. 'Tiny panties, I suppose. Exciting! Black? White with red trim?'

'Fu-chan, you're really dirty! But wait till tonight—then we can have some fun!' The conversation had reached a point where Midori believed she could dodge his attacks.

Suddenly, Fujio struck her hard on the side of the head with his hand; the blow sent her reeling.

'What are you DOING!?'

Midori crouched down with her hand to her ear and screamed. 'WHAT'S SO BAD ABOUT BUYING PANTIES!?'

'You whore! You think you're fooling me? All that buying is a lie!'

'My ear hurts!' Midori cried in pain.

Fujio stormed out of the apartment, leaving his wife crying loudly. From that time on, Midori had been deaf in her left ear. As compensation, when they divorced, Fujio had to pay her a lot of alimony.

His mind returned to the present. 'What are you going to do with all that soy sauce?' he asked Yoko.

'I told you. It was on sale, cheap.'

'You sound just like an ordinary housewife!' Fujio said, laughing.

'It makes my mother happy if I get a bargain for her.'

'Dear me! Aren't you the filial daughter!' Fujio said in mocking admiration.

'Not really,' Yoko said. 'Can I put this stuff on the back seat?'

'Sure, of course,' Fujio said politely, opening the back door of the car for her. But Fujio's emotions were seething.

—*What was all that strict stuff about her parents? I reckon she is married after all. Even when she's going out with another man, she can't resist buying soy sauce on sale, and she rides in a stranger's car to do her shopping! She's accustomed to playing with fire...*

But Fujio managed to control his temper. Recently, he had found that interesting things could happen if he let his anger simmer. So when he closed the door, Fujio added innocently, 'Whatever makeup you bought, aren't you going to put it on?'

'No. I've got heavier eyelashes than most people, you see, so I use a lot of mascara.'

'But that's not very economical. You know, when I see a woman with long eyelashes, I get turned on.'

Fujio's forte had always been his ability to adapt his attitude toward the woman he was with; watching her face, he would change how he listened and how he used words. He would use increasingly more suggestive language and, finally, his speech would become intimate, even vulgar. And recently he had become quicker, so that usually within an hour he could read the woman's character. The point was that women were like cats—happy when you stroked them. But if you made a mistake, just like twisting a cat's tail, you had to be careful that they didn't bite you.

'How about something to eat? It's one o'clock. My stomach's empty. I didn't eat any breakfast.'

His suggestion was fine with Yoko, but Fujio knew there was a trick in choosing the right place to eat.

—*With Yukiko Hata, the morning glory lady, I chose tempura. She seemed to be the kind that would go for tempura. But with this girl 'Yoko', perhaps some place with a livelier atmosphere would be better...*

Fujio actually disliked the word 'atmosphere.' However it was said, the word could never sound evil. Even if it was said quite carefully, he thought it was the kind of word only some foggy-brained fool would use. At any rate, this woman seemed the type to like 'atmosphere.'

—She's probably accustomed to eating instant noodles leaning with her elbows on a cheap kitchen table, or going to a place set up in a corner of a store like Asano-ya that couldn't even be called a restaurant and maybe having chirashi-zushi with ghastly red ginger on a styrofoam plate—or an oily-smelling American hot dog. And yet many girls who live that way make a big fuss about 'atmosphere'!

As usual, Fujio headed toward the west side of the peninsula where the scenery was good; it had the kind of feel about it that attracted visitors from outside the area. He had decided from the start on the restaurant he wanted to visit, a place called 'Eden'. It was built on a cliff and offered a view of the sea. It has originally been constructed in the style of a resort home, and there were always flowers in the windows. For some reason, women couldn't resist going to a window with flowers in it.

But the food there remained as terrible as it had been the last time he had brought a woman there. On that occasion, he had accidentally caught a glimpse of the kitchen. He had noticed a huge commercial soup can that had been discarded, along with a box—with flour still on it—that had contained frozen fried prawns. At the time, Fujio decided it was probably better that the cook faked it with canned soup, fried prawns and curry with rice rather than try to prepare anything himself.

'Is this all right with you?' Fujio asked.

There was some small difficulty about whether or not they could sit at a table by the window, because the place with the best view had a 'Reserved' sign on it. Fujio complained, but Yoko intervened and said anywhere would do. Finally, they settled into seats where they could see the ocean.

'You know, it's really nice not to go to the library today,' Fujio said, just as the waiter came to take their orders.

'I'll have the beef stew,' Yoko said, and Fujio said he would have the same.

'Will that be with salad?'

'Yes,' said Yoko.

'I thought it already came with salad?' Fujio said, indignantly.

The flustered waiter explained that some guests didn't want the salad.

'Well, the menu says 'with salad', so just bring it without grumbling, will you?' said Fujio. He thought it likely that the waiter would add the price of the salads to the bill without saying anything if he thought they hadn't noticed.

Yoko watched this performance with an expression of unconcern. When the waiter went away, she said, 'Maybe I've done something bad, preventing you from studying?'

'It's said that studying people is much better than studying books,' Fujio said, to change the mood.

'Who said that?'

'I think it was Descartes,' Fujio said, which was complete nonsense.

'I think so, too. If I'd only stayed at home, I wouldn't know much at all.'

'So when did you begin to study people?' Fujio said with his sneering smile.

'What do you mean?'

'Studying men.'

'Oh, that. From when I was about seventeen, I suppose.'

'When you were in senior high?'

'Right.'

'Wow! I wish I'd met you then. Where were you living?'

'Near where I'm living now.'

Fujio was silent, but he understood clearly from what Yoko said that she at least had a place near her parents' home. Yoko tried to strengthen her story.

'When I graduated from high school, my mother and father built a new house and moved there.'

'So they have money,' Fujio said, simply as a statement.

'Not all that much.'

—Ah, someone who answers like that really doesn't have much money...

The beef stew arrived. Just as Fujio had expected, it was greasy, tasteless and included only a few bits of dry meat. It was probably made from the canned stuff they used here, so it couldn't be helped.

Yoko, obviously dissatisfied, said, 'This place isn't so good.'

'Last time I was here it was alright,' Fujio replied, 'but this is bad. They probably changed cooks.' His face reflected complete bewilderment.

'It's all right, we'll get by. The view's good.'

'Listen, Yoko. There's something I want to ask. There's something special I like.'

She frowned and looked at him. 'What's that? I'm not into SM at all.'

'Nothing like that. Strictly straight.'

'So what is it?'

'I know you're living alone, but, when we're together, I wonder if you would mind pretending that you're married?'

'Why would you want something like that?'

'I'll tell you. If I think you're married and that I'm pulling the wool over someone's eyes—I don't know how to say it—somehow, it gives me the feeling of being the hero in a novel or something. I'm no good. You see, it turns me on just to think that I'm sticking it to your husband.'

'Well, if you're turned on by something that simple, it makes no difference to me at all.'

'Great. Then it's settled. So let's go on with that in mind.'

A look of relief appeared on Yoko's face, which was just what Fujio was aiming for. He could make her tell the truth while telling lies.

'So what time does your husband usually come home?' Fujio asked casually.

Yoko lit a cigarette and said, 'You mean we're beginning now?' She then added smoothly, 'Generally about seven o'clock.'

'He's an office worker, right?' Fujio asked. 'And you met and got married. It wasn't an arranged marriage?'

'Mm, well, that's what I thought then,' Yoko answered.

'Good! I like it. That's the spirit...,' Fujio laughed. Then he added in a whisper, 'Yoko, on the way back let's go to a hotel, shall we?'

'Well...'

'Because of him?'

'No, not that, only...'

'So why not? I'd like to think that I'm stabbing him in the back. You know.' And then in a slightly louder voice, continuing the make-believe, he asked, 'So, what kind of a person is your husband?'

'What kind of person? He's mild and quiet...He's OK.'

'Sounds pretty boring. Describing him as "mild and quiet" is just like stabbing him in the back.'

'He comes home and doesn't say much. I hear there are lots of husbands like that.' Yoko seemed to have all but forgotten that this was supposed to be play acting.

'Yes, but if he was a real husband he'd come home and talk to you. If I were married, I think I'd come home and talk all the time during dinner. I'd tell my wife everything I'd seen during the day.'

'That isn't the way it is with us. He waters the flowers, feeds the fish...'

'Really? You raise fish?'

'Sure. My husband would like to have a dog or cat, but the apartment block won't allow it.'

'You know, you're pretty good at acting,' Fujio told her. 'When you speak like that, I really believe that you're married. You ought to become an actress. You're good-looking and...'

'Please don't ruin the mood,' Yoko said. 'Not when I'm just getting into it.'

But she had volunteered that she lived in a box-like apartment with her office worker husband who raised goldfish, and that was that.

'How many fish do you have?'

'Five. And four little ones in a separate bowl. They were hatched at home.'

'I didn't know it was that easy.'

'Eleven hatched, but they got eaten. So now we have four.'

'If it was me, I'd throw away the other four.'

'Why would you do that?'

'It's obvious. Cannibalism is a crime.'

'But they're cute! When my husband feeds them, they dash to the surface and make little sucking noises.'

'At least *you* should feed them. You *are* married, right?'

'But if *I* feed them, I give them too much.'

'That's because you're so sweet. It would hurt me to stab your husband in the back,' Fujio said, staring fixedly into Yoko's face.

'No way! He's too dull. If he's happy, then he thinks that other people are happy. He's that kind of fool.'

Fujio looked at her and said, with a tone of admiration in his voice, 'You really ought to be an actress.'

'Yeah. When I was in high school, I thought about going to acting school. Someone from a production tried to invite me when I was on my way to school one day.'

'What a waste! What university did you go to?'

Fujio didn't really think she had been to a university; it just that seemed a suitable question to ask.

'I'm too bashful to tell you. It was a college for...you know, for young ladies. But everyone makes fun of places like that.'

'I have a young girl cousin who graduated from Gakushuin Academy.' Fujio's mendacities were now flowing effortlessly. 'Since I dropped out of college, she's had nothing to do with me.'

It seemed that Fujio spoke nothing but lies to women, but in fact he thought otherwise. Even in casual conversation, he could convey a sense of interconnection with women that at the same time affirmed his own life. And yet Fujio himself well understood the fault in this, that his 'extraordinary talent' could not be sustained for long. As soon as he began these fabrications, they started to crumble away and become foolish.

To top it all off, he hadn't told Yoko that this place—a restaurant in name only—was the absolute worst. The salad he'd insisted upon having was nothing but shreds of old lettuce, and even the ice-cream dessert and coffee were not worth mentioning.

The woman called Yoko agreed to go with him to a hotel afterward, but Fujio's mind had returned to Yukiko Hata. He paid the absurdly high bill—something close to outright fraud—went to the toilet and then made the second phone call of the day to Yukiko.

'Hi. It's me, Fujio,' he said in a low voice. From where he was calling, he could see Yoko. There was no danger that she might hear him. However, he had given her a false name, so he preferred to be cautious.

'Again? What now?'

'Nothing important. I just wanted to hear your voice.'

'Hello...'

'What did you have for lunch?'

'Me? The usual simple things. When I'm eating alone during my work, I always have leftovers or something.'

'That's fine, really. What kind of leftovers?'

'Well, I broiled two dried sardines that were in the refrigerator. Someone came to see the old lady next door and brought them, and she gave me half. And, let me see...I picked some mustard spinach from the garden and boiled that for three minutes...and a little dried bonito with soy sauce...'

'Uh-huh.'

'And a slice of yam...just one. Women like to clear things up, you know.'

'To tell you the truth,' Fujio said, 'I'm with a woman right now...because you chucked me.' There was no answer from Yukiko. 'We're at a crappy restaurant—really bad stuff. I'd really like to be eating some of that mustard spinach you boiled.'

'Oh? Do you like that kind of thing? Isn't meat better?'

'Let me tell you, the stuff that we were eating just now was really disgusting. You can't imagine.'

Fujio was ill at ease when it came to long phone conversations. He soon hung up and returned to his seat. He asked Yoko what kind of hotel she preferred and she replied that one of the small, pension-like hotels would be fine, if they rented rooms by the hour. Fujio knew that even the better places would grab the business if you asked for 'a room until evening.'

When they arrived at the hotel, Yoko casually popped on a pair of sunglasses as they got out of the car.

'Always prepared, eh?' Fujio commented casually, and with equal nonchalance put a hand on her shoulder. Yoko brushed it aside in silence.

You could see the ocean from the windows of the hotel as well. Fujio felt there were too many places in that area where the rooms were poor and the food worse but which offered an ocean view. Nonetheless, he was in a good mood. He sat down in the overstuffed chair near the window and eyed Yoko. He was certain it was better to gaze at a woman; compared to a woman, the ocean was nothing at all.

'You take a bath first,' he said.

Yoko grunted.

'Does your husband like sex?' he said, continuing the game.

'Yes, he's hornier than you'd think.'

Her answer was not what he expected.

'Take your clothes off,' he said.

'I'll just do that,' Yoko said. 'Otherwise I can't take a bath!'

Her one-piece dress fit her body closely. As she removed her dress, the thick hair under her arms showed and gave off a slight odor of sweat.

'That front desk clerk...' she began, and then hesitated while she took off her panty hose. 'Do you know who he is?'

'The owner or the manager, I suppose.'

'He's got a tattoo on his chest.'

'Really?'

'Yes. I caught a glimpse of it when you were getting the key. But I couldn't see the design.'

'Right. If you say so. Just get undressed, please. You've got a nice body, so don't be afraid to show it.'

The bit of lace on Yoko's slip was frayed and slightly dirty. Her hips under her tiny pink panties were a bit different from what he'd expected, but they were good enough to stimulate Fujio's appetite. Yoko slipped into the bathroom without giving him time to satisfy his admiring perusal of her body.

Fujio sat in the chair, smiling. He was trying to forget anything unpleasant. He said nothing, but lingering in a corner of his mind was the image of Yukiko sitting at home, working away at her sewing.

Chapter 4

SAGGING POCKET WATCHES

WHEN the time had come to leave, the woman had told Fujio that her name was Yoko Miki.

Their encounter that day had left Fujio hot with desire. Recently, Fujio had felt starved for a woman, but he had had a persistent cold, and, feeling down, had stayed at home. And when he did go out, he had no luck finding a woman. That was how it went. He felt as though he was still standing on the edge of his youth, even though from the point of view of young girls he was more likely to be seen as just middle-aged. Or so they made him believe. When he tried picking up a couple of schoolgirls dressed in sailor suit uniforms, he only succeeded in making them giggle. 'Really, Dad, really!' one of them had said. That didn't amuse Fujio at all, especially as had carefully chosen the color of his shirt and worn a short jacket to look younger.

It had been a while since he'd had a young body like Yoko Miki's. Against his better judgment, Fujio indulged himself in the taste of what had become a rare pleasure. He thought Yoko was quite good-looking, but there were a lot of things about her talk and her actions that irritated him, including the way she made love.

During their encounter in the room at the small hotel overlooking the sea, Yoko had displayed a bold and exciting character with her panting and her long hair flowing wild. Although the sweaty odor of her body had become more noticeable as they went on, Fujio had rewarded Yoko for her enthusiastic service by leaving little bite marks on her upper arm. It had been quite a bout.

But as he thought about her afterward, Fujio had his doubts about the authenticity of Yoko's passion. He suspected that her actions were simply the product of being experienced in seduction plus whatever she had learned from gossip, stories, and from her own vanity. He suspected that she was basically frigid. Fujio kept that idea in mind; it was proof that his own skill was no better than anything in the realm of her past experiences with men. That was humiliating.

Of course there were some saving elements. Yoko almost certainly had a husband, and that indeed heightened Fujio's pleasure. There were plenty of her kind around town these days. For them, it was a thrill to deceive their husband

and slip out to sleep with another man. Yoko thought her stupid affair was proof of how beautiful she was, and when Fujio thought about her frantically lying to her husband and to everyone else, he could only smile.

After they had finished making love, Yoko sat cross-legged on top of the bed. 'Maybe you don't realize it, but this particular girl is very popular with men,' she said, blowing smoke from her cigarette. For no particular reason, Fujio thought it would be no problem to do just about anything to a woman who used an expression like 'this particular girl.'

—I wonder why I don't commute to my seduction work every day? I should encourage myself to try harder since all the conditions are consolidated—I have the time and I have some money available...

It was now late January and the heat of the sun's rays was encouraging the onset of spring. Fujio was out riding in his car. As he hunted for game, he glanced at the wild narcissi blossoming on the curve of a hill. Some of the insects already out of hibernation had begun spinning their cocoons, a process that usually went on in March. But such things happened a month earlier than elsewhere in this part of Japan.

Then, at the end of January, Fujio came across something interesting in town. He slowed his car beside a girl in a sailor suit. She was walking along briskly with her eyes lowered.

'Hey, how about going for a drive with me?' Fujio called out.

In Fujio's experience, it was only the girls who walked along slowly who were easy to pick up, so he expected this one to cut him off. But the girl stopped and then, without the slightest hesitation, nodded. Fujio was slightly shocked. During the few seconds it took to open the door, Fujio even thought of driving away without her. When it dawned upon him that he would have to spend a couple of hours with her, he was immediately chagrined.

She sat down with her navy blue school book bag on top of her pleated skirt. The dyed bag was worn on the edge and the color of the base leather showed through.

'Senior high school student?' Fujio couldn't help but ask.

'Yes, I am.'

'What year are you in?'

'The 2nd year.' Her eyes were narrow.

'Where shall we go?'

'Anywhere's OK.'

'Do you always say 'yes' to an invitation?'

'I'm not invited much.'

This was more like an inquisition than a conversation; talking with her didn't go very smoothly.

Fujio flinched and said, 'I see. What kind of things do you like?'

'Dogs, you know, and Jun-chan of Cutie-Cutie, you know, and...'

She accented the end of her words. 'Cutie-Cutie' was the name of a group of four teenage boy singers that had recently become popular.

'Hey, the manager of Cutie-Cutie's a friend of mine. Really. I know Jun pretty well. I've met him lots of times.'

Fujio spoke without the slightest reticence.

'What? Really?' the girl exclaimed with sudden emotion in her voice, and Fujio nearly let go of the wheel.

'Would you like his autograph?'

'You bet! But...'

'But what?'

'Well, you know, a shirt would be better.'

'Sure, of course. That's no problem.'

'Really?'

'Of course.'

At that instant, Fujio decided he would give her one of his own T-shirts. He smiled broadly and said, 'Jun wouldn't mind doing that. After all, I've worked enough for him.'

'And could you get him to sign it, do you think?'

'Sure I could.'

Fujio had never even seen the singer's autograph. However, a girl like this who wouldn't even know where the capital of the United States was, would certainly know what Jun-chan's signature looked like. That was something you couldn't make light of. Fujio thought that if he told her that, what with Jun-chan being so busy and all, arranging for the shirt and an autograph too would take a little more time, then he could stretch this thing out a bit.

'I can get them both for you, but what about something for me?' Fujio asked suggestively.

'What would you like?' the girl asked seriously.

'Just what you think I'd like. You. Do you suppose I need money?'

'Yes, sure.'

'No, I don't want money. I'll buy the treats. All you have to do is take off your clothes. I don't want any money.'

The girl seemed to be thinking it over carefully.

'You know, it's just common sense.' Said Fujio. 'If you like the show business world, you'd be foolish not to go along with the ways of that world.'

'Will you introduce me to Jun-chan?'

'Actually, that might be hard to do. I'll give it a try. Jun-chan's really a prince in the entertainment world, but he's got to be careful about meeting women one-on-one, you know. I might, though, if you promise you absolutely won't tell anybody. Jun-chan really hates women who go around talking about that kind of thing.'

'I wouldn't tell anyone, honestly. I don't want to disturb anyone.'

'That's right. You really understand, don't you? Anyway, how about going for some tea?' Fujio said lightly. 'Afterwards, in bed, I'll teach you what kind of sex a girl who likes Jun-chan should do. What's your name?"

'Yoshiko Yamane.'

'Now that's a coincidence! Jun-chan's first love was named Yoshiko. But that's a secret, and I'm the only one who knows about it.'

Fujio stopped at a family restaurant where it was easy to park and asked the girl pleasantly what her father did. She replied that he was a junior high school teacher. Fujio felt a shock, as though he'd fallen backwards off a bar stool.

'Oh, that's nice,' he said, showing great admiration. 'And what does your dad say when you tell him about Jun-chan?'

'I don't tell him.'

'How come?'

'You know! He just wouldn't understand.'

'Sure, I know,' Fujio said. 'After I grew up, I hardly said anything to my parents, either.'

Fujio only intended that as a distraction, but the girl was not the kind to announce anything of importance to her parents or teachers. From his own experience, Fujio knew that perfectly quiet people might do anything without any kind of advance signal; it was the talkative types, who just couldn't keep quiet, who never did anything significant.

'Is your father always after you about things, like studying or what kind of boys you're seeing?'

'No.'

'What? Really? Doesn't he say anything?'

'We just don't say anything to each other.'

'But you must say *something*?'

'What do you mean?'

'I mean you have to say something to him at home, don't you?'

'No, not much.'

'Well, what does your father do at home?'

'He reads girls' comic books.'

Fujio hesitated about the meaning of that.

'Don't you think he reads those because he teaches girls and he needs to know the kind of things they read too?'

'Oh, *I* don't know.'

Fujio felt a slight chill run down his back.

—*Something's wrong there... The father of a high school girl would usually be in his forties. But when her father gets home, he doesn't talk much with his family but looks at comic books for girls!*

'That's all right. I'm going to teach you all kinds of things,' Fujio said to get back to the subject.

'Thank you very much. Please do.' The girl sounded like a member of a sports club talking to her senior. For an instant, Fujio was quite turned off.

They left the family restaurant. Fujio began to have qualms about taking a girl in a sailor suit to a motel.

'I suppose there's nothing we can do about what you're wearing, is there?' he said uneasily. 'You know, it's a little tough to talk about show business when you're wearing your school uniform.'

'I've got a change with me.'

'You do?' Flabbergasted, Fujio looked at the girl's beaten-up leather bag. 'In there?'

'In a locker at the station.'

'Then get it. I don't go much for sailor suits.' He didn't know whether she really understood what he was saying. He turned the car toward the train station. 'You're really prepared, aren't you?'

The girl made a strange sound, not quite a laugh. Her voice gave Fujio an odd feeling, as though he'd heard the cry of some night bird.

'You're into a lot of bad things, aren't you?' Fujio thought she would somehow protest that remark.

'So-so...' she said, dragging out the sound.

It was not a denial; it gave Fujio the feeling of something she had learned from someone and that had stuck with her quite unnaturally.

He stopped in front of the station and sent her inside for the things in the locker. He felt dazed. Fujio liked dumb women, but this one could not really be classified as dumb. The situation reminded him of a painting by Salvador Dali that a man who worked in the hotel had showed him a long time ago. It depicted four pocket watches, all of them looking like under-cooked hotcakes—one on the back of a beached whale, one hanging over the edge of a desk, another sagging over the limb of a tree, and the last one face down on the table, with a lot of ants crawling on it. The title of the painting was *The Persistence of Memory*. According to the fellow at the hotel, who wanted to be a painter, it was an important piece of art. But Fujio had no idea of what was so good about it; he only remembered that the painting was strange. And when he met a girl like Yoshiko, he associated her with those peculiar, totally non-functional watches.

Yoshiko returned half running with her things from the coin locker. She had been gone for only a brief time, yet Fujio imagined that perhaps she had run off. And Yoshiko seemed to have been fearful that Fujio would drive away, leaving her there.

'Change your clothes before we go to the motel,' he told her.

'Where?'

'Here in the car. Just the top will do. They won't notice the skirt. I'm taking you to the right kind of place.'

He drove for about ten minutes and then stopped the car next to a long wall that might have belonged to some kind of research facility. There was a residential district on the other side of the street and hardly a soul in sight.

'Now you can do it,' he said.

He had stopped where he could enjoy watching her change, but he was more than disappointed with what he saw. She was flat-chested and put on an ugly red sweater. She even changed her skirt because she had it with her and thought she had to put it on. Perhaps she considered her green skirt as something special, but Fujio noticed her legs were chapped like a chicken's legs in winter.

'Unpropitious,' he said aloud. 'Do you know what that means?'

'No.'

'It means unlucky.'

Fujio was thinking of this girl he had picked up.

'I don't get it,' she said.

'I mean, there are people around you who say their luck is bad, right?'

'Sure. Like when somebody said he had a car accident.'

'Oh? What kind of an accident was that?' Fujio asked.

'He thought it would be all right for a little while to lend someone his car who didn't have a license, but the guy had an accident.'

'Yeah. Right,' Fujio said. 'But something like that is not exactly an accident.' There was a stunned look on her face. 'How about school? Do you like school?'

'I hate it.'

'Sure, I know. Girls like you don't have to go to school or anywhere else.' He intended to be cutting, but Yoshiko showed no particular anger. 'I mean, you do what you like.'

'What *do* I like?' she repeated.

'Don't do that, questioning every little thing. Sometimes you like things, right?'

'I like this. Riding in a car...this is pretty new, huh?'

Her pleasure was evident.

'About six months old,' Fujio told her.

'Cars really have a good feeling when they're new. They really move, too.'

Fujio remembered his humiliation when he'd bought the car. When Fujio said that he was going to get a newer car, his brother-in-law Saburo had strongly opposed the idea to his mother. He said that Fujio could still use the old one and that they shouldn't buy a car for a person who was just playing around. But the old car was ten years old and they'd bought it second-hand. These days, the young girls he was trying to pick up wouldn't want to ride in a car like that. Fujio was a man who placed great importance on harmony.

—Compared with this Yoshiko Yamane, Yoko Miki was really something else! I wouldn't have minded in the least if Yoko had wanted to go to one of those fancy hotels. But this Yoshiko girl…as far as I can see, she has no emotions at all. Any place at all will do for her…

Fujio had been to the motel called 'The Skyscraper' before. Though the place was the same, the motel's name had been different then. Maybe the manager had changed. But he just couldn't remember the old name.

'Which room shall we get?' Fujio asked.

The lamps outside indicated that two of the rooms were empty.

'What kind of rooms are they?'

'Well, we can have either 'New York' or 'Los Angeles'.'

Every room had a name.

'New York, of course! No question about it.'

'OK. That's the one then.'

They drove into the carport, and with a practiced hand Fujio placed a cover over the license plate. Nothing had happened in the past, but still Fujio never failed to cover the plate. After all, he was a bachelor.

Even in this area close to the big city, there was lots of open country. The boys from Yokosuka would go down to the love hotels in Zushi; so around here, Fujio might meet someone he knew. Even Fujio's brother-in-law had stories about guys encountering one of their male relatives as they pulled out onto the road from a motel.

Fujio and the girl went up the private stairway to the 2nd floor room. To the right of the bed, there was a night scene of skyscrapers with a river in front and a bridge. The bed seemed to be right on the water's edge.

Yoshiko was thrilled and said, 'Oooo, that's neat!'

Fujio was abashed. 'Eerie kind of room, isn't it? I get the feeling that the dirty river's going to wash over us.'

'But it looks just like New York.'

The scene was no more than a huge photograph glued to plywood.

Fujio said, 'Hmm. The bridge is jam-packed.'

'How come?'

'People are throwing their garbage over the side.'

'Do you always come to neat places like this?' Yoshiko asked.

'Yeah, generally.'

The bedcover was printed in a pattern of red and white Budweiser beer cans.

'Well, what do you think? How many times have you been to a place like this?'

'This is the first time,' Yoshiko said.

Fujio imagined that before this she had always gone to the guy's house, or even to her own house when her parents were away.

'So before it was with one of your classmates?'

'Before?' Yoshiko asked with a straight face.

'You've had a boy before, haven't you?' Fujio said impatiently.

'Well...a few, actually.' Yoshiko laughed without any happiness in her voice, leaving only the echo of a sneer.

'Quit bragging,' Fujio chided. 'Just take off your clothes.'

He sat watching her in a chair. He had watched women disrobe many times, and every time he found the process interesting. Usually the woman took off her coat first, then her skirt, and then the rest from top to bottom. This girl was different. First she removed her skirt and then her tiny pink panties. She left her red sweater on and the slip underneath that hung down like a modest curtain.

'Hey, that's enough! Don't take the rest off.'

From the previous glimpse he'd had of her, he knew that she had no breasts; the imbalance between top and bottom was rather interesting.

—*In fact, it might be even better if she put on her sailor suit again—not that it would make that much difference...*

Without another word, Fujio pushed her down on the bed. Her hair was short and sparse, and her pubic hair was just as meager. It was like staring at a scraggly chicken.

'You're not fully developed, are you?' Fujio said as he peeled off his clothes.

Yoshiko closed her eyes and remained silent.

Fujio's next experience was totally incredible. While watching her face, he explored her body for a while with his fingers. When her eyelids curled and little lines appeared between her brows and her body began to twist, she suddenly tried to push him off.

'Yoshiko!' he exclaimed. 'You're not still...?'

'No, I'm not. I'm not! I told you!' she insisted.

But as she said this, she was trying to escape from under him. Using his weight, Fujio pinned the skinny body to the bed. Suddenly he felt as though he was in a dense forest. He'd heard of the sea of trees and brush on the lower slopes of Mount Fuji, but he'd never been there. Now he felt as though he was trying to run through that forest. He was at war, on a mock battlefield, and though it might be just be a kind of war game, he knew he had to run hard, this way and that. The shells were coming at him, he couldn't stop. He heard the bullets and crouched, covering Yoshiko's body. Yoshiko bucked and muttered. Still the shells came, getting ever closer. They paused and together they bent their bodies to avoid the bullets. And then, amidst the thundering sound and the flying shells, the uproarious game ended.

—God, if I could only smoke...

Fujio had tried cigarettes several times, as well as alcohol, but every time he smoked it hurt his throat, and he couldn't make himself do it.

'Honest,' Fujio said to the girl, who had gone into the bathroom. 'I didn't think it was your first time.' He didn't know whether she had heard him or not; he thought she probably hadn't.

It was the first time he'd had a virgin. His divorced wife had been a hostess in a snack bar and, having known many men in her past, she was not overly delicate. But Fujio thought it would be boorish to be hung up on her past. He had never placed much value on virginity. It was like making pickles in a new wooden tub; a well seasoned tub works much better. However, this occasion could be regarded as an unexpected bonus.

Fujio grinned and called out, 'Are you OK?' Standing in his open robe, he glanced inside the little refrigerator and then called again. There was a faint response from the bathroom.

'When you come out, there are some hotcakes. Would you like some?'

'You've got some hotcakes?'

'Yeah.'

The room provided a small microwave oven. You put the packaged hotcakes into the oven to warm them, and then ate them with syrup. Yoshiko came out of the bath in a purple robe. Her eyes sparkled when she saw the hotcakes.

'Are these for me?' she asked.

'Sure. Hotcakes and coffee are on the house. Please enjoy yourself. I'll take a shower.'

'OK. I'll start the microwave,' Yoshiko said.

When Fujio returned to the room, there were two hotcakes ready on a plastic plate.

'Eat up,' Fujio said. 'I know you're hungry.'

'This is such a great room. I wish I had a room like this,' Yoshiko said.

'How big is your room at home?'

'Real tiny. About four meters square, and there are two bunk beds in it. My older sister and I share it.'

'You shouldn't put any furniture in it. If you used futons, you could use the whole room.'

'But we don't want to tell people we're sleeping on futons and not using beds. It'd be embarrassing.'

'You're worried about that?'

Yoshiko changed the subject. 'It's so great to make your own hotcakes like this!'

'You didn't make them, you just warmed them up.'

'If I go to a place like this with Jun-chan, I'll make hotcakes for him.'

'Don't talk about Jun-chan. You make me unhappy just talking about him.'

Fujio was suddenly in an extremely bad mood.

Chapter 5

SMOLDERING

VIRGINITY is often talked about as a matter of interest and people make much of virgin girls, and yet for Fujio Uno personally it came as a shock to realize it wasn't much of anything at all. No matter what, he could only think of Yoshiko Yamane as a chicken. She wasn't even a pig. She couldn't talk at all; she was like an alien being. All the same, Fujio didn't neglect to get her telephone number.

'OK. Listen. When can I call you?' he asked.

'If you call at suppertime, I'll probably answer. I sit near the phone.'

'And if you don't answer, I'll just hang up.' Fujio laughed.

—So if I say anything, that means her parents will remember my voice! It seems that if a man answers, I'm supposed to just hang up the phone...

Fujio was trying to keep himself together, and seducing women worked well enough for that. He wasn't at all disposed to lead his brother-in-law's dull sort of life, stuck in a shop for twelve hours every day, from 9 to 9. But the time came when his barely tolerable relationship with Saburo became a lot worse. It had to do with some alterations at the store. Ever since he'd arrived, Saburo had been suggesting changes to the building; and now the plan was to add to the corner where Fujio parked his car, put up an awning and a display case, and lease it out as a shop that would sell pastries and cakes. Saburo's idea would provide additional income from the rental area, and customers who came to buy pastries could be expected to stop to buy fruit and vegetables as well.

Fujio opposed the whole thing because it was clearly designed to deprive him of a parking place for his car rather than merely increase their business income. But he pretended otherwise. 'Sure, go ahead if you want to,' he said. 'I'll rent a place for the car instead.'

'You'll have to rent a place with your own money,' Saburo said. 'The business won't pay for it. After all, it's only a car for your pleasure.'

'Oh, no. I can't go along with that,' Fujio said. 'If you say you're going to build an extension, then I'll just drive the car into whatever you put up and wreck it!'

Fujio was speaking with a big smile on his face, but he was aware that would make the threat even greater.

'In that case, how about doing some work?' Saburo replied with empty bluster so as not to acknowledge the implication of Fujio's words. 'Do you think I'd have to say this if you were actually doing some work?'

'Look, this is my house,' Fujio said, 'and I'll do what I please.'

'Are you going to put up with his notions?' Saburo asked his mother-in-law.

She was flustered. While looking at Saburo, she said, 'Fujio, you rent a place and...'

That was as far as she got. Fujio abruptly kicked over the kerosene stove. He knew very well that it was the old model used in a room at the back of the shop. It had been in the family for ages, and was not one of the newer types that automatically shut off if it was tipped over in an earthquake.

Fujio's mother gasped once; she stood there looking at the kerosene spread out from the stove over the *tatami* mats, burning as it went.

'Fujio!' she cried out.

Naturally, Fujio himself did not move. He didn't care whether the house burned to the ground or not, and his lack of action showed it. Saburo moved quickly, all but flying to a place under the stairs to grab the fire extinguisher. When he returned to the room, the flames had already reached the futon spread over the low table. He drenched them with foam and they went out immediately. As this went on, Fujio's father was left standing in a corner of the room, while his mother stood by crying.

A bit of something white seemed to be stuck to the corner of Saburo's mouth. For a moment, Fujio thought it was a fleck of foam from the fire extinguisher. Then he realized that it was saliva, the result of his brother-in-law's excitement.

His eyes squinting, Saburo was heading for the telephone.

'Saburo! What are you doing?' his mother-in-law cried out. 'Isn't the fire out!?'

She caught Saburo's hand as he was dialing.

'Let go, please! He's a pyromaniac! I'm calling the police.'

'But the fire didn't spread much! If the police come, there's no proof. I'll just tell them Fujio tripped and bumped into it.'

Saburo and his mother-in-law stood face-to-face, both panting.

'You've no idea what might happen, protecting him like that!'

'Go ahead and turn me in if you want,' Fujio said. 'I've got the time. I'll go with the police or anywhere.'

Fujio was grinning and sat down in a corner of the room where the foam hadn't reached.

'Mother, listen,' Saburo said. 'Fujio is going to kill us all one day. Is that what you want?'

Fujio laughed mockingly. 'Oh, don't exaggerate!'

'Saburo, please, just think,' mother pleaded. 'Arson, starting a fire...If that gets about, then the ones who'll suffer most are Michiyo and Sachiyo. What will they do when other children say, 'Your uncle started a fire'?'

Saburo was silent.

'Right,' Fujio said. 'You all do whatever you want. Anything's all right with me. But don't be so arrogant, OK? You think you can get away with anything, but you can't. Just remember that.'

When Fujio had finished his speech, he slowly got up and went up to his room on the roof.

It's said that quarreling and fighting are not much fun, but Fujio didn't feel that way. Starting a fire and seeing the room splattered with foam made him feel sick. But after his fierce encounter with Saburo, a pleasurable excitement charged through his body, proving to him that he was alive. People don't quarrel without reason, but rather out of necessity. When that need is frustrated, the body suffers; the individual can feel like a total liar. People might think Fujio was a liar, but Fujio himself never lied naturally, unconsciously. He only lied deliberately; he would invent anything, say anything. If that was bad, then Fujio was in the same class as people like novelists.

He whistled as he went straight up to his room. But Saburo had not calmed down at all, and soon Fujio crept quietly back down the stairs to a place where he could hear the others' voices.

'What do you think, Father?' he heard Saburo ask. 'For a long time now you haven't said a thing when it's most important. Why's that? Do you think things will clear up if you behave like a coward?'

'Well, I don't particularly...' Fujio's father began.

'Look. If this were anybody else, I'd report him to the police for setting the place alight, no matter what you say. Starting a fire isn't just arson. If someone dies, then it's murder, don't you see? This is the same as Fujio stopping just one step short of murder.'

'Well, I don't know. Fujio was excited...If he wasn't excited, he wouldn't do...'

'Everyone gets excited,' Saburo broke in. 'But most people keep it under control, don't they? But getting excited like that...What kind of upbringing brought that about?'

Fujio's mother said, 'I just don't know any more. It's not that he wasn't loved, you know. Fujio was raised full of love.'

She used a tissue to noisily wipe away the tears that seemed to have gotten to her nose.

Of course, Fujio had become excited because someone had threatened his car, and the car was Fujio's indispensable means to preserve his sex life. He had got excited because he had been informed that the outlet for his sexual desire would be shut up—and he regarded that as his right.

'Wasn't coddling him and spoiling him your mistake?' asked Saburo.

Fujio couldn't hear the answer.

'I really thought the day might come,' Saburo went on, addressing the parents, 'when you'd see clearly what kind of person Fujio is. But you really don't understand at all, so all I can do is give up. What will happen? Will he kill us all first? Are we hoping that he dies first? There's just no other solution. And it's your fault that the situation has reached this point.'

Fujio listened calmly to what Saburo was saying. He was not conscious of the slightest anger in himself.

—Saburo's hinting only that I might kill them, not that he will kill me. I suppose that's his idea of fairness. In practice, he won't do anything. All Saburo wants is for them all to stay alive and, somehow or other, for me to die before them. According to the magazines and newspapers, most people pray for the happiness and long life of other people. But I've doubted that for a long time. It's perhaps not surprising that a large number of people in the world wish for someone else's death—or at least think about how nice it would be if someone died. I have a vague idea that Saburo might even wish me dead...

It was extraordinary for Fujio not to get angry. He felt calm. His instinct would have been to grab Saburo by the neck and slam his head against a pillar without the slightest hesitation. And if Saburo really wanted him to die, then that would have given Fujio a nice, bittersweet feeling. Oddly, the present scene gave him a feeling like being loved.

'How about letting Fujio live separately from us?' his father suggested.

It was rare for him to speak; now, his intention was nothing more than to escape being scolded into doing something by his son-in-law.

'Well, yes, I really couldn't ask for more than that,' Saburo replied. 'But only within the amount of extraordinary salary that he is getting already,'

Fujio was receiving 150,000 yen a month. Saburo called that money paid to someone who didn't do any work 'extraordinary.'

—I wouldn't work every single day for that kind of money!

'Even if he said he'd work, I wouldn't believe it.' Saburo went on. 'Mother here would be slipping him money on the side just to keep him happy, wouldn't you?'

Saburo knew what he was talking about. There had been a time when Mother would give Fujio 50,000 yen whenever he said he needed some pocket money. Saburo deeply resented that: he couldn't trust anything she said about money.

'Now pay attention to this,' Saburo said to his in-laws. 'You're thinking that there will be no problems if we don't have any contact—but that's a naive attitude.'

Saburo's high-pitched voice reached Fujio up on the stairs.

'And if we lived in a completely separate place, do you think that Fujio would work peacefully and seriously like other people? If there isn't someone to stand over him, he'll get mad all the easier, and then what do you think he'll do? When he's around here, I'm the one who has to put out the fire promptly. I'm always ready to run for the fire extinguisher. In most families, even though the fire extinguisher is kept in a corner of the room, when they need it they don't even know how to operate the lever. So what if Fujio does something like today at a boarding house, and burns up the whole place—not just one room—and some poor people are killed? Then Fujio would be a murderer, that's what. As far as I'm concerned, Fujio will still be a problem even if we let him go and live somewhere else. I'm certain of that. If he's at home and starts a fire, then we'll be the only ones burned up. It's this family that will be burned to death. Well, that's probably for the best. If you keep a guard dog and the dog bites and injures somebody, then the owner is responsible. Well, it's the same thing with Fujio.'

Mother had only a weak argument against all this. 'But Fujio's an adult. So if he does something, that's his own responsibility.'

'Sure it is—in court. But will people excuse that? Do you think that the papers and television are going to be so careful about how politely they deal with our lives? Are they ever considerate about not hurting the feelings of the parents, the kids, the wife? In the name of morality and propriety, the media go wild. Haven't you seen enough of that? That's the way the world is. At the kids' school, they're already talking about us. 'Is your uncle out of work? What does he do every day?' Just that much is enough to give other kids an excuse to tease our kids.'

On hearing that, Fujio came pounding down the stairs. He had heard everything and he wanted everyone there to know it. If Saburo hadn't been there, his mother would surely have run after him. *Fu-chan! Where are you going?* she seemed to want to say, as though that would stop him. But under Saburo's glare she remained silent.

Fujio went straight to his car. As he opened the door, he was thinking of where he would go. There was nothing good on at the movies. And it was still only nine o'clock in the morning. At this hour, there was only one person who he knew would be at home for certain.

—*What was her name? I can't remember...the woman who sews, the woman at the morning glory house...*

Perhaps it was because he was excited, but all the way to Yukiko's house he still couldn't remember her name.

—*Will I be able to recognize the house? It won't stand out without the morning glories. From the start, I didn't have any very serious intentions regarding her. I just talked to her on a whim, even her, so will I be able to find it...?*

But at last he did find the house, and when he saw the name 'Hata' on the gate sign he naturally remembered the name Yukiko.

The front door was open, but Fujio left the door just as it was and first rang the bell.

'Yes?' came a voice from inside the house and then the sound of light footsteps approaching. Yukiko was wearing a beige sweater and a grey skirt; as usual, she seemed to wearing no makeup.

'It's me, Fujio,' he said. The idea of not using a phony name here delighted him.

'Oh, it's you.'

'I happened to be passing this way again. How are you?'

'Fine.'

'If you're busy, I'll be on my way...'

'Well, I'm busy working on a lot of kimono for a graduation banquet, but if you don't mind talking while I work, please come in.'

'OK, but please carry on with what you're doing.'

The last time he'd come here and been in this room, there had been no place for him to sit. Graciously, however, Yukiko placed a cushion for him on the *tatami* mats and Fujio sat there quite at ease.

'Has your work been going along well since last time?' Yukiko asked him.

'I'm afraid not,' he said.

'How come?'

'I just said it was going all right for the sake of appearances, but actually, even from the start, there hasn't been much real work. I suppose it's my fault.' Fujio laughed. Actually he was in a slight sulky mood, but he spoke with perfect calm.

'Still, you're living pretty well, aren't you? Most people don't eat if they don't work,' Yukiko remarked, frowning slightly. The collar of the white blouse poking from the top of her sweater matched her serious expression.

'My family's in business. I just help out when I feel like it. So now I'm a bachelor just living at home where it doesn't cost me anything. And since I'm out of work, my mother doesn't even ask for any help with money for food...'

Fujio said this all easily.

'That's why I think you're spoiled.'

'Spoiled? No! Everyone treats me like I'm a nuisance. In fact, that's why I've come to see you.'

'Why do you think that? No one in this world is a nuisance.'

Fujio was distressed by the earnest tone to Yukiko's voice. 'No,' he said. 'There are a lot of people out there that other people would be glad to see dead. And I'm one of them.'

'If that's the case, so be it,' Yukiko said calmly. 'If a person hasn't had to face that kind of terrible fate, they'll never become much of anything. So what you are saying has some meaning in it.'

'That's an interesting outlook,' Fujio remarked.

'Do you think so? Looking at the world, I can't think any other way.'

Yukiko paused for a moment and then said, 'Now, what's become of those morning glory seeds?'

'The seeds? They're at home. I'll plant them in the spring.'

'Don't lie about it. You threw them away in front of my house and I picked them up myself. I don't care whether you keep them or throw them away, but it's hard on the seeds, you know.'

'Well, I'll tell you the truth,' Fujio said. 'I mean, morning glory seeds or anything would have done. I just wanted to make a connection with you, that's all.'

'I wondered whether you would lie about it, but at least now you're being honest. It was my mistake to think bad things about you,' Yukiko said.

'No, you were right. You've got to be careful. I'm a liar from way back.'

Fujio took considerable pleasure in saying that.

'I noticed,' Yukiko remarked. 'Your saying "I'm a liar" is really funny, and also so human. Yes, but there's nothing more honest you can say than that. If such a person really is a liar, then he's speaking honestly about himself, and if he isn't, then it's a clever joke.'

'Hey, that's enough! You're making fun of me,' said Fujio, feeling that she really was. A conversation like this was something he'd never had at home, and of course not with any of the women he'd picked up in town.

'After you turned me down the other day...'

'You had a great time, right?' Yukiko said simply, her hands still working away at a regular speed.

'Yeah. I can't get along without a woman.'

'There's nothing odd about that at all. But I don't really understand men's feelings.'

'I see a woman and I talk to her. That's it.' Fujio said, and then, agitated, he added, 'But you're special. You're like the morning glory.' Fujio frowned deliberately. 'Since I saw you last...I screwed a virgin. I mean, she lied to me. She said she wasn't a virgin. It was awful.'

'Is it so important whether she was a virgin or not? For a young person like you?'

'I didn't say it was important, but I was sure surprised. She's the daughter of a teacher. I just don't understand what that kind of girl is thinking.'

'But if you liked each other, it's all right, isn't it?'

'How could I *like* a thing like that?'

'Well, what is clear is that for her you're going to be someone she'll never forget.'

'It's not a big deal. And she wasn't so delicate, either. Like it was nothing at all.'

'Well, if it was me, I think I'd like the person who had such a relationship with me for the first time to spend a happy life. Even if I didn't remain with him.'

'It's no joke, honestly. She doesn't know my name. If I told her I was the Prime Minister, she wouldn't get it.'

'Somehow, you seem to be wasting your life...' Yukiko didn't finish her thought, and Fujio said nothing. 'You don't understand what you get, and you remember only about what you don't get.'

'No, I know just what I have.' Fujio grinned. 'My brother-in-law says I ought to be dead—I can't forget that. But you said 'what you get.' Well, I made it with another woman, too. But that was before the virgin.'

Yukiko listened to his boasting calmly, her hands still moving at the same tempo.

'She was pretty well-equipped...and she knew it.' Fujio went on. 'I guess she thought she could have any guy she wanted. But the best thing was that she was a genius of a liar.'

'How do you know that?'

'She talked as though she was single. I let her think I thought it was true, and I suggested that she should pretend to be married and taste the thrill of a love affair. But then she smoothly went on about her real married life.'

'And you're a liar, too, aren't you?'

'That's what I told you.'

'Right. Just a moment ago,' Yukiko said a bit pointedly.

'I even forgot that I said that. Irresponsible, that's me.'

'People...They're all the same,' Yukiko said.

'Have you ever had bees build a nest around here?' Fujio asked.

'Bees? Yes, once, a long time ago. Why do you ask?'

'It's dangerous if they make a nest, you know. I heard a story about how to get rid of them and I was wondering it if would work or not.'

'I don't know about that. But certainly they were a nuisance. Anyway, a person I know came along and saw the nest and said that something had to be done. We waited until winter, and then one day he came by and knocked the nest down for me. That was that. He didn't smoke them out. Do you have a bees' nest at your house?'

'No, we're in the middle of town and they don't come in that far. I'm the only bee, and my brother-in-law has chased me away.'

'You know what they say: 'Brothers are stranger after all'. Have you heard that?'

'Sure.'

'Well, if you've heard that, you shouldn't be surprised. There's a warning for almost everything in this world. But, really, it's unbecoming for a grown-up to fret like you do. If there was something really sad, it would be different. Even if you know that someone is going to go away or die, there's no way to undo that kind of thing.'

'If I died in an accident or disappeared, my brother-in-law would throw a party. That's the kind of human relations we have.'

'I really doubt that. I don't know you very well, but if you got ill or died, I think that I'd certainly remember you while I did my work.'

'How about *your* parents? What kind of people were they?'

'What kind? Father was just an office worker. Why do you ask?'

'Nothing. It's just that people often use the expression 'taking after their parents' in a bad sense. But when I look at you, I wonder what kind of good parents raised you. I'd like to meet them.'

As it turned out, Fujio remained at Yukiko's house for a couple of hours that day. In the midst of her work, Yukiko went to the kitchen and brought back some *amazake*, a sweet drink made of *sake* lees. That kind of thing was usually distasteful to Fuji; he was not much attracted to sweets. Nonetheless, when he came to this house before he even ate sweet dumplings without complaint. Fujio thought how strange it all was. At home, if his mother served *amazake*, he would deliberately upset the cup. His mother knew perfectly well that Fujio basically didn't like sweet things, but every now and then, quite unreasonably, she served sweet things because *she* liked them. She was incorrigible. 'There, now, this is delicious,' she would say, putting some cake in front of him.

It was time for Fuji to leave, but he was reluctant to go.

'It really puts me at ease seeing you,' Fujio said, putting on his shoes in the hallway.

'Oh, *I'm* not the reason for that. It's just because it's quiet here.'

'Quiet?' Fujio muttered and laughed in a low voice. 'An explanation like that is ancient. It shows your age. Don't you realize that our generation likes noise?'

Yukiko was not in the least flustered. 'Is that really true?'

'Well, not all the time.' Fujio was saying what he really meant.

'It's nice when it's quiet. You become human then.'

'And what do people become if it's noisy, then?'

'They become objects, things.'

'Look, I want to ask you something. Could you always be here?' Fujio himself could hardly believe he had said such a childish thing. 'I mean, just be here and not meet anyone but me? I'll never ask you to go to a hotel. Would you just see me when I want and never change?'

'Well, there's not much that's going to change. I don't go anywhere with my needle box. And since not many people come here, I hardly meet anyone.'

'So be here for me. I want you to be here just for me.'

Fujio was standing on the concrete floor of the hallway. While he was speaking, he unconsciously took hold of Yukiko's hand and pressed it to his cheek. He had seen the foreign custom of kissing a woman's hand; but he didn't kiss her hand, he only held it. He told himself this was just a pose, but he also knew it was even more than that a spontaneous act of emotion.

'They're pretty rough...'

Indeed, her hands were not silky smooth. The back of her hand was lined, and there seemed to be some chalk dust on it.

'I'm embarrassed that they're not so delicately looked after that you might want to cherish them,' Yukiko said, slowly withdrawing her hand from Fujio's. 'It takes a long time to sew silk with rough hands, but I do have to look after all of those plants outside.' Her tone of voice suggested she regarded them as people.

'OK. Goodbye. I'll see you again.'

Fujio went slowly to his car and got in. Instead of starting up the car, he sat thinking for a few moments.

—Ah, for a few hours I've been able to forget that lousy Saburo and the whole miserable household! But if I go home now, there's no way to kill time. I think I'll go and eat some noodles at that place called Shinano down the road...

With the eye of a bird, Fujio saw everything but his food in black and white. Just as he was getting out of the car, the distant figure of a woman walking flickered into his awareness. Usually, at that distance, she would not have caught his attention. She was wearing a grey coat and carrying a black purse and a shopping bag. Her style would have passed unnoticed anywhere. But the sight of her raised a question in Fujio's mind.

—I wonder where she's going? The road ahead of her only leads to the ocean. It may be true that a big development company really has bought the land and is keeping it for some recreation project years in the future, but right now the road only goes to a wild bit of coast where there's nothing...

For a few seconds, Fujio fixed his eyes on the woman's movements, considering whether to approach her or just forget her. He disliked interfering where he didn't belong. People chose their path and took responsibility for it, that was the usual thing. And this woman was, literally, walking her chosen road. Maybe she didn't know that it was a dead end; for some reason, Fujio didn't believe that was so. He felt she had something else in mind. He waited a few minutes before starting the car; then he slowly drove after her along the road.

'Hello there,' he called, easing the car to a halt beside her. 'This street comes to a dead end. I wonder if you know that?'

'Is that right?' she replied. It would have been normal then for her to ask directions to someplace or other, but she didn't.

'There's only the ocean up ahead,' he said, and then added pleasantly, 'That's great if you're intending to drown yourself, but not for anything else! If you'd like to go back, let me give you a lift.'

She made no response.

—*Perhaps she has made a mistake? But, in that case, wouldn't she then have said, 'Oh, dear! A dead end?'...*

Fujio had jokingly added the bit about drowning. Then it occurred to him that he might have hit the nail on the head, and he began to regret his invitation.

—*She might be totally honest or a complete fool desperately trying to retrieve herself—someone to seduce and drop immediately. Should I take her back, or leave her to go to her death, as she seems to be heading?*

'Where do you want to go? Where's your home?' Fujio asked.

'It's all right.' The woman was still distraught; her response was still not coherent.

'Please, get in if you want,' Fujio said. 'I'll take you. Just say where.'

The woman said, 'I'm sorry', and then, for the first time, raised her eyes and looked at Fujio.

Fujio realized then that there was something really distressed in the woman's looks—her sunken cheeks and her eyes wide open. Her hair was straight, drooping over her forehead, but trimmed short at the back. Scrubbed up a bit, she might have been one of those Takarazuka show girls who took male roles. She wasn't tall—rather slight, in fact—and she gave Fujio the impression of resembling some kind of foreign monkey, but he couldn't remember the name. She seemed to be in her mid-thirties. From a distance, she looked like one of the local farm wives. But, looking the way she did, she was certainly an interesting type.

'Are you in a hurry today?' Fujio asked as he waited for her to get into the car. It was a crude invitation and intimate to a degree; the woman looked rather startled.

'No,' she replied. 'I'm not in a hurry.'

'To tell you the truth, a woman just dumped me. And if you wouldn't mind, I'd like someone to keep me company.' Fujio was putting on a cheerful front. 'My name's Wataru Miura.'

'Keep you company...?' she asked.

'Nothing serious. We've only just become acquainted, but that's no reason we shouldn't spend and hour or so together, is it?'

'No, not really.' The woman's eye were large to begin with and now, with her tenseness, they had grown larger.

'To tell you the truth, I'm out of work just now. Enforced leisure. How about coming along?'

Fujio knew from experience that this kind of clumsy approach often worked.

'Out of work? Did your company collapse?' She seemed to be staring into Fujio with her huge eyes.

'Yes, right. It was a small company and doomed to fail from the start. I became a target immediately because of my character and was wiped out. Some people say it's the same in business or in government. You know, it's the people who never say anything or make any decisive commitment who really get ahead in the world. My mother keeps telling me to just take it easy and be like everyone else, and not say anything that will be misunderstood.'

Fujio been speaking this line about himself for less than a minute, so what he said about his character could mean absolutely nothing to the woman. Fujio always shifted his story to deceive his audience, to control the way a woman thought about him. But this woman seemed not to notice anything peculiar about him.

'You're very pretty,' Fujio observed as he started up the car.

'Don't joke, please,' she murmured.

'I can't help it if you think it's a joke. It's just that I really like people with big eyes.'

'My eyes look like that because I'm nearsighted and pop-eyed, that's all.'

Fujio couldn't decide whether her clumsy way of talking was more laughable or pitiful.

'Married?'

'I have a husband...I suppose you'd say.'

'Mmm,' was all Fujio said, as though talking to himself. Then he added, 'Bad type, that kind.'

'How can you say that about someone you haven't even met?'

'Are you offended?' Fujio seemed to be amused. 'Please don't get angry with me. I get very weak when a woman is upset.'

There was a silence.

'Well, if I were your husband,' Fujio went on, 'I'd never stop telling you how beautiful you are with those big eyes. Does your husband ever tell you how pretty you are?'

'He's never said that.'

'Ah, obviously a bad type, just like I said.'

Fujio let some moments pass in silence, then put his hand lightly on the woman's shoulder.

'Well, today, you and I can have a little fun. Then I'll take you home. Understand? I'll make a beauty of you.'

'Are you a beautician?'

—*Absolutely typical, humorless woman!*

Fujio laughed quietly to himself. 'Not even a beautician could do what I can do! By the way, what's your name?'

'It's Hitomi,' she replied. Her name sounded the same as the word for 'pupil of the eye.'

'No kidding? That's a perfect bull's-eye of a name for you! Shall we go, then, Hitomi-chan?' he said. He thought that using the intimate term '-chan' might make her angry, but she didn't show any such reaction.

'Actually, I was thinking of taking you to a hotel. I like you and was thinking I'd like to go to bed with you, but I've changed my mind.'

Fujio would study his companion's face; and bit by bit, he would bring about a change. It was Fujio's line.

'Where are we going?'

'Oh, to a hotel, naturally,' Fujio laughed. 'But not to a hotel *room*. We'll just have a quiet meal in the dining room. You're so thin, I feel I should feed you.'

He let go of the wheel with one hand and took hold of Hitomi's hand. He didn't look at her face. She made a hesitant, tense movement, as though she might withdraw her hand; then slowly, in the warmth and moisture of his hand, there came the feeling she would entrust it to him.

After that, Fujio took every opportunity to touch her until they reached a hotel next to the harbor in Yokohama. He touched her when they stopped at lights and he touched her while driving along. Not that he took much pleasure in it. She was one of those women you just can't tell where their breasts swell.

At one point on the way, Hitomi said, 'May I ask you a question?'

'Sure. Go ahead.'

'Why were you out in Miura?'

'Why?'

Fujio knew, far back in his consciousness, that there was something he ought to remember, but he ceased pursuing that.

'I'm out of a job, you see, so I can go anywhere. I really don't know why I went there today. It was just by chance.'

A couple of hours ago, when he'd met Yukiko, he'd asked her to see only him and no one else. Conveniently, that thought came into his mind from somewhere far removed.

'And that's the only reason we met.'

'I suppose so.'

From the restaurant on the top floor of the hotel, they could see a luxury passenger liner approaching the pier.

'What's the name of that ship, I wonder?'

'I don't know,' Fujio said. 'My eyes aren't that good.'

'I'd like to go somewhere on that!'

'Really? I wouldn't.'

'Why not?'

'I know that if I traveled on that kind of ship, there would only be old folks, and I've met people who say it's awful. When you see all of those passengers together, they say it gets to you. It's like seeing your own future. It takes all the fun out of the trip.'

'But me...I've never had a dream come true,' Hitomi said.

'You mean you want to travel on a floating casket that much?' Fujio sneered.

'No, that's not the reason, but I have the feeling that I'll never travel on that kind of luxury liner in my whole life.'

'If you really want to travel on a ship like that, I'll go and commit a burglary to get some money to buy you a ticket!'

Her eyes seemed to fill her face as she looked at Fujio.

'Honestly?'

'Sure...well, almost!' Fujio laughed. 'If it's just thinking, a human being can do anything. But there are some people who won't even think about things. They amaze me.'

The waiter had come to take their order.

'Whatever you want,' Fujio said. 'Order plenty of something good.'

'I don't eat very much.'

'Now, don't say that. Just look at the menu.'

Hitomi couldn't decide what to have.

'I'll have whatever you have,' she said.

'Fine. Then we'll split an order. Let's have the Chateaubriand. I feel that today we should share everything. I'd even be happy to wear matching clothes!'

Fujio was quite at ease with the waiter standing there.

'And how would you like it done, sir?'

'Medium rare.'

That abysmally serious look was still on Hitomi's face when the waiter left.

'I've never been taken much to restaurants like this, so I don't know about the menu or anything,' she said.

'You know, my father always used to say that it was a crime not to take a woman to a restaurant. There's no other way to learn about good cooking, or improve your taste in clothes. If you don't go out to restaurants, where else can you wear good clothes? Wearing good clothes all alone in a tiny apartment would make no sense.'

Fujio smiled as he said that, but it was a lie related to his own real life, the same old script he was sick of.

'Your father sounds wonderful!'

'Well...' Fujio demurred.

Fujio's mood improved all the more as he thought that his indecisive and irresponsible father could never talk that way.

'But what were you doing walking about in a place like that? Tell me that, at least, OK?'

He didn't have to treat most women or buy anything for them. All he had to do was listen to their stories and they would melt in his arms.

'I didn't know just where or how, exactly, but I...I didn't want to live any more...I intended to die,' Hitomi said.

'Just as I thought,' said Fujio. 'My intuition was correct.' He smiled naturally, feeling as though he'd bought a winning ticket at the races.

'But that's the worst way, dying in the ocean,' he said. 'When they find you, your body is all decayed and swollen. That's the truth. I'd be glad to hold you when you're alive, but I wouldn't lay a hand on your dead body.' Fujio believed that he was honestly expressing himself. 'Even if you're going to die, you should think about things after that. If you die in the sea, they say the best place is inside a coral reef. Maybe your bones will be chewed by a shark, but, aside from that, your remains will be washed by the waves and coral and turn pure white.'

No matter whether this information was true or false; it was the product of Fujio's days working in a hotel as a bellboy.

'How come you don't want to live?' he asked.

'He found a girlfriend,' Hitomi said.

Just at that moment, Fujio had to yawn and didn't try control himself. It was a big yawn.

'And what's more, she's had a child.' Hitomi continued. 'At first, he was hesitant about it and tried to dismiss the matter, but I'm sure that later on he'll become fond of the child, and then he'll want to live as a family, the three of them. Then I'll just be in the way. You see, I can't have children and there's just nothing I can do about it.'

'I understand. It's a case of no change for the better.' He appeared to be thinking about the matter. 'But after listening to your story, I've another idea.'

'Oh? Please tell me.'

'Well, because of what's happened, you're going to kill yourself to spite him, I suppose. It's worth dying if you *can* spite him; that's the best way to make him suffer. But if this guy is the kind who'll think, 'It's good that she's dead! That gets rid of a real nuisance...', then you only lose all the more by dying.'

Fujio was enjoying this immensely. There are times when someone's else's suffering is bitter to see, and other times when it is certainly a pleasure. Fujio thought what a positive delight it would be if his brother-in-law Saburo was suffering from terminal cancer.

'What kind of person is your husband's girlfriend?'

'All I've heard is that she runs a coffee shop near his office.'

'And the child? Is it a boy?'

'He said it was a girl.'

'Ah, better yet. On Saturdays she'll be doing things like carrying home a bag from the supermarket with celery ends sticking out of the top, with him and the child in tow. Grand! No one wants the little one to grow up in a situation where she's saying, 'How come my father's never at home?''

The ample steak greatly satisfied Fujio. Moreover, Hitomi gave him a third of her portion, so Fujio felt limp with the delicious meat.

'Now, today,' Fujio whispered to her, 'you must have some dessert to finish off the meal.'

'You like sweets, don't you?' Hitomi laughed.

'That's right.' Fujio raised his eyebrows in admission.

'I saw some tarts and cheesecake on the dessert wagon,' Hitomi said.

'Yes, those are fine, but for after the meal *you* would be even better. You'd be the perfect dessert for me!'

Hitomi's gaze took on a distant look.

'Maybe you've forgotten what cake tastes like?' continued Fujio.

'Oh, no. I remember.'

'It seems to me that a kid who knows the taste and can't buy it is more pitiful than one who doesn't know to begin with—right?'

Hitomi said nothing.

'It's really all right. You're not betraying anyone. Your husband is the one who broke the trust first. I'm not telling you to do that. This is really just a natural thing, like eating three times a day. It's a cruel life if you can't do that.'

'Where shall we go?' Hitomi said, in a small, calm voice.

'We'll get a room here,' Fujio told her. 'I'll say my wife doesn't feel well. It will be all right.'

Fujio asked Hitomi whether she wouldn't like cake or ice cream, but Hitomi declined both. 'Then let's get to the real thing,' Fujio said, ordering just coffee for them.

When they left the dining room, they took the elevator directly to the front desk.

Fujio made his explanation. 'We've just finished eating at the 15th floor restaurant and my wife isn't feeling well, she said, so we'd like to take a room for a rest.'

'Yes, sir. If you wish, we can arrange for a doctor...'

'No, that's not necessary. She suffers from Ménière's disease and is often ill after a trip. It's not life-threatening. All she needs is a little rest when she gets dizzy.'

Fujio had learned about Ménière's syndrome from the hypochondriac guy he'd worked with at the seed store.

'Then you'll be staying until about 3:30 or 4?' the desk clerk asked.

'Yes, that would be fine. She'll recover if she lies down for a while,' said Fujio. He turned to Hitomi, who had just returned from the bathroom. 'Are you all right?'

The two were shown to a room on the 3rd floor. The bellboy gave Fujio the key and left.

Fujio laughed. 'My, but you look quite ill. The medicine for that is steak and sex!'

After Fujio had stripped off Hitomi's skirt and blouse and sent her to bathe ahead of him, he tore back the covers on the twin beds. While stretching out on one, he imagined the contours of Hitomi's body. But that was only from seeing her dressed in a slip. Her underwear hanging from her skinny hips showed that nowhere was her angular figure smooth or round.

It was Fujio's experience that there were not many women in the world who liked sex as much as the characters in stories and comic books did. In fact, most of them rather disliked it.

—I expect Hitomi's like that. How many casual encounters have I had with women? Hmm, let me see…

Of course, some women he'd approached just dashed off without a reply the moment he spoke to them, and he let them go because he didn't need them that much.

—If I'd been more serious, I reckon I could have netted those women every time…

The reason he was trying to think clearly like that was that someone existed in his life who was different; but Fujio was trying not to make that part emerge and become too conscious. So he was operating very deliberately, stirring up the mud at the bottom of the pond in his mind.

Hitomi was taking a long time in the bath. He couldn't hear the slightest sound of water. Concerned, Fujio called out, 'Hello. Are you all right?' He wasn't concerned about her health, but if she had changed her mind and taken poison that would really make a mess.

'I'm coming,' she called back.

'That's OK. No need to rush,' Fujio told her.

She came out with a towel wrapped around her, wearing a shower cap provided by the hotel. Her painted eyebrows had vanished; beneath the cap her face resembled a ghostly cat.

'Please take that bed. I'll just have a shower, too,' he said.

Fujio had something like a bird bath. After about thirty seconds of splashing water over himself, he came back and slid in beside Hitomi.

'Waiting?' he asked, in a voice not overly sincere. At such an animal moment, it was natural that there were no appropriate human words. Fujio noticed that the corner of her eyes were wet, but not from the bath.

'Have you been crying?' he asked.

'Yes.'

'Why?'

'Because I'm still alive...'

'Oh, don't be upset by every little thing,' he replied, feeling himself becoming irritated. But when his hands had roamed over every part of Hitomi's body, Fujio closed her eyes with a kiss on her eyelids and murmured thickly, 'Go ahead, cry. I'll let your whole body cry...It's good for you to cry.'

Chapter 6

COUNTERATTACK

THEN it was March, and Fujio felt that the enemy attack had begun. The 'enemy' was Saburo, his brother-in-law. It was as though everyone—his sister Yasuko, his mother and his father—was caught in the net cast by Saburo and was forbidden to move.

One day, returning from an excursion, Fujio found his parking space filled with piles of things like concrete blocks, bags of cement, and a variety of building materials. There was no room for him to park.

'Mother!' Fujio shouted, his face crimson. Saburo was not in sight. 'Mother! Didn't you say anything when they put all that stuff in my parking place?'

'But Saburo said that he'd talked with you.'

Shingo, Fujio's father, in a corner of the room as always, stood like a limp, hanged body that had simply been left there.

'Well, he hasn't talked with me. What's he done with my parking place? And what did *you* do?' Fujio said to his father. 'I suppose you don't have the guts to say a word, no matter what that bastard Saburo does around here?'

'Well, I...'

'Shut up, you fool! I'm going to throw that stuff into the street.'

For a moment, he thought of throwing the blocks and bags of cement into the middle of the street. On second thoughts, however, he realized that would be heavy work. Vexed enough just by the idea, he retreated instead to his castle on the roof. His car was left parked in the street.

In the evening, he heard voices out on the street. A patrolman from the nearby police box was there and seemed to be warning Fujio's mother about the car that had been left in the street. Mother explained that the materials had suddenly been delivered that day, and from now on the car would be parked at a friend's house. She apologized and thanked the policeman for his concern and trouble.

Fujio tried to think about how things had gotten to this state. It must be that he had failed to recognize his enemies in other people. At that time of day, there was usually no reason for the patrolman to appear, so why had he come around and why was he so industrious? He could think of only one reason. Without a doubt, the old woman at the Wakana shop across the way had secretly complained. His car presented no obstacle to cars going to Wakana. The old woman only knew that it was illegal for cars to be parked on the street, so she immediately reported it.

'Fujio...' his mother called meekly after a while. 'Fujio...'

'Don't bother me!' he called.

'Dear, you should put your car in the empty lot. If you don't, the police will come again and we may have to pay a fine.'

'What about the police? I don't care about them.'

What his mother had to convey delicately to Fujio, at Saburo's request, was the matter of deducting the price of a rental parking space from Fujio's allowance. Fujio had already been informed of this and the fact that there was a rental lot close to the house that still had space. However, while he had delayed replying, all the spaces there had been taken up, and now the only space available for rent was located about 500 meters down the road. If they delayed any more, that too would probably be filled up, so Fujio had to be carefully informed of this. As for renting the space, Saburo could go and settle everything. These were the messages Fujio's mother had to carry between the two men.

'If that's what Saburo wants to do, let him do it!' Fujio coolly declared to his mother. 'Anyway, I'm not doing anything. I won't ask. I don't have to bow to that creep.'

Mother went back and forth between Fujio and Saburo with the messages, but they were not her own words and she lived in constant fear that one or the other would get angry. As she did her best to continue with her messenger work, her husband did nothing whatsoever. He voiced no opinion, nor did he do any work around the house. He simply hoped that none of this argument would come down on his head.

Of course, Fujio did nothing to negotiate the parking space, simply parking his car wherever it suited him in the neighborhood. Finally, mother obtained a sketch map from Saburo with the rental agreement attached and told Fujio he could park in space No.13 and that he would have to pay for it.

'I'm not going to pay for it,' Fujio declared. 'The one who rents it has to pay. *I* don't have any contract with the parking lot. Just tell Saburo that.'

Fujio decided, however, to go and have a look at the lot. It wasn't even paved; it was just an empty lot with gravel spread over it. There was no one around and no houses close by. He liked it. He reckoned that the story about there being no more rental places if he didn't take it immediately had just been so much propaganda, and even after a few days, no cars had appeared in the spaces on either side of No.13.

—*But what a space to choose—No.13! I think I'll go somewhere to take my mind off this unhappy mess. If I stay at home, the noise of the construction will go on and on, disturbing my afternoon nap. And the construction sounds will be as bad as Saburo spouting off that he's won. Besides, I think my luck with women is definitely going to improve this year. Thinking only in terms of quantity, it's certainly been a lucky year so far. I've pulled in plenty of housewives and college students—though of the kind whose names I really didn't want to know!*

For him, such casual situations—irresponsible sexual encounters that could hardly be called affairs—were nothing more than meetings with dressed-up, walking vaginas. And, as far as Fujio was concerned, and to the extent that he remembered the women at all, the experiences left a bad taste. The principle reason Fujio felt as he did was that, despite the women being too dumb even to speak Japanese properly, they made themselves out to be quite above most other people. Clearly they wanted to show that it was their own charm that had provoked sex with Fujio, and that made him feel sick.

—If they're only stupid but not self-conceited, then that's kind of balanced and cute. But the more stupid they are, the more conceited they get. And self-conceited women are all stupid! That's a strange phenomenon, but it's true. And yet, if the contest is judged on quantity rather than on quality, the odds are pretty fair. Considering the money spent in return for the sheer quantity of sexual pleasure gained, I'm perfectly satisfied with the bargain!

However, his composure regarding the economic balance soon fell to pieces. 10,000 yen was deducted from his allowance that month for the rent on his parking space. That was the same as the price of a motel and other necessities when he took a drive out of town. He knew it was his argument with Saburo that had resulted in this family decision.

Fujio challenged his mother. Afraid, she took 10,000 yen from her apron pocket, slipped it to him, and said, 'Just keep this secret, that's best.' But Fujio then got angry with her over the matter of losing face.

His feeling of uncontrollable irritation needed to be soothed, and he thought of calling Yoshiko Yamane. He remembered her saying that she usually answered the phone around supper time.

'What happened? Is that you? I've been waiting for you to call.' It was her usual scatterbrained voice.

'Are your parents home? Are they close to the phone?'

'They're not here. Everyone's out today.'

'That's good.'

'I've been waiting for you. What happened with Jun-chan?'

'It went fine. He'll send a present you can show to all your friends.'

'Honestly?'

'Oh, he wouldn't forget you, for lots of reasons.' Fujio said, smiling at his own exaggeration.

'But when can I meet you?' Yoshiko pleaded.

'When's a good time for you?'

'The day after tomorrow?'

'That's fine. We'll have some fun. It was really something, you know. Jun has been terribly busy. Did you know that he's doing a concert in Kyushu?' Fujio had read the entertainment news at the barber shop.

'Oh, I already know everything about Jun!' Yoshiko replied.

Fujio arranged to meet her in front of the video rental store behind the station where there were always all kinds of people coming and going. It was unlikely they would attract any attention, and it was better than in front of the train station.

He parked the car a bit early and waited. In a little while, the nondescript girl came into view, eyes lowered, approaching from a distance. Fujio was pleased.

'Good to see you,' he said as he opened the door.

Yoshiko grunted.

'Is everything all right?'

She grunted again.

'I've been wanting to meet you again,' Fujio told her.

'How about Jun-chan? How is he?'

'I meet you and all you think about is Jun-chan! How about me?'

'I'm thinking.'

'Sure, but *what* are you thinking?'

'I'm thinking about whether you could fix me up to meet Jun-chan.'

As he drove, Fujio thought of the pleasure lying ahead. No matter what, he'd discover the difference between the first time and the second time, and that would be fun.

'Did you like the hotel we stayed at last time?'

'The New York place? Yeah, that was neat.'

'Then let's go to a place like that again,' Fujio said. But in fact he intended to change the scene this time.

He'd read about the 'Sunlight Hotel' in a specialty magazine he subscribed to so that he could become an expert on these matters. According to the magazine, its special feature was its Japanese-style baths. Apparently the room interiors resembled old Japanese cottages and beyond the traditional-style *engawa* verandah there was a rock bath.

'You mean I can really have a hot-tub bath?' Yoshiko said, surprised, when they entered the room.

'Of course. Take a look. There's a bucket and soap, isn't there?'

'It's a natural hot spring!'

'No, it's not a hot spring.'

'How come?'

'Look. See the ceiling and the glass door?'

'Oh, yeah.'

'First we'll do it. And then I have a reward for you.'

'Oh, great. Shall I prepare the bath?'

Even though she made the offer, Fujio was the one who actually had to do it. Yoshiko didn't even know where the taps were, let alone how to adjust the temperature of the water in the bath. She was not at all shy when the water was ready, slowly easing herself in without first rinsing her body using the bucket.

Settling himself in the water, Fujio said, 'Young lady, didn't your parents even teach you how to take a bath?'

'Why do you ask that? I know how to get into a bath.' And then, as they were lying at ease in the bath surrounded by rocks, she said, 'Oh, this is such a nice feeling. I really wanted just once to see what a natural stone bath is like.'

'Do you really like it?' Fujio asked.

'It feels terrific. Imagine getting into a neat bath like this on the way home from school!'

'Well, don't go to school or anything, just stay in the tub! That's the best thing for you,' replied Fujio. Yoshiko said nothing. 'Except that if you go home with that shiny, scrubbed look on your face, your mother will see through you pretty quick.'

'Then I won't wash my face. It'll be all right.'

'Listen,' Fujio said in a patient tone. 'You've been up to something, haven't you?'

'Yes.'

'Have you slept with someone else since then?'

'Well...just someone in my class.'

'You mean lots of guys?'

'Sort of.'

'A regular veteran, aren't you?'

Yoshiko chuckled.

'So if you have to report what you've majored in at school, it will be Sex, won't it?'

'Did you get to meet Jun-chan?' Yoshiko asked.

'No, I didn't have time to meet him in person, but I talked with him on the phone. I told him about you, and when I said your name was Yoshiko, he said, "Wow, that reminds me of something a long time ago," and he really choked up.'

No matter what the woman's name was, Fujio always managed to say that her name was the same as his or someone else's first love.

'But is he going to meet me?' Yoshiko asked.

'Sure. Only right now he's incredibly busy with concerts outside of Tokyo and with recording sessions. He said just to wait a little while. But I get the feeling it might be a little bitter, you know, for Jun-chan to meet a girl with the same name as his first love.'

'I'll just change my name, then,' Yoshiko said.

'That's dumb! The only reason Jun-chan wants to meet you is that you have the same name as his old girlfriend.'

—That's the best story I can offer! I'm making it up all for you. Why are you trying to wreck it with trifling stuff?

Last time he'd held Yoshiko in his arms, it was like having a trumpet blowing in his ear. But today there was nothing like that at all. She had her eyes closed and her eyebrows knitted together, and she just moved her body lightly.

'You're really calm this time, aren't you?'

Fujio wondered whether he should comment on how she'd matured.

'Go have a shower,' Fujio said afterward. 'In the meantime, I'll get out the present I brought from Jun-chan.'

Yoshiko just grunted compliantly. While she was in the shower, Fujio took his own old blue T-shirt out of a paper bag. When she returned, he held it out, saying, 'This is Jun-chan's.'

Yoshiko stood motionless, gazing at the shirt respectfully, not even putting out her hand.

'It's OK. You don't have to be like that...,' Fujio said, relaxing his face. Fujio had always like to fool people, and he was in a good mood fooling this young girl with something so worthless. 'What was the name of that last film Jun-chan was in?'

'Running to Inoshishiyama?'

'Right. Well, this is what he wore on location. He said that he'd send it to you after he washed it, but I told him not to wash it.'

Yoshiko was silent.

'He said he was a little busy to autograph it, so please just wait a while.'

The girl had taken Fujio's blue shirt in her hand. He was expecting her to at least press the shirt to her cheek. That would mean she was putting his sweaty shirt to her face and nuzzling it.

For a while, Yoshiko seemed to be dazed, lost in her thoughts. Then suddenly she took aim at Fujio, who was just moving his face closer to hers in a familiar kind of way. She hit him with the shirt. It was such a quick movement, he couldn't duck, and a corner of the cloth hit Fujio squarely in the eye.

'Hey! What was that for?' he said roughly.

'You liar! Jun never wore this shirt!'

Fujio could still feel the sting in his right eye.

'He didn't wear a blue shirt in that picture. I'm not fooled by your lying.'

'Listen, on a film location, don't you know that they wear different clothes rehearsing and shooting?' Fujio was thinking up reasons fast, trying to control the situation.

'I know that. But this shirt isn't Jun's!'

'OK, have it your way. Next time you say you want something, I won't bring it.'

'A shirt like that isn't Jun's. Jun isn't that chubby.'

Indeed, Fujio had no idea that she knew that much. But this near-imbecile of a girl had a strangely good nose only for that kind of thing.

'OK. Now, take it easy,' Fujio said. 'I just passed along what Jun sent to me. If you think this isn't Jun's shirt, then he must have sent someone else's by mistake. But *I* don't know anything about that, understand?'

'Yeah. Well, there's something else I want you to do,' Yoshiko went on in an oddly calm voice.

'And what's that something?' Fujio replied.

'Well, you see, it's about our thing last time. I talked with some friends of mine, and they all say that I should get some money from you.'

'And why should I pay you?'

'Because I was a virgin, that's why.'

'I'm tired of that 'virgin' stuff. You did it because you wanted to.'

Fujio paid no attention to what she said.

'Right, but I'm underage, and if I complain about you, you'll be in a lot of trouble.'

Fujio began to feel a hot mass growing inside his head.

'Complain? And *how* would you complain? Listen, sweetie, do you know my name?' Fujio smiled.

'No, I don't. I don't know, but that's all right.'

'Oh? Why's that?'

'Because I know your car's license plate number. I can find it from that.'

Someone had put her wise, that was certain.

'That's pretty good,' Fujio replied. He pretended to be unmoved.

'Where did you write it down? In your notebook? If it's in your notebook, then bring it out and you can write down my name and address.'

'No, not in my notebook.'

'Then you wrote it here? On the palm of your hand?'

Fujio seized Yoshiko's hand violently and opened her fingers, but there was no indication of an ink-smear on her palm.

'You're hurting me! Do you think I'd write it there?'

Yoshiko resisted, pulling away from Fujio.

'If you didn't write it there, then there's no other place,' Fujio said her.

Yoshiko pointed to her head and said, 'I wrote it in here.'

A momentary chill ran over Fujio's skin. His license plate number could be easily remembered by anyone; all they had to remember was *ku-i-na-shi*, the first syllables of the numbers 9-1-7-4. Put together they formed the word *kuinashi*, which could mean both 'no regrets' and 'no food'. Within a few seconds, the chill changed to something more unpleasant; he felt he was now enveloped in the hard scales of a reptile, just as though he was no longer warm-blooded and, through fear and anger, scales like armor had been raised on his skin.

He tried to analyze the situation. What irritated him most was the possibility that this girl, who seemed so stupid, might tell someone else about his license number and completely turn the tables on him.

Fujio calmed his breathing and said, 'What about a complaint? That doesn't matter to me. I really loved you.'

'I'll say I was raped.'

'Raped?'

'So just pay me. I couldn't say it was rape if you paid me.'

'You want money?' Fujio exclaimed.

'They say you should pay me a lot because I was a virgin.'

'And suppose you do get that kind of money. What will a schoolgirl like you do with it? It would be hard to know how to use it,' said Fujio. He was stalling, probing for her real intention. But at the same time the anger he'd suppressed was building, this time to an explosive level.

'It would be hard to know how to use it?' Yoshiko raised her smiling voice, but it was totally lacking in emotion. 'Is anyone put off by getting money? I'm not put off at all, not a little bit. I could buy an apartment.'

'And then what would you do?'

'If I had my own apartment, I could do what I like, right? And if I bought it with my own money, my folks couldn't say a thing.'

'Didn't you say your father was a schoolteacher?'

'Yes.'

'Even a teacher is like that?' Fujio's tone expressed his total disgust.

'That's the way it is. It's my right. This is a democracy.'

'Oh, sure.' Fujio waited a moment to catch his breath. 'How much do you want? To begin with, I don't have any money.'

'My friends say I should get three million yen, but if you don't have that I'll take one million.' Her tone seemed to suggest she was giving him a discount.

Fujio felt suffocated.

—If I send her away like this, she will keep on wanting her million, I'm sure of that. And the situation I'm in with Saburo was not from him asking anything like a million yen!

'But you can't buy an apartment for a million yen, can you?'

'I don't have to buy it right away. I can save up.'

'By doing the same as you've done with me?'

'Well, yeah.'

'You mean, to get the money, you'd turn into a whore?'

'Or whatever. I don't care a bit.'

'Listen. If you don't stop talking like that, I will go to your school and tell them just what you're up to, believe me.'

'But I'm still underage, and you're the one who made me do it.'

Fujio felt something like a plan or a decision taking shape, as though his head was growing thick and heavy.

'A million yen is a lot of money.'

'I know that. But I only get to lose my virginity once.'

'I'll have to raise the cash.'

'Well, that's your problem.'

'OK. But we have to talk about how I'll pay it—like, how long you can wait, things like that.'

'That's all negotiable,' Yoshiko said, sounding completely in control.

As they left the hotel with the natural hot spring décor, Fujio saw the room with entirely different eyes. When they'd arrived here, his mind and body had been elated. There they were, a man and a young woman just right for each other, setting out to discover mutual pleasure. But now it was different. If he left this weak, squint-eyed, thin-browed little twit, she'd cause trouble. He looked at his watch. It was just past six o'clock.

'How about if we go for drive while I do some planning?' Fujio kept his rage under control. 'What time did you tell your parents you'd be home?'

'I didn't.'

'And won't they be concerned?'

'Everyone has their own key. My mother gets home late.'

'Why's that?'

'She runs a coffee shop. I go there sometimes.'

'Oh? And when do you study?'

'I don't study much. I hate it.'

'Do you help out at the coffee shop?'

'Now and then. When I'm there I learn a lot of things. You know.'

'Mmm, a great place to study the world!'

'My mother closes up the shop and...well, if you want to know, there's a guy who stays around. So we go home at different times.'

'Doesn't your dad say anything about that?'

'Him? He's just her second, anyway.'

'What do you mean, "her second"?'

'I mean he's her second husband. He's not my real father. He's got no connection with our life. My mom runs the coffee shop to pay for my board at home. And since her husband doesn't support us economically, he doesn't say anything, no matter what.'

'But they're formally married, aren't they?'

'Sure...I suppose. But when they got married, Mom made him a promise. She told him that her child wouldn't be a drag on him.'

'So she runs the coffee shop and sees other guys?'

'She's just fooling around. Her husband isn't dependable.'

'Proof of the pudding. So whoring is in your blood.'

Fujio said this without especially thinking, but he was surprised when Yoshiko laughed delightedly.

The street lights outside the hotel could barely compete with the evening glow.

'Do you like this car?' Fujio asked.

'It's OK. But it's not particularly wonderful...' Yoshiko said condescendingly, haughtily, eloquently. The uncertainty she had shown when they first met was nowhere to be seen.

'Now, listen,' Fujio began, 'let's do it once more, eh? Because we've started being lovers. I really like you a lot, you know.'

Fujio slowed down the car and put his face to her neck like a puppy.

'Stop it! That tickles!'

'But you like it, don't you?'

'Sure.'

'Let's just forget about the money.'

'As long as I get it, I won't ask for any more, that's settled.'

Her craftiness and stupidity made Fujio's blood boil.

'And in spite of all I've said, you still want the money?'

'Don't give me that. If you love me, it's only right that you should pay.'

'Who told you that?'

'A...friend...of...mine,' Yoshiko said, childishly stretching out her words.

Fujio made up his mind instantly. 'OK. I'll pay,' he said. 'But not a million yen. What do you say to half a million?'

'You said before that you didn't have any money.'

'I'm going to rob a bank and bring you the money. All for you!' Fujio laughed. 'And then you will be an accessory to the robbery. You'll be sent to a reformatory, at least.'

'I said I'd take a million.'

'You'd *take*, you'd *take*! Right. Don't hesitate. How about *taking* TEN million! How about THIRTY million? Then you could buy an apartment. Wouldn't that be just peachy?'

Yoshiko was not quick to reply.

'You said you knew the license number of this car,' Fuji went on. 'But do you *really* know it?'

The sky had darkened. Fujio was thinking that if she was bluffing he would just drop her off somewhere and be rid of her. He would stop at a convenience store, send her in for a bottle of fruit juice, turn off the car lights and speed away. If he did that quickly enough, she wouldn't have time to read the license number.

'OK. Let me see if you know the number,' Fujio said cheerfully. 'If you know it, it won't be very useful anyway. After all, this is a stolen car.'

Yoshiko bowed her head low.

'Do you know it? I guess you don't,' Fujio told her. Yoshiko made no response, and when Fujio glanced over at her face for an instant he saw that she was in tears. 'Hey, what's this crying stuff! Let's see if you know the number is all I said.'

Yoshiko was sniffling. 'I don't know the first part.'

'Then what's the second part?'

'91-74.'

'That's pretty good; you have a good memory,' Fujio said. He felt a chill run through his body, as though something big and slimy had slithered down his back. '*Ku-i-na-shi*...right? 'No regrets.' You don't have any regrets, do you? Up to now, you've been spending quite a selfish life. That's enough, isn't it? You should give up the rest of your life.'

'Take me home, please,' Yoshiko said.

Fujio felt the sharp change in Yoshiko's tone.

'I really wish that you'd take me home,' she repeated.

'Sure. Of course. Right away.'

As he spoke, Fujio made a secret move. He threw a switch that locked all the doors and windows. When he had bought the car, he knew that women would be riding in it, and he chose one that came specially equipped. Of course, the manufacturer had not intended that the device would be used to prevent women from escaping. Fujio had assumed his most ingratiating manner and told the salesman he was getting married soon and would be having children and wanted to be able to lock the car for safety from the driver's seat so that they couldn't get into any mischief with the doors.

Fujio stopped for a red light at a crossing; he expected Yoshiko to be watching for her chance to open the door. It had been amusing for Fujio to see women's responses when they found out that it was impossible to open the doors. But Yoshiko only hung her head, looking as though her hair was growing from her knees, and went on crying.

'Come on now, don't cry. I said I'd give you three million yen, so there's nothing to cry about, is there?'

Fujio was no in high spirits. A short while before, she had been on the attack, without any counterattack. Now he was turning the situation around again. Awareness of victory sent a feeling of intoxication running through his body. Nothing was resolved in this situation, but as far as those numbers wedged into the girl's thin gray matter was concerned, there was only one way to erase them.

Fujio stopped at the intersection. Ahead, a star shone in the sky, their only witness. He didn't yet believe in the reality of the action he was about to take.

—In order to start threatening her, I'll have to make her fearful. I must go to some lonely place to do that. But if she changes her mind, I don't want to be rough with her. Some lonely place would do, even somewhere near where I picked up that girl with the big eyes, Hitomi. That's very close to Yukiko Hata's house. A lonely, bleak stretch of coast would be best...

'Where are we going?' Yoshiko asked after a while.

'To a pretty stretch of coastline, that's where. To kiss you. I don't like kissing you where there are other people around. Just the two of us alone.'

'But we just had sex, didn't we?'

'Hey, don't say dumb things like that.' Fujio didn't conceal the smile on his face. 'There's no limit with sex. Now with food, you mustn't eat too much or you get fat. But with sex, there's no problem. And there's no tax to pay, either, no matter how many times you do it!'

Yoshiko's uneasiness was apparent from the break in the conversation.

Fujio had been to this area countless times, to park and just spend time taking a nap, or simply to relieve himself. Now he drove some distance from the main road, stopped the car at the edge of some deserted woods and turned off the headlights. The sound of the ocean should have reached them, but he couldn't hear it.

'I need to pee,' Yoshiko said.

'Sure, right. Pee all you want.'

Magnanimously, Fujio unlocked the door. Yoshiko got out slowly and walked noisily over the dead leaves into the woods. Then suddenly there was the sound of running.

'Hey! Where do you think you're going?'

Fujio strode in the direction of the sound.

—If she gets away now, she could really get back at me later...

Apparently, Yoshiko thought it was impossible to run in the woods because a few moments later she came back out onto the road. Her screams froze Fujio's heart.

'Help, somebody! HELP!'

Fujio's chest nearly burst with anger; his heart felt as though it had jumped into his throat. Hew could hear his muscles tensing as he ran furiously in the direction of the screams. Luckily for Fujio, shouting and running are different actions and Yoshiko chose to escape from Fujio. She didn't cry out again. But less than 30 meters from the car, Fujio caught up with her, grabbed hold of her neck and shoulder from behind and pulled hard.

Yoshiko was unexpectedly agile. She tried to swim out of Fujio's hold and then fell to the ground. Fujio attacked instantly, glad that he had overcome her. But Yoshiko kicked out at him as she lay on the ground, and Fujio felt a sharp pain in his thigh.

—*She's strong, a woman's strength...*

Fujio renewed his attack. Yoshiko got to her feet, but now, before she could move, Fujio drove his fist hard into the pit of her stomach. The girl was already too weak to cry out. Her body bent over two or three times as Fujio pounded her with his fists. Then she fell to the earth on her knees. Fujio was on fire; he quickly dragged her to a less visible place. He thought he could easily carry a body as thin as Yoshiko's, carry her someplace to hide. But when he tried to lift her up, he found that to be impossible. He was out of training. She seemed to have taken root in the ground, as though this was her way of getting back at him. Out of breath, Fujio simply dragged her by the shoulders.

—*Now there's no turning back! If she recovers, she could charge me with attacking her and beating her unconscious. Then she'll want more than a million yen...*

Fujio's mouth was dry. His heart was pounding in his throat. He was breathing frantically. One hand was clasped over the girl's face, and with the other he continued squeezing her throat, using the full strength of his body.

Someplace, far beyond the awareness of his own hand, Fujio seemed to have taken hold of the universe. Darkly, silently, whatever it was, it conveyed a sense of some enormous turning, like the commotion of revolving stars.

What Fujio could feel was rather the echo of resistance against his violence coming from every cell in Yoshiko's body. Her blood was still flowing, and there was a scream struggling inside her lungs. Her body moved slightly several times. Fujio was enveloped by fear. He had reached the limit of his strength, and yet he had to continue the fight. Blood rushed to his head. If he failed, he would be devoured by Yoshiko. Now he was breathing like a frantic animal. Then he changed his position of his hands, using his upper arm on her neck, pushing with the full weight of his body. The radial artery of his own forearm was at right angles to Yoshiko's neck and he could feel a terrible reverberation from his own pulse.

The crushing whirl of stars went on. Only when he loosened his grip, did the stars come together again to form the stream of the Milky Way, just as though they would envelope him and bury him alive.

—Somehow or other, I must stop that flood of stars in the universe...
Time passed.

Suddenly, the feeling of holding the boundless universe disappeared from Fujio's hands. Yoshiko had become limp. Every sound seemed to have stopped as Fujio crouched there in the darkness. Kneeling beside her body, he stroked his hair; in a while he was breathing normally again.

He had no idea how long it had been since he'd left the car. During that interval, his eyes had grown accustomed to the darkness, and now he could see clearly. One of Yoshiko's shoes had fallen off a few meters away; he picked it up and put it back on her foot. He was not acting out of any feeling of sympathy. He knew he had to hide the body, and he didn't want to carry a shoe in his hand while he was doing that.

—You can take care of the shoe yourself...

Even while he was bringing Yoshiko here, Fujio had been working out a vague plan for if things went completely wrong. He knew there used to be a refuse pile in a thicket out in the woods, a place where they dumped cow manure.

—It'll be soft and digging there ought to be easy. And so much the better if there's an odor. No one will be suspicious. The biggest problem is whether I can drag her that far or not. Cutting through the bushes carrying her weight will probably be too hard. And although there'll be an element of danger to it, I think maybe it'll be easier to just take her the 20 meters or so in the car...

As he dragged the girl's body to the car, Fujio noticed how very bright the night was. He couldn't see the moon itself, but the area was awash with light.

Fujio had never felt so grateful as now for all the things that he'd stored in the car: a small shovel, ropes, army cotton gloves, a safety helmet, raincoat, rubber boots, a bucket, wires, and so forth. They were just things that had caught his fancy, and some of them he'd never actually used. He'd acquired them working at odd jobs. He had placed them all in the car without giving it much thought, but feeling they might be of use someday in his work. Now they would indeed be useful.

Fujio stopped at the place he remembered. Then he struggled as though swimming though the grass of the dark woods. He recognized the manure dump and saw that the grass was growing thick. It was an irritating business, dragging the girl's body from the car and then carrying it 15 meters or so. He encouraged himself to be as crazy as possible in order to get it done. This time the shoe stayed on.

—I took care of your shoe...Now, don't forget to throw her schoolbag away!

His work at the seed store had given him some experience, and he could dig a hole more easily than most people could. Not many people know how hard it is to do. And digging a hole with a small entrenching tool is the most irksome kind of work.

—I just pray I can stay cool and calm. And I mustn't forget to bury her leather bag!

Fujio wanted to prove that he was a careful, thinking person, not at all like other people.

The combination of the small shovel and being out of breath with digging made Fujio think that perhaps he'd chosen the wrong place. He remembered the layout of this manure dump well enough. They'd piled some soft earth on a small slope to contain it all, but just a bit closer and you ran into the old hard surface of the earth. There it was difficult to dig down to the required depth. But if you went too far out, where some rotten boards held the earth dam, there was a danger of the corpse sliding down and becoming exposed. For a moment, Fujio was afraid that this was a bad spot.

The Miura Peninsula was full of hidden places where people seldom went—small valleys and thickets close to old forests, caves and shrines. If you were looking for somewhere to bury a body, there were plenty to choose from. It was foolish to think that this was the only spot. However, the work was already started and the hole had to be deep.

—That's all there is to it. If it's just a bit too shallow, the body will be found...

For Fujio, the hole could hardly be deep enough. He wanted it to be at least one meter deep, but he reached the limit of his strength at about 60 centimeters. He'd hoped that the ground would be soft, but it turned out to be harder than he'd expected. He'd neglected to wear his gloves, and so his hands, long unused to hard work, began to blister.

When he'd reached a depth of about 70 centimeters, his temper began to boil and he decided to stop.

—God, all this has happened because of this stupid girl!

Her body was face up, as though she was sleeping. Distasteful as it was to be face-to-face with her, Fujio still had to put her into the hole. He picked her up under his armpit and tried to get her in like that, but the body doubled over and fell bent into the pit.

That moment, it seemed as though his heart had stopped. Far off down the dead-end road, but heading toward him, Fujio could see the gleam of approaching headlights. He crouched down immediately.

—If it's a police patrol car, that's the end of me! If it's just a couple of lovers looking for a dark place, then it's unlikely they'll stop near some suspicious car. But there's just an outside chance that someone will remember my license number...

Fujio bent down, just like Yoshiko in the hole, lowering himself against the approaching lights broken by the trunks of the trees. He tried to hold his breath. Seen from his position, the lights seemed persisted and immoral. It was like being enveloped in a sandstorm.

Suddenly the lights stopped moving and remained motionless. Fujio's car was caught in the beams of light. For a moment he thought fearfully about the license number again, but a second later the lights were gone, appearing again only as the car smoothly changed direction.

'Scared off,' Fujio murmured and returned to his work.

The arduous task of digging the hole finally came to an end. All that remained was to fill it in.

—*What about burying her leather bag? No, that would be stupid. If I bury it with her, that will help in identifying the body. I should get rid of it somewhere else. On the way home, just a little out of the way, there are lots of wooded places. Not that the forest there's so deep, but with the dense growth of evergreen oaks, camellias and so on, hardly anyone goes in there. If I rip the bag apart and throw it away in pieces, it'll probably never be discovered...*

The work of burying the body was easier than digging the hole, but the most unpleasant part was trampling down the little mound of earth remaining on top to make the grave inconspicuous. His feet felt strange. He knew it was physically impossible, but Fujio had the sensation that he could feel Yoshiko's body pushing up against the bottom of his feet. He decided to replace the grass he'd torn up so as to further disguise the disturbed earth. He put it back so that the roots would quickly take hold.

His work done, Fujio went back out to the road, shaking the dirt from his trousers. He wiped his hands with a rag that was under the seat in the car and then sat down in the driver's seat to clean his shoes, carefully shaking out the soil that had gone inside.

His earlier baptism of fire in the car's headlights now gave him a peculiar calm. Yoshiko's leather bag was on the back seat. Fujio stretched his arm back to get it and check the contents. He thought he would dispose of anything with her name on it, but there was almost nothing of that sort. Her notebook contained mostly simple scribbling in the *hiragana* syllabary.

—*Maybe she slept during her lessons? No one would steal this...*

In fact, the only item with Yoshiko's name on it was her railway pass, which was attached by a string to the handle of her bag. Fujio removed only that and put it into his back pocket as a keepsake. Then he started the car.

His mind was blank except for thinking about a place to discard the notebook and bag. After disposing of her body, he even ceased thinking of those things as an urgent matter. His mind was occupied by his relationship with Yukiko Hata. It gave him a tremendous thrill, the greatest of his life, to think of her, and, at the same time, bask in this sweet calm after a brutal murder.

Fujio glanced at his watch. It showed 20:50.

—*I wonder whether this is a suitable time to visit? Yukiko said she often works late and that her younger sister working for a publishing company sometimes stays at her one-room apartment in Tokyo instead of coming home. At those times, Yukiko works into the night without stopping. I like that term she uses for her proper job—'moonlighting'. It's just the right phrase for Yukiko, with her modest, affable way of speaking. Well, at least I can go round to her place and see...*

The dirt remaining on his hands was hardly noticeable, and, for better or worse, he was wearing brown trousers and dark brown socks.

—If I say nothing, she probably won't notice. And if she does, I can simply say I happened to go into a rice field this afternoon...

Fujio put Yoshiko's bag on the back seat and placed some old newspapers on top of it. Anyone passing by who looked in would see only some scattered sheets of newspaper. With that simple precaution taken, he then opened the car window. There was no sound of waves, but the feeling of sea air filled the car.

—Sometime, I'll take Yukiko for a moonlight drive, and together we'll watch the moon set while standing on a bluff overlooking the sea...

Along the western side of the Miura Peninsula, you could only watch the sun or the moon setting, not rising.

—I don't know whether that kind of thing would be possible with Yukiko or not...I can hardly believe I'm thinking of such things just ten minutes after burying a body!

He started the engine and made a U-turn. His luck was holding. A patrol car might have come along, but it hadn't. Timing was on his side.

It was only a minute by car to Yukiko's house. As he approached it, the car's headlights picked out the darkly-dressed figure of a well-built woman walking in his direction. By chance, or because of his keen natural awareness, Fujio felt a warning shoot through him.

—That's probably Yukiko's younger sister coming home...

He continued driving slowly. When he noticed that the woman had indeed turned in at Yukiko's gate, he gave up and drove away.

Fujio reached his parents' house a little after 10 p.m. Instead of discarding the bag somewhere in the woods, he'd scattered pieces in a pond half covered with a lot of dry grass. It was close to a daytime bus stop beside the highway. He'd thrown what remained down the old well of a tumbled-down house a few miles from the burial site.

His parents were sitting up late, still watching the TV.

'I'm home!' Fujio called.

'Where have you been, Fujio?' his mother replied, coming to meet him with a worried expression on her face.

'Everything's OK. I was visiting a friend, that's all.'

'You know I worry when it gets late. I think that you might have had an accident with the car...'

'It's OK. I don't drink, so I won't do any drunken driving.'

'Yes, I always think what a relief that is.'

—*That's right. Be relieved by anything trivial!*

Instantly, Fujio started feeling angry again.

'Would you like some dinner?'

'I don't need any.'

Fujio hadn't eaten anything proper, but he wasn't thinking about food; nor did he feel hungry. He thought he must be under pressure from that other business and went upstairs. In a corner of his room was a basket his mother had put there for his dirty clothes. While Fujio was taking off his trousers and socks, the idea flashed to him that his mother would notice the dirt and say, *Fu-chan, how did you get all this dirt?* He wondered what he could tell her.

'Oh, I was playing in the sand, Mama,' he muttered to himself and laughed.

Fujio was in the habit of examining his pockets before putting things in the basket. It wouldn't do for his mother to find a 100 yen coin, a condom wrapper, or something like that. Now he found Yoshiko's train pass in the back pocket. In the plastic holder, there was also an ID card with Yoshiko's picture on it. He thought he would be scared when he looked at it, but in fact he didn't feel anything. Yoshiko stared out at him with her slits of eyes and her slack, expressionless mouth.

'Even if you'd stayed alive,' Fujio said to her, 'you'd only have had a worthless life!'

However, when he saw her address, his curiosity was aroused. He knew the area and even the actual apartment building. Some kid who lived there had once stolen his bicycle and Fujio had gone round to beat him up. The boy's parents had said they would bring assault charges against Fujio, but he had replied that he would tell everyone that their son was a thief if they did that, and so they had given up.

Presently, Fujio's mother came up to his room and told him that the bath was heated. Fujio said he would take a bath, thinking how he must totally destroy the evidence of his work. His hands and feet were quite dirty.

Submerged in the hot bath, Fujio felt rather strange. In spite of the violent deed he had committed, and the scrape on his left hand from the bushes that testified to that, there was no real feeling in him of what he'd done that day.

—*Was it only a dream? No, because I have proof that it wasn't—Yoshiko's identity card hidden in my room under a cushion. But without that, it could have been just a few hours' fantasy...a hallucination...a dream...*

Fujio enjoyed his bath and then went back to his room. His feeling of calm remained a mystery to him and he thought that somehow or other he needed to confirm reality. Perhaps the girl's parents were already making a fuss about her not returning home. He wanted to check on that situation. Fortunately, having once been there once a long time ago, he could recall the location perfectly. He knew just where the apartment block stood. It was built in one of the steep little valleys that dotted the Miura Peninsula. It looked like a stage prop and could be seen clearly from the road that wound around the cliff below. Fujio very much wanted to take a look at it. As luck would have it, the road below the block was a busy commercial street, and lot of cars passed by even this late at night. There would be nothing peculiar about his car being there.

Before that, however, Fujio burned Yoshiko's ID in an ashtray. He didn't smoke but just had the ashtray there for convenience. He flushed the ashes down the toilet and then cut up the plastic train pass with scissors, putting the pieces into a paper bag. Then he waited for his parents to fall asleep.

Fujio didn't make a move until after 1 a.m. He went quietly down the stairs and out of the front door. Once in the street, he felt refreshed. He swung his arms and stretched, breathing in the heavy smell of spring. On his way to the parking lot, he threw away the remains of the plastic card bit by bit, discarding the paper bag itself in a trash bin.

He got in his car and started the engine. As he drove along towards the valley, Fujio imagined the flashing red lights of the patrol cars that would be stopped outside the apartment block. Then the dream would become reality. Yoshiko's apartment was on the first floor and he expected all the lights to be on.

But when he reached her place about ten minutes later, there were no patrol cars to be seen and not a single light visible anywhere on the first floor.

Chapter 7

FROZEN GROUND IN SPRING

F UJIO slept exceptionally well that night and awoke early the next morning to the sound of a bush warbler's song. His whole body tingled with an extraordinary feeling; it was a mood that told him he had absolutely nothing to fear, nothing to have misgivings about in the whole world. It was because there had been absolutely no response to yesterday's incident.

Of course, Fujio opened the morning newspaper somewhat nervously. But he couldn't find anything relating to what had happened. Nor was there anything about it on TV. As he considered the matter, it seemed quite natural for it to be that way. If they made a news story about every person who didn't come home, it would be a 24-hour-a-day program. He felt a twinge of disappointment, but he soon managed to recover his good spirits.

These days, when girls don't come home for a night or two, their parents don't immediately assume that they've been murdered. That was just as well, since someone as notorious as Yoshiko would have had many such occasions, and if her parents had called the police each time, they would simply have got a scolding from her.

However, such reasoning was too elaborate for Fujio. He had come to believe he'd hallucinated the whole business. It's said that if you kill someone they will appear in your dreams, bent on revenge, and attempt to crush your chest or wring your neck, or something like that. But Fujio's refreshing sleep the previous night had been the same as usual; he had been totally undisturbed by nightmares.

And today was a spring morning at the height of perfection, filled with sparkling golden light. Fujio had always regarded the bush warbler as a talkative kind of song bird, but the one he could hear today was really crying out incessantly.

Fujio decided he would visit Yukiko Hata during the morning and take her a huge armful of spring flowers. She was always at work, sitting in her quiet house that seemed to exclude the world outside, and he wanted to show her how gorgeous was the coming of spring. He would grasp the very world of spring and give it to her.

While eating his breakfast, Fujio realized that there might be a problem with Yukiko's difficult sister, the editor.

—If she's off work today, then she could be at home. And if that's the case, then the best thing will be just to hand the flowers to Yukiko, thank her for the morning glory seeds she gave me, and leave...

Most of the time, Fujio couldn't stand the usual polite, silly talk that such moments required, but he could perform well enough when it was necessary.

He left the house a short while later, taking a kitchen knife with him. It didn't concern him in the least that Saburo, who was always so precise, would notice it was missing and would likely spend the whole day searching for it. He drove to a place he'd been to in the past, where he could gather some flowers. He knew where just the right daffodils grew in part of a field on a hill overlooking the sea along a twisted road. The daffodils on the Miura Peninsula blossomed only from January through February, and the ones growing in abundant wild clusters on the slopes facing the ocean were the most fragrant, even though their season had already ended. The flowers in that field resembled the wild daffodil clusters, but, due to the lateness of the season, both their color and size varied somewhat. Only the fine fragrance was the same. He reckoned it would not be bad simply to pick some flowers; but to cut them down with the knife that he had brought along would really amount to theft.

—No other flowers are as cheap and as fresh as these! In the shops they sell larger flowers, but they totally lack the real daffodil fragrance—and daffodils without fragrance are a fraud...

Fujio had neglected to tale along any wrapping paper; he could only lay the flowers on the floor of the car as though .they were a bunch of onions. But the flowers soon filled the car with a dizzying fragrance.

As he drove towards Yukiko's house, Fujio passed close to where Yoshiko was buried. That worried him a bit, but it was no problem as long as he didn't actually go to the spot.

Just as he was approaching the house, he knew he was in luck. Yukiko's younger sister was just leaving on her way to work. He could hardly imagine better timing—both this morning and last night—but so as not to attract her attention he drove on past the house at normal speed. It was about 10:30.

—Nice work she has, that lets her set out this late! It'll be noon by the time she gets to Tokyo...

Her clothes were slightly peculiar for going to work. In spite of the lovely day, she was fluttering along like a bat in a black coat. The sleeves and body of the coat were sewn together in a way that was rather difficult to fathom out. She was smoking a cigarette.

—That's hardly a look that would find approval with the locals, even if we were closer to the city! It takes a lot of work to become popular and it's so refreshing to see someone who starts off badly and doesn't seem to curry popularity.

The world censures the good person who makes a mistake, but heaps praise on the wicked person who does something good! She must already know that kind of thing and doesn't mind being adversely criticized. Notoriety first is the best way!

Fujio waited until the figure of the bat had completely disappeared around the corner before he approached the house. He stepped inside the front door feeling as though he had come home, and announced himself with words that came spontaneously and naturally to his lips: 'I'm back!'

Inside, there was a kind of human presence but no answer. Then Yukiko's face appeared at the end of the corridor and he called out again.

'I'm back! I've brought you some daffodils,' he said, holding out the flowers without even a string tied around them.

'Oh, how magnificent! Thank you so much,' Yukiko said.

'Can I come in? The daffodils are only an excuse. I really just wanted to talk with you.'

'Yes, of course you can.'

'I won't interrupt your work and I won't stay long.'

Yukiko put out a cushion for Fujio in her usual workplace. He sat down, asking if Yukiko had air-dried the cushions.

'Yes, so you noticed?'

'I really wanted to see you. A lot has happened since last time.'

'Oh?' Yukiko said without further inquiry. 'Where did you find such marvelous daffodils at this time of the year?'

'I got them from a friend who grows them at his place.'

'Thank you very much,' Yukiko replied, apparently believing him. 'You say a lot has happened. What kind of things? Good things?'

'No, not so many good things happen to me.'

'Well, let's hear about them. You'll feel better if you talk about them.'

'I can't talk about them to you. I could tell some guy, perhaps, but not you. I won't tell you.'

Fujio was excited. He realized immediately it was very simple: what he *wouldn't* say would keep Yukiko as a friend.

'Why can't you tell me? I mean, didn't you come here to talk?'

'I just can't. I'm a showoff, that's why.'

Yukiko lowered her head slightly, but said nothing.

'Where were you in February, on Valentine's Day?' he asked.

'Where? At home, I suppose.'

'I guess I should have come to see you then.'

'Why? Did you want some chocolate?' she teased.

'No. But if I had come, you might have proposed to me,' Fujio replied.

'I'm an old-fashioned kind of woman.'

'What do you mean by that?'

'Just that it's not my style for the woman to propose.'

'Then I suppose the proposing is up to me.'

Yukiko was silent.

'As a matter of fact, I had a dream,' Fujio said.

'What kind of dream?'

'I dreamt that you said, "Let's get married."'

'I hardly ever dream,' commented Yukiko.

'I wonder why not? I often do.'

'Shall I tell you why you dream?'

'Sure.'

'It's because you sleep too much. If you only sleep for six hours or so, you won't have any time for dreaming. I only sleep for a short while, and so I don't dream. Sometimes, though, I think that I'd like to dream about my dead father. It's sad that he never appears in my dreams.'

'Now that you mention it, I probably do sleep too much. And my dreams are full of guys I don't want to meet.'

'Are there so many people you don't want to meet?'

'There sure are.'

'Well, not me!' Yukiko exclaimed, surprising even herself.

'But even for you, there's that guy who jilted you for another woman he married. You don't want to meet him, do you?'

'Not especially, but I really don't care either way. If he's living a happy life, that's fine; that makes me think that it didn't have to be me, after all. And if he's *not* happy...'

'*Not* happy?'

'...then it's all the more sad. But I'd leave him alone.'

'I guess you often treat things that way.' Fujio said. 'Myself, I couldn't do that. I used to fight when I was a kid, you know. Now, someone I can't stand...Well, I'll fight against the other guy until he shuts up and agrees with my way.'

'Until he shuts up? You mean you hit him?' Yukiko asked, quite amazed.

'Yeah, sometimes,' Fujio said. 'There are too many damned fools in this world. But I suppose you think I'm a fool, too.'

'We're all fools, not just you.'

'You know, if someone else said that I'd get mad. But it's strange. When *you* say it, I don't get mad; in fact, it gives me a kind of nice, warm feeling.'

'That's because your heart's becoming more compliant,' Yukiko replied. 'I don't think that 'being a fool' is necessarily bad. After all, geniuses have both happiness and mishaps; fools have the meaning of their own existence and the happiness of being a fool.'

'I wonder...'

'What I mean is 'Let it be,' or 'Let that person be as he wishes,' Yukiko continued. 'Those are words I learned from the Bible. Jesus used to say that kind of thing all the time.'

'Let it be?'

'Yes. There are other ways of putting it, like letting go, not interfering, leaving something alone, postponing a problem, overlooking something, not obstructing, forgiveness, releasing, leaving as it is, leaving and dying...The words are wonderful and include all those meanings. It was an expression Jesus liked and it's used lots of times in the Bible.'

'Wasn't he kind of passionate and strict—the type who would force people to do the right thing by grabbing them by the back of the neck?' Fujio asked.

'No, nothing like that!' Yukiko replied. 'The words I was just saying are something different from 'love for God.' I think we humans are all corrupt anyway and we leave God. Irresponsibly, I thought it was like my case—'leaving the state where love existed'—but my interpretation was wrong. I didn't want to leave; I was abandoned. I left, thinking things would be better. For me, no matter how things go, if the result is good I'm satisfied. I didn't leave him out of anger or spite.'

'That's not true!' Fujio exclaimed. 'If someone stabs them in the back, anyone will get mad and feel bitter,' Fujio said. 'When that guy threw you over for another woman, I'll bet you were really upset?'

'Maybe,' Yukiko said. 'But I still knew that walking away from it was the best thing to do. And that enduring the pain itself was a gift from the man who left me.'

'I don't want to argue,' Fujio said, agitated. 'But you say to leave things alone when there are things in the world you just can't leave alone.'

Yukiko was silent. It seemed to Fujio her silence was encouraging him to say more.

'You know, come to think of it,' he went on, 'I once had a child, even though I said I didn't.'

'You *once* had one? What do you mean?'

'I mean my wife was pregnant. I was looking forward to her having the baby, but then in about her fifth month she had a miscarriage.'

'That's terrible...' Yukiko murmured.

'It was bad. I didn't really feel like a father then. And I was moving from job to job, so I wasn't home very much. Then, when I learned that she was in hospital and I got back, she's already had the miscarriage. I suppose I wasn't really so broken up about it.'

'But your wife must have been disappointed, wasn't she?'

'I doubt it. She told me later that she got pregnant around the time she was anyway thinking about divorcing me. But then she thought it wouldn't be right to raise a child in a home without a father, so she started thinking of not divorcing. Anyway, about then she had the miscarriage. After it was all over, she was relieved and said she felt free to divorce. But it was a strange story. If it was all over and emotionally settled, she could have had a divorce right away. But she stayed with me, looking as though she wouldn't even kill a bug. At the time, she was fooling around with some guy on the side. I only realized that later.'

Yukiko said nothing. Fujio, looking into her face to find a reason for her silence, saw traces of tears in the corners of her eyes.

'Hey, what's this?' he said.

'Nothing, really. Only...I always think how cruel life is.'

'Well, mine is just ordinary, not especially unlucky. I think women are all like that. My wife wasn't particularly bad or anything. It's just that you are different, really special.'

'Was the baby a boy or a girl?'

'A boy. The Head Nurse told my mother. She said "How sad for your son. But his wife can have another soon enough." Only that's not about to happen.'

'Well, you don't really know about that. At your age, you will have lots of chances to have children.'

'I just can't get rid of one strange idea,' Fujio told her.

'What's that?'

'Well, I feel that I shouldn't have another kid. If I did, it would really be a shame about that other kid. Especially if he was really mine. He didn't even get to see his father's face. He wasn't even held once by his mother. Didn't get to eat or run or laugh or sing...or hold a girl. Just ended his life right there. Not breathing one gulp of the air of the world. That's really too cruel for a human being! Would you say I should just 'let it be' for that matter, too?' Fujio said fiercely.

'How did she come to have a miscarriage in her fifth month?' Yukiko asked. 'I haven't had a child, so I don't really know, but I've heard it said that that's the safest time in a pregnancy.'

'She said she was riding on the train and that it was shaking a lot, and she hit her stomach against a partition between the cars. That's what I heard, anyway.'

'Did the train stop suddenly?'

'To tell you the truth, I wasn't much interested in that, and I didn't ask any caring questions. She blamed me a lot because of that. Hey, that's enough talk about that. I mean, even if the kid had lived, there wouldn't be much for him, would there—what with his father out of work and his mother sleeping around?'

'But if you are alive, there are always some wonderful things for anyone, you know.'

'Oh, yes? Tell me what's wonderful for *you*? You want to marry someone, don't you?'

'Not at all. It's nothing like that. With me, it's just tiny things, really—things like the flowers blooming, or walking along a hill where you can see the ocean at sunset. Just tiny things like that. No matter how rich you are, you can't buy any work of art that's as splendid as that.'

'I don't know about things like that,' Fujio replied.

'No, men generally don't. They have other pleasures, like bicycle races or mahjongg or drinking.'

Fujio laughed and then said, 'Anyway, my life has been terrible recently.'

'Has it?' Yukiko said, looking him steadily in the face. 'You have to pardon me. I really don't like giving advice on other people's lives. My mother told me a long time ago not to hand out advice to people. She said that men seldom consult with others about their personal affairs, and women should never take the role of a listener too easily. It's just not good manners.'

'OK. From now on, I'll come here as little as possible.'

'No, that's not what I meant. Please come and have tea, any time. I can't give you any alcohol, however. The only liquor we have here is my sister's. And I don't secretly give that to my guests. Even people who are close need to keep their manners.'

Sooner than he'd expected that day, Fujio said he would be leaving. As he was getting up, Yukiko said, as though she just remembered, 'You came at just the right time.'

She went off to the kitchen and returned with a 'Honey Pot' brand jar of jam.

'Can you get the lid off this jar for me?'

'What's the matter with it?' asked Fujio.

'Well, I stopped by to visit Mrs. Iwamura who lives next door, and she asked me if I could open this jar for her. She said that it was something her daughter left for her, and when she was going to use some of the jam she couldn't get the lid off. Her daughter had just carelessly left it there without loosening the lid for her. The old lady tried all kinds of things, but she wasn't strong enough, and she says that she had to eat her bread for three days without any jam.'

Thinking that it would be nothing to open the jar, Yukiko had told the woman that she should have asked her sooner and tried to open the lid then and there, but it was stuck hard with sugar and would not move at all.

'I told her that I'd open it and take it back, so I brought it home and did everything I could, even putting it under hot water, but it didn't work. I'm sure you're strong enough to open it easily.'

Fujio took the jar and twisted the cap. His hand slipped; the lid didn't move.

'Let me have a damp towel,' he said to Yukiko.

He took the towel from her and eventually succeeded in twisting the plastic lid.

'Yes, it's true! Men *are* strong, after all,' she said in thanks. 'Usually, I think *I'm* pretty strong.'

'Hmm. Fancy making this kind of unfriendly lid!'

Fujio's brow wrinkled as he read the maker's name on the label—'Shimada Foods Company'.

'The manufacturer ought to be more careful for the sake of the elderly,' Fujio said. 'It's really bad that old lady spent a whole three days without jam on her bread.'

Fujio looked sullen as he went to the hallway.

'Will you be by this way again?' Yukiko asked.

'I'll try not to. My reason for coming round here never seems to be very good,' he said, smiling. 'Still, I suppose I will.'

Fujio examined the newspaper every day and became gradually more confident that the business about Yoshiko Yamane would not appear.

He would come downstairs for breakfast when Saburo had already started bustling about opening up the store for business. And every morning when his eye caught sight of the pages of the newspaper scattered on the dining table, he briefly felt as though a thorn had pierced him. However, although nobody thought it unusual if he didn't read the newspaper, it wasn't so easy to turn off the TV. He braced himself ready for the news broadcast about a missing person, but nothing of the kind appeared, even as spring steadily ripened.

—*In this warmth, Yoshiko's body will quickly decompose. And pretty soon— perhaps in ten years or so—even if her body's unearthed, no one will know who she was or where she came from...*

Fujio truly felt that the whole matter had no significance at all. If he thought of it at all, his act merely justified the kind of life he had led thus far. Fujio wanted to return to the kind of sex life he had led in the past. Clearly aiming at him, Saburo had started talking about working in the shop with his father, but Fujio chose to ignore such talk.

One morning, Fujio dragged the telephone over by the *kotatsu* heated table where he'd just finished his breakfast and dialed Yoko Miki. The last time he had met her, she had told him she couldn't give him her telephone number because her parents were so strict. Of course, it wasn't really her parents she was talking about—she was thinking of the bad scene that might take place if her husband was there.

'I understand that much,' Fujio had told her as they parted. 'If a man answers, that will be your father, and I'll hang up without saying anything. But if I want to meet you, what can I do if I don't know your number?'

Finally, she had given it to him, but he was somewhat concerned whether it was right or not. However, after five rings, a woman's voice answered the phone and Fujio smiled in satisfaction.

'Yoko? It's me.'

'Who's calling?'

She knew perfectly well who it was and her voice was slightly tense.

'Wataru. Have you forgotten? That's all right. At times like this, I have to say "Has your husband gone out?"'

'Come on! Are you still playing games?'

All of a sudden her voice had warmed up. It now sounded as though it could melt polar ice.

'That's right. Last time when we were together, you said you'd had a chance to become an actress. Well, a long time ago, I wanted to go to acting school myself. I'll tell you, there aren't many people who can play along with as much feeling as you give it. That's the truth,' Fujio said smugly.

'And why didn't you go to acting school?' Yoko asked. It was clear from the time of day, and also by her tone of voice, that her husband had left.

'Do I have to tell you?' Fujio murmured. 'I just don't have the looks for it.'

'Mm, that's not true. These days what they want are character actors.'

'And if there were more people like you around me who said such nice things, my life wouldn't be so messed up.'

Unluckily, Saburo appeared at that moment. Hearing this talk about the theatre, he said in a deliberately loud voice, 'Hey, are you going to be on the phone all morning?'

Fujio felt a sudden desire to fling the telephone at Saburo so hard it would break up and couldn't be used for a while. But then he completely reversed his feeling.

'Oh, OK,' he said, quite controlled. And then, to get Yoko's sympathy, he said, 'I'm being scolded by someone around here. In fact, I wanted to call you earlier, but this winter I caught a really bad cold.' Lying came perfectly naturally when Fujio talked with her.

'Well, I had a cold, too. Were you coughing a lot?'

'Yes. I thought I was about to come down with pneumonia and I'd have to go into hospital. The doctor told me to be very careful until the weather warmed up. Still, I can't afford to take it easy at home. They're always after me to get to work. When I was on the verge of pneumonia, I thought how bad it would be if I died and couldn't meet you, so I just held on and got better. Really.'

Yoko said nothing.

'Just hearing your voice today makes me feel better. I wouldn't mind dying, even.'

Convincing people that he had a weak constitution had long been one of his tricks for getting easy work.

'Can we get together today?' Fujio finally said.

'Sure,' Yoko replied. 'My parents had to attend a Buddhist service for a relative in Shizuoka; they'll probably stay there overnight.'

'Is that right? What luck! I'll pick you up this afternoon at the same place as last time. About 4:30?"

'All right.'

'Thanks,' Fujio answered. He was smiling as he put the telephone down.

—*That fool Saburo will be mucking about in the shop today, working, but I'll be out with a woman!*

The thought satisfied Fujio as a way back at Saburo for annoying him. But he still had to pass the time until his date at 4:30, and there was no reason to stay locked up in his castle on the roof. He needed something to amuse himself and there was nothing very amusing at home. He finished his breakfast and set out in his car a little before noon.

Generally, this time of day would be too early to find students wandering about, but it was the middle of the spring vacation. Fujio decided there would be plenty of young women with too much time and no money walking about and wondering if there wasn't something interesting to do somewhere. The girls liked to go shopping and watch movies with their friends. They knew that it was best to go out alone when they were looking for a man, but they were afraid of rumors. They would figure that a guy might buy something for them—even just one shoe—and they knew perfectly well that it was difficult if two girls went out together.

Actually, for Fujio, buying one shoe was not a fiction. A few years earlier, he had bought one shoe for a girl he picked up on the street; and even though he only took her to a hotel, she was terrifically happy. On the way home, she had told him he could call her any time if he would buy her another shoe.

But today, Fujio couldn't even find anyone like that. He tried calling to a couple of girls on the street, but they ran off without a word and looking back at him with a weird expression. He decided that he would have to change his tactics, and so he turned his car south and out of town.

For Fujio, apartment blocks were great hunting grounds. It might seem that there would be lots of eyes watching, but the reality was that people in apartment blocks knew nothing about one another's lives.

For a while, Fujio cruised about. Then he suddenly spotted a woman carrying a child going up the stairs and into the furthest door on the 2nd floor of a block. He drove around the corner to the next block and stopped the car.

As he got out, he looked around inside the car and found a bag of pamphlets that the clerk at a prefab housing show had given him when he was walking around one day to cool off. With a stroke of genius, Fujio thought of using them as a device.

On the door of the second floor apartment there was a plate with a man's name written on it—'Yoshimi Kanaya'. He read the name, listened for a moment to the sound of a baby crying somewhere at the back of the apartment, and then pressed the buzzer.

'Who's there?' came a voice.

'Excuse me, but I've come with a questionnaire.'

He rated his chance of success at only fifty per cent, but the woman half opened the door.

'I'm sorry to disturb you when you're so busy, but I'm doing a survey for the CCC Company.'

The name was completely Fujio's fabrication. He reckoned that the letter 'C' had some healthy associations with vitamin C. And recently there were companies with three-letter names like 'CCC' everywhere.

'I wonder if I might come in?' Fujio said in his most ingratiating manner.

'Yes, all right,' the woman replied.

As Fujio stepped inside, with a smooth manner and without revealing the slightest evil intent, he slid the bolt closed on the front door.

'Actually,' Fujio began, 'my company is doing an opinion survey of wives in this apartment complex.'

The woman probably thinking that it was impolite for her to just stand there, kneeled down on the edge of the hallway step.

At that moment, Fujio attacked her.

He heard the sound of the bones in his hand as they struck her. He was afraid she would cry out, but he realized that because of his suddenness she could barely catch her breath. There was no time for him to consider the shape of her nose or whether she was ample-breasted or not. Roughly, he tore her skirt up to the waist and heard the sound of its buttons popping. With her skirt in his hand, he covered her face.

'Now don't make a sound!' he told her. 'If you do, everyone will come and see you like this'.

The woman struggled with the free lower half of her body, but the movement simply helped Fujio do his next work more easily. Even in his boiling excitement, he felt a cold fear gripping him: his awareness seemed numbed, and all the feelings of a normal person were frozen. He veered from light to heavy, from hot to cold, all the movements of his diseased body dictated by something from millions of years ago. At that moment, he was only dimly aware of himself, and his senses only seemed to be half present. His angry fight against that eventually gave an extra edge to his pleasure, but he felt the woman was insulting him by letting him be in that condition.

Finally, the woman was still as death. Fujio knew he hadn't killed her. He removed the skirt covering her face. She was breathing, but her gaze was fixed and her face expressionless.

The baby had stopped crying some time earlier.

Fujio stood up, quickly arranging his clothes. From his crib placed inside an enclosure, the baby was looking directly at him, his face strained but smiling angelically and making a pleased 'Ahhh' kind of sound.

Fujio quickly opened the door and went outside. Luckily, he didn't meet any neighbors. He ran down the stairs without attracting attention. Silently, on his rubber-soled shoes, he moved along rapidly, keeping close to the wall. Then he walked slowly to his parked car. He started the car and drove away.

'Busy, aren't we!' he muttered to himself.

He felt depressed that the woman had made no sound at all. Of course, he was thinking only of himself, and if she had made a sound it could have caused a lot of trouble. He would have promptly smothered her, and that would have stopped her breathing. If he had killed her in an apartment block in the middle of the afternoon, he could have done nothing but abandon the body and flee.

When he picked up Yoko at the appointed time, Fujio was still deeply fatigued and said very little.

'What's up? You don't seem very well,' Yoko said.

'I've only just recovered from an illness,' Fujio told her, slick as always with his lies.

'Will you be all right, out like this? Shouldn't you be taking a rest?'

'It's OK. Hearing your kind, sweet voice I feel better already. How about you? Did your husband go out as usual?'

'Yes.'

Incredibly, she had answered naturally to Fujio's genuine question.

'Really? So you *are* married?'

'Don't be like that! We just promised to act in that way.'

'Of course, that's right,' Fujio said, repairing the lapse. But he was beginning to get disgusted by her viciousness. 'We have lots of time today. Where shall we go?'

'Anywhere's fine, but...'

'But what?' he asked.

'The other day, a friend of mine said there was an interesting hotel just outside Fujisawa.'

'You have great friends.'

'Well, she's married. She said her husband is so busy at his company that he doesn't come home every night until early morning. So in the evenings she goes to the culture center and...enjoys herself.'

Doesn't her husband notice?'

'No. He's proud that his wife is studying *The Tale of Genji.*'

Normally, Fujio would be swift to ridicule such a simpleton of a husband, but today he deeply despised the wife who was stabbing that kind of naive husband in the back.

'I think my friend's to be pitied. A husband should come home every night, and not too late,' Yoko said.

'You mean, if he comes home early, there's time for some leisurely sex?' Fujio said with a smile.

'No, I don't mean that. But when there isn't even time for having dinner, I think there's something wrong. But that guy is just in a hurry to go to bed.'

'Well, it's really good that they go to bed as soon as he comes home!' Fujio laughed salaciously.

'On the other hand, if they have sex, then he has less time for sleep, and his house is a long way from where he works.'

'Mm...'

'So the wife doesn't feel like she's really married; that's the problem.'

'But isn't her kind of solution cruel for her husband?'

'But not coming home is bad of *him*,' Yoko insisted.

'What's bad is the company or government that creates such a system.'

'Yes, but there are husbands who come home earlier, too.'

Her reply cut off any rejoinder from Fujio.

'This friend of yours. Tell her she ought to marry someone like me.'

'Yeah, you're right. I'll tell her there's an available unemployed guy.'

Fujio was often reminded that an unemployed man was liable to be treated as barely human. When Fujio heard that line from Yoko, he felt the blood start pounding though his temples. The idea of going to a hotel with her was barely enough to sustain his patience.

Yoko guided them faultlessly through the maze of roads that had probably once been just paths through the paddy fields, until they reached a white building called the 'Hermitage Hotel.'

'Let's try Room No.15; she said it was really fun,' Yoko said. But only three or four of the more than twenty rooms in the building were empty.

'No.17 is vacant,' Fujio said as he drove slowly along to select one.

'OK. Shall we try that? I wonder what it's like?'

While Fujio was locking the car door, Yoko, with her experienced hands, put a cover over the car license plate.

'I wonder what it's like?' Fujio said as he walked behind her up the stairs that led only to that room. Then, as he stepped from the landing into the bedroom, he exclaimed, disappointedly, 'What is *this!*'

For a moment, he could only stare. He thought there had been a mistake. The hotel was the kind with rooms decorated like a stage to create the atmosphere of one scene or another. The hotel where he had first gone with Yoshiko gave the impression of a room with a view of New York from over the Hudson River, some pastoral spot under a bridge. And for Fujio, the Hudson River was certainly preferable to this.

'What the hell is this?'

The room duplicated a school kindergarten. Large dolls of a pierrot, a bear and other figures were suspended from the ceiling. The walls were painted yellow, and on one there was a whiteboard. On another, there was a board with various papers for writing practice stuck on with little magnets. The letters were in Japanese and in the Western alphabet, written in bright colors to please children. But what really caught Fujio's eye was the 'jungle gym' play frame in one corner of the room.

'Could *I* climb on this? It looks pretty frail,' Fujio said, testing its strength.

'Isn't it cute!' said Yoko. 'I really like this room.'

'Like it's full of little brats?'

'Why not? I might even have been a kindergarten teacher!'

Fujio stood there bewildered. Yoko went to the board and arranged the letters to spell out his phony name and hers, side-by-side—'Wataru' & 'Yoko'.

'Now, Wataru-chan. Sit down,' she said, pushing him down with her hands. 'So, Wataru-chan. What did you do at home yesterday?'

Fujio replied at random. 'I massaged Dad's back, I pulled out Mom's gray hairs, I kicked my big brother's leg and I burned the cat's whiskers.'

'Oh, you mustn't kick your big brother's leg, Wataru! And it's awful to treat the cat like that. And did you brush your teeth before going to sleep?'

'Look, look...' Fujio said, imitating a child and opening his mouth wide. Yoko approached him, pretending to look. Fujio grabbed her arm and roughly pulled her down on his knees.

'Now, now, you mustn't do that to teacher!' she said, and Fujio kissed her. 'Come on, Wataru-chan, take off your clothes and have your bath!'

'But I don't know how to take them off,' Fujio replied.

'Oh, that can't be true! You're in kindergarten now, and you have to be able to take off your own clothes.'

'Show me how, teacher, please! If you do it first, then I'll know how.'

'Oh, what a child! Well, I suppose I'll have to do it. Teacher will show you how, and then you'll be able to do it properly.'

Fujio watched dutifully as Yoko proceeded to remove her clothes. But he felt dissatisfied that his level of stimulation didn't match the enthusiasm of her play acting.

'And will Wataru-chan take a bath, too?' Yoko asked him.

'You go first,' Fujio replied abruptly, dropping the kindergarten game. He was tired of playing the fool.

'OK. I'll go first.'

Naked and on tiptoe, Yoko disappeared into the bathroom.

While he waited, Fujio stood up and went over to the play frame. He examined its construction.

In a little while, Yoko returned, wrapped in a bath towel.

'Hey, how about dropping that towel and getting up on the jungle gym?' he said with a laugh.

'Won't it collapse?' she said, frowning.

'So what? There's no sign saying not to climb on it. I can't tell whether it will break or bend, but, anyway, this room is ours until morning.' He seemed to be inciting her on.

Yoko accepted the challenge and began to perform. She was very athletic. Wanting to please Fujio, she climbed inside, climbed on top, straddled it, sat high up and looked down on him.

'Nice view from up here!' she said, striking a pose.

'From down here, too!'

'I'm just light enough. The poles won't bend or break.'

But Fujio was getting more and more depressed. He felt no compunction about Yoko's husband; you could call it the husband's responsibility—or just bad luck—that he had an immoral wife. That was all there was to it. But, for a while, Fujio saw in Yoko the image of Midori. He wondered what she had been doing secretly in that quagmire just before they divorced. When he looked up at Yoko, he felt that he could just about guess.

—*Without her husband around she can be marvelously lively, but in front of her husband she's a living corpse. For men other than her husband she can be on fire sexually. A wife like that might be cheerful and lively with a guy she meets on the side, but only has a dull attitude toward her husband. To the other man, she presents her husband as someone to laugh at. She cheats on him, takes the money he earns and hides it away to use on her lover. She thinks of herself as being irresistibly charming because a guy speaks to her. She's haughty, and yet she thinks that she's kind and generous when she does anything at all for her despised husband...*

'What's the matter?' Yoko asked, noticing Fujio's somber mood. 'What are you thinking about? Don't you feel well?'

'I'm OK. But that's not the point. It's just that, all of a sudden, I'm not so interested. When I think of you doing all that provocative stuff in front of your husband, I start losing my interest.'

'But I don't do this kind of thing for my husband,' Yoko replied lightly.

'Why not?'

'I keep up the usual front. If I didn't, he'd be asking me where I learned all that. You know how it is.'

'Do all women deceive their husbands like that?'

'Mm, well, not *all*. But most women like to have fun.'

'And it's not fun with their husbands? Wouldn't it be better to get a divorce and live with someone you can have fun with?'

'No, no. I can't do that,' Yoko said in a loud, flurried voice. 'The reason he's my husband is that he's better than a playboy. He's got an income and a stable social position.'

'And you just exploit that, you mean?'

'What's wrong with that? Everybody does it,' Yoko said.

'That's not for me. I think a family should be pure, existing without calculations like that.'

'Only a man without any means says something like that,' Yoko said.

Fujio was at a loss for words.

'What's the matter? Why so quiet all of a sudden?'

'I want to leave,' Fujio said.

'You mean you're that offended by what I've just said?' Yoko said with a big smile on her face.

'No, not particularly. But even though we made it together last time, now it just doesn't seem like much. That's what I feel.'

'All right. Sure. I can take myself home any time.'

'OK. Do that. You can go back alone. Since I'm here, my mood may change and I can find someone else who's more fun. I'll stick around.'

Yoko exploded in anger.

'Listen. Don't joke around with me! You brought me out here, and now you're telling me to go back home alone? You'd better not try making a fool of me.'

'It's your doing. You told me this was a good hotel.' Fujio laughed. For some reason, he always became very calm at this point in an argument.

'But you were the one who asked where I wanted to go,' Yoko said.

'You mean I should take you home? OK. Then I can go somewhere else, to another woman's place, after I take you home,' Fujio said.

Without saying a word, Yoko began to dress. Fujio paid the bill using the payment equipment set up in the room. A voice emerged from the machine, sounding like a parrot. 'Thank you very much,' it said in a strange tone, 'We hope that you will visit us again. Please take care as you leave.'

Yoko rode in the back seat of the car, far away from Fujio. As soon as they were away from the hotel, Fujio said in an agitated voice, 'How about I let you off at the nearest station?'

'Stop kidding. Take me back where you picked me up today.'

'Now, just a minute. I told you I wanted to find another woman tonight.'

'That's no concern of mine,' she shot back.

Fujio glanced at her in the rear-view mirror. She was looking out of the window with an angry expression on her face.

'OK. Better yet, I'll take you to your house. And I'll give a gentlemanly greeting to your husband.' Fujio grinned at his own witticism.

'More than kind of you,' Yoko said.

'Then get out right here.' Fujio braked to a stop, but Yoko was in no such mood.

'I'm not getting out,' she shot back.

'No? Then do as you like,' Fujio told her.

It was not so much that Fujio wanted to call up another woman immediately, but with Yoko still sat there he began to feel that she had destroyed any chance of a date with another woman that night.

'You really talk wild. You tell me that you have a husband and then you turn around and do something bad and don't even seem to realize it.'

'Everyone does it. And I get taken out more than you think. Some famous guys have fallen for me. Sorry I can't tell you their names.'

'So why haven't you switched over to them?'

Yoko said nothing, but Fujio could feel her anger.

'Men all fool around. A woman has to be pretty dumb not to know that. It's hopeless!' Fujio laughed. 'Then how about it? I'll make a clean break and you stop this wild kind of life.'

'You're a pest! I hate that kind of meddling. It's my business what kind of life I lead.'

'In spite of having a husband?'

Suddenly, Fujio realized clearly how much he was discovering his former wife in this woman named Yoko. At that moment he was playing the roles of husband and adulterous lover at the same time.

'I want to tell you something,' she began. 'If you don't want to lose your wife, don't be so domineering. Even if you find out she has a boyfriend, don't make a big fuss. Otherwise, you're sure to lose her.'

'So even if a guy knows, he shouldn't mention it to her, but just put up with it?'

'Sure. From the wife's point of view, there are lots of cases where she just goes on living with him out of pity.'

'Oh, really? Out of pity?'

Fujio fell completely silent. He was thinking of his ex-wife. He had still been young when he and Midori divorced, and he hadn't understood a lot of things. It depressed him to think of that.

—*At the time, I didn't have a regular job and I was having relations with other women. It wasn't that I didn't support her. I considered Midori incomparable and I'm sure I was satisfying her enough sexually as well. I didn't understand why she would want to divorce me. And now, several years on, Midori's actions and psychology have re-emerged in my life, and I understand it all for the first time. I have no idea what kind of person Yoko's husband is, so I can't compare myself. And even if I did make comparisons, there's nothing I can do about my past. But one thing is clear: out of dissatisfaction, the woman was coolly cheating on me. Either she didn't think it was bad, or she considered it a kind of punishment...*

'What are you thinking about?' Yoko asked, uneasy with Fujio's silence.

'Nothing.'

'If you have another woman besides me, there's no reason to feel so depressed,' she said.

Fujio still said nothing.

'What's the matter?'

'Nothing's the matter,' he said.

'OK. Then drop me off at the nearest station. No problem.'

Fujio felt that Yoko sensed the muddy flow of dark, thick feeling collecting in his heart. Fujio knew that he couldn't easily change his own plan.

'Where are we going? Tell me the truth,' Yoko said.

'You said to take you back to where I got you, and that's what I'm doing.'

With that, Yoko relaxed slightly.

As though drawn in the direction, Fujio headed toward the grave of the girl he'd murdered. To him, it was also the shadowy grave for something he had never been given in this world—a thing that was true, sincere, honest, and decent.

—*If my wife had been faithful, I suppose everyone would have sneered and blamed me. And in that case, they might have asked if I had been faithful...*

Deep inside, he was aware of many questions like that. Perhaps his education was to blame: perhaps the circumstances would have been different if he had been taught perseverance. But in so far as he was no longer a child, his actions had to be his own responsibility, no matter what.

When Fujio turned off the main road and on to a dark street, a look of fear touched Yoko's face.

'Tell me where we're going!' she demanded.

Fujio laughed. 'I have a little errand to do.'

Yoko understood by his smiling face that he was looking for a place where he could relieve himself.

'You can stop anywhere; you don't have to drive into the woods.'

'I'm the bashful type,' Fujio said. 'And the moon is out.'

He stopped the car precisely at that familiar place.

—It's now spring, and Yoshiko is sleeping in the frozen ground right here...

Fujio looked out of the car window. He felt as though the light of the moon, just past full, was making some kind of sound.

'Hurry up,' Yoko said.

'Don't rush me,' he replied.

Fujio got out of the car and walked into the woods, pretending to attend to his need. He was making sure there was no strange odor where he stepped. He felt in his pocket for the thin rope he had brought with him. He determined that there was nothing out of place in the forest and then returned to the car, still hesitating to take the final action.

'Listen. I've thought it over; let's try to get along,' she said as she lowered the back of her seat.

'That's good.'

'But you came out here thinking the same thing, didn't you?'

'Well, yeah,' Fujio replied.

Yoko took off her sweater and unzipped her jeans. Her breasts shuddered seductively.

'That's enough, really,' Fujio said again, in a flat tone. 'You don't have to be totally unreasonable.'

'I'm not being unreasonable. Isn't this the right thing to do?'

'What do you mean, "the right thing"? You're still in that mood, I suppose,' Fujio said, laughing. Yoko seemed to take it as one of Fujio's jokes.

Suddenly, Fujio leaped on top of her, smiling. For a moment, he just stared at her face. Then he struck her violently in the solar plexus. He was still smiling; he had no idea whether or not she cried out. All he heard was the sound of air being ripped from her lungs, or perhaps it was the pounding of her heart.

Then he was holding the rope in his hands. He was aware of himself calmly thinking that the slender rope was not the best, but with a rope that thick there would be no pain.

For seconds, or maybe minutes—he had no idea—Yoko moved hardly at all, even though Fujio was fully prepared for the terrible struggle which would drag them to the depths of hell. His muscles were tensed as hard as rock.

He waited a long time and then opened the car window. Yoko's face was as white as alabaster in the moonlight.

'Now you won't be cheating on your husband any more,' he said out loud.

Chapter 8

DISTRESS SIGNALS

TO celebrate Easter, Yukiko made some rice dumplings with bean jam, which was an unusual thing for her to do. This year, Easter came on the first Sunday after the spring equinox. Combining Easter with the preparation of these rice dumplings was an odd mix of East and West. Yukiko was not a Buddhist, but she felt her cooking was appropriate for a Japanese. She had boiled the beans and roasted the sesame seeds. For a true Easter feast, she would make colored eggs at her church along with the other members.

Tomoko had said that it would be all right to buy the rice dumplings at a confectionery shop. However, the oddly-shaped dumplings made at home always seemed tastier, and because they were homemade she was in the mood to take some to Mrs. Iwamura who lived next door.

Yukiko went to Mass on Easter Sunday. It was attended by twice as many people as usual, and that was her weak point. Attending church was fine, but she found meeting people and saying a few words a strain and so she slipped away and returned home a little after 11 a.m. She expected Tomoko to still be asleep, but in fact she was already up and about to go out.

'Where are you off to?' Yukiko asked, surprised to meet her in the hallway. She had intended to prepare brunch for them both.

'Something's come up all of a sudden,' Tomoko replied. 'I expect I'll be back by dinner time.'

Yukiko said goodbye and saw her sister off. She had the feeling that Tomoko was *not* going to meet a man, but, since that was a possibility, she didn't inquire further. Yukiko was a little concerned because it looked more likely that Tomoko was going off to visit a sick friend. She decided she would save the sea bream sashimi she had prepared for them for dinner, and for brunch she would make an omelette for herself instead.

She ate alone, listening to the cries of the bush warblers in her garden.

Tomoko returned just before 7 p.m.

'You're late,' Yukiko observed. 'I was beginning to think you wouldn't be back for dinner.'

Tomoko looked exhausted. She went straight to her room and stretched out on her sofa without even changing her clothes. She told Yukiko that she'd planned to return home earlier but that something had come up and she couldn't make it.

'Then have a bath; there's nothing better when you're tired.'

'Yes, I think I will,' Tomoko said. 'There's something I want to talk with you about afterward.' It was rare for her to say something like that.

When she finished her bath, Tomoko put on a robe over her nightgown and joined Yukiko at the dining table.

'Was someone ill?' Yukiko asked her, starting the conversation as she poured a glass of beer.

'Actually, someone has a problem.'

'Who is it?'

'That girl Mitsuko Kawahara who used to work at the office. Haven't I mentioned her before?'

'Is that the one you always call 'Mitchan?'' Yukiko asked, recalling the girl who had been Tomoko's capable assistant.

'That's her yes. But she got married and is now Mitsuko Kanaya. She's living in Yokosuka.'

'What does her husband do?'

'He works in a bank. A solid type. At first she didn't find him very interesting, so she wasn't too keen.'

'And things aren't going well?'

'Well, he improved after they had a child. But something's come up,' Tomoko sighed, lighting a cigarette. 'I want to hear what you think about it.'

'About what?'

'She was attacked by a psycho.'

'A psycho? Where?'

'In her own apartment.'

Yukiko couldn't quite grasp the situation.

'It was an incredible mistake for her to make,' Tomoko went on. 'She thought he was a salesman, you see. He was really calm and convincing about it, and so she let him inside, and then he suddenly attacked her.'

Yukiko turned and served Tomoko a bowl of miso soup with crab in it; but, beyond that action, she wanted to avert her face on hearing such a story.

'How awful,' she said.

'And her baby was there. It's too small to talk yet. Mitsuko says her milk has dried up completely. She called me on the phone and her voice sounded like a mosquito buzzing. I almost didn't recognize her.'

'Did she call the police?'

'That's the trouble. So far, she *hasn't*. And her husband's against telling them.'

'So he knows about it?' Yukiko said, thinking that half the problem would be cleared up if the husband knew the details.

'Yes, but his thoughts seem to be going round and round. I told her to inform the police. It's no good for anyone if she keeps quiet—and since her husband knows, I couldn't see any problem.'

'I would have thought so, too.'

'But her husband is thinking about appearances. And Mitsuko herself isn't all that strong.'

'Did she get a look at the man's face?'

'Yes, she did. But she can't say what kind of person he was. When she thinks of it, she starts shivering and feels sick, she says, and so she can't be pushed too far.'

'She should have called for help. Was she in danger of being killed?'

'She said she was afraid to scream and be seen in that state by the other people in the block, so she didn't.'

'Well, I've never been married, so I can't say much, but at least it's good that she wasn't hurt or killed,' Yukiko said. For a while she made hardly any response, trying to compose herself.

'Yes, that's true,' Tomoko replied. 'I said the same thing. If the child had been hurt or taken away, there wouldn't be any question of keeping quiet about it. But since nothing like that happened, she calmed down and told herself it was just an unfortunate mishap—something like that—and she should just get on with her life.'

'Maybe she ought to think of it as something like being hit on the head by a sign board that blows down outside on a stormy day. I've heard of things like that happening to people.'

'It could have been worse if she'd fallen for another guy and was having sex with him—only she hadn't, and so it wasn't really a big deal. But her husband doesn't seem to see it that way.'

Absent-mindedly, Tomoko put down her chopsticks and stubbed out her cigarette. Almost immediately she took out another.

'At a time like that, I would imagine you really become husband and wife,' Yukiko said. 'The husband is the only person who can help an injured wife like that. It would be really great if he could say: "Don't think anything of it. Don't make a big thing of it."'

'Ah, Yukiko. What a dreamer you are!'

'But something like that isn't such a big thing, is it? Surely it's a lot easier than paying off the loan on the apartment?'

'These days, men aren't made of such strong stuff,' Tomoko said, sounding a bit masculine.

'Nobody's that strong,' commented Yukiko. 'I think I know how I'd want to be treated by my husband if I was in a situation like that. When you think of what really bad things could have happened, you can be grateful.'

—*If the criminal had reacted to Mitsuko's ineffectual resistance, it would have been unbearable for Mr. Kanaya to have lost both his wife and child…*

'It would help if he could be strong,' said Tomoko. 'Anyway, he's saying that he can't go to work at the bank tomorrow. But he can't get a doctor's diagnosis saying he's sick. He keeps repeating that if he takes time off without good reason, he'll make a bad impression at work. In that kind of situation, there's not much that can be done. And, being Mitsuko, she's sure to worry that this guy will come after her again and cause trouble until they move out of their apartment.'

'Of course, it's a terrible situation.' Yukiko said. 'But I'm sure the best thing they could do is inform the police.'

'We went round and round on that. She says she can't sleep at night thinking that a person like that is on the loose. But when it comes to being questioned about everything by the police, she thinks it's best not to say anything.'

'You can give up one thing and make sure something else takes it place; isn't that the way life goes?'

That night, Yukiko perspired in her sleep; a thing that rarely happened to her. Perhaps it was because the temperature had risen. Usually she slept soundly through to morning. The days when Yukiko had worked in her garden, it was not unusual for her to sleep solidly for eight hours. But a little after 2 a.m., after dreaming and perspiring, Yukiko got up. She supposed that there was no direct connection between her perspiring and her dream, that it was merely that her futon was too heavy for the temperature.

And yet her dream had had a peculiarly coherent—if frivolous—plot, and the odd thing was that she should remember it so clearly. Mr. and Mrs. Kanaya had been the main characters. She had never even met them in real life, but it seemed that the husband was short and had a bald spot in the middle of his head. Mitsuko was taller than her husband and wearing a light blue apron. She was holding her second child in her arms. Somehow, her first child didn't appear in the dream, and Yukiko knew that the baby was the one conceived in the rape incident.

—*They say you had a child?* Yukiko asked, confused in her dream.

—*Yes.* Mitsuko answered in a casual way, a gold tooth shining through her smile.

—*And whose child is it?* Yukiko astonished herself at her outspoken question.

—*Why, my husband's, of course!* Mitsuko replied with a vulgar laugh.

—*Do you really think so?* Yukiko had no idea why she asked such an impertinent question.

—Well, at first it wasn't his, but later it became his. That's because we're husband and wife.

—Oh, yes, of course, Yukiko agreed.

And that was the end of the dream.

Yukiko imagined that this absurd dream was some fulfillment of her own wishes; it involved really terrible problems.

She remained seated in bed, waiting for the memory of the dream to clear from her mind. Even so, it took a considerable while for her to get back to sleep.

The next morning, while she was preparing breakfast for Tomoko before she went to work, Yukiko asked, 'That Kanaya couple—is Mitsuko bigger than her husband?'

'No, the opposite. The husband's medium height and build, and Mitsuko's small.'

'Is the husband going bald?'

'Not in the least; he's not that old.'

After seeing her sister off, Yukiko decided to make one of her rare shopping trips to Misaki. She was out of kitchen cleanser, and the scrubbing sponge was old and dirty. Also, Tomoko had asked her to get some mocha coffee beans.

Yukiko always went shopping in the morning. She couldn't really say that she didn't like places where there were crowds, because there were not so many people on the edge of town where she lived. But if the supermarket happened to be full of people when she arrived, she always felt like going home immediately without doing any shopping.

The bus came along, and in about ten minutes Yukiko reached the busy shopping street where she could generally get everything she needed. While she was walking around the supermarket, she suddenly remembered that her gardening sandals were about to fall apart. Even in a household consisting of only two sisters, and with no one else likely to see, Yukiko felt uncomfortable using something ragged.

She was looking for some new black sandals when suddenly she heard her name being spoken from behind her. Turning, she saw a small, girl-like woman with round eyes standing there.

'Oh! Hitomi!' Yukiko said.

'How are you?' the woman asked.

'I'm well, thanks, and yourself?'

'I've often thought of calling you, but time just slips by. How have you been?'

'I'm getting along as always, just doing the same things.'

Hitomi Sakata used to be in the choir at Yukiko's church. Her father worked at the fish market. A pleasant woman, she had willingly helped out at the bazaar and other social activities. People said that after she married she had stopped attending church. The rumor went that her husband wasn't fond of the idea of her going there.

'Where are you living now?'

'Do you know the apartment just beyond the water tank?'

'I think I've seen it as I've passed by.' Yukiko said.

'Well, my husband bought a place there three years ago, just when it was built.'

'The scenery around must be nice,' Yukiko said, 'because it's quite high.'

'I wonder,' Hitomi said, 'if you have time to come back with me for a chat? I have my car here, and afterward I'll take you home.'

Yukiko had an unusual psychological habit: although it always annoyed her to have to make an appointment to visit someone else's house, it was no burden on her if she was invited through a chance meeting.

'Alright, just for a while,' Yukiko said. 'I'd like to see your new place.'

'It's not so new. It's three years old now.'

Hitomi went around with Yukiko as she shopped and then led her to the parking lot and her small red car.

Hitomi's apartment was on the top floor of the building. In spite of the thin clouds that day, they could see all the way across Koajiro Bay to Sagami Bay. There was no division between sea and sky; the perfect stillness of the clouds and the waves deprived the scene of any feeling.

'How lovely!' Yukiko said. 'I can't see the ocean at all from my place, even though I'm next to it. You never get tired of looking at the ocean.'

'That's right. But I understand what people mean when they say that the sky and the sea are fearsome and sad, and that they disturb them. Man-made things aren't so sad, but nature seems to reflect your life back at you right into your heart.'

'But some people say they are saddened when they see the lights of the city,' Yukiko said.

'Which type are you?' Hitomi asked.

'Oh, from my house, I can't see either the town or the sea.'

'You're lucky.'

'Yes, perhaps I am.'

A moment passed. Then Hitomi asked, 'How's everyone at church?'

'Nearly everyone is well, I think, but Mr. Tashiro lost his voice because of an operation for throat cancer. And Mrs. Ashida has vision problems due to her diabetes. She doesn't come to church very often.'

'That's too bad,' Hitomi replied.

'But she's cheerful enough. She jokes a little and says that since her eyes went bad she's been thinking that the day of her death will be a pleasure, because on that day it will be so wonderful to recover her sight!'

'She's really quite a character, always full of hope.'

'I don't know if it's hope or what, ' said Yukiko. 'But truly, when she lost her sight, she thought she wanted to die. I heard that when she said that to the priest, he told her that life didn't belong to her and that she mustn't do anything foolish. He said it's not something you own by making or buying it, so you don't have a right to do whatever you want.'

'Mm. I wish I'd heard that a month ago,' Hitomi said.

'Why do you say that?'

'Well, a month ago, I learned that my husband had a child by another woman.'

'How did you find out?'

'Someone called me on the phone, without saying who it was. When I think of it, I suppose the woman herself must have asked someone to call to say that. That person said I could find out the facts for myself, and then hung up before I could say anything.'

'And was it true?'

'For a while, I didn't say anything, but I could guess. Up to then, my husband said he didn't want any children, but sometimes when he saw a little child in town he would stop and stare. I was going insane.'

'I don't mean to pry into your marital affairs, Hitomi, but couldn't the two of you have children?' Yukiko asked.

'That's the problem. A year and a half after we were married, I thought of going to see a doctor. But my husband said that was no good. It might seem reasonable to know exactly what the problem was, but he didn't want us to blame each other. He said that what happens between two people is their joint responsibility.'

'You have a very good husband.'

'That's what I thought. But it seems that the result of his affair was to show that I'm the one who is at fault. All that talk about it being two people's responsibility...that was just decoration.'

Hitomi explained that about that time she had learned the name of the person on the phone. She recalled the name because her husband had made many calls to the woman. She owned a coffee shop called 'Erica'.

'He was talking about her one-year-old child. I thought everything was all right and never imagined that the child was *his*. I thought that maybe her husband had died, or that she was divorced.'

After receiving that strange telephone call, she had thought about it a lot. Then one day, at the time her husband left the bank, she had watched the place from a little distance away. Pretty soon her husband had appeared and gone directly to the Erica coffee shop.

She thought he would just spend half an hour or so inside and then come out. But in fact he didn't leave until after 10 p.m. While the woman was locking up the door of the shop, Hitomi's husband was holding her baby, who was wrapped in a padded blanket, and nuzzling it. Then they had gone to the woman's apartment. Hitomi went to the train station and returned home directly. Her husband had finally returned about midnight.

'At a time like that, a woman can be cruel. I put on a straight face and asked him where he'd been. He said he'd been playing mahjongg with some people from the office. I asked him where he'd played and he said, it was a place near the office where they often went. Then he asked why I wanted to know in a perfectly straight way.'

'That's the way it goes,' Yukiko replied.

'It's just so pathetic. Hiding the fact that he has another woman...I respected him and married him, and I've respected him all this time we've been together. Respect...I know, that's when you feel warm and close. I'm just so bitter now that it's all fallen apart. I don't despise him. I only feel that I hate what has happened, that it's destroyed my dream.'

'I understand,' Yukiko said. 'Something like that happened to me, but I wasn't married and so the hurt wasn't so deep. It healed, eventually.'

'I thought of you, all of a sudden, at that time—really—and thought I wanted to talk about it with you.' Hitomi said.

'I'm flattered that you thought of me, and if you had come to that messy place of mine I would have been very pleased. But, to tell you the truth, I'm not very qualified to help you. I mean, I've never even been married.'

'Oh, that doesn't matter. When you need someone's help, you don't think about whether they went to college or not!'

'Well, Hitomi, you're certainly not at a loss for words.'

'During that time, I thought about it around the clock. I thought I was in hell. It was so bad that I even fell asleep in the bath tub.'

'Now, that's dangerous. You might drown!' Yukiko said.

'I wasn't so distressed about the triangle relationship. Even after he lied to me, my husband said that he loved me. And I didn't feel like handing over my husband to the woman at the Erica. Either way, they know that I'm here. They have their relationship, even though they can't really get married. Anyway, I try to put it out of my mind.'

'Isn't that the best thing to do?'

'Yes, it is. But when I thought of the child, I nearly went crazy. The child thinks he's just like other children, of course, with a mother and father at home, and that at night they will all have dinner together, and on Sunday father will be at home watching television and napping. But one day, when he asks why things are not like that...Well, anyone would feel sorry for the child then. Who's responsible for putting him in an environment like that? When it comes down to it, I am. But I'm not the child's natural mother, so I thought that if I withdrew myself from them, everything would be all right.'

Hitomi was speaking in a low voice. Perhaps she was afraid of stirring up her own emotions. And yet, even though she was nearly speaking in a whisper, Yukiko could hear her just as well as if she'd been shouting.

'And did you do that?' Yukiko asked calmly.

'No. It would be the Christian thing to do, I thought, but I just couldn't. I was worn down, and just handing him over like that was too bitter. I thought of dying. If I died, then there would be no obstacle to my husband and the woman from the Erica being together.'

'That would be the worst kind of revenge you could inflict, to involve them in causing your death,' Yukiko said.

'Yes, I know that. But *I* didn't begin this conflict.'

'Of course not.' Yukiko paused. 'Living is such an agony,' she added in a murmur.

'You are the first person to hear what I'm going to say. The priest at church hears confessions, but since I'm not a Catholic any longer I would rather have you hear it than a priest I don't often see or really know,' Hitomi said. It seemed that her mind was made up.

'There's nothing to recommend me; all I can do is not repeat what you say. And that's because I live on a dead-end road in an out-of-the-way place,' Yukiko said pleasantly. She tried to put Hitomi at ease. She didn't intend to deceive her. She had long thought that when she wanted to speak about something, oddly enough she put on psychological brakes. Silence was best.

Hitomi went on. 'And then one day, I saw my husband off, just as usual. I went out, intending to die. Just as you said, there was another element in it all, but on the one hand I intended to die for the child's sake, and so I wanted to be as casual as possible. I wanted something heavy just to seem as light as possible, that's what I thought. I thought that making a big production out of it would be too shameful.'

'How did you intend to do it?'

'I was going to drown myself in the ocean.'

'Why that?'

'I felt it was dirty to die on land. I took along two umbrella holders. I can't swim very well, and I intended to fill the sacks with little pebbles and tie them around my body to weigh me down. If I'd succeeded, then my body wouldn't have floated up. I remember once some university yacht ran aground on the rocks and none of the dead came up. I thought that if I went along that road to the beach no one would notice.'

'I'm sorry I didn't meet you then. If I had, you might have changed your plan because of me.'

'Well, something like that did happen. A man I didn't know at all appeared. He said that if I walked straight on as I was going, there was only the ocean, and that was fine if I intended to drown myself. He laughed and said that if I had anything else in mind, that was not so good.'

'And you hadn't said a thing?'

'Not a thing.'

'What a strange person. I wonder how he knew.'

'I wanted to be inconspicuous. I just wore ordinary, plain clothes, and I walked along looking straight ahead—with my usual shoes, my handbag...'

'Of course.'

'Then he gave me a ride in his car. And we went to Yokohama together.'

'Was he young?'

'No, a little under forty, I felt. He told me his name, but I forgot it. I wasn't interested, either, since I intended to die that day.'

'Of course. When you encounter someone without knowing their name or anything, you can see their real character.'

'He amused me, I suppose you could say, and tried to raise my spirits, and... well...did all sorts of things...' As for the rest, Hitomi spoke through the intensity of her large eyes.

'Yes, I understand,' Yukiko laughed. 'You can do anything, say anything, if it is to save someone who doesn't want to live.'

'Yes, you understand. He told me all kinds of lies. He took me for a fine meal at a nice hotel where we could see the harbor, and said I was pretty and praised me, and finally got around to saying, "There are lots of men like your husband. Don't think twice about turning him over to his mistress." He just laughed.'

'Really?'

'The way he talked...I felt repelled. There is one thing I know and that is that only my husband would say he likes me, and, secondly, that man said it only as a joke. Even so, ever since that day, I've changed. It's not because I thought that something better would come along if I discarded my husband. Can you understand?'

'Yes, of course I understand, because it's you.'

'So even if life attacks me like a some bad dream, I'm not going to worry about it. They say that love is like getting hit by lightning. But this thing is like three of us getting hit by lightning and being electrocuted. It's bad luck, but it's just part of living.'

'Very likely that's because you felt as though you died once. If you think you've died, then no matter how you live you will still be calm.'

'I still haven't consented, and I've not said that I will give my husband a divorce. Our life is going on as usual, and he comes home looking a bit embarrassed. And then on Mondays he goes off happily to the office. And on the way back, he's probably delighted to get a look at his child's face. On Saturdays, he comes home very late. I think he gets a little taste of being a parent. I sympathize with him, but I don't say a thing. We look out at the ocean and we seem to be like idiots facing each other as we eat our meals. We don't even know what we're eating, and we don't speak at all. Of course, we don't quarrel, either— but somehow that's even sadder.'

'You've been experiencing quite a life,' Yukiko said. 'And I have to congratulate you.' She walked out to the balcony. 'How many apartments are there in this building?'

'Sixty, I believe,' Hitomi replied.

'I imagine that in every home in this beautiful building with its view of the ocean there's a story like yours. No one could write it all down, never.'

Yukiko's voice was as sincere as her words were naive.

Chapter 9

A Woman on Display

FUJIO found it impossible to remain at home. All day long there was noise from the construction work in the family store. His mother said that since Fujio's little house was up on the roof, if he went up there and closed the door it wasn't likely he would hear much. But Fujio had nothing to do, and when he sprawled out, the sounds echoed through the floor and walls as though they were slicing into him.

Mixed in with the building noise, he could hear Saburo's tense voice giving directions to the workmen. For many years, Fujio had started to felt sick whenever he observed someone behaving or talking with total conviction. And to make matters worse at such times, even his mother chattered happily out front, either to humor Saburo or out of happiness with the household prosperity. When Fujio saw women wagging their tails that way for the boss, he became very displeased.

From time to time, Fujio's thoughts turned to the women he had known. He couldn't comprehend why there had been no commotion about the two who had disappeared. That was something he hadn't anticipated at all. As the days passed, he felt more and more regret for having killed them.

First there was Yoshiko, killed because she was going to raise a fuss. And yet she had been so happy to take a hot tub bath on the way home from school. Even though she hated school, he felt that she might have had some kind of life ahead if she had enjoyed getting into a bath so much.

Then there was Yoko. Clearly, she was one of the better girls that Fujio had laid his hands on. And while he had found her pretensions disagreeable, he thought it would have been all right to have left her alive and meet her now and then. When he strangled her, it was a surprise how much easier it was than with Yoshiko. He would have thought that Yoko would cling more strongly to life than the young girl.

But when he thought of the woman named Hitomi, he considered himself to have been truly incompetent. He had felt so good at the time that he had failed to ask for either her address or her telephone number. She was such a naive and pleasant woman; he deeply regretted not being able to contact her. And, quite by chance, she thought of Fujio as the benefactor of her life. At least it was he who had saved her from suicide. When they were about to part, she'd said, 'I'm quite a different person from what I was this morning.' He thought that was generally true, even if a bit exaggerated. But there was no way to contact her, and he could hardly expect to meet her on the street by accident.

Fujio was also thinking remotely of Yukiko Hata, and that was like being in a village and dreaming of the mountains. Lately, he began to have the feeling that she was more remote and not a person he could easily go to meet.

If Fujio remained at home, he vented his ill temper on his mother, and so he wheedled as much money from her as he could and tried not to stay home. At the same time, both his mother and father felt relieved when Fujio was not there. Yokosuka was a small city, and Fujio was afraid that he would meet some talkative friend. As a result, he extended his radius of amusement as far as Yokohama.

Possibly because his life had become so irregular, Fujio had recently been suffering a lot from diarrhea. He wasn't aware of having eaten anything bad. The likely reason was some case of nerves that he couldn't guess at.

That day, he slept until past noon, and then, on the way to Yokohama for amusement, he experienced severe cramp in his stomach. He got out at the next station, ran to the toilet, and relieved himself. Then he went back up the steps to the platform where a warm breeze was blowing, redolent of the scents of spring. He stood enjoying the breeze for a while.

Then, as he waited for the next train to arrive, Fujio ambled to the end of the platform. There he came across an interesting scene. At the same level as the platform, there was the open window of a beauty salon. It was generally thought that the best place for a beauty salon was close to a train station, and in this case it seemed that the place had been constructed with the idea of exhibiting its customers to people waiting for a train.

Fujio grinned, finding this quite amusing. He had once heard that the women in the Yoshiwara brothel district used to be exhibited to customers behind wooden lattice windows; it would make a good story to say that he had seen something so very like that. Fujio was not the only sightseer: there was also a young man wearing a kind of farmer's trench coat, with the belt pulled tight, and sunglasses that concealed the expression of his eyes. Fujio was certain that he had casually strolled about the platform and then stopped at that spot with the specific idea of peeping into the beauty salon window.

The shop appeared to be fairly busy with customers; around 3 p.m. was a good time for women at home to visit the beauty salon. Fujio was amazed at the nonchalance with which the customers came to the place.

—*I don't really think they should display themselves without putting on some makeup! Wrapped up in a towel or a sheet to their necks, with things like chicken bones stuck in their hair for the permanent, and calmly showing themselves to strange men...It's like saying 'Sure!' when someone says 'Please take your clothes off'...*

Fujio was not in a hurry to do anything else, so he enjoyed gazing at the scene. He let several trains pass and toyed with the idea of stationing himself at the entrance to the beauty salon to pick up any woman that caught his eye. But just as he was thinking that, one woman came to a seat before a mirror next to the window. Fujio couldn't see his own expression, but he felt his face was twitching. He was looking straight at Midori, his ex-wife.

She appeared to have put on some weight since he had last seen her, and her face looked more lustrous. He hadn't noticed her until then because she had been over in the hair washing area. Her hair was still wet, and it was longer than it had been when she lived with him.

For a moment, Fujio felt that he should hide somewhere. But from where he stood in relation to the sunlight, *he* could see *her* perfectly well, while from her position it would be difficult for *her* to distinguish *him*. His old anger flared up again. He decided to stay and view her impudently for a while.

Fujio noticed that all the hairdressers working there were male. Midori was having her hair cut by one of them. Perhaps they were on close terms, for it was clear as could be that she was chatting with him in a most friendly way. Was it about her hairstyle? The man took a bundle of her hair and piled it on top of her head. Midori looked pleased to be fondled.

—*Hmm. I've seen some breed of dog that looks just like that—when it's petted on top of its head, it yelps with pleasure...*

Fujio was managing to remain calm.

—*Today we put animals behind glass in the zoo. That's as bad as it was for the girls on display in the old brothels of Yoshiwara. The same thing, really...*

Just like Fujio, the guy in the trench coat had let the next train pass; he continued to stare at the beauty salon window.

Then an old man with a cane added himself to the group of voyeurs, and that sent Fujio into a sudden rage. He was of medium build and was wearing a tattered old jumper. He carried a stick because of a leg that seemed to be lame. He took extremely short steps, and that alone conveyed a feeling of age. His mouth hung open stupidly as he stared, blank-faced, at the women in the show window. To Fujio, he seemed to be the archetype of a dirty old man, even though the look on his face was not particularly lecherous.

—*Ah, I know those types from the time I worked in the hotel! Both the old man and the guy in the trench coat look calm on the surface, but they're the kind with revel in secret, erotic pleasures...*

Fujio sketched a scene in his mind of waiting outside the beauty salon to catch Midori. Smiling, he would call to her:

—*Hey! Aren't you pretty! Got yourself all polished up at the beauty salon?*
—*Mind your own business! What are you doing here, anyway?*
—*Oh, I was just thinking how you liked being treated by that hairdresser. You looked so pleased. I thought I'd take a closer look to check how pretty you are.*
—*Well, don't tag along! There's nothing between you and me now at all.*

Fujio suddenly envisioned burying Midori in the grave along with those other women.

—*It's not such a lonely spot; I buried Yoko there—No.2—and there's still room for one more...*

That cemetery from which you could hear the sound of the sea was Fujio's secret harem. Fujio hated the women who were buried there, but at the same time he also loved them.

—*The light of the setting sun never reaches them, but they're forever stroked by the wind blowing through the scattering of trees. And in that beautiful place at night, the stars came to look down on them...*

Fujio abandoned the thought of seducing Midori. It would take some time before her wet hair was finished, and, no matter what he did, Midori wouldn't go along with him. He boarded the next train to Yokohama.

He didn't find anything very entertaining there. However, as he walked around a department store, he slipped a cassette tape into his coat pocket, and then a small, folk craft glazed dish priced at 7,500 yen. As soon as he stole the dish, he began to wonder where in the world it might find a suitable home.

—*I suppose the best thing would be to give it to Yukiko rather than let it fall into the hands of some stranger. Yes, I'll give it to her as a present the next time I meet her...*

Without much interest, he made a cursory tour of the store. Then he went to the rooftop flower and garden shop and looked at the orchids. One rather arrogant-looking specimen in a pot seemed to be urging to be picked, but just as Fujio was about to put out his hand, he felt the presence of someone behind him and he stopped himself. He bought a cup of cheap coffee from a vending machine and sat down on a bench to drink it. He thought about the shameless scene at the beauty salon and the sensibilities of the women who went there.

—*It wouldn't have had to be Midori; anyone else there would have been fine. I would have approached the first woman who came out, simply to amuse myself...*

But Fujio was not in the mood to put that idea into action, not immediately. He hadn't brought his car, and without a car he was like a snail without a shell.

Fujio had an early supper of noodles. Then he killed some time playing pachinko and going to a game center. It was one of those days when nothing seemed to go quite right. He hadn't been very hungry when he ate the noodles and the idea was to save money by eating something cheap, but in a while he began to feel hungry again. He went into the train station building and ate some tasteless Chinese-style fried noodles. After that, he thought he would have been better off spending his money on a steak to begin with.

Fujio avoided returning home, having no wish to encounter his brother-in-law. Saburo's schedule changed from day to day, and there were times when he remained in the shop until 10 p.m. to finish up his work. Fujio's mother did everything she could to make things go smoothly for her hard-working son-in-law, like taking him tea and snacks during the day. When Fujio arrived home, they would all suddenly fall silent. His mother, while attending to Saburo, would only ask if 'Fu-chan' wanted some tea.

At last, Fujio boarded a train for home about 9.30. At that time, he would probably not have to meet Saburo.

Most people got off at the stations along the way, so the car gradually emptied and it became possible to walk down the central aisle. Fujio decided to change seats for one more convenient for getting off. The trains on this private railway line had the reputation of swaying violently, and perhaps that was why Fujio suddenly stumbled over something in the aisle.

He managed to avoid himself being thrown to the floor but, because of the shaking of the train, he was unable to recover his posture and was thrown in an ungainly manner toward the exit. His wrist slammed into the metal support pole. As an automatic reflex, Fujio looked around to see where he had blundered. He expected to see some bundle in the aisle, but all he saw was a high school girl in her school uniform with her feet stuck out in front of her. She was looking toward Fujio with a stupid expression on her face. Her fat ankles in their white socks were still not withdrawn, and she sat there blankly with room for at least half a person on either side of her. Fujio slowly walked over to her.

'Could you move up a little bit, so that I can sit down' he said to the girl in a moderate way.

The girl moved up without saying anything.

'I banged my chest badly,' Fujio whispered. 'Your feet are sticking out. I've probably broken a rib. Would you please do me the favor of getting off at the next station?'

Several other passengers had immediately turned to look at Fujio when he stumbled. They had lost all interest when they saw him calmly taking a seat.

'What do you want me to do?' the girl said, perplexed.

'Well, that's what I want to talk to you about,' said Fujio, smiling at her.

For the first time, Fujio felt that he had met the culprit responsible for his child's death. When Midori was pregnant, she had fallen down in a train as Fujio had nearly done just then, and as a result of the hard blow to her stomach she had miscarried—or so she had told him. Fujio was working away from home at the time, and since their marriage had psychologically been half broken up already, Fujio had received no detailed explanation about the circumstances of the miscarriage.

In any case, this girl must be pretty insensitive. She was a senior high school student, and yet she had no idea of how to sit in a train. Until someone like Fujio came along and pointedly told her, she would sit there sublimely at ease without noticing that she was taking up the space for two people.

Of course, it was a lie that Fujio had anything like a broken rib. But if a pregnant woman had stumbled like Fujio did, the same tragedy could have befallen her son as it had to Fujio's. He said nothing more, and the two of them got off along at the next station like strangers, one after the other. Fujio waited until the platform cleared and then took the girl to one side.

'Now listen, young lady,' he said. 'Do you always sit that way in the train?'

'What way?'

'With your feet stuck out so that you trip people up.'

'I don't know,' the girl answered, with a faint smile on her face as though she was perplexed.

'How many tickets do you have?' Fujio asked.

'Huh?'

'Tickets. I asked how many you bought.'

'I didn't buy a ticket. I've got a pass.'

'And you have just *one* pass?'

'Yes.'

'Then how about sitting properly in *one* seat, eh?'

'But nobody else has said anything,' the girl explained.

'It's too much bother, that's why no one says anything. People would rather stand than tell you to sit in your own seat. Right? When it's not a day when the car is really empty, you should sit with your elbows touching the people next to you. Don't you understand that, my dear?'

The girl said nothing, as though she was sulking.

'Tomorrow, I'm going to have a doctor look at me. If there is some clear injury, I will have to claim some compensation.'

'But...'

'But what?'

'I can't pay compensation. I don't have any money.'

'Don't give me a story like that. If your foot hadn't been there, I wouldn't have stumbled. If it had been a car and you hit me, I think that you'd pay for the damage—you know that.'

She was silent.

'What does your father do?' Fujio said.

'It's just my mother and me, and we really don't have any money.'

'What kind of work does your mother do?'

'She's like a 'companion'—do you know what I mean?'

'Like at banquets?'

'Yeah.'

'So she must be pretty.'

'Oh, no, she isn't.'

'Do you have any brothers or sisters?'

'Just a little brother.'

'Well, if your mom's a companion, she's got some money. But if she doesn't, let's talk it over.'

'You mean a monthly payment?'

'No, you don't have to pay monthly. Some other kind of payment,' Fujio said with a smile. 'Well, I'll tell you what, you come to my place and we'll talk to my wife and decide.'

The girl seemed to relax a bit at the implication of Fujio being married.

'Where's your place?' the girl asked, since Fujio was about to get on the train again.

'The big condominium on the ocean side of Tsukuihama. Do you know where that is?' As always, Fujio said the first lie that came to mind.

'No. I don't.'

'That's OK. I left my car in the parking lot of a friend of mine just a little walk from the next station, and if I don't take it home, my old lady will get mad.'

Fujio continued playing the weak-willed husband, and so the girl consented.

'What's your name?' he asked.

'Kayo Aoki.'

'My, what a nice name. You say your mom's a companion? Which hotel does she usually work at?'

'I don't know.'

'I suppose she gets home late?'

'I don't know what time. I go to sleep before that.'

'So you only get to talk with her in the morning?'

'We don't talk in the morning, either. I go to school before she gets up.'

'Some family!' Fujio commented, but his sarcasm failed to reach the girl.

Fujio had not been particularly deliberate in his action. As he boarded the train, he glanced back to see if the girl called Kayo Aoki was behind him or was perhaps getting ready to run off. But in fact she was walking docilely after him.

They stood side-by-side in the train, but both remained silent. As Fujio got off, he gave her a wink. She followed him off the train. They passed through the ticket gate and she went with him out into the night.

Fujio was glad, now, that his car was parked at a place some distance from his house. If it had been parked as it was before, then when he started the engine at this time of night and prepared to leave, his mother would have thought it strange, and the old woman next door might have peeped out through her window. But no one would notice the car's movements at this distant parking lot.

'Sorry to make you walk,' he said, looking up at the sky as he entered the parking lot. Kayo walked silently on without the slightest expression on her face. Her way of walking could have been interpreted as though she was making an effort for his sake. There was no moon, and the stars appearing like sand between a scattering of clouds offered only a dim light.

Fujio let Kayo into the car and started the engine.

'Shall we go for an elegant night drive, then?' he said.

Perhaps because Fujio's words were trivial, Kayo said absolutely nothing.

'So there's just your mom and you? Where's your father?' Fujio asked as he pulled out into the road.

'He's not here.'

'Is he dead? Divorced?'

'Dead.'

'Had he been ill, or was he injured?'

'He drank a lot and died of a brain hemorrhage when he was thirty-four. Mom said she was relieved when he died.'

'Relieved?'

'It wasn't a severe stroke at first, but eventually he couldn't talk and he just turned into a vegetable.'

'Yeah, well you might say he was a fool, but he was her husband and your father.'

Fujio felt a fierce anger filling his body as he responded.

—*People like this are just accustomed to getting rid of unnecessary people, so the sick father was a burden to them. It's the same as Saburo thinking it would be fine if I was dead. When they ride on a train, they take up a couple of seats, and just casually stick their feet out so that people trip up. And if that results in a pregnant woman having a miscarriage, they just say: 'It's your own fault that you fell down!'*...

'Does it take this long to get to Tsukuihama?' Kayo asked uneasily when they had gone some distance along the dark ocean shore road.

'It's under construction. Usually I take the direct road, but now we have to take the roundabout route.'

He had passed the turn for Tsukuihama, and was now heading in the direction of Kenzaki.

'I've been thinking,' Fujio began. 'My wife is really tight about money. If I tell her that I've broken a rib and that you can't come up with compensation money, she'll probably raise quite a fuss, and that wouldn't be so good. So before we get to my place, I think it would be best if you and I just talk about it together.'

'How do you mean, "talk"?'

'Look. You're in senior high school, so you must understand. If you treat me right, we might get around the matter of money. What do you say?'

Kayo looked at him with dull eyes and said, 'If you say this will be the end of it and you won't want any money later, I don't mind. If you write a note like that.'

She spoke in a low voice and without any modulation. To Fujio, this was the same kind of impudent manner she had shown when she stuck her feet out in front of her on the train.

'Of course I will, if that's what you need,' he said.

To Fujio, this part of the coast road was like his own garden. He drove slowly along the coast and then turned into a narrow farm road that headed steeply down towards the shore. Though he thought of it as a farm road, recently it had been completely paved. And yet the farmers in the district still carelessly discarded cabbage and radish leaves along the road. They were always demanding that the city government should surface the roads, but in their minds this was still a dirt track.

Still some distance from the sea, but where one might expect to hear the sound of waves, Fujio stopped the car, rolled down the window, and looked at the land. In the darkness, there was neither human voice nor ocean breeze. He turned off the headlights.

'It's dark tonight,' he muttered. Then, when his eyes grew a bit accustomed to the dark, he said to Kayo, 'Put the seat back.'

With a big noise, Kayo lowered the back of the seat. Fujio climbed over the separation and approached her, but she pushed him back with her hands.

'Write the note first, as you promised,' she said.

'Isn't afterwards OK? It's hard to write in the dark.'

'You can write it if you put on the light.'

'What if someone sees us?'

'I don't care.'

'Well, *my* nerves are a little more delicate than *yours*,' Fujio said, and then added, in a softer voice, 'If I write a page, then you must, too.'

'Write what?'

'I want you to write, 'I'll never stick my feet out in the train again and I'll always sit close to other people.''

'And what will you do if I write that?'

In a corner of Fujio's mind, there was a small blue flame burning, and suddenly he felt it burst into a conflagration.

'Yeah. Right. That wouldn't mean a thing to a simpleton like you.'

'You said your rib was broken, but it isn't. And your face doesn't look like you're hurt at all. I'll do it if you give me proof that your rib is really broken.'

Kayo said this with a lizard-like lack of expression on her face.

Fujio turned his eyes away from her. Until then the sky had been clouded, with nothing visible, but suddenly the stars peeped through and Fujio felt as though they were whispering to him. Until then, he had never thought he could understand their words, but now he felt that he could clearly interpret what they were saying.

—*Strictly!* one star said first, rather solemnly. *Strictly, lives,* it went on, its language a little different from that of humans.

—*Do what strictly?* Fujio asked the star.

—*Count. Do not forget!*

Suddenly, Fujio laughed.

—*They say that there are as many lives as there are stars in the sky. I can't be bothered with that.*

—*Count. Do not forget!*

—*Is that the way it is in your world? The human world is full of unnamed lives, like my child.*

—*One who got rid of unnamed stars.*

—*What happens to those who get rid of unnamed stars?*

—*To cease existing.*

—*Punishment?*

—*Execution has to be carried out before dawn. The Dance of Dawn. Before the sun steps forward to death.*

—*I cannot oppose your command, but I'm so saddened.*

—*As in the transfigured rule.*

—*At dawn you will be extinguished in death. That is the fate of stars.*

—*To be remembered.*

—*Yes. It's so human a thing to say 'I'll remember.' But that is so irrelevant to this kind of woman.*

Suddenly, the star ceased speaking. Fujio looked up; he couldn't see a single star. Perhaps it was because of the clouds.

'I'll write a note,' he said to the girl. 'I suppose you have something to write on? Get it out.'

Like a 40-year-old woman, Kayo popped open her school case and took out a ballpoint pen and some paper.

'What shall I write?' he asked. ' "I have received your body as compensation for my broken rib bone, so I shall not hereafter request any money." How's that?'

Fujio laughed. He was sure that Kayo would be disconcerted to hear that.

'All right,' she said calmly.

'Really? Then that's it,' he replied.

He thought she was throwing a last suspicious glance his way. Instead of stretching out beside her, Fujio drove his fist violently into the pit of the girl's stomach.

It took a long time for her severe convulsions to stop, with his hands pressing into the base of her throat. By the time she grew quiet, Fujio was quite out of breath, more than ever before.

'You were indifferent even when men were staring at you at the beauty salon...' he muttered.

Fujio immediately corrected himself.

—*No, there's absolutely no connection between Kayo and the customers at the beauty salon. My hatred for her was momentarily confused...*

For him it was better that the area was so utterly dark that he couldn't see the dead face of Kayo in the seat next to him.

Fujio would do anything except dig a hole for burial. He hated that kind of work so much that he began to tremble at the very thought. Also, from here to the sea there was nothing but trees. The forest seemed as dense as the woods below Mount Fuji. The local people hardly ever came to the place. If he got rid of the body here, no one would be likely to discover her soon.

Fujio immediately thought of a good spot. He would have to move ahead about 300 meters. He turned the running lights on low and set the car in motion. No one could see inside the car because of the lights, but he didn't want anyone over the ridge line of the hill to notice their glimmer as he drove along the road.

The top of the hill was not a bad place, but, to avoid being seen, Fujio chose to stop in a little hollow. He got out of the car. With only that small distance he'd driven, the waves had become audible. He opened the trunk and took out an old bath towel. He used it to pull out Kayo's body; he was fearful of having contact with it. Having strangled her, he now had to carry her, and it had occurred to him that he might come into contact with her vomit and excreta.

He knew this place from having once spent more than half a day sleeping in the midst of its primeval woods. No one ever came here. He had lain there perfectly still, waking with the thought that in future he would have neither goals nor desire. On that day, Fujio's world had been at rest.

His eyes gradually grew accustomed to the dark and he walked cautiously down the steep slope. Kayo had not appeared to be thin, and yet her small frame was not so heavy. Finally, the slope turned into a cliff. Fujio felt beneath his feet that he had come to a rock outcropping, and there he used all his strength to throw Kayo's body out toward the ocean, losing his balance in the effort. He expected the body to go a long way, and, but it only rolled a short way down the cliff. Fujio returned to his car and brought back Kayo's school bag. He gripped the handle tight and flung it hard. He heard it land in the distance a few seconds later.

'Don't sit with your feet out! And sit in your own seat!' Fujio intended to shout toward the dark sea, but his voice was no more than a tiny, servile whisper.

Chapter 10

THE COLUMBINE

FUJIO awoke the next day to the thought of visiting Yukiko. It had been a long time since he had seen her. Just to think of this made him feel better, and he wanted to whistle. He considered calling her on the phone and asking if he might stop by immediately. But if she refused to meet him, he would feel bad, and so he decided to stop thinking about it and just go.

Fujio had a present for Yukiko today—the little glazed dish he had swiped at the department store in Yokohama. He'd wrapped it in a scrap of newspaper from his room, but suddenly he noticed that it was from a horse racing sheet. He didn't think that was anything to be ashamed of, or that horse racing was no good, but when he realized that Yukiko might notice the paper, Fujio went to the unusual length of re-wrapping it in an ordinary newspaper.

He arrived at Yukiko's house early in the afternoon. When he found that the front door was locked, Fujio was very disappointed. He remembered, childishly, that she had said she was always at home.

Ah, but I suppose she sometimes has to go shopping, or to the post office or the bank. And, if she has some illness, she might have gone to a doctor...

With that thought, he became uneasy.

—I could look in at the major hospitals and clinics in Miura, but she might well return home in the meantime. I think I'll just sit in the car in front of her house and wait for a while...

He parked the car on the other side of the street facing the opposite direction. He had no particular reason for doing this, but he would like to be able to see her face for a few moments before she noticed him.

He lowered the back of the driver's seat completely and adjusted the rearview mirror. Then he stretched himself out, having decided to wait for her no matter how long it took. Yesterday, Aoki Kayo's dead body had been stretched out on the seat next to him, like a sleeping cat. It was not something that troubled him.

—There's no doubt that the three women I've killed so far are dead in a place even their families know nothing of, and not one of them has become a matter of social concern. While the police and the newspapers are always saying that human life is precious, in this way, in one corner of society, people die, and *there's not the slightest whiff of anything extraordinary. It's said that people who kill someone don't sleep well afterward and have other difficulties, but I reckon that's nothing but superstition! I'm sleeping well at night, and I have no loss of appetite. And this morning, just like the gentle sun of this spring day, I sprang out of bed at the thought of meeting Yukiko and my heart was bouncing like the wind!*

Some cherry blossom petals had settled in one corner of the front windshield.

—Hmm. They said the cherry trees would blossom a bit early this year, but some rather cold days stretched into the end of March and in fact the blossoms appeared at the same time as always. So it's a bit early for the blossoms to fall, really. But I suppose there are blossoms that die young, even amongst cherry trees...

As Fujio was thinking such thoughts, he glanced in the rearview mirror and immediately felt his body go tense.

At first glance, she looked like a girl in a white culottes and a red jumper jacket. But in fact it was the woman called Hitomi...and she was going up to Yukiko's house. Fujio wondered what he should do.

—Surely there wouldn't be any problem if I spoke to her? That matter of going to the hotel was just a situation between two adults...

Fujio remained still, holding his breath and keeping an eye on the entrance to Yukiko's house. A minute passed and then Hitomi left the house again. At that moment, she looking curiously in the direction of Fujio's car. Fujio sank his body lower in the seat.

—If she comes over, I'll pretend to be asleep...

He watched Hitomi through narrowed eyes. She turned to look back two or three times, but she was going back the way she had come.

Simply knowing that Hitomi was an acquaintance of Yukiko's was a marvelous windfall. Later, when he wanted to reach her, very likely he could easily find out her address.

An hour passed while Fujio was waiting in the car. When he finally caught sight of Yukiko in the distance coming along with her shopping, he went up to meet her immediately and took her packages from her.

'Have you been waiting for me?' Yukiko asked.

'Well, you said you were always at home, so I took you at your word,' Fujio said in a child's tone.

'I really am always at home. But today I ran out of food and had to go and buy some.'

'Please tell me if I can help you anytime with your shopping. I'm a man of leisure and I can drive over here in my car any time.'

'Thank you very much, indeed, but I only buy what I can carry myself, so it's quite all right.' As she went inside, Yukiko added, 'Have you had lunch?'

'I had a late breakfast,' Fujio replied, 'so I haven't eaten lunch yet. But I don't need anything. I'm not hungry.'

Fujio felt refreshed by this kind of conversation.

'Everything I bought was for myself—only very simple things. But, if you like, let's eat together.'

'Can I help you with anything?' he asked.

'I'm not making anything that involved, so just relax.'

Yukiko's workplace, where they usually talked, wasn't cluttered with sewing things today.

While listening to the echoing kitchen sounds of pot lids clashing and the tea kettle boiling, Fujio noticed a plant with a peculiar white and purple flower growing in a pot in the room.

'What's the name of this flower?' he asked in a loud voice. 'The strange one that looks like a confetti ghost.'

'Oh, that's a columbine—or maybe a Western columbine. It has a large, showy flower.'

'I like it,' Fujio said in a loud voice directed toward Yukiko in the kitchen. 'I like everything I see at your place,'

'The usual ones aren't blooming yet. I think that one was raised in a hot house. When it finishes blooming this year, I'll plant it outside, and then next year it will blossom outside.'

'Fine,' Fujio murmured. Yukiko couldn't hear him. For a moment, Fujio envied the columbines that would always be in this garden, and he tried to convey this feeling to Yukiko, but the very tone of his raised voice defeated that idea.

'But there is something I don't like about columbines,' she said.

Fujio got up and went to the entrance to the kitchen. He leaned against the doorway.

'What's that?'

Yukiko was using chopsticks to lift some fresh, green mustard spinach from a saucepan.

'They're not so pretty when the flowers scatter,' she said. 'Just when you think they're doing fine, they suddenly scatter all over the place and stick to the leaves and the soil. I can clean them up, but it's a nuisance.'

'You're very particular, I suppose.'

'Not so much about decorating inside the house. But it's refreshing to gather up fallen leaves and get rid of rotten ones.'

'Oh, I've brought you a little present today...'

Fujio went to get the package wrapped in newspaper he'd placed with his jacket. 'I found it on the way here. Even though I'm out of work, I could at least buy this for you.'

When he saw it again, the dish looked like something well worth shoplifting.

'Oh, what a nice color,' Yukiko said.

'But I think you have much nicer ceramics in the house.'

'No, not in the least. I just use things I get at the supermarket.'

In fact, Tomoko had a rather fine set of cake dishes and tea cups, but she kept those in her room and Yukiko didn't use them unless Tomoko had visitors.

'I'll use it at once,' Yukiko said.

Fujio, feeling strangely pleased, returned to the workroom. For the first time, he had involved the unknowing Yukiko in one of his dirty acts. He felt like embracing her shoulders for the first time.

'What have you been doing since we last met?' Fujio asked when Yukiko came in and delicately set out some plates and small bowls on the table.

'Oh, nothing special. My work's usually the same. But now and then something different happens.'

'Like what?'

'Like something totally unexpected happening to someone I know.'

'Totally unexpected? Such as?' Fujio asked her as she set out the food. She had prepared boiled sardines, boiled bamboo shoots, *miso* soup with clams, and mustard spinach with soy sauce on the dish Fujio had stolen.

'What do *you* think would be totally unexpected?' Yukiko asked.

'Well…if it was me,' Fujio replied, 'I suppose it would be something like being diagnosed with cancer.'

'Would that be an unexpected matter to you?'

'Well, yes.'

'What I think of is something like being directly under someone who is committing suicide by jumping from a building.'

'And what happened to the person you know?'

'She was raped,' Yukiko said.

'Where?' Fujio asked as calmly as possible.

'On a dark road, it seems.'

Yukiko was being cautious. She was anxious that even though she didn't even give a false name for the victim, no one could guess who she was through a similarity of circumstances.

'But rape isn't such a big deal, is it?' commented Fujio. 'The man likes the woman, that's all.'

Fujio felt relieved, but at the same time he felt that Yukiko was foolish to make a problem of such a trivial thing.

'Well, if that's true, I think the man is stupid,' Yukiko said.

'Why do you say that?'

Fujio was speaking as though it was nothing to do with him. But because he was having to suppress his real thoughts, he felt fiercely uncomfortable.

'If a man does that, then he can't meet the woman again, of course,' Yukiko said. 'But you want to meet someone you like again. So if it was me, I would do whatever would please that man.'

'I'd do the same, then,' Fujio said, and took a rice bowl from Yukiko, resolved to keep both his expression and his mind calm.

'Please start,' she said.

'Thank you,' Fujio said, and began to eat.

Fujio felt distant from himself. At home, he never said thanks, nor did he use any of the polite formalities.

'Until the other day, that woman had led a quiet life,' Yukiko said. 'But suddenly all that collapsed right from under her. It was like when someone suddenly snatches away your bag, right? And her husband's not a person to get over something like that.'

'Then maybe it would be good for her to make a change? Now she understands clearly that her husband isn't much of a man.'

'No, it's not that, and it isn't necessary for her to understand that. We are all foolish. It's cruel to force others to realize how foolish they are. It's just like having to carry a scar from a wound to your hand or foot all your life.'

'I'm surprised,' Fujio said, putting down his bowl. 'When I talk with you, you sometimes say things I've never thought of. You get me confused.'

'I've been thinking all morning about the woman who was raped,' Yukiko said. 'What would she do if she got pregnant? What do you think she should do if that happened?'

Such an idea had never before entered Fujio's mind, and it caused him a shock of surprise. Clumsily, he put down his chopsticks.

'I've never given that a thought,' he replied. 'I suppose she should get an abortion; that would end the problem.'

'Yes, that's an adult's point of view,' Yukiko said. 'That would solve almost everything. But it would still end the child's life.'

'But the woman won't let the child live, will she?'

'Do you think that, too?' Yukiko sighed a bit.

'What would you do?'

'But it's not my business, so I can't ask about that kind of thing And yet, even at my age, I continue to have sweet dreams. So my sister is always laughing at me. But even if the husband was bitter toward the father of the child resulting from such an incident, he should struggle with himself to make the child—who has no responsibility—happy. My sister says that's foolish, but I think there are people like that. Without anyone knowing about it, I'm sure there are people who just take it upon themselves to hold no grudge against the child and love it with all their heart as their kind of lifework. Life is life.'

'Well maybe, but perhaps that woman has already done away with the child. I think that would be the natural thing to do.'

'Yes, I suppose so.'

'But the woman has killed someone. I suppose that killing someone is worse than rape,' Fujio said, his breathing barely under control. 'Anyone could commit a murder. Like the guys involved in the courts. Having an abortion...or neglecting elderly parents. Some of those incompetent, damn fool lawyers are like that too.'

'You really hate them, don't you? Do you know them that well?' Yukiko asked.

'More or less. I heard some stories when I worked in a hotel. You see the underside of life there.'

'Well, I think everyone has some things they would like to hide.'

'Everyone except you, right?'

'Oh, in my case, probably something like tax evasion!' Yukiko said.

'You do that? That's interesting.'

'Well, only as a result of not keeping my books properly. I take in work that I do myself, and sometimes I just forget—or I can't recall some of the details. For one thing, I don't think it makes bit of difference in this world at all.'

'I know I'm not welcome to be here...'

Fujio said this innocently and was even playing up to Yukiko.

'That's not true,' she replied. 'You are one of the few people who come here to visit me.'

'Well, not really. While I was waiting for you outside in my car, some woman came and rang your bell, and because there was no reply she went away.'

'I wonder who it could have been?' said Yukiko. 'Not that it matters. If it was someone with work, she would have telephoned. Probably someone selling something.'

'I guess I'm making a nuisance of myself coming here, but, you know, when I talk with you I begin to feel that I'm straightening out a lot of things in my mind. I'm not too smart. There's a lot that I don't understand about what I do, and what other people do, too. But when I come to see you, I really feel better.'

'Of course. Someone else can always see another person's problems clearly enough. But when it comes to ourselves, we just can't see our own situations clearly.'

'Then you don't mind listening to me again?' Fujio coaxed. 'Still, I suppose sometime you'll give up on me.'

'Why do you say that? I'm listening to you now, aren't I?'

'That's not what I mean. I mean in the future. When you understand that I'm really a good-for-nothing, you'll lose patience with me.'

'I will never know whether you are good or bad,' Yukiko said.

'Why is that? Anybody will know that when they're betrayed by believing in me.'

'Even then, nobody knows what you will do at the end.'

'At the end?'

'When you die.'

Fujio laughed. 'Right. I am going to die, that's for sure.'

'Well? Have you ever thought about that?'

'Actually, no.'

'That's too bad. It seems that no one ever taught you to think.'

'Who did you learn from?'

'I worked it out by myself. That's the way I am. I'm timid, and so I'm always prepared for the worst. I couldn't get by if I wasn't that way. So I can't get excited about happiness or pleasure, either.'

'I'm really happy meeting you,' Fujio blurted out. 'You think you'll be able to say this kind of thing anytime, but somehow or other the opportunity always slips by—that's how it goes. So now I've told you.'

Fujio finished his meal and left Yukiko's house. He remained in good humor afterward. It had been a real pleasure for him to have a heart-to-heart talk. He had even eaten the little sweet cake that Yukiko offered him for dessert. Fujio usually didn't care much for those Japanese confections with sweet red bean paste inside.

He drove off slowly in the direction of Yokosuka and left his car in the parking lot. Then he walked to the train station and headed for Yokohama. He had recently felt a strong attraction to Yokohama when he was going out on 'business.' However, it was difficult to kill time there without spending a lot of money. Today, it had been a great pleasure for him to give Yukiko the little colored plate that she believed he had bought at some curio shop. He thought he might steal something else, too, if that would make Yukiko happy, but he didn't feel like approaching the shop he'd visited before. There was some danger they might recognize him if he went there again so soon.

Instead, Fujio went to have a look in a bookstore. From time to time, as the mood struck him, he bought books, even though he rarely read them all the way through. But Fujio hated the popular comic books, and when he saw men in suits on the train reading comic books he wanted to spit on them. He didn't feel quite so bad about children and high school kids reading them.

That was why he had hardly been able to restrain himself when Yukiko had said that she liked comic books on one occasion.

'You mean you buy stuff like that?' Fujio had asked her, feeling betrayed.

'I don't buy them, but they're always lying around when I go to the doctor's or the beauty salon or the bank. Sometimes they're pretty good. Some of the stories could even be made into novels.'

Since then, Fujio had looked on comic books with different eyes. But at the moment he had no intention of buying anything. Quite simply, if he went to the area where they sold books, it made him feel intellectual, and in that mood it pleased him to look disdainfully at other people.

A woman wearing glasses caught Fujio's attention. She looked around thirty. It appeared that she had deliberately dressed in a light brown suit to give her a boyish air, rather than wearing something youthful, which would probably have had the effect of making her look older.

'Excuse me, but...' Fujio began in a deliberately mild tone. 'I'm looking for a book on a certain foreign city—not a travel book, but something on houses, local festivals, food, a general information book. And I wonder if you know which shelf I should look on?'

Noticing the slightly confused look on her face, Fujio added, 'I hope you'll pardon me, but I don't read much and I don't know about such things. When I asked one of the clerks, he wasn't kind at all...'

The woman in the brown suit seemed to be paying him little attention, but Fujio noticed that, behind her glasses, her slightly severe look had softened.

'Which city do you want to know about?,' she asked in a dry tone, polite though abrupt. She conveyed the impression that it was simply a human obligation to respond when asked about a book.

'Venice,' Fujio told her.

'Well, they'll certainly have something on 'Venezia.' Everybody goes there—it's an old, historical city.'

'Ah, not 'Venezia', but Venice,' Fujio earnestly insisted, demonstrating his sincerity. But he could just as easily have said New York or Miami—someplace he'd seen on the enlarged photographs of American cities in that love hotel.

'In Italian, Venice is called 'Venezia.''

'Oh, I see,' Fujio said, with an expression of innocent surprise. 'And is Venetian glass made in Venice?'

'That's right.'

'Ah, I thought it was a completely different city!'

'It might be over there, in the 'Geography and Society' section,' the woman said, walking over with Fujio.

'I'm sorry to trouble you. You're looking for a book too, are you?'

'No, I've already found what I wanted.'

'You're really helpful, but I don't know which book to buy.'

'Here's a collection of Tadaomi Yamada's photographs...And there's *A Thousand Years of Venezia...Venezia, Nation of the Sea...* and *Venezia and the Crusades,* but I think they're a bit specialized. How about *Poetical Venezia*—that seems to be a travel book?'

'I don't know which to take.'

'What do you want it for? For travel reference, I think something a bit more concrete would be best.'

'Well, I know a guy who died in Venezia. I wanted to know a little about the place where he died.'

'In that case, I think Yamada's collection of photographs would be fine.'

It was a big book and seemed to be expensive.

'I think I'll get them one at a time. My reading speed is slow, and I'd be ashamed to buy one and not read it. Maybe I'll read one and then come back and buy another,' Fujio explained.

The woman neither agreed nor disagreed; only her eyes showed her amusement.

Fujio chose *Venezia, Nation of the Sea.* As he took it to the cash register, he said to the woman, 'Excuse me, but are you in a hurry just now?'

'No, not particularly,' she replied.

'Then if you don't mind, may I invite you for a cup of tea? I'd like to talk with you a little more about the man who died in Venice—I mean, Venezia.'

Some time ago, Fujio had come up with a kind of running leitmotif centered around people dying at the end of a journey somewhere in the world; sometimes it was a story about a man, sometimes it was about a woman. The Japanese travel all over the world these days and there was nothing odd about such a story. It wasn't perhaps as dramatic as dying on a mountain, but it was something that touched people's hearts.

'Do you know a good place?' Fujio went on. 'I live out of town and I don't know this area very well.'

'There's a place called 'Windsor' on the 8th floor. It has a rather ordinary name, but in fact it's a quiet place—a little snobbish. Would that be all right?'

Fujio hesitated, looking perplexed. '*Su-no-bi-shu...*What does that mean?'

The woman had used the English word. She explained it meant something like 'sophisticated.'

'Then let's go. But I'm pretty ordinary myself.'

The woman looked at him with a pitying smile, but Fujio pretended not to notice.

Just as she had said, the tea shop wasn't crowded.

'So...Some tea, and perhaps a cake or sandwich or something like that? They have a kind of English high tea here in the afternoon, the standard menu.'

146

'Never had it, but that would be fine,' Fujio replied.

'What kind of tea would you like?'

'Oh, you mean green or roasted?'

'Well, actually, they don't serve Japanese tea here, just foreign tea. You have to choose a type of black tea—Darjeeling or Ceylon.'

'I see. Makes no difference to me.'

'Then some Darjeeling?'

Without giving him the chance to say he'd have the same as her, she ordered Darjeeling for Fujio and Ceylon for herself.

'Did you say "high tea"?' Fujio asked her. 'Does that mean the price is high?'

The woman's expression hardly changed, although she was trying hard not to laugh.

'Yes, I suppose so. They serve cake and little sandwiches with it, so the price may be high, but in fact in English the expression 'high tea' means tea with extras,' the woman explained.

'Uh-huh. So that's it. Sorry, I haven't introduced myself,' Fujio began, just like a proper gentleman. 'My name is Wataru Miura.'

'Mine is Goto,' she replied, without giving her first name.

'Thank you for helping me choose a book.'

'Not at all. I only directed you to the bookshelf. I didn't select the book,' the woman said very accurately. 'And just who was it who died in Venezia?'

'A cousin of mine. The son of my father's younger brother. Unlike me, he was born in the house of a professor at Tokyo University, and, since he was so bright, his parents expected him to follow in his father's footsteps and become a scientist, I suppose. But the boy liked art and said he wanted to become a painter. His father was upset and it ended up in a big argument at home. I'm no genius, so I took the boy's side. In those circumstances, I was the relative who got on best with him. His father is the only genius in our whole family, far above all the rest. None of the rest of us are involved in any kind of intellectual work. My family runs a china shop in the country; it's good because china doesn't go rotten! My father's younger brother runs a factory in town.'

This kind of story was Fujio's specialty. The china shop idea was inspired by associations from the ashtray in front of him, and the idea of managing the factory arose from the tin bud vase holding a salmon pink rose on the table.

'And did he go to Italy?'

'Yes. I don't know much about art, but for painting I thought he'd go to Paris. Then they said he was in Venice. He sent a picture postcard of a gondola. He seemed to be completely happy. Still, in less than six months, he died in one of those ditches or canals, or whatever they're called.'

'When was that?' the woman asked coolly.

'Two years ago. So, counting in the Japanese way, the third anniversary of his death just passed and it occurred to me that I should read something about Venice. His death made me so depressed, I didn't feel like doing that till now. At first, for some reason, there was a rumor that he might have been murdered, but the autopsy showed that he wasn't poisoned, and there were no injuries...'

'So why did he fall into the canal?'

'I don't know. There were some fantastic rumors, like the story that he was involved in a love triangle and was pushed in. Who knows? It was Italy and he was a painter, and some glamorous ladies or some cute girls might just have been walking along a canal with him, and...'

At that moment, the waiter brought them each a silver teapot, with some tiny sandwiches, cakes, and muffins of three kinds on dishes stacked like tiny pagodas.

'Wow, this is something!' Fujio exclaimed.

'The tall dishes make it high tea,' the woman replied.

Hearing the stiffness in her voice disappear for the first time, Fujio looked into his companion's face.

'Would you mind telling me your given name?' he asked.

'Isn't it enough to know my family name?' she replied calmly.

'Sure. But I'd just like to know your given name. I was wondering what kind of name an intellectual like you might have.'

'A name is just a sign.'

'Still...'

'Well, it's Hanako.'

'Fine, that a nice name, even if it's not true. I suppose you've been to Venice?'

'Yes, but only passing through. But I don't seem to recall anything in the newspapers about the body of a Japanese being found floating in a canal.'

She seemed confident that she would have remembered everything written in a newspaper two years earlier.

'It was there,' Fujio said, 'but since it wasn't a crime, not much was made of it.'

'Really? Probably it was when I was away traveling. I travel a lot.'

'Pardon me for asking, but what kind of work do you do?'

'Me? I'm just a woman of leisure!'

'Of leisure?' Fujio was puzzled.

'I spend my time playing,' she said.

'That's great! So you just live to enjoy yourself?'

'And you?'

He felt that she was not really interested, but was asking simply because he had asked her.

'Like I told you, I run a china shop. Just cheap new things. They don't spoil, so if I don't sell them one day, I can sell them the next. I get along somehow and that's enough for me. So I'm not particularly encouraged to have higher ambitions. I'd have to struggle if I had a housing loan like people in the city, but I've got my father's old house, you see. I can get by pretty well. But it's nice for you. You can buy books at a place like this on your parent's bill.'

'No, I have my own money.'

'Are you in the stock market?'

'I do translations. I can support myself with that. But there is no set time for that kind of work, so I can work any time—day or night, today or tomorrow, whenever I like. So I'm a woman of leisure.'

'Mm, next time I go book shopping I'll look for the name Hanako Goto. What do you translate? Detective stories?'

'I use a pen name for translating.'

'That makes sense. I knew you were an intellectual. But it's good you don't work someplace. Sometimes I lie and tell people I don't work. I've got free time but no money. That's no good at all!'

'I wanted to work at a foreign company where there was a good position as a secretary, but my father prevented me. He said that if I worked he would lose my maintenance deduction and there would be a tax loss.'

Fujio noticed that Hanako hadn't touched any of the food that came with the high tea.

'Why aren't you eating anything? It looks bad for me to gobble all this up alone,' he said. 'I asked you here for a treat, but I'll probably eat it all myself.'

'Please do,' Hanako said. 'I'm not in the habit of eating between meals.'

'Have you always been like that?'

'Yes. When I was a child, I may have eaten snacks, but my father thought that it was bad manners to eat between meals. Japanese children, especially, think nothing of eating things on the train, you know. Or they are fed to keep them quiet. He said that was gross and was really strict about it.'

'And you don't take sugar or cream with your tea,' Fujio suddenly noticed.

'No, but that's just my preference. You can taste the flavor better if you don't put anything in it.'

'I'm pretty low-class, the kind that thinks you ought to eat everything that comes with your order—sugar, cream, lemon, whatever. I was once laughed at for being a bumpkin who put both cream and lemon in his tea!'

Hanako smiled faintly. 'Now that is really a mistake. It makes the tea taste bad, doesn't it?'

'Right, it does! I learned that much.'

The whole tale was Fujio's invention. His intuition was excellent. In order to ingratiate himself with this conceited woman, it was better to play the fool than to display how much he knew.

'So, is Venice a really good place? If I ever get the chance, I'd like to see Venice and then die.'

'Don't die until you see Napoli,' Hanako replied.

'Oh, I see,' Fujio said.

His mistake could hardly have been more appropriate, but Fujio had not intended it as such; it was a genuine misunderstanding.

'It depends upon the person whether Venice is grand or not,' Hanako went on. 'Some people go there and feel a kind splendid, dream-like decadence, what with there being no way to save the city from sinking into the sea. People say that when you go to Venice, you understand why Italy is not modernized. Anyway, it was the home of Venetian businessmen; it wasn't a very moral city.'

According to Hanako, the canals of Venice were terribly polluted. All sorts of filth was deposited on the stone landing places for boats at the house entrances and the water itself smelled putrid. The houses were always standing in that water and the buildings, as well as the people who lived there, were all rheumatic.

As she went on with her lecture, Fujio, while pretending to take it all in, was in fact thinking of something else.

—*Do I want to sleep with this conceited woman? Would she be worth the trouble? It's hard to imagine she'd be easy to seduce...*

All the while he was making the conversation go smoothly, he was actually thinking about the significance of making the effort to seduce her. What drew him out of his daydream and back to what she was saying was not the fact that she was such a great conversationalist but something in what she was saying that struck his ear.

Earlier she had admitted that she'd only visited the city briefly, but she was like an encyclopedia. She seemed to know all kinds of things that Fujio had no idea about, whether it was about the origin of the name 'Venezia' after the old city had been devastated by the Huns, or the fact that both Marco Polo and Casanova were natives of the city. But what attracted his interest was the story that—because of the slavery system in Venice—until the 16th century there had been 10,000 or more prostitutes in the small city. Women held a very low social position and they were sometimes counted in the list of possessions of a wealthy household. And one of the interesting things about Casanova was the presence of 'nuns' who often acted as high-class prostitutes. Further adding to the disparagement of the name of Venice were the widespread practices of homosexuality and bestiality.

The woman talked about this kind of thing coolly and precisely, setting Fujio's teeth on edge. But she never used such clear terms as 'homosexuality' and 'bestiality.' She preferred some kind of circumlocution such as 'sodomy,' which was more shocking because it suggested 'unnatural sexual relations.' While she was talking, Fujio suddenly realized that her interpretation of 'sodomy' was something a little different from what he had thought.

'Decadent beauty—that seems to have a bad odor about it. Venice's most famous incident—I think it was in the 15th century—was the case of a number of men molesting an adolescent boy and then killing him. After that incident, the prostitutes of Venice were ordered to stand on street corners all together at night with their breasts completely bared...'

As he flicked through the book of photographs, Fujio imagined how voluptuous and humorous the women with their bare breasts must have looked under the street lamps of a city piled high with stone monuments encrusted with human malice and desire.

'The idea was to sate the desires of the men of Venice of that time for unnatural sex.'

'Do you think the sodomy thing was because Venice was full of poor guys who couldn't afford a woman?' Fujio commented. 'I read somewhere that even now there are a lot of countries where if you don't have money you can't get a wife.'

'Still, according to the records,' Hanako went on, 'it seems that what was wrong with Venice was not between men but rather with the prostitutes. The people who bought women were the aristocrats, wealthy foreigners, and the priests. Religious rules aside, the ordinary people didn't take to perversion because they were poor. It seems that they just lost interest in the usual pleasures. The people who were obliged to bring accusations about perversion were the doctors and bathhouse keepers who could see clear signs of disease.'

Fujio was gradually taking in the situation.

'You really have the details down,' he said. 'For having been there for just a short time, you really got to know a lot about it!'

'That was an accident. The truth is I translated a book about Venezia.'

Expressing admiration in his eyes, Fujio asked her whether the book was on the shelf they'd just seen.

'No, that was five years ago; I suppose there are copies in the publisher's warehouse, but you won't see it in the usual bookstore.'

'I'd like to read it,' Fujio said, adding in a lowered voice, 'It's rare for a woman to talk about sex like that. Was that on purpose? Are you a feminist?'

His question was partly to tease her. It seemed as though he was baiting a hook with rotten meat. It was his trick to see if she would take the bait.

'No, not particularly. Venezia is just that kind of city. You don't think that talking about sex is limited to males, do you? Women are sexual, too, you know. But I'm not a feminist.'

'No need to be since you're a woman,' Fujio said.

'Well, all women are feminists in so far as they advocate equal rights for men and women, or expansion of women's rights.'

Fujio was only aware of the particular Japanese meaning of the word 'feminist' as a man who was kind to women, so he became displeased that the term had made him lose face.

'I don't know exactly what that word 'sodomy' means, but it sounds interesting,' he said.

Hanako said nothing.

'Listen,' he went on, 'it kind of seems we were fated to meet like this. Would you like to try it together?'

Fujio poured a second cup from his own teapot. Since he'd been told that there was separate hot water for a formal tea, he thought it would be a waste not to drink it all up. His final cup of tea was as thin as rainwater and caused Hanako to laugh silently.

Since he had eaten Hanako's portion of the sandwiches, cakes and muffins, and he thought it would soon be time for them to say goodbye, he had thought up the suggestion of them trying sodomy as a parting line. He expected her to refuse with a word, but she made no objection to the outrageous proposition. Fujio felt a real thrill of interest when she didn't refuse.

'I couldn't say this to just anyone, but my cousin who died in Venice was a complicated person.'

Hanako stared into Fujio's face, saying nothing. It seemed as though she wouldn't express her feelings without a precise understanding.

'I was the lowest member of the whole family and so he confided in me about sexual matters, but meeting you today had helped me to understand the whole thing.'

'And just what is that?' Hanako asked.

'Well, that he was, er, a philanthropist.' Fujio felt he was being infected by Hanako's way of speaking. 'What I mean is that he loved both men and women—truly. And he suffered for it. He wondered why you couldn't love both men and women, and that was the root of his pain. Since I didn't understand then what I do now, I couldn't give him any good advice. If I'd met you earlier, things might have been different, but I suppose that's fate. He once said that he felt better after talking with me. We weren't brothers, but—even though I had no education—he talked to me as though we were brothers.'

There were times when Fujio felt that his lies were the actual truth about his life. He had seen too many movies. Because he didn't know whether genuine bisexuals really existed, he had to make a rough guess about that too.

'He told me there were times in bed when he didn't look at his partner's face. With him, every woman immediately became the Virgin Mary. He couldn't see the saint and the animal as the same; he couldn't have sex with someone who was a spiritual personification. I really understand that feeling now. If I were to have sex with an intellectual like you, I would feel like your pet dog. The people of Venice were sure full of emotion. It's not that they were degenerate. Why weren't they understood like that? There must have been a lot of intellectuals there...'

Fujio paused for a moment.

'Is your whole family intellectual?' he asked.

'Not particularly what you would call intellectual, but a lot of them graduated from Tokyo University. Three generations of Tokyo U., in fact.'

'That's pretty good,' Fujio observed.

'My grandfather graduated from Tokyo Imperial University and went into the Ministry of the Interior. His sons were my father and his younger brother. The two were expected to go to Tokyo University College of Law, but my uncle liked literature and took French literature. He passed the examination, of course, but he knew that my grandfather would be angry, and for a while all he would say was that he was at the University, without giving any details. Anyway, it leaked out eventually. Grandfather was the kind of person who thought literature wasn't a real university subject, so for a while my uncle was spurned by the family. But as time went by my grandfather got older and eventually resigned himself to it.'

Inside, Fujio was gagging on all this. But, in his most admiring voice, he said, 'What an accomplished bunch of people!'

'One of the boys in our family got a quite high post in the police department. He's good at judo. In our family they say that he's the physical one rather than having brains.'

'That's hard to imagine. In my family, except for the father of my dead cousin, they was just one who managed to get into an *ekiben daigaku*—a local national university. That's the beginning and end of it.'

Even that was a lie, but Fujio was completely immersed in his theme. The woman's mention of 'a quite high post in the police department,' might—for all he knew—mean Superintendent-General of the Metropolitan Police. The woman had that affected way of talking.

'He wouldn't be Superintendent-General, would he?' Fujio asked.

'Does it really matter?' she replied.

'Well, no, but an ordinary guy like me is particular about those long titles. I'd get the shivers if I had to show up in front of someone with a title like that.'

As he spoke, Fujio was excited by the good luck that his target might be either a former or present police Superintendent-General. Involving a relative of a Superintendent-General in a crime would offer him the exciting challenge of the power of authority.

Hanako took the sense of Fujio's words seriously and allowed herself only a cool smile.

'Well, he's important, but it's not an enviable job. When foreign VIPs come here, there mustn't be any kind of incident. If anything happens, he's the one responsible.'

'The Japanese police are pretty good at avoiding blunders that allow something to happen.'

'The result is 'super-protection' of whoever or whatever it is. 'Safety first' is what they say. In fact he likes to drink, but at times like that he's sober 24 hours a day.'

'Well, now, where do you live? Yokohama?' Fujio asked in his most offhand tone.

'No. I have a little apartment in Roppongi in Tokyo these days, just for me. I came down here just to see a friend's ceramics show.'

'That's great. Places in Roppongi are expensive.'

'That's right. For a while it made me feel uncomfortable, but I feel right about it now, and it turned out to be a good place to live. There are good things to eat and smart shops, and—most of all—the district stays awake late at night. You don't get a feeling of freedom in a place that shuts down early.'

'That sounds really good. In small towns, everything shuts down by 9 p.m. "Simple and pure, but no food for the spirit" is what my cousin used to say.'

Fujio had never considered whether it was healthy for a town to close down early or whether it raised the cultural level of a place to stay up late. But he was determined to go along with this woman for an hour or two at any rate. According to that policy, all that remained was how he could act to give an impression of sincerity.

'I really admire people who live in the middle of Tokyo. If it's all right, I wonder if you would let me take you home? I'll probably never have another chance to visit a high-class apartment.'

'You'll have to excuse me, but I don't let other people know where I live,' she replied.

'Oh, I'm disappointed,' Fujio said. At the same time, he was offended by the term 'other people', that in part discriminated between himself and her kind. He calculated that if he let his feelings show on his face it would be the end of this business. 'And yet your father allows you to be independent, doesn't he?'

'I don't want to live with my father. You might think it would be good if I stayed with him because I would get a lot of gifts. But at times like mid-summer and at the end of the year, the door bell never stops ringing; the whole day goes by just receiving gifts. And no one at our house eats things like the packaged ham that we receive as a present. Even our dog turns up his nose at it! Even when we give some to our housekeeper's sister, we have to ask them to take it away! It just seems to keep coming...'

'That's really something. There aren't too many people who bring ham to *my* house. But ham in a can or a jar isn't very good anyway.'

Fujio was trying to maintain an attitude that would please her, but the truth was that he'd only eaten canned ham once in his life. When Fujio said it wasn't very good, Saburo go angry, saying that in Africa kids were starving and Fujio shouldn't say wasteful things about food. So he had boiled the meat with cabbage and eaten it all by himself. Fujio's mother had no skill with such things as boiling bad meat with cabbage.

—*How unpleasant she is, this woman in glasses called Hanako Goto!*

The thought stiffened Fujio's smiling cheeks.

Everything she says displays her knowledge and her family's talents, as well as her material superiority. Compared with her, even Saburo—who's just too stingy to throw away food that he doesn't like—wasn't really so bad when he brought up that stuff about starvation in Africa and made me cook cabbage stew with ham, even though I couldn't take more than a bite of the stuff...

Fujio's gut feeling was for some simple act that would smash this woman's stuck-up attitude.

'Shall we go?' he suggested. 'Let's go somewhere and do it Venetian-style.'

Of course he had said that he would pay for the high tea, but when he went to the cashier and looked at the bill, he was further put out by the exorbitant cost.

'To tell you the truth,' Fujio said in a gentle tone, 'I thought that an intellectual like you wouldn't go with a person like me.'

'Oh, in my way of thinking, I'm a very free spirit,' Hanako replied.

'Yes, of course,' Fujio said, his teeth on edge.

'How about taking the Keihin Kyuko to where my car's parked?'

'All right, that's fine.'

'I'm glad you said that. It makes me feel better.'

As they walked along, Fujio put his hand around her and felt the tension in her thin shoulder bone.

'I get plenty of propositions,' she said. 'But it depends on how I feel that day whether I take them up or not.'

'So what determines your feeling?'

'Mostly something existential.'

'Oh? I don't quite understand what you mean.'

'Have you ever heard of Kierkegaard?'

'Never. A politician?'

'No. A philosopher.'

Hanako smiled her tiny smile. 'Kierkegaard said that only the person himself could know whether or not he was free.'

'I don't understand, except that I think it's a big thing for you to be free from your parents.'

'That's right. Kierkegaard saw the problem as an oppressive sense of guilt, and that's what I struggled with. Now, I think that I'm really free.'

'Wonderful. Simply marvelous,' Fujio said in his most artless tone. But Hanako seemed to evaluate his awkward expression mildly enough. 'You are the most educated person I've ever met,' he added.

'I'm not surprised. I was raised in quite an academic atmosphere.'

Faced with this kind of arrogance, there was hardly anything that Fujio could say in reply.

—*Could I retaliate through sexual pain? I could even bury her in that place in the cosmos, that final place at the end of all space. And I won't be the one to take her there; she will do it of her own choosing...*

The train was crowded. Hanako was pressed against him. 'You're pretty, you know that?' Fujio said.

'Just say individualistic.'

'But you know that yourself.'

His smile was sweet but full of contempt, a nuance that did not reach Hanako. They rode mostly in silence. They got off at Fujio's station and left the garishly-lit commercial street to enter the dark residential byways that led to the parking area.

Some people were out doing their evening shopping. As they walked past a convenience store, Hanako suddenly said, 'Please wait a moment while I do some shopping.'

Fujio asked her what she needed, but Hanako ducked into the store without answering. Curious, he followed her inside, believing that since she hadn't told him otherwise, she could hardly object.

Hanako walked straight to the refrigerated case, gazed inside and removed some dainty packages of fried bean curd. She took them to the cash register.

'What are you doing with fried bean curd?' Fujio inquired.

'I'm staying at my parent's house tonight and I promised Mother I'd bring some as an alter offering to Inari-san.'

'The fox deity?'

'Yes, there's been a little Inari-san shrine in a corner of our garden for ever so long.'

'Oh, I see, of course. A faithful believer.'

Without showing the least sign on his face, Fujio had a good laugh to himself. But at the same time he suddenly felt a fierce pressure, as though the air inside him had been jerked out.

'Are you a believer in Inari-san?' he asked Hanako.

'Sure. Whenever we pray to him, we all have good luck.'

They reached the car park and Fujio's car. Standing on the driver's side and opening his door across from the waiting Hanako, Fujio said, 'I've had a change of mood. I don't feel much like going to a hotel with a person like you. I'm going home alone.'

For a moment, Hanako couldn't believe what she had heard. Her face drained of expression.

Fujio looked her in the eye and said, 'You're a damned fool...you bitch!'

Chapter 11

THE 2ND MOVEMENT

FUJIO, in the best of humor, slept well into the morning on April 10th. It had rained buckets the day before, but today the sky was brilliant. As he looked out from his 'prefab castle' on top of the house, Fujio felt as though he was sitting in a mixed green salad. He'd always thought that the city was only man-made structures, but as he looked out across the blossoms of azaleas, Japanese roses, and Chinese redbuds the color of peonies, he could smell their scents wafting into the air.

It was already past 10:30 when Fujio went downstairs.

'Fujio, dear, would you like some toast?' his mother asked. 'If you like, I'll warm up some rice. Would you like rice? There are some bamboo shoots and new potatoes. And I could roast some salted salmon for you.'

'Whatever you have,' Fujio replied casually, a sign of his good mood. On a day like this, he felt that anything would be fine.

For no particular reason, Fujio looked out into the store area. The slightest tingling in his nerves told him instinctively that there might be something out of the ordinary. The store was about to open. He couldn't see Saburo. At first glance, nothing seemed outside the ordinary, but then Fujio realized his intuition was correct. There was a black-and-white poster stuck on the wall near the entrance. Fujio felt sure he recognized the face in the 30cm x 30cm photo.

In large letters underneath the photograph were the words 'HAVE YOU SEEN THIS PERSON?'

Her name was Yoko Miki. Fujio knew she was definitely a married woman, but the poster described as an unemployed girl who helped her parents.

This woman has not been seen since March 22.
Anyone with knowledge of her whereabouts,
please contact the address below.
Height: 4'10". Weight: 106 lbs.
Distinguishing mark:
leaf-shaped burn scar on left arm.

'Hey!' Fujio shouted angrily. He was calling to Saburo, but it was his mother who answered.

'Who brought this poster?' he demanded.

'I don't know,' his mother apologized. 'Someone asked Saburo if it would be all right to put it up.'

'Is this the sort of thing to put up in front of customers?' Fujio retorted.

He slid into sandals, stepped down into the store and roughly tore down the poster.

'If you want to do that,' his mother said, 'perhaps it would be best to ask Saburo first.'

'I don't have to ask his permission for everything, damn it!' Fujio declared.

Saburo came in. He noticed at once that the poster had been torn down and discarded. He looked severely at Fujio and said, angrily, 'Just why did you take it on yourself to tear down the poster that was here?'

'I don't recall giving permission to put up that sort of thing.' Fujio shot back.

'You might talk like that if you worked here every day, but I don't need your permission,' said Saburo. 'Why should I ask someone who doesn't work in the store?'

Fujio was furious but silent.

'I'll tell you why it I put it up,' Saburo continued. 'The wife of a friend of mine asked me to. She said the parents of the girl are worried sick. I thought it was terrible, so I let her put it up. What's wrong with that?' Saburo was staring at Fujio. 'The family doesn't know where she's gone. I don't know how many of these posters they had printed up, but it cost them something, you can be sure. The neighbors felt so sorry about it, they've been walking around and asking shops to put up the poster where as many people as possible will see it. It seemed to me that I might help a little bit. It was the natural thing to do.'

'A woman like that is probably just a slut who's run off with some guy. You can't take it seriously,' Fujio said.

'She might be a slut, but her husband and parents are still worried,' Saburo said. He was picking up the torn pieces of the poster when Fujio charged in from the side.

'What are you doing?' The veins on Saburo's temples bulged.

'I'll tell you why I don't want this poster up,' Fujio said, laughing. 'I killed her and buried the body, that's why!'

Despite Fujio's laugh, Saburo stood open-mouthed for a moment, staring at Fujio with all the lines of his face drooping, expressionless.

'Fujio, dear, are you still making jokes like that?' Fujio's mother said. Fujio didn't respond to his mother's earnest query. 'Even if you're joking, what would people think, hearing something like that? Really, Fujio dear, making a joke like that! You worry your mother when you say things like that. Please say that you're only joking.'

'You mean you can't trust your own son that far?' he said.

'No, that's not it at all.'

'It was a joke,' Fujio said. 'Just a bad joke that seems true. What I mean is—don't do anything that annoys me! I hate people who don't mind their own business, pretending to be a good person.'

Fujio maintained a calm expression on his face and went to his room on the roof. His mouth tasted dry and he was trembling. He tried to persuade himself that it was really nothing that there were now two or three fewer people in the world. But in fact it did mean something to him.

That afternoon, Fujio observed the mood in the house, noticing first the reactions of people close at hand. His mother had received a shock when, for a moment, she'd believed that what he said was true. But, at any rate, he'd said that it was a joke and she seemed to be relieved and had recovered her good spirits—like someone getting over a serious illness.

—Women are such simpletons! If there's something they don't want to think about, they just disregard it and let it pass. As if her cute little 'Fujio dear,' couldn't possibly do anything so terrible!

Saburo was another matter.

—His attitude seems unchanged. He's treating the customers as always. But he's not saying much, and I know that he's thinking things over to himself. He will think, 'What if Fujio wasn't joking?', and that it's not beyond me to do something like that. In that sense, Saburo understands me better than my mother does. The idea that 'No one sees the child like a parent' has long since gone. Saburo knows that if what I hinted at was true, it won't just end with me, but will involve the whole family. He'll soon come up with some plan to deal with it all. Evidence of that is that he didn't piece the poster back together and hang it up again. If the person who asked him to put it up asks him why he took it down, he'll be put in a bad position, but it suggests that not wanting to have anything to do with it is more important than that...

Fujio felt that something was starting to happen. The struggle was not yet openly joined. He suspected that his enemy was sneaking up on him from behind. At a time like this, it wouldn't do to just stay home. He decided to go out after 4 p.m. Today, for the first time, he used his nest on the roof of the house to check out the neighborhood streets. He looked for some clue: something like a man standing in the shadow of a power line pole, or possibly someone sitting too long in a parked car. But all the shadows were moving, and no cars stayed parked for long.

Fujio felt somewhat foolish as he left the house; he was not in his usual good mood. As he rode the train into Yokohama, there was a group of junior high school girls standing in front of his seat, chattering, oblivious to the people around them. They talked about their teachers, about the father of one of their friends buying a motorbike, about a church bazaar that someone's mother had participated in, and about a cat catching a baby bird someone was raising, and how the girl wanted to find the cat's owner in order to complain.

Fujio pretended to be dozing, but he was listening to every word.

When he half opened his eyes once, he saw that, as he had expected, it was the girl with a large mouth and prominent jawbone who was doing most of the talking. But the girl he wanted to get a good look at was the one her friends referred to as 'Tomo-chan.'

'Last time, you know, at the church bazaar, you know, Tomo-chan's mom, you know, gave us things like Shimada Foods' jam and stuff like that, you know.'

'I don't know anything about that,' said Tomo-chan, dully.

Fujio got a brief look at her face. She was wearing glasses and her hair was tied back behind her head. Her face was so lacking in expression that Fujio imagined she never laughed. Then he experienced one of his strokes of genius. He sometimes couldn't remember vital things, but he could recall every detail of things that didn't seem so important. In short, it seemed that this 'Tomo-chan' was the daughter of the owner of Shimada Foods. And that reminded him of the old lady who lived next door to Yukiko, who had to eat her bread without jam for some days because she couldn't open the lid of a jam jar. The jam had been made by Shimada Foods.

Fujio continued to monitor the situation. The group of girls got off at the next station, leaving Tomo-chan standing alone at the car doorway. Fujio continued his feigned sleep. When the girl got off some three stations later, Fujio followed her on to the platform, deliberately letting her get ahead of him. He waited a full ten seconds and then ran to catch up with her. As he went past, he looked round at her.

'Excuse me, but aren't you the daughter of Mr. Shimada, the President of Shimada Foods?'

'Yes, that's right,' she replied.

'And your name is Tomoko, isn't it?'

'Yes.'

'Well, at the church bazaar the other day, I met your mother. My name is Tanaka. I'm a member of the church. I wanted to thank her for that occasion.'

'Not at all,' Tomoko replied.

'They sold quite a bit then. I don't know the total, but everyone was very grateful.'

'You're quite welcome,' she replied appropriately, but rather abruptly.

'The truth is I've been hoping to meet your mother since then, but, since I've run into you, that's really lucky. Although, of course, I'll ring your mother later, but now you're here, I'd like to outline my favor, and then after that if I ring her, that would be ideal. So I wonder if we might talk somewhere?'

'I have a piano lesson just now,' Tomoko said.

'Oh, I'm sorry. I couldn't possibly disturb your lesson, but what time does it end?'

'Well, I'm going to the teacher's house now, and then it will be about an hour and a half,' she replied trustingly, believing that Fujio was a member of the church.

'That's a long lesson,' Fujio said. 'Oh, now I remember. Your mother once said that she wanted you to become a pianist.'

If Tomoko Shimada's talent was quite minimal, his talk about her wanting to become a pianist could sound very phony. Still, he felt that a 90-minute lesson was very serious, and many earnest mothers, even though lacking a sense of their daughters' real talents, have them take such lessons, imagining they will develop their skills to some degree or other. When Fujio saw that Tomoko didn't make a face about this story—whether or not the mother had actually said such a thing—Fujio was pretty certain that he understood the atmosphere in their house. So, in that sense, the way he'd approached her had been appropriate.

'Myself, I work in a bank and I have to go and meet a special customer at his home on business. The meeting will take about an hour. Where is your piano teacher's place? If I can, I'd like to meet you in front of the house...or at the station ticket booth. If we can talk for just five minutes, that would be fine.'

Fujio said all this in a light tone. He was merely cultivating her trust, and there was nothing insistent in his behavior. Mention of the ticket booth was a trick to put her completely at ease.

—Still, it must be obvious that I'm not a bank employee—I'm wearing a sweater, whereas all bank employees wear suits. I hope my young friend here is not that observant...

'My piano teacher's house is straight ahead along this street. There's a bakery on the corner of the second block. Turn right there and you'll see the Aoi Apartments. It's on the 2nd floor,' Tomoko said.

'Well, I don't want to go inside, so I'll wait for you downstairs. And, besides, I can't promise to be there in an hour and a half. I'm meeting a customer and if it goes on a long time, I won't be able to make it.'

'That's fine.'

Fujio said goodbye and then, as though just remembering, asked Tomoko what she was playing on the piano.

'Mozart's *Piano Sonata No.8 in A, K.310*,' she said.

'Ah, that's a good one. I'm very fond of the 2nd movement,' Fujio said, waving his hand and walking away. The girl looked after him blankly, but there didn't seem to be any trace of suspicion on her face.

Of course, Fujio had never listened to anything like a Mozart sonata. With this talk about the 2nd movement, he was simply putting to good use some information he had acquired from the boiler-room man at the hotel, who had been crazy about classical music. He reckoned that if she played stuff with a heavy title like that, she must be quite talented for a junior high school student.

The boiler-room man had already been about 40; he was single and he spent nearly his entire salary going to concerts and on audio equipment.

'It's really great, to be involved with something like that,' Fujio had once told him.

'No, it's nothing,' the man had replied. 'It's the musicians who are great. My specialty is just listening. It's like being an alcoholic. The people who make *sake* are great, but the people who drink it are not particularly great. No matter how poor a person is, if he can just listen to music he feels rich.' The man seemed to laugh at his own absurdity. 'I don't have any education, you know. I don't know about fine arts and I've never read any philosophy books. But when I listen to music, I feel as though I've read books like that, even though I haven't. It's strange, isn't it, but the 2nd movement in a piece of music tends to be especially good. I wonder why that is? You see, the 1st movement has tension and structured passages. But the 2nd movement takes that tension and structure and sets it free. It's like the skin getting warm and the fat swelling up. The psychological topic is cleared up in the 2nd movement. It moves along to a conclusion simply, without any strain.'

'The 2nd movement?' Fujio murmured as he watched Tomoko Shimada walk down the street. Then he turned back through the station ticket gate.

He hurried to where his car was parked and then drove straight back to await the end of Tomoko's piano lesson. Without a car, he wouldn't be able to carry out the rest of his plan.

His meeting with Tomoko had been quite fortuitous. Usually, if you're angry with a jam jar that is difficult to open, you will just mumble something about the kind of company that would produce such a thing and forget about it. But it was in Fujio's nature never to forget the name of whatever provoked him.

—*The Shimada company should have something in mind when it makes its products. The population of the elderly will be increasing in future. The strength of elderly people's fingers is only the same as children's. So making jars, cans or packages that the elderly can't open is the same as starving them...*

An hour and a half was hardly enough time, and Fujio had to rush in order to get to the piano teacher's house. He was by nature extremely cautious, so he didn't take his car directly in front of the Aoi Apartments.

—*If the piano teacher or Tomoko's friends come out with her and saw my face and the car, that will ruin everything. But if I park where I can keep an eye on the apartment building from a distance, there'll be a lot of people passing by and there are lots of cars parked illegally anyway, so this car won't be outstanding in any way...*

At ten minutes past the appointed time there was still no sign of Tomoko. He thought that she might have slipped away. But then, another ten minutes later, he spotted her. It was already getting dark and Fujio remained watching her without moving. He thought she might look around for him, but she didn't seem to be doing so.

—*Perhaps she's forgotten our appointment?*

With that thought, Fujio's temper flared. He started the car with a jerk, drove ahead for about 50 meters and slammed to a halt in front of the startled girl.

'Ah, there you are!' he said through the window. 'The meeting went on for a long time and I thought I'd missed you. Have you been waiting?'

'No. I just came out,' Tomoko replied.

'Great! Get in. I'm really sorry you had to wait.'

The girl was overawed by Fujio's performance and got in the seat next to him.

'Do you like taking piano lessons?' Fujio asked as he drove off and quietly set the locks on the doors and windows.

'Yes, I like them,' she said, falling silent without any elaboration. A few seconds passed and then she asked, 'What did you want to talk about?'

Fujio's tone completely changed.

'Your family runs the Shimada Foods Company, right?' he said very roughly. 'Who's the president, eh?'

'My father is.'

'And he sells 'Honey Pot' foods, like jam and other things, right?'

'Yes, he does.'

'Well, did you know that the lids on those jars are so tight that even a man can't open them?'

'I've never opened one,' replied Tomoko.

'Who opens them at your house?'

'My mother.'

'Hasn't she ever said how tight the lids are, eh?'

'I don't know.'

'Well, your grandfather and your father make bad products and sell them, even if old people can't eat the jam they buy!'

'Uh-huh? I'll tell my father about it.'

'Just talking about it won't solve it! Do you know what happened to one old lady who couldn't eat the jam?' Fujio asked. As he drove along, he glanced over at Tomoko and saw that she was pressed against the opposite door. 'She didn't get any nourishment and she died! She was old and couldn't go for help. The police assumed that she had died a natural death because of her age, but the woman next door had bought her some jam made by your father's company and the jar was standing there unopened. After the funeral, the woman next door tried to eat the jam but the lid wouldn't open. She had to ask a carpenter who regularly helped out at her house to open it with one of his tools. The woman was in tears because she should have opened the jar herself for the old lady before she gave it to her. After all, a jar lid that even *I* couldn't open would be impossible for the old lady. So you see: thanks to your grandfather and your father's management, a person died!'

As usual, Fujio had made up most of this story, but, while he was talking, he began to believe that this kind of incident had really happened. Of course, Yukiko's next door neighbor—the old lady—ate other things besides jam, and she hadn't died because she was deprived of jam made by Shimada Foods, and had suddenly lost her strength because of acute malnutrition. But it could have happened. Whenever Fujio had rambled on emotionally in that way about things were apparently true, he was accused of lying. But Fujio just regarded himself as being in the same boat as those who, for example, have the occupation of 'novelist.'

When he looked over at Tomoko, he saw that her head was down and she was crying.

'Hey! Stop that!' he said. Fujio was immediately angry. He hit Tomoko's head with his free hand, knocking off her glasses. Quickly he picked up the glasses and kept them in his hand. He had realized she was very nearsighted, and without her glasses she was less likely to remember his face or run away.

'Let me have my glasses back!' Tomoko said, sobbing. Tears streamed down her face.

'Don't worry. I'll take your hand,' Fujio replied.

'Please stop the car.'

'Sure, but first we have to discuss what your family is going to do about that incident?'

'I'll tell my father to go and apologize.'

'Fine. But you're fourteen or fifteen, right? At your age, do you think that telling me something like that is enough? The old lady was childless, and now she's dead. What are you going to do? Who will he apologize to?'

Tomoko was quiet for a minute. Then she asked, 'Then what should we do?'

165

'We'll talk that over somewhere. Besides, you wouldn't want it known around that your company makes jars that won't open and you've been someplace with a guy like me, would you? So we'll have our talk, and we'll do it so that there won't be any harm to your family name, understand?'

Quickly, a wild plan formed in Fujio's mind.

'Where do you live?' he asked Tomoko.

'In Miura Kaigan.'

'OK, I'll take you there.'

Immediately, Tomoko looked relieved.

'Tell me the way. What part?'

'Do you know Miura Kaigan Station?'

'Sure I know it.'

'It's on the hill just five minutes from the station.'

'That's a classy district.'

'It used to be just farmland, my mother said.'

'Where's your dad's company?'

'In Kurihama.'

'Yeah? I didn't know that. Got any brothers and sisters?'

'There are four of us.'

'And which one are you?'

'I'm the third.'

'And the oldest? A brother?'

'Yes.'

'At school?'

'He's studying at a college in the States.'

'And the next one? A sister?'

'I'm the only girl.'

'I'm asking what your next brother does?'

'He entered medical school this year.'

'And your younger brother?'

'He's a year younger than me; he's still in the 2nd year of junior high.'

'I know that,' Fujio fretted. 'What's he like?'

'I don't really know. But since Father bought him a computer, he's been using it very skillfully. Even my second brother said he couldn't beat him. He also uses it to communicate with foreign countries.'

'A kid like that won't amount to much,' Fujio said. 'He'll probably become a hacker and steal some confidential stuff from the American Secretary of Defense, or maybe even disrupt a bank's on-line system.'

Fujio knew nothing about computers and so he couldn't do a proper job of criticizing, which exasperated him. He soon switched on the headlights, and for a while that made it harder to see their faces from outside. By the time half the cars on the road had their lights on, they had reached Miura Kaigan Station.

'Go up that street all the way, please,' Tomoko said.

Fujio drove up the street as he was directed.

'Turn left at the next street...then go straight.'

The area was complicated. Just when it seemed to turn into a valley, they suddenly came out on level land. The road passed through a cut and then snaked along to one side. Shortly after, an extremely bright ball of light hit Fujio's eyes. The source of the light was behind the ridge line of a hill and so he couldn't make it out in detail, but it seemed as bright as the lights of a baseball field seen from a distance.

'Is it beyond that light or this side of it?' Fujio asked Tomoko.

'That bright place is our house.'

'*That's* your house?'

She made no reply. There was no time for an explanation. The car was now passing in front of a wide guest parking area lined with palm trees and gorgeous double-flowered cherry trees in bloom. The trees contrasted strongly with each other, but standing in front of this unimaginably luxurious house, they were in perfect harmony.

'Well what a surprise!' Fujio said. 'It looks like some Hollywood actor's place.'

'Why didn't you stop?' Tomoko said breathlessly. 'You said you'd take me home.'

'Sure, but later. I'm not quite through with what we need to discuss. Anyway, I know where your house is now, so I can bring you back easily.'

Tomoko seemed to go along with that.

'How long have you been living there?' Fujio asked.

'My mother and father have lived there for 25 years. My father likes the water and said that he wanted to live where he could see the ocean, and so they decided on this place. They had it rebuilt three years ago.'

'Business is doing well, eh? I suppose there's a swimming pool, too.'

'Yes, there is.'

'10 meters? 20?' Fujio was in a good mood.

'It's oval. It's 20 meters at the longest part.'

'Do you swim every day in summer?'

'From the middle of May, my father swims on warm days. He was a swimmer in college. He's so busy now that he doesn't have time for golf, but he can swim at home...Where are we going?'

'Take it easy. I'm not going far. Just someplace where we can park for a while. If we park on the street, someone may hit us or come along and complain about illegal parking.'

It was not a street with that much traffic.

'What kind of a car does your father drive?'

'A Governor.'

'Wow! A big engine—6000cc. How about your mother?'

'She has a Hummingbird.'

'A sports car?'

'No, a two-door hard-top.'

'That's a sports type. How about your eldest brother?'

'He's in the States and has some kind of Italian car.'

'An Alpha Romeo? How about your younger brother?'

'He doesn't have a car. He's busy with his studies and so he lives in a boarding house in Tokyo and doesn't have a license yet.'

Fujio persisted in his questioning of Tomoko.

'That's a pretty big place your dad has. Just how big is it?'

'About two acres. It used to be half farmland.'

'Your mother farmed it?'

'She hired people.'

'Your mother is nonsense!' Fujio muttered.

'What do you mean?'

'People ought to take care of their own farm,' Fujio snorted.

Tomoko was silent as Fujio went on questioning her about the luxurious life the family led, such as eating steak every day.

'If you don't answer me, I'll hit you,' he demanded.

'I don't like meat,' Tomoko told him, breathless and afraid.

'How much pocket money do you have on you?' Fujio demanded.

'10,000 yen.'

'Yeah? Well there are old people who live a whole month on 50,000 yen. Aren't you ashamed to spend 10,000 just playing around?'

'But my mother gives it to me and...' Tomoko protested, almost in tears.

'I'll bet your father spends a lot of money. What does he tell you?'

'He says to live frugally because he has to pay a million yen a day in taxes.'

'A *day*?'

Tomoko was silent.

'A *day*? Not a *year*? Answer me!'

'That's what he said. I don't know much about money.'

'Paying a million yen a day in taxes, he must earn twice that.'

Fujio was hardly confident about tax matters; he was merely letting himself grow angry. When he was angry, he became confident about almost everything.

'And you think nothing of it that every morning when your family wakes up you're all two million yen richer overnight?'

'I don't know. Ask my father.'

'Don't tell me you don't know. You live by money. You live in that palace, you take piano lessons and you have a grand piano, I'll bet. How about it? Answer me!'

'I don't practice on that. I use the upright piano, made in Japan.'

'So you have *two* pianos? Many people can't even afford *one*! And even if they can afford one, they don't have enough space to put it. I suppose your family paid out a fortune to buy your brother's way into medical school? Where do you think that money came from? Huh? It's because your father employs hundreds of people and takes it out of their labor. That's stolen money.'

As he talked, Fujio was gradually approaching the area of steep cliffs by the shore.

—A family like hers must take in 60 million yen a month, and at the same time they cause starvation among the elderly! There are a lot of people who don't earn 60 million yen in their whole life. And in one year that's more than 720 million yen. No one can do work worth that much in a year...

Fujio was trying to remember the name of the ill-mannered girl he'd thrown off the cliff, but it wouldn't come back to him.

—She said her mother was a 'companion,' but she didn't even know how to sit properly inside a train. Now she's dead, and even if she didn't know how to sit in a train, she won't be a burden to the world any more. That's just fine...

Suddenly, relieved, Fujio remembered the girl's name—Kayo Aoki.

—If I've already started growing senile, I wonder what it would be like to live for 80 or 90 years? Ah, this is Kayo's lonely grave. Soon she will have a friend around the same age. The two will become very close friends after tonight!

Fujio gave a big yawn. At a time like this, he wanted to seem casual, even bored.

'I'm asking you...please. Take me home!' Tomoko said.

'Shut up!' Fujio snarled. 'I said after we've talked.'

He stopped the car in the same place as before. Tonight, unlike last time, the thin moon was just sinking into the sea. The ocean seemed calm enough, but the woods here were filled with its soft rumbling.

'How about talking here?' Fujio said.

He saw her try to open the door, and fail; he laughed, but he didn't tell her it was locked.

'What is it you want?' she asked.

'Your body, of course.'

'No!' She thrust his hand away, an action that gave Fujio a clear target.

'Take your clothes off!' he ordered.

'No. I won't!'

'If you don't, I'll kill you,' he told her calmly. 'So just take your clothes off and you won't get hurt.'

Tomoko paused for a moment and then removed her school uniform.

'Your skirt, too. And your underwear!'

Fujio folded his arms and sat back to enjoy watching.

'Take your shoes off, as well...and your socks. It's against the rules to keep your shoes and socks on while you're getting undressed.'

Fujio gathered up each item of her clothing, one by one, and put them on the back seat. When he got to her shoes and socks, a new idea occurred to him. It would be good to make Shimada suffer, that president of a company that made faulty jam jar lids. To do that, there would be no need to kill the girl, or even to lay a hand on her body.

'Now, I'll open the door, so get out!' he ordered.

Fujio secretly released the door lock; when the girl tried the handle, the door opened easily, as if by magic. Tomoko got out, but she was unused to walking barefoot and seemed to be in pain.

'I'm going to turn the car around, so get out of the way!' Fujio bawled through the open window as he started backing the car.

At that moment, Tomoko thought she saw her chance. From the moving car, Fujio saw her white figure dash into the underbrush. She seemed to think that he hadn't noticed, but Fujio saw it all in his mirror. Still seated in the car, he laughed soundlessly. The car was now completely turned around. As though intending to her, Fujio gunned the engine and then sped out along the narrow farm road. He was still laughing as he joined the main highway and drove away.

—*Now, I wonder what that buck naked girl will do next?*

Her clothes were scattered all over the back seat of the car. Fujio stopped about a mile down the road. He gathered the clothes and stuffed them into a paper bag he got from the trunk. Then he drove to the east along the shore road, looking for a place to discard the bundle. When he came out of the woods at the long sandy beach of Miura Kaigan, he stopped the car and placed the bag with Tomoko's clothes in a large trash container left there for the use of visitors. All kinds of people came to the beach from Tokyo and Yokohama. From having once observed the trash being collected here, Fujio knew there was always an unimaginable pile of trash thrown away at a spot like this: everything from underwear, bags and shoes to baby baskets for strolling, glasses and cameras. His bundle would hardly be out of place.

Fujio whistled in the night air. He felt refreshed, but also sad. He intended to visit Yukiko again, and he would need an excuse.

After throwing away the clothing, Fujio bought a small glass cup of *sake* from a vending machine in front of a liquor store. He turned the car around and headed toward Yukiko's house. As he passed near the place where he had already buried two of his victims, he felt an unearthly cool evening breeze pass over his face. It was a ghostly touch. To rid himself of that, and to create an excuse for seeing Yukiko at this unusual hour, Fujio stopped his car in front of her house and took several mouthfuls of the *sake*. It tasted worse than some bitter medicine. After waiting until the 'poison' was rapidly hitting him, he went up to the house and rang the door bell. He knew that the *sake* would hit him any moment.

Yukiko opened the door and immediately saw how ill Fujio looked.

'What's the matter?'

Fujio was pretending a bit, but not all of it was an act.

'Are you feeling ill? Come in and lie down,' Yukiko told him.

'No, I'm not sick,' he replied. 'I had to...drink some *sake*. I...really bad for me... I feel terrible...But I'm not ill...Be all right in a while...I'll leave before your sister returns...don't want...to cause...trouble...'

'She's not coming home tonight. I just talked with her on the phone.'

Yukiko supported him and guided him to her workroom.

'Now loosen your belt and lie down. I'll bring you some water,' she said. She folded a cushion to make a pillow for his head. 'Do you feel like vomiting?'

'No...It's just...my heart hurts,' Fujio told her.

'It could be alcohol poisoning.'

'Only had three cups,' Fujio said. Actually he had drunk only part of the glass of *sake* he'd bought from the machine and then thrown the glass and the rest of the *sake* on the rubbish heap where he had once discarded the morning glory seeds.

'Only a little drop...Thought I'd go home...Didn't want to come by here so late...but after I had the drink I felt sick...and I stopped here.'

'You shouldn't go home, not in your car. Think of what might happen if you drove after drinking. You can leave your car here if you wish.'

'I need my car tomorrow so I have to take it with me.'

'Why did you drink *sake*?'

'Why? I'm a man. The guy I was with said I should have a few cups, even though I don't drink. I was offered one drink. Other people think it's OK to have five or six cups. There were three people there. I didn't want to upset the mood. And this is what happened.'

Fujio delighted in making up this story.

'Why did they insist on you drinking, I wonder?'

'It's part of most jobs, drinking...for men, anyway.'

'What kind of job is that?'

'Real estate. I can't play around forever...Occasionally, unless I earn some money...I feel uneasy about staying at home.'

'Well, it's your work and so there's not much I can say, but instead of trying to get rich all at once, I think you might pay more attention to the family business.'

'Sure, when my brother-in-law isn't there. I get an ulcer when he's around.'

'And I suppose you affect him the same way?' Yukiko responded.

'I suppose so,' Fujio chuckled, feeling a little better. 'It's funny, isn't it?'

'When you come down to it, every serious matter is humorous. Or, to put it the other way round, there's something not very funny in humorous things.'

'I heard an absurd thing today,' Fujio said, still lying down. His heart now seemed to be under control again and he was feeling better. 'They say that some people earn enough to pay one million yen a day in taxes. That's just *one day*. If that's the tax, imagine what their income must be!'

'Aren't there a lot of people like that? Are you envious?' Yukiko asked lightly.

'Living in a grand house—two acres of land. Ordinary people could never buy anything like that.'

'Some people are lucky,' Yukiko said. 'Still, from my long observation, I think people who have things are also hard put. In their business, they have to work and sacrifice themselves for decades. And money like that is their reward. You don't accumulate that much in one day. You're envious of a house on two acres, but to keep a place that size clean is a big job. If I was asked to take charge of such a house, I'd refuse. I wouldn't want to devote my whole life to a house.'

'People like that don't take care about their garden the way you do. They're just arrogant. They employ a gardener to do the work for them.'

'It's still quite something. Other people can only do superficial things; it takes the *owner* of the garden to make the plants grow,' Yukiko told him.

'Doesn't that mean they're just cherishing themselves because they value their own belongings?'

'You're being strangely idealistic! Everyone cares the most for their own child. You'd see what a nice place the world would be if people brought up their own children properly within their responsibility to be selfish about it. It would be unnatural or unreasonable to be forced to think more about other people's children than our own.'

'And you don't think its a contradiction that you make expensive clothes, costing thousands of yen, for other people? Don't you think its funny that some people can afford such extravagance and others can't?'

'Not *thousands* of yen. The other day I made a kimono worth nearly ten *million* yen,' Yukiko told him, as though it was something interesting.

'Ten million yen!'

'Exactly. I was a little nervous working on material like that. I couldn't get a refund if I ruined it. But I wasn't unhappy about doing it. If someone wants to sell it at that price and someone wants to buy it, what's the matter with that?

Thanks to such people, the weaver and the dyer make progress in their arts. Human society involves a lot of waste, but without that people become very trifling and mean-spirited.'

Fujio was still not satisfied. 'But is a kimono really worth that much money? Some rich fool was cheated into paying out that kind of money, wasn't he? At least you wouldn't buy it, would you?'

'That's not my kind of dream. But being deceived is all right, isn't it? It's a dream—and there's no price on dreams.'

'You know, you're pretty generous about life,' Fujio told her.

'Not so much generous as easygoing.'

'No, that's not true. You're very sincere.'

Yukiko was amused and started laughing.

'Well, maybe I'm boasting when I say that I'm easygoing,' she said. 'You know, there are some people who can hit just the right thing by roughly measuring things out by the spoonful or checking the temperature of the water. They don't carefully measure or adjust things or have any ethical idea... It's like having the ability to cook well. In that sense, I might be able to boast about being easygoing!'

'Listen, I want to ask a favor.' Fujio kept his eyes closed to avoid meeting Yukiko's look. He knew she was looking straight down at him. 'I'd like to rest my head on your lap, just once. I'd feel reassured if I did that.' He spoke as though she had already refused him.

'Of course, but I think you'd be more comfortable with pillows.'

'Why's that?'

'I'm all bones, that's why.'

'Fine. I don't like fat women,' he replied, but it was no more than a pleasantry. If Yukiko had been plump, Fujio would certainly have said that he didn't care for skinny women. 'Well, no matter. It's just that it calms me when I put my head on a lap. Sometimes I just want to be calmer than I can ever say. I suppose it's because I'm timid and childish.'

Yukiko said nothing. But, just as he'd requested, she settled his head on her lap.

'What is it that's been disturbing you?' she asked.

Fujio's eyes were closed. His cheeks twitched slightly.

'Nothing,' he said.

'That's good, then.'

Fujio was still for a while. Then a tear rolled from his eye.

'I was going to say I wanted you...to sleep with you...but I was afraid.'

'Why?' Yukiko asked, her face serious.

'Oh, you told me before that if I want to be with you always, I shouldn't do anything bad to you...'

NO REASON FOR MURDER

'That's nothing bad. Being loved isn't anything bad, is it?'

'Is that really true?'

'Yes. I meant that rape was shameful, that's all.'

Fujio loosened one button on Yukiko's blouse, but there was no strength in his hand.

'Just once,' Fujio pleaded, 'let me see you. I want to see you without clothes. I want to remember you...And if I see you once, I'll remember—I'll remember until I die. I think I'll remember you at the moment of my death. I don't want to die without seeing you.'

Yukiko smiled.

'Don't you think that's exaggerating a bit?' she said. 'You're still young. Why are you thinking about death?'

'You said it once yourself. We should always think about death, you said.'

'Yes, you're right; I suppose I did say that. And I think about it all the time myself. But you're so completely disillusioned. I'm not young anymore, and even when I was young, I wasn't pretty.'

'I'm not in love with you because you're pretty. My dead mother wasn't pretty at all, but even now I can't bear to think of her—I love her so.'

'I thought your mother was alive?' Yukiko said, surprised.

'Right. I haven't told you the details of that yet.' Fujio said this to support the string of lies that had become habitual.

'The fact is that the woman who is now my mother is not my real mother, because my father re-married. She's been good to me, but she interfered a lot in my marriage.' Fujio said with the air of some special, hidden meaning. 'Some people say that because I'm not her natural child I ought to consider how she has treated me, but I think that she's been good to me. I feel badly when I think about my real mother, who didn't do anything for me...Look, I'm asking you, just once, OK?'

'Do as you please,' Yukiko said. 'Because I still don't know what you want me to do.'

Fujio was silent as he continued to unbutton Yukiko's blouse. Simple as the action was, it didn't go smoothly. Her removed the blouse and put it to one side. Then he tried clumsily to pull off her slip as well with his right hand, while holding her with his left. It might have gone more easily if he'd used both hands, but Fujio didn't want to let go of her.

'I just had a bath a little while ago,' Yukiko said softly. 'Don't I smell nice?'

Instead of replying, Fujio slipped aside her bra and shyly buried his face between the mounds of her firm breasts.

'The garden was full of scattered orange blossoms,' she continued, 'so I put some in the bath water along with some orange skins.'

Yukiko held Fujio's head still against her breasts. Her whole being was a fragrance that came not just from the orange blossoms. They remained motionless; finally there was the sound of Fujio's tears. Softly, Yukiko stroked his hair, keeping his head close to her chest.

'What's the matter?' she asked.

'I can't. I...I wanted to take you...to force you...but I can't.'

Yukiko continued to stroke his head. 'I wouldn't do anything if it wasn't the right time.'

'I don't like that idea!'

'No. It's simply human that you can't do some things. I'd feel bad if you could do everything.' There was a peculiar echo in Yukiko's voice.

'There is nothing I can't do,' Fujio murmured.

'That's remarkable. Ever since I was a child, there have been so many things I couldn't do. But when I run into something I can't do, I duck my head and tell myself, "You still can't do it." That's all.'

'I'm so miserable.' Fujio said.

'That's because there's something inside that's got you all tied up, you know that. When you're free of that, you'll be at peace.'

Her words hit home and he tensed. 'I don't want to be at peace.'

'Then I'm sorry I said it. I've never understood something as complicated as men's stubbornness.'

'It's better that you don't. Believe me.'

'You and I don't understand each other fully. But we are happy understanding each other only a little bit. It's because of that we can enjoy each other so much.'

'How can you be so natural like that?' Fujio said.

'They say that naturalness is just doing nothing,' she said humorously.

'Who said that?'

'My sister, the editor. She's talented and she reads books and I don't. It's strange. She say things exactly the opposite of what's in the magazine she works on.'

'For me, your naturalness is frightening.'

'When I was a child, the sea and the woods used to frighten me. But out here on the Miura Peninsula, there are no real rivers and so I never became afraid of rivers.'

Thoughts of the sea and the woods drifted into Fujio's agitated mind: the dark woods by the sea where the bodies of two girls lay buried, and the sea where the corpse of one girl floated, and beside which he had set the naked girl free.

'Now would you do a favor for me?' Yukiko said.

'What's that?'

'May I put my head on your arm? I let you put your head in my lap and I've always wanted to sleep in someone's arms. I've never done that, and I think it would be very comforting.'

'Sure,' Fujio replied.

'If your arm begins to hurt, let me go right away,' Yukiko said.

Fujio lay there and Yukiko snuggled her face into his side, her eyes closed and a soft smile on her lips.

Chapter 12

HALF A PERSON

F UJIO awoke early the next morning with bittersweet thoughts in his mind. He supposed that he'd missed his chance with Yukiko, but his feelings of regret and humiliation were eased by the memory of the girl he'd sent naked out of his car.

—*She must have looked for help from some passing car or the nearest house and got them to take her home, or maybe asked them to call home to ask someone to go and get her. An incident like that will be quite a shock to the girl and her family. Whoever picked her up will spread the story around, and even if they don't, her family will live in deadly fear of it getting out. Though she wasn't actually hurt, that was revenge enough...*

Still, Fujio regretted that he couldn't speak to Yukiko about it. A more pleasant thought, however, was the slender hope that his frustrating relationship with Yukiko might someday bear fruit.

—*You can never tell about a woman. Even if you fail once, you don't know what will happen next...*

He tried saying this aloud, but his own words stung him.

Yukiko had fallen asleep in his arms. Fujio rarely opened a book, but long ago, as a child, he had read some Greek myths, and by chance he still vividly remembered some of them. Each Greek goddess in the myths personified some entity over which she ruled: Nyx personified night, Psyche personified the human soul, and Echo was said to be the spirit of trees. In spite of her name, Yukiko was not the spirit of snow but rather, as in a Greek myth, the personification of calmness and dependability. She trusted Fujio and slept in his arms; she was the only woman who had done so.

Fujio gently freed his arms. He had been holding her for a long time. He wanted to stay the night, but he was afraid that if he did so he wouldn't again be able to visit there again. He spread a large towel he found in the bath over Yukiko so that she wouldn't catch cold, and quietly left the house.

He was uneasy that someone might try to enter the house, since there was no key with which he could lock the door, and so he stopped his car a short distance away and remained there, watching the house. He remained parked for some two hours until he saw the entry light extinguished from inside; only then did he start up the car and go home.

The previous day had been rather cold, but today the sky was clear. Fujio could feel the first hint of summer in the air. He remembered that he had to buy some lightweight underwear. He didn't like keeping underwear until it was ragged, and with the change of season he felt like wearing brilliant white.

He ate lunch and then immediately headed for the supermarket across from the train station where Yoko Miki had bought the soy sauce on special sale. He knew just where men's underwear was sold, but he ambled through the music department first. Someone there caught his eye. It was a girl in her late teens, just the age that Fujio liked. She was wearing jeans, a thick white sweatshirt, and had a healthy, but sensitive and sharp expression on her pale-skinned face. She was only selecting a CD, but her eyebrows were knit in concentration under her pageboy hair cut.

—I don't think she's a working girl. What day is it?…Tuesday…April 11th. It's the beginning of term in every school. If she was a 1st year student at elementary school she could be out shopping for a CD at one o'clock in the afternoon, but that seems unlikely for a senior high student…

For a minute or so, Fujio stood across the CD rack, observing her while he pretended to look for a CD himself. Then he spoke. 'Say, I wonder if you know where the Camellia Fonti records are?'

'Camellia Fonti? They must be in the 'C' section, so I guess that's on this side,' the girl replied.

'Oh, then they're arranged alphabetically? Whose stuff are you looking for?' Fujio asked, moving over to her side of the rack.

'Edwin Montaigne.'

'Really? Never heard of him. Is he good?'

'Yes, of course,'

'I'd like to hear him.'

'Yeah, you really should.'

'What are his best songs?'

'*The Night We Die, Judas Tree, Swingin' in the Rain, Confession…*' she recited.

'What's a 'Judas Tree'?' Fujio asked.

'I don't know, but the words say it blossoms with a blood-red flower.'

'That's news to me,' Fujio told her.

'Is Camellia Fonti any good?' she asked.

'You've never heard him?'

'I know the name, but he's older.'

'Yeah, well…' he said, realizing that would be true; it had been ten years since he'd worked in the hotel.

'Are you in senior high?' Fujio asked, getting to the point.

'Mm, yes, I suppose.'

'What do you mean?'

'Just that I don't go to school that much.'

'You dropped out?'

'Yeah, that's about it.'

Fujio empathized with the girl immediately. 'When did you drop out?'

'Well, I went to junior high now and then, but I think senior high's really lousy,' she said.

'To tell you the truth, I dropped out, too,' Fujio told her seriously, although it was a lie.

'Really?!'

'I thought we were alike immediately.'

The girl didn't reply.

'If it's OK, how about a cup of tea or something? My treat.'

'If it's all right with you,' she replied.

'Sure thing. It's great to talk to someone like you.'

'Fine. Let's go,' she said.

Fujio forgot all about buying any underwear.

'How about a little ride in my car?'

'Cool. I'd like to see the sea.'

'Great. I'm parked a little way from here. Do you mind walking?'

'No, not at all.'

She loosened up easily.

'By the way, what's your name?' he asked.

'It's Jun Yuzuki. 'Jun' is just written in the *katakana* syllabary. I was born in June you see. I know it sounds like a Takarazuka stage name, but it's my real one.'

'The hydrangeas bloom in June, don't they?'

'Gee, you know that, too?'

'And not much more,' Fujio admitted.

He had watered that plant when he worked at the seed store. It's a plant that likes moisture, and the roots don't rot, no matter how much water you give it.

'My dad isn't interested in any of that. He doesn't know the difference between a chrysanthemum and a rose. How about you, sir?'

'Hey, leave off the 'sir' stuff! Just call me Mr. Miura. I'm only thirty-two.'

Today, surprisingly, Fujio gave his right age.

'I'm seventeen,' the girl said. 'But the father of a friend of mine is thirty-five."

'Oh, yeah? So when was she born?'

'He was only seventeen when he became a father.'

'I bet her mother was older, right?'

'Right. She's four years older than him.'

'Seventeen...Older women all look good then.'

'Anyway, my friend's mother is older. She thinks her mom is sure to lose her husband, but her dad says that her mom is the best-looking woman in the world.'

'I like some older women, too,' Fujio allowed.

'Gee, that's neat. Are you going to get married?'

'I'd like to, but I'm not really up to it.'

'What kind of work do you do, sir?' she asked.

'My work?' Fujio pretended to be perplexed. 'It's hard to explain, really. It's like dealing with the whole globe.'

'Are you in finance?'

'No, finance is only part of it. I'm a poet.'

'Oh! Wow!'

'It's not so much. I've only published one collection. Under a pen name.'

'What's the pen name?'

'I'll tell you later, OK?'

'I write poems, too,' she said, 'but I've never shown them to anyone.'

'Same with me. When I said that I wanted to be a poet, everyone was against it. I mean, my mother says it was good. Even when I dropped out of school, she said I had talent.'

'I envy you. My family was the opposite. When I said that I wasn't going to school, they said everything would be ruined.'

'So how come you don't want to go to school?'

'Just because...'

'Don't be so bashful. I've had some experience.'

'I know, but I couldn't go on studying English and all that. I was picked on, too. If I was left alone, I would secretly have studied the parts I couldn't do later. But in the class the teacher kept calling on me, as if I was a kind of target. I got scolded when I couldn't answer. And then I just didn't want to go any more.'

'I know just what you mean,' Fujio agreed. 'There are always some sadistic teachers like that.'

'I don't mind that they thought I was dumb, but nobody seems to read books much. After I quit school, I began to read a lot. Whenever my mother hears music coming from my room, she thinks that I'm only listening to music, but I'm reading, too. You know, she thinks you can't listen to music and read a book at the same time.'

'I do that, too,' Fujio said. 'And I write poetry the best when I'm riding on the train.'

'I really know what you mean. I don't even like to talk with friends because they only gossip about other people, or talk about clothes, or complain about the teachers. And they can't even speak proper Japanese. When the teacher used to ask them to explain something, most of them couldn't. I could, but they said

I was pushy and so I shut up. They probably thought I couldn't do it.'

'There are too many grown-ups who can't see a thing.'

'Everybody talked during assignment time and the teachers never tried to keep them quiet. They just said it was natural. I tried to explain why I didn't want to go to school, but they just said I was rebellious, and so I decided not to say anything at all.'

Jun Yuzuki was cool and composed, and she walked along cheerfully. Fujio imagined that people looking at them would think they were brother and sister. They reached the car. Fujio opened the door and they got in. But Fujio had failed to clean out the inside and so there was an odor of mildew inside that made Fujio gasp.

'I apologize for the smell,' he said to Jun. The odor had nothing to do with a dead body, however.

'Doesn't bother me. Cars smell bad whether they're new or old,' she told him.

'You say nice things,' Fujio replied. 'I just wonder why they couldn't see that at school.'

He began to drive. Jun's face showed not the slightest doubt that they were going off to look at the ocean.

'I can't talk with anyone at school,' she said.

'Yeah, I was the same,' was Fujio's reply. 'But in my case it wasn't at school—it was outside in society.'

'So you write poetry,' she said admiringly.

'Yes, because a poet has a free spirit.'

'You know what my dream is?' Jun began. 'I want to have a little house in the mountains.'

'The mountains are cold, you know that?'

'I don't care if they're cold. When I was younger, someone gave me a calendar with pictures of the Alps. I really liked that scenery and I wanted to go and see the Alps. Ever since I dropped out of school, I've wanted to be in a place where I could see the mountains. Even if everybody says that's weird, I would be able to remain calm there. The mountains make people forget their small problems. And anyway, there wouldn't be many people like that in such an environment.

'Then I'll come and write poetry in your hut in the mountains,' Fujio suggested, honestly feeling that such a day might come.

'There's a guy I was in love with,' Jun told him.

'I see.'

'Unfortunately, he's not in love with me.'

'Then he's a fool. What's his name? I'll talk with him.'

'No, that's OK. I'll live alone on the mountain and think about him. That way he'll belong just to me.'

Fujio looked at her and said, 'Meanwhile you could fall for somebody else.'

'Sure, that would be all right. It's just that I can't see why graduating from school is so good for me, like Mom and my teacher say it is.'

'Neither can I.'

'When a grown-up says that, I really wonder about them, but they can be wrong, you know.'

'Of course. But you say a grown-up...'

'They're childish.'

As he drove along, Fujio's spirits were lifted by this banter. When he had first spoken to her, he was thinking where he could take this girl—perhaps some restaurant that wasn't too expensive and had a nice view. And he'd been thinking of finding some novelty love hotel. But after talking this way with the girl, for some reason those ideas dropped out of his mind.

In a quite different tone, Jun said, 'Hey, is it OK for me to consult you about something?'

'Sure, go ahead,' Fujio said.

'It's just that recently I've really been down. There's a big fuss at home every morning. Every night, I think that I'll go to school the next day and I get ready and everything. But when I get up in the morning, I just can't seem to do it. My mom asks me why I can't go, and when I try to explain, my whole body just feels dull. My mom says I'm just being selfish, but I'm not. And my dad just doesn't want to hear any of it, so he stays in bed until the last minute, gobbles down his breakfast and tears off to work. Mom gets mad and says that he's irresponsible. Things go on and on like that. You know, I don't have any hope that anything will change, and when I'm at home—day or night, summer or winter—it's like time has stopped. That's what I feel like, and I can't even taste my food.'

Fujio thought his situation was the same as Jun's, but he said nothing about that.

'What were you doing out today? Just slipping away? Or did you say you were going out to buy a CD?'

'I can tell anything to my mother. She was going to a memorial service for some relative and I told her I was going to look at CDs in the afternoon. She didn't say anything.'

'Well, you don't have to go to school,' Fujio said casually. 'You have things that you want to do rather than feeling guilty about not going to school. Isn't there anything else you would like to do—I mean, since you can't build your cabin in the mountains right away?'

'Sure. I like to cook. I think I'd like to teach cooking if I lived in town. It's like I get involved with one thing in particular. Now I'm doing salad dressings. When Mom buys some salad dressing, I make the same thing or something better myself. I really think I could be good at teaching cooking.'

'Then you can study a lot on your own. You can read cookbooks, and if you want to do French cooking, you ought to learn to speak French. All the names of foods are in French, like historical things. It's like the culture of the French court. You could go to France and study, wouldn't that be great? This is turning into the age of female chefs, you know.'

Fujio's air of knowing all about French cooking came from the time when he worked at the hotel.

'I felt good about it because I thought I wouldn't have to go to school,' Jun replied. 'I'm comfortable now and I feel I can do anything; I don't mind studying.'

'People don't have to do things if they really dislike them. I mean, you don't *have* to go to school or anything else.'

'Is that true?' Jun asked.

'There's a reason for saying you don't want to do something. You can't fight that. If you fight it, later there will be some repercussions, and that can be scary.'

'My mom says I have to do things I don't like. She says you can't do anything if you're the kind of person who can't face up to doing things you don't want to do.'

'I don't know,' Fujio said. 'My brother-in-law is that kind of jerk, he really is. The kind of life he spends doesn't interest me at all. The god of self-control, that's him. He thinks you have to look out for your reputation all the time. 'The virtue of a coward', they call it. It's a pitiful thing.'

'My dad's a little like that,' Jun told him.

'Me, I'm just the opposite. I do only what I want to do. So my brother-in-law hates me and jibes me. Not that I'm bothered by it. I've always been a poet and no one understands me at home, that I know.' Fujio was rambling.

Jun said, 'I read somewhere that you have to take responsibility if you want to be free.'

'Oh, yeah. That stuff's pretty tedious. People should just enjoy themselves is what I think. That's just what I do, and so I can face death at any time.'

'Oh, sir, you mustn't die,' Jun said.

'No, I don't want to die. I'm still young,' Fujio said, but he felt a twinge in his heart.

Suddenly, Jun exclaimed: 'Please, stop the car!'

Fujio slammed on the brakes, thinking that she wanted to buy something.

'What do you need?' he said.

Jun opened the car door and nimbly hopped out, speaking to Fujio through the open window. 'Goodbye, sir. I'm going straight home, right now, to tell my mother that I'm not going to school any more and that I'm going to do something else. Thanks for everything. Goodbye.'

Amazed, Fujio watched as she scampered off like a young child. 'What the hell...?' he said to himself.

He couldn't get out of the car and chase after her. Some cars had already come up behind him in the narrow street and were urging him to drive on.

When he awoke the next morning, he immediately thought of Jun Yuzuki, and how absurd that all was. He knew he shouldn't really have got excited about a narrow-minded, anti-social high school dropout, but in fact he had, and he knew that he had given her some psychological lift in her despair. He should have been able to get on with his usual amusements without all that silly emotional stuff. By following the usual procedures and inviting her to a hotel, he could have helped that miserable, school-hating girl by teaching her that there was pleasure in life outside of a CD.

It was nearly noon when Fujio went downstairs to eat; his parents and Saburo had already eaten. His father had finished first and had gone out to the store to relieve his son-in-law while his mother was sipping tea and idly watching TV. Saburo was holding the newspaper open in front of him and was absorbed in reading, but when he saw Fujio enter the room he quickly folded the paper and put it down beside his knee.

'Fujio dear,' his mother said, 'Saburo has just had some curry and rice. Shall I make some nice broiled barracuda for you?'

'I don't feel like curry. Yes, broiled barracuda would be fine,' Fujio answered, wondering at the same time what Saburo's altogether too casual movement was all about. He had deliberately put the newspaper where Fujio couldn't easily reach it, tucked under the low table. Fujio thought about that for about ten seconds.

Saburo didn't get up immediately. He paused long enough to take one long breath and then stood up and escaped to the store, so that Fujio couldn't criticize him for leaving the moment he saw his face.

Instantly, Fujio grabbed the newspaper. A moment later, the look on his face froze like ice, the chill spreading to the tips of his fingers. The headline announced that the battered body of 15-year-old Tomoko Shimada, eldest daughter of the President of Shimada Foods, had been discovered on the cliffs near Matsuwa at the tip of the Miura Peninsula.

Fujio was dumbfounded.

—*How could something like that have happened? When I left her, she was certainly alive. The article says the police have found none of her clothes in the vicinity, so rather than considering it as a suicide, they've opened a murder investigation! But who could have done that?*

The question burst into Fujio's mind. He didn't notice when his mother brought him his broiled fish. He concentrated intensely, trying to recall the night he had left Tomoko Shimada naked and alone. That night on the coast there had been no cars stopped where he'd been, nor had he noticed any stray cyclists in the area. That was precisely why he had left her there.

—If there was no one around to help her, she probably became confused. But there was no one around to push her over the cliff. And what's happened to Kayo Aoki's body? There's nothing in the paper about the police having discovered another body...

Fujio thought through it all again and again. He was surely in the clear in the matter of the death of the Shimada girl. It was a matter involving the upper class, and so there would likely be no indictment.

—It was just a prank! But the girl saw my face. If she was still alive, she could have run into me somewhere and informed her parents. Then there would be some retaliation. Shimada Foods is a famous company, but who knows what it is on the inside; maybe the president has connections with gangsters...

As he thought about it all, Fujio realized how dangerous it could have been to ride on the same train if there had been a chance of encountering Tomoko Shimada as he went out on his daily pleasure rounds. Whatever the circumstances, Fujio now felt relieved that the girl was dead. Then, like a bolt of lightning piercing his heart, Fujio remembered that Tomoko's school case was still in the trunk of his car exactly as he had left it there.

—Why I did a thing like that was because I didn't kill her. I didn't even touch her naked body. And I thought I'd return it some day. Anyway, my plan would have been unfinished if I hadn't deliberately thrown away her clothing and left her naked as a statue. But her school bag didn't matter...

'Fujio dear, is anything the matter?' his mother asked. 'Don't you feel well?' She was presumably peering into his face because he wasn't answering any of her questions.

'Shut up. Sometimes I need to think,' Fujio said.

'If there's something the matter, it's best to discuss it, you know. You always used to talk things over with your mother when you were worried.'

Fujio didn't reply. He looked steadily at his mother's face and laughed harshly. He imagined the sight of her face if he were to say *Mommy, I've just killed three women and buried their bodies, so what can you do for me?*

Instead, he said, 'No, nothing's wrong. I was in town yesterday and helped a kid who'd dropped out of school. All Saburo thinks is that I'm a loser, but now and then I do something pretty good.'

That was the version he gave to his mother, but all his talking had probably done nothing more than encourage the girl's laziness.

'You've always been such a gentlemanly boy,' his mother sighed.

'Yeah? You think so?' Fujio replied.

'And even though you used to hate carrying the portable shrine at festivals, you always did it in the end like a good boy.'

'Yeah, that's right.'

Just to think about all that made Fujio cheerful. In fact, he had never carried the shrine at all, but just pretended he was holding it up with his hand and shoulder. He only touched it when they were turning it around, and then it was to push in the opposite direction.

But in those circumstances, he couldn't afford to be in a good mood. At home, it seemed to him he was surrounded by enemies. The motive behind Saburo's hiding the newspaper was now obvious; he had wanted to conceal the newspaper article from Fujio. And that only went to reveal that Saburo's suspicions had been aroused that Fujio himself was somehow involved in the incident. Of course, there was absolutely no proof. But that constant shadow of fear had showed in Saburo's eyes since the day Fujio had reacted to the poster about Yoko Miki by joking about having killed her. Hiding the newspaper could be explained as an expression of that fear.

—Saburo knows that someone like me is capable of doing such a thing, and he's thinking that if by chance I discover some evidence linking me with the Yoko Miki incident, I might go wild and cause trouble at home. He's knows I'll eventually find something, but he's trying to avoid that! That's the type of character he has—like a cowardly rat. Anyway, from now on, no matter what happens, I'll have to keep on deceiving Mother, who's always been a burden because of her naive character, as well as Saburo, who's turning into a wily observer...

Fujio went up to his rooftop castle and lay down on the *tatami* mats to work out a plan.

—There's now a pressing need to get rid of that school bag that's in the trunk of the car. The death of the Shimada girl is a big matter, and without doubt the locals will all be on the alert, looking everywhere for anything like a clue. When something like this comes up, the garbage collectors will even notice a discarded notebook or anything that might otherwise be overlooked. I think the safest thing to do is to keep the bag at home until the public excitement has calmed down. I'll put it somewhere where it won't be found...

A short while later, Fujio went downstairs. He called to his mother in a way that Saburo wouldn't notice, and when she replied he said, in a voice inaudible to Saburo, 'Could you please come upstairs?'

'Yes, of course,' his mother replied.

When they were in the prefab room, Fujio said, 'Listen, Mother, I need to ask something of you. I want you to keep something for me a while.'

'What is it?' his mother asked.

'It's just a small leather case, and to tell you the truth I don't even know what's inside it.'

'Well, whose is it?'

'It belongs to a friend of mine. Someone named Fujiki who I know through some real estate work asked me. It seems he's in the middle of a messy divorce.'

At dinner, in order to put Saburo off the trail, Fujio had deliberately mentioned that if a certain real estate deal went through, there might be something in it for Fujio. Of course, the story and Fujiki's existence were wholly fictitious.

'We had an experience like that, you know. You were so concerned that Midori would come round and turn my room upside down at one time, right? It's just that kind of situation. I mean, the two of them are still living in the same house, but there are a number of documents and letters that he doesn't want to hand over to his wife. He said he knows that she's been through his desk while he was away, and he asked me to take care of his things so that no one could get hold of them. It could be messy if he asked some close friend to do this, as most probably his wife will go around and inquire. So, since we haven't been associated for very long, and since he's never mentioned my name at home, I agreed and took his things so that his wife wouldn't have any way of sniffing them out.'

'It's an easy enough favor,' his mother said. 'I can keep it as long as you like.'

'Then I'll be off to get it,' Fujio said and left the house at once.

At his usual supermarket in front of the train station, Fujio bought a small travel briefcase. It was just big enough to put Tomoko Shimada's school bag inside, and it couldn't be opened unless you had the right combination for the lock. It was the cheapest one he could find.

Fujio walked to the parking lot where he'd left his car, checked to see there was no one about, and quickly put Tomoko's bag inside the briefcase. He closed and locked the case, and headed home with the price tag still on the handle. On the way, he met the young woman who ran the Japanese cake shop near his house. She was the one treated so badly by the old crone who was always so annoyingly nosy about Fujio's movements.

'Oh! Are you going on a trip?' she asked instead of a simple greeting.

'Right. I'm going on an overnight trip with members of my junior high school class, so I bought this travel briefcase.'

'How nice. You'll have a pleasant time, I'm sure.'

Fujio was in luck with his timing, for Saburo was away making a large delivery to a nearby company dormitory when he reached home.

'Here it is,' Fujio said to his mother.

'Then I'll put it away immediately, and only you will know where it's hidden.'

Mother was clearly enjoying hiding something. From the closet, she removed a large cardboard box that had once held something like an electric fan.

'I'll just put it in here,' she said confidentially. Without really intending to, Fujio noticed what was inside the box. It was full of his mother's old underwear: tattered brassieres, slips that were once white but now yellowed with age to some indeterminate color, and panties that wouldn't bear close examination were all thrown in together.

'Nobody ever looks in here,' she said.

Fujio couldn't even say that would be for sure.

'You really ought to think of throwing all these old rags away,' Fujio told her.

'Well, they may be of some use sometime.'

'What? How could they be of use?'

'Well, if there's an earthquake, or a fire, or a war.'

'If anything like that happens, you'll just die. You won't need this dirty old underwear!'

But, at least for the moment, Fujio felt relieved.

The morning weather report had indicated worsening conditions, and by the time Fujio had shaved again and left the house, the sky had darkened and it looked as if it was about to rain.

Previously, Saburo's attitude toward Fujio had been threatening, and when he was aware that Fujio was going out he would look daggers at him, but today he didn't even turn his head. It was not only today, for recently Saburo seemed to be intimidated by Fujio's very existence.

As he walked toward his parking lot, Fujio turned over in his mind this change in Saburo's attitude. He had just decided he would drive his car to Yokohama rather than ride the train as usual. At the same time, he was wishing it would start raining so that he could he could put up his umbrella. Those two thoughts seemed, to Fujio, to be connected by some mysterious thread tugging both ways, something from the depths of his dark soul. And while he had no wish to bring the connection to light clearly, there was something there he felt he had to make clear to himself as a matter of course. He was avoiding people as he had never done in the past. Or, rather, he didn't want to create any situations when he might be seen by the police or have to pass by a police box. It was completely different from being at home; simply by walking out like this, Fujio felt a clear intimation of danger.

—*Nothing's clearer than the fact that I didn't kill Tomoko Shimada. But because her clothes had not been found nearby, the police have initiated a murder investigation. Perhaps, after I left, if someone raped her, wrung her neck and left her there naked, the police might have decided that whoever stripped her also killed her. And, since the distribution of that poster, I'm sure that the case of Yoko Miki is also under investigation. As far as her family was concerned, it would have been just too strange for her to have left the house and consented to go along with someone...*

Fujio felt his situation becoming more tense. His emotions were divided between anger and fear. He sat in the driver's seat of the car and looked at his own face in the rearview mirror; there was a flash of lightning and a roll of thunder. What he saw in the mirror was the expression of a man gripped by what he had once thought were incompatible emotions.

Until then, Fujio had been confident he would remain unaffected by any external worries. But now the face in the mirror had a parched expression. It wasn't thin and there was still a glisten of oil by his nose, but all animation was gone; its whole expression seemed dry and dead. Fujio had betrayed himself. He was gripped by a dizzying rush of blood to his head.

—On a day like this, I could very well cause an automobile accident—and that would mean I had lost. I must be careful. I will be the quiet, ordinary, inconspicuous citizen. Then, after a time, the woman on the cliffs and the women sleeping in the ground will all return to earth. It's impossible to count how many billions of human beings have lived and died since the earth was formed, and no matter how many bones are excavated from construction sites, I can't be connected to any such reality. Those women too will blend into the earth, just like the numberless dead of history...

He set the windshield wipers for the intensity of the rain and started the car. As the wipers started beating steadily, the distant thunder drew gradually closer and the flashes of lightning became more frequent. Somewhere he'd read that lightning was evidence of life. It was in a short essay in a magazine he'd picked up in the barber's shop. He'd forgotten the author's name, but the writer had chartered a small plane in Mexico or some warm country and crashed in the jungle amidst a rain storm and fierce lightning. The pilot was killed in the crash and the author had suffered serious injuries, lost consciousness, and was not even aware that he'd been taken to a hospital. For three days and nights he was between life and death, and then miraculously he regained consciousness on the evening of the fourth day. Those two incidents—being pushed to the brink of death and then pulled back again—were both attributed to the fierce rain, the thunder that shook the earth, and the purple lightning that pierced heaven and earth.

However, Fujio could not regard the thunder as being something favorable as it was for the man who had crashed in the small plane. With rain like this, the roads soon began to get congested. Fujio struggled to calm his sensitive nerves, especially so as not to get involved in an accident.

There was only one place where Fujio could regain his composure, and that was at Yukiko's house. He wanted to take her a present of some kind, and he intended to make that his work for the afternoon. He had often thought how a department store was a support to a person's spirit. It was like an opiate. It was frequently the destination for housewives who couldn't stand staying at home. For anyone, the department store, the shopping mall or the supermarket was a public place, free of charge, where the climate never varied, and where you could remain for an unlimited time.

That night he'd spent with Yukiko, holding and covering her, he didn't know where she kept her blankets. He could have opened a closet, but he was hesitant and it would have made a disturbance.

—*I'd like to give her a blanket with a fine feel to it, one that's soft and light. But I think Yukiko would certainly be annoyed if her younger sister—who I've never actually met but looks so ill-tempered—began to question her about the gift of a blanket from a male acquaintance. And it's not yet even mid-July. It's the time when you might be expected to send some traditional summer gift— ordinary things like a towel, eau de Cologne, or slippers...*

Fujio spent nearly an hour driving to the department store in Yokohama, and then he had to wait a full twenty minutes to get into the parking lot. He went directly to where blankets were sold and looked over the offerings. However, the prices of the goods brought a revision to his plan. He never knew when he might pick up a woman and take her someplace, and he had no wish to dig into his capital reserved for that. The matter was settled. He would find an apron or something like that. When Yukiko came to the door, she usually had her rolled-up apron in her hand, and he had also seen an apron hanging on a nail in the kitchen.

The blanket section was next to the towels, where there were no customers. A rather square-faced and bony-jawed female clerk stood there glancing toward Fujio. She was obviously suspicious and keeping an eye on him. Just in retaliation, if the goods had been a bit smaller, he'd have give her a lesson in the art of shoplifting a blanket. Instead, he spoke to her.

'Excuse me. Where are the aprons?'

The name tag she was wearing had 'Suga' written on it.

'Just a moment, please,' she said, going to the cash register and consulting some kind of a chart. She returned and told him that aprons were on the 3rd floor. Fujio was then on the 6th floor.

'The 3rd floor?' Fujio repeated.

'Yes, next to ladies' underwear,' said the square-jawed Ms. Suga.

Fujio thanked her and went to the down-escalator. From the escalator, he could see the music section on the 5th floor and he suddenly remembered Jun Yuzuki, the high school dropout.

He muttered softly, 'If I knew where you lived, I'd buy you an Edwin Montaigne CD.' He felt so comfortable speaking of a kindness that he didn't have to put into practice.

On the 3rd floor he went once around the underwear area that seemed to be awash in waves of lace, but he didn't come across a place selling aprons. A male clerk was passing by; Fujio asked him where aprons were sold.

'Aprons are on the 6th floor,' the man replied.

'But I asked on the 6th floor and I was told they were on the 3rd floor, and so I came down here.'

'I'm very sorry,' the man replied. 'There is a towel section on the 6th floor and the aprons are just behind that...'

'I see,' Fujio replied and went back up by the escalator. When he reached the blanket section, he said to Ms. Suga, 'I was told that the apron section is on the 6th floor.'

'Really?'

'Yes. Behind or next to the towels.'

'If it's the towel section, it's over there.'

It was hardly any distance from her counter.

'Haven't you ever walked around the 6th floor?' asked Fujio.

Ms. Suga didn't reply to that, but stared at Fujio and said, 'Our chart says that aprons are on the 3rd floor.'

'But they're on *this* floor. Haven't you seen the goods sold on the same floor as you work on?"

'I'm in the blanket department and that's not my responsibility.'

'You don't have eyes in the back of your head?' Fujio remarked.

'Well, no one has,' she told him.

'As a matter of fact, I do,' Fujio said. 'I know immediately when a finger is pointed at me from behind.'

He laughed. This woman didn't even have eyes in the *front* of her head. Possibly she was relieved that he was not really angry, for she abruptly turned and walked away.

Fujio was aware himself that he was living without any clear purpose. Not that there was anything particularly shameful in that. And it was unbearably tedious for a self-confident person like himself to lecture another person on everything he or she did. Yet, to the same extent that a cat will catch sight of a small animal and runs toward it, Fujio instinctively felt himself envisioning a target for action.

A fierce rain was now falling. It was due to continue through the night. Fujio couldn't hear the noise of the rain from inside the department store, but when he descended to the 1st floor of the building, he was struck by the stuffy odor of the rain that filled the inside.

Fujio was by no means lying in ambush, and it was surely mere chance when, in the congestion of people he felt a human presence sending him a signal. It was the woman named Suga who worked in the blanket section.

'Thanks for just now,' Fujio said to her from behind. 'Thanks to you, I bought an apron, a nice one, with a kind of foreign style design.' Fujio lifted the department store bag he was holding and smiled happily. 'Are you going home?'

'Yes,' she replied.

'Let me give you a lift in my car. This rain is something else. Which way are you going?'

'Kami-ooka,' she replied.

'That's not far from my house. In fact it's on the way, so I'll take you there. You'll get soaked just walking from the station in rain like this.'

'Really?'

After his complaint a while back, Fujio thought she might get embarrassed and refuse his offer, but she gave no hint of that. Together they moved toward the parking lot beneath the store where Fujio had left his car, but there was no conversation as they walked along.

'It sure is nice to get into a car, isn't it? It's your own personal world,' Fujio said with a pleasant expression. 'And your husband?' he added.

'I'm not married.'

'Oh? Divorced?'

'No, just not married yet.'

'How come you're not married?' he said with a surprised expression on his face.

'Well, I can make a living without getting married.'

'So you think marriage is only for making a living?'

'Well, isn't it? If the husband earns and all the wife has to do is stay at home, then it's great for women!'

'What are you interested in?'

'My hobby, you mean?'

'Yes, surely you have some kind of hobby?' Fujio said.

'Nothing in particular. I save money.'

Fujio's nerves began to tingle when he heard that—not an unpleasant sensation. He had always thought that an attachment to money is as straight as an appetite for food and sex, so that was good.

'I can understand you liking money. Do you like sex?' Fujio asked.

'It's just like food,' Ms. Suga said.

Fujio laughed happily. 'Then let's go and have something to eat.'

Ms. Suga grinned, saying nothing.

'Let's see, your surname is Suga, right?' Fujio said.

'That's right.'

'What's your given name?'

'Reiko. The characters mean 'lovely child.''

'A pretty inappropriate name!' Fujio mumbled as if to himself, but loud enough for her to hear. Then he asked, 'Are your parents living in Kami-ooka?'

'No, I've got an apartment there. My parents live in Kyushu.'

'Really? I guess you've had quite a lot of experiences here, then.'

'Sure.'

'The place where you're working isn't bad, but I don't think that department suits you. If you were to move into neckties, you'd get fed every day.'

'Oh, I never miss a meal.'

'Oh, sorry. My mistake.'

'The blanket department isn't much fun, but it's better than staying at home.'

'I suppose your parent's place is pretty boring?' he suggested, half teasing.

'My father is seventy-five and senile. He soils himself, and when we have meals together he's always coughing and spitting his food all over.'

'Seventy-five?...He's too young to be senile.'

'I was the last child, you see,' Reiko said.

Fujio calculated that she must be about thirty-five years old.

'Then who's looking after your father?' he asked.

'My mother. She's seventy-two, and it's hard for her. She wants me to quit work and go home.'

'You could live in the country and adopt a husband,' Fujio said.

'Oh, that's not for me at all—living in the country with a senile old man. If someone has to look after them, my older brother lives nearby and he can do it. After all, he's the oldest son and he'll carry on the family name.'

'So you're thinking of getting your fair share of the inheritance and yet you let your brother take care of your dad?'

'Yes, I think I have a right to it.'

'You know, you're really shameless,' Fujio told her. He expected that she would get angry at this criticism, and he was half hoping that she would get out of the car in indignation. Instead, she merely giggled. Fujio was rather disappointed.

'So, how about it? Where shall we go? Which do you like better, Japanese food or Western?'

'Well, for me something Japanese.'

'I'll bet you like a futon more than a bed,' Fujio smirked. 'So let's go straight for Japanese. Then we can eat the futon!'

With that remark, the two of them enjoyed a dirty laugh together.

'And what's your name, sir?' Reiko asked as though she was addressing a customer at the store.

'Me? I'm Wataru Miura.'

'And what kind of work do you do?'

'I'm a poet.'

'Oh, yeah? Can you live by poetry?'

'Not usually. But in my case, my parents had some money, so it doesn't matter whether the poetry sells or not.'

'Poetry,' she said. 'What do you write?'

'Well...I write some poems about happy things, but mostly I write about grief and unhappiness. My nerves are more sensitive than most people's, so I grieve and suffer more than most. Poets...a lot of them really lead unhappy lives, you know. Unhappiness brings out your artistic talent, really.'

'Then it's a loss for you. I mean, you can't work unless you're unhappy. I just want to forget awful things as fast as I can.'

'But isn't forgetting that a loss for you? Grief, unhappiness—they're your personal capital. No one can forget their personal capital.'

That idea was merely something Fujio had taken in from words he'd caught as he had zapped across the television channels.

They came out of the underground parking lot, the windshield wipers struggling fast to remove the rain water.

'I'm glad I'm not alone! When it rains like this, no matter where I go, it's like the car isn't moving. I get irritated when I drive alone. I really like women a lot. I always feel in a good mood when there's a woman around.'

'Are all poets womanizers?' Reiko asked.

—*I reckon that whatever answer I give to this woman who asks such stupid questions will be accepted as the truth!*

'No, that's not it. There's one poet I know who likes lizards. He says the coolness of a lizard is inexpressible...'

'Doesn't he have a woman? A wife?'

'His wife left him. One day she stepped on one of his lizards by mistake and squashed it. "What a dumb lizard!" I said to him. "It might as well die if it's stupid enough to get trodden on by a human!" But the poet didn't see it that way. He got mad with his wife and hit her in the face—so she divorced him.'

Fujio took Reiko to a love hotel located in a bamboo grove in the hills just west of Oppama. Fujio had long wanted to check out the place, which was made up of a number of separate cottages that could be entered through curtained garages; he thought it would be a good spot for a rainy evening like that.

'This hotel isn't so tasteful,' commented Fujio, 'but I think its atmosphere is good for a woman like you who is fond of Japanese food. And a bamboo grove in the rain is very attractive.'

From the small hallway, they entered a six-mat living room where a *kotatsu* heater was lit under the low table. Fujio thought it would be pleasant to be there with someone in the winter, touching knees under the table and playing around. He slid back the door that separated the sitting area from the next room; marvelously, a futon with two pillows was already spread out.

'So, shall we drink some green tea and get some sushi sent in?'

As he spoke, Fujio sat down at the table. He was used to his mother preparing tea for him, so he sat at the end of the table furthest from the red thermos bottle of hot water and the round container with the tea-making equipment. Reiko sat at the other end.

'What a cute thermos bottle,' she said as she looked around. The thermos was red with a pattern of childish white and pink roses painted on it.

'Really? You like this sort of thing?' he asked.

'It's cute, don't you think?' was her reply.

'To tell you the truth, a thermos like this looks to me like cheap stuff made in some underdeveloped country. This kind of rose pattern is an attempt to hide socialist poverty, but it just doesn't succeed. That's what it says to me.'

Fujio mouthed this wild criticism without the slightest conviction.

'But you look like you could make a nice cup of tea,' he added.

Reiko burst out laughing.

'No, I've hardly had any experience with that.'

'What? Come on!'

'Green tea's expensive, so I always buy a big jar of oolong tea when it's on sale and drink that; it's cheap. When I've drunk about a third of it, I fill the rest of the jar with water. I put it in the fridge as it is and then it saves me the trouble of having to boil water for tea.'

'Do you ever cook rice?'

'Sure, I do—about once every four days. I put it in the freezer and then heat it up in the microwave.'

'I'll bet it tastes terrible.'

'Not at all. I've been living like that for years here. When I'm home in the country, I can eat freshly-cooked rice all the time, but I haven't been back home for a long time.'

'Not even to see your senile old father?'

'Because he's senile, there's no point in going home. He doesn't talk; he doesn't even know who I am.'

'Just as well he doesn't know who you are!' Fujio replied sarcastically. Reiko still took no offence.

'You're right,' she agreed. 'That's just what I think.'

With such banter, and after failing to get Reiko to prepare the tea, Fujio pulled the red thermos and the tea set to his end of the table and ended up making the tea himself. Reiko excused herself on the grounds of being no good at it and stubbornly refused to pour the tea.

To tease her, Fujio poured tea only for himself, pretending to forget about her. Since she had not shown any offense at what he had said in the car, Fujio was at this point planning to deliberately provoke her and send her home. But Reiko wasn't angry. She simply poured her own cup of tea with a calm look on her face.

When it became evident to Fujio that this woman had neither pride nor sensibility, it seemed more and more foolish to him that he should be with her at all.

While they were going back and forth about the tea, Fujio discovered something amusing. Next to the table there was a small pink refrigerator, and lined up next to it was a small safe.

'I wonder if rich people come here?' he said, pointing with his chin at the safe.

—*No…A very rich customer would stay the night at one of those inns near Izu where it costs about 100,000 yen a night per person…*

'I can't believe that after they've taken off their clothes and gone to sleep, a thief would slip in and take their money! It's more likely your partner would steal it while you're asleep.'

'You have to be prepared for everything,' Reiko said with a serious look on her face. 'There are bad people in the world.'

Fujio tried to endure her comments without bursting into laughter.

'Look, I'm just a poor poet; I don't have money or anything. But it wouldn't hurt if you were to put something in the safe—I mean, you seem to be pretty well off.'

Fujio said this as a joke. Indeed, with the two of them naked together in the room, the idea of her putting money in the safe was like a scene straight out of a comic book.

But Reiko was in earnest. 'OK. I'll put something in.'

'You mean you have that much money?' Fujio exclaimed.

'Not that much, really, but I worry if I don't have 100,000 yen with me.'

'Wow! A guy like me doesn't carry that much money very often!' Fujio said. He was laughing, but his eyes studied all Reiko's moves coldly.

From her handbag, she took out a thick batik-dyed purse which she put into the safe, locking it and putting the key in her handbag.

'Are you always so careful?' Fujio asked.

'It's just that I live alone, you know. And there's no rental fee for this safe.'

Fujio liked money, but it didn't excite him as much as sex. Still, today, that money in the safe weighed on his mind. He could not have said just why it made him feel vaguely apprehensive. It was a similar feeling to not wanting to meet up with the police and wishing to walk about with an umbrella hiding his face.

At some point, he knew, he would have to escape.

—*I've left no evidence, but what would I do if I had the feeling that some stranger was standing in the street in front of the house? He might not be particularly looking at our place, of course. It would turn out to be a joke if I thought the fellow was looking at me, and the truth was that the cake shop owner had cheated someone or done something bad and was being followed! But if something like that happens, I might have to get out of the house for good. I could probably get a little money from my mother, but if it came to fleeing, I couldn't tell her that I needed three times that much because I'd killed three people. 100,000 yen extra would certainly make things different...*

'After you come home from the department store, what do you do? What do you like? Do you have some special hobby?'

'No. I don't do anything special.'

'Just guys?'

'Yeah, well, now and then. Actually, I have some shares and I read up on that in a magazine I get on the financial market.'

'That's pretty smart. How much are you trading? Three million yen?'

'No. You used to be able to play the market with that, but no more. You need at least five million now.'

'You're really into it!'

'Five million yen isn't all that much. That's the kind of money you just forget about. If you don't have a little risk money, it's not much fun. How about you, sir? Do you play the market?'

She was still referring to Fujio as if he was one of her customers.

'No, I don't invest in the market, but a friend of mine is a broker and I get the news from him.'

'How come? You can have fun and make some money.'

'It was in my parents' will.'

'Have your parents kicked the bucket, then?'

When Fujio heard the expression 'kicked the bucket' instead of a more polite expression like 'passed on,' he thought for a moment he was talking to a foreigner trying out idioms.

'They weren't rich' he replied. 'Before they passed away, they just told me not to do that.'

'So when did they kick the bucket?'

'Five or six years ago. My father passed away first, and then Mom passed away the next year.'

'So now you're free of obligations,' Reiko observed.

—If my parents were to die and I came into some money, I would leave home immediately and live the rest of my life without ever having to look at Saburo again. And I wouldn't give Saburo one yen of his share. But a woman like this, who uses that kind of language and says I'm free to do what I like because my parents are dead, really makes me angry...

'You may not believe this, but I really respected my parents. I'm not like you.'

'Oh? Is that so?'

'My father was in hospital for a month, and my mother was there for six months before she died, and I stayed with both of them all the time.'

'That's pretty good. What did you do about your work during that time?'

'I'm a poet, and I can write anywhere. And staying up all night until dawn while one of your parents is on the verge of death is the best of conditions for composing poetry.'

'If I stay up all night I can't work the next day. I couldn't sit up with a sick person at all.'

'Hey, it's not a 'person' but your *parents*—looking after your *parents*.'

'But I don't have a special sense of obligation to my parents.'

'Do you mean they did something bad to you...your parents?'

'No, they never did anything *bad*! They sent me through high school and gave me spending money...That was it.'

'But when you were ill, they took care of you, didn't they? And if you were depressed, wouldn't they worry and ask what the matter was?'

'Yeah, I suppose so,' said Reiko. 'But for some reason I hated my parents.'

'Well, there's nothing you can do about that, and there's no argument against "for some reason." You're just an ungrateful egoist.'

'Yeah, I guess you're right,' Reiko said, without any feeling of anger.

'You know, you're a really crummy woman,' Fujio told her. 'I bet nobody likes you much—no man...nor your friends.'

'There's not much you can do about being liked or not,' Reiko said.

'That's true,' Fujio replied.

'It's more a matter of whether *I* like someone than whether someone else likes *me*.'

'And if you like someone, everyone will be overwhelmed, right?'

'Not necessarily!' Reiko laughed, with no trace of sarcasm.

'There are some pretty strange people in this world. Anyhow, today, let's get on with it without falling in love, OK? Somebody's always in love with me, so I'm afraid of looking at a woman. How about a bath first?' Fujio said, aware that the bathroom was at the other end of the futon.

'Yeah,' Reiko said, 'I'll do that.'

Unlike other love hotels, the construction of the bath area of this place was in the style of a country inn. It wasn't too wide or novel; in fact it was just a plain farmhouse-style bath. Some pink and purple tiles were set midst the light brown tiles as decoration. But, despite it's looks, the room was professionally done. There was no wall between the bedroom and the bath, only a sliding glass panel. That set Fujio to guessing about the construction. Reiko went into the changing area, and when he reckoned a minute or two had passed, Fujio brusquely slid open the sliding paper door that had been hung in front of the glass panel to make it look like a closet. He could then look directly into the bath while lying on the futon, like looking into an aquarium to admire the sights.

Reiko had just taken off her clothes and was about to enter the bath area. Just as Fujio had imagined, she had a thick waist and her center of gravity was a bit low. She was not particularly bow-legged, but her figure was hardly lithe.

When Fujio opened the door and looked through the glass, Reiko glanced his way. Her expression was not one of surprise, embarrassment, pleasure, or even amusement. Fujio was disgusted. Even a slightly startled look from her would have been something. But her blank look of seeing and not responding was impossibly inept. She gave not the slightest sign she knew he was looking at her. Instead, she went through the process of washing every corner of her body, without embarrassment, just as she always did, douching herself with the little wooden bucket like an elderly person.

—*The controlled movements of fish in an aquarium are something beautiful. There are no fat fish, and even old fish can swim. But a zoo's another matter. A hippo or a rhino will shake its mud-covered behind and go in and out of the water—and no matter how you look at it, it's hardly a thing of beauty. Reiko's like that. Not that her body's especially inferior. There are few women in the world with bodies that are a real pleasure to look at. On the other hand, Yoko Miki's body was worth looking at...*

He couldn't see the changing area, but Fujio confirmed that when Reiko went into the bathroom she took her handbag with her.

—*I could understand her taking her makeup kit, since I picked her up suddenly on her way home from work. But that wasn't the reason—she's afraid that if she doesn't have her bag with her, I'll open the safe!*

He felt foolish. He neither smoked nor drank, and there was no way he wanted to be with this short-legged, pot-bellied woman. Some alcohol or a cigarette can help if you're appraising a woman, but just looking at her unadorned body can be a miserable business. More precisely, however, what made Fujio feel miserable was not so much that Reiko's body was so poor but that, with the exception of Yukiko, all the women that he had met had been worthless.

—*They were all either liars, sluts or simpletons...They were greedy or selfish...only partial human beings. The woman contemplating suicide was a little better than the others, but I must admit I took advantage of her distressed state of mind the day we met. That conceited woman who knew something about Venice, and the lively girl who had dropped out of school—they were both pretty good, but the one didn't really suit me and the other split so fast I can't really tell. The only one left is this short-legged, uninteresting woman who I've bad-mouthed and made a fool of. She doesn't seem to care...nor has she run off and left me. She has coolly stood her ground...*

To change his mood, Fujio went to the door of the bath and called, 'Hey! How about I order some sushi?'

'Fine,' Reiko replied.

'Which do you prefer, *nigiri* or *chirashi*?'

She seemed to be thinking about the choice and delayed answering.

'I'll have *nigiri*,' Fujio said.

'That's fine with me, too,' Reiko called.

'Would you like plain or fancy?' Fujio asked.

'If you're paying for it, sir, then *you* decide.' She was still addressing him like a customer.

'OK. Then I'll just order something.'

Fujio turned away and sat on the futon, feeling disgusted with his life.

—*Being with her is getting worse by the minute. My delusion about having any fun with her is fading rapidly. I can't go on living if I don't put up a fight against the miserable aspects of the world...*

He telephoned the sushi shop at the number listed beside the phone.

'One plain, one fancy,' he ordered. 'But no shrimps with the fancy. They give me hives.' He spoke in a low voice so that Reiko wouldn't hear.

He recalled the first time that he'd taken a drive with Yukiko. When he'd ordered *tendon* at the Tenko tempura restaurant, Yukiko had said 'No shrimps for me.' That day still sparkled in his memory.

—*That was before I became a murderer. I immediately threw away the seeds Yukiko had given me—the morning glories called Heavenly Blue. If I had lived an honest life, I would still have had a chance as a human being. Now, everything has changed. Now what lies ahead is only a dark road leading straight into oblivion...*

The sounds of water splashing went on and on. Reiko was taking her time in the bath. Fujio imagined that the sushi wouldn't arrive until she had come out of the bath, but in fact he soon heard the voice of the delivery man at the special delivery box.

Deliveries could be taken through the small door located next to the entrance to the room at a height of about one meter. When you opened the door, there was a space inside just the right size for two dishes. The whole thing was arranged so that the delivery person outside and the customer inside couldn't see each other directly when the delivery was made.

Fujio paid the delivery man as requested. 'Shall I just leave the dishes in here when we've finished?'

'Yes, please,' came the answer.

Fujio sent the delivery man off and carried the sushi to the table in the middle of the room. He promptly ate the *uni* sea urchin and the most expensive cut of tuna that on the fancy plate. Sure enough, there was no shrimp.

'Oh, sorry. You were so long in the bath that I helped myself to a couple of pieces of sushi,' he said to Reiko when she came out slovenly dressed in a hotel bath robe.

'I didn't drain the bath water. Is that all right?'

'Drain it, please. I'm hungry, so I'll eat first,' he replied, but in fact he didn't at all like the idea of getting into the bathwater after her.

'Come on and eat. I don't drink any kind of alcohol, but if you'd like beer or something, I think there's some in the fridge, so go ahead.'

'No, I don't need anything,' Reiko said.

'How about if it's my treat?' Fujio suggested with a snicker.

'Well, I do drink a little beer,' she said.

'Look, don't you feel cheap talking like that?'

'Not particularly...' she said.

'Not...?'

'I just think it's good to be clear.'

'I mean about paying for this place. I'm paying for the sushi, but how about sharing the room bill?' Fujio said without hesitation.

'Well, I've heard that when a couple does something in Europe and America, the man always pays,' Reiko said.

'But you're an independent woman. The women's lib people would be in tears to hear you talk like that.'

'I'm not a women's libber!' Reiko told him.

'Just practical,' Fujio said.

'That's true.'

'You know, I'm a man who dreams. You're a woman who counts her money.'

'So, what would the poet think of that?'

'I think it's like a painting by Picasso: a good combination.'

Whether Reiko understood or not, she made a silly laugh.

'I'd like you to become my patron. Would you do that?'

'What does a patron have to do?' Reiko asked.

'You give me money because you have faith in my talent.'

'Give *you* money?' Reiko said, licking her chopsticks. 'Actually, *I've* been looking for someone who would agree to a monthly contract.'

'A monthly contract? So you want to become a kind of mistress?'

'Well, it wouldn't have to be as much as for a mistress. I could only meet the guy on the days when I don't work, because, as you know, I'm a working woman. I'm hoping for the guy to pay for my loan.'

'You? With that face?'

'It's not so bad,' Reiko said.

'And you've just bought a condominium?'

'I've had it five years so far; it's to be paid for in yearly installments spread over the next 20 years.'

'So still a long way to go! You're stingy but have bought an apartment and you like it. I'm sure it must be a good one,' Fujio chided.

'It's not bad, not too far from the train station, and it's quiet, a nice place.'

'It sure would have been better to go to your place today instead of a crummy hotel like this.'

'My place? We couldn't do that.'

'Why not?'

'I just don't let men come to my apartment.'

'You certainly are meticulous. Are you afraid the neighbors will see?'

'I'm not worried about the neighbors a bit. I just don't like the nuisance afterward when I tell a man my address.'

'You're really careful.'

'I'm just concerned at present.'

'What about?'

'They're putting up an institution near my place, and we've got a protest movement going.'

'What kind of an institution?' Fujio asked, 'An old people's home?' He remembered that Reiko had said she disliked her parents.

'It's a rehabilitation facility for disabled children.'

'But that's a good thing, isn't it?'

'I don't like it. It gives a bad impression. It will lower the property value immediately.'

'What kind of people are objecting? Are you the leader?'

'Oh, no. I don't have that kind of strength. I was just relieved that someone asked me if I'd join them in opposing it.'

'Then who instigated it? Who's the leader?'

'A university professor, a junior high school teacher and the wife of a businessman are the main people.'

'That's a funny collection.'

'Yes, they're all intellectuals.'

'You call those intellectuals?'

'They're all university graduates.'

With some effort, Fujio had kept up his attitude of lazy disinterest, but inside he was now boiling mad.

'Well, I'm not like you and I would welcome the rehabilitation facility. I'd be put out if it were a pachinko hall or something noisy like that. But even a pachinko hall wouldn't be a problem if it was soundproof and there was no noise escaping.'

'Uh-huh.'

'A prison would be fine, too; they're quiet. Or a garbage incinerator; they're really clean. They grow flowers and plants like crazy there.'

'Really? For me they'd both be bad.'

'Then where do you suggest they build prisons and incinerators?' Fujio asked, putting her on.

'Well, I wouldn't know about that,' Reiko said.

'So you wouldn't mind if they were built near someone else's house, so long as they're not near *your* house.'

'I don't know. Aren't the politicians supposed to think about things like that? I mean, maybe they could be built on reclaimed land where there aren't any houses.'

'Well, if just building things like that on reclaimed land solved the problem, they wouldn't need to ask greedy people like you for their help or understanding.'

'Anyway, I think we have a right not to have our lives violated. That's the basis of democracy.'

'Sure. But democracy is the enemy of poets. Democracy is just when everybody gives in a little—that's what I learned.'

Reiko had nothing to say to this.

'Now, don't get excited!' Fujio said, laughing. 'Let's get excited with something else! I'm going to have a shower. Meanwhile, please brush your teeth. I just lose interest in kissing if someone's mouth isn't fresh. As a poet, I'm terribly sensitive to that kind of thing.'

'All right,' Reiko said.

Fujio turned on the shower.

—*This hotel isn't that great, but at least the water pressure in the shower's strong...*

He placed a little plastic stool beneath the shower and sat there lazily enjoying the stream of hot water. The sound of the downpour outside mixing with that of the shower made him feel he was sitting in the rain. Being like this, Yoko Miki's parents searching for their daughter, and the discovery of Tomoko Shimada's corpse, and even the activities of the police—all that business seemed to be part of another world.

Suddenly, Fujio thought of a way to get at this stupid woman, Reiko. He planned it all inside his head, put on the hotel robe, and went back into the bedroom in good humor.

Luckily, Fujio had long been aware that the main force of energy for sex was disdain, or a passion for destroying something. That's why, in spite of his intentions, he had not been able to perform while holding Yukiko in his arms.

While he had been talking to Reiko, however, Fujio had found himself thoroughly despising her. He was not posing as a humanist, but it angered Fujio that a facility for disabled children, trying to help them overcome their handicaps, should be shunned because property values might drop if there was such a building in the neighborhood. And Reiko had the nerve to oppose publicly what had best been thought of in secret—if at all—and that angered him. He'd made friends with many women, and he thought he knew some sure techniques for impressing women, but he totally refused to please a woman like this. So he proceeded with his plan to please himself.

Outside, the rain still pounded fiercely. Fujio, dully aware of Reiko's angular and unmade-up face and her short, untidy hair on the pillow, pulled himself away from her and fell relieved onto the futon beside her.

'You said you made love a lot, sir,' Reiko said, 'but is that the way you always do it?'

—*I gave her a name—false as it was—but she just can't stop addressing me like a customer! I wonder if she's expecting to be paid afterward?*

'Right. I'm indifferent to everything when it comes to life,' he replied.

'I don't think you're *indifferent*. You're just below average.'

—*Sure, and a fool like you chatters on about what everybody already knows...*

He folded his hands under his head and looked at the ceiling.

'Sorry I wasn't any good,' he said.

'I've never been so disappointed,' she replied.

'You're really a fine critic on these matters.'

'I've had a lot of experiences, that's all.'

'I'd hoped to take my time here today, but I just don't seem to be able to make it with you...So shall we leave?'

'Whatever you like. *You're* paying for it.'

'And if *you* pay for it?'

'If *I* paid for the hotel, we'd stay until morning. Otherwise it would be a waste of money.'

Fujio thought about that for a few moments. Then he said, 'You know, you're really trash.'

'Oh, really? Well, I don't much care if I am.'

'Let's go. I'm a poet and there's nothing about you that inspires me.'

'Have it your way. You brought me a long way out here, so you can just take me home.'

Hearing her talk about being brought a long way, when she had readily consented, made Fujio feel sick. But he hadn't yet carried out the plan he'd thought up in the bath, so he showed only a look of agreement. It was already 11 p.m.

'It's still raining heavily. A day like this really makes you depressed. I thought I'd try to forget disagreeable things and come here with you, but it didn't go very well. Actually, I came her wanting you to listen to my story.'

Fujio muttered this nonsense as he was fastening his seat belt in the car.

'What did you want to talk about?' Reiko asked.

'The fact is, I'm not really formally married, and what I wanted to talk about was the girl who is going to have my child.'

'That's all right, isn't it? Why don't you get married? Your parents are dead and so there's nothing standing in the way.'

Fujio started the wipers and drove the car out.

'I don't know where to begin. Until about six months ago, I was living in San Francisco.'

Reiko said nothing.

'Well, I don't believe in thinking about the future, so when I got that little inheritance from my parents, I took it and went to San Francisco and I started living with someone there.'

'That sounds great...I mean, for a poet and all.'

'Yeah. My friend was a great person, too—talented, good-looking. But it was a man. He was going to be an actor.'

'Was he?'

'We lived together, fooling around and enjoying ourselves, for three years. I mean, we got along, but all the time I was thinking that we couldn't continue like that. There were a lot of things. Anyway, I came back to Japan to break off my relationship with him. And then I met this woman. I was really happy with the idea of returning to a normal, straight life. Even though she wasn't my wife, I thought we'd get married. And then, when she said she was pregnant, I really wished that my parents were still alive.'

'Of course.'

'At first, I thought that we could have a relationship just as man and woman—without getting married—but, when she told me about the child, I thought that we ought to get married just like everyone else. And then, just at that time, I found out that the guy I was living with in San Francisco had died.'

'So? That was good, wasn't it? I mean, it's not something that sir would like people to know about.'

Reiko was still addressing him like a customer.

'Yeah, that's right, but it's not quite so easy. It seems that he died of AIDS, and so I'm afraid that it will be transmitted to the child.' Fujio held his breath and glanced at Reiko. 'Somehow, I just can't bring myself to tell this to the woman who is going to have my child.'

'You say you're afraid the child will have AIDS? What about yourself?'

'I don't know. I haven't had any examination myself,' Fujio said, carelessly.

'But that's *totally* irresponsible!' Reiko said, a murderous edge to her voice.

'When I heard that he was dead, the very first thing I felt was that I should be dying, too. I loved him. According to what I heard, he suffered a lot when he died. And I felt that the same fate should happen to me. And then there's the child. A completely innocent child could die because of me, and then I would have to die as punishment. My girlfriend was so happy when she knew about having the baby. I just can't tell her that the baby may have AIDS. I can't say it. I'd die before saying that.'

'Well, do you feel any different? Do you feel anything strange about your body?'

'No, today I'm fine. It's just that I've had a lot of colds lately that I don't seem to be able to get over, which is strange for me. I've also lost some weight lately. Until a while ago, I was quite chubby, I felt, and I tried dieting lots of times. But this time I suddenly lost about 15 pounds. I felt weird, so I stopped dieting. But I'm still losing weight. I pretend to her that I'm still on a diet, and she tells me she's worried that I'm going too far. I don't think I'll be able to go on lying for much longer.'

'And just what the hell were you doing to *me*, knowing all this?!' Reiko exclaimed.

'I'm sorry. In my condition, I've lost the normal sense of consideration for other people. If you're angry about it, do whatever you wish. I'll agree to anything, honestly. No matter what happens, I don't have very long. Do whatever you wish with me.'

As he told this story, Fujio began to feel that it was true.

'I just want to spend at least one more day without this unhappy shadow,' he went on. 'Tomorrow, I'll go to her place. I thought I'd take her an apron. I even bought one. Look—I put it on the back seat.'

By this time, Fujio's voice was nearly in tears.

'I can't just shut up now and go home,' Reiko said. 'Not after hearing all that. What you've done is just too awful.'

'You know, in the past I was intimidated by women, and I was afraid,' said Fujio. 'But now, it's nothing at all. Because I'm going to die in a little while, there's nothing that frightens me at all.'

'Where do you live, sir?' Reiko asked.

'I don't have a home right now. A friend of mine is letting me stay at his cottage, and sometimes I stay the night at a rehearsal hall where some friends practice, or sometimes I spend the night with her.' Fujio spoke in a way that made it clear that he would not tell her his address.

'Well, I'm not going to stay quiet,' Reiko said. 'I'm not going to pull out of this. There's no way to withdraw silently when I've been treated like this.'

'That's all right. Do what you want to. You understand now why I was so cheerful and why I performed so badly that you got angry tonight, because you thought I was a playboy. It's true I'm trying to forget my troubles, it really is. And it's also true that my body is getting weaker and my mind is caught up in my illness to the extent of not even bothering about sex.'

'This is the first time I've ever met anyone as messed up as you,' Reiko muttered to herself.

'But I told you I was a poet. If you can't forgive me, maybe we should die someplace together. We could fall off a cliff, or crash into a tree, or drive the car off a pier and sink into the ocean. I'll take the responsibility for us dying together.'

'Oh, that's a very nice idea, but somehow I don't feel like dying with *you*.'

'Ah! You said it! I've been waiting for you to say that. It don't care whether you hate me or despise me—I've been waiting for you to call me something better than 'sir.' I've been thinking what useless things I've had in mind since I realized I might die soon.'

'You should pay me some money', Reiko said. 'I deserve some consolation money at the very least.'

'I don't have any. I gave it all to my boyfriend when we split up. Even when I met my girlfriend a while ago, that's what I told her. I said I couldn't see her because I didn't have any money. She was really mad at that. But not like you. She said that if it was a money relationship, I should leave immediately. That made me happy because I knew she loved me.'

As far as Reiko was concerned, what Fujio was saying was just a lot of defensive smokescreen.

'Listen!' Reiko declared. 'I'll think it over. I'm going to talk to a lawyer. You're going to take responsibility. So please tell me your address.'

'I'll call you on the phone, honestly. You can trust me. Even if you're not at the store, I'll get in touch with you.' Fujio was maneuvering. 'I'll tell you. I'm not like the usual kind of AIDS patient; I'm not in the least bit afraid of people knowing what I have. I don't care if no one comes near me. The people in the theatre group know about it and they accept me. I don't care if everyone shuns me. My friend in San Francisco was like that, too; he was found dead where people in the final stage all lived together. I should die abandoned like that, too. So I won't try to escape or hide. Couldn't you change your point of view in this situation?'

Fujio looked over at Reiko. The car was dark, but for a moment he could see her clearly in the light of another car's headlights. She was looking extremely agitated. And though she said nothing, her lips were moving as though she was speaking.

'In the first place, 'Fujio went on, 'we don't know whether I've given you the disease or not, so let's think about that later.'

'You lying bastard!' Reiko suddenly blurted out like a man. 'Saying that so calmly!'

'But if you aren't sick, you'll just be so happy you'll weep for joy,' Fujio said. 'You'll take a whole new view of people. It will be all right to put up a rehabilitation facility for disabled children in your neighborhood, that's how you'll think, I'm sure of it.'

'You've said enough! You *murderer!*'

Suddenly, madly, Reiko was at Fujio's neck, choking him. He could hardly control the steering wheel but he managed to stop the car beside the road. When he heard the word 'murderer', Fujio had become enraged. He hit her face with all his strength. Her saliva flew against his cheek. Then, in that cramped space, to silence her emerging screams, he drove his fist hard into the pit of her stomach.

'Don't give me any trouble...' he growled.

He looked at the now quieted woman and wiped the sweat from his forehead. He lowered the seat as far as possible. The woman looked as though she were drunk and asleep.

—*That settles it. It'd be a bad idea not to throw away any things that could later lead to trouble, like the last time. I'd better throw her handbag beside her in the road. Then, when she notices it, she'll get home somehow. She might complain or say something, but I'm not afraid of that. Even if I run into her now and then around Yokohama Station, she won't say anything about AIDS for fear of what might happen if people learned about it. And if she's worried, she can go to a doctor and find out there's nothing at all wrong with her...*

What Fujio was aiming for was exactly such a foolish series of procedures.

—*Anyway, now she can take a little nap in the rain. It isn't winter; she's unlikely to freeze to death. In fact, it's rather good weather for sleeping in the rain. Her clothes will be ruined, so she might decide to demand compensation from me. But she'll find out it's much too optimistic to think that she can buy new clothes that easily...It won't do to be seen throwing her out of the car and driving off. I need a few minutes in the dark to find a place where there are few cars out driving...*

As though by some homing instinct, Fujio once again headed the car towards the south along the Miura Peninsula.

Chapter 13

NOTHINGNESS

WHEN Tomoko stayed at home on her days off, for Yukiko it was rather like having a somewhat troublesome husband around. However, from time to time, she thought that perhaps it was good to have that kind of tension sometimes.

When Tomoko was there, Yukiko continued working as usual; her sister rarely stayed long in her workroom. Even so, Yukiko felt confined; she couldn't scatter things about as she usually did. For her it was quite all right not having a place to put a foot down in the room, but she felt that it was an inconvenience for others.

'Maybe I'm getting old,' Tomoko said. 'After a late night, I'm really tired the next day.'

She had got out of bed at around 10 a.m. and was now smoking a cigarette at the kitchen table, her coffee cup in front of her. In earlier days, Yukiko had worried a little whether Tomoko's coffee was just a prelude to breakfast or whether that would constitute the whole of it. But recently she had stopped thinking about things like that. She realized she need only start preparing food if Tomoko showed some clear intention of wishing to eat. She'd come to understand that this ambivalent morning interval, when she was neither asleep nor properly awake, was an important time for Tomoko to relieve her stress.

'What time did you get in last night?' Yukiko asked. She had woken up when she had heard Tomoko coming in the night before, but she hadn't even looked at her clock because she had been afraid that she wouldn't be able to get back to sleep.

'Around 2:30, I suppose,' Tomoko replied.

'That's early morning rather than late at night!' Yukiko responded.

'I was a bit worried about Mitsuko Kanaya, so I stopped by her house. You know, it looks like they're doing just fine. Her husband came out to say hello. He said that it was Mitsuko who was to be pitied. And as for the child...they can handle that. It seemed to me that since he could talk so calmly about the problem, they would work it out between them—psychologically, I mean. Or so I thought. But then Mitsuko broke down crying.'

'Do you think she was just glad, or relieved?' asked Yukiko.

'For a moment I thought so, but it wasn't that,' Tomoko replied. 'I felt they were trying to make things look all right.' She added that the husband had less to say than ever and went to bed without saying anything, even though it was only 9 p.m. Tomoko knew about his insomniac tendencies, but she could hear him snoring in the next room.

'Maybe he was especially tired from something?' Yukiko suggested.

'Yes, that's what I thought, too, but then all he had to say was "I'm really tired because of such and such, so I'm going to bed." He's the kind of person who would normally do that—but he didn't.'

After Mitsuko's husband had gone to sleep, Tomoko felt more at ease. But the apartment was hardly spacious, and, unless the snoring continued, Tomoko felt that she ought to be careful about what she said.

'Even then, I had my doubts,' Tomoko said.

'What about?' Yukiko asked.

'I'm such a suspicious kind of person, you know, and I wondered whether he wasn't just pretending to be asleep while he was listening to us all the time.'

'Wouldn't it be strange for him to be making a snoring noise if he was listening in?' Yukiko imagined the scene, envisioning something out of a comic book. She couldn't help laughing.

'It's my evil nature that makes me so suspicious.'

But it was only when they were alone that Tomoko and Mitsuko had got down to talking in earnest.

'His demeanor hasn't changed since the incident,' Tomoko reported. 'He hasn't said, "After what happened, let's get divorced". I said, "I think that's fine. It's like slipping and grazing your skin; it doesn't heal quickly. If it doesn't turn into anything decisive, I think it'll resolve itself naturally." That's what I feel and that's what I told her.'

'I feel the same way,' Yukiko said. 'Human beings forget.'

However, the relationship between Mitsuko and her husband was not so calm. Although there was no outward change in her husband, Mitsuko had to endure his unresponsiveness. He neither blamed her nor said anything cruel; he was just extremely quiet.

'Has he always been untalkative?' Yukiko asked.

'Well he's a man; it's not like a woman. He was the very picture of adequacy. He's not a chatterbox, but, you know, the kind of person who can say what's on their mind. Although there were times when I thought his adequacy was a bit problematic.'

—I've always thought that Tomo-chan and I are very different, both in appearance and character. But these things she's saying really strike a chord with me. How funny it is that we are definitely alike in a way! When a person comes up against something shocking that can't be avoided, they have to curl up and

endure it. There are drugs for a wound to the heart, but there's no medicine. You can only cling to the healing power of nature itself...

Tomoko said that Mitsuko's husband was quite nervous immediately after the rape incident, but after a short time he simply became silent. At first, Mitsuko was grateful, but then she began to detect a dark change within the silence.

'Mitsuko says she felt he wasn't saying anything because he was feeling calmer about the situation and he felt some compassion for her,' Tomoko recounted. 'But if I were her, from the beginning I wouldn't feel like that.'

'Neither would I,' said Yukiko.

'It's not as though silence is being polite,' Tomoko went on. 'After all, they're husband and wife. Naturally, there would be times when they would touch on the matter. Not discussing it at all is just evidence that they're concerned about it.'

'But she's not being as analytical as that?'

Tomoko slowly lit her cigarette and said, 'I suppose her hunch is the same as yours.'

Mitsuko felt she couldn't ask how her husband's work was going at the bank. He had been there for many years, and was probably continuing his duties without any noticeable change. But at home he had definitely changed. As before, he watched baseball and sumo on TV, and sometimes a quiz show. When Mitsuko gazed at his back at those times, she told herself that she should think everything was all right, that their day-to-day life had not crumbled in the slightest. But she realized from time to time that her husband hadn't the slightest idea about what was happening on the programs he was watching.

'Who's winning today?' she would ask about a baseball game, trying to make polite conversation, but her husband couldn't even answer what inning it was, let alone who was ahead.

She couldn't help asking, 'Darling, what are you watching?' It took all of her strength not to make her inquiry a rebuke: 'Don't you even know the score?'

'Well, I was thinking about something else,' he would reply.

'Don't you feel well?'

'No, no, I'm OK,' he would reply.

Mitsuko had heard that the recent health check conducted by the bank had showed that there was nothing wrong with him.

'Men have to continue worrying about their work on the train and at home, you know,' her husband said.

There was nothing unreasonable in her husband's explanation. Mitsuko herself, when she started to think about something as she was riding on a train, often passed two or three stops without noticing. She admitted as much to herself, but she was not satisfied with what her husband had said. She hardly thought he was being untruthful, and yet she couldn't believe he was so immersed in his work that he could overlook who was winning or losing a baseball game.

It was true that he had a habit of bringing work home. Mitsuko never knew what it was about, just that there were a lot of documents, and that he said that he was preparing for a meeting. Then he would stay up late at night working at his desk. It was routine kind of work—nothing that demanded much extra mental effort.

Her husband was by nature an intelligent person, eager about everything he did, even when at leisure. But recently, no matter what he was doing, he seemed to be acting without thinking. With sports, spectators can just sit back and relax, although the actual sportsmen are very serious abut what they're doing. Mitsuko's husband really enjoyed watching sportsmen in action, and so it was all the more odd that he was unaware of the score.

Yukiko listened to these and other details of Tomoko's report. Then she remarked, 'It sounds like there's something a bit worrying in all that.'

'Exactly. Things are not going very well. But it's not yet time to reach any conclusions. Mitsuko said she had the feeling they would lose the most important time of their young lives if things went on like this.'

'But there's nothing they can do about it, so that's the way it is.'

'That's right. I stayed up late last night with her, but not with the intention of trying to come up with any solutions. She seems to feel a bit better after talking with me.'

'Then you did something good,' Yukiko said. At the same time, she was thinking of her own situation and the times in your life when you have to wait.

—*People often say there is no special time to marry. While that certainly is not a lie, neither is it meant to console someone lightly. It's merely a fact. I can see myself living my whole life without any chance of marriage. Nothing can change that, and so there's no need to give much thought to something I can't do nothing about. Of course, if something doesn't work because you don't make enough effort, then you need to reflect on it. In the real world there's usually some element of being able to influence your own fate. But in the schools these days, education doesn't seem to recognize any such thing as 'fate.' I've heard that students are taught that suggestions about someone's 'unhappy fate' are only really an admission of poor government or some social evil. But personally I can't imagine anybody not being influenced by fate...*

At that moment, there was some commotion outside the front door. As it slid open, she heard a voice calling out, 'Miss Hata! Hello? Miss Hata!'

Startled, Yukiko sprang to her feet. It was the voice of the liquor store owner who sometimes delivered things.

'Anybody at home?' he called.

'Yes, coming!' Yukiko replied, and in a moment she encountered the young man. He was looking very tense. He was dressed in blue jeans and a casual shirt.

'It's Mrs. Iwamura, next door...'

'What's happened?'

'She's not dead, but I went next door and there was no answer, and when I looked in she was just lying there on the floor,' he said.

Yukiko quickly stepped down into the hallway and slipped on her sandals.

'When I spoke to her, she answered. She said she was tired and decided to lie down. But she didn't have any futon laid out and she was wearing her street clothes. She was just lying on the floor. It's strange...'

Yukiko dashed out without answering.

At the entrance to Mrs. Iwamura's house, Yukiko kicked off her sandals and went straight into the house. Just as the liquor store man had said, Mrs. Iwamura was lying face up on the door sill between two rooms, in a peculiar position.

'Mrs. Iwamura, what happened?' asked Yukiko as she slid the old lady onto the *tatami* mats, which would be less painful for her to lie on. She felt she had to do something.

'I was feeling a little weak,' Mrs. Iwamura answered in a thin voice, 'so I'm resting.'

'When was that? How long have you been lying here?' Yukiko asked.

Mrs. Iwamura made no answer.

—*Well, she's breathing alright. Perhaps she feels relieved somebody's come...*

'We shouldn't leave her like this,' said the man from the liquor store.

'That's right. We don't even know if she's eaten recently or not,' Yukiko replied.

'Shouldn't we call an ambulance?'

'Yes, let's do that,' Yukiko said.

—*I'm sure she can hear us, but she hasn't objected. So I suppose that's OK...*

Listening to the man telephoning the 119 emergency number and giving directions to the address, Yukiko went to have a look in the kitchen. There was hardly any sign of food having been prepared and it didn't seem to have been cleaned up for a while. Neither were there any food scraps about. But when Yukiko looked inside the rice cooker, she found a bit of dried rice at the bottom of the pot. From the amount there, she could guess nothing. It might have been cooked recently and these were the leftovers, or it might have been cooked four or five days ago. It was hard to tell.

Yukiko had a look in the chest of drawers, thinking Mrs. Iwamura would need a nightgown if she went to hospital. But the drawers contained only kimono that she had probably been wearing for years, and Yukiko couldn't find even a well-worn nightgown.

Speaking close to the old woman's ear, Yukiko said, 'Mrs. Iwamura, we're going to the hospital for a bit to let the doctor have a look at you, so you'll need a nightgown. Can you tell me where to find one?' But, as she had half expected, Mrs. Iwamura didn't answer.

'Were you going someplace after this?' Yukiko asked the liquor store owner.

'No, I was just walking around today collecting the money,' he said. 'But that doesn't matter.'

'Then could you ride with her in the ambulance? When you reach the hospital, please give me a call and let me know where she's been taken to. If you can do that, I'll prepare her things and bring them to the hospital right away.'

'Sure, that's fine.'

Yukiko had never telephoned to Mrs. Iwamura's daughter, but she felt she should try to contact her now to tell her about her mother.

In a few minutes she heard the ambulance siren and then the sound of the men coming into the house. The man from the liquor store started explaining how he had found Mrs. Iwamura.

When one of the ambulance men saw Yukiko, he said, 'Are you her daughter?'

'No,' Yukiko told him. 'I'll try to contact her immediately.'

Yukiko watched as they went out with the stretcher. Then she went back in. She vaguely remembered the old lady saying her daughter's name was 'Naoko.' Fortunately, the first name on Mrs. Iwamura's telephone memo book was 'Naoko Fujita.' Yukiko tried calling, but there was no answer.

Yukiko went to the closet and opened it. It exuded a foul odor. She found two rolled-up nightgowns inside. But when she took them out and examined them, she found that they were both soiled and had been stored away like that. They were not simply dirty from wearing; there were signs of incontinence on the material. In spite of that, the garments had been put away. Right away, Yukiko went to put the two robes into the washing machine. When she opened the lid, she found that there was already a robe floating there like a body in the water.

As quickly as possible, Yukiko returned to her own house.

Tomoko was sitting on the sofa in the living room smoking a cigarette. It was just like her to have heard the sound of the ambulance but realize there was no need for her to do anything because Yukiko had gone next door.

'Is she dying?' Tomoko asked.

'No, she's still alive. But she's not fully conscious,' Yukiko replied, thinking that for the time being there was nothing else but to take one of her own nightgowns to the hospital.

The man from the liquor store called about half an hour later. He reported that they had taken Mrs. Iwamura to the emergency room and then into a regular ward, and during that time she had been able to say one or two words in response to questions.

'She's in the Miura Hospital in front of the train station.'

'Not the municipal hospital?'

'No. Apparently it was full.'

'It seems her daughter is still out,' Yukiko said. 'I couldn't reach her. That's a bit worrying, but anyway I'll go right to the hospital with the things Mrs. Iwamura needs.'

'If you'll excuse me, I think I should be getting home soon,' he said.

'Of course. You've been a great help in taking care of her,' Yukiko said.

'I'll just stay for a little while, and then I'll leave if there's no change,' he said.

'Well, it's all thanks to you she's there. If you hadn't come by, she might have lain there unnoticed and died,' Yukiko said.

'If that had happened,' he said, imagining what it would have been like to find Mrs. Iwamura's dead body while making his rounds, 'I think I'd have fainted away with shock.'

Yukiko returned to the now empty house next door. She collected a small wash bucket, the toothbrush and comb from the bathroom that Mrs. Iwamura seemed to use, some well-worn slippers that were cast off in the hallway, a glass, a pair of chopsticks, and so forth—all the things that caught her eye that Mrs. Iwamura might need. She also copied down the daughter's phone number and returned home.

'Will you write the daughter's telephone number on the notepad?' Tomoko said. 'And the number of the old lady's hospital room. While you're at the hospital, I'll try to reach her daughter.'

'That would help a lot. But I don't know the number of the Miura Hospital,' Yukiko replied.

'Just leave that to me,' said her sister. 'My only professional skill is getting around obstacles like that!'

Without saying anything, Tomoko would probably consult the business section of the telephone directory, cigarette in mouth, and write down the hospital's number along with other necessary data. She left no doubt that she would get through to the old lady's daughter.

Mrs. Iwamura's ward was on the 6th floor of the hospital. There were six beds in the room; her bed was nearest to the hall. She was sleeping. There was an intravenous drip-bottle on a stand beside her. The occupant of the bed near the window was out of the room somewhere, and in the next bed a woman in her fifties was half sitting up reading a magazine. She was plump and in good color; it was difficult to guess what was wrong with her.

Yukiko entered the room circumspectly. But the patients immediately sensed someone different, and she was subjected to inquisitive looks.

'I'm sorry to disturb you,' she said to the woman in the next bed and to the one opposite.

'Are you her daughter?' asked the woman in the next bed, her voice suggesting that she came from the Kyoto-Osaka area.

'No, I'm just a neighbor. But she does have a daughter,' Yukiko replied. 'This happened suddenly and we called her, but there was no one at home and we haven't been able to reach her. But I expect she'll be here today.'

Actually she had just had an unpleasant experience related to the daughter. There was nothing specific to reproach the hospital about, but when she'd approached the room where the nurses were and explained why she had come to the hospital outside visiting hours, the fact that admittance papers had not been completed and no health insurance forms had been filed engendered some complaint. Of course, Yukiko had no idea where the documents might be in someone else's house, and she could hardly search for them before the daughter arrived. The nurses didn't seem to care.

'Well, it's good of you to take care of her,' the woman said. She was more pleasant than the nurses. Yukiko read her name from the tag at the head of the bed—Sakae Mukai—and that of her doctor—Joji Nagata.

'Excuse me, but is your physician also Dr. Nagata?' Yukiko asked.

'Yes, that's right,' the woman replied.

Yukiko had learned from the nurse that the examining physician for Mrs. Iwamura was named Nagata, but he was not available just then.

'It seems this old lady's doctor is also Dr. Nagata. I wonder if he's here today?' Yukiko inquired.

She wanted to obtain as much information as possible to pass on to Mrs. Iwamura's daughter.

'Have you asked the nurses?' the woman asked.

'Yes, they said that he was visiting the wards just now, and so I thought that he might be here. It seems he's the internal medicine specialist.'

'He hasn't been around yet today. In fact he doesn't often come by.'

'That's all right; I was just anxious about what I should tell her daughter so that she'll feel relieved. Either her daughter or I will visit tomorrow.'

'He's so busy, he's really hard to get hold of,' the woman said.

It was not a general hospital, but the six floors seemed to have internal medicine, surgery, plastic surgery, obstetrics and pediatric departments. Yukiko was rarely ill. When she was a child she had had pneumonia, but as far as she could remember she had not been hospitalized, and so she wasn't familiar with hospital procedures. She was convinced that she could come the next day or later, meet the doctor, and find out about Mrs. Iwamura's condition. She assumed that the results of whatever tests had been done would not yet be available since the ambulance had only arrived a little while before.

Yukiko's day had already been busy, and when she finally reached home and looked at her watch it was already past 2 p.m.

'You couldn't get her on the phone?' Yukiko said, seeing that Tomoko was silent. It seemed unlikely that she'd spoken to the daughter.

'No. There was no answer. I checked with the operator and she said the line was in order.'

It was just like Tomoko to be laidback like that—but in fact she had done everything that was necessary.

'Thanks, anyway. I wonder where she's gone? She probably didn't go on a trip,' Yukiko said.

'You think not? Listen, Yukiko, there was a study that showed housewives hardly ever stay at home.'

'Where do they go all the time? Surely not out cheating on their husbands?'

'Sure, some of them. But it's the working women who want to relax at home as much as they can when they're not working. The high-spirited women who don't work are out by 9:30 in the morning.'

'What's the significance of 9:30?'

'If they leave home by 9:30, they can get to the department stores by the time they open at 10.'

'But they don't go to a department store every day, do they?'

'Well, the elder sister of someone in our editing department says she goes every day.'

'Is she that rich?'

'I wouldn't say that. But that doesn't make any difference. She just buys some food for the day, or, if not food, then some trifle that satisfies her needs, and then she goes home.'

'What do you mean by *trifle*?'

'Oh, you know, just something like a basket to hold things, or a cover for the telephone, or a knife that cuts vegetables into various shapes. She buys useless things like that every day so that the things pile up in their small apartment until there's no place to put your foot down. Even when she's told she should give things away, or throw them out if she doesn't use them, she says that she may use them someday. Her younger sister says she thinks that's sick. But I hear its not just her, it's widespread, and she says it's really like a sickness.'

'I suppose it's all right if it somehow manages to satisfy them,' Yukiko said.

'One way of thinking is that it's good for Japan's economy. If people like that buy useless things, domestic demand increases, and we look better vis-à-vis America. That's what I said to cheer her up.'

Yukiko telephoned to the young man from the liquor store who had been the first person on the scene, but he hadn't yet returned from his deliveries.

Yukiko described the hospital room and so forth to his young wife.

'Oh, that's a relief, I'm so glad,' she repeated several times.

Finally, a little after 8 p.m., Yukiko managed to reach Naoko Fujita. The daughter took in what information Yukiko could offer.

'Oh, I see. Thank you very much,' she said.

But Yukiko noticed that she didn't say that she would go to the hospital.

'The fact is, my husband is also ill,' Naoko said, as though to excuse herself. But she didn't say what was wrong with him, nor whether he was resting at home or in hospital.

'Yes, well, she says her husband is ill,' Yukiko muttered as she hung up the phone 'but it seems that she was out all day anyway.'

'Just forget it,' Tomoko said in a cool tone. 'There's no way to know the circumstances of other people's lives. When I think that one side is definitely to blame for things, it usually turns out to be both sides.'

'That's really true,' Yukiko agreed.

'Yuki-chan, you're so kind-hearted and you get so worried each time anyone gets hurt in some way! But I think that whether people are old or anything else, everything that happens to them does so because they choose it themselves. It's the result of fate.'

Recently, Tomoko's magazine had put together several special features on the elderly. She had written the title 'Even Though Obviously Recovering...' for a report she had done on cases where the stubbornness of elderly people had proved very troublesome to the people around them even though their situation could be greatly improved if they put in just a little effort. Top of the list of examples of problems were: 'Meddles in Other People's Affairs,' 'Dirty!' and 'The Affluent Miser Who Pretends Not To Notice Money Spent On His Behalf.'

'Meddles in Other People's Affairs,' referred to the excessive number of old people who wanted to impose their own way on everything from the education of their grandchildren to the tempo of a son's married life, how he and his wife spent money, and who their friends were.

'Dirty!' looked at the problem of the detailed living habits of the elderly. Grandchildren complained that grandparents licked their finger to turn the pages of magazines and so they didn't want to read the magazine after that. Or they didn't wash the sheets for a month. Or they didn't change their underwear. Or they left tissue paper around that they'd spit into. Things like that bothered others.

Of course, there was a reason for the elderly not contributing money—they were worried about not having any income, and if they spent money now they knew they would have to depend upon the younger generation later. If parents wished to be regarded respectfully by their children, they should rid themselves of all feelings of dependence upon their children. If the Prime Minister goes abroad and is given a banquet, then without fail he will hold one in return. If your children treat you, then it's only to be expected they would think that next time you should be the host. But in the real world that was often not the case. There were a lot of lax 'middle-aged children' who thought it only proper that if they went out to eat with their parents the parents should pay every time.

Even though Hatsu Iwamura lived next door, it was a different house, so nobody knew much about her habits or could say whether she fitted into any particular category of 'difficult elderly person' or not.

The next day, when Tomoko went off to work, Yukiko's thoughts again kept returning to Mrs. Iwamura. The average person regards hospitalization as a kind of imprisonment—although it's said that some people go there through choice as a form of escape, or even as a kind of hobby. But thinking of all the inconvenience and loneliness involved, it seemed only natural to Yukiko to visit her and take a gift.

Yukiko left the house and bought some strawberries and milk at the shop by the bus stop, assuming the hospital visiting hours were in the afternoon. It was unlikely that the daughter had visited yet, but Mrs. Iwamura had been brought in as an emergency case so the hospital might have allowed her a brief visit in the morning.

When Yukiko peeked in at the records room on the 6th floor, she couldn't see any nurses. She thought she would probably meet someone on the way to the ward to ask if it was alright to visit at that time. She walked in that direction. In front of the laundry room, she bumped into someone with a familiar face—it was Sakae Mukai from the bed next to Mrs. Iwamura.

'Good morning,' Yukiko said. 'How is she today? Did she disturb you last night at all?'

'Well, she was fretting a little. She said she wanted to go home. But I think they gave her something, because after that she was quiet.'

This comment caught Yukiko's attention. She half pulled Sakae into the laundry room since there was no one else in there.

'You mean they gave her sleeping pills to keep her quiet?'

Sakae tried to evade Yukiko's earnest question.

'Well, I couldn't say that for certain, of course. But they had her take some medicine that was the same color as the stuff they give me when I can't sleep.'

Sakae's manner of speaking suggested that she was the kind of boss figure you find everywhere.

'Last night, we finally got in touch with her daughter,' Yukiko said, 'but she lives a long way from here and I don't suppose she's come yet, has she?'

'Not yet. I haven't seen anyone looking like a visitor besides you.'

'Her daughter's husband seems to be ill. She must be very busy dealing with invalids here and there.' Although it was not her duty at all, Yukiko spoke in a way that seemed to protect Mrs. Iwamura. 'I'm going to see her now, but I don't know any more about her condition since yesterday and I haven't met the doctor in charge yet.'

This time it was Sakae who stepped back further into the laundry room and away from the entrance, drawing Yukiko with her. She spoke to her in a low voice: 'You seem like a nice lady, so I think I should tell you something. About that Dr. Nagata. On the outside he looks as though he was born with a silver spoon in his mouth, he's so gentle and unassuming. But in fact, he's a tough customer. I didn't realize it at first. I had to ask him a lot of questions, because I didn't understand my condition.'

'But you look healthy,' Yukiko said. 'What is your illness?'

Sakae didn't seem disturbed by being asked to name her condition, and she replied, 'It's my liver. But it's not an illness that hurts or itches, and it hasn't made me feel lethargic at all, so it doesn't seem real. Maybe my questions are funny, but Dr. Nagata doesn't answer them. He just stares me in the face.'

'That's not so good,' Yukiko said.

'Mm, I thought he was a peculiar kind of doctor, but I decided that's the way he is. And then I've heard things from people—whispered in my ear, you know. People have told me that even if you have medical insurance, you have to tip him on the side or else he won't do a thing.'

'So you've given him some money?'

'Couldn't be helped. I'd be in trouble if my liver wasn't cured, wouldn't I?'

'How did you pay him?' Yukiko asked.

'I just sent cash in a registered package to his house. Of course, he never said thank you or even said that he'd received any money. Anyway, it hasn't been returned, so I presume it got there.'

'And after that, did his attitude change?'

'Oh, sure. He even started cracking jokes, like "Do you come from a samurai family?"—as if something as dumb as that would be taken as a compliment nowadays!'

'Really? And he isn't in the least ashamed of such a complete change of attitude?'

'I think a person like that is less than human. Nobody thinks politicians are clean these days, but they still talk politely to voters, don't they? That Dr. Nagata is the worst, without even a trick like that. I can't believe he got into medical school!'

'But even if you hadn't given him any money' said Yukiko, 'surely he would have treated you anyway?' She was thinking of the daughter who seemed cold toward her mother and whether it would mean anything for her to go to the trouble of conveying such a message.

'Well, I think I might have said too much about it...' Sakae said.

'Not at all,' Yukiko told her. 'I'm grateful for the information. And please pass on Dr. Nagata's address if it becomes necessary.'

With that she left and went straight to Mrs. Iwamura's ward.

Mrs. Iwamura seemed to be sleeping, but she responded when Yukiko spoke to her.

'Good morning, dear. It's Yukiko from next door,' she said. But although the old lady looked at her face, she didn't seem to recognize her, nor did she offer any thanks for the day before. Yukiko thought that perhaps she was still dulled from the sleeping pills they had given her earlier. The IV bottle was still connected to a vein in her arm. Perhaps when you get to her age, Yukiko thought, a sudden change was too much to keep up with. She recalled the adage about old age being like a tea cup with cracks in it. It won't break if handled carefully, but the slightest strain or change of environment and it falls apart.

Yukiko hadn't looked in on Mrs. Iwamura since the matter of the jam jar. She felt that, no matter how old a person was, if they were in reasonable health it was impolite to be nosey, especially if you had no particular business there. Furthermore, someone she knew had told her that people who weren't blood relatives and who frequently visited the elderly people in their neighborhood were disliked by the rest of the family who lived separately. Some restraint was best, otherwise it would seem as though you assumed a visit was necessary because the real family was neglectful. Another person, a stranger, might easily became a 'good person' in that situation; the family might feel there were some things they couldn't discuss, and they might well wish that no one had interfered.

'Mrs. Iwamura,' Yukiko said, 'don't be concerned about your house. I've shut off the gas and locked up well.'

'Yes. Thank you,' the old lady answered softly, but there was a hollowness in her voice.

'Do you know who I am?' Yukiko asked again, even though she had introduced herself a moment earlier.

'I'm sorry, I just don't recall,' was her reply.

'I'm Yukiko Hata, from next door.'

There was no positive reaction. Yukiko thought the situation had made Mrs. Iwamura nod even slightly only through her feeling that it was impolite not to recognize her.

'Isn't the drip uncomfortable?'

'No.'

'You'll soon be better and then you can return home. Please try to eat properly.'

'Yes.'

It was one of those moments where a conversation grinds to a halt. Mrs. Iwamura had been more herself until just a short time before. Even when she had asked Yukiko to open the jam jar lid, she was able to express her feeling that it was an imposition to ask something like that. There was nothing like that today.

At that moment a doctor appeared. His eyes were large and a child-like expression remained on his face.

'Mrs. Mukai isn't here?' he said, looked over at Sakae Mukai's bed.

'Oh, just now she was walking in the hallway,' Yukiko said. She grabbed the chance and added, 'Excuse me, are you Dr. Nagata?'

'Yes, I am.'

'I'm Hatsu Iwamura's next door neighbor. When she fell, I had her brought here in an ambulance. Since her daughter doesn't seem to have arrived yet, I was wondering if you could give me some idea of her condition? Then I could pass it on to her daughter.'

'Well, she's advanced in years, but, as you can see, she's quite conscious.'

'Yes, perhaps, but I have the feeling that's she's undergone a big deterioration recently,' Yukiko said.

The doctor was unaware that her level of consciousness had declined.

'At present we're doing some tests on her condition. I'll speak with her daughter when she arrives.'

'Oh, yes, please do. Thank you.'

Dr. Nagata was not as wordless nor as impolite as Sakae Mukai had implied, but he had nothing more to offer Yukiko. There are some confidential things that are kept only for the patient's family. Anyone other than a close relative who asks about the person's condition is not told anything. And no matter how much Yukiko persisted, there was nothing to talk to the patient about.

When Sakae Mukai returned to her bed five minutes later, Yukiko stood up to leave.

'Please give my best wishes to the Mrs. Iwamura,' Yukiko said.

'You're leaving already?' Sakae asked. 'Oh, let me give you Dr. Nagata's home address,' she added in a voice loud enough for everyone to hear. She shuffled open the drawer of the night table next to her bed and gave Yukiko something written on the edge of a newspaper advertisement.

'May I keep this?' Yukiko asked.

'Yes, please do. My daughter-in-law has already written it down properly.'

Yukiko didn't remember asking for the address when they had talked. She'd only meant to suggest that she would give Mrs. Iwamura's daughter the address if she needed it. But the idea was in Sakae's head, so Yukiko couldn't refuse.

'I'll pass this on to her daughter,' Yukiko said. 'Mrs. Iwamura probably can't eat something like strawberries and milk yet,' she added, wondering whether to put down the contents of the bag she had brought.

'She said that she doesn't want to eat anything yet,' Sakae replied.

'If she sees her daughter, I expect she'll feel relieved and will want to eat then. But won't you please take these for yourself?'

'Really? Are you sure?'

'Certainly. They would be heavy to carry home.'

—*Sakae might think it's a gift in return for receiving Dr. Nagata's address. But at least it will have served a purpose...*

When Yukiko reached home, she washed her hands. She turned over in her mind what the last 24 hours had meant. She had heard about Mr. and Mrs. Kanaya from Tomoko, helped Mrs. Iwamura to the hospital, and then been to visit her. That was all. She felt it had been a day of fruitless labor. It wasn't because she had earned nothing; nevertheless, it had been a somehow suffocating and airless day, like grasping at thin air.

She had done no sewing, and her work was left lying about. The kitchen was clean, but the dishcloth that she washed every day was still dirty. Yukiko liked having a sense of 'doing one good deed every day.' It wasn't an ideological thing, but she ordered herself to attend enthusiastically to just one task each day. For example, today she would go to the dentist—something she had been putting off. Then tomorrow she would pluck out the new shoots of the azaleas she had noticed by the front gate for some time. That was enough; she let herself off easily. One thing was enough. If she became over-eager, doing two or three things, it would amount to nothing. But if she did one thing, at least that was something cleared up. Without that one task to do, Yukiko would somehow feel her spirit was growing soft and weak.

She was just thinking she would first clean up the kitchen through and through, and then try to move the work along, when she heard the voice of the liquor store man at the door.

'How is Mrs. Iwamura?' he asked as soon as he saw Yukiko.

'Well, she's pretty hazy, but she's stable.'

'I suppose at her age it's better to be hazy,' he said, and then continued in a more somber tone. 'Actually, I intended to come by to ask about her earlier, but a friend of mine ran over someone in his car yesterday, a woman who worked in a department store. It was in the papers because he's an elementary school teacher.'

'Oh, that's terrible!' Yukiko said. 'And was the other person killed?' Yukiko asked, recalling that she hadn't read the paper since yesterday.

'Yes, he hit her straight on. The woman was lying on the road, so there was no way to avoid her.'

'How strange! I wonder if she'd been drinking, lying on the road like that?'

'I can't imagine. I know the person who hit her very well. He's a very serious person, not like other teachers these days.'

'What a tragedy,' Yukiko said.

'Yes, and that's not the end of it. When he hit her, he panicked and drove on a couple of kilometers. In the meantime, another car found the woman who'd been run over. It was a hit-and-run incident. And he had drunk a glass of beer before. He wasn't drunk or anything. But if he caused an accident, it would be a drunk driving charge.'

'Yes, I suppose so,' Yukiko said with a deep sigh.

'His wife said "It was all the fault of his job—the psychological pressures for him of being a teacher must have rattled his judgment." But people won't take it that way at all. I know they'll blame him, saying that a person who can injure someone and lose his judgment doesn't have the right to be a teacher. But everyone makes mistakes, and I think it's pretty cruel.'

'Will he lose his job, your friend?'

'I don't know, but if he goes to jail because of this, practically speaking he probably won't be able to teach again.'

'But if he's a good teacher, won't the parents of the students plead for a reduced sentence? People who make a mistake and suffer become really good people. Of course, it will make him a good teacher, too.'

'Yes, that's what a woman in my neighborhood is saying. But they say there are some funny parents who say that a teacher involved in a hit-and-run accident shouldn't be excused for any reason. There are a lot of righteous fools around these days, you know, people who think that if they clamor for justice it will raise their own status. But I think that half of our lives is determined by fate. It was raining hard at the time of the accident and it was hard to see very far ahead. If it hadn't been raining, I think he might have avoided hitting her. Apparently, he also said that he skidded.'

'It's true that bad luck piles up,' Yukiko said, 'and at times we're right in the middle of it.'

I was talking with my wife about that the other day. She thinks that we're neither lucky nor unlucky, just in the middle. So I told her we ought to be grateful. We've got no right to complain. Look at the people around us who really have bad luck. But what can we do for those people? Some say you ought to change your name or find a luckier 'direction' for your life.'

'I'm terribly simple,' Yukiko said. 'I would try and make that person feel happy, even for just an hour or a day.'

'That's great. It's true that when we're happy we become strong. You know, when I eat some delicious cake and drink some good tea, I suddenly become happy.'

'Ah-ha,' Yukiko laughed. 'Is that what liquor store people do to become happy? Eat cake?'

'Well, there just hasn't been anything good happening around me these last few days.'

'Me, neither,' Yukiko said.

'I suppose there are days like that. I told my wife it must be a trembler before the big earthquake, and she said that earthquakes come along just when you think you're happy. So I told her that was unscientific.'

'Yes, but my feeling is that disasters always come like that.'

'Then we must be safe right now.'

'Anyway, please be careful with your own driving,' Yukiko said.

As she saw him off, Yukiko couldn't help wishing that these days full of meaningless news would come to an end.

As soon as the liquor store man had gone, Yukiko realized there was someone else at the front door. She hadn't heard any footsteps; nor had she seen anyone. But she felt that there was someone outside the door.

'Who's there?' Yukiko called.

'It's me,' came Fujio's voice.

Yukiko opened the door and for a moment looked inquiringly at him.

'Did someone make you drink again?'

'No, nothing like that,' Fujio said, looking gloomy.

'Well, why don't you come in?' Yukiko told him.

'Is your scary sister at home?' Fujio asked in a low voice, pretending to peek into the house and making Yukiko laugh.

'How do you know she's scary?'

'Oh, I can understand what she's like from listening to you.'

'You have good intuition,' Yukiko said.

'Nothing but intuition, all my life. That's me.'

Fujio stepped slowly into the house and then looked out at the garden.

'That's really nice.'

'It's just hit-and-miss really, nothing planned,' Yukiko replied. 'When there's a place for something I want to grow, I plant it. The flower bed's very cramped, so the plants may be indignant!'

'The roses are blooming...'

'They're very small flowers, aren't they? That's because they have a lovely scent. The ones with good fragrance seem to insist on being small.'

The blossoms were yellow and white.

'When do you plant the morning glories?' asked Fujio.

'In early June.'

'I hope they blossom.'

'Oh, they will, certainly. Morning glories are quite hardy. Still, I'm not a gardener who uses natural techniques when it comes to morning glory seeds.'

'What do you mean?'

'Well, I cut the shell a bit with a knife, soak them in water, and don't put them in the ground until I've made sure they've sprouted.'

'Really?'

'Some people say you shouldn't do that, but I cheat, just because...'

'Just because...?'

'I like the easy life! I don't really like working, living a hard life. It's the same for morning glories; it's pitiful to see them struggling for days to sprout. If there's an easier way to grow, that's better. I said that to my scary sister once and do you know what she said?'

'What?'

'She said, "Yuki-chan, it's good you don't have a child." '

'Oh, really?'

'And then she said, "You would spoil the child as much as you could, and who knows what an awful brat it would have become!" But didn't you come around to talk about something that's troubling you?'

'Well, you might say that...or you might not. I'm used to leading an uneventful life, so this is nothing special.'

'But there is something, isn't there?'

'Nothing important. The other day, while I was out, I picked up a cat on the spur of the moment. Then I put him in my car.'

'Did it stay still?'

'No.'

Yukiko couldn't help smiling. 'You've never raised a cat—that's why you thought of doing that.'

'Hmm, maybe you're right.'

'Cats become attached to houses. So, the day you're moving, when you try to put them in a basket, they'll run off and you won't be able to catch them. There are people who have to leave them behind.'

'You really know about cats, don't you?' Fujio said.

'Oh, that's just something basic about cats. Once a cat that was pregnant came here and stayed. She liked people and when I held her, she would stay and chat with me forever. That was a Visiting Cat. The other day I was riding a bus and looked over at a car where a cat was riding in the back just dozing and looking out at the scenery. It was something exotic, like a Persian, with long hair, a very classy type. Now that's a Riding Cat.'

'But the cat I picked up was a pure Japanese Cat—short legs, you know.'

'Huh? Are there really differences in the length of cats' legs?' Yukiko said, and Fujio giggled. 'And are you going to take care of this cat at home?'

'No, it didn't work out that way. It escaped along the way. It was raining hard. I picked it up because it was wet.'

'Cats hate rain, but you don't have to feel so sorry for animals, you know. Besides, was it really lost? It would be a kidnapping if it had and owner and you took the cat with you. Just pity the person who raised the cat.'

'No one would own a cat like that. It was the kind that will go along with anyone who feeds him. I put it in the car, but it was squealing so much I got tired of it, and threw it out along the way. And then the stupid thing was hit by another car...'

'Oh no! Did you see it?' Yukiko exclaimed.

'Not clearly. But the car behind me did something or other. It hit the cat, I'm certain.'

'And you're concerned about it?'

'Some people say it's bad luck to hit a cat.'

'Well, I don't believe in that at all. It's how *you* feel that's the problem. Even though you don't intend to hit it, a cat will often run out in front of a car. A cat can't back up. It's a shame for the cat, but it's not that bad. Recently, there was a person lying on the road who was run over by a friend of someone I know,' Yukiko informed Fujio.

'Oh?' Fujio said in a mocking tone.

'Didn't you see it in the papers? A schoolteacher ran over a woman who was lying in the road.'

'I don't read newspapers much these days,' Fujio said, 'and I don't much care for teachers, so I'm not very sympathetic.'

'What do you have against teachers? I had many good teachers in school,' Yukiko said.

'I had one in junior high who wrote 'Stick Up For Your Rights!' on the blackboard as the 'Goal For The Week.''

'And you think that's bad?'

'I don't say it's bad...but I hated it. As far as I was concerned, he was always just boring. They don't have to teach that stuff. Leave people alone and they'll still desperately defend their own rights. I thought he had an entirely bad attitude and I didn't respect teachers after that.'

'It's a tough problem,' Yukiko replied, 'but I would also feel uncomfortable with a teacher like that, and I couldn't possibly respect him.'

Fujio was both angry and relieved with how his connection with Reiko Suga had turned out. He was angry because she had been killed by mistake, which was not what he'd calculated.

—*Who did that unnecessary thing? That department store clerk was so oppressively calculating. But the reason why I played around with her was to keep her alive and jerk her around with the threat of AIDS. And then, while I was having my meal, I heard repeatedly on TV that some fool of a schoolteacher had hit her. But I'm also relieved because—unlike the business with the daughter of the Shimada Foods family—it's clear who ran her over. If that wasn't the case, by some odd chance I might be a suspect...*

Fujio couldn't complain, but at the same time he couldn't forget the eerie outcome of the coincidences in the past few days. If he were to name what was on his mind, it was that he wished to talk to Yukiko about this 'accidental malice,' but he couldn't quite put it into words. True, he'd stripped the Shimada girl naked, but he hadn't pushed her over a cliff. And he'd only wanted the woman from the department store to lie down in the rain for a while. But, for quite different reasons, both of them had died, although not directly by Fujio's hand. Perhaps they were just women with bad luck. But it was also annoying for Fujio, and in truth he had come to see Yukiko hoping to dispel his pent-up feelings.

'So. How have you been since last time we met?' Fujio asked.

'Perfectly fine,' Yukiko answered. 'I never get sick.'

'How do you manage that?'

'Because I'm single. When I'm old and get ill, there won't be anyone to look after me. And so, from now on, I can't afford to get ill. That's what I tell myself sternly, and so far it's worked.'

'Don't worry. If you get sick, I'll come running and take care of you all the time,' Fujio said in the tone of a promise too easily made.

'Thank you very much,' said Yukiko. 'But I can't hold you to a promise about the future.'

'Do you think I'd lie?'

'Well, yes. People do, you know. Suppose you have a family then. Do you think that your wife would give you permission to come and take care of me? And besides, people's lives generally don't follow their wishes and expectations. If you promise something like that now, it means you won't be able to do it.'

For a moment Fujio was seized by sadness. It was something he felt only when he confronted Yukiko.

'I've failed in life. I think you've already understood that without my repeating it.'

'Why's that?'

'Oh, someone who can't help you when you're in trouble has failed for that reason alone.' Fujio confidently supposed that Yukiko would be moved by those words.

Yukiko laughed. 'It's rare in this world that a person can really help someone who is in difficulties. I think I told you before about the old lady next door who couldn't open the lid of the jam jar and had to make do with eating her bread plain?'

Fujio went tense. He felt that the name of the Shimada Foods Company was about to come up.

'Well, the man from the liquor store found her yesterday, after she collapsed in her house, and we had to send her to hospital immediately. But the attending physician is difficult. The woman in the next bed told me that he's the kind who won't even explain a patient's condition properly without getting a gift.'

'What an insolent doctor!' Fujio said.

'There are a lot of people like that. As soon as they get money, their treatment of someone improves. People who are nice to famous people but callous towards everyone else are the same type.'

'How much did you pay him?'

'That comes later. For the moment I only have his address.'

'Oh? Does he live around here?' Fujio asked casually. He felt like one of the black kites that flocked in that area. He hadn't caught any game yet, but it was as though his hawk-like eyes were fixing on his next catch as he went soaring overhead.

'I think he lives towards Yokosuka,' Yukiko said.

'Let me see the address, will you? If by some chance I run into him, I'll be sure to turn him down.'

Without a word, Yukiko showed Fujio the scrap of paper she'd just received.

'Well, fancy that!' Fujio said. 'It's right near my house.'

Chapter 14

THE HOUSE ON THE CLIFF

FUJIO simply had a cup of green tea with Yukiko that day and returned home. Yukiko had no idea why he had come by, and her expression showed as much. Of course, anyone would have felt that way.

Actually, the moment Fujio saw Dr. Nagata's name at Yukiko's house, he recalled the house where the doctor lived. Although he seldom helped out at the family store, he was certain he remembered it from the summer of the previous year. He had been in the back of the shop one day when a gorgeous-looking woman had come in and bought a watermelon.

'This is too heavy for me to carry,' she had said. 'Would it be possible to have it delivered to delivered to Dr. Nagatas' home?'

Fujio had agreed to her request on the spur of the moment. But when he delivered the watermelon, it was not the same beautiful woman who appeared at the entrance to the house but a rather rustic-looking woman with a peanut-shaped face. He wondered if that could have been the doctor's wife. It had been careless of him not to have asked Yukiko how old the doctor was, for somehow he couldn't picture that woman as his wife.

The next day, Fujio went off to confirm that the white house he remembered was indeed the doctor's house. When he'd delivered the watermelon, he'd gone in his own car, but this time he decided to walk to have a look. Fujio looked up at the building from the park just below.

—This is the kind of house you can't forget!

It was situated up a hill on top of a cliff, like a terrace that projected out. The part below the house had been turned into a park, with one area equipped with swings, a slide and other equipment for children, while the remainder had been left natural, overgrown with trees and shrubs. Just a day or two ago, the cherry trees there had been in full blossom. There were still a few remaining flowers on the treetops.

'Damn!'

Fujio felt envious that from the doctor's white house you would be able to look out over clouds of blooming cherry blossoms. An expansive square bay window without pillars projected from the 2nd floor and Fujio imagined that the inside of the room would be like a goldfish bowl. Lace curtains, probably made of thick material, hung behind the glass, and he could make out nothing inside.

The air was calm. Perhaps there were no elderly people living in the neighborhood—certainly there was no one killing time sitting on the park benches. Children's voices could be heard coming from the direction of the park, and Fujio was drawn to have a look. He would like to have seen a young woman with a child. Fujio mulled over the excitement of that violent embrace the time when he'd forced his way into the apartment of that young woman holding a baby—the one he'd noticed as he passed by.

—*She would probably say that I attacked her, but now I think that I actually loved her, if only for a moment. There was no question of her naive innocence. I didn't analyze it clearly during that brief encounter, but now I think I'm envious of that woman's husband. That woman is living an ordinary human life. I suppose anyone in the world would tell me that if I tried hard like an ordinary person, then I would gain the happiness that comes to such a life. But that's not true. I think there are a lot of people who have those elements inside them that prevent them from leading a normal life. But I'd better be careful about making a move on the doctor's wife. This time I should be discreet about what I do. I don't want to draw anyone's attention to me and arouse suspicions about what I'm doing around here...*

That is why, when Fujio heard the voices of some young women approaching from behind him, he immediately walked nonchalantly away. There would be people around on the street after he left the park, so there would be nothing suspicious if he walked off in the same direction that the women were headed.

Fujio made his decision and went up to ring the doorbell of the Nagatas' house. He could hear the bell chime its little song at the back of the house, but there was no sound of anyone coming to the door. For a while, Fujio stood there at the entrance, smiling. He was sure that Mrs. Nagata was in the house.

—*I can only imagine three reasons for her not answering the door if she's at home: she's sleeping, she's in the bath, or she's sitting on the toilet!*

Any one of those reasons was enough to bring a smile to Fujio's face. He waited longer than was really necessary, then gave up and decided to leave.

—*It's 3 p.m. This is the time when there's the greatest chance of the lady of the house being out shopping for the evening meal. I don't know whether there are any children here, but the appearance of the front entrance is rather too neat for that. Housewives these days liked to play tennis and golf, and a lot of them frequent culture centers. If I leave now, I should at least try to find out where Nagata's wife has gone...*

But Fujio didn't return home directly.

—*I have plenty of time. If Mrs. Nagata isn't at home, then I could try looking for her husband instead...*

He walked back to his parking lot, got into his car, and set out for the hospital where the doctor worked. It was a good time to pass himself off as a visitor.

Along the way, Fujio had a sudden thought and turned toward Yukiko's house. But, instead of stopping, he drove straight past. He quietly confirmed from the nameplate on the gate next door that the old lady's name was 'Iwamura.'

He then drove to the hospital and asked at the reception desk which ward 'Mrs. Iwamura' was in.

But Fujio had no intention of visiting Hatsu Iwamura. He got out of the elevator on the 6th floor and walked down the hallway to what he took to be a waiting room or smoking room. He went in and sat down silently.

There was a sad-faced couple in the room talking quietly, as though some relative had just been confirmed to have a fatal disease. And in the corner, a man dressed in pajamas and smoking a cigarette was using the public telephone. He was obsequiously giving excuses about why some business deal had fallen through and repeating his apologies, presumably to some important client.

As Fujio listened to the man on the telephone, he surreptitiously read the name tag of every doctor who passed by in the hall.

The man in pajamas finished his call and immediately put his phone card in the machine to make another call. This time his voice turned ugly and brusque: 'It's me...Yeah. I just talked with him. I'm sick and so he had to agree...But he said he didn't want to hear any more excuses. So you tell Yamada for me, and you make sure he gets the message!'

After that, he seemed to be asking about how some stock was doing, whether they could get it at the right price, the results of stock dealings, and so on.

—*I bet he's a fake patient! But, even if he isn't, a patient with that kind of greed will live through any illness...*

At that moment, he saw the name tag 'Nagata' on the lapel of one of the doctors. The doctor's face was expressionless. Although he was medium weight and height and had regular features, he seemed stolid and arrogant. He in no way created an image of brightness. Fujio imagined that perhaps among the sly, middle-aged nurses who were unpopular with their colleagues, there might be some deep secret sympathy for his darkness, but he was not the kind of person who would be popular at the workplace.

—*Now I've seen his face, my work here is done...*

He returned to the 1st floor entrance. At the information desk he said, 'A friend of Dr. Tanaka's asked me to bring his car around for him. Could you tell me what exit he might use when he leaves?'

'Dr. Tanaka?' the woman said, a doubting look on her face. Fujio thought he might have lost the game this time. He had speculated that at a hospital of this size, there would be at least one doctor with such a common name.

'Isn't there a Dr. Tanaka at this hospital?' he inquired.

'He's not here any more,' the woman replied. 'Dr. Tanaka was the former Director of the hospital, but he retired last year.'

'Oh? That's strange, but I'll check it again. Where should I wait, once I've got the name right?'

'Well, the doctors generally use this entrance, but those who park their cars at the back entrance of the hospital use the space near the boiler. Some doctors use the exit next to that.'

Fujio thanked her and walked away. He carefully looked around the parking area of the hospital. There was a garage at Dr. Nagata's home and so Fujio thought it likely that he used a car to commute to work. The receptionist had given him enough information, and when he walked to the back of the hospital, he found there was only one way for cars to exit.

—All I have to do is to hang around where I can catch Dr. Nagata leaving in his car. I may have to wait a long time...

The idea that he had nothing but time on his hands had recently echoed through Fujio's mind two or three times a day. Now he sat in his car at ease, the seat fully reclined, observing people and cars as they passed.

—There's no place like a hospital parking lot for people paying no attention to others! Everyone's totally wrapped up in their own affairs...

Suddenly, Dr. Nagata emerged from the rear parking lot in his grey Mercedes-Benz; it was just after 6:15 p.m.

'That was close,' Fujio murmured. It was getting late, and even though the days were long, it was becoming difficult to see the faces of the drivers.

The doctor's car headed in the direction of his house and then turned suddenly in another direction down a curving street.

—Now where's he going?

The car stopped in front of the Keihin Kyuko Line train station. Parking places there were rare, but there were some spaces reserved for customers shopping for a limited time in the nearby supermarkets, boutiques and pharmacies.

Without so much as a sideways glance, Dr. Nagata headed directly for one of the supermarkets. He took a shopping basket rather than one of the carts and went briskly inside the store. He seemed to know exactly where everything was. He picked up some tomatoes and cucumbers near the entrance, milk and yogurt at the dairy products counter, and then a container of tofu from the frozen goods case next to that. He went straight past the meat counter to the fish counter where, despite the variety on offer, he unhesitatingly selected a pack of salmon containing two pieces and placed it in his basket. He seemed about to buy a pack of sweetfish as well. He took a careful look, but didn't take it. He also picked up a six-pack of canned beer—apparently uninterested in the brand, he simply took the nearest one.

—*Perhaps he clearly knows what he likes, but it's strange to see a man shopping like this. It's the last thing I'd expected to see from the likes of him...*

But Fujio's doubts took an interesting turn. After leaving the supermarket and putting the bag of groceries in the trunk of his car, Dr. Nagata went into another store, a shop specializing in women's nightwear and underwear. Fujio felt he would be too conspicuous if he also entered, so he settled for simply waiting in his car and observing. The shop window had a kind of lattice on it, but the interior was brightly lit. He could see that the doctor was buying a pair of brief bikini-style panties with some lace, in what seemed to be a light porcelain blue color.

—*Uh-oh! What kind of shopping is that? Looks like Dr. Nagata has a girlfriend! And if that's the case, then next he'll be heading to her house with the things he's just bought. Yes. And if such a woman does exist, there'll be no end to his need for secret money...*

Fujio couldn't keep himself from smiling; he had begun to like Dr. Nagata. He liked anyone who did immoral things. Or, to put it exactly, he could trust a person like that more than someone who always said the right thing and regarded other people too critically.

Dr. Nagata came out of the shop, looking pleased, and got directly into his car without glancing around.

—*And where is your other house, dear doctor?*

Fujio smiled again as he started his own car.

But the doctor didn't stop along the way. On the contrary, he drove straight to his own house and put his car away in the garage. The door appeared to close by itself behind him. It was solid and Fujio could see nothing on the other side.

'Damn!' Fujio mumbled, but he still didn't give up hope. The fact that the bags with the groceries and the underwear had been placed in the trunk before he went home suggested concealment from someone. In an hour or two, if he waited, the man would surely return to the car and go to the other woman's house.

Fujio parked his car some 50 meters from Dr. Nagata's house and settled into a war of attrition.

—*There are both good and bad points to these days of long sunlight. They're good for observation, but they also mean people can see me better. But because this is a quiet residential neighborhood, at least no one passing by will be annoyed that I've stopped in a no parking area...*

As usual, Fujio lowered the back of the driver's seat and pretended to be resting, occasionally opening his eyes slightly to watch the street. A middle-aged woman walked by with her dog, and a housewife or two who seemed to be returning from shopping. Fujio started thinking about marriage as he watched the women passing by.

—*Perhaps one day I'll get married. But I wouldn't want a beautiful wife— that's for sure. There's nothing satisfying about a real beauty. There would also be the danger of someone like me choosing a beauty to attack. Anyway, a woman who's just a bit proud of her appearance is intolerable, and the changes are more dramatic and hopeless as a woman like that ages. Yes, I'm sure the best thing would be to marry an ordinary woman...*

Suddenly, Fujio wondered why he had never thought of marrying Yukiko. He imagined that she wouldn't regard him as a prospect, so he was protecting his feelings by deliberately not considering her in that way. But although it meant there was something of a contradiction in his mind, Fujio also felt he quite liked the idea of her saying she wouldn't marry him.

—*Of course, if she said that she was going to marry another man, I'd be deeply hurt. I think it might be best if she just goes on living forever alone in that house with its Heavenly Blue morning glories and the scent of the small roses...*

The front door of the Nagata house remained firmly shut.

—*Perhaps she came home while I was at the hospital? I wonder if she's been out to buy materials for the evening meal?*

From time to time, a few noisy elementary schoolchildren passed by. They were like a stream of ants as they came out from a three-story building about 100 meters down the street from the Nagatas' place. They were probably attending the cram school that had opened here recently in response to the demands of the ambitious children of the neighborhood intelligentsia.

Fujio remained watching the Nagatas' house until nearly 8:30 p.m. Then he decided to leave. He was not satisfied. Something was going on and he didn't know what.

The next morning, around 11, Fujio drove to the house again. This time he was fully prepared to get inside the place that exuded such a profoundly 'closed' feeling.

He put on a cap with the logo of a motorbike company that he had got from Saburo and hung a hand towel from his belt. In that outfit, he trusted he looked like a stalwart farmer of the district. He stood outside the front door with its general air of gloom and rang the bell. He had the peculiar feeling that the house had been empty for a long time. A minute or two passed and there was still no response from within.

—*Just as I expected!*

Then he sensed something moving slowly from the back of the residence, coming toward the door. There was neither a peep hole in the door nor a TV camera to survey him. When the door opened, Fujio was startled.

It was the woman with the peanut-shaped face who had once received the watermelon that Fujio had delivered here. She was wearing a white blouse and a grey skirt with a slanted check pattern. Fujio reckoned she was about five years older than Dr. Nagata.

'Are you the lady of the house?' Fujio inquired.

'Yes,' she replied.

'Excuse me for calling on you suddenly like this, but I'm from the Miura Agricultural Cooperative.' Fujio had concocted this story the night before, while lying in bed. 'I've come to introduce the fruit distribution association.'

The woman seemed to study his face carefully for a moment and then said, 'Please come in.'

'Thank you.'

This was hardly something Fujio had anticipated. No matter how well things might go, all that had entered his head was that she might listen to his story at the front door. When she asked him in, he was disconcerted; he could do nothing but comply.

He went through into the sitting room, which was furnished in Western style. It had a marble mantelpiece and an executive suite sofa. In one corner of the room there was a glassed-in cabinet of shelves that extended to the ceiling, obviously a fitting that had been specially designed and built. The shelves supported some 20 to 30 dolls, both Western and Japanese. To Fujio, it felt as though the glass eyes of every doll were staring straight at him; it sent a chill down his spine.

'What charming dolls,' he said, in spite of what he felt. Since childhood, Fujio had detested dolls. He thought they were like corpses. When he was young, he had done things like scalding the hair and pulling out the hands and feet of his sister's dolls and secretly throwing them into the drainage ditch beside the road. His sister used to cry terribly, but his mother would merely explain that 'Fu-chan is jealous because you treat your dolls so nicely.'

Fujio had not seen a big collection of dolls like that since he was a child. While there were more than these to be seen in the toy section of any department store, they were the cheap kind, and to Fujio they were only slightly distressing since they resembled humans so little. But the haughty eyes of the dolls in this collection seemed to be staring straight into his soul. And that was rude; to stare at people without their permission was impolite. Fujio wanted to sweep them all up into a great bonfire and destroy them.

'They seem to be quite expensive dolls,' Fujio observed, trying to get a normal conversation going.

'Oh, yes. It took me a long time to collect them,' she said.

'And are there any children in the house?'

'No, we have no children.'

'Then these are like your children?'

'Yes,' she said, suddenly laughing. Until then she had not even smiled, and her laugh now felt all the more mechanical because there was no real reason to laugh. It came as though a switch had been thrown, and her quick change of expression again sent a chill through Fujio.

'Well,' Fujio began, 'we've organized this system of distributing fresh fruit directly from the farm to consumers...'

The previous night he had actually written out a set of rules for the distribution association and had made copies at a nearby shop, making an effort to make it look more convincing. Such distribution groups had recently become numerous, bringing fruits like pears, peaches and watermelons from the areas all over Japan where they were a specialty. The Miura Peninsula had a lot of fruit to offer— extremely fine watermelons, tangerines, kiwi fruits, melons and pears. And the really important point was that they were fresh. There was considerable difference in the taste of the fruit from different producers. Experts would gather and judge the taste, and then the farmers would ship only the selected fruit to their special customers. In season, any number of fruit stands appeared beside the roads, selling watermelons, but buyers couldn't tell which ones would be delicious. People would stop their cars to buy and take the watermelons home, anyway, but not only were they heavy to carry, they could easily get damaged. However, the distribution association would bring the fruit to the kitchen door on a day convenient for the customer so that they could enjoy a product that had been picked that day.

Fujio's story was that he was going around explaining the association and signing up buyers.

'I see,' Mrs. Nagata said, but she didn't attempt to read the order form and commit herself to the 5,000 yen monthly fee—another detail Fujio had added.

'Well, then, how about it?' Fujio urged.

'Hmm...'

At that moment, Fujio felt the frustrating reaction that foreigners sometimes have toward Japanese ambiguity. Mrs. Nagata neither accepted nor rejected; nor did she ask for any further explanation. While he was wondering just where the conversation might go from there, she suddenly spoke: 'We've met before, a long time ago...'

Fujio felt as though she'd made the first attack.

—Surely she can't remember me delivering a watermelon that day?

'And where might we have met?' Fujio was forced to ask.

'At this house.'

Fujio was struck dumb.

'You once came here to take pictures, didn't you?' she went on.

'I sure don't remember that,' he answered.

'But it *was* you. You set up a hidden camera. But I can't give you the film you took. I deliberately took it from your camera.'

'Hey, that's enough, lady,' Fujio said, annoyed. 'So where are the pictures now?'

'You would have taken the film to a processing shop in town. I knew you'd do that. You went to the shop to try and get them from the assistant, didn't you? Then the photographs would have been lost. But I had them developed by an acquaintance of mine, a Professor at Tokyo University.'

'So what did you do with the pictures that the Tokyo University professor developed? I wonder how they came out?' Put off as he was, Fujio asked this with some amusement.

'They came out well,' she said.

'I'd like you to show me the pictures,' Fujio said.

'But you got rid of them, didn't you?' Mrs. Nagata again gave her hollow, mechanical laugh.

'*I* got rid of them?' asked Fujio.

'There was heavy rain one day last month, right? You destroyed the pictures then.'

'How did I destroy them?'

'That's easy on a rainy day—you said so yourself, remember? You did it by psychokinesis.'

'And the camera? What did you do with that?'

'I had my husband take it away.'

'But that was *my* camera, and if you don't return it, then that's theft,' Fujio said to her.

'He took that to the police, too. He knew it belonged to the same person as the tape recorder.'

'Tape recorder?'

'Last year, you attached it under the eaves and secretly recorded our voices.'

Fujio had no reply.

'Yes, you collected a lot of information that way. For instance, that my husband treated a Russian high official. And because my husband cured him, the Russians pulled out of Afghanistan.'

Fujio took another look around him. For the first time, he recognized the peculiarly unhealthy atmosphere of the house. Nothing moved. There were no windows open and so no wind blew through the house. Even the lace curtains were unnaturally still in this room shut up so tight. But it was not only that there was no wind. There were no decorative plants growing in pots, either, nor any cut flowers that might fade and wilt. And there was no music and no television turned on. Nothing was out of order, but on the surface of the furniture there was a film of dust.

'Excuse me, Mrs. Nagata, may I get a glass of water from the kitchen?' Fujio asked.

'Yes, please do,' she replied.

He didn't think Mrs. Nagata would trust a man she didn't know, a man she believed had done such things as install a hidden camera and a secret recording device. So he expected her to follow him. However, she remained calmly seated there on the sofa.

Fujio went into the kitchen. There, finally, he detected a lingering trace of some daily life going on. The plastic carton of the tofu that Dr. Nagata had purchased the day before had been thrown into a corner of the sink, along with some tomato stalks and a bit of something that might have been salmon skin.

When Fujio left Mrs. Nagata, he felt as though he'd just fled a haunted house. He felt tired in a strange way. The moments of crushing struggle to throttle those hated women and the long, muddy struggle with the ground to dig a hole and fling the bodies in—those two jobs had filled him with horror, and yet he was able to do it because of his anger. But even immediately after those deeds, Fujio had never felt as awful as he did right now.

As a layman, there was nothing definite he could say, but he thought that Mrs. Nagata was clearly mentally ill. During the time he'd worked at the hotel, a few guests had complained angrily that there were hidden cameras in their rooms. Fujio had been a porter then, and he supposed that men who made accusations like that were used to love hotels, and they might simply be paranoid about hidden cameras. But after talking with the experienced front desk clerk, he learned that when a guest thought there were both hidden cameras and recorders, it meant he was mentally ill, and the only thing to do was to say nothing and move him to another room. From those days, Fujio had first learned how tough schizophrenia could be. There were people who always suspected they were being secretly photographed and that some hidden device was recording their private conversations. Their minds would never be at ease.

In spite of all that, what was especially odd about the Nagata house was that time seemed to be standing still. Everything was fixed; there was no change and there was no atrophy. Everything that existed there was like a mummy from the beginning, and the dolls were a symbol of that. If they didn't grow, then neither did they age. The dolls looked out coldly upon whatever happened in the house.

—*What is Dr. Nagata thinking? What kind of a person is he? Does he look for secret money because he thinks he needs it to protect his sick wife? And who were the panties bought for? At first, I thought they were for some other woman. But since Mrs. Nagata no longer goes out shopping for food, perhaps she doesn't buy her own underwear, either. If Dr. Nagata is one of those rarities who is so devoted to his wife, then the malice that his patients bear him is ill-founded...*

Fujio felt that perhaps his own uneasiness was a presentiment of that side of Dr. Nagata.

He returned home exhausted and telephoned to Yukiko. But she didn't answer, no matter how long he let the phone ring.

The evening newspaper reported that a garbage collector had come across some clothes while emptying the contents of a trash box. Thinking it a waste to destroy them, he had sorted the things out. Then later, reading about the discovery of the naked body of Tomoko Shimada, he had taken the clothes to the police. The Shimada family had confirmed that they belonged to their daughter.

Chapter 15

PLAYING REVENGE

THE fact that Yukiko hadn't answered the phone was enough to make Fujio worried; she had said she wasn't going out. She was *always* at home, and any time he went to visit her she *had* to be there to greet him. Fujio wanted to believe only that and nothing more.

—*Where could she have gone?*

He persistently continued trying to reach her. When he finally heard her voice on the phone, about 8 p.m., he was so relieved that his mood turned to anger.

'Where have you been? When you don't answer the phone it worries me, you know that.' He spoke like a complaining child.

'Old Mrs. Iwamura from next door died this morning.'

'What?' Fujio gasped.

'At first she seemed to be getting better, but when the nurse went to look in on her this morning, she had died. Even the patient in the bed next to her hadn't noticed.'

'It's that hospital's fault!'

Actually, Fujio intended to say 'A peaceful death,' but the opposite came out of his mouth.

'Perhaps it was, perhaps it wasn't. When people reach a certain age there is the possibility of them dying any time. And recently I think she had lost her will to live.'

'Did her daughter get there?'

'Yes, but somehow she seemed relieved that it was all over. That's the sad truth of it.'

'That doctor probably didn't treat her properly.'

'Maybe. I just don't know. There are a lot of doctors like that, but I just don't know about him.'

Fujio wasn't too keen on her cautious tone.

'Actually I enjoy listening to rumors, but I choose not to trust them,' Yukiko went on. 'That doctor didn't get any money out of Mrs. Iwamura directly.'

'Maybe he skimped on her treatment because he thought it unlikely that she'd give any money? I'd go after a doctor like that,' Fujio said.

'How would you do that?' Yukiko said. She spoke as though she had found out a child who was planning some mischief.

'I'll give that some thought later,' Fujio said.

'If you have time for that,' Yukiko told him, 'it would be better to think of more pleasant things.'

'For me that is pleasant. It's like a war of justice.'

'I don't like wars of justice,' Yukiko replied.

'Why not?'

'It's just that I prefer people who think that they are doing something bad over people who think they are doing something righteous—they're nicer.'

'You are a strange one, aren't you?' Fujio said. 'This is the Age of Justice.'

In fact, since Fujio learned of the existence of the crazy wife, he had begun to feel he wouldn't have anything more to do with Dr. Nagata. Insanity was a troublesome thing. Doing some injury to a healthy person had some meaning, but not to someone who was ill like that. And yet, after hanging up the phone, Fujio changed his mind. Call it her age, or that her time had come, but either way the old lady was dead. She had died suddenly, when it seemed that she was about to recover. And her own daughter was relieved as if she'd got rid of a nuisance.

Fujio wanted to do something that would leave a bruise on the daughter's cheek. But, for the present, the one who had to be punished was the doctor who had conspired in such a crooked fate. It was only a question now of how to bring definite harassment down on Dr. Nagata. He was irritated because he couldn't immediately hit on just the right plan for this case.

—I don't want to seek money particularly; not that it would be bad if money were involved, but that's not my main purpose. Not treating people kindly when they have no money is something that has to be punished. And so there should be some kind of knockout punch that will fleece that doctor of a lot of money...

Until now, Fujio might have come up with some interesting plot immediately, but this time there was a complication.

—Since she's crazy, she might think of it before I do and start the ball rolling before me. That will never do. Then she'll have the initiative and I won't be able to play out my scheme...

Fujio stopped thinking about all that and went to a video shop after 10 p.m. and brought back two particularly stimulating porno videos. It was nearly morning before he went to sleep.

Fujio got up after midday...it was nearly 3 p.m. He went downstairs feeling cheerful and ate some cold pork cuts that his mother had bought at the supermarket with his rice. Then he slipped on his sneakers and went out. Just knowing what he was going to do today put him in a good mood.

Before getting into his car, Fujio bought a copy of a weekly comic book called

Slip. A magazine like that wouldn't occupy him for long, but it was better than listening to the car radio.

He stopped his car at the same place as he had the day before and gazed at the closed curtains of the Nagatas' house.

What doubly confused Fujio was that even if he involved the doctor's wife in some incident, the doctor himself might not be disturbed in the least. He suspected that the doctor had already set things up so that his sick wife could not make free use of all that money. If he planned it so that a fire were to break out in the house, the fire insurance would cover it; and if his wife committed some sexual indiscretion, the doctor would not be driven mad by jealousy. And if his wife died, that might be just what the doctor wished.

'Come to think of it, she's the best wife in the world!' Fujio said to himself, laughing out loud at the idea.

Inside the parked car, Fujio was tormented by these useless thoughts. If he were to ring the doorbell to the house, two things might happen; for no reason at all, he might be invited again into that weird house; or there might be no answer at all.

'This is getting on my nerves,' Fujio muttered. No matter how long he waited, he couldn't expect too much from a sick woman.

Fujio hadn't set foot in Yokohama recently. He began to think warmly of Reiko Suga, the woman at the department store. He thought fondly of her greed, her egoism, her foolish self-confidence, and her lack of shame.

—She was the archetype of the Japanese woman. She was emotional, hated suffering a loss, and was foolishly honest to the point of being indifferent to how she appeared to others. She was absolutely dependable. Without Reiko, the world has become a pretty dull place...

Fujio didn't feel like going to Yokohama.

For a while he read his comic book and then he dozed off for a bit. When he awoke, dusk was beginning to settle over the neighborhood. He felt that he had to do something wild to break out of his submerged feeling. He had to be able to assert himself, analyze himself, and express himself freely.

Like a divine revelation, he found an interesting line in the magazine:

Look at the history of Rome. Emperor Caligula said, "To the Emperor all things are permitted." And not just to the Roman emperor, but to all men of cunning and meanness—even to four-legged beasts—all things are allowed.

Of course, the words were neither philosophy nor the invention of the comic writer. They came from a book on the Russian Emperor Peter the Great and Fujio was much impressed. Many things could be solved these days if one became an animal. Humans are no longer animals, so they destroy nature; and because they have become just a little cleverer than animals, they cause trouble by making nuclear weapons.

The evening darkness was beginning to envelop Fujio's soul, and still there was no light from the house on the cliff. He was sure Mrs. Nagata was there, inside.

Suddenly, Fujio felt something strike the car. It was not a big shock, just the unpleasant sound of metal scraping against metal—enough to jangle Fujio's nerves when, psychologically, he was submerged in a kind of fetus-like ease.

'Hey!' He looked through the partly-opened window on the opposite side of the car into the face of an elementary school boy. 'What did you just hit against the car?'

Fujio had already guessed what had happened. The boy was carrying his school rucksack in his hand instead of wearing it on his back. He had most likely been idly swinging it about as he walked along the street.

'You've damaged my car!'

'Not much,' the boy answered casually, glancing over the car as he spoke. His features were regular.

'That's for me to judge!' Fujio said as he got out of the car and carefully examined the door on that side. There was a slight scratch, about five centimeters long, around the height of the boy's shoulder.

'Hey, come on and have a seat,' Fujio said to the boy, smiling. He opened the door. 'Your rucksack hit the door, right?' he said, after sitting down next to the boy.

'Well, yeah, you could say that.'

'Aren't you going to say you're sorry?'

'Sure, I can do, if you want,' the boy answered in a surly tone.

'No, that's alright,' Fujio said.

'No one would be that serious with kids, would they?' the boy said, chewing some gum.

'No, but I'm different,' Fujio said. 'I'm always straight with kids. Making allowances because a kid is a kid is insulting. Tell me, what grade are you in?'

'5th grade. If you want me to apologize, I will.'

Again, for no reason, a feeling of unpleasantness swelled in Fujio.

'No, I'll just think it over carefully later on,' he said with a smile. 'Do you go to that cram school?' He was making idle conversation.

'Yeah.'

'I would have thought that a bright kid like you wouldn't need to go to cram school.'

'But the standards at my school are so bad. That's not much fun, don't you think? So if I don't at least go to cram school, I don't feel like I'm making a serious effort to study.'

'Is that the way it is?' Fujio said, trying to keep his inner feelings from showing.

'Were your grades good at school?' the boy asked.

'No way! I couldn't even go to college.'

'That's a problem,' the boy said like a grown-up.

'No, not a problem at all.'

'But if you don't go to a good college, people don't treat you like a person. You don't make connections...'

'Is that what you think?'

'My father says so, and I guess it's like that when you look inside a company.'

'And later, which college do you want to apply to?'

'Tokyo University, of course.'

Inside himself, Fujio could hear and feel the usual anger and excitement of his begin to flow up to the ends of his veins, which had been quite dull until a few minutes before.

'That's what I figured! How about going to a place like Meirin University?' he said to the boy.

'What's that? I've never heard of it.'

'My cousin went there.'

'I bet your cousin didn't study much.'

'I suppose so. Anyway, he's my cousin.'

'They say you should be grateful to people with bad grades.'

'Why's that?'

'Because thanks to people with bad grades, kids with good grades can go to a good university. If everyone had good grades, they would sure get in the way of me going to Tokyo University.'

'What an idea!' Fujio said, deliberately showing he was impressed. He even gave a laugh. 'Until you said it just now, I never thought of it like that. Who told you something so smart?'

'My mother.'

'Mm, what a mother! My mother used to be happy for my friends when they got good grades.' Fujio was lying again.

'Sure. It's all right for your friends to study...but not everyone can. Don't you think it's good that people are different like that? If everyone went to Tokyo University, the school would be too small and they'd have to rebuild it.'

'Have you ever been there?' Fujio asked. 'Which department are you gong to apply to?'

'Science. Because I'm going to be a doctor.'

Fujio felt the tingle of coincidence.

—Buddha is surely controlling fate! Doctors are appearing everywhere today...

'Did you know that they're saying the medical school of the Science Department of Tokyo University will be moved to Miura?'

'No, I didn't.'

'By order of the Ministry of Education—five years from now. The Hongo and Komaba campuses have become too small, and so just the medical school will move to a hill with a nice view in Miura City. But it's still a secret.'

If he had been a bit older, the business about 'by order of the Ministry of Education' would have sounded like the lie it was, but a boy in the 5th grade would hardly have the capacity to question it.

'How do you know about it?'

'Oh, a relative of mine works in the Ministry. In the future, medical students will probably be rooming around Yokosuka, so he let me in on the business secret, suggesting I should prepare for that by setting up in the rooming business.'

'Gee, I bet the price of land will rocket up!' the boy said.

'Of course.'

'I bet we could make a bundle, too.'

'So, since I know where the medical school is going to be built, I could take you there and show you if you like,' Fujio said, anticipating that the brat probably wouldn't go along with the idea. He thought the boy might even get out and leave. But, on the contrary, he didn't move at all.

Instead, the boy said, 'Come on, start the car! If we don't get going, it'll get dark and we won't be able to see, will we?'

Fujio's anger surged at the tone the boy used to order him about—he sounded as though he was used to giving orders.

'Hey, take it easy!' Fujio said.

'I just don't like guys who are slow to act.'

Fujio could not easily overlook the boy's innocent bluffing and boldness.

'What business do you work in?' the boy asked, busily continuing to chew his gum.

'I'm just an office worker.' Not knowing just what to say, Fujio had seized upon the easiest answer.

'Hmm. Which company?'

'A fertilizer company.'

'Wow, stinky!' the boy said, holding his nose.

'You don't know a thing, do you? Fertilizer doesn't smell—it's chemical.'

The boy was into the idea and said, 'The fields get bad with inorganic farming because you sell that kind of stuff.'

'Then we should go back to the Japan of 50 or 100 years ago. We were spreading shit on the fields then. It bred intestinal worms and people got polio. But it sure was organic farming.'

'Stinky!' the boy said, still holding his nose playfully.

'What kind of work does your father do? Is he a doctor, too?'

'Mm, well...'

'Is he a banker?'

'No, nothing like that.'

'How come you want to be a doctor?'

'A politician would be OK, too.'

'So you just want to be something snobby?'

'I guess you think that's not so good. But everyone wants to be proud of what they do, don't they?'

'I don't like kids being so power-oriented at such a young age,' Fujio said.

'There's no difference between grown-ups and children, is there?' the boy asked.

'But it's so obvious and shameful, isn't it?'

'Not at all! Nobody follows you unless you have power.'

'What does your mom do?'

'She's pretty good—except for one thing,' the boy said in a way that fed Fujio's vulgar interests.

'You mean she plays around with men?' Fujio asked with a toothy grin.

'Oh, no, not that,' he answered roughly.

'Are you mad because I'm talking like that about your mom?'

'No I'm not mad.'

'So what's the one thing?'

'Well, it's not something immediate. She tells people that "I'm going to have him take care of me when I'm old." I don't remember promising anything like that.'

'Are you saying you're not going to?'

'I'm not saying I won't. I might not. I probably will, but I think it's weird when I hear "It's natural for a parent to have their child look after them." '

'But that's only natural to the one who gave birth to you, isn't it?'

The boy grinned, so Fujio expected to hear the usual tedious line about not asking to be born in the first place. But the boy quietly came back at Fujio with another question.

'Are you grateful to your mom for having been born?'

'Sure, I am.' Fujio had to say that to keep consistent. 'Aren't you?'

'I don't know. If you were me, would you be grateful?'

'Of course it's good you were born. You have a smart mind and motivation, and your family seems to have a lot of money...And you've never been bullied, right?

'Not by my friends,' the boy said.

'So who else might have bullied you?'

The boy laughed a little. 'Fate.'

'Don't be a smart-ass,' Fujio said.

'I think I'll only answer your questions after I'm married and have kids,' the boy said. His cheeky replies were beginning to irritate Fujio.

'Are you going to get married?'

'Yeah, probably.' The boy reverted to his fearless and innocent questioning. 'Are you married?'

'No.'

'Not married at your age?'

'Oh, I get enough women,' Fujio allowed.

'But surely you want kids?' the boy asked.

Fujio had gone sullen again. He couldn't stand other people leading him in what he thought.

'Well if you don't have kids,' the boy continued, 'there's no one to pass on your work to, or your feelings.'

'That's why I'm not afraid of anything in the world,' Fujio said. 'Since I don't have a wife or a kid, there's no one I have to worry about.'

Fujio's replies to the boy had become more serious.

'Really?'

'You doubt what I say?'

'No, nothing like that. But I think anyone who says that is a fool.'

'Well, I'm sorry I'm a fool. But I'm probably more a man of action than your father. I'm not afraid of anything because I've got nothing to lose.'

'I'm afraid of a lot of things,' the boy said, thinking.

'For instance?'

'Like graveyards, because there are ghosts.'

'You're pretty silly.'

The boy seemed smart, but this comment was appropriate to his age. The whole conversation was getting a bit stupid.

'I promised my mother.'

'Promised what?"

'Well, I made her promise that she wouldn't haunt me as a ghost if she died. And in return, I promised her that if I die first, then I won't haunt her, either. But she said that if I die first, she *wanted* me to haunt her. And she wouldn't mind meeting my ghost sometimes.'

'So you'll appear as a ghost?'

'Sure. I promised.'

'Don't! You'll be all tired out doing that. It's a long distance between this world and the next, you know.'

'But it's all settled that I've got to appear. Then I can tell my mother about what's in the other world. Do you want me to tell you, too?'

'Ah, no, not particularly. I'm not much interested in that kind of thing,' Fujio said.

'How come you're not interested?'

'No reason, really. I'm just not interested.'

'Gee, that's a pity, not being interested. I mean, that's the most pitiful thing.'

Fujio again felt his anger rising.

'Just be careful what you say, pitying someone like that to his face.'

'But if you aren't interested, you can't do a thing. You're just alive, that's all.'

For a while Fujio was silent. Then he said, 'So just living is no good?'

'That's right.'

'Then what kind of people are 'just living'? Tell me that.'

The boy thought about that for a few moments. 'The guys on the train who read comic books and the horse racing news.'

'Did you get that from your mother?'

'No. I thought so myself. I feel ashamed of them. It's OK to read, but they should read that stuff at home.'

'Look, do you know how much the comics and the races amuse people?' Fujio said roughly, wondering whether the boy had noticed the comic magazine he'd thrown on the back seat of the car. It was almost as if the boy had guessed right.

'I hate drunks,' the boy said, not quite answering Fujio's question. 'Do you drink?'

To match his unpleasant mood, Fujio decided to counter whatever the boy said. So he replied, 'Oh, sure I do. But I bet your dad doesn't drink?'

'No, he doesn't.'

'A guy who doesn't drink has got to be pretty dull.'

—Isn't that myself I'm talking about? The razor of words I'm trying to cut the boy with seem to have come back to cut me!

'Well, you're really hard to understand,' the boy said.

'I don't much want to be understood,' Fujio said.

The boy showed his disgust by throwing his head against the back of the seat.

'Aren't we there yet?'

'Just a bit more,' Fujio replied.

Actually, during their conversation, Fujio had mistaken the road. But there was still a way out. It didn't matter if it was a wheat field or a cabbage field, any kind of wide open area would do. He needed to find a spacious place where he could say, 'This is it.' Fujio had passed the same place twice.

—The boy didn't say anything; I suppose he didn't notice...

They went on in silence for a few minutes.

'You lied,' the boy finally said.

'What about?'

'There's no such place, is there?'

—Perhaps he did notice that we've passed the same corner twice?

'Well if you think it's a lie, let it be a lie. But that's got nothing to do with me.'

'You shouldn't tell silly lies like that. You're the one who'll get in trouble later.'

'You're quite a meddling kid, aren't you?'

'I want to go back right away. If there isn't any land to see, then there's no point going there.'

Fujio kept right on driving in silence.

The boy was also silent, as though he'd guessed what was happening. Fujio stopped the car beside a field on a knoll. At that time of day, it was unlikely there would be anyone out working the field or any cars passing.

'This is the site. They're going to build the medical school here.'

'OK. This is enough.'

To carry the charade one step further, Fujio got out of the car to gaze around the place in the dim light just after sunset. The boy remained seated in the car.

'Come on, let's go back,' the boy called.

'You don't believe me? Suit yourself.' Fujio spoke coolly, but his curiosity was vaguely aroused. 'Why don't you think it will be here?'

'Because as soon as I said "Let's go back", you said this was the place, right? You shouldn't tell such an obvious lie! I can tell because my dad's a prosecutor.'

A volcano seemed to erupt deep in Fujio's gut, as though from the depths of the sea. Yet he managed to produce a frozen smile.

'That can't be true! You shouldn't feed adults with stuff like that.'

'It's true. I wouldn't lie to you with bull like that.'

Accustomed as he was to putting out a string of blatant lies, the boy's words sounded like painful sarcasm to Fujio.

'So he earns his money as a prosecutor by sending people to jail?'

'Sure. Doing bad things is bad. What would happen if they didn't prosecute bad people?'

'Do you know what the Bible says?'

The boy was silent.

'It says you mustn't judge people, that's what.'

This was a bit of something he remembered hearing from Yukiko.

'I wouldn't know about that sort of thing. My family is Shinto.'

'Let me tell you. Because of guys like your father, innocent people are sentenced to death, or suffer all their lives because they're falsely accused.'

'No, it's right to punish bad people. If we didn't, then good people would be murdered.'

'Really? So you think bad people deserve to be killed?' Fujio said. The boy seemed to guess what was on Fujio's mind. 'If they do that, then guys like you wouldn't be alive,' Fujio said. 'I bet when you grow up, you'll go to Tokyo University, start a war of aggression, make trials stricter, cater to rich people and make weak people suffer. You know, the only thing to do to guys like that is to kill them.'

Struggling to get up from the car seat, the boy tried to keep a clear, dignified tone to his voice.

'It would be a loss to the country to kill me,' the boy insisted.

Those words were the final straw for Fujio.

He leapt to the attack, clamping his hands around the boy's throat. The boy put up a surprising resistance and Fujio was caught off guard. The boy pulled away from Fujio and grabbed the rear view mirror. He tore it off in his desperate strength.

Fujio changed tactics. He let go of the boy's throat, and as he heard a gurgling sound from the boy's windpipe, like water going down a drain, he smashed his fist into the boy's stomach. Nothing would be more dangerous than the boy coming back to life. As a prosecutor, his father would certainly seek the death penalty for someone who attempted to kill his son, and, out of sympathy, his friends would all help in getting such a verdict. Fujio knew that any court would be set against him from the start.

He put his hands firmly around the boy's throat again. Letting anger take over, he clamped down with the full strength of his whole body.

Even after the boy seemed to be finished, Fujio remained uneasy. It had turned dark. In spite of knowing the boy was dead, Fujio nervously imagined that he hadn't completely stopped the boy's breathing, but he was determined to remain icy calm. He decided to confirm that the boy was finished. He had no inclination to go through anything as unpleasant as digging another grave. He had to be certain the kid was dead and wouldn't come back.

The boy still gave off a sunny odor that reeked of life; he seemed smaller now, leaning there sideways in the seat. After a while, Fujio brought his face close to the boy's, confirming that his breathing had completely stopped. Their cheeks touched and Fujio realized it was like an affectionate greeting.

'Take me for a fool?' Fujio muttered. His words had no meaning at all. There was not the slightest sign of life from the boy.

At that moment, Fujio felt something strange that made him crouch in fear. Was there someone just outside his window, someone looking in upon him? Fujio readied his whole body and then snapped around—but there was no face looking in. There was no one at all outside. Fujio's nerves were so razor sharp he was twice as aware as usual of noticing the presence of others. He opened the door and looked out, feeling suspicious. Perhaps the person was still crouched down, hiding behind the door? Fujio made certain no one was anywhere about.

Only then was he free of the fear and tension that had gripped him.

'Take me for a fool?' Fujio muttered again, and though he took it for an illusion, he asked himself whose eyes they might have been out there and what kind of eyes they were. What surprised him was the height of the position of the eyes he thought he had seen. They gave no feeling of bending over; their arrogant, cold stare made Fujio think of the eyes of the dead boy beside him.

—*Did the boy see them from inside the car? No, nothing like that could have happened. I must keep cool if I want to put my mind at ease. There's nothing to be afraid of, and there's no chance the boy will come back to life...*

To check the boy's breathing, he put his face to the dead boy's cheek again. Unable to stand the horror of this action, Fujio lowered the window. At that instant, he was gripped by another fear. With the window open, he had the curious feeling that someone's existence could freely fly in and out of the car. He started the car. The only thing on his mind was to get rid of the boy as soon as possible.

Fujio was fairly familiar with the area around there, but he couldn't recall in detail where there was a grove of bamboo or some thicket of trees.

—*This isn't the city; I'll be able to find a place to get rid of the body almost anywhere...*

Despite his frenzy, Fujio had driven less than one kilometer when he found a suitable place. A steep slope fell away from the gentle curve of the road, dropping into an inconspicuous bamboo grove. No one would think of going down there to gather bamboo shoots. It was just right. He parked the car at the highest point where an old farm road wound off.

—*It offers no concealment, but I'll be warned by the headlights of any approaching car from a distance, especially at this time...*

Fujio scanned the vicinity to check that no car was approaching. Then he opened the passenger side door and pulled out the boy's body. If he could just get him as far as the bamboo, then, even if someone did come by, they would only think that a man had stopped there to relieve himself.

The boy's body was oppressively heavy in the way a dead person shows their bad intent by trying to drag you down into the depths of the earth. The weight pressed on him like some evil thought.

—*Is this how much an elementary school kid weighs? I suppose boys have heavy bones. If he'd been in junior high school, it would have been an incredible strain just to lift him...*

It was hard for even one person to get through the bamboo grove. Fujio let go of the body, trying to think of a better way. Three cars passed by, seeming to pay no attention to the crouching Fujio nor to his car. The bamboo grove was a filthy and depressing mass of litter—probably the work of passers-by, or maybe the local farmers chucking things down there. The place emitted a foul odor; it was piled up with vinyl sheeting used in the fields, bits of rope, plastic containers, empty cans and cabbage shreds.

Fujio kept stepping on rotting things that felt most unpleasant and he had to pull his feet free, like a person drowning. He struggled to where the slope fell away and put the boy down on the ground. Fujio was hoping that the fallen bamboo leaves all about would allow the body to slide down the slope. He threw the body forwards and down the hill, but the bamboo stopped the fall after only abut 50 centimeters.

—*Still, even if I'd succeeded in sending the corpse three meters down the slope, anyone would easily discover it if they were looking carefully...*

He went back to the car and brought out the boy's rucksack, using his handkerchief to hold it to avoid fingerprints. He threw it toward the body. But the rucksack also got caught in the bamboo and fell short of the spot where the body lay.

Fujio decided not to think any more; he was still feeling dazed, as if in a dream. He was afraid that if he didn't stay alert, he wouldn't be able to get out of the thicket. He was panting as he returned to his car. He turned the key to start the engine, only to find that his hand wouldn't work smoothly. He put the car in gear and released the brake. But his ankle had lost its flexibility and the car set off with an unnatural jolt.

Fujio headed in the direction of his house, but after a few kilometers a small incident occurred which had nothing to do with the discomfort he was feeling in his hands and feet. Totally by coincidence, a man riding a bicycle at great speed suddenly turned out from a narrow side road, hit Fujio's car, and spilled over.

'Stupid jerk!!' Fujio shouted without thinking.

Fujio was the one driving on the straight. He immediately despised the man for just blindly hitting his car like that, whether it was due to a lack of caution or to annoy him.

In the side mirror, Fujio could see that both the man and his bike had flown through the air and landed on the side of the road. But the man was not down and out on the ground: he had picked himself up and was standing. The impact that Fujio felt had not been hard, only as though the man had hit the car's tire; his spectacular fall was simply in response to the motion of the car. If he had hit some metal part of the car, Fujio would certainly have stopped immediately to make him apologize and find out where to bill for the repairs to the car. But Fujio knew he could do nothing of the kind right now. No matter what, he couldn't afford having anyone notice his face and his name; he must avoid anything that might set the police looking for him. Fujio drove off smartly to perk himself up. He felt extremely excited, as though he was putting a whip to a wild horse.

—I suppose that fool will just reluctantly pick up his damaged bike and go home, perhaps limping. But if it comes to a question of who was in the wrong, then it would be the cyclist who came out of a side road without slowing down. An idiot like that should be grateful to have escaped with his life and just put up with it. Even if there's an investigation, there'll be no reason to suppose that I was involved in anything more than that accident. This is not like the time involving the Shimada girl. This time I discarded the rucksack and the clothes and everything in the bamboo grove. And it wasn't a matter of drunken driving, nor driving with a suspended license. So there's absolutely no reason for complaint...

The area was totally dark when Fujio returned his car to his parking place. Finally feeling relaxed, he remembered something he ought to do.

—Just in case, I should wipe away any fingerprints the boy may have left on the door or the broken mirror. Also, since I can't be sure, I'd better wipe the whole area around the passenger seat where the boy may have touched with a chamois leather. If someone sees me doing that, they'll only suppose I'm cleaning up the car after a day out driving...

But there was no one around to see.

The spring night was quiet. Fujio detected the odor of broiled fish coming from somewhere. When he returned home, his mother was clearing the tea table.

'You haven't eaten yet, have you, dear?' she asked.

The TV was noisy; his father was watching a quiz show and didn't even look in Fujio's direction.

'No, not yet,' Fujio blurted. 'Is there anything?'

'I went to the supermarket today and there were dried sardines on sale. Your father said they were delicious.'

As Fujio's mother announced this, there was a sudden look of fear in her eyes. Fujio well knew the reason why. Last time when he was in a bad mood and his insensitive mother had gone on about what a bargain in delicious mackerel she'd bought that day at the supermarket, Fujio had thrown his plateful of fish onto the floor under the table. Since then, whenever his mother got something cheap like fish at the supermarket, rather than being pleased about the price, she seemed to be afraid that her son would get angry.

'Sardines'll be fine,' he replied.

'Then I'll broil some right away,' she said. She went off busily to the kitchen.

'Eight yen each?' Fujio called after her.

Good fresh sardines used to go for that price.

'Not that cheap!' his mother called back. 'About 12 yen each.'

'Oh, not too bad.'

'But you can't really tell until you cook them,' she said. 'The other day, they seemed to be fatty, but when I cooked them they were too dry. These today are fine. Do you want two, or shall I cook three?'

'Two's fine.'

'Have three, anyway, since they're salted just right.'

Fujio didn't answer. In a little while, his mother brought in some pickled vegetables, *miso* soup with fried bean curd and chopped radish, and rice along with the sardines. The fish burned Fujio's tongue.

As he as using his chopsticks, Fujio noticed his father's profile in front of him. His father was absorbed in the TV program. He said nothing, and there was no change of expression on his face to suggest to Fujio any human need to talk about what he was watching or about something that moved him.

The way the sardines had been salted was excellent—neither too sharp nor overly sweet, perfectly bringing out the flavor of the fish itself.

'That was delicious!' Fujio said, finishing.

'Food at home is absolutely the best,' his mother said. 'Home cooking is best.'

'Well, you can't exactly call broiling dried sardines home cooking,' Fujio answered.

'No, no. Hot food straight from the oven is real cooking, for sure.'

His mother looked quite satisfied.

But Fujio couldn't stand his mother's chatter. He quickly went up to his room on the roof, his private castle.

Chapter 16

THE TRAP

FUJIO'S peaceful sleep that night may have been due to the rare event of his having dinner at home. Despite the fact that the conceited boy—whose name he hadn't even learned—had stopped breathing forever, some slight afterthought was pressing on his memory. At the moment, he was trying not to have to deal with it.

—How conceited could the boy have been to think that his death would be a loss to the nation? He was the kind of person I don't want to be living in Japan today. That's what made me want to kill him...

When Fujio was angry, he had to struggle to restore his equilibrium. But precisely because of his anger, Fujio slept peacefully that night. At an absurdly early hour for him, he awoke, sensing the presence of someone downstairs. He looked at the clock. It was just 7 a.m. There seemed to be someone at the entrance to the store. It wasn't yet time to open, and since the person was speaking in a low voice, Fujio couldn't make out the words. He was trying to listen when his mother came up the stairs, stepping lightly for her age, and he heard her outside the door to his room calling his name in a reserved kind of way.

'Fujio...'

'What is it?' he demanded.

'Are you awake?'

That was obvious, so he didn't respond. But his mother slid the door open and slipped into the room.

'I really don't know what this is about, but there's a policeman downstairs,' she said.

'What does he want at an hour like this? Does he want me?'

'Yes. He said he wants to ask you something about a car accident.'

Fujio was relieved, but he didn't hide his displeasure.

'Idiot! Can't you say I'm not here?'

'I said you weren't here at first. Then he asked where you were and said that he would wait until you got back. I said that you might have come in late last night and still be sleeping and that I'd have a look.'

'It's no good lying. What's he thinking, getting someone up at this hour? It's ridiculous.'

'Shall I ask him to come back? I'll tell him that you're still asleep and ask him to come back later.'

'No, I'm awake now, anyway, so I'll meet him,' Fujio said.

'I wonder what it is? Was there some kind of accident?'

'No, I've no idea at all. Probably just some mistake.'

'Oh, then it's alright.'

Fujio went downstairs, still in his pajamas. There was a uniformed policeman standing at the entrance. He was about forty and had a prominent chin.

'I'm sorry to disturb you this early in the morning, sir,' he said after showing his police notebook and identifying himself as being from the Miura Traffic Investigation Section. 'It seems that last night, about 7:30, there was a traffic accident near the Takada intersection. Were you by any chance in that neighborhood about that time?'

'Takada? Don't know it,' Fujio answered. It was true—he had never heard of the place.

—*There's no reason for me to know the name of some little intersection, or the name of some village just because I happen to live in this area. Probably it has to do with where that damned cyclist hit me...*

It was a perfect chance for Fujio. In a very natural tone, he could apply his ignorance to the accident as well.

'Did you go anywhere yesterday in your car?' the office asked.

Fujio was a little flustered about how he should deal with the accident, but the tension of this encounter aroused his fighting instinct—it was almost like erotic pleasure.

'I went out, yes.'

'Where did you go?'

'Well, do I have to tell you that? I mean, there are some things that as a human being you don't want to speak about in front of your mother,' Fujio said, looking over at his mother who was peeping at them from behind a pillar.

'Well then, would you come down to the station and explain the matter?'

'Explain what?'

'As I said, there was a traffic accident yesterday. And if you were there, we'd like to have an explanation.'

Fujio took a few moments to think and calculate the turn of events.

—*If it's nothing to do with all the other incidents, there's no need for me to do what they say. But I don't want to spur things on right now...*

'Sure. I don't know anything about this, but if you want, I'll go,' he said reluctantly.

'Yes, please do. Do you know the Miura Police Station?'

'Yeah, I know it.'

'What time will you be coming?'

The officer didn't indicate any particular time, which put Fujio at ease.

—If the matter was serious, he wouldn't say any time was alright...

'Well, I've just gotten up...I'll eat something and then go there. Let's say about 10 o'clock, all right?'

'That will be fine, sir. I'll be waiting for you then...I apologize for disturbing you so early in the morning.'

The officer's last words were directed to Fujio's mother who was still peeking from behind the pillar.

'What's that about wanting you go to the station?' his mother asked after the officer had gone.

'I don't know,' Fujio told her, 'Some accident I know nothing about.'

Fujio had little appetite, not because of being summoned to the police station, but because he was never up this early in the morning. He ate the fried eggs and *miso* soup his mother served him in silence.

—The only way to overcame the dangers ahead is a carefully-planned strategy. I told the officer I knew nothing about the accident, so I can't confess to hiding the truth and ask to be forgiven. In any case, for now, I'll insist that I didn't notice a bicycle striking the car. If I insist, I've heard that the police can easily get offended and do mean things to you. So, in the end, I might have to say that the person in the wrong was that guy who came out from the side road and hit me...

Fujio opened up the newspaper; he'd not read a paper in a long time.

—As far as I could see in the mirror, the guy on the bike slowly picked himself up and was OK. But, of course, after that he might have died in hospital. The cop didn't say anything about that; maybe there's something in the paper...

But there was nothing about it on the front page, the local news page or anywhere else in the paper. Not only was there nothing about a bicycle accident; neither was there anything about the boy who wanted to go to Tokyo University. The thought flashed through Fujio's mind that the boy had somehow managed to get back home on his own. He always remembered his actions like that, as though they had taken place in a dream.

After everything was considered, he decided that if it was just a matter of a traffic accident, nothing much would come of it.

—But it angers me that I might have to pay a doctor's fee or consolation money to that stupid cyclist! The screwed-up system will plod along because the other guy who broke a rule was only on a bike, but I was in a car. For that reason alone, it will be the operator of the car who's at fault. If the truth were told, I was simply drawn into that calamity, but I'm the one who'll have to pay a fine, in spite of deserving to receive damages. I might even get something like having my license suspended...

He was not satisfied that he should receive any punishment. At other times, Fujio would have felt no reason to put himself at the disposal of the police. He wouldn't have bothered to go and discuss anything ordinary with them, or apologize. However, not wishing them to explore those other matters, he thought it was the best policy to avoid antagonizing the police.

When Fujio had finished his breakfast, he returned to his rooftop castle and changed from his pajamas into a suit. He thought he might go in a sweater, but that would be too informal and might cause an unnecessarily bad impression.

Before going out, he looked around his castle. His bed was unmade, as though someone had just got out of it. There were three issues of a swapping magazine lying around beside it. Although he had no wife to make it possible to go on swapping adventures with another couple, Fujio had joined the group a few years earlier to enjoy the stimulation of looking at the nude pictures of those ordinary, down-to-earth women with their long bodies and short legs pictured in the catalog that was sent out every other month.

As he left the house, Fujio was thinking of driving to the Miura Police Station, but then thought better of it. He wanted to be safe. His car was nowhere dented, and he wouldn't mind showing it to the police, but it was safer not to encourage them by doing that. He had a car, but that didn't mean that he necessarily had to ride in it.

The Miura Police Station was not right on the coast but set back some 30 meters from the highway on a small rise near the end of the peninsula. From the entrance, you could look out across the ocean to the hazy horizon.

As he stood for a moment at the peaceful station entrance, Fujio thought he would visit Yukiko after the questioning. A sweet sense of anticipation stirred his heart. He went into the lobby of the new building that had been there only two or three years.

The officer with the prominent chin, the man who had been to Fujio's house earlier in the morning, was standing down the hall speaking with another officer in uniform. He looked toward Fujio and came forward immediately.

'Ah, hello,' he said. 'Thanks for taking the time, sir. Would you come upstairs, please?'

Fujio was led first to large room, and then to a smaller, windowless room at the far end of it. He sat down.

'I'll be back in just a moment. Please wait here,' the prominent chin told him.

Fujio was amazed as he looked around; he'd never seen a room with so little to look at. It was a only about 4 meters square and contained nothing but a steel table without drawers and two chairs. Fujio felt he had been seated at the end of the room like a guest, but he noticed that the chair he'd been asked to sit in behind the table lacked armrests, while the chair nearer the entrance—the one for the person who would question him—did have them. Fujio had never worked in a regular company, and so he couldn't be certain, but he reckoned that would be considered as the difference between a regular employee and a section chief.

'They're making a fool of me,' Fujio said to himself in a barely audible voice.

Just then, with timing that would allow no further mumbling, a man entered the room without knocking. His face was as round as a dumpling, quite different from the large-jawed guy of a few moments earlier.

'I apologize for calling you here,' the dumpling said in a ridiculously nasal voice, plunking himself down in the other chair. 'Last night at about 7:35 there was a collision involving a bicycle and a passenger car at the Takada intersection. Do you have any knowledge of that?'

'Don't know anything about it.'

'Where were you at about that time?'

'About that time?...I think I was on my way home.'

'In whose car?'

'My own car.' Fujio was determined to answer as truthfully as he could.

'License plate number?'

'Miura S-55-9174.'

'Where were you coming from?'

'From Miura Kaigan.'

'Where had you been in Miura Kaigan?'

'Well, officer, I have a kind of secret life, you see,' Fujio said with a grin. 'I don't like to discuss it with other people.'

'So you went to a woman's house?'

Normally, Fujio might have been satisfied with the officer's convenient chain of association; today, however, he was momentarily flustered, because the officer with the face of an over-steamed dumpling reminded him audaciously of the time he had held Yukiko's hand.

'Don't meddle with my life,' Fujio said, 'It's none of your business.'

The officer's expression didn't change.

'Were you at the Takada intersection about that time?' he asked.

'Where's the Takada intersection? If I don't know where it is, I can't tell you,' Fujio said.

The officer produced a piece of paper and drew a simple map that showed where the intersection was relative to the Keihin Kyuko Line train station. He showed it to Fujio.

'I don't know. I may have passed it, or I may not have. That's all I can say. I don't really know where I am driving round there—it's so easy to get confused.

There are a lot of farm roads you can't easily describe, but if I know the general area I eventually find a place I recognize.'

'All right,' the officer said. 'But about that time you were headed home, correct? Did anything out of the ordinary happen? Didn't you feel that you'd struck something?'

'Absolutely not.'

'What time did you reach home?'

'Well, I didn't check my watch, but it was about 8, maybe 8:30—something like that.'

'Where did you eat dinner? Along the way?'

'No, I didn't eat out. I ate at home.'

'Your mother said that you came home late.'

Fujio was suddenly angry with his mother for telling such an unnecessary lie.

'Mom's a little out of it these days,' he said. 'She often gets the days mixed up, you know. She's not that old, though. I wasn't late last night. I ate supper at home. Mom broiled sardines for me. My dad was there, too.'

—*It's probably a good idea to leave the impression that anything Mom says might not be accurate...*

'Yesterday, where did you go in your car?' the officer asked.

—*This dumpling looks stupid, but he's persistent...*

'Well,' Fujio began, 'you'll probably laugh, but now and then I write poetry. So, I sometimes take a drive alone for inspiration. I listen to the waves and spend half a day lying by the shore, or sometimes, when the moon is out, I take a walk in the woods.'

'Oh? That's a really fine hobby. Have you published any of your poems?'

—*Was that a twinge of envy on the dumpling's face?*

'Not anything worthy of showing,' Fujio said modestly.

'What's the title of your work?'

'Oh, it's not out yet. A publisher offered to publish it. It's being planned, but I don't want to publish it until I'm confident about my collection of poems. I'm thinking about it,' Fujio said grandly.

'Well, tell me about the drive you took yesterday for your poetry. What time did you leave your house?'

'It was in the afternoon. I think it was about 3:30. I left the house and went first to Hayama. Then I drove south along the west coast.'

—*That sounds safe. Surely there's no problem with driving along the western shore of the peninsula to write poetry?*

'Was the road crowded yesterday?'

'No, not so bad,' Fujio said.

'Did you stop along the way?'

'I didn't stop anywhere. I go out there to be by myself, so I only stop where there aren't any people.'

'For example? Tell me where your favorite spots are. I'd like to go there myself on my day off.'

'Oh, Sajima, or Arasaki...or even Mitohama. They're all quiet places. But you probably know all about those spots. They're in your district, right?'

'But I've never been to those places for pleasure.'

'Ah, I suppose not.'

'Now, about the accident. I think you must have some recollection about it.'

'Nothing at all.'

'You see, we had a report.'

'What kind of report?' Fujio asked.

'From the man your car hit. The report was that you knew there had been an accident and just left the scene.'

'*My* car?'

'Right. The man remembered the license number.'

—*What? A stupid guy like that cyclist was quick enough to notice the number on the car that hit him?*

'Is...Is that right?' Fujio's true feeling came out and was noticed by the officer on the other side of the table. 'I don't know how that man was injured. But I wonder how he knew my license plate number? Maybe he got hurt hitting a tree or something, and since my car was passing by, he's blaming it on me to get paid or something?'

'Don't tell us a cooked-up story. There was another witness.'

'Eh? No matter what they say, I didn't hit anyone.'

'Where is your car now?' the dumpling asked.

'Where I always leave it. There's no parking space at home, so I rent one.'

'Then I'd like you to show us the car. I'm sure we'll clear up things immediately after that.'

'Sure, fine. Look all you want. There aren't any dents or marks from any collision.'

'Where's the key?'

'I have it here.'

'I want to bring the car here for examination; is that all right?'

'Sure, sure. That will be perfectly OK. I'll use it to ride home. I'll draw you a map to the parking space.'

'No, the police can't bring it over here. *You* ride with us and drive it over here.'

'Really? You won't have to look hard for the parking place in that case. I can show you where it is any time. By the way, I don't possess a personal seal. I don't have any interest in money, you see.'

'You won't need a seal. You can sign with the forefinger of your left hand.'

'Sure, that's fine with me,' Fujio joked. 'I always have the forefinger of my left hand with me!'

The document presented was a voluntary submission form.

'All this is just a lot of fuss,' Fujio said to the dumpling as he put his fingerprint on the paper.

'Yes, that's how it goes with the police department. Well, let's go.'

The dumpling got up first and left the interrogation room. Fujio went out to the back of the station and was put into another car with a uniformed officer.

In the car, Fujio said, 'You have to work hard for just a little traffic accident, don't you?'

'That's what we're looking into—whether it's just a little accident or not,' the officer replied.

When they arrived at the parking lot, Fujio pointed out his car and looked at the back wheel on the left hand side. There was just a slight mark which might have been from that incident, but otherwise no dents or scratches in the paint. He had checked it over the previous night, and while he had still harbored some slight doubt, looking at it now in the daylight there was no trace of an accident visible. Fujio felt relieved.

'So, are you going to drive? If you want, I'll drive it,' Fujio proposed, when he saw that the uniformed officer was going to drive the police car.

The dumpling said, 'It's all right. The car is evidence.'

'Then please drive the evidence carefully,' Fujio jokingly admonished. Once the car was moving, he asked the dumpling, 'How long have you been in the police department?'

'Ten years.'

'That's pretty good. Married?' Fujio asked.

'Are you?' the officer responded.

Fujio chortled. 'No, I'm not married or anything. But I never run short of women. Artists are popular with women, you know.'

'So how many girlfriends do you have?'

'Mm, that's hard. The total would be a lot. But I just have one at a time.'

'But it must be hard sometimes to get away. What do you do then?'

'Yeah, that's a problem. Not to boast, but I've never paid one of them off.'

'Is that the way with artists?'

'Yeah, something like that.'

'What do your parents do?'

'They just have a tiny business, selling fruits and vegetables. Oh, I could've dropped by home and had something to eat. I'm hungry this early in the morning!' Fujio said.

The dumpling made no reply.

When they arrived back at the Miura Police Station, Fujio's car was put in the parking area in the back courtyard. They went up to the same interrogation room as before. Fujio said that he was really hungry and would like to get something to eat.

'Sure, we can do that. We can have noodles or *tendon* delivered.'

'I don't go much for noodles,' Fujio said. 'I'd prefer *tendon*.'

A quarter of an hour later, the delivery man was paid 750 yen and Fujio ate his meal in the interrogation room. Looking at the bowl of rice with prawn tempura, Fujio recalled the restaurant he'd first gone to with Yukiko.

—I must let Yukiko know about coming here. As soon as the questioning's over, I'll have to tell her that I'm coming over...

He finished eating and remained sitting at the table. There was no sign of the dumpling coming back. Fujio stared at the calendar on the wall; there was nothing else to look at in the room other than the two chairs and a table. Probably, some businessman in the area had left the calendar as a New Year greeting. He looked at the printed name—*Yamafuji Construction Materials, Ltd.* The flower for this month seemed to be a short, white chrysanthemum painted in the Japanese style by an artist he didn't know. Its name was given as *African Kinsenka (Cape Marigold)*. There was also the scientific name, *Dimorphotheca*. Fujio turned to the page for July—as he'd expected, the flower of the month was the morning glory. It looked very much like the blue morning glories he'd seen in Yukiko's garden.

Fujio suddenly stood up and said to the man sitting close by in the large outer room, 'Where can I make a phone call?'

'Just a moment,' the man answered, 'the inspector's coming.'

But he didn't go and call the dumpling-faced officer. There were any number of phones close by; presumably there was a public phone amongst them. Fujio thought the man might have told him which he could use. He could only go back to the interrogation room.

Moments later the dumpling appeared, clumsily as always.

'Would you let me use the telephone?' Fujio asked.

'Where do you want to call?'

'Just in Miura.'

'Then you can call from here. What's the number?'

Fujio gave him the number from memory. The dumpling first wrote it down in his notebook, and then, looking at his notebook, dialed the number from a phone on one of the nearby desks.

'The office complains about personal calls. It's a lot of trouble to call someone outside of the city; so we have to dial out ourselves,' he explained.

'The police can't trust anybody,' Fujio said.

'If we don't watch it, things get messed up.'

While Fujio was on the phone, the dumpling sat at his desk close by, apparently looking at papers and writing a memo. Then he stretched his back as though tired.

Just hearing the calling sound of the phone to Yukiko made Fujio's heart tighten with joy.

'Hello...' came Yukiko's voice, and Fujio tried hard to keep a calm tone.

'How are you?'

'Fine thanks. And you?' she replied.

'Yeah, fine I suppose.'

'You suppose? Don't you feel well?'

'I'm out just now,' he told her, 'but when I finish up, I thought I'd stop by. Are you going to be at home?'

'Just as I said, I'm *always* at home! I go shopping only once every three days. But otherwise I'm home—unless I'm sick and have to go to see the doctor.'

'I was worried that you'd fallen ill and might not be at home.'

'Thanks, but I'm fine.'

'Anyway, I thought I'd like to see you today to get some of the morning glory seeds.'

'But you really don't have any interest in them, do you?'

'Well, no. But I want to try planting some. Don't get mad at me about that. Won't you give me some more seeds?'

'Yes, of course I will.'

'I haven't planted any since elementary school. So I'm wondering whether they'll bloom.'

That was one of Fujio's neat lies. Even in elementary school, when Fujio had been asked to plant seeds, all he had done was kick over a pot of morning glories—that a friend had proudly brought in—when nobody was watching. He had damaged the flowers in the process.

'Where are you now?' Yukiko asked.

'I can't tell you,' Fujio replied in a cheery voice, 'but if you knew, you'd be surprised.'

'That's fine. It's your private business. About what time are you coming? If I need to go out for something, I won't go then.'

'I can't be sure, but I think I'll be done in an hour or two. I'll come right after that. I think it's about 15 minutes from here to your house.'

As he said this, Fujio's glance strayed to the dumpling's face. Although the officer was certainly within hearing distance of his voice, Fujio was relieved that he showed no sign of hearing his end of the conversation. Rather than wishing to give Yukiko a time when he would arrive, he wanted to see whether the officer might say, 'We won't be through with you in an hour or two.'

When he hung up, the lunch break seemed to be over, and the room suddenly filled up with people returning to their desks. There was nothing Fujio could do then but go back to the interrogation room, and once there he waited a long while for the dumpling. The strange, artificial quiet of the room was quite exasperating. This new station had been built only two or three years earlier; Fujio imagined that the interrogation room had been specially soundproofed. Nonetheless, if he could have heard any sounds from outside, he might have realized that the state he was in was neither especially quiet nor tranquil.

At a little past 9 p.m. the previous evening, a message had arrived at the Yokosuka Minami Police Station to the effect that Ken Okada (11), 5th grade student at Yamate Elementary School and the oldest son of the Prosecutor for the Yokohama District Investigative Unit, Sakae Okada (45), of Yamate 3-chome, Yokosuka City, had failed to return home from his cram school.

According to Shigeko, the boy's mother, Ken had a good record and a cheerful personality, and had until then never been late for supper, always returning home by 7:30. On the rare occasions when he went to a friend's house and might be late for supper, he always called on the telephone. His parents had demanded that he should do that, but it was in his conscientious character to do so without complaint.

When a child did not return home, four possible reasons were considered by the police: a kidnapping, a runaway, getting lost, or an accident. In Ken's case, there seemed no reason for him to be a runaway and he was not of an age or mental condition to get lost. Moreover, on the 10-minute walk between the school and his house, there was nothing like a river, a bridge, an open manhole or an excavation materials dump where he might have had an accident. Even if there had been, Ken was a very careful child: when his friends wanted to go into dangerous places, he was the kind of boy who warned them of the danger and cautioned them to stop.

So a specialist in kidnapping had already been sent to the Yokosuka Minami Police Station from the main prefectural office, and in case there was contact from kidnappers regarding exchanging the child for money, recording equipment and call tracing facilities were already in place. The parents waited, sleeping hardly at all that night. But they received no phone call of any kind that was outside of the ordinary. Ken's father, Prosecutor Okada, stood by in his study, and Shigeko eased her concern by saying that what with all this commotion, Ken would get a severe scolding when he came home.

About the time that Fujio was visited by the traffic officer from the Miura Police Station, the Yokosuka Minami Police Station had begun its search with inquiries to the teacher at the cram school and the children who studied there with Ken, as well as checking the streets where the boy walked between his house and the cram school.

There had been nothing in the least out of the ordinary regarding Ken that day; he'd taken his mathematics and language lessons and then left the school at about 6:50 p.m. The last person he had spoken with was his classmate Mamoru Yamada. As Ken had requested as they had left the school, Mamoru had returned three sticks of chewing gum that Ken had given him. Mamoru had given him three sticks of the same kind of chewing gum that Ken had lent him because he thought that Ken was quite meticulous about such matters. The gum was a product called 'UFO Laser Gum.'

The Yamada boy had felt like going home with Ken, but Ken had forgotten something in their room at the cram school and gone back for it, so Mamoru went on home alone. Ken had not asked him to wait, and Mamoru was hungry; he would be late getting home if he waited for Ken.

After that, no one had seen Ken Okada. The office worker who closed up the school saw no one lingering about. It seemed that Ken had left the school not long after his friend. Thereafter, no trace of the boy could be discovered.

One of the investigators from the main office had inquired about the license numbers on cars parked in the neighborhood around that time and he learned that among them was a white car with the number '74' at the end. It was scant information, but the person who saw it was a 65-year-old man in the neighborhood by the name of Saburo Kaneda who had recently received a letter from an old high school chum. Apparently, the man who had sent the letter had gone through a lot of changes in his life, but finally—he had written in the letter—he had bought a *nashi* pear orchard in Gumma Prefecture and was going to spend his remaining years there. Mr. Kaneda was a little envious of his friend. However, he was concerned that the work of caring for the orchard would be quite a task for someone their age.

All that day, Mr. Kaneda had thought about *nashi* pears. Consequently, when he took his dog out for a walk his attention was drawn, quite by accident, to the number on a car license plate that was parked on the other side of the street. The number ended in '74,' which could be read *na-shi*, the same as the word for Japanese pears.

Mr. Kaneda didn't know the make of the car. His 7-year-old grandson would probably know all about it, but for a man in his 60s who didn't drive, the make of a car was hardly an object for his attention. He recalled, however, that it was a Japanese make, white, and of a standard kind of size seen all over Japan. It was around dusk at the time, and he couldn't recall whether there was anyone inside it or not.

When this kind of partial license plate number that might have some connection to an incident was recalled by an eyewitness, the police noted it as a 'partial', but just the last two numbers were insufficient data. A lot of people might have seen a car license with those last two numbers; it was rather like a lottery postcard with the two digits '74' at the end. Since there were so many cars that fit the description, it was impossible to sort them out immediately. Furthermore, a car that had just stopped there at about that time of day raised the question of whether it was really worth the labor to look into exactly which car it might have been.

But one event that day accidentally quickened the investigation. A detective from the Miura Police Station's Investigative Division went to the toilet during the afternoon break. He happened to glance down into the parking area behind the building as he unconsciously breathed in the fresh spring air through the open window. As he was sweeping the familiar scene below with his professional eye, he noticed one car that started his nerves buzzing.

Several faxes had been sent from the Yokosuka Minami Station to the Miura Station in connection with the disappearance of Prosecutor Okada's oldest son. Included was a list of items to be on the lookout for. The Criminal Investigation Division at the Miura Station had already passed its contents to all its members. The officer had a strange feeling about that car parked outside—it was the same kind of white car with the same last two numbers.

He went downstairs and had a look at the suspect vehicle. There was a card on the front windshield that said 'Held for Traffic Investigation.' After checking again, he went promptly to report this news to the Chief, and at that juncture the investigation jumped to a new level of intensity.

Shokichi Hara (48), owner of the land where the body of the murdered boy had been thrown into a bamboo grove, paused there in his labors to relieve himself. The time was a little after 1 p.m. Shokichi had often felt annoyed that passers-by discarded things in the bamboo grove on his land. The crowd that came down from the city for a drive angered him by throwing away empty juice and beer cans there. But even people in his own village did the same thing, not realizing that Shokichi had seen them. When he met them later, Shokichi was not at all inclined even to greet them.

That day, while he was in the bamboo grove, he suddenly felt strange. At first sight, his impression was that someone had gone into the bamboo to get rid of something like a futon or some old clothing. But the thing was too small for a futon; it looked about the size of a loosely rolled-up judo uniform. Since he was already there, Shokichi went to check on what he'd seen. When he got near the steep part of the slope, he felt his hands and feet go rigid. Not only that; he felt as though his tongue was frozen in his mouth. His wife was working in the field where she might hear if he shouted in a loud voice, but he was totally unable to call out. Right before him was the collapsed body of a dead boy.

Due to the tumbled position of the body, which he was viewing from behind, he could not at first see the head or face, only that it was dressed in a sweater and jeans. As he approached, he caught a glimpse of the boy's face, all yellow and swollen. Shokichi could hardly bear to look directly at it.

As Shokichi struggled from the grove, not only his tongue but his whole throat seemed to have frozen stiff. He couldn't run; he could only walk haltingly to where his wife was.

Finally he was able to speak. 'A dead person...' was all his hoarse voice could manage.

'Where?' his wife asked. Shokichi could only point in the general direction.

He could remember only a few things about what happened next. Certainly, he felt, his wife was calmer than he was. She told him to get in the car and ride in the passenger seat. It was odd, when he considered it later, that at the time he had not thought of driving himself. Without fail, he always drove to work in the fields. When he thought of it later, it seemed he felt that he would have gone off the road if he'd attempted to drive then, and so it was wise for his wife to take the wheel.

His wife drove them to the first house in the village. The family there was also named Hara, and the house belonged to a man named Manzo, who was something like a second cousin to Shokichi. Manzo and his wife, and a young, newly-married couple, were out in the fields, but the 92-year-old grandmother was seated there alone on the veranda. Shokichi had somewhat recovered by then and felt that his wife's communication to the police was rather fragmentary.

'It's the bamboo grove straight on from the Jizo statue on the hill,' she'd gasped out, after calling the 110 number.

Within just 10 kilometers of the village—not to mention the entire Miura Peninsula—Shokichi could not possibly count how many Jizo statues there might be. And no matter how many police patrol cars might be covering the district, they would never get to his bamboo grove with directions like 'Go straight on from the Jizo statue on the hill'. Presently, Shokichi took over the telephone and gave clear instructions about reaching the scene.

The voice of the man on the emergency 110 number was calm, much to Shokichi's astonishment. He asked about the condition of the body, approximate age, clothing and so forth, but all Shokichi could say was that the child was wearing jeans. He couldn't say anything about the color of the jacket, or what kind of shoes it had.

'It was a child, that's all. A schoolchild has been killed. Please come quickly!'

After the call, the man and wife left the old lady—who couldn't hear the phone conversation—and went back to the scene of the discovery in the bamboo grove.

Within a few minutes, around 10 patrol cars and some unmarked vehicles suddenly gathered in the field at the top of the slope. In Shokichi's mind, at least, during the next hour at least 100 officers in uniform, along with men in civilian clothes, gathered there, cordoned off the area, and stomped through his cabbage field. They were not only from the Investigative Unit of the Miura Police Station but belonged to everything from the Prefectural Police Station and the Mobile Investigation Squad to the Identification Unit.

The media people also arrived in cars flying their company flags in front. And, as if that wasn't enough, a helicopter appeared to take photographs from the air. The noise of the machine prevented Shokichi Hara and his wife from communicating with the police who were questioning him about the circumstances of his discovery.

In the interrogation room of the Miura Police Station, Fujio still knew nothing about these other activities on the Miura Peninsula.

'Officer,' Fujio asked, 'when will this inquiry be through? I promised to visit my girlfriend.'

'We'll be done just as soon as we get all your story.'

Meanwhile, the Traffic Investigation Unit of the Miura Station had discovered a number of very interesting things in Fujio's car. The most conspicuous thing was the broken rearview mirror that had been left on the passenger seat. It was certainly not normal for a rearview mirror to be broken off so easily—an explanation was certainly needed. They also found some discarded chewing gum on the metal beneath the passenger seat. It had almost certainly been put there secretly by someone sitting in the passenger seat. The investigators felt there was a possibility of lifting a fingerprint from the gum. Further, from the charcoal-grey seat—and hardly noticeable because they were about the same color—they extracted a few strands of soft hair, not really black but with a slight reddish tinge, looking as though they had been forcibly torn out.

In addition to those items, the Investigative Unit discovered an entrenching tool in the trunk of the car. Most of the tool had been washed clean, but in a cavity in the handle there were still some bits of earth that had been missed.

During this time, the dumpling-faced officer frequently left the interrogation room. But not once when he returned did his attitude toward Fujio change. However, in the Chief's office, the question had arisen of whether or not there might be a connection between the newly-discovered body of a murdered boy, that had just come to light through a 110 call, and the car parked at the back of the station.

In the first place, at the time the boy Ken was returning from his cram school, a white car had been parked in the neighborhood. Only the last two digits of the license plate—74—were certain. But the last two digits of the license number of Fujio Uno's white car parked at the back of the station were also 74.

Secondly, the scene of Fujio Uno's hit-and-run accident was just a few kilometers—and only a few minutes by car—from where the body of the boy had been discovered. Of course, it was not being discussed that there was a direct connection; only the hit-and-run case was under scrutiny at the moment. But because of the proximity to the scene of the crime, the police could not totally rule out a connection.

Until that afternoon, the charges used by the Miura Police Station to request a warrant for the arrest of Fujio Uno were simply 'A Violation Of The Road Traffic Law' and 'Inflicting Bodily Injury Through Professional Negligence'. The Traffic Section Chief appeared in the Station Chief's office. He had been pursuing the matter of Fujio Uno's hit-and-run departure from the scene of an accident. At that point, the Station Chief told him to delay turning Fujio Uno loose.

It would be necessary for the dumpling to employ delaying tactics until an arrest warrant could be prepared. At the afternoon session of questioning, he began a leisurely inquiry.

'Now, about your movements yesterday afternoon, we'd like a slightly more detailed account.'

'Look, I've already told you,' Fujio said. 'I'm a poet. I come and go as the mood strikes me, like the wind.'

'Then if you will just give us a general idea of your coming and going that will be fine.'

'You're really persistent, aren't you? I don't like people much, so I didn't talk with anyone and I didn't go into any store. When I buy something to drink, I get it from a vending machine.'

'You bought something to drink?'

The dumpling was seizing on Fujio's every word.

'Yeah, I bought something. What was it...? It was somewhere on the Sajima side. A shop with some bitchy old woman. Ah yes, I bought some fruit juice to drink. I didn't go inside. There was a vending machine outside the door. I was glad that the old woman was inside. But I don't like the dog that's always outside.'

'What kind of dog?'

'I don't know much about kinds of dogs. It looked like that dog by the statue of Saigo in Tokyo, but bigger. A Doberman, perhaps...or maybe a mongrel. Anyway, it isn't leashed up; it's always out in the street. Isn't that against the law? Next time you go by there, you should give the shop a warning.'

Fujio had been by there often, so he could describe the scene with confidence.

'That shop—where is it located? Could you draw a map?' The dumpling put a piece of paper in front of Fujio and went on. 'By the way, what were you doing in Mitohama?'

The dumpling gave the feeling that he was in no hurry, that he had all the time in the world to ask questions. Fujio was getting more and more irritated.

'I didn't do anything! I stopped by the shore and went to the beach.'

While Fujio was answering, the officer slowly took out his notebook.

—Ah, I suppose this guy's going to finish his day's work by slowly recording everything. They'll be sending me home soon. There's something else he has to do. That's enough for one day...

'Did you see anyone?'

'Yeah, I saw some woman before going on to the rocky foreshore. But she was wearing a stupid outfit and had on some kind of dirty farm-work hat. I've no idea of her face or whatever, whether she was young or good-looking...'

'Tell me about the sea.'

'The sea?'

'Was it rough, was the tide low...?'

'Mm, I don't know. It was out, I suppose. Some young guy and a kid were fooling around the tide pools.' Fujio was having to use his brain carefully.

—I suppose a scene like that is plausible?

'Where did you go after that?'

'I dozed on the beach for a while.'

'On the swimming beach?'

'No, there's a small, sandy beach just beyond the rocky part. Don't you know it? There's a little freshwater spring there in a hole in the rock. People often camp there. Camping there is prohibited, but as the weather gets warmer, people camp there more and more. You ought to arrest them. You guys are lazy. You ought to patrol your area better and check things out.'

'Did you see any campers there yesterday?'

'I don't remember too well.'

'Just where is that, exactly? It would help if you drew a map.'

'Sure, sure. I believe in cooperating with the police.'

Fujio drew a map on the paper the officer gave him. Then the dumpling said, 'There's a village here, right? Which way did you take to get to the rocky part?' Fujio pointed.

'Uh-huh. And where did you take a nap on the beach?' He got Fujio to mark the place.

'You guys don't even know that?' said Fujio.

'There are a lot of beaches,' the officer replied.

'Don't you ever go to the seashore on patrol?'

'Sometimes we do, but sometimes we just stay on the road.'

'Well, you ought to have a look at the rocky parts. There are more problems on those than on the sandy beaches.'

'How's that?'

'Well, the sandy beaches may be good for burying dead bodies, but a rocky seashore is better for hiding.' Fujio said.

—Uh-oh, maybe that wasn't a very good idea to touch on the matter of dead bodies? But, in fact, I've never buried a body on a sandy beach, so maybe it sounds quite natural to say something like that...

'Have you ever buried a body on the beach?'

'You must be joking! If I *had* buried a dead body, I wouldn't have said that, would I? But there was an incident like that in Zushi recently. Don't you remember?'

'Where did you go after that?'

'After that? I went home.'

'Which road did you use?'

'Look, I told you. The one that winds through the fields and comes out at Misakiguchi Station, not the one through Hikibashi.'

'And about what time was that?'

'Excuse me, officer, but, unlike you guys, poets like me don't look at their watches all the time. We say *'The dawn brightens and the flock of stars has disappeared'*—things like that.'

'Mm, "the flock of stars"?'

'What about them?'

'Well, isn't that word used only for animals?'

'If you say that, it means you haven't studied enough. You police ought to learn a little more about literature.'

'OK. But on the way home you hit a bicycle, right?'

'I don't know.'

'Sure you do. The man who was injured, and another person, too, saw your license number. When a car hits something, the occupants always know it.'

'Well *I* didn't know! You're really pushing, aren't you? Was the guy on the bike hurt badly?'

'I think they're still examining him. They already gave him an X-ray and they say they have to do a CT scan as well.'

'So you're telling me that the guy wants money or something? If he's poor and can't afford the treatment, you can tell him I'll give him a little money. It's not my fault, but I feel sorry for him now that I know about it.'

'It's not money. It's just getting the facts straight. Anyway, you passed close by there.'

'Sure I did. On the way home, I had to first go east and then north.'

'And during the drive, were you alone all the time? I mean, on your drive yesterday, were you alone all the time?'

The dumpling's question slightly alarmed Fujio.

'Absolutely alone. When I'm writing poetry, I like to be alone.'

'And you didn't give a ride to anyone on the way?'

'No one. If I pick up a girl, it's bad for the poetry,' Fujio said with a grin.

'Doesn't have to be a girl. But didn't you pick up anyone else? Maybe a kid, or...?'

'A kid?' Fujio's face showed his surprise. 'I don't have any kids.'

'Not *your* kids. I mean, did you pick up a kid outside?'

'I'd rather pick up a woman than a kid!' Fujio said, smiling.

'How about chewing gum?'

'Huh? Do you mean now?'

'No. Do you like to chew gum? That's what I'm asking.'

'No, I don't chew gum. I'm not a dumb brat.'

'Did anyone riding in your car chew gum?'

The faces of numerous women swam before Fujio's eyes.

'I just can't recall. Maybe someone I gave a ride to once chewed gum, but I just never noticed.'

'Who did you have ride with you lately?'

'Lately? Well, let me see...'

'Just whoever comes into your mind. You can probably remember who rode with you during the last month, say.'

It was a question Fujio would prefer not to have heard; it would take some effort to calculate.

'Well, my mother, first of all...and my brother-in-law...and my nieces...Then I gave a ride back to the main street to a woman who was lost. That was about two kilometers. She got out at a bus stop and thanked me and then went off...And the person I called on the phone just now.'

'Your girlfriend?'

Fujio said nothing.

'You keep a shovel in your car.'

'Oh, that?' Fujio said, smiling.

'What do you use it for?'

'Actually, I don't use it; it's just for appearances.'

'How's that?'

'Well, an acquaintance of mine went on a race in the Sahara Desert—but it wasn't the Paris-Dakar Rally. While I was listening to his stories, I thought I should get a shovel.'

'What's the name of the person who told you about going to the Sahara?' The dumpling's questions were slow, but he gave the impression that he could go on forever.

'I don't know. It was just a guy I meet at the sauna. I never got his name.'

'Which sauna?'

'The place called 'Oasis', right in front of Yokosuka Station. Haven't you been there?'

'I don't have time to go to places like that,' the dumpling said in a regretful tone, but he didn't sound as though he was catering to Fujio's wishes. 'Do you go to a sauna often?'

'Well, I'd like to go more, but I'm probably too egotistical. The guys I like to talk with are all right, but the other guys…Inside the sauna, there's a chummy kind of feeling, what with everybody naked, you know, and a lot of them talk on endlessly. I don't like that.'

'When was the last time you were there, approximately?'

'I don't write down that sort of thing,' Fujio said in a mocking tone.

'Do you write memos?'

'No. Nothing.'

'But as best you can remember, when did you go to the sauna?'

'Let's say it was during the last six months. If I was talking to other people it wouldn't have to be so exact, but I wouldn't want to make a mistake with the police.'

'And the person you said you met at the sauna: was he there at that time?'

'Sure, he seems to go there a lot—he's a person of leisure.'

'Since you've been keeping that entrenching tool in your car, have you used it?'

'Once, maybe.'

'Where? At home?'

'There's no soil at home. But I helped a friend of mine at his place. He likes flowers.'

'What's his name?'

'I won't tell you,' Fujio said in a childish way. He hadn't really helped anyone, and Yukiko was the only person he knew who liked flowers. 'That person has no connection with the police.'

'I will ask you once more. When you went through the Takada intersection, didn't you feel something touch your car? I want you to think about that.'

'Nothing! How many times do I have to tell you? If you want me to write it down, I will. You can confirm it. Come to think of it, I have insurance, so if this is a chance for the guy to collect some money, that's fine by me. My insurance will pay for it. That's something to write down in the official record.'

'The matter's not about money,' dumpling said, with peculiar stubbornness. 'You don't want to be difficult, do you?'

'So, what do you want from me?' Fujio said.

'We'll be here until you tell me the truth.'

'Hey, ease off! What are you thinking of, using people's time like this?'

Fujio felt a dangerous anger beginning to surge inside him.

'I think *you're* the one who's dragging this out,' the officer said. 'We'll be done when you give us the story without hiding anything.'

Just then a uniformed policeman came into the room and handed a slip of paper to the dumpling. Fujio was too agitated to pay any heed.

'I'm leaving,' Fujio said. 'I'm sick of you asking the same questions over and over again. From now on, you can think whatever you want.'

Fujio stood up, but he wasn't able to leave the interrogation room quite so easily. The officer who had come into the room was blocking the small space beside the table in the narrow room.

'We aren't letting you go,' dumpling said. 'There's a warrant for your arrest.'

'A warrant?' Fujio felt a dangerous pressure inside his head, as though an artery was about to burst.

'The warrant's right here. Do you want to see it?'

Fujio snatched the paper held out by the dumpling, tore it up and threw the bits down before the dumpling and the other officer could stop him.

'What kind of evidence do you have to arrest me?' Fujio demanded.

'It's better not to tear up things like a warrant,' the dumpling said deliberately, watching the other officer collect the pieces of torn paper. 'A warrant is a public document. If you destroy it, you're liable for imprisonment for more than three months but no more than seven years under the crime of 'Destruction Of A Public Document.''

As the dumpling placed the torn pieces of document out on the table, he read it out loud in a perfectly level voice.

Fujio stood at right angles to the table and listened with a faint grin on his face. But his temples were throbbing with resentment. The charges were 'A Violation Of The Road Traffic Law' and 'Inflicting Bodily Injury Through Professional Negligence'. Concerning the reasons given for arrest, Fujio heard the details of a hit-and-run accident to a certain cyclist, but the totally automatic tone in which it was presented failed to move him.

—I've been trapped! The dumpling knew that well enough, and yet he let me telephone and make an appointment for when I left. All the while they've been preparing things ready to arrest me...

'I can make a phone call, right?' Fujio said in a dry voice after a few moments of silence.

'For what purpose? Do you want to ask for a lawyer?'

—*Huh? I remember the dumpling saying something earlier about hiring a lawyer...*

'No. I made an appointment and it would be rude if I didn't cancel it.'

'You can't do that. Your family will be informed.'

Chapter 17

MORNING CONVERSATIONS

YUKIKO was startled by the jarring sound of the door bell. She looked at the clock: it was 06:50. The ringing of the door bell at a time like that would have shocked her if her parents were alive, or even if she had parents-in-law. But her parents were already dead, and Tomoko, her only remaining close relative, had come home last night and was probably still asleep in her room.

'Who's there?' Yukiko called before she opened the door, thinking it was lucky she had just got dressed.

'Pardon me for disturbing you this early in the morning. My name is Higaki. I'm from the Miura Police Station.'

Yukiko was still a bit doubtful as to whether he really was a police officer, but she decided to open the door, reassured by a certain ease in the loudness of his voice.

'I'm sorry to disturb you, coming at a time like this in the morning...Are you Yukiko Hata?

'Yes, I am.'

'Well there's a matter I wish to ask you about. May I speak with you now?'

Yukiko thought his voice had an honest ring to it, and when he took out his police identification from his coat pocket for her to look at, she could only feel that she was in a scene from some movie.

'Yes, please come in,' she said.

'Is it all right?' Higaki said.

'Sure.'

Yukiko was relieved that she had straightened up the small Western-style reception room the night before.

'Now, what can I do for you?' she asked as she sat down on the sofa.

'I believe that a man by the name of Fujio Uno was due to come to your house yesterday...?'

'Yes, that's correct, but he didn't appear,' Yukiko said.

'Then the visit yesterday...was an appointment made earlier?'

'No, he just called on the phone.'

'About what time was that?'

'Yesterday...? I'm not sure of the time. I think it was early afternoon.'

'And what did he say at that time?'

Yukiko fixed her eyes on the policeman's face. 'I think it would be irresponsible of me to discuss such a thing unless I know for what purpose...?'

'Of course, I'm sorry. He has been detained as the result of a traffic accident in which someone was injured. We are asking people who know him concerning the time of the accident, that's all.'

'An accident? Was someone killed?'

'No, but the investigation is still going on. I heard there was a bone cracked in the person's hand, but I don't think it's serious.'

'Are people arrested for every such traffic accident?'

'No. The person in question did not realize there was an accident. But the injured person and someone passing by saw the license number on the car.'

Higaki spoke to Yukiko in a tone suggesting that meant there was some trouble.

'When was it that you became acquainted with Mr. Uno?' he asked.

Yukiko was about to answer when Tomoko called her name from just outside the doorway. Her voice signaled that she was aware of the visitor's presence.

'Yuki-chan,' she said, 'Excuse me, but before I go out there's something I want to ask you. Do you have a moment?'

'Yes, I'm coming.' Yukiko answered. 'Please excuse me,' she said to Higaki. 'My sister works at a publishing company in Tokyo, and since I take care of the house, she needs to talk with me. Excuse me for a moment while I see what she wants.'

'Yes, certainly.'

It was probably the first time Tomoko had ever been up so early. But Yukiko supposed that, hearing a strange visitor in the house, her ears were burning to hear the reason. Just as Yukiko had expected, Tomoko was sitting at the kitchen table in her pajamas, smoking. She turned on the NHK morning television news as Yukiko came in. Yukiko immediately realized that she wanted to cover their conversation with the sound of the TV, and also that it might arouse the suspicion of the officer. She sat down opposite her sister.

'Who's that?' Tomoko asked.

'A police officer from the Miura Police Station,' Yukiko replied.

'What does he want?'

She sounded as though she already knew and was just checking.

'He said he wanted to ask about Fujio Uno. You know. He's been here a few times.'

'The one who sells fertilizer or something?'

'Right.'

'What did he do?'

'He said it was a traffic accident. But the other person wasn't killed, just a slight injury.'

'Well, I don't know a thing about it,' Tomoko said in a half-whisper, 'but to tell you the truth, I thought that Uno guy was dangerous. It'd be best not to say you know him very well. It might turn into a problem, later.'

Yukiko thought for a moment, and then said, 'We were never all that close. I really don't know much about him.'

'That's just as well, too,' Tomoko said.

There was a sense of slight opposition in the moment of silence that followed.

Then Yukiko said, 'Thanks for your concern, Tomo-chan. I really don't like maneuvering things like this.'

'Maneuvering?' Tomoko asked quietly, but as though in disagreement.

'I mean, I say what I know, what I've heard and not heard, that sort of thing.'

'There's nothing so dumb as saying you know something when you don't know,' Tomoko said. 'On the other hand, it's wise to say you don't know when you do know. At least that's what I've always thought.'

'I think you're right about that. But *you* can do that because you've got a sharp mind. I just fall to pieces when I try to get by with that. I'll just face it honestly.'

Yukiko spoke softly, but she sounded insistent.

'Look, it's your problem. I can't say anything more. Just remember what I said about getting involved; that would be really bad.'

It was Tomoko's style to warn, and then, if her warning was not accepted, to leave the matter alone. Yukiko thought that her advice was good worldly wisdom. And Tomoko knew that she couldn't put her own words into a grown person's mouth.

Yukiko added just a small amount of water to the tea kettle to boil and returned to her guest.

'I'm sorry to have kept you waiting.'

'Oh, excuse me for intruding when you're so busy in the morning,' Higaki said.

'Not at all. My sister doesn't usually get up this early in the day, but she works as an editor and sometimes she has to get up to collect material or something, even when she hasn't had much sleep the night before.'

Tomoko had said nothing of the kind this morning, but Yukiko was suggesting that was the situation.

'Then I'll finish up as soon as possible. There are just a few things I'd like to ask.'

'Certainly, whatever you wish.'

'First, when did you become acquainted with Mr. Uno and where?'

'That would have been last summer, when the morning glories were at their best,' Yukiko said.

'The morning glories were blooming?'

'Yes. He said he thought the morning glories were pretty. That was the first time I heard his voice, through the garden hedge.'

'What kind of work did he say he did?'

'I think he said he was a fertilizer salesman.'

'His family runs a greengrocer's shop. Didn't he say anything about that?'

'I don't usually ask anybody about personal matters,' Yukiko said hesitantly. 'I don't have much need to know how people earn their living. If I like someone, I spend time with them, and if I don't like them, I put some distance between us.'

'And did you like Mr. Uno?'

For a moment, it seemed more that he was enjoying a morning conversation than questioning her. But the question made Yukiko think carefully.

'I'm not quite sure what to say if you ask whether I like him or dislike him,' Yukiko said, looking at the officer's face inquiringly.

'Well, answer any way you feel is appropriate. For instance, did you like him as a friend? Did you like him as a man, or whatever?'

'There were times when I thought he was an interesting character, a bit dangerous even. And sometimes I thought he was just an ordinary weak person who wanted to be liked. Sometimes he seemed to be wavering and insincere...a kind of bankrupt personality.'

'A bankrupt personality? When did he get like that?'

Yukiko told him about the incident of Fujio coming to ask for morning glory seeds and then immediately throwing away the seeds she had given him at the edge of the rice field.

'Then you found the seeds he'd discarded right away? Didn't you say anything to him?'

'Yes, after a little while I mentioned it,' Yukiko said.

'And what was his response?'

'I don't remember exactly. I don't think I expected a really satisfactory answer from him. I'm not concerned about whether someone is either insincere or lying; that's the way he or she is. He seemed to reflect on his action immediately, so his answer wasn't anything to take notice of, either in a good or a bad sense.'

'Why do you say "He seemed to reflect" rather than "He reflected"?'

'Well, it could have been a misunderstanding.'

'What made you think it was a misunderstanding?' Higaki asked.

'He said that next time he would surely plant the seeds and asked me if I'd give him some more.'

'And did you?'

'No, I didn't. I knew that he really didn't like them. It didn't make any difference at all to me whether he planted them or not. And that doesn't just apply to Mr. Uno. Some people are just too busy to plant seeds. I'm rather timid, you see, and I'm afraid of being deceived. So I draw a line with people by not expecting anything of them.'

At that moment, there was a light knock on the door. Yukiko heard Tomoko's voice: 'Yuki-chan, the coffee's ready.'

'Ah, thank you.'

Although Tomoko always spoke in a very straightforward manner, she was a very considerate person at heart. She opened the door, looked at the officer for a moment and smiled. She had changed from her pajamas, but her hair was still mussed from sleep. Yukiko took the coffee from her sister. The aroma brought a relaxed look to the policeman's face.

'Thank you. I'm afraid I'm delaying your sister's departure,' he said.

'No, I think she made some for herself,' Yukiko said, 'but she's always thoughtful towards others.'

Obviously pleased, Higaki helped himself to a lot of cream and sugar.

'Mm, this is delicious,' he said. 'What blend is it? It's as good as what they serve in a coffee shop.'

'I don't care for coffee that much,' Yukiko replied, 'but my sister is very particular about it. I don't know what it is at all.'

Higaki continued: 'There is one more thing I'd like to confirm with you. You said that Mr. Uno showed some interest in your morning glory flowers, but that he really had no interest in plants. Is that your impression?'

'Yes,' Yukiko said, 'that's what it seemed like to me.'

'If that's the case, do you think his admiration for the morning glories was just an excuse to approach you?'

'It may have been, I don't know. At any rate, he certainly didn't get very far.'

'Did he show any interest in any other plants here at your house?'

'What do you mean?'

'Oh, just anything. Did he talk about any plants in particular? Did he help you plant any flowers? Or...'

'I think that we once talked about columbines,' Yukiko said.

'Did you plant some columbines together?'

'No. He saw a columbine in a pot and he said that he liked the flower. I think that was it.'

'So he never planted any flowers with you, and he never helped you—is that right?'

'That's right. He never did anything like that. I wouldn't think of having a person do something they didn't like.'

'Miss Hata, what kind of tools do you use with flowers, working in the garden?'

'Tools?'

'Yes. For doing garden work, you have some tools, don't you?'

'You mean something like scissors? I have several of them...for cutting high branches, you know, and for trimming grass...I don't have any grass, but I use them for trimming the azaleas. Then I have a hoe, and something with three prongs I use for turning the soil—I don't know what it's called...'

'How about a shovel? Do you have one?'

'Well, I only use it occasionally, but I do have one, yes.'

'One of those short entrenching tools?'

'An entrenching tool? I don't know what that is. I've never heard of one of those.'

'It's a little shovel used by the American army—just a short, rather pointed thing.'

'No, I don't have anything like that in the house,' Yukiko assured him.

'Hasn't anyone helped you in the garden using one of those?'

'No. If they had, I would have been interested and asked what it was called.'

'Mr. Uno said he once helped you in the garden,' Higaki said.

'Here? Never,' Yukiko replied, and then remained silent. It was a deliberate silence of the kind that she occasionally fell into, immersing herself in her own world. But Higaki seemed suspicious.

'What's the matter?' he asked.

'Oh, nothing. I was just wondering why Mr. Uno told such lies. He might have some deeper reason, but I'm afraid I can't understand that.'

'You don't really have to worry about it too much. People often tell lies without much reason.'

'Yes, I know about that,' Yukiko said.

'Anyway, he has never done any garden work for you?'

'No. Aside from hiring someone, it has never occurred to me to have anyone do manual work in the garden if they didn't want to.'

'I see. Well, thank you very much indeed. You have been a great help.'

'Not at all,' Yukiko replied.

She seemed distracted. She wanted to divert her mind from her feeling of dissatisfaction. She was holding her coffee cup in the palm of her hand.

'If he caused an accident, I wonder why he didn't admit it? An accident is an accident. No one likes to have an accident or fail in some way, but it can happen to anyone. Isn't that so?'

Higaki didn't seem accustomed to Yukiko's way of talking.

'Well, yes, I suppose that's true.'

'But if he said that he didn't do it, don't you think that's true?'

'However, at the scene of the accident, both the person who was injured and another person passing by saw the license number.'

'Then he should have admitted it right away. Please tell him that.'

'There is just one more thing. Have you any idea why Mr. Uno contacted you about coming here yesterday? Do you know why he wanted to come here?'

'Not at all,' Yukiko said firmly.

'You can't even make a guess?'

'I've hardly made any effort to get inside his head.'

'When you say "hardly," does that mean you might have a little?'

'I didn't ask him to tell me this, but it seems that once his ex-wife was pregnant, but she lost the child.'

'And he regretted that?'

'He said that he felt he couldn't have another child. He said he felt sad that any child he might father after that would be at a disadvantage compared with the other one.'

Higaki left after no more than twenty minutes.

There was no sound either from the kitchen or from Tomoko's room, but Yukiko was sure she hadn't yet left the house. She locked the front door and then returned to the kitchen. Despite her big physique, Tomoko appeared as quiet as a cat, holding her coffee cup.

'Thanks for making coffee,' Yukiko said.

'Not at all.'

They both sat down at the table.

'Would you like some toast?' Yukiko asked.

'No, thanks.'

Reluctantly, Yukiko began making some toast just for herself. She didn't put a piece of bread in the oven toaster because she had any real appetite; she just wanted to do things as usual.

'You know,' Tomoko began, 'that accident and all...Maybe it's just a case of hit and run. But a lot of people we know have been involved in accidents, and not one of them was a hit and run. I think there's something wrong with his character.'

Tomoko lit her cigarette, speaking quite precisely. For a moment, Yukiko took in what her sister had said. A faint smile of embarrassment touched her face.

'I think so too, Tomo-chan. I understand what you mean. But I've thought about people who run away from an accident, and I know it's strange for me to say this, since I don't even have a license, but I can certainly understand the feeling of wanting to escape from the scene of an accident. If the victim died and you attended the funeral service and the family said something like, "Go away, you murderer!" I don't think anyone would know what to do or what to say. I know I'd want to escape—absolutely.'

'Don't think every hit-and-run driver is so good-hearted,' Tomoko said. 'It's more likely that they don't want to pay any money, or they caused the accident because the victim was incompetent or maybe just a damned fool—so it would be absurd for them to deal with it seriously. People feel like that, don't you think?'

'Of course that's true for some people. But this way of having the person who hits someone immediately going to the family of the injured person and apologizing—that ought to stop. When a person's killed, if the driver is honest, then he shouldn't have to face such a thing. If it's a murder, the murderer doesn't have to go and apologize to the family of the victim, does he?'

'No, but this was an accident, and he's the one who caused it. He has to accept some bad feeling towards him, since he has some responsibility.'

Yukiko wanted to say that that was probably the reason he ran away, but she kept silent.

'It's just better not to be around someone like that any more,' Tomoko said. Yukiko thought that was natural advice to give. 'I don't want to pry into your affairs, Yuki-chan, but how close were you to him?'

'I don't know if we were close at all. We went for a drive once, and he came to visit a few times, that's all.'

But Tomoko's question set Yukiko to thinking about her own feelings.

'Did you enjoy those times?'

'Yes, I suppose I did. There were some moments of fun, but I also thought that he was really insincere.'

'But you continued to see him.'

Cigarette smoke hung around Tomoko's body like a veil as she spoke.

'Yes. I wasn't looking for anything, really. I don't mind how it goes with anything. If someone wants to come around, that's fine—I won't stop them. And if they don't want to come, I won't call them in. Besides...' Yukiko seemed bewildered.

'Besides?' Tomoko said.

'Oh, it's just that in your kind of work you meet a lot of first-class people, I suppose.'

Tomoko laughed and corrected her in a low voice. 'That's a slight exaggeration!'

'All right. Even if they aren't first-class, I still think you do have a chance to meet a lot of peculiar individuals. But in work like mine, that's impossible. The people I see are all very proper. They're people who are all calculating in an ordinary way, and cunning in the same way—emotional and weepy, lazy and simple. Even though they lie a little and promise anything at the moment, if I don't have contact with them, then I don't have contact with anybody. That's the way I am myself. I don't have the talent or the education to work for a company, and I'm not a beauty, so I stay home and do my sewing. If a man keeps company with a model, he can boast of that to his friends, but with me there's nothing special to boast about. That's what I think and that's why these days I value every chance I get to meet people.'

'I understand,' Tomoko said. 'And I'm all for you getting a male friend. But there are some real bad ones out there, you know. An acquaintance of mine let a salesman into her house and while she was making some tea he stole the money that was in the cupboard.'

'Mr. Uno once gave me a nice piece of porcelain. I thought he had good taste,' Yukiko said.

'It may not mean much, but when I first meet people I make it a rule not to trust them.'

'I guess you have to in your kind of work.' Yukiko opened the door of the oven toaster and removed the toast. 'By the way, the policeman said he liked your coffee.'

'Perhaps I should open a coffee shop when I quit my job?' Tomoko said, her expression finally softening.

In another place, another officer from the Miura Police Station was having another morning conversation.

The police were starting to trace Fujio's movements on the day of the accident, opening their investigation with the Yamanakaya Tea Shop in Sajima, a place that had been in operation for many years. Fujio had mentioned it as a place with a disagreeable old woman. In the old days it had been a real tea shop, but some years ago the business part of the structure had been rebuilt, and now it had the look of a coffee shop. The rear part of the building was kept as a residence in the old pre-war style.

The shop was closed at that early hour, but luckily, before the policeman knocked on the back door, an old woman appeared, dressed in a tattered robe. She might have come out to collect her newspaper, but she appeared to be merely taking in the morning air.

'Good morning,' the officer said. 'Pardon me for disturbing you so early.' He introduced himself, showing his identification.

'From the police?'

'Yes. You know the Miura Police Station, I'm sure.'

'I went there once when a bicycle was stolen,' she told him as though she could smell a suspicious odor.

'Yes, well there's something I'd like to ask you.'

The woman was silent.

'The day before yesterday, was the shop open as usual?'

'Yes,' she replied.

'A man told us that he bought some juice from your vending machine and drank it without going into the shop. We'd like to know a little about him.'

'What's happened?' she asked.

'You wouldn't be able to remember his face by any chance, would you?'

With a photograph of Fujio Uno in front of her nose, the old woman looked blankly back at the officer.

'I don't know about people who don't come into the shop,' she said.

'Right. Of course,' the officer acknowledged dryly. 'Do you keep a dog here?'

'We *did*, yes.'

'*Did?* You don't still have it?'

'He died last week. Quite a relief it was, too. We took care of him for such a long time. He used to growl every time he saw me, the bad dog.'

'Then the dog wasn't here the day before yesterday, for sure?'

'No, he wasn't. I thought we could bury him someplace close by, but my son said that was against the law. He had to pay I don't know how much to the city to come and take the body away.'

'I see you don't like dogs much, eh?' the policeman asked good-humoredly.

'Oh, I don't dislike them, but that stupid dog was wicked. He always bared his teeth at me—part of the family—and he wouldn't make a sound at people he'd never seen and didn't know.'

'Was it a big dog?'

'Oh, yes. The only thing he was good at was eating.'

The officer put the same questions to the woman's elder son, the manager of the Yamanakaya shop, who appeared a few minutes later. He confirmed that the dog had died about ten days earlier. The old woman seemed to be clear-headed, but the officer had run into some other doubtful cases where he had suspected the person was senile.

The son explained that the shop had kept the dog for some 12 years. These days dogs lived for 15 or 20 years, so their dog was not so old when it died. But recently it had grown very thin and had not been eating much of its food. It had been listless, and had had a sad a look in its eyes. They had planned to take it to the vet, but the morning they went out to the dog's kennel, they discovered it had already died. What to do with the body of a dog that size and weight had turned into something of a major discussion among the family. The son calculated that the whole business must have happened exactly 11 days ago.

'And until then, where *was* the dog usually?' the officer asked.

'Where?' By the look on the son's face, it might have been the first time he'd thought of it. 'Well, he was always sleeping on the road. Come to think of it, it's a wonder he wasn't run over.'

The road was quite narrow and not well-defined. Only the section right in front of the Yamanakaya shop was a bit wider. Perhaps the roadside shrine close by, the one that protected them from automobiles, had also protected the dog's sleeping spot in front of the shop.

'While Kuma was alive nobody paid much attention to him, but when he died a lot of people asked about him.'

'His name was Kuma?'

'That wasn't his real name. His name was Koro, but people who didn't know him called him Kuma, so we used that at home, too. He'd wag his tail either way.'

'Thanks,' the officer said. 'Sorry to bother you so early in the morning.'

Fujio Uno's story about seeing the unleashed dog in front of the shop dozing menacingly was clearly a total fabrication.

On the way back, the officer stopped by Mitohama. He had relatives there and so he could enjoy a pleasant chat about whether anyone had been that way. A man named Noboru Tanaka, who ran the Uozen fish store, was a member of the family his cousin had married into.

Here the officer spoke with the local accent. 'There's something I want to ask you.'

'Sure, come on in,' said Noboru. 'But have something to eat first.' He was sitting at the back of an 8-mat room. He was watching TV while eating breakfast. The morning sun was pouring into the room.

'Please do,' added his cousin Tatsue. 'You can listen to him over the meal.'

The officer said he would just do that; he could smell the appetizing aroma of freshly-cooked rice drifting from the kitchen.

'It's just some *miso* soup with radish—not much to speak of really—and some boiled sea bream.'

The officer started eating. 'Hmm, delicious, really delicious! Every time I have your *miso* soup, I forget all my troubles,' he said, enjoying the taste and aroma of the soup made from fish bone stock.

'That's right. You can live a pretty good life anywhere,' Noboru said, laughing.

'And his hobbies are baseball, sumo, soccer, swimming and the marathon!' added Noboru's wife.

The officer laughed at this and said, 'Yes, he does just about everything, doesn't he?'

There were no children around, and there was no hard work to do. Noboru had let it be known that his leisurely lifestyle centered on going to market a bit in the morning, then taking a nap at home and watching television, and enjoying the sunlight and the moonlight shining on his pillow.

'Now, then, what's today's problem?' Noboru asked as the officer held his rice bowl out for a second helping.

'Well, the day before yesterday, there was a guy who walked from the beach here out toward the rocky foreshore. I'm investigating him.'

'From here towards the rocks?'

'Yes, that's what he told us.'

'The day before yesterday? About what time?'

'Late afternoon. Maybe around 5 or 6. Earlier, maybe. He said he went from here to the rocks and then took a nap on a sandy spot there and composed.'

'Some kind of musician?'

'No, no, he writes poetry.'

'Eh? With his back getting wet?' Noboru said, sounding very doubtful. He looked in a small calendar-like book.

'What do you mean by his back getting wet?'

'Well, the day before yesterday...the tide was full at 4 o'clock and almost all the beach would have been covered. After 4, the sand was still wet. If he was taking a rest, then his backside would have been soaked!'

'At high tide all the sand of the beach here would have been wet?'

'Not all of it, but nearly all. The bits that aren't covered by the tide are up on the rocks, but that's not so good for taking a nap.'

'Yes, I see,' the officer said. 'Then it looks like the guy didn't come here after all,' he said softly.

Noboru didn't follow that, but said, 'Looks like you boys are busy just now. A prosecutor's son was killed, right?'

The Investigation Headquarters for the murder of the boy called Ken had been set up at the Miura Police Station the previous afternoon, immediately after the discovery of his body. There was an instant flurry of activity. Since the station's jurisdiction included Misaki, it was naturally their case, but for them the kidnap and murder of a minor was an unprecedented affair. Not only that; there was also the feeling that it had started off peculiarly. In most cases, there was a long process involved in discovering the culprit. However, in the present case, the culprit may already have been caught. It was very strange. It gave the police, the professionals, an odd premonition. Most people would think that if the perpetrator was already in custody, then the case was halfway won. But in a situation like that there is an atmosphere of foreboding that it might take considerable time to gather evidence and obtain a confession. A suspect smoothly confessing with evidence easily obtained was not the way things usually went. The suspect, Fujio Uno, was hardly silent; indeed, he was more than talkative. At times he was explosively emotional, but then he would get control of himself and his good humor would return.

Furthermore, the officer who had visited Fujio's home had had no problem going in to meet Fujio's parents. Fujio's mother had telephoned to Saburo Morita, her son-in-law, to have him come by, and he arrived within 15 minutes. During the interval, the officer was able to gain some understanding of Fujio's day-to-day life.

'You certainly came quickly to the station yesterday,' said the officer, whose nickname was 'Pop.' He was not actually so old, but the nickname had stuck to him since he had gone bald in his late thirties.

'Yes, I was so surprised. I took his underwear and nightwear immediately'.

'I suppose he's had a number of accidents in the past,' Pop said casually to Fujio's mother.

'Oh, no, not at all, never. He was once hit from the side by another car, but it was the other car's fault and they paid for the damage immediately, so nothing unpleasant came of it.'

Pop took a quick look around. Fujio's father was sitting right in front of him like a wooden statue, silent. He couldn't expect much from that quarter. Uno's mother talked readily, but in general she didn't seem to have a very good hold on reality, and so he couldn't accept what she said at face value. Saburo sat quietly to one side, and Pop observed that he was sharp and attentive. He wondered what psychological relationship existed between him and Fujio. He would have to determine that as quickly as possible.

'So Fujio's a skilled driver, is he?' Pop said, gratefully sipping the tea he'd been offered.

'Yes, I'm sure he is,' his mother said. 'But of course, I don't have a license, so I can't really say. Saburo, what do you think?'

'Yes, well, I suppose he's a bit better than average,' Saburo replied.

'And do you ride with him often? In his car?' Pop asked Saburo.

'No, we each have our own car. But I've seen him driving around town.'

Pop thought that Saburo was hardly naive. There are two types of people; the ones who aren't excessively clever and are careless about what they say; and the smart ones whose brains work fast but are very careful about what they say. Generally, it was the ones who selected their words carefully who tended to leak out some meaningful truth rather than the careless speakers.

'Have you ever been for a drive in his car? This is such a pleasant season for that, you know.'

'No, never. I have my own car, and Fujio doesn't like to be bothered by children.'

'Oh, no, that's not so,' mother interjected. 'It's just that the nieces are so busy with school and classes at the cram school these days.'

Saburo made no expression of agreement with his mother-in-law.

'And does Fujio do any deliveries or the like?' Pop asked, addressing Saburo.

'No, he doesn't, at least not more than several times over several years.'

Mother said, 'No, it's more than that, Saburo. If we get a call after you've gone home, he delivers things.'

Saburo made no effort to challenge this, but by his expression he showed his doubt about whether it could be believed.

'Then does he work in the shop?'

'Not much,' Saburo replied.

'Then what *does* he do?' Pop asked, the look on his face showing he couldn't imagine how this strange person lived.

'Didn't he tell the police?' Mother said. 'The boy writes poetry.' For a moment Fujio's mother's face shone, and Saburo lowered his eyes. 'You see, officer, Saburo has no interest at all in things like poetry. He works very hard, of course. But Fujio...well, from childhood he wasn't interested either in the business or in school. I took a pencil and a notebook to him just yesterday. He just has to write, that's his nature.'

'Where does he write?' Pop asked, showing interest in the life of the poet. 'I suppose he walks, looking at flowers and the ocean...'

'No, there's a little room on the roof of the house, one of those pre-fabricated 'study rooms' they call them. It's too noisy down here. That's his very own castle up there. He stays up there when he has time, you know.'

'And do you ride with him in the car very often?' Pop blandly asked Fujio's mother.

'Oh, yes, he often takes me to the hospital.'

'Which hospital is that?'

'Do you know the Ogura Clinic? The one on the 4-chome corner?'

'Have you been there recently? Do you recall?'

'Recently? Let me see...I'm quite a healthy person, you know. Despite my age, I don't normally go to see to the doctor. Even when I think I might have a cold, it's cured by medicine I get from a peddler who comes from Toyama. It fixes me up right away.'

'That's fine, just fine,' said Pop. 'And do you ever take a drive anywhere else besides the doctor?'

'I get a little ill in cars—a bit dizzy, you know—so I go on the train as much as I can,' Mother said.

'They say that a cuttlefish broth will cure dizziness, but I don't know for sure.'

'I've tried several things, but nothing seems to work,' Mother said.

'And do *you* sometimes go for drives?' Pop asked the wooden figure next to him.

But before Father could open his mouth, Mother answered for him.

'Fujio and his dad haven't talked together in years.'

'Oh, why's that?' Pop asked, surprised.

'Well, Father just doesn't talk, you see. Fujio's like I am—he loves to talk. But Father answers very slowly, so Fujio gets annoyed and talks to me at mealtimes. He doesn't talk to Father.'

Fujio's mother said all this with a sense of amusement.

'And how about with you? Is he like that with you, too?' Pop asked Saburo.

'No, not at all. Father worked a long time in the business, you know. If there's something I don't know, I ask him and he tells me right away.'

'About the day before yesterday,' Pop said to Mother, 'I just want to ask you something. What time did your son come home that day?'

'Mm, what time was that...' Mother said, trying to think. 'I think it was late, but I couldn't say exactly what time it was.'

'Your son said that he came home about 8 o'clock and had dinner here. Was that a lie, I wonder?'

A look of relief came over Mother's face. 'Oh, yes, now I remember! He *did* come home early, just a little past 8. I broiled some sardines for him. It was the day before that when he came home really late.'

'I understand that happens sometimes. If I don't look at my notebook,' Pop said, 'I often can't remember what I ate even the day before!'

'You write down in your notebook what you've had to eat?'

'Yes. It helps my memory to write things like that down.'

'Well, we'd appreciate it if you could help us about something,' Mother said cheerfully to Pop. 'Yesterday, when I received a call from the police, I was told that my son had asked the police to tell us to find a lawyer for him. But so far there's been no one around and that's a problem, you know.'

Pop listened to her in silence.

'Of course we were so surprised and we took his toilet things and a change of clothes right away. We wanted to meet with Fujio and find out what had happened, but we weren't allowed to see him. He was telling us here at home that he didn't know anything about the accident at all. So then we came back and talked with Saburo, and Saburo went off immediately to consult with the Director of the Association. And he said that he had a friend and he would contact him. I expect that he will call this morning. He seems to be a much older man. Is that alright for us to decide on someone whose reputation we don't know about? After all, if it was a doctor, we'd want to know something about his reputation.'

'We don't have much to do with that,' Pop said. 'I can't tell you much. But I think that a lawyer who has some connection with you would probably be the best for you.'

Pop was more interested in Saburo Morita's silence during all this. Saburo appeared to be very careful about what he said. He seemed to know a good deal about his brother-in-law and the family situation here. But he was not saying anything extra to the police.

'What's your feeling about this?' Mother asked. 'When will Fujio be coming home? Everything will be cleared up, I'm sure.'

'Well, the police can't tell you exactly. If you talk with a lawyer, I think that will be a help for you.'

'We just don't know which lawyer, so we're anxious. I think all this has happened because Fujio isn't married.'

'Oh, I don't think that has much bearing on it.'

'No, that's the way the world is. If he was married, he'd be treated as a solid person. I know. But being alone after the age of thirty, when something happens, there's always some question. When he comes back, I think we'll just have to find somebody for him.'

'Well, excuse me for bothering you so early in the morning,' Pop said.

After leaving the house, the officer turned back and looked up at the Uno family's house. But he was too close to the building to see the room on the roof. He went over to the other side of the street to get a better look. From there, he could just see some blue roof tiles. Then he went on his way, quite satisfied.

Chapter 18

SUN, WIND AND SKY

FUJIO lay in his cell, counting the hours of the night. On the other side of the bars, the night duty officer was reading a sports newspaper under a desk lamp. A theme of anger played through Fujio's mind like a refrain about cheap love in a popular song.

That day, questioning had begun just after 9 a.m. and Fujio had returned to his cell sometime after 10 p.m. He had experienced hard labor often enough before, but he had never felt so exhausted as he did now. His skin seemed to be tingling all over. The ends of the nerves in his skin felt as though they were exposed and knives were slicing into him; his defenses against attack had all been consumed.

His irregular-shaped cell was about 6 mats in size, just adequate for one person. Its floor was surfaced with hard cork. Fujio thought that the usual police cell would have wood or *tatami* matting, but the guard explained that the flooring of this new police holding cell provided insulation from heat and noise and didn't absorb spilled liquids.

The light in the cell had been dimmed for the night, making it somewhat darker. Fujio was used to sleeping in total darkness, so it was still disturbingly bright, even when he shut his eyes. But it wasn't bright enough to read—not that Fujio had any reading matter.

The cell was windowless. Perhaps that was what irritated him most. He felt caught in a trap. Since the day after the warrant had been issued, apart from a few minutes of exercise, he had had no contact with the outside air. Other than that, he had had contact with the sun, the wind and the sky only for a few seconds as he walked along the corridor to the windowless interrogation room. The only variation was when he was sent to the Public Prosecutor's Office in Yokosuka—and that day it had rained.

Four officers were handling the questioning: one inspector, one assistant inspector, and two sergeants. The assistant inspector, Kazuo Takarabe, had described this station holding cell as a paradise.

'Why do you say that?' Fujio had asked quite blankly, intending to do anything to let others speak rather than him.

'Well, the weather is nice now,' Takarabe replied, 'so you may not notice anything. The cell is neither hot nor cold. It's a new, air-conditioned building. Even your home may not be so well-equipped, right?' He might have been boasting. 'Think how nice it will be in here during the summer. Do you have air-conditioning at home?'

Fujio didn't answer; he was not inclined to compare the cell with his home life. The officer might be threatening, or just sarcastic. Either way, life in a man-made box—cut off from the sun, the wind and the sky—grated on his nerves, even with the air-conditioning.

That morning, Fujio had been informed that the police had evidence he had killed the prosecutor's son, the boy who was going home from the cram school.

'Hey, that's an interesting story!' Fujio said with a laugh. 'What's all that about the boy? I haven't even read the papers here, so I don't know anything about it.'

'The child left a testament. Don't you remember?' Takarabe said.

'A testament?'

Takarabe's face showed no expression. Sergeant Shiro Higaki was sharp-eyed, closer to the style of the detectives portrayed on television.

'And what did the kid write?' Fujio asked.

'He felt he was in danger and so he left a testament. He was riding right next to you. Didn't you notice?'

'How could a boy write in a moving car?' Fujio said.

'You're sure he didn't write anything?'

Fujio felt as though he had almost been caught. He'd denied knowing anything at all connected with that schoolboy. But in that moment of give and take just then he had got a bit flustered. It sounded as though he had almost admitted to taking the boy for a drive

—*Water will drip out of your hands, no matter how skilled you are! But there's still room to recover...*

Fujio put all his nerve into the effort.

'Don't you think the boy might have been kidnapped? A criminal isn't going to have him write some kind of testament. That would be dumb.'

'You said you often gave your relatives a ride in your car, but isn't your memory wrong?' Takarabe asked.

'There's nothing wrong with my memory. When my mom visited the hospital, I always gave her a ride.'

'What was wrong with her?'

'Just little things, like a cold or her stomach or a toothache—you know, things like that. And we went to have her blood pressure checked.'

'As far as your mother can remember, she hasn't been sick at all. That's what she told us.'

Fujio felt as though a volcano was about to erupt inside of him; a dark pressure was building in his head.

'Tell us a bit about the dog.'

'The dog?'

'Before the accident, you went alone on a drive to Sajima. You didn't go into the shop where the old lady was; you bought some juice from a vending machine in front of it. And next to it there was a large dog that belonged to the shop. Isn't that right?'

'How many times do I have to tell you!'

'Is that right?'

'You know it's right.'

'But there wasn't any dog. The dog had died. 11 days before that.'

Takarabe left the room, and Sergeant Higaki took over. There were playing an unpleasant game of tag and Fujio was in the middle.

'OK. Now, would you tell me a little about when you gave the kid a ride?' Higaki asked.

'What kid? My niece?' Fujio said.

'Yes, your niece would be fine. Tell me something about your niece. What kind of a girl is she?'

'I don't know, I haven't seen much of her recently.'

'Oh, I'm sure that's not so. A fine uncle like you, you must have taken her for a drive, surely?'

Fujio was silent.

'And you took a schoolboy for a drive, right? A boy in about the 5th Grade?'

'I've never given a ride to any kid like that.' Fujio was pretending to be thinking. 'I give rides to old ladies a lot. There are some places where there aren't many buses. I like to drive them to the edge of the village.'

'Splendid. But not just old ladies; you drive the young ones, too.'

'Young ones? Like my mother?'

'No, no, other women.'

'I've driven with Yukiko Hata. She went for a drive with me. She'd promised me some morning glory seeds.'

'I've been to Miss Hata's place.'

'You have?'

'Yes.'

'Did you mention my name?'

'Of course. I went to confirm whether you were telling the truth or not.'

Again Fujio was overwhelmed with anger. He rose to attack Higaki, but he was quickly restrained.

'Sit down, sit down! the officer commanded without getting agitated. 'Tell me about your connection with Miss Hata.'

Fujio sat with his fists clenched beneath the table, feeling totally abashed and miserable. He felt that explaining about Yukiko to this man would be a disgrace, and so he said nothing.

After a period of silence, Higaki spoke. 'The shovel you kept in the back of your car—where did you use that?'

Fujio was silent.

'Where did you dig a hole?'

'I've never used it. It's been there all along.'

'Ah, but you *have* used it. And you didn't wash it very well. You used it, all right, but not at Miss Hata's house.'

'OK, then you tell me about it. My memory isn't too good. I'm really up against it when you ask me about the past. It would help if you'd remember for me.'

'By the way, Miss Hata sent you a message,' Higaki said. 'She said that you should tell the truth at once. She also said that you had never done any work in the garden there.'

During the last few days, Fujio had been desperately turning over in his mind how he might best put his story together. He would have to pull back at some point, and he was concerned with the timing.

'Did she say that I should tell the truth?' Fujio said feebly to Higaki.

'Yes, she did.'

Fujio pretended to think for a while. Then he murmured, 'I see. So that's the way it is.'

'Well?'

'I'm thinking about the accident.'

Higaki's gaze urged Fujio to continue talking.

'I looked in the rearview mirror. The guy on the bicycle had stood up and seemed to be all right, so I got out of there. The truth is that *he* hit *me*—that's honestly what I felt.'

'You saw him in the *rearview* mirror? But it was broken off. Who broke it off and why?'

'I told you that the other day. When I was parking the car, I got too close on the right side and so I couldn't get out that side. I slid over to the left side and I grabbed hold of the rearview mirror to help myself out, and tore it off.'

'Really?' Higaki said. 'The boy didn't tear it off, did he?'

'A kid? A kid wouldn't be strong enough to do that, would he?'

Higaki said nothing more.

—Ah, I reckon he would have continued if he knew any more. Perhaps he doesn't think he's got enough evidence yet? But during the questioning, both

297

Takarabe and Higaki have been rubbing my nerves raw by touching on unpleasant facts...

'Yeah, I had a reason to run away,' Fujio said.

Higaki was staring at him to urge an answer.

'That day...I'd been drinking. I was drunk.'

'The story is that you don't drink,' Higaki said.

'Usually I don't. But that day I thought I'd drink some *sake*—it would be good to change my mood. I've only really wanted to drink about three times in my whole life—that was one of them. So I drank some *sake*. I was afraid I'd be arrested for drunk driving if I stopped and the police came.'

'Where did you drink it?'

'I bought some from a vending machine along the way.'

'Even though you hate *sake*?'

'I thought I might feel better if I drank some. It's a kind of bitter medicine.'

Higaki was silent, thinking.

'How much did you drink?'

'Not very much. Not more than half a bottle. But the accident isn't connected to my drinking. I wasn't that drunk. It was only a small accident. The guy who ran into me got up immediately, and I wanted to avoid a drunk driving charge and conceal what had happened.'

—Well, Yukiko wanted me to tell the truth, so I should confess. And that's just what I've done. I'm happy she said the right thing. Her advice has come in handy. Now I have my scenario. I think I've done pretty well for putting together a story on the spur of the moment...

'Then your story about a drive was a lie. What did you do all day?' asked Assistant Inspector Takarabe, who had just returned to the interrogation room. Fujio started getting angry again.

'I went for a drive, that's the truth.'

'But the dog was dead.'

'Assistant Inspector...' Fujio said. 'Do you think there's only one big dog in that village?'

—At least that will put them to the trouble of going out to the village again!

'What about the soil on the entrenching tool? Miss Hata said you didn't use it to do anything at her house.'

'I told you what I would like to do. I'm a poet. I said it would be a pleasure for me to do something for her.'

'Answer the question!' Takarabe shouted, 'I'm not asking you about poetry!'

'Assistant Inspector, have you ever read any poetry? Just read some poetry, please. It's bad for a person to think only about crime.'

Higaki looked at Fujio. 'You may not be aware of it, of course, but Assistant

Inspector Takarabe is well versed in Chinese poetry. He is the leading calligrapher here at the Miura Police Station.'

'Oh my! Then I've been very impolite,' Fujio said.

'Tell me whose poetry I should read,' said Higaki. 'I don't get to read poetry. I've only been into sports since my school days.'

'And boss of all the other kids, I bet?'

'Yes, I've always preferred action to thinking.'

For just a moment, Fujio stared at Higaki. The sergeant's whole body was like a coiled spring.

'Where did you use the entrenching tool?' said Takarabe, pursuing the question.

'I got stuck in the mud once.'

'Where?'

'Let me see. Up at a bluff where you can see Koajiro Bay.'

'*Why* did you get stuck in the mud?'

'You mean you've never got stuck on a muddy track while out on patrol? To make one more row of cabbages, the farmers cut into the farm roads any time they want.'

'Maybe in the old days they did,' said Higaki, unmoved, 'but these days most of the roads are paved. Where you got stuck in the mud—what kind of field was it?'

'Sorry, but I don't have much interest in agriculture,' said Fujio. 'To me, a field is a field—it's not a pond, right?'

Two days later, Fujio was jolted when Inspector Takarabe suddenly changed his tone during interrogation.

'How did you kill the boy?' he shouted.

'I don't know anything about a boy,' Fujio replied, satisfied that he would be able to keep a calm attitude.

'That boy was so deeply attached to life, he left a lot of things in your car—a piece of chewing gum, hair from his head, and partial fingerprints scattered around.'

Fujio was silent.

'Now tell me, how did you kill him?'

From that point on, Fujio remained silent. He had remembered the term 'the right to remain silent.' Sergeant Higaki said little; his eyes remained fixed on Fujio almost as though he was doting on him.

The stalemate continued for about three hours. Fujio had decided to shut himself up within his own private world of thought. The only intrusion was the booming voice of Assistant Inspector Takarabe.

Fujio was trying out a number of tactics in his mind.

—*If Higaki begins to threaten me, I'll demand to have a lawyer. I asked for one a long time ago, but there's no sign of one yet. And if they don't let me consult with a lawyer, the police will be in a bad position regarding a charge of a coerced confession...*

Fujio remembered this much information from his work at the hotel. He had been on good terms with the man who delivered polishing wax to the hotel. In the evenings, even though Fujio didn't drink, he often went with him to a bar to hear his stories. The man had once been arrested. He'd been sued after giving some sleeping pills to a 17-year-old girl who worked in his shop and having intercourse with her.

'They said the crime was fornication with a minor in my care,' the man had told Fujio. 'But I'd promised to buy her a handbag and she was quite willing to have sex. Believe me, I learned a lot from that. Lawyers! It's 'Yes sir, yes sir' to them all the time, but a lot of them are real scum.'

'But prosecutors aren't corrupted like that, right?' Fujio asked.

'Oh, they're the same. They were sucking up to the lawyers.'

'Why would they do that?'

'Well, you see, there's a kind of professional game to change your job from a prosecutor to a lawyer—a lawyer like that is called a 'lawyer-from-prosecutor.' So a lawyer is a prosecutor's senior. Even the young prosecutors flatter the lawyers, because they're planning to quit the prosecutor's job and become lawyers to make some money. They want things set up for their convenience ready for when they switch jobs.'

Fujio didn't know how far to believe the man, but what he'd said about not counting on a lawyer stayed in his mind. He stated that his basic principle was to fight his own battles.

The previous day, Fujio had been told that a lawyer had appeared, and he was taken into the consultation room. Maybe the police thought he was about to confess because he had said he would think about lots of things if he could meet a lawyer.

The room was rather like the interrogation room, with the addition of a plastic panel separating the two sides. Voices could be heard, but nothing could be passed between them.

'My name is Yuzo Tagami. I will be your lawyer. Sit down. No one else will be here with us.'

With that, the guard who had accompanied the visitor slowly left the room. Fujio sat down in the chair on his side of the plastic panel, studying the face of Yuzo Tagami. He supposed that the man was over seventy. He was somewhat bald and he peered out at Fujio over the top of his reading glasses.

'I'm here at the request of Mr. Saburo Morita, who is the guarantor in this matter. Mr. Morita is the husband of your elder sister, I believe.'

'Yes.'

The lawyer seemed to be speaking with some kind of accent, but Fujio couldn't place it.

'I received a request from Mr. Morita to come here. Later, I'll ask you to sign a formal request for representation. However, in the interest of your own defense, it will be difficult if you do not speak quite honestly with me.'

Fujio stared at Tagami without speaking. He noticed a grain of rice stained with soy sauce that had stuck dry on the collar of the lawyer's jacket. It was a very ordinary, everyday kind of detail. Fujio almost never wore anything formal, or even a necktie, and he'd even come across guys who said that a necktie was just to catch splashes of noodle soup. So while the bit of rice on the lawyer's jacket was not particularly odd, it brought a chill of disappointment to Fujio's heart.

'According to the indictment,' Tagami began, 'about 7:30 on the evening of April 18th, in the neighborhood of the Takada intersection, you were involved in an accident with another person, and you left the scene immediately. Is that correct?'

'Yes,' Fujio grunted.

'Why didn't you stop? Surely you saw that the man had fallen?'

'Look, that guy came out and hit *me*. He got up immediately. I don't need to meet every damned fool in the world, do I?'

'When you were questioned by the police, why didn't you tell them you did that?'

'Counselor, I've had enough of this! In the first place, I don't trust this room. You seem to believe the police won't come in, but I'm not so naive. The police probably put a listening device in here. In a place like this, I just don't feel like talking.'

'However,' Tagami said, 'this is the only place we have to meet.'

'So let's leave all the details aside, shall we?'

The lawyer had finished and left within about 20 minutes. He had not been at all perfunctory, but Fujio, in his arrogance, failed to answer directly even once. The lawyer and the accused left the consultation room by separate doors, so Fujio couldn't really study the departing figure of Counselor Tagami. But for the few seconds he was able to watch him, the lawyer gave him the impression of being a totally wrung-out human being. There was no vigor to his walk any more than there was to his voice and mind. As he walked, his two bent legs caused his upper body to totter as though he was a child walking. He was not so very old, so possibly he had suffered a stroke, but Fujio was not interested in any such reason. Whatever the case, Mr. Tagami gave the impression that for health reasons it was time for him to retire. Fujio became ever more angry when he thought of his brother-in-law Saburo sending around such a useless lawyer.

After a little while, when Fujio was again called to the interrogation room, the guard following him brought a single sheet of paper. Assistant Inspector Takarabe entered and said, 'The lawyer left this document saying he represents you for you to sign.'

'I don't want him,' Fujio said.

'Why not?'

'Nothing major. Just that his eyesight isn't very good.'

'I don't think that's so, is it?' Takarabe said quizzically.

'The man's blind. That paper he brought—he was holding it upside down and didn't notice when he pretended to be reading it. He's physically decrepit and should be told to retire.'

'There's another warrant issued for you,' Takarabe said. 'You know the boy named Ken Okada, I believe? You gave him a ride in your car on his way home from his cram school. You killed him, and threw his body into a bamboo thicket. This is a warrant for your arrest for the abduction and homicide of that boy. You had better think carefully about getting rid of the lawyer.'

For a moment, Fujio was silent, but he was not thinking about whether or not to retain the lawyer. Then he said, 'For sure, I'd be better off without that kind of old man around. There's not much point in having a lawyer who won't work hard and is just grubbing for money.'

'In my experience,' said Sergeant Higaki, who had been silent until then, 'it's best to sleep on it overnight before you decide. You shouldn't decide things in a hurry. With anything important, I make it a habit to sleep on it overnight before I decide.'

'Thanks for the advice. If you say so, I'll do it. But that old guy is really too much.'

It had long been Fujio's practice to confide in no one, and he hadn't done so now, either. His reticence was nothing to do with being in jail, and he didn't feel he was suffering particularly. Of the two interrogators, he thought he could probably trust Higaki more.

—But I'm not going to swallow his every word like a cormorant swallowing a fish...

That night, about 10, when another interrogation session was almost completed, Higaki said, 'Mr. Uno, you probably don't know what's going on outside, do you? The mass media is kicking up a big fuss. Even at this hour, there are probably 30 newspaper reporters at the front desk. They even came round to my house—five or six of them. We've got a small house, and my wife can't get any sleep on account of them.'

Fujio listened carefully, but he couldn't hear any noise.

'If you knew what was going on outside' Higaki went on, 'you'd appreciate how protected you are being in here. The mass media would kill you if we sent you outside. I should think you'll be begging the police for protection.'

'Yeah, I'd sure be grateful for that.'

'Well, you'll be going to the office of the Public Prosecutor the day after tomorrow. The media will be waiting for you both outside here and in front of the Prosecutor's office like a swarm of black flies. You ought to be ready for them.'

'They're probably at my house, too, those bastards...' Fujio muttered. His whole body was gripped with the urge to kill.

'I heard today from one of the officers that the shop has been closed and your mother and father have gone to Shizuoka. What you do think of that?'

His mother's younger brother ran a pachinko hall in Shizuoka.

'And your sister's family can't stay in their apartment. The media are after them, too, and the two children are both suffering nervous disorders and can't go to school.'

'I don't know anything about that,' Fujio replied. 'Complain to the media.'

'Now, about going to the Prosecutor on Monday—you need to be a bit prepared. We can hide the handcuffs with a handkerchief if you want. But I don't want to hide your face. There was one guy who said he wanted to hide his face, so we put a jacket over his head. He couldn't see in front, and he couldn't walk up stairs. The only thing we could do was grab him by both arms and carry him into the Prosecutor's office. He banged his shins on the stairs pretty badly and was complaining a lot. So I decided not to try hiding your face. If you don't want your photograph taken, you should be prepared to walk with your head down.'

Fujio had no idea what time it was. Even in jail, he suffered no insomnia. In the past, the night had been a time of wild dreams. They were mostly erotic, and, somewhat reluctantly, he took an obscure pleasure in them. But now, in his imagination, he was only concerned about what kind of figure he would cut in front of the battery of media cameras on Monday. He imagined himself walking proudly, with his head held high. Hostility would be the only force supporting his straight back.

But, on the actual day, he knew that his posture might well become all doubled up—like a monkey.

Chapter 19

A MAN OF MANY FACES

E VEN at this point, Yukiko's life hadn't changed at all. She got up early every morning, and went out to tend the garden for a while so as not to wake Tomoko up. Like it or not, there was no pause in the care of plants, children and other living things.

However, for the past few days, going to the garden had become a way for Yukiko to maintain her composure. There had been no ransom demand in the matter of Ken Okada's disappearance on his way home from cram school. It was now being described as a cruel murder case with the sudden discovery of his dead body. The place was not far from where Yukiko lived, and the people who lived on the snug peninsula were talking a great deal about what kind of terrible person might do such a thing.

On the afternoon of the day that the detective visited her to talk about Fujio's car accident, Yukiko went to the supermarket to buy some bread and milk. The girl at the cash register remarked what a terrible thing it was to kill a child.

'Yes, it really is,' Yukiko replied, and for a moment she thought how infantile a person must be to do such a thing. Her depression wasn't at all because of the death of the boy; she was actually thinking of Fujio, but she had no idea of the extent of what was happening with him. Just the matter of the accident was not something that happened to anyone around her. She vaguely thought he would be sent to some traffic jail. However, the victim hadn't died, and she wondered why Fujio was under arrest. It was not something she could comprehend simply by thinking about it, and she didn't really have to, except that it weighed darkly and heavily on her mind as if pieces of lead had been put in her heart. She felt a growing sense of uneasiness.

It was Sunday, April 23rd. Some fearful if intangible premonition made her glad there was no evening newspaper on Sundays; it provided a moment of escape. Yukiko decided she would not even watch TV that evening.

That day, the father of one of Tomoko's colleagues died, and Tomoko thought she might have to spend the night attending the wake in Tokyo. She told Yukiko not to stay up for her and then left the house in the evening.

Rain was falling, and the sound of rain on the eaves spread throughout the quiet house. Yukiko sat alone, wondering what a normal household did on a night like this.

—Even Fujio might have had a normal home life with children if he hadn't got divorced. On a rainy Sunday night like this, he'd be at home, playing some TV game and being scolded by his wife for wrestling with the kids in a small room. Perhaps if I'd been just a little closer to Fujio, he might not have been involved in that hit-and-run accident...

Immediately, Yukiko felt ashamed of her sugar-coated, girlish imaginings. A few moments later, the telephone rang, startling her.

'Hello? Is Miss Hata there, please? My name is Mitsuko Kanaya.'

Yukiko remembered the name. Mitsuko used to be one of Tomoko's subordinates. She was the woman who had been raped by some weird man who went to her apartment while her husband was away. Yukiko had taken any number of telephone calls from people at Tomoko's office who talked like Mitsuko. There were two people named 'Miss Hata' in their house, but it usually referred to Tomoko. The voice at the other end was out of the ordinary, rather excited and like a synthetic, mechanical voice that wasn't quite human.

'I'm sorry, but if you wish to speak with Tomoko, the father of someone at her company has died and she's attending the wake. She said that she'd probably stay in Tokyo tonight.'

As she spoke, Yukiko was guessing ahead what the other woman would say. Because she and Tomoko had worked in the same company, surely she would want to know whose father had died. She would say that she was surprised by the news and would call again later. But the woman gave no sign of any formality, and on the other end of the phone she began to weep.

'Hello? Mitsuko, I'm Tomoko's sister, Yukiko. I've heard a bit about your situation from Tomoko. Can you tell me what the matter is?'

But Mitsuko seemed unable to speak.

'Mitsuko-san, has something happened?' Yukiko continued, softly. 'If you like, you can tell me about it. I'm here alone, and I won't speak to anyone else about it. Tell me if you want to. It's all right if you cry, but if you talk to someone you may feel better, you know.'

For a few seconds, Mitsuko couldn't stop herself crying. Then she seemed to get hold of herself.

'I'm sorry. When I heard that Tomoko wasn't at home, I couldn't control myself. But I would like to talk with you, if you don't mind.'

'That's fine. Just talk with me as you would to Tomoko. I'll pass on what you say, and later you can talk with her yourself. I'm sure there is something you need immediately and you wish to tell her?'

'Well, yes, there is. That time, when that man came in and...and raped me— well, now I know who he was.'

'How do you know?' Yukiko asked.

'Didn't you see it? The news about that little boy, Ken—it was on the TV just now. The man who came in here was the same one, that man called Fujio Uno! I remember his face perfectly. I wanted to tell Tomoko at once. What should I do?'

Yukiko clutched the receiver tightly in her hand, her mind spinning wildly. Fujio had been arrested as the suspect in a mere hit-and-run accident. When had he become the accused in the murder of the boy? She had to fight with all her might against her own trembling. She had to continue in a calm voice, keeping her words logical. Her mother had never properly lectured her on a situation like this, and there was no one else who could have taught her how to handle such a moment.

The tips of her fingers had suddenly gone cold, a feeling that was completely different from the effect of cold weather. Through fear and surprise, her capillaries were contracting; she felt as though there was no circulation at the tips of her fingers.

'Mitsuko,' she said. 'Please excuse me. Could I call back in just a moment. I have some oil heating on the stove. I don't want it to burn. As soon as it's done, I'll call you back, all right?'

It was totally untrue, but the timing was right, and nothing else came into Yukiko's head as an excuse for hanging up.

'Yes, that's fine,' Mitsuko said. 'I'm really sorry to disturb you. But I have no one else to ask and I don't know what to do. My husband hasn't been here, and...'

'He isn't ill, I hope? Or his parents, perhaps...?'

'No, it's not that,' Mitsuko replied.

'Then I'll just turn off the heat and call you right back,' Yukiko said.

'Yes, thanks. I'll be waiting for you.'

As soon as she hung up the phone, Yukiko turned on the TV. It was between news broadcasts, but at 5:30 she caught the news bulletin on a private broadcasting station. What Mitsuko had said was correct.

Fujio Uno, the suspect in the murder of the boy Ken Okada, had fled the nearby scene of a hit-and-run accident involving a bicycle immediately afterward on the same day; he was arrested the next morning by the police in connection with striking the bicycle. The police had examined Uno's car and found some of the boy's hair and a piece of chewing gum with saliva matching the boy's, along with other evidence. Fujio Uno had offered an explanation for the killing. He said the boy was on his way home from school and did some damage to Uno's car, which was parked in the street. Because of the boy's smart aleck attitude, Uno had got angry with him and forced him to ride in the car. Along the way, the boy had said that he was going to attend Tokyo University and so Uno, who had no proper education, became enraged and strangled the boy in the car. Then he had thrown his body into a bamboo thicket. The boy was in the top group of his class, and his mother had urged him to take it easy and enjoy playing more sports. But she said that, in spite of that, he went to cram school of his own volition in order to do some more advanced study.

When the news finished, Yukiko switched the set off and again listened to the sound of the rain.

—That person? HIM?!

Without making sense, the words echoed again and again through her mind.

—How many days in a human life are spent in such depressed thoughts, listening from the depths of sadness to the sound of falling rain?

She suddenly remembered the story Tomoko had once told her about a man in the Auschwitz concentration camp. He was suffering from 'starvation edema', although Yukiko was not quite sure what that was. There was no food in the camp or medicine, and no way to cure the man. But he survived that terrible situation. When a psychiatrist, another prisoner in the camp, asked him the reason for his survival, the man answered, 'It's because I just wept and wept.' His starvation edema was cured, not by getting food secretly, but by looking pain in the face. He was ashamed of weeping, but he recognized that weeping was not in itself shameful. The sincerity of his distress had actually been a source of help.

—Now the chorus of criticism will swell against Fujio Uno, the villain. The mass media will swarm around him like hyenas, tearing him to the bone. Even so, I'm sure he won't complain. He's unlikely to cry out his pain. Even if his reasons for killing the boy have been described in the media, he will never suffer as long as he remains in a state of anger with the world...

Tears came to Yukiko's eyes when she thought of this as something merciless. Her sense of the word 'merciless'—a bit different from the normal meaning—gnawed at Yukiko's heart. But she allowed herself only a few minutes of such sentimentality. Composing her feelings, she went through their list of telephone numbers and called the number for Mitsuko Kanaya.

'I'm sorry for the delay; there were a lot of things frying on the stove,' she explained.

'That's all right. I just don't seem to be able to think any more. My husband isn't here...and when I try to think, my head just feels numb.'

'You say he isn't there. Is he away on business?'

'No, it's not that. Since that incident, our marriage just hasn't worked any more. I don't think he blames me for it, but he had so little to say, and now he stays at his parents' house nearly all the time.'

'Does he want a divorce?'

'No. He says that he feels pity for me. He says that he wants to help me. But his spirit won't follow what he says. He...' Mitsuko stopped.

'I don't know what Tomoko said to you,' Yukiko said, 'but our feeling about it was that with time everything changes. You will gradually forget it, and you will come to see that even things that you thought were so very terrible at the time aren't so big after all.'

'Oh, please, don't say that, about time passing and things seeming less!' Mitsuko was by then almost shouting. 'It's not something I'll be able to forget in time—I'm pregnant! I'm pregnant with that man's child! And, at the same time, the child is mine!'

The sound of the violent rain covered Yukiko's abashed silence.

'What do you think I should do?' Mitsuko went on. 'That man invaded my house. Should I inform the police? But then the police will investigate everything and it will go to court, and it will be like being naked in public. Is enduring all of this my obligation?' Yukiko could hear Mitsuko crying through the telephone and she closed her eyes. 'Maybe because of all this, my husband hasn't even touched me since then. And now I know what his plan was. He's always right. But being right isn't always the human thing at all.'

Yukiko held herself back. 'Mitsuko, I know that you are suffering, but we are all suffering. In this incident, that man is the only evil person, no one else. But someone who is not evil can also make someone else suffer. Such nonsensical things do exist in this world. Did you ever imagine, when you were young, that such strange things could happen in this world? I'm a little older than you are, and I've just now begun to understand things like this. But perhaps neither of us ever learned all this from anybody? It's not written in any textbook. Our parents didn't teach it, did they? But the world is different from a textbook. We're both thinking the same bitter thoughts, aren't we? Please forgive your husband by understanding that suffering. We forgive everyone except the criminal. Your husband and yourself, too.'

From the other end of the phone, there was only the sound of weeping. Yukiko let a few seconds go by.

'I'm sorry,' Mitsuko said finally. 'I forgot something important.'

'What's that?'

'I forgot that you were already concerned about me.'

'Yes, I am concerned, but there is nothing I can do. And I didn't understand that, either, until I grew up. Tomoko's very concerned about you and your husband. Please tell her if there's anything she can do, anything at all. She is much more worldly than I am, and stronger. She will fight for you if need be.'

'Thank you so much,' Mitsuko said.

'When Tomoko isn't here, please call me instead. It isn't good for you to do anything alone.'

After the call was over, Yukiko wished to be alone for a while to compose herself. But a moment after she put the receiver down, the phone rang again, the sound jangling against her nerves.

'Yuki-chan,' came the voice of Tomoko.

'Yes. How are you doing in this nasty rain?' Yukiko was telling herself that she'd have to say the words as though melting into the rain.

'I'm at a public phone near the place.'

Yukiko was silent.

'I saw the news about that man Uno. So the police coming the other day meant they were suspicious about that case.'

'The officer who came that day said he was asking about the car accident.'

'But the police had caught him about another matter. It often happens that way.'

'Tomo-chan, don't be too surprised, but just now I had a phone call from Mitsuko Kanaya.'

'Why, what's happened to her?'

'She saw the news on the TV just now, and she recognized Fujio Uno as the man who forced his way into her apartment. Please give her a call, she's in a terrible state. Shall I give you her number?'

'It's OK, I know it.'

Neither of them spoke for a few moments.

'Yuki-chan,' Tomoko said finally, 'it's so lucky you weren't murdered.'

'No, I wasn't. I don't know about the rest, but I never once thought that I would be killed.'

'Why not?'

'Because he talked to me all the time. People don't kill you while they're talking with you. I remember someone writing that if a burglar comes in, you should keep talking to him.'

'Look, no matter how late it is, I'll come home tonight. You're such a good-natured person, Yuki-chan, so please be careful. I have a feeling that this isn't going to be resolved so easily.'

'Yes, I think you're right. The hit-and-run thing, plus the rape, that's two. And who knows what else he's done to other people.'

Yukiko hung up the phone and sat down on the cushion she used in front of her sewing work, the only place where she could think about so many things.

—Maybe I should write a letter to Fujio? But even if I just suggested doing that, Tomoko would certainly scold me. I suppose I should forget everything about Fujio? Yes, it would make good sense to be completely silent...

But Yukiko was afraid of such a judgment. It would be the same as regarding someone as not being there when they fell into some difficulty, even though they were there right before you in the world.

—Yes, it might make good sense, but is that proper human behavior? The

Bible offers any number of clear examples of the relationship between Jesus and evil-doers. He made an achingly rational choice from the depths of intense grief. The legal scholars of the Pharisees, seeing Jesus sit down to eat with criminals and Roman tax collectors, said to his disciples, "Why does he eat with tax collectors and criminals?" When Jesus heard this, he said, "Those who need a physician are not the healthy but rather the sick. I have not come to invite the righteous but rather the criminals." But I'm not Jesus; I'm an ordinary citizen, afraid of being killed if I invite a criminal into my life...

The idea remained in her mind as she took her evening bath and spread her futon to prepare for sleep. It was a cool evening. She wore a cotton robe over her favorite nightgown, but even then, she felt the damp cold. She sat down at the *kotatsu* table and turned on the tiny electric heater underneath.

—I'll decide everything tomorrow. There's nothing for me to do immediately...

While she was waiting for Tomoko to return, trying to calm herself, she decided to do something she hadn't done since she was a little girl: she would write a letter. She was thinking that she probably wouldn't send it, and even if she did, she doubted if it would be delivered.

Dear Mr. Uno,

Your name and face appeared prominently on television just now. But it was a face of yours that I didn't know. For a moment, I was shocked and I caught my breath. Most people would say that what you've been accused of is an incredible thing to do, but I know that people are capable of doing anything if the situation so demands.

I don't know why you had to kill the elementary school boy, nor do I think that people will generally understand that. If the victim was an adult, you might want to do that out of hatred. But does killing a child mean that you have no more patience with the world than a child does?

I think that with one part of you, you haven't given up with your life. If you realize how impolite people are, and how cruel your fate has been, you will not expect anything from anybody. If you don't expect anything at all, then you can't be betrayed or feel anger.

The sound of the rain on the roof came piercing down.

A police inspector came to my house inquiring about your car accident. He wanted to confirm whether what you had told them was true or not. Why did you tell them that you had helped me with the gardening at my house? I know pretty well that you really disliked gardening work. And I know you even had no intention of planting morning glory seeds, and you threw away the seeds that I'd given you.

I answered all the Inspector's questions quite directly. I'm one of those people who can't calculate my responses very well. You might expect me to lie for the sake of friendship, but let's stop any petty tricks like that. Living isn't a matter of tricks; I think it has some kind of greater scenario to it.

I have the feeling that I wouldn't be surprised at anything you do. People in the past have done magnificent things as well as despicable things to such a great degree, and sometimes those extremes go very far. But there is no reason why either you or I should behave like monsters. We are both insignificant people. And simply because you are insignificant, you did a thing like killing a child.

This letter is also to let you know about another matter. Some time ago you followed a young woman at an apartment block in Yokosuka. And you raped her in front of the woman's child—actually, it was still a baby. She has now become nearly insane, and she knows who the person is who attacked her. Until you invaded that woman's home, the husband and wife enjoyed mutual trust and were a pleasant couple getting along well in life. But now that home has fallen apart. The husband has left home, and he blames himself for holding bitter feelings against his wife. And there is nothing he can do about that feeling.

It is possible that the couple won't bring charges against you. They don't have the strength to endure any more pain than they have already, which is why I am writing to you about this. Regarding the rape, I read in some magazine or other that so long as those people don't file a complaint, your crime cannot be punished. Even though the police know about it, there's nothing that they can do to you.

You simply don't realize what killing a child means, do you? If he was alive now, he could laugh, play, love, work, cry and be happy. He would live his life for many years like that. But you took that away from him. Where did you find the right to do that? I simply cannot imagine why you killed him.

And it is also terrible thing to think about the way you have destroyed the life of a young couple. That husband and wife will never regain the mutual trust that they started out with. You took part of their lives away from them, too.

I have no intention of telling you to find a change of heart. Though the world probably demands repentance, I think that what is necessary for you is to suffer, rather than offer some superficial repentance. But in so far as you can't truly grasp what you have done, perhaps you are totally incapable of suffering.

It's truly pitiful that you do not know how much it means to feel sadness and suffer.

There was a sound at the entrance to the house. The sound of a key in a lock has its own peculiar sound, and Yukiko realized that Tomoko had returned home.

She called a greeting, and Tomoko, still in her black raincoat, came into the living room without answering.

311

'Some hot tea?' Yukiko asked her.

'Coffee, if you're offering,' Tomoko replied. She would happily drink coffee even just before going to bed.

'Did you call Mitsuko?' Yukiko asked, when she returned with a cup of coffee from the kitchen.

'Yes.'

'Was she a bit calmer?'

'More like an imbecile. I didn't think she was like that. When she got married, I thought what a shame it was to lose such a good editor. But it's turned out that she wouldn't have been worth thinking about.'

'Did she tell you she was pregnant?'

'Sure.' Tomoko lit her cigarette and spoke in a muffled voice. 'All she needs to do is get an abortion and that's the end of it. I told her to go get it done right away.'

Tomoko's atheistic logic was commonplace, but Yukiko thought that to act as she recommended would be to perpetrate another crime.

Yukiko's letter was casually folded on the *kotatsu* table. Yukiko had written:

> You simply don't realize what killing a child means, do you? If he was alive now, he could laugh, play, love, work, cry and be happy. He would live his life for many years like that. But you took that away from him. Where did you find the right to do that?

The person who had snatched away that boy's life was a brutal stranger from the start. But now it was a mother herself who would snatch life from the child in her womb. Yukiko felt giddy and closed her eyes for a moment.

'That man Fujio Uno—I thought that I would write a letter to him to tell everything. Anyway, the police know he came to this house.'

'Do you think he's going to confess because of that?' Tomoko asked with a trace of scorn in her eyes.

There are countless numbers of things people don't experience in the world. Through the cases connected to Fujio, Yukiko realized that there were also sounds in the world that remain with you forever. One of them was the sound that accompanied Fujio's appearance before the cameras of the media as he was being taken to the Office of the Prosecutor. Yukiko told herself that she shouldn't be afraid about Fujio appearing on the screen. She tried to look at the TV now as she had in the past, but it was unnatural to both follow him and avoid him on the TV.

There was nothing out of the ordinary in Fujio's expression when he came on the screen. He looked neither ashamed nor arrogant. His face was not particularly hard. Of course, to maintain such an attitude must have involved an incredible amount of control. What struck Yukiko as remarkable was the sound of the camera shutters that came pouring off the screen. It was a sound new to her world—*basha, basha, basha...*

That unique sound of the motor-driven shutters had become the usual accompaniment to such scenes. But this time the sound of the shutters was surrounding *Fujio*, continuing without interruption; it was like the chilling sound of a fierce downpour, un-moderated even by wind. Fujio passed through this odd curtain of sound without any change of expression to his face. In the newspaper next day, Yukiko read such phrases as *'Uno faced the cameras calmly'*, *'No hint of repentance'*, *'A dauntless smile on his face'...*

Yukiko questioned whether such phrases were appropriate.

—*As far as I could see, Fujio's expression merely expressed that, as far as he was concerned, no one else was present, that he was alone. I suppose the fact that he ignored the gaze of so many people could be interpreted as 'dauntless.' But if he had lowered his eyes, would that have been a sign of contrition? I don't think he was smiling. Perhaps, for an instant at some point, the combative Fujio might have shown a slight sneer. But no one could know for certain whether that reflected any daring on his part...*

Yukiko had simply been writing the letter to him to try and put her thoughts in some kind of order—they were not even rough notes ready for rewriting. And she was not intending to add anything more. She remembered what Tomoko had said and decided to sleep on the matter overnight. But what finally brought her around to secretly completing and mailing the letter was a development the next day that she could not have anticipated.

Yukiko wasn't fond of leaving the house, and she went out only every few days when she ran out of vegetables or fish. It was slightly overcast when she went out to the supermarket. She started filling her basket—tofu, *miso*, leeks, ginger, sardines, bread, lemons...Then suddenly she heard someone calling her name. It was a woman called Hitomi Sakata. She had once been a member of the choir at Yukiko's church, but since her marriage she had ceased attending out of regard for her husband's wishes. But now he had found another woman and had a child by her, which Hitomi knew about. In her distress, she had even considered suicide.

'How have you been?' Yukiko said to her.

'I've been fine, thanks,' Hitomi said, 'but all that other business still isn't resolved. He's not seeing her as frequently as before, but I feel bad, now, about the child, and I sometimes tell my husband to go and visit them. I've come that far. He seems a little unwilling, but he goes with a relieved look on his face.'

'Well, I think you're marvelous, doing that,' Yukiko said sincerely. 'I suppose that's what is meant by real love.'

'No, not at all. I don't love my husband the way I used to.'

'But still, you've struggled with yourself, and you're thinking of the child. It may be bitter, but at church that sort of rational love is taught as real love.'

'Yukiko,' Hitomi said, 'do you have time to talk? How about having a cup of coffee at that place across the street?'

Yukiko had time and agreed. Together they went in and choose the seats furthest from the entrance and the counter.

Hitomi began her story. 'I haven't seen you for a while and so I wasn't really intending to tell you, but since I've run into you...When I found out about the other woman and was thinking about committing suicide, I didn't want to talk to the priest about it. But since I did talk to you, I think I ought to tell you the rest.'

'Of course,' Yukiko said. 'I'm glad we met.'

'Well, that day, when I was thinking of killing myself, a man I didn't know gave me a ride in his car, and we went toward Yokohama, and...well...because of that, I gave up the idea of killing myself. I told you about that, remember?'

'Yes, and I thought it was fascinating, that it ended all right. I'm an easygoing kind of person, so I love a story about changes coming about by accident. I'm so glad that things worked out, no matter what, even through just a chance encounter.'

'Well, that man—I didn't know his name or where he lived—I owe my life to him. But now I know who he is.'

Yukiko was silent.

'I thought there couldn't possibly be any reason for me to discover who he was, but now I've realized that *he's* the one—that person...' Hitomi bowed her head. 'The man who killed that boy, Ken Okada...Fujio...'

Moments before, Yukiko had begun to anticipate his name. When it was confirmed, she felt slightly faint.

'The night I found out about the man who treated me so well that day,' Hitomi went on, 'I couldn't sleep at all.'

'Were you afraid?' Yukiko asked. She controlled herself and was able to listen quietly.

'No, not that. I didn't think he was going to kill me, not then, no. I know a different face of that man. I wanted to tell somebody about it, but I lacked the courage. And now, I'm so terribly sad about it all.'

'Everybody lacks courage. But I think it's sadder that there are so few people who regret lacking courage these days. Hitomi, I'm relieved to hear your story, and I don't care whether the person who saved your life is a devil or a saint.'

'But I wonder,' Hitomi sighed. 'Is that a good way to think?'

'As far as you're concerned, it's the same thing,' Yukiko replied. 'After all, there are a lot of wonderful people who *couldn't* help you.'

'It's just so odd. I now think that if I had died then, I would have committed suicide for something very trivial.'

'Listen. Since you've told me this, there's something I ought to say too. I knew that man, too. We belong to such a small community, don't we? But I didn't know him as a murderer—just as an ordinary person.'

'Is that true? Well, would you—if you ever get the chance—just say thanks to him for me? Just thanks. It's sad, somehow, that there's nothing I can do for him—with the trial, I mean. I can't have my name involved because of my husband. I'm afraid. I'm a coward, aren't I?'

'I don't think I'll be meeting him, either,' Yukiko said. 'But there is nothing for us to do anyway. His mind is twisted. If he knew who you were, he's one of those people who would think how he could use you.'

'I'm not sure about that. I'm just confused when I think of him. I knew the part of him that was not a killer, but everyone now says he's a murderer.'

'Are you feeling bitter?' Yukiko asked.

'Maybe I am. But I'm a little happy, too—as if my heart is dancing...'

'He's just not honest,' Yukiko said. 'I think his emotions are strange, and that makes him dangerous, you know. But he's not some inhuman devil.'

'Yes, I know. That one day—he made me happy. I can't understand him killing a child. A child is certainly more attractive and unquestioning than I am.'

That evening, Yukiko continued the letter to Fujio; only now she was more clear about what she wished to say.

I intended to post this letter yesterday. However, today, there is one more thing that I must add.

You once met a woman near my house, I believe. If you don't recall, I think that what I have to say will bring it to mind. The woman was walking toward the ocean, and when you saw her, you thought that she might be intending to commit suicide. You were quite right. When you spoke to her, she was just on the verge of heading into the water to die, and you stopped her. She says that she was saved that day because of your concern. I think that she enjoyed being with you. You may not have felt the same, but it was something important.

I've lived for more than thirty years and I've never had the merit of saving anyone who wanted to die. And I would hesitate to say that I ever made anyone happy even for a short while. So I want to thank you for what you did.

The woman I refer to is well. The reason for her losing her will to live is not completely resolved, but I don't think that the pain that was tormenting her mind will again lead her to seek death.

I think you are basically a perceptive person. To me it's strange that you didn't use that talent in a meaningful way. I think that you still have that strength. Please be aware of that, and from now on think of a way to use it.

Regarding the woman whose home was so totally shattered by you, and the one whose life was turned back from the edge of death—even if the police ask me, I do not intend to reveal their names.

I don't know whether this letter will reach you or not. After all, the police have their rules. But I want to send it to you, anyway, so I will send it to the Chief of Police at the Miura Police Station asking him to hand it over to you.

I've heard that it's possible to send things to prisoners. If I can do something for you, I shall. You have a family and a fine mother and so I think there's no need for me. However, if there is something that, because of the circumstances, your family can't do for you, I'll do what I can. You can contact me through your lawyer if you wish.

If you were a relative of mine, I would say this—Please use whatever time you have to improve yourself, however and wherever. I pray that you won't lose your own self.

Yukiko Hata

Yukiko didn't want to delay any longer. The night had already worn on by the time she finished copying the name and address of the Miura Police Station from the city directory and sealed the envelope.

Chapter 20

THE SPIDER'S WEB

YUKIKO Hata's letter was destined to reach Fujio Uno, but not until circumstances had changed once again.

The police investigators had already searched the Uno house. In a cardboard box in Fujio's mother's closet, they discovered something highly revealing—a student's school bag. And since there were no children in the Uno household, the police became curious.

Of course, Fujio's mother said that the school bag belonged to a friend of Fujio's who was going through a divorce and who had asked Fujio to take care of it until all the fuss was over with. Naturally, Fujio was not responsible for what might be in the bag. If the police would ask the friend, she went on, everything would be cleared up. But, for the police, the school bag was a treasury of evidence.

Inside the bag there were textbooks and notebooks bearing the name 'Tomoko Shimada' and her initials. The Shimada family confirmed that these things belonged to their daughter, and on the bag itself the police discovered many of the girl's fingerprints. They also found several strands of women's hair inside Fujio's car; along with the hairs from persons unknown, there was one from Tomoko Shimada.

Fujio had said that he sometimes took his sister's children for a pleasure ride in his car, but according to his elder sister, Yasuko, it had been years since they had gone out with her brother. That being the case, the police seized as powerful evidence the matter of which women the hairs they had found in his car belonged to.

The task of investigating the school bag fell to Inspector Masamichi Nomura. He looked like a trading company employee and he worked with Sergeant Higaki, head of the patrol unit. Nomura had a soft manner about him, but he was clearly very able and Fujio judged he must stay on the alert with him.

'A guy I used to meet at the game center asked me to take care of his bag for him,' Fujio answered to Nomura's question. 'It belongs to him. I never looked inside. You have to be keep faith with someone about things that he leaves with you.'

'What's his name?' Nomura asked.

'His name? I don't know anything like that. He's in his late 20s, thin, glasses. About 170 centimeters, I suppose.'

'You don't know his name and yet you kept his things for him?'

When Fujio heard about the two officers finding Tomoko Shimada's bag at his house, he responded casually, as though their questions to him were somehow peculiar.

'That's right. But he was no fool. He gave me some money and said that when he needed the bag he'd give me a call, and that I should just forget about it until then.'

'How much did you get?'

'I think it was about 30,000 yen.'

'So you took care of the bag without knowing what was inside, and you didn't think that might be dangerous?'

'What's so dangerous about it? Isn't that something the other guy should think about? We can't clear other people's possessions. It's not for someone else to say whether there's anything dangerous about someone's marriage to a woman, right? We can't interfere.'

'There's a letter here for you.'

'Oh, yeah?'

'I'll give it to you if you want to read it,' Nomura said, looking over his glasses at Fujio. 'But if you don't want it, I won't insist.'

'Depends on who it's from. If it's about returning money I borrowed, then maybe you can keep it and not show it to me! I don't need to see it, right?' Fujio said cheerfully.

'You borrowed some money?'

'Not that I remember. Haven't you? It seems to me that a person forgets about money he's borrowed as best he can. I'm a man full of cares, you know.'

'It's from Yukiko Hata.'

'Oh? That's a surprise. I never thought she'd send me a letter.'

'Why's that?'

'I think, for her age, she's a fool. She's too straight. I'm an oddball and I have been since the moment I was born—like a dwarf pine tree. I'd get tired of dealing with her.'

'OK. Then I'll get rid of it.'

'You police just do what you like with people's things, don't you?'

'No, that's not it at all. If you say you don't want it, there's nothing to do but throw it away.'

'Let's see it,' Fujio said. 'It'll be tough for you later if you don't deliver a letter sent to me. It's your responsibility, right? So I'll read it.'

Fujio ran his eyes over the letter. Nomura, bored, tapped the table with the end of his ballpoint pen. Higaki stood against the wall, his arms folded.

This was the first time Fujio had seen anything written by Yukiko. Her sewing was precise and he supposed her handwriting would be the same. In fact, he thought it was rather childish. For a few minutes, however, it was as though Fujio could hear the sound of Yukiko's voice. Of course he wouldn't be planting the heavenly blue flower seeds this year. He had promised, but now, with her letter in his hand, he realized, with a dizzying sense of loss, that he would never again see the blue of those flowers.

As his eyes scanned her letter and the sense of her being failed to seep into his mind, he grew irritated. Day after day in jail, he'd heard the same kind of thing. It was like some slimy oil running into his brain and coagulating there. He felt as though he had been robbed of the ability to take in anything delicate.

To begin with, having to read Yukiko's first letter before the gaze of other people was humiliating. Fujio kept up his pose of bitter toughness, but then real anger and contempt began to invade his mind.

—No one could say that I've never felt despair in my life. There've been many times, I'm sure, when I've been treated scornfully, when I've been humiliated. It's like being vomited on by a drunk, being showered with humiliation. Half my life, I've held a monopoly on that kind of treatment. How could anyone say such foolish things to me? I expect nothing from life. I have no faith in humanity. And I wonder who is the more realistic—that goody-two-shoes Yukiko or me?

But Yukiko's letter brought back the memory of the day that he'd forced his way into the young mother's apartment in Yokosuka, a day in the full tide of spring. The cherry blossoms had been about to fall and the fragrance of flowers was everywhere.

—I wanted to make love. Isn't wanting to make love believing in the other person? I was a bit forceful, but force is part of the man's role. Yukiko said I should be suffering. That's a great recommendation! I've been suffering. It makes me feel sick. Ah, yes! I did meet another woman. She was walking toward the sea and I made her change her direction. I took her to a hotel in Yokohama. Thin, small frame. She wasn't very hot about doing it. But I was in a good mood then and I thought she shouldn't do anything as crude as committing suicide. Right. I was looking at the sea that day. Someone raised by the ocean, whether he can directly see the water or not, can always feel the ocean. The ocean is close to this police station, but from this closed room I can't smell the ocean or see sunlight. The ocean is becoming a distant memory. I wonder how far it is to the ocean on the other side of that wall?

In his imagination, Fujio was walking totally free on the hill road, bathed in light.

'All right,' Nomura broke in. 'How about the letter?'

'I've read it,' Fujio said, plunking down the letter on the table.

'And that's all?'

'Dripping with her sermonizing—that Christian stuff is crap.'

'Would you tell us a little about the woman she mentioned?'

'Which woman?'

'Both of them were true stories, then?'

'Don't joke,' Fujio said, throwing himself back on the chair. 'She's misunderstood. Of course, it was just a chance meeting. But I didn't rape her. It was sex by consent—you know, consensual sex.'

'Well, how did you make the connection with her?'

'No problem with that. She was a beauty, and so I followed her. She kept looking back at me and then, at the entrance to her apartment, she said, "Please come in." So I was interested and went in with her. Afterwards, it was just like asking the baby to turn the other way.'

'How about the other one? I heard that you rescued her.'

'It wasn't quite like that,' Fujio said modestly. 'But I perceived that there was something wrong with her, so I said, "How about going to Yokohama, for a change of air?" And so we played around together for a night.'

'What was her name?'

'Hitomi, I think. I don't know her family name. You know, it's bad manners to ask a girl's name like that on a one-night stand. You don't need her name or life history.'

'You're a literary person, aren't you?'

'Sure. I'm a poet—you know that.'

'But that first woman—that wasn't consensual. You forced your way in; you wrecked her life.'

'Inspector, look. You're no simpleton, so don't ask me to add such a naive explanation. She might've said that because she couldn't avoid being discovered by her husband. It's an old trick for that kind of woman. She even made tea for me. "Take it easy," she said to keep me there. But I'm not used to adultery. When I thought about her husband coming home with a cold or something, I got jittery and wanted out of there. But she was just as calm as could be, nothing to it. I mean, she'd been around.'

'How about telling us where she lives, then?'

'Inspector! Is that any kind of a question to ask me? Talking like that, and in jail, too! If the news media heard of this, you'd have a problem.'

Inspector Nomura fell silent. His expression was closed and extremely displeased. Sergeant Higaki took over the questioning.

'No problem at all. We're just trying to get to the bottom of your story, nothing more. If you aren't lying, your woman probably wouldn't mind if you give us her name and address.'

'Like I told you, officer, I didn't hear it like that. A woman like that—I could drop in during a coffee break and have some fun, that's what it felt like. Even if I may look like this, I'm a poet and I'm sensitive to language, so don't try to deceive me!'

Fujio looked with some pleasure on the unhappy faces of the two interrogating officers. When he was succeeding in a fight with someone, even his voice seemed to grow more refreshed.

'I understand how it is,' Fujio went on. 'Someone like that is a big liar. If you went to her, she'd start crying and complaining that I forced her to do it. She's really good at a performance like that. So you'd believe her right off. It would be dangerous for me to tell you where she lives.'

'Then how about the woman whose life you saved. Is that a lie?' Higaki asked.

'Come on, Sergeant,' Fujio replied in a good mood. 'You've got it in for me, haven't you?'

'You think so?'

'Sure I do.'

'Then have it your way.'

'And you won't change that?'

'Even if *I* try to change, for a poet that's not likely, is it?'

'Uh, you're right.'

'That's fine. Then you'd better stick to being a poet.'

Fujio's spirits sank a bit when he heard that.

'Wouldn't it be better if you told us the name of the woman whose life you saved?' Nomura asked. 'She's happy about it.'

Turning to look at him, Fujio said, 'Inspector, you probably think that I'm a dunce because I didn't graduate from a university? But I'm not. People have secrets. If I sent the police to her, she'd panic. I have to keep my mouth shut, that's all.'

'Then tell us about the other women.'

'Which other women? I've known a lot of them. I can't remember each and every one.'

'We just want to hear about the ones who were with you that you killed.'

'Killed?' Fujio laughed. 'Yeah, thanks a lot. I may have been a lady-killer and known a lot of women, but this is the first time I've been called a lady-murderer!'

Suddenly, Fujio felt as though a blaze of sparks had struck his cheek. Inspector Nomura had slapped his face with his open hand. He staggered, but remained seated in the chair. Trying to take in what had happened, he put his hand to his cheek and tried to pull himself together.

'Hey, this is a surprise!' Fujio said. 'The police still using the third degree?'

'Then stop fooling around.' Nomura said. 'The police are human, just like you. They don't train our feelings out of us, you know.'

Fujio was trying to be casual, but inside he was undergoing a change. This was the first time he remembered ever having been hit.

'Mr. Uno, listen to me. Stop your transparent lies. These days you can't get off with lying. The Identification Section checked out every dust speck in your car. We've searched your house. We retrieved a lot of material from that. The evidence speaks loud and clear.'

For some reason, Sergeant Higaki referred politely to Fujio, whereas Nomura simply called him 'Uno.' It was a small difference, but Fujio felt it as a friendly opening on Higaki's part. But no matter how good Fujio felt about him, he reacted to Higaki's next words in an unexpectedly harsh tone.

'It will be better for you to come clean about killing Tomoko Shimada. We're at the stage of getting down to details.'

'Don't joke, please, Mr. Higaki,' Fujio said. 'I didn't kill that girl.'

'We want you to tell us how she came to fall off a cliff, naked. You threw her clothes in a trash bin in Miura Kaigan, and you gave her school bag to your mother to keep.'

'I don't know who pushed her off the cliff. OK, I admit I stripped her naked. I stripped her out of revenge.'

'Revenge? This is the first time you've mentioned that.'

'I'm a nosy type of man. Shimada Foods Company sold jars of jam that you couldn't get the top off easily. I wanted to give the president something to think about after making that old lady nearly die.'

'A story that inflamed your sense of justice? But if you don't give us a little more detail, we won't get what you mean.'

'OK, I'll tell you the whole story, all the details,' Fujio said.

At that point, Fujio began to empty his heart out—not to Nomura, who he kept to one side, never meeting his eyes, but to Higaki, his eyes fixed on him alone.

As Fujio talked about the Shimada girl, he naturally touched on the circumstances of the death of the old lady Iwamura who lived next door to Yukiko. He developed his story even to the crazy incident connected with the doctor named Nagata of the Miura Hospital who had become the old lady's primary physician. And then the young lad named Ken appeared in the story for the first time.

'What did you think you were going to do to Dr. Nagata?' Higaki asked.

'I don't know. I hadn't decided. I'd only gotten a look at him.'

'Extort money from him, maybe?'

'I wasn't thinking about money. To harass him, I might have got at his wife—something like that.'

'And did you?'

Just recalling the sitting room of the Nagata house and the stare of all those dolls lined up on the shelves sent a chill down Fujio's spine.

'You ought to take a look at that house,' Fujio said. 'If Nagata's weird old lady stripped herself naked, you'd feel sick and come running out of there. Don't they have a psycho ward at Miura Hospital?'

Fujio's whole body positively shone when he was lying. But when he was silent, the chair in the interrogation room caused him continuous and heavy pain. In spite of that, it was a fact that when he told the truth, the pain became slightly less.

'I took another look at Nagata,' Fujio said to Higaki.

'What do you mean?'

'There are a lot of them. Unethical doctors who come right out and require bribes. I thought he was one of those. But I took another look.'

'Say what you mean.'

'Taking care of a wife like that. He does the shopping himself and brings it home and feeds her. She probably doesn't clean or wash or cook or do anything. How many husbands would put up with that, I wonder? But it's not fair if you don't take care of your own wife.'

'Now, Tomoko Shimada. How did she die if you didn't throw her over the cliff?'

'How should I know? I let her out on the road naked so that she could look for help. Maybe she stumbled toward the cliff?'

'Why did you take the girl there?'

'Because I knew the place.'

'How often did you go there?'

'What?'

'I'm asking how many times you did that kind of thing out there?'

'I've known that place well since I was a kid in school. I've no idea how many times I went there.'

'But you go to department stores a lot, right?'

'Department stores? Sure. I'm unemployed and I have time. I suppose I go more than the usual guy. I like to walk around and look at the goods. The new things are interesting, you know.'

'And not just the things on sale. You seem to have an interest in department store women.'

'Sure, don't you?' Fujio shot back. 'Sometimes there are some real beauties in department stores.'

'Would you tell us about the time you took a woman from a department store for a drive in your car? We know that you did that. Did she comb her hair in the car?'

'How should I know? I was driving. I didn't look at her face.'

'Do you remember that woman's name?'

'Just lay off it, OK?,' Fujio said, suddenly in bad humor. Higaki ignored him.

'Oh, so you remember her name?'

'Yeah, I heard it, but it's not a name I want to recall.'

'It was Reiko Suga,' Higaki said. 'You remember that now?'

'She...'

'What was your relationship with her?' Higaki pursued the point.

'No relationship at all. She left an impression on me because she wasn't anything but a dumb, uneducated department store clerk. I mean, she came on with, "How about going to a hotel?" That's pretty forward. She was really unpleasant the whole time.'

'So, after the hotel, what did you do?'

'You already know I didn't kill her. I read in the newspaper that she was hit by a teacher in his car and died. I'm not responsible for her actions after I let her out of the car.'

'How did you let her out of the car?'

'It was nothing special at all. I didn't want to stay at the hotel, so we left. Up to then, things hadn't gone too well. We even argued in the car. The only thing she thought about was money. I began to feel bad about it and so I stopped along the road and told her if she felt like that to get out.'

'Where did you let her out?'

'Actually, when I think about it, it must have been close to where she got hit. I don't know the place. It was raining and dark. I was angry and I wasn't thinking much about where I was. I just stopped the car and told her to get out.'

'Did she get out by herself?'

'Of course,' Fujio laughed. 'Do you think I'd carry out a woman I didn't like? Come off it!'

'The woman had a cracked breast bone and a broken rib. Did she twist herself and get out of the car without saying it hurt?'

'I don't know about any stuff like that. If she was hit by a car, maybe her rib was broken then, right?'

'As a matter of fact, no. I told you: the corpse says a lot.'

'She was in a rage when she got out. I don't know what happened to her after that.'

'Had she been drinking?' Nomura asked.

'While I was in the bath, she might have taken something for herself from the refrigerator. I don't drink, and I don't remember what she did. When I read about it in the newspapers, I had an impression that she'd been drinking and was sleeping in the road when she was hit. To tell you the truth, I don't feel all that sorry. A woman like that isn't much interested in anything, and she isn't much loss to the department store. She was part of the movement opposing a facility for disabled people in a spot near her apartment. A really cold person. You ought to feel sorry for the teacher who hit her. It's better for the world and everybody if a woman like that is no longer alive.'

In a fierce tone, Nomura said, 'Reiko Suga hadn't been drinking.'

'Oh? Is that right?' Fujio said. 'I thought she was the kind that drank like a fish. Hey, I don't really want to think about that woman.'

'We know perfectly well what you thought about her. But why did you kill the child? There wasn't anything to hate about a child,' Nomura said.

Suddenly, Fujio turned to face Inspector Nomura.

'Oh, yeah? Well, I'm not one of those love-everybody guys like you,' he said indignantly. 'Some kids give me chills.'

'What did the boy Ken do that you had to kill him—a studious, motivated child like that?'

'That's the problem. What do you think that kid said to me? "If you kill a child like me, it will be a loss to the nation and to society." When he said that, I knew that if I let him live he'd be a cancer on society.'

'Your thinking is shallow,' Officer Higaki said. 'It's not so important whether a person turns out good or bad. But, of course, it's better to be good.'

'You think so? Well, someone like Tojo sure brought a lot of grief to Japan during World War II.'

'Tojo alone didn't change Japan's fate. There were thousands like General Tojo in Japan then. I think it's a mistake to pin the responsibility on him alone.'

'Well, then it's not so important what kind of guy I am,' Fujio murmured, half in sarcasm and half expressing his real feelings. 'The court probably won't see it that way, but that's what I think, as an individual.'

'Really?'

'An individual is pretty small. I've never thought of it until now, Mr. Higaki. I've always thought that the individual's life and fate were pretty important. I've heard that they say the individual is heavier than the earth.'

'Ken-chan's father is a public prosecutor,' Higaki said.

At that moment, Fujio felt a shock as though a hot iron rod had pierced the length of his body.

'Oh, is that so? So he'll make sure I get the death penalty, won't he!'

'It has nothing to do with that,' Higaki said.

'What has the world ever done for me? They've never treated me fairly!' Fujio shouted emotionally. 'Thanks a lot! Just at a time like this, the world takes it all seriously and punishes me.'

'Mr. Uno! Cut it out!' Higaki said.

Suddenly, there was a current of feeling in Higaki's voice that Fujio had not known before.

'You have no right talking like that,' said Higaki. 'I was a foundling. Your parents loved you and raised you. But my parents, both of them, rejected me. It wouldn't have meant a thing to my real parents if I'd died. Don't you think *I've* been treated unfairly? But I didn't go wrong. I don't think like you do. Until we met and I asked the reason, I thought I shouldn't judge them. There was surely some reason why they had to give me up. That's what my foster father, who had a bicycle shop, told me when I was young and he adopted me.'

'Don't tell me lies like you were a foundling,' Fujio said, as though he could no longer bear to listen to Officer Higaki.

'Yeah, it's a lie,' Higaki admitted, and suddenly his usual smile returned to his face.

'What? You mean the police can say something like that?'

'It's not a lie,' Inspector Nomura said, a tone of disgust in his voice. 'Do you think that Sergeant Higaki would lie about something like that?'

Fujio was exhausted and said nothing.

'I wonder where you learned that trick of hitting them in the pit of the stomach and then choking them?'

Fujio remained silent.

—*Today, I won't open my mouth even if it kills me!*

'Do you know a woman named Kayo Aoki?'

'Kayo Aoki?' Fujio was simply repeating the name like a parrot, for an instant not recalling her. 'Is she a porno star?'

'No, a student in a girls' senior high school.'

'I don't know any girl like that.'

Fujio hid his feelings and tried to remember her.

—*Yes. The girl in the train who sat with her legs thrust out into the aisle. I stumbled over her feet, and instead of getting some apology money to cover medical expenses, I said that I'd sleep with her and she agreed if I didn't demand any money later...*

'You know her alright! The girl rode in your car. The Identification Section takes in a lot of information. Her hair was recovered from your car.'

Fujio still said nothing.

—*Well, if you know that, isn't that enough? There's nothing I have to say...*

The difficult thing was that when he was silent, there was no way to mitigate the pain of sitting in that chair. No matter how he changed positions or sat another way, even the space of a minute seemed terribly long.

—*Some people might think if that's how it is, I'd as soon die. And if I die, well, at least my ass will stop hurting...*

Fujio tried thinking of something pleasant in order to ignore the questions from the policemen. He could think of nothing then except meeting with Yukiko. In his imagination, he was once again looking at the blossoms of the

Heavenly Blue flowers as he approached her front door. The door was open and from the back of the house came Yukiko's relaxed voice, but she didn't come out for a while. When her face appeared at last in his mind's eye, Fujio suppressed his pleasure and, putting on a severe expression, complained to her.

—*It's dangerous not to lock the door.*

—*Do you think so? But no one comes here,* Yukiko replied.

—*I've come, haven't I? Be careful. There are a lot of bad guys in this world.*

Fujio thought it was an odd kind of conversation, but in his imagination he was happy and laughed. At that moment, he didn't want to think about whether such a day would ever come again or not. If it did, he thought, it would be in the very distant future.

Fujio felt the strength utterly drain from his body. It didn't occur to him that Yukiko wouldn't want to meet someone who had lived the life of a murderer. That was surely his greatest blunder.

Perhaps sometime in the future, circumstances would allow him again to visit the house where the morning glories bloomed—but that was a big 'if,' and then Yukiko herself might be dead by then. The thought was unbearable. If Yukiko was not in that same house, Fujio would be likely to lament loudly in front of the house.

—*Isn't there some way I could meet Yukiko? Or if I can't meet her, couldn't I just once see her house? I can well understood the feeling of the prisoner who thinks of escape. Even if it's impossible, he still starts thinking of ways he might free himself...*

About his own case, he maintained his silence.

That night, the interrogation finally ended just before 10 p.m. Fujio tried to stand up from his chair, but the pain in his stiff muscles was such that he couldn't. Yukiko's letter was there in front of him. He tried to pick it up and take it with him so that he could read it once more.

Higaki stopped him short, saying, 'We'll keep that for you.'

That made Fujio mad.

'It's *my* letter!'

'So we'll just keep it for you. We put your documents in custody,' Higaki said in a soothing voice.

'Custody?'

'To keep them for you. A file on you.'

To control his anger, Fujio sat down again. He paused for a moment in the chair.

'That reminds me,' he said. 'I haven't settled on a lawyer yet.'

'What about the lawyer who came the other day? Didn't he suit you?'

'He's a spy sent by my brother-in-law. He'd have him get me the maximum sentence,' Fujio said, going back to a bantering tone. 'In the letter, Yukiko Hata wrote that she could send food and other things for me if I needed them, so would you ask her to find a lawyer for me?'

'Does she have a lawyer among her friends?'

'I don't know about that, but I'm sure she'll find one for me. I can depend on her.'

There were five holding cells like Fujio's in the Miura Police Station. Each cell was about 12 square meters and had cork flooring, the new police department standard. So that the outside world would not be able to say that the prisoners were made to live on wooden boards, the police noted that it was the same safety cork as used in kindergartens. The cell guard pointed out that this was expensive material, as though Fujio should be grateful. But Fujio thought that was a lie. From another cell came the muttered comment that cork came in various grades.

Fujio was in a cell alone. The cells were arranged in an L-shape with the guard's desk situated where he could see every cell. The rules required prisoners to remain silent in their cells, and the guard was always present, leaving only occasionally for a few moments. Brief as such periods were, Fujio learned a lot in those intervals.

One of the prisoners there called the guard 'The Person In Charge.' He seemed to be quite familiar with the jail. In addition to him, there was the strange fellow who called the guard 'Professor,' regardless of what anyone said to him. Fujio had only had a brief look at his face, but he seemed to be about forty years old, with a bald patch on the top of his head. Once, when the guard was out of the room, Fujio heard a voice from the cell next to his.

'Hey! Your butt hurts, right?'

At first Fujio thought the words were meant for someone else.

'You, next door,' the voice continued. 'You were groaning during the night.'

'Sorry to disturb you. They kept me sitting for a long time.'

'Make a fuss—say it's killing you. They'll take you to the doctor. While I've been here in the country villa, I've had all my bad teeth fixed! It's a free service.'

The messages all had to do with life inside the jail. From one anonymous prisoner, Fujio learned the phrase 'take care of', meaning that if you got on the Inspector's good side by confessing directly, he would take care of you by providing some of the things you wanted. One prisoner said he was served coffee and all the cigarettes he wanted after confessing. He said he'd even had some cakes. Fujio felt a tingle like some long forgotten sweet on his tongue.

'And then they let me come home at five o'clock', the prisoner added.

'Home' would be his cell, and 'coming home' at five and lying down would surely be a pleasure.

'Look, old timer,' Fujio said. 'When you go to the dentist, do they use handcuffs and a waist cord?'

He knew that he would be handcuffed on a trip to the doctor, but he hoped that perhaps they might not use a waist cord as well. The other prisoner chuckled.

'What do you expect? You're not paying for the treatment, so of course there's strings attached—attached to *you*!'

It seemed to be intended as a joke. However, Fujio gave up the idea of going to the doctor when he heard that. It fired up his anger just thinking about being put in front of the media cameras and the reporters. Fujio knew that this guy who was used to jail took pleasure in a walk even though he was handcuffed and well tied by the waist. In fact, Fujio was like an animal in a cage, but he preferred to think it was the guards who were on display. Unless he thought that way, he would feel he had been destroyed.

The guard named Tanaka liked to talk, but when he was on duty at night, he tended to doze off. He would sit at the desk, dozing with his arms outstretched. Anyone who glanced at his back from the doorway would think he was looking at some documents. And whenever he seemed to be about to fall from his chair, he would straighten himself up with perfect timing. When awake, he was a non-stop talker.

'These days it's distressing how the character of the clerks at the supermarket where my wife goes shopping has declined. In the past, we could rely on them, but one day when she thought something was amiss and looked carefully, the sales slip was all wrong. Since that, unless she checks what she bought against the receipt, there's always some mistakes, so she's always on the lookout for something wrong...'

Time after time, Tanaka went on like this.

'This New Year, for example, I was returning with my family from a visit to Niigata and we stopped off to see the wife's family in Komoro. But when we transferred at Takasaki, instead of taking the Shinkansen tickets we had used that far on the Shinkansen, they took the tickets we had for the Shin'etsu Line. It was lucky we noticed that on the spot, because if we hadn't, we wouldn't have had time to go back to the Shinkansen gate when we realized that we had no tickets for the Shin'etsu Line...'

This story about how the railway had slackened under private management seemed to be a major incident in his life recently, and ended up with a 'Things like this happen and so you need to be careful' kind of admonition. Fujio thought it peculiar that people in jail should need to be careful when they rode on trains.

However, Tanaka took a special interest in Fujio.

'Hey, Mr. Uno! If you were outside now, you'd be the most famous man in Japan! Everybody knows you. I commute on the Keihin Kyuko Line, and your face was on the advertising posters of at least three weekly magazines hung up in the train this morning!'

Tanaka went on without noticing that Fujio would have liked to kill him for saying that.

'They said that a teacher named Ota was in charge of you at junior high. In his interview with a weekly, he said he thought you'd turn out better. But he said you had no patience, although you had some pretty bright ideas. Don't you think he sounds like a good teacher?'

'Ota wasn't in charge of me,' Fujio said. 'He just pretended to know...'

'That woman you're sweet on, what's her name?'

Fujio made no reply.

'She lives around here, doesn't she? Sergeant Higaki, the one from here, he's gone over there a lot. He's a nice kind of guy.'

Whatever Tanaka's real motives may have been, Fujio wanted to kill him. Still, it was true that Higaki had been to see Yukiko several times. Tanaka didn't have the character for tricking a prisoner into giving any information with all his chatter.

Officer Higaki's visits to Yukiko were to gather information she might have about Fujio, since he thought she knew him best. What Higaki found was that Fujio didn't have any close friends at all. He didn't have any friends among his school alumni and had no connections though leisure activities in the local area. Nor did he drink, so he didn't frequent any bars or pubs. He also had no lasting romantic associations. But, from long years of experience, Higaki felt that there was something deep in Fujio Uno's background related to his criminal acts.

Higaki also felt that he ought to avoid the constant importuning of the mass media. After the incident that led to this case, every media company had opened a field office near the Miura Police Station. On top of that, reporters from the weekly news magazines and other publications were coming around constantly. Every reporter knew the license number on Higaki's little Japanese car, called a 'Taro.'

It was impossible for him to go to Yukiko's house by car, and so, one morning before 8 a.m., Higaki, dressed in a jumper, set out for her house on his bicycle. On arrival, he apologized for visiting at such an early hour; he explained that was the only way to avoid being seen.

'I realize this is an inconvenience for you, Miss Hata, but there are still some things that are quite incomprehensible. But the weekly magazines are writing it all up as if they know perfectly about him, and in some ways I feel sorry for him because there are some doubts about the truth of what they write. All that aside, I want to try and understand him, and I can't do better than to depend upon you. And, besides, I have a request from Mr. Uno for you.'

Of course, Higaki did not suppose that his words would be all that well received by Yukiko, and he knew that she was fully aware that he was using police techniques all the time.

'There's no need to apologize,' Yukiko replied. 'I'm an early riser. My sister stayed in Tokyo last night. I was just about to start my work.' Her face suggested that she had, indeed, been up quite a long time. 'Please come in,' she said, sounding slightly distressed. 'I have to start work on a rush job. It's rather a rare case. I do Japanese sewing and one of my regular customers said she wants something finished by the end of the month. She's taking it with her on a new job abroad.'

'Would it be all right if we talk together while you work?' Higaki asked.

'If that's all right with you,' Yukiko replied.

By the look on her face, she seemed relieved. Higaki thought to himself what an honest person she was. He had no way of knowing, but the cushion and the place he was given were exactly the same that Fujio had used right next to where she did her work.

'Since my sister isn't here today, I didn't prepare any morning coffee, but I do have tea.'

In spite of Higaki telling her not to bother, Yukiko soon brought in a cup of tea for him and urged him to sit comfortably.

'About Mr. Uno,' Higaki began, as he made himself comfortable, 'was there anything annoying about him?'

'No,' Yukiko replied, as she took up the sewing in front of her. 'This is the first time I've known anyone who has killed someone, except in an accident. People say it must be a frightening experience. But what disturbs me most was that I didn't understand Mr. Uno's feelings. No matter what it was, good or bad, you feel relieved if you understand. Not getting along, or something you can't forgive, that's something later, after the fact. But not to *understand*, that's so sad. Of course, what I mean is not *really* understanding him, but at least to *think* you understand.'

'So you mean you didn't understand him, either?'

'That's right. I didn't understand him.'

'And yet you associated with him...' Higaki said carefully, so that he would not sound sarcastic.

'He came here, that's all—just like you. I appreciate visitors coming any time. It's not that I'm a lonely old maid, but I regard it an honor when someone thinks of me and comes to visit.'

For a moment, Higaki was overwhelmed by Yukiko's naive words.

'Well, please forgive me for these personal questions,' Higaki said, looking toward the garden. 'Please try to remember whatever he did or told you.'

Yukiko was amused and smiled. 'He came by just as you're doing now. He sat there and had tea and ate some dumplings. And he talked about picking up a cat and letting it ride in the car. Then the cat got out and ran off along the road. And before he saw what was happening, he said, it was hit by a car. At least that's the story he told me.'

Higaki was thoughtful; the matter of a cat in Fujio's life had not come up before.

'He was quite amiable with me,' Yukiko said. 'Possibly because I basically stay here all by myself. He even said that if in future I fell sick, he would take care of me.'

'It seems that he was really fond of you,' Higaki said.

Yukiko smiled softly.

'Well, there was no reason for him to hate me. He didn't have to treat me in a special way because of my age. He has his own way of thinking and I didn't challenge him. And I wasn't a burden to him financially. Even though it's not much, I earn my way, and so there was no need for him to be extravagant.'

Higaki had not encountered many women who spoke the way Yukiko did. While she expressed her own thoughts, she seemed to be looking at herself from the outside.

'I said that I was in no way a burden to him financially, but there was one exception. He once bought a present for me.' Yukiko added this as a correction to her statement that she had never been indebted to Fujio financially.

'And what did he give you?' Higaki asked.

'A little Gosu dish. It was old and struck his fancy, and so he bought it for me. Shall I show it to you?'

'Yes, please do.'

It was a small dish, about 15 centimeters in diameter, with a soft pattern of peonies on it.

'Is it valuable?' Higaki said. He had never in his life laid hands on something like this and was confused.

'Actually, I don't know about it, either. When I showed it to my sister, she said that while it wasn't cheap, neither was it so very expensive, nothing like tens of thousands of yen. Until a little while ago it would have been cheap, she said. But there's a boom in that kind of thing now and prices have gone up wildly. She said that when her magazine did a special issue on them, she was quite surprised.'

'What did he say when he brought this to you?'

'Oh, I've forgotten. Just that he'd seen it when he was walking by somewhere and bought it—something like that.'

'What kind of wrapping paper was it in?'

'I think it was newspaper. I had the feeling that he didn't buy it at a regular shop. It seems to me it's the kind of thing you might buy in a second-hand store.'
'Did Mr. Uno speak to you about any of the people he associated with?'
'There was his former wife. He said that his mother was so upset about the divorce.'
'And he first came to your house...?' Higaki asked.
'We began to talk over the fence about how pretty the morning glories were, and he came to get some seeds.'
'Did he say why he was out here so early in the morning? It doesn't have to be anything particularly about that occasion, but I just wondered why he was on a little used street like this where so few people pass by?'
'Yes. Where and on what business he came round? Well he said something about he used to deliver fertilizer to the agricultural cooperative in the past.'
'In fact, there was nothing like that,' Higaki said.
'Yes, I know. Isn't it odd that at his age he speaks such nonsense? Did he say he was thirty-two? He told me he was thirty-five.'
'May I ask you a question which doesn't have anything to do with my police work?' Higaki said. 'I wonder why you always use polite language when you speak about Fujio Uno?'
Yukiko thought about the question for a moment. 'I suppose, because he has murdered people, it doesn't seem appropriate to speak that way. But a long time ago, my mother taught me that I shouldn't change my speech according to the person I meet. She said there was nothing more despicable than to calculate the professional and social position of people and then speak politely to some and speak down to others. What she taught me seeped into my bones. The only people who are entitled to insult Mr. Uno are the parents of the boy he killed.'
After a moment she added, 'But, Sergeant Higaki, you yourself refer to him as 'Mr. Uno' when you speak of him, don't you? I thought the police didn't use polite language.'
'There's no rule about that sort of thing,' Higaki said. 'It depends on the person. Some of my bosses just use the surname without a 'Mr.', but I think that for me it's natural to use 'Mr.' before a name. So I use it for everyone. Our Chief lets us do as we like in that matter.'
'Yes, there's a difference between strictness and arrogance.'
'Indeed there is,' Higaki said, appreciating her words. 'Did your mother teach you that, too?'
'No, that's just from living to this age.'
'My feeling is that strictness and gentleness have to go together. If you have both of those things in one person, that's pretty good. But there's a tendency to lean one way or the other.'

'Why is it that you are gentle?' Yukiko asked him.

'I didn't know my parents; I was a foundling. My adoptive father took me and educated me. He was a gentle man. I learned gentleness—or rather the strength of gentleness—from him.'

' "The strength of gentleness"—that's clever. What a happiness for you to have discovered something so marvelous in the world.'

Higaki laughed diffidently. 'There is one more thing in connection with the case. If it's distasteful for you, you may refuse, but Mr. Uno said he wanted you to find a lawyer for him.'

'A lawyer?' Yukiko parroted.

'Yes. He refused to accept the lawyer that his brother-in-law sent. Instead, he asked that you select a lawyer for him.'

'That's a surprise. I wonder if he isn't mixed up and thinks that I'm acquainted with some lawyer. I've never had the slightest connection with the courts.'

'Then should I tell him that you refuse? Because the court will assign him a lawyer, of course.'

'Wait just a bit. I'll think about it. I probably won't be able to help him, but it wouldn't be right for me to refuse without thinking about it.'

Yukiko hesitated, weighing possible motives for Fujio saying that he wanted her to find a lawyer for him.

Against the background of rejecting the lawyer sent by his parents and his brother-in-law, there would have been trouble since it was really Fujio's business. According to the weekly magazines, his father had already been taken to a home for the elderly and was not responding to anything anyone said, and Fujio's mother had entered hospital with a bad heart. The Uno greengrocery store had been closed, and Fujio's elder sister and her family had moved to a friend's place in another prefecture in the countryside. It seemed there was no one left to assist Fujio.

Among Tomoko's business connections there would surely be a lawyer or two. On the other hand, Yukiko imagined what Tomoko would say if she consulted her about such a thing:

I told you not to get in any deeper! I don't mind introducing you to a lawyer or anybody else, but do you think that man can pay a lawyer? It looks like his family is through with him, and they're not about to pay anything. If he rejected the lawyer his brother-in-law introduced, then it will end up with the family telling him to do whatever he wants on his own.

Yukiko could not guess how much a lawyer would charge to handle a serious case like this. However, if she went out and found a lawyer, then she would be committed to paying the fee herself.

—You cannot get anything without discarding something. People expect too much good fortune without paying the price. I think I've become like a thread in

the spider's web for Fujio. I am not the Savior Buddha come to assist people. I am only a slender link with him, but he has no other way of crawling through the web than having me at the other end of the thread as his guide...

Yukiko did her work with a heavy heart that day. She decided to give herself three days to think the thing over, and if she met someone who might be able to help her, she would ask whether them if they knew a lawyer. But she had no faith in such a possibility. In fact, when she imagined the surprise and fear on the face of anyone she might ask, she could well imagine what they would say:

'If it was some other matter, that would be all right, but something like that man's case you should avoid. It would be terrible for you to be known as any kind of acquaintance of his, and there's no chance of his winning in court. Besides, the man is a fiend. Why do you have to support a devil like that by finding a lawyer?'

The day passed without incident. Yukiko would like to have consulted with Tomoko, but she hadn't come home. Yukiko diligently devoted herself to her work. More than finding a lawyer or anything else, Yukiko told herself, it was necessary to complete sewing the kimono in time for the woman who was going abroad. Her shoulders grew stiff with the intensity of her work. She thought she should apply some ointment, but Yukiko didn't want to think of herself as an old woman and so she didn't keep anything like that in the house. However, on the second day of the discomfort, Yukiko went to the pharmacy to buy some medicine and also get some exercise at the same time.

The pharmacy she was accustomed to visit was in the narrow alley a few steps from the supermarket. A deaf old woman usually tended the shop. She was difficult to communicate with, and some people said they didn't like to buy things there, but Yukiko felt supportive of the old woman's stubbornness. The shop didn't have any of the medication Yukiko intended to buy for her shoulders, but she bought a substitute she thought would do as well and left.

As she walked through the narrow, twisting alley, a teenage boy on a bicycle came riding through too fast and knocked over a younger, kindergarten-age boy wearing short pants who was playing there. Yukiko, who was just a few meters away, went to help the boy.

'Are you all right? That's good, you didn't cry at all,' she said. But then she noticed there was some blood on the boy's knee, and decided that she shouldn't leave him alone.

'Where is your house?' she asked.

The boy stood stiff and straight, perhaps feeling pain. He responded that it was just nearby.

'Can you walk? Here, take my hand.'

The boy nodded, keeping a stoic look on his face. He seemed to be accustomed to being brave about such things, and still he didn't cry. Yukiko wanted to carry the boy on her back, but she felt she should be cautious. In the recent social atmosphere, she might be mistaken for a kidnapper if she did that. He dragged his leg along like a stick. She felt a degree of trust in the strength with which he held her hand, and when they finally reached a white plastered building, the child opened the door and called out for his mother.

Two things stopped Yukiko from leaving immediately. One was that if she left without explaining the situation, it might look rather suspect. But more than that was the sign nailed to the door of the house saying 'Kazami Legal Services.' After the child had gone into the house, Yukiko stood in thought at the entrance for a few moments. Then she called: 'Hello! Excuse me!'

'Yes!' came a voice, and then a woman of about Yukiko's age appeared. She was thin and wearing glasses. She was wearing a brick-red sweater and under that a white blouse with its collar over the top.

'Please excuse this intrusion, but I wonder if I might have a word with Mr. Kazami the lawyer? My name is Yukiko Hata and I was at the scene when your boy was knocked down by a bicycle and slightly injured. I was a bit worried, so I brought him home.'

'Thank you very much, that was most kind of you. He's all tears about it now.'

'Is this the lawyer's office?' Yukiko asked.

'Yes, that's right,' the woman said.

'Please excuse me for bringing this up so suddenly—you'll probably laugh— but I'm looking for a lawyer. Is your husband at home? I'd like to have a word with him if I may.'

'Actually *I'm* the lawyer,' the woman said. 'My name is Nagisa Kazami.' For a moment, a mischievous smile touched her face.

'Oh, *you* are...' Yukiko said, a bit distracted.

'Please come in,' Kazami said. 'I'll just put some antiseptic on the boy's scratch; I'll be with you in a moment. It's nothing to worry about.'

Yukiko was shown into a small reception room just inside and to the right of the entrance. On the other side of the hallway, a plump girl was working, amidst the sound of electronic equipment, in what appeared to be an office.

The reception room held only a small conference table and a sofa. On the wall was an oil painting of a beach, a small boat and a promontory; on the table stood a bowl with pink azaleas. The sound of the child's crying soon stopped and Yukiko heard only a sweet nasal voice:

'Mommy has a visitor just now. It's the lady who was worried about your knee and brought you home. So I mustn't keep her waiting. Don't you think it's wrong to keep someone waiting?'

'I don't think so.'

'Really?' came the mother's cheerful voice.

'Well, I think it's wrong a little.'

'Yes, I think it is. I'll go in now.'

In a moment, the woman appeared. 'Sorry to keep you waiting. He's in his first year at school and is still a little dependent...'

'That's quite all right. I heard you and him just now and I felt a little envious. I'm single and I've never been married.'

'Do you live near here?'

Yukiko thought that the lawyer might need to know in future, so she explained in detail where her house was located.

'Oh, isn't that the house with the lovely morning glories?'

'Yes, that's the one.'

'Of course. I went walking there once with my son. I was so surprised to see such beautiful flowers, I stopped for a while to look at them.'

'Yes, they're a strange variety of morning glories. They attract a lot of people, not just you. One day, a man stopped to look at the flowers and spoke to me. I'd like to consult with you about him if I may.'

'Yes I suppose a lot of people take an interest in those flowers. They are certainly quite lovely.'

'I shouldn't really consult you until I know your specialty.' Yukiko hesitated to mention any details to Mrs. Kazami.

'Well, it may seem odd, but I do all kinds of cases—civil and criminal, divorce, inheritance,' Kazami said. 'In a location like this, I've even handled public order cases about disturbances at the Yokosuka base where the defendants kept perfectly silent. If you wouldn't mind telling me, who does this matter concern?'

'You've probably heard of him. It's Fujio Uno. He's been in the news.' Yukiko spoke with as level a voice as she could manage.

'Oh, yes, his first offence.'

'Eh?'

'He hasn't previously been arrested by the police.'

'I think that's true,' Yukiko said. 'Still, I don't know much about the details. I don't even know why he asked me to do something like this.'

'Doesn't he have a lawyer already?' said Nagisa. A tone of some surprise had crept into her voice.

'His brother-in-law sent someone,' Yukiko told her. 'But they didn't get along, he said, and he turned him down.'

Kazami Nagisa laughed lightly.

'Oh, he's a strange one, all right.'

'If you consider taking this case, there are two things I must tell you. One is that I don't know much at all about the man. It's not that I'm pretending ignorance because he's a criminal. It's just that he visited my house when he chose to and without any announcement. I didn't chase him away, nor did I refuse him to come. I sew Japanese-style clothing and people very seldom come to my house, so I appreciate any visitor. But I was not his woman, so to speak. The second thing concerns me somewhat more. If you take on this rather large matter as a lawyer, I can't foresee whether I shall be able to pay or not. I've put a little money aside, but I don't know whether that will be adequate.'

'And the suspect himself? I suppose his family can't pay?'

'I have no idea about that. I've never visited them, and so far he has told me nothing but lies about his work. However, my feeling is that his family has been very indulgent with him from the start, and since he rejected the lawyer that they sent, he will have to make do on his own.'

'There is no fixed standard of payment,' Kazami Nagisa said. 'I don't think that should be a big concern.' She was then silent for a moment. Yukiko assumed that she was having doubts about the case, and so she continued.

'You must think it strange that I take an interest in Fujio Uno, someone I don't really know. He's famous just now, and for most people he's someone they would not want to be involved with. But some people will say they are friends no matter what, if the person is famous. My younger sister works for a magazine publisher in Tokyo, so she knows the world much better than I do, and she often tells me about that kind of thing. Anyway, before anything else, I would like you to ask Sergeant Higaki of the Miura Police Station about all this and how I came here.'

'Oh, but I know Sergeant Higaki very well,' Nagisa said. 'He used to be based in Yokosuka and I met him in connection with my work. He was transferred here about six months ago, and that pleased me very much.'

'I see. Then perhaps it would have been nicer if he had recommended you when I was at a loss not knowing any lawyers?' Yukiko said.

'Not doing that is like him. Well, I should say it's a kind of police rule. As long as the authorities haven't assigned a lawyer, the police may go with your selection of a lawyer, but they will refrain from suggesting a particular lawyer. That's the usual procedure.'

'I understand what you've said, but I wonder if you could telephone directly to Sergeant Higaki about all this?' Yukiko asked.

'Yes, I should eventually do that anyway. It's not that I have any doubts about you, but, if I take the case, then as soon as possible I should go and meet with Fujio Uno. I'll call Sergeant Higaki about that and some other matters. Actually, he's a good friend of my husband's.'

'Does your husband have some connection with the police?' Yukiko asked, surprised. For a moment, the lawyer's face showed her amusement.

'No, my husband is a potter. It's actually better that they have such different kinds of work. My husband might have heard about Fujio Uno in connection with all the commotion lately, but he wouldn't have any interest beyond that. He hasn't the slightest interest in judging people. He became friends with Sergeant Higaki in connection with a previous case, and since then just the two of them go drinking sometimes. But, from what I hear, they don't talk about anything very practical—just about clay and fire or Zen ideas. The two of them are eccentric that way, somewhat distant.'

'May I tell you another concern of mine, as an outsider?' Yukiko said.

'Please do.'

'As far as I can see, Mr. Uno's case in court will not be easy. It may be obvious, but at first glance he doesn't seem to have much chance of winning. And so the lawyer who takes this case may lose their reputation. Isn't that so? If a lawyer's reputation is made through skill and a not guilty verdict, then I think that you will be taking on a defeat right from the start.'

'Well, yes,' Nagisa said, 'there are certainly such people in my profession. As far as possible, they take cases that are showy and attract media attention; some even say they won't argue cases they can't possibly win. But there are still some pleasant aspects of this work. It's interesting that to a degree your lifestyle is reflected in the way you choose your work.'

'So do you make it a rule to handle cases that you *can't* win?' Yukiko asked.

'No, nothing quite so magnanimous. You see, I'm not like a great doctor in a big hospital; I'm more like a doctor in a country clinic. After all, the truth is that in my surgery I can't refuse to see a patient just because they come in saying, 'Doctor, I have a sty in my eye.' I mean, I'm a doctor, so I can't turn away an old lady who has a cold. Of course, if something is too much for me, I send the person to a specialist, but basically I don't turn down anyone who comes to me. You may wonder why. Well, if the suspect doesn't like his lawyer, he turns him down, just like Fujio Uno did. It doesn't take a lot of high-powered lawyers to calm a crying child, so I take on cases like that and plod along with them. I take on any kind of case that the client thinks I'm capable of handling. The only exception for me is someone I feel is putting on airs. But when I turn down a client like that, someone else will take them on, so there are no repercussions.'

'But if you do that,' Yukiko said, 'there must be a lot of work and few cases at court that bring success? What with criminals lying and not earning much money.'

'Oh, almost 100 percent of people lie,' Nagisa said, her smiling face suddenly looking younger, despite her glasses. 'In fact, I'm quite used to being lied to. And about money: my husband told me when we married that if I was going to be a lawyer, I should do it for mere pleasure, like a hobby. He would be responsible for making a living. So it wasn't a question of money, but whether my involvement with the case was meaningful for both me and the defendant. That was my husband's view.'

'That's very fine, indeed.' Yukiko was impressed and somewhat envious as well. 'I didn't really understand what he meant at the time. He thinks that making ceramics is a kind of pleasurable occupation, so I thought he was only thinking that there should be a balance between us. I'm also a bit selfish, so if I was guaranteed a minimal kind of lifestyle with marriage, I thought I could well take cases like that. But when I thought about it later, it's hard to take cases just as a hobby. It's too simplistic, and it's hard to say whether a case has any meaning for me or my client. I was really confused at first. I thought about every little thing. Would something be a plus for me? I wondered. Even if it was, I wondered whether it was for the client as well. But there wasn't really any way to know that. And so, between the two, I gradually got lazy and found a good way out. I simply let the client choose.'

'We seem to think alike,' Yukiko said. 'I'm a Christian, and in my faith I make decisions on the basis of whether something is the will of God.'

'I'm sure that's a comforting way to think.'

'Yes, I do like comfortable things,' Yukiko admitted.

'And so do I,' Nagisa said. 'They say that people who pass the bar examination are hard workers, but my basic outlook is really just to enjoy myself. Still, from what you've told me, I think I've made a discovery. Because of various circumstances, my husband was raised by his grandmother. She's dead now, but I heard that she was a Christian. My husband wasn't baptized and he hasn't any inclination toward that in the least, but, come to think of it, his devotion to pleasure must be from his grandmother's influence.' Kazami's expression suggested she was thinking this over. 'I've answered your questions. Now I'd like to ask you a question, if I may?'

'Of course, please do,' Yukiko said.

'Just a moment ago, you were concerned above all with the lawyer's fee. Well, frankly, lawyers' fees are more than a box of candy or a new suit. Why are you prepared to pay for someone who lies to you about his work, a person you only know casually, who has just spoken with you in passing? I wonder if your religion has anything to say about that? Is it because you have to respond to anyone who asks, or is it because you felt especially sorry for this man Uno? If that's the case, he may well be grateful to you, but if he's not grateful, then spending money on him is nothing more than taking the money you've put aside over the years and throwing it into a ditch.'

Yukiko hesitated. 'I'm not very worldly, and my sister thinks I lack the common sense of her workaday world. If I tell her I'm spending my money on a lawyer for

Fujio Uno, I think she will really be hard on me. She'll say the money is wasted, and by doing something like that, people will think that I have some kind of special connection with him. My sister's a journalist and she knows very well how awful the mass media can be. I know she would criticize me about doing something so obvious. But, in fact, if I pay your fee, I will be doing that for myself and not for Fujio Uno.'

'Excuse me. I don't wish to pry into your affairs, but why do you say that's for *you*?' Nagisa asked, obviously interested.

'I just met Mr. Uno by chance. You know, with rain or snow you can just wipe it off yourself. That's just life. I think my taste in spending is different from other people's. Rather than spending money on clothes or travel, spending it on Mr. Uno's trial would be much more worthwhile. We don't often have a chance to spend money on someone else's life, or for some effort that will clear up what the world doesn't understand. A thing like this...is something really important, and in this way I'm involved with someone's life, and I haven't been involved before, nor will ever be again in the future, I suppose. So spending money just to know how this will turn out may be paying a high price for a ticket to a great drama...if that's not too rash a way to put it.'

'Yes,' Nagisa said, 'I understand. Still, the main characters on stage are the liar Fujio Uno and an amateur actor like me. The prosecutors and judges are not the stars in the drama as you might think. I wonder if that's all right with you?'

Chapter 21

A House Awaiting Death

A S Yukiko left her house and walked the short distance to the bus stop, two cars, passed by her. They were both flying the flags of the newspapers they belonged to. Although such cars had nothing to do with her, when Yukiko saw them she automatically turned her face away.

Since the Fujio Uno case had begun, her small town had been in a state of commotion, just as though a fire had been lit under it. First there had been the cruel death of the prosecutor's son, followed by the discovery of the nude body of a junior high school girl thrown from a cliff. Then a woman who worked as a department store clerk had been beaten and thrown onto a dangerous roadway where she was later run over by another car. These were all barbarities that shook the local people. But the furious pursuit of the case by the mass media brought about an astonished reaction at first, and then, finally, some humor.

Tenzan, the closest noodle shop to the Miura Police Station prospered greatly because of the newspaper and magazine reporters covering the Miura Police Station. There was even a rumor that the shop would soon be rebuilt.

The same prosperity hit the 24-hour convenience store located just a few shops away. Instead of the usual empty space in front, there was now a fleet of mass communication vehicles parked there. The apartments and rooms at tourist guest houses, situated just one kilometer from the police station, were usually only rented out during the summer to people who came there on the weekend. Now those places were available on a monthly contract basis. And, of course, with all the media vehicles in the vicinity, there were complaints about the roads being too narrow.

Yukiko waited five minutes, boarded the bus, and soon passed in front of the Miura Police Station. Automatically, she turned to look. There were at least half a dozen news media vehicles parked conspicuously near the entrance.

Yukiko wondered what Fujio was doing at that moment. She had gone there to take something to him two days earlier. It was the first time she had completed the forms and gone through the red tape of a visit. Since she didn't know what she could bring, she asked the clerk at a window inside the office. She was informed that jam rolls and comic books were popular. Yukiko brought what was recommended; she was so nervous, she couldn't remember Fujio's tastes or even her own.

For several days, Yukiko had felt extremely tired. When she told Tomoko that she might be paying for Fujio's lawyer, her sister had slapped her face for the first time in her life. What surprised Yukiko was not the fact that she had been slapped, but that Tomoko, who didn't normally lose her cool judgment, was in such a frenzy. Yukiko was speechless when she saw her trembling in rage.

Yukiko took the slapping incident as something of a necessary evil. But Tomoko seemed to feel that it was a weighty matter that impinged on her. Grasping that she couldn't fight against Yukiko to avoid it, she decided to remain in her apartment in Tokyo. Yukiko thought that Tomoko's opinion was entirely appropriate from a common-sense point of view.

As Tomoko said, Yukiko spent her life at home and was hopelessly naive about the world. Tomoko thought that was fair enough, but she was totally opposed to her sister comporting with a suspicious person like Fujio, and because she was not a child, she could only deal one way with Yukiko's decision. After Fujio Uno's crimes became clear—especially since Yukiko was not related to him by birth—the fact that she would spend hundreds of thousands of yen on his legal expenses struck Tomoko as displaying very little sanity. In the first place, if any of this should become public knowledge, then Yukiko would inevitably be regarded as Fujio's woman.

'Why is it necessary for you to spend money on a lawyer for someone who is going to get the death penalty? There would be some sense to it if the charges against him were false and might be dropped, or the death penalty could be avoided. But even so, you shouldn't have to pay at all. Besides, you may be hiding something from me. Were you Uno's lover?'

'No, absolutely not. I thought he was odd right from the start.'

However, Yukiko could not dispute the logic of her sister's argument.

The second reason why Tomoko was angry was that Yukiko neither followed her advice nor argued her point. This was not on purpose; she was still turning it over in her mind. Yukiko realized that she was not being reasonable, that people would think her action quite foolish. She was trying to find a reason why what she was doing was bad.

Tomoko was deeply distressed that her sister didn't think about what she had said and change her course immediately. She remained in Tokyo and didn't return to Miura.

Yukiko got off the bus at the far end of Misaki and walked to the right toward the ocean and the nearby Catholic church. She didn't attend church every week. She liked to pray and was fond of the mass, but she found meeting people she knew there and making conversation painful.

She knew the pastor of the church very well. Father Izumi was a quiet man in his fifties who was fond of fishing. In fact, if there was anything to criticize in him, it was the fact that he went fishing at every opportunity. Some people said his fishing made him unavailable to administer the last sacrament even if a parishioner became seriously ill. The day was fine and clear and Yukiko thought the priest just might be out fishing. She was taking her chances on finding him in. But when she rang the bell of the rectory, the priest appeared at the door, wearing his sweater with its stretched-out elbows.

'I wonder if I might have about 10 minutes of your time?' Yukiko said to him.

'Yes, of course,' he replied.

Yukiko was conducted to the small, dreary, Western-style room beside the entrance. She was welcomed by a small statue of the Virgin with a beatific expression.

'Is your sister well?' Father Izumi asked Yukiko.

'Yes, thank you. She's fine, but she's been angry with me recently and has left the house.'

'Oh? Some argument?'

'Yes.'

Father Izumi had once said that a parish priest in a small town can't do his work unless he himself had suffered hardships. As succinctly as possible, Yukiko told him about Fujio Uno. She didn't like the way most women told a long story about something connected with themselves.

'I think what my sister said is reasonable, but I seem to be the only person in the world that Mr. Uno can call upon. It's not at all that it makes me feel good or conceited—it's a truly pitiful thing for him...'

'Of course' replied the priest. And how you use your money is your own business. But even if you don't pay for a lawyer, the government will provide one for him.' He spoke as though Yukiko was not aware of the fact.

'Yes, but I'm afraid that if it comes to that, they will get someone who treats his case just as a formality.'

'I'm not speaking just for the sake of contradicting you,' the priest said, 'but I wonder why you feel the way you do. Frankly speaking, there is no chance of him being found not guilty. Just think about it. There is also every chance that he will receive the death penalty. In such a situation, the question is why you are willing to spend a considerable amount of money on a lawyer.'

The question was the same one that Nagisa Kazami had put to Yukiko.

'Of course, I don't think that it will help save Mr. Uno's life,' Yukiko said. 'And I think it's especially hard for the mother and father of little Ken Okada, because he was their only child—not that it would be any easier for them if they had another child. The truth is that Mr. Uno completely stole that family's future. And it was not simply a blunder, but deliberate...I think that a person might well atone for that with his own life.'

As she said this, she thought of people at this church in Miura who were involved in the movement to abolish the death penalty.

—*Yes, it would be better if there were neither those to execute nor a system to put the sentence into practice. But I don't like the idea of Fujio getting used to prison life and becoming a prison boss, nor the idea of him coming out of prison into the world again and blaming the justice system for keeping him in prison for so many years...*

As she imagined such things, Yukiko could see the very Japanese posture of atonement by death. It was difficult for her to handle her own torn emotions.

'But if it's the same death sentence, the important thing is what it takes to reach that point, I think. No one should be cast off to die. Mother Teresa always used to say that.'

Yukiko's recalled Mother Teresa gathering up the homeless people of Calcutta, people who were on the verge of death, and taking them to her hospice. There, the dying could receive humane treatment for the first time. People who had fallen in the street and were covered with filth and the dust raised by the hooves of oxen—those people were washed, dressed in clean clothes, and given a bed in a room where they were attended to by a nurse. Of course, treatment was provided for the seriously ill as far as possible, but it was acknowledged that half of the people taken there died. They had been undernourished throughout their lives, and so they were prey to tuberculosis, liver disease, parasites, malaria and other illnesses, until in the end their strength was mortally sapped. That was the reason the place where they were taken was called 'The House of Those Awaiting Death.'

In Japan, a place like that would never be called by such a name. Even though half of the people brought in might die, it would certainly be called something like 'The House of Hope.'

But for Mother Teresa, it was a self-evident principle that human beings die. Death itself was not extraordinary; the important question was whether the life had been worth living or not. In a life worth living, a person should have certain proof that they are loved by someone, whoever it is. Persons who are reduced to a condition in which no one knows whether they are alive or dead need to be attended by a nurse in their final days. What was important was that they might breath their last in a state of joy such as they had never known before.

Yukiko had read the journal of a doctor who had worked in India treating leprosy. Because of the numbing effect on their sensations, many lepers felt no pain, even when some limb was injured. Because there was no pain in the injured area, they didn't feel the need for it to be protected or treated. In the past, people used to say of lepers that their fingers and noses rotted. That did happen in the second stage of the disease if it was not cured, but people confused the disease with its symptoms. But nowadays, Hansen's disease is a simple skin ailment, more easily cured than athlete's foot, and it is now worthwhile for doctors to attack it.

According to the physician who had worked in India, when a patient was receiving treatment for a hand or a leg, then the larger the bandage, the happier the patient would be. The doctor thought that Japanese patients would prefer the smallest possible bandage on their hand or foot so as not to impede movement. But in India, even though the bandage stayed sparkling white for only a few hours, patients were happy with a thick bandage. The reason was that the bandage was a sign that they were loved as human beings. A white bandage showed that someone had looked after them, and that was important emotionally. The bandage might be the only pure white thing in their world, and so it became a proof that they were loved in this world.

'Father, I happened to open the Bible yesterday,' Yukiko said, tacitly conveying to the priest that she almost never looked at the Bible.

'Yes? I'm interested in what caught your attention,' the priest said, suggesting that he took this confession of hers lightly.

'Well, it seems that everyone right now thinks that its proper to despise Mr. Uno, and I wanted to know what the Bible might say about someone like him,' Yukiko said in a low voice.

Only a few days earlier, the grandmother of the murdered boy was quoted in one of the weekly magazines as saying, 'I think I would kill with my own hands someone like a monster who would murder an innocent child.'

Yukiko tried to smile at last. 'I happened to notice a strange passage that said "I seek not sacrifice but compassion." But I wouldn't want to bring up those words, because something like that from the Bible would be put to evil use by Mr. Uno, and the next thing, people would be talking about what foolishness the Bible contained.'

Social justice seems to require a blood sacrifice from those who violate society. Phrases like 'Judge not,' and 'Judge not people by their crimes' have no power before the loud cries for justice. On the contrary, Yukiko had discovered that, unless she cried out for it, she could find herself in the same class as the criminals who don't acknowledge justice.

'The passage that supposes the world wishes to forget that probably is especially meaningful,' the priest said. 'There have been people who complain of the passage that says, "I have not come for the just but for the sinner." They say it's unfair.'

'I remember that you once gave a sermon on where God exists in the world,' Yukiko replied,

'Really? Did I?' Father Izumi seemed to have forgotten.

'Yes. Until then, I thought that God existed up in Heaven. And so, ever since childhood, I've always looked up to pray. I was quite surprised when you said that God exists in the people right in front of me.'

'Yes,' Father Izumi said, 'that seems to surprise everyone. But it's quite to the point. The Bible says "These are my brothers; as you do to the least of them, so you do unto me."'

'Yes, and later I felt bitter about the sermon you gave that day,' Yukiko said. 'If I hadn't known the reality, I still wouldn't have been affected. I wanted to continue disliking people I despised. That's the natural and sure way. But to think that God might be among the people I despised really confused me. And to think that God might exist inside of Fujio Uno is just about inadmissible to a humanist.'

'If God exists in him, it will eventually be perceived,' the priest said in a quiet tone.

'Yesterday, in the letters column of the newspaper, there was a note that said how people shrank away when the name 'Uno' was called out at hospitals or banks. Owing to the emergence of that kind of person, everyone in Japan named Uno feels uncomfortable now,' Yukiko told the priest. It was an immature and childish thing, of course, and she was quite saddened when she read the article.

The priest said, 'Yes, and, as an outsider, I thought how wonderful it would be if the name 'Uno' were taken biblically. It means 'one' in Spanish and Italian.'

'You mean the number 'one'?'

'Exactly. And in English, the word 'one' means a person, in the sense of 'one can do something.' The word 'uno' has the sense of 'people,' or 'humanity in general.' I thought that, as a name, it is the most modest and most general. Especially for a criminal who commits such a crime, the name 'human being' is very appropriate. At least I think so. He's not unique, after all.'

Yukiko said that she knew nothing about such things.

'What I remember best out of my seminary training,' Father Izumi went on, 'is that people who do evil are not a special kind of being, not at all. Take me, for example. Even if I thought of committing a crime that no one had ever done in the past, it would be nearly impossible. And being a warmed-over second, it would be impossible for me to gain the glory of being first, you see.'

'You mean you study such things...?'

'Of course. In fact, someone like me—not very talented, just a fellow with a modest record at some country school—gets his first hard lesson in religion that way. No matter what you try to do, good or evil, it is within the sphere of 'being human.' That's the lesson, and with that, for the first time, you won't fall into making simple judgments like 'That person is evil,' or 'I am good.' You can easily become one of the other kind. Do you see that?'

'But that's different from being foolish. Mr. Uno committed the most pointless crimes. And now I'm about to do the same thing. It's was quite understandable that my sister got angry.'

'Well, it's like this. I can't tell you to pay or not pay for Fujio Uno's lawyer. Let me put it clearly: what you do is something between you and God. It's a relationship that has existed since antiquity. The Jews also recognized it as a relationship that no one may intrude upon. They thought the basis of justice does not lie either in fairness or human society, but in the rightness between God and humanity. I was taught that there is only prayer for realizing that relationship...'

Yukiko left the church and walked slowly along the road by the sea. Her usual quick pace was slow now, and she hoped the fresh wind would clear away her confused thoughts and put her mind in order. While she was with the priest in his reception room, Yukiko felt there was something cowardly about him. He had answered nothing for her. She was thinking of the special sense of the pastor, the shepherd who leads a flock of sheep, and how it suggested the role of a priest who takes care of his parishioners. But the priest had not told her anything about which path she should take. Yukiko was far from satisfied; she paused for a while beside the sea wall.

The unspoken words 'How foolish!' were on her lips, and now for the first time she felt that she could say the words, at least to herself.

—*But what kind of foolishness lies concealed inside Fujio? Whatever it is, it's not merely something like a poor school record, far from it. At least from the point of view of his ability in mathematics, as well as his experience of the world, Fujio has a good deal of the knowledge you'd expect of an adult. And yet Fujio has closed off the road to his own future. People die at some point in time, but until that time they have any number of things to do. And those things are not only making money and getting ahead in their work. What can a human being do until taken by death?*

There in the sea wind, Yukiko felt a tear roll down her cheek. She knew even less about Fujio's past than what had appeared in the newspapers and magazines. But in so far as Fujio had told her about himself, it seemed that he had never once tasted the fullness of human life. To feel pity for that would reflect on how silly she had been. Once in the past she had allowed herself to be betrayed by a man she loved; she had no capacity to be sympathetic.

—*Different from Fujio, somehow I feel that I do know something of the fullness of human life. The people who are taken to Mother Teresa's 'House of Those Awaiting Death,' people living properly for perhaps just one day before their end, might taste a deep satisfaction before they die. My heart reaches out to them. No matter how much sadness fills the world, the sea heaves its great sighs, and the flowers and trees continue to blossom in all their sumptuous splendor. Every human is invited to take part in that transcendent relationship, and through that secret feast reach in time to a universe of thought. But Fujio has foolishly denied himself that fate. He has sunk into an abyss from which he cannot climb out. I can try to extend my hand to help him, but I won't be able to reach to his depth. And seen from the depth of Fujio's unhappiness, surely everyone in the world is living in light. How will Fujio deal with that?*

To avoid passers-by thinking her strange, Yukiko kept turning her face upward and looked at the sea, keeping her back straight. But her tears continued to flow. She thought now of how the person who is killed is so much more wretched than the one who kills. Because of Fujio, Yukiko could see the wretchedness of human life for the first time. During those few minutes, Yukiko's mental vision changed. She began to see Father Izumi's profound solicitude in dealing with her. He had given her no opinion of his own, but in a world of people who readily meddle in the lives of others, the priest had merely asked her to pray for guidance.

Yukiko walked to the Misaki bus stop and in that frame of mind called Nagisa Kazami from a public telephone.

'I wondered whether you might have gone out,' Yukiko said.

'I just got home,' Kazami said. 'This is a good time.'

'Then if it's all right, I would like to talk to you for just 10 minutes or so...'

'That's fine. Actually, I was thinking of getting in touch with you.'

'Then I'll be there in a few minutes.'

When Yukiko arrived at the lawyer's office after a walk of about one kilometer, Mrs. Kazami was at her desk in the office with her assistant. Yukiko could see her from the small hallway. When she sat on the sofa, she saw that the number of pink azaleas had decreased.

'I've been to meet Mr. Uno,' the lawyer said, 'and I thought I'd give you a report.'

'I suppose he was being stubborn. He simply doesn't know how to be grateful.'

'I really don't know how he felt, but he seemed cheerful enough. Not exactly full of thanks, but grateful. He seemed to be rather manic, high...'

Yukiko was again on the verge of tears. 'He's so pitiful. No matter how sad or how terrible something is, it doesn't seem to get to him.'

'I think he's bluffing. I was sure of that when I saw him. He's a familiar type.'

'Was he frank in talking with you?'

'No, he was pretentious. He said that he would talk gradually, that if he told it all at once I would be confused.'

'How foolish. He has no idea of reality. This is not the time to say something like that.'

'I didn't know whether I could get interview time with him all that freely, and so I told him that from now on he ought to decide whether he was going to use the meetings profitably or not.'

'Has he turned down your services?' Yukiko asked.

'He didn't go that far. Anyway, he signed the lawyer selection papers.'

'Asking you this may be beside the point, but I wonder if you really want to represent him? I suppose any lawyer could take on a case like this. He's certainly a miserable client.'

'It's not totally irrelevant whether a lawyer likes a client or not, but I don't think that it's such a big problem.' Nagisa said to Yukiko with a certain coolness. 'Nor is it a matter of hating the sin but not hating the sinner. My younger cousin is a doctor, a dermatologist, and when I talk with him I often think that our work has a lot in common. Though I'm not very fond of hearing it, he says that he doesn't remember much about a particular patient's face or name, but he does remember the ringworm, if that was their ailment. When he looks at the ailing part, he remembers when the patient came to see him and what kind of complaint they brought in, but he doesn't remember the actual person.' Nagisa smiled. 'Of course, my cousin says that it's different when his patient is some really beautiful woman! So whether I have a personal connection with the client or not, it's all the same thing. I'm just concerned with the crime itself, what it means legally, and how much I can uncover of the background—but that's not usually so clear.'

'Speaking of that,' Yukiko said, 'I wonder whether Mr. Uno really opened up to you? If he's going to make use of your services, I think that he'll have to open up his feelings completely.'

'Well, I think he has too much distrust. He's being very cautious—especially about the interview room. There's only a plastic panel between us, and absolutely no decoration. You can meet with your lawyer without anyone else being present. But he doesn't say much at all because he's convinced that there's a secret listening device hidden in there.'

'That's possible, is it?' Yukiko said.

'There's not much chance. There would be a huge fuss if word about it got out.' Nagisa smiled softly. 'But I wouldn't guarantee it 100 percent. Anything's possible in this world.'

'I wonder if he intends to keep hiding the facts?'

'Well, it's only my intuition, but I don't think so. He's trapped and I think he's just playing around. He gave me the feeling that in part he's watching to see how skillfully the police can uncover what he's done. Of course, the interrogation wasn't all that easygoing—so far he's being very stubborn.'

'My other reason to be here is to consult with you about a totally different matter from his defense. The other day, for the first time, I took him some things. It seems that his own family is not sending him anything. I wonder if the fact that I'm taking things in is producing any kind of good reaction in him?'

Yukiko felt more fragile than ever before when she realized she was asking about such trivial things.

'I don't know whether it's good to talk to you about this,' Nagisa said, adopting a gossipy tone, 'but he seems to be extremely dependent upon you just now. He said that he had received a cake from you as soon as we met. And it was funny. He said he'd eaten cake like that when he was a child but hadn't bought any since. He kept saying how delicious it was. They don't get any sweet things to eat in the jail, so it was a real treat.'

'They don't have any sweet things?'

'No, they're regarded as luxury items, so they're out.'

'If that's the case, then to punish him, he mustn't be given sweet things,' Yukiko said, her eyes downcast.

'No, that's not it. For him to return to a real person, he needs to experience a number of things, some of them pretty intense. His mother was always coddling him, saying things like, "Fu-chan is such a *good* boy," and "Fu-chan is really quite bright, but the teachers at school just aren't smart enough to see that." Naturally, he can't get along with those comments for ever. But if he only has a feeling of isolation, that will drive him into a corner. So I think the things you took to jail for him were just fine.'

The stories about "Fu-chan is such a *good* boy," and "Fu-chan is really quite bright" had appeared in the newspapers and weeklies after interviews with Fujio's mother.

'From now on, how about taking him things a day or so after you hit on the fact that he may want something? Since you're the one who always brings things, he'll surely start taking it for granted. But some days, I think, he should feel isolated and defenseless, of course, and other times you can encourage him and that will be tied to his confession.'

'All right, I'll do as you suggest,' Yukiko said.

'He hasn't said so quite so clearly, but besides you he seems to like Sergeant Higaki. He said a lot of bad things about the other people at the interrogation, but he didn't say anything specifically about him. That's the way the police play the game. They want you to trust someone, and so Sergeant Higaki might be playing that role just because of the way he naturally is.'

'I wonder if my letter reached him? I sent it to the Chief of Police at the station.' Yukiko said.

'Yes, it reached him. He seemed very happy. He said that you were naive about the world and seemed to preach to him like an elementary school teacher, but his face showed that he was pleased.'

351

'Can you take letters to him for me?' Yukiko asked.

'I can if he'll read them through the plastic barrier between us. You did that publicly last time, so it would be better to do the same thing again. Of course, letters are always inspected.'

'That's quite all right with me.'

'And besides—although this is just my intuition and it may not be correct—I think that he's holding something back. I don't mean from the magazines. He said something to the effect that since he was destined to Hell, I didn't have to be too serious with him. I said to him, "Then you do think that the matter of the boy was bad enough to send you to Hell?" And he replied, "Oh, I'm not thinking of that impudent brat." And so I thought that it must be something else he did. What do you think?'

Nagisa clearly spoke as though urging Yukiko to confide in her.

'He's just so much more clever than I am at fitting together lies and facts,' Yukiko replied. 'He wants to show how clever he is at putting his story together.'

'And he said that he didn't kill the two women who ran away after he let them out of his car and abandoned them. I asked him why he tormented them so much. He said that, in the case of the daughter of the president of Shimada Foods, the company put out jars of jam that no one could get the lids off. He said that he heard that story from you. The reason was that the old lady who lived next door to you died. He said, "Didn't they kill the old lady when they sold those jars of jam that you couldn't get open? I gave them something to think about." That sort of talk.'

'That's not the reason at all!' Yukiko said. 'She couldn't get the lid open for a few days, and so she had to eat her bread without jam. But why in the world did he have to take any revenge? If the jam jar is hard to open, then next time you just wouldn't buy it. Right? It's certainly no reason to murder the daughter of the head of the company.'

'Well, he insists that he did *not* kill her. But he feels enormously resentful about all that. "Those damned company heads. That bunch never open their own jam jar in the morning, so they don't know what kind of stuff their companies are making." He says things like that all the time. And he says the same thing about the woman who worked in the department store. He said he asked about where something was sold. And she had no idea about it, even though it was sold just 20 meters or so from where she was standing. He said she told him it was on a completely different floor. "I can get around," he said, "but thanks to that damn fool woman, I had to go downstairs. That's nothing to me, but if it was an old and weak person, or someone disabled—what then? If it didn't relate to her, she didn't pay any attention at all." He said it was no loss to the department store when someone like that gets run over.'

'Do you think he would speak like that in front of the judge?' Yukiko asked.

'I really couldn't say. Purely from the point of view of tactics, when it comes to a case like Mr. Uno's, it doesn't matter how he talks. Personally, I think he can talk just about any way he wants to.'

Yukiko felt the calmness in the lawyer's words. She spoke in a tone that made it clear she was involved in a business communication.

'One more thing,' said the lawyer. 'He asked me to find out when your birthday was.'

'My birthday? What for?'

'He doesn't understand what he's done, but I think he feels obliged to you and he wants to give you some kind of present.'

'Please tell him it's June 10th. Nobody makes any fuss about it. Since I passed thirty, I don't feel much like celebrating each birthday. I prefer to forget it. What do you do for your birthday?' Yukiko asked Nagisa.

'I feel the same way you do about birthdays,' she said. 'And most of the time I'm busy with my work. But my husband seems to like that sort of thing. If that day is no good, then the next day, or even the following week, he always takes me and our son out to some good restaurant in Tokyo.'

'I think that's wonderful,' Yukiko said.

'He likes to eat, so every year about that time he asks around and finds out some good Japanese or Western restaurant and makes a reservation for us. He doesn't really ask me what I would like, but the truth is I'm not very critical about food.'

'I just remembered,' Yukiko said, 'that Mr. Uno once gave me a little dish. He brought it one day wrapped in a newspaper. I wonder if I should tell the police about it.'

'Yes. He's spoken to me about that already. It seems that he saw it at a department store curio sale. He just stole it and gave it to you. He said "I trust you. That's why I'm telling you about this." That was the story he gave me. It seems to have been the department store in Yokohama where the woman named Reiko Suga worked. He told me the story and then said that anything he said to me I could tell you, too. His reason was that you are sponsoring him.'

'I wonder if he thought it would make me happy to hear about the dish? Aside from the content of what he said, should I be happy to use something that he stole?'

'You know,' said Kazami, 'it might be that he really doesn't consider what other people will think. If he feels all right about something, then he thinks that other people will, too. If he's unhappy, he just doesn't consider other people, or he wipes them out of his mind. It might be his nature to do that kind of thing, or maybe he was just never taught any differently. I don't know.'

Yukiko said, 'I always thought that such things were simply human nature even without being taught.'

'If I weren't in this business, I might think like that, too. But these days, things are a little different. In the past, no matter how uneducated the parents were, they would tell their children, "Even though no one sees you, if you do some evil you will end up in Hell," or "That's not what a man does." Something high-minded like that. But our world today isn't quite so brave. Nobody says anything like that. It's a world where children are turned out wild, like stray dogs.'

Chapter 22

A WALK AT DAWN

F UJIO was woken up a little before three in the morning by the guard knocking on the door of his cell.

'It's time.'

'Damn! You never let a man sleep in peace! You didn't let me get to bed until 11:30,' Fujio responded arrogantly.

'Weren't you the one who wanted this?'

The prisoners in the cells next to him were deathly silent—perhaps fearful of drawing the attention of the guard, perhaps still asleep. Only one snored on earnestly, unperturbed by the sounds around him.

'It's raining, isn't it?' Fujio asked the guard while getting himself ready.

'Do you want to postpone this because it's raining?'

'No, that's not it, but the place will be easier to find if the weather's good.'

'I didn't see any stars around nine o'clock.'

'Shit,' Fujio muttered in a low voice. 'It'd be easier to show them if it was clear.' Fujio said this in a voice so low the guard didn't hear.

It had been a long while since Fujio had taken notice of how the weather was for going out. He wanted to breathe the outside air. That was all that he had given much attention to during the past weeks. He had told people that he was a poet and that to stimulate his imagination he walked in natural settings; but in truth he despised anything to do with nature. Sitting on the ground got your backside wet, and if you walked in the forest you were attacked by mosquitoes. He knew nothing about walking in the mountains or sailing a boat, the pleasures other people enjoyed even though they weren't their work. He had once been out on a yacht, but he'd been shaken by the waves and the heat of the sun had soon broiled him. And the moment the sun went down, the sea wind was cold. He had felt nauseated on the small, light craft, and he wondered how anyone could take pleasure in all that.

However, in that small space of steel and concrete, Fujio had changed; he wanted nothing more than to breath the outside air. It was not even that he wanted to go somewhere that had lots of green; if only he could walk around outside there a little. There was sunlight at every corner in the towns on the Miura Peninsula, and the odor of the sea wind, the grasses and the trees filled the air. Aware of such things now, in his prison cell, he thought vaguely of the people walking about outside who noticed none of it.

Fujio was not even certain what day of the week it was. He had no calendar, and his watch with the day and date had been taken from him. He had been questioned for nearly two months, without any holidays and no Sundays off. The interrogation often went on until 10 or 11 o'clock at night. When he stood up, it was as though he was stuck to the chair; he could hardly straighten his legs to walk. The interrogators were a team of specialists who took turns, like human-wave tactics. For them, the work was nothing; but Fujio was alone on the receiving end of the ordeal.

He didn't know how they had discovered the place. As far as he knew, there had been no eyewitnesses. But something strange was going on, because the police investigation had already connected him with the three women he'd killed.

Fujio knew about the waist cord they would use on him, and he thought it was always black. But now it seemed that the rope had been changed; it was either blue or grey in color, he couldn't tell which. It was thought that this slight modification 'reduced the psychological sense of oppression on the prisoners,' and helped democratize the police.

—*Probably just some timid guy's childish rationale!*

'A morning walk. What grand treatment!' Fujio said as he was taken from the back entrance of the station to the motor pool. His comment was offered in general to the unexpectedly large number of people there, but he didn't feel like saying anything more. He walked the few steps from the door to the car with deliberate slowness. It was important for him to draw in deep breaths of the ocean air, the odor of the Miura Peninsula.

In that brief space of time, Fujio looked up at the sky. He was aware of the handcuffs, but he could convince himself they were a minor irritation, confined to one part of his body. The guard had said that it had been cloudy the previous evening, but now, thankfully, the clouds had blown away and the sky was full of stars.

Two vehicles set out. In a short while, when they reached the main highway at the top of a small hill, the stars filled the sky nearly to the horizon.

Along the way, the two vehicles were joined by two more, making a convoy of four.

'I'm surprised,' Fujio said, turning to Sergeant Higaki, who was sitting next to him. 'Are those for me, too?'

'That's right.'

'Really something! On the scale of protection for the Prime Minister, right? But those other two cars weren't with us to begin with, were they?'

'We had them wait elsewhere and join us. You said you wanted to get rid of the newspaper reporters, so we tried to made it inconspicuous.'

'That was really nice of you,' Fujio replied.

'Which road did you take?' asked Takarabe, his voice far from joyful.

'Let's see, which road was it? Let me think...' Fujio said in a jocular tone.

'Bastard!' said Takarabe jerking Fujio's body. But beyond that he did nothing more physical to him.

'At the train station, take a right,' Fujio said as though he was imperiously directing a cab driver. It had been a long battle to come this far, Fujio fighting long hours against 'the third degree' of sitting in a chair without being allowed to stand.

'Could you roll down your side window a little?' Fujio asked Higaki. 'Then we could see the shape of the land better.'

Fujio thought Higaki might refuse, but he opened his window more than half way and Fujio gulped in the odor of the sea he had missed for so long, filling the deepest corners of his lungs.

—In order to get them to bring me on this outing, I've had to do a lot of maneuvering! But I just can't imagine how they connected me with Yoko Miki, Yoshiko Yamane and the disappearance of Aoki Kayo. How could that have been? Let's see...Well, they probably found out that I had a meal with Yoko at that restaurant called 'Eden' and that we stayed at the hotel called 'Côte d'Azur.' I said that I had no memory of the name Côte d'Azur, and that I thought it might be a seaside rooming house. When the officer said, "The two of you stayed there—the manager said so," I recalled for the first time what Yoko said about the manager having a tattoo on his chest. But it's strange that they found out about me going to the 'Skyscraper' love hotel with Yoshiko Yamane...

'Officer, why do you say that I went to that hotel with Yoshiko Yamane?' he'd asked the new sergeant whose name he hadn't yet learned. 'To tell you the truth, I meet a lot of women. But it's all been perfectly legal. I ask them, 'How about it?' and they say 'OK.' So we do it. I'll tell you what I think. Both sides like sex. But it's odd that only the guy pays, right? If men and women are going to have equal rights from now on, I think it would be good if the woman pays sometimes. I mean, from the woman's point of view, maybe she just wants to sleep with a guy, you know?'

'Did you or didn't you go to the 'Skyscraper'?'

'I don't know. I go a lot to those love hotels. Some I like especially. Sometimes the woman puts on airs, and then finally says 'Sure, it's OK.' At times like that, I just pile into the nearest place before she changes her mind. I mean, I don't remember the name of each and every place like that. You know how those joints are set up, officer—on duty or off, right? Most of them are built so you don't meet anyone else: you pay the bill like at a hospital, send your money in a tube and get your change the same way. That's how it works. Now, with a system like that, can anyone testify that it was *me* who was there?'

'How about in your car?'

'You mean making love?' Fujio smiled at Higaki's question. 'Sometimes.'

'And there wasn't a woman you might have lent your car to, just to get to know her better?' Higaki asked in a commiserating tone, implying that Fujio shouldn't have been such a dupe.

'No such thing,' Fujio replied. 'My car's the one thing I don't lend out.'

'You really don't lend your car to anyone?' Higaki asked.

For a moment, Fujio wanted to say that he had lent his car, but, sensing that there was some hidden motive in all this, he told the truth.

'I don't lend my car. If there's an accident, things get too damned complicated.'

'That's a commendable policy,' Higaki said.

'Let's suppose you've forgotten about the 'Skyscraper,'' Inspector Takarabe said. 'But you probably remember the 'Hotel Sunlight.''

'And just what is that all about?'

'It's the love hotel you went to with Yoshiko Yamane.'

'Officer, the term 'love hotel' isn't very popular these days, you know,' Fujio said. 'It's better to say 'leisure hotel.''

In spite of the fact that Fujio himself had used the term 'love hotel' just a moment earlier, he made a point about Takarabe using it.

'I'm not saying I never went to that hotel; I just don't remember. I've told you that over and over.'

'You picked up Yoshiko Yamane at the video shop in front of the station, right? Someone saw you.'

'Oh?'

Takarabe related how someone, a regular customer at the coffee shop that Yoshiko's mother managed, was surprised to see Yoshiko get into the car of a man he didn't recognize. One day, when Yoshiko was working rather clumsily at the counter, she had been introduced by her mother as her younger daughter.

'We know that your car was parked at the Hotel Sunlight in the late afternoon,' Takarabe said in a loud voice next to Fujio's ear. 'The hotel has a record of it.'

Fujio was silent. He wanted to say, 'You don't have to be so loud. I'm not an old man; my ears are still in good shape.'

'And there's a record at the 'Skyscraper,' too. They take down the license numbers of all the cars. You entered the 'Skyscraper' at 3:43 in the afternoon of January 31, and you left at 5:50.'

Fujio said nothing.

'The next day, Yoshiko Yamane told some of her friends about going to a love hotel called 'New York' with a man.'

'Maybe it was some other guy, OK? I've never been to a hotel called 'New York.' I'd remember if I'd been to a place with a name like that.'

'Oh? But we checked out that hotel, the 'Skyscraper,' and we found a room there called the 'New York.' And in the hotel record for that day, we found the license number of your car.'

Fujio could not conceal the jolt it gave him to hear about his license number being on the hotel register.

'OK, you win,' he said. 'I'll tell you about Yoshiko Yamane. I really regret meeting up with that girl. She was the worst. I must have been blind to pick her up. After I left the 'Hotel Sunlight', I let her go immediately. She kept telling me how she had an appointment later. It sounded as if her next date was the main thing for that day and she'd only picked me up because she had some time to kill. Anyway, the guy looked to me like a gangster, that was my impression. I was really afraid that I'd picked up his girl. Believe me, I was shaking and got out of there right away!'

—That lie went over well enough for an improvisation! And since it concerns a gangster, the police will have to investigate the connection...

'And would you tell us about Kayo Aoki?' Higaki said. 'You see, we have an eye witness.'

The words came as another shock to Fujio. Suddenly he felt like denouncing Kayo to the world.

'You killed her, didn't you?' asked Takarabe.

There was a stunned silence in the car.

'Where did you put the body?' Takarabe demanded.

Fujio was willing to talk about Kayo Aoki to Higaki, but he resisted at the sound of Takarabe's voice. 'I do know a little about Kayo,' he said, 'but I don't feel like talking about her just now.'

'Did you kill her?'

'Yeah. A woman like that doesn't deserve to live.'

'Something about her put you off, didn't it?' Higaki said. 'Tell me what it was.'

'Everything. Even riding on the train, that simple twit didn't even know how to sit. She'd dangle her legs out in the aisle so that people would stumble over them.'

'There are lots like that riding on the train, I guess.'

'Shit! I'd like to kill them all,' Fujio said.

Higaki smiled briefly at Fujio's response.

'Why are you laughing at me?' Fujio asked, but it was clear that he was not really disturbed.

'It's nothing. I was just thinking of how much work it would be if you killed every one of them.'

'And you think that's funny?'

'No, no. But it would be quite a job to do that.' It was like a pleasant conversation between the two of them. 'You'd feel better about things if you did that. But you'd have to send the bodies home afterward. And you can't put a whip to a corpse.'

'Sergeant Higaki, you're too optimistic!' Fujio replied in a good-humored voice. 'I won't become what you want me to be so easily. Believe me, I only get tough when I run into a bad time. Then I give it right back.'

'What do you mean by "get tough"?' Higaki asked.

'I've got a grudge against the world,' Fujio said.

'The world? What do you mean by that?'

'The world is the world: the police pigs who are always judging people; the mass media, who are always writing nonsense; those who picture me as an ignorant bumpkin; my brother-in-law and his wife, who think I'd be better off dead; and those stuck-up women, too—the bitches! That's who I mean. They're my enemy.'

'Yukiko Hata, too?'

'She's different.'

'Then she's the only one who's human?'

'No. She's a morning glory. Not that you would know about that.' For a moment, Fujio was nonplussed.

'I just wanted to give you something fresh to think about,' said Higaki. 'We'll send the girls' bodies back to their mothers. I wanted to let you show us the place.'

Fujio's expression conveyed that he wondered why he was saying such self-complacent stuff, but he was encouraged to go along with it. When he was still free, he had noticed beautiful things: the transparent light of dawn; the soft golden sunlight of morning; the sounds of the ocean; the soughing of the wind in the pines; evening light tinting the waves like a flaming memory; the evening star; the white of moonlight on a landscape. How long had it been since he'd last seen these things? When he said he would show them where the corpses were, he imagined he would be taken to the place. He could be outside. He could see the ocean. And only then would he decide whether to show them the real place or not.

Fujio had thought about it for several days before saying he would show the police where the bodies were if they accepted his conditions.

'What conditions?' Takarabe had asked.

'Write them down. I've got them in my head, so just write them down nicely.'

'The police don't make deals,' Higaki said.

'Sure. But, before you say no, just write down the conditions, because you might want to study them.'

He had hardly slept the night before, thinking of what he would propose. Now, Fujio dictated his conditions smoothly. They were simple enough:

1. *When I show you where the bodies are, no reporters will be present.*

2. *I will not prepare any maps or detailed descriptions.*
3. *When the burial place is confirmed, I will be allowed to meet with my parents and Yukiko Hata.*
4. *An agreement of consent will be signed by my brother-in-law and his wife saying they will be responsible for my body after my execution.*
5. *I will be given the time and the means to write down the facts for the media.*

Fujio thought there was a chance that the police would accept all five conditions in exchange for showing them where the bodies were. But he had miscalculated: all but one were instantly rejected by Higaki.

'I promise that we will keep the reporters at a distance.'

'I supposed you would. You couldn't fool me about that,' Fujio said as a test of Higaki's sincerity.

'The reporters are swarming around the police station. We'll have to think of some way to fool them.'

'It would work if it's late at night or very early in the morning. But I couldn't agree to provide you with a detailed description or map before going out,' Fujio said.

'Then forget it. There's no sense talking about it,' Higaki said in a tone that ended the plan.

'OK. But even if I tried to write something down, I can't remember very well. It was at night. I couldn't draw something if I tried.'

'So you're saying from the start that you don't know where the place is? You don't know, right? You're only pretending to know.'

'I *do* know where it is! But I have to go and look to make sure,' Fujio said. 'If we drive the same way I went that day, I think I'll recognize the area, more or less.'

Higaki said nothing, as though he saw through Fujio's plan to be on the outside.

'All right, then we'll follow the route you tell us. But it won't do any good if you don't give us a rough map.'

'I can do a rough one. Then if I go there and have a look, it might be different from what I remember.'

'OK. Agreed.'

'And will you let me see my mom and dad, and Miss Hata?'

'We can't negotiate,' Higaki replied. 'Look, I've got a letter for you here from Miss Hata.'

Fujio felt the blood rushing to his face. 'She only sent a lawyer. I haven't heard from her since then. I thought she'd given up on me.'

'Now hurry up and draw the map. Then you'll get the letter.'

'So you're negotiating on the letter?'

'Nothing like that. Just everything in sequence. You can't do two things at once. Only a damned fool thinks he can put *miso* soup and a sweet roll in his mouth at the same time.'

Higaki spoke in a low voice. Fujio didn't mind if Higaki treated him as a fool, but he decided to play it straight.

'But you will let me see the letter today, won't you?'

'If you don't cause any trouble, you will have time to read the letter, because it means we'll soon get our investigation of the scene over with.'

Fujio showed them on a map where Kayo Aoki's body was buried, but of course he drew a place quite separate from where he'd let the naked Tomoko Shimada out of his car.

Fujio received Yukiko's letter from Higaki later that day:

Somehow I can't think of appropriate words to write when I communicate with you. It seems unnatural to begin with a conventional 'How are you?'. Having killed people, there is no need for you to be in good health.

I can't imagine what your daily life is like. Scattered all around me are magazines and newspapers with articles about you. If you saw them, I suppose you'd find some truthful things, but most of it false. Until I hear from your own lips, I won't trust any of it. Even if you say the same things, I want to hear them from you. There's a great difference between hearing things directly and hearing something from an unreliable third party.

People should not have to let others explain about themselves. First of all, it is an impoliteness to you. If you want to say that you've been dull-witted since birth, then you have to trust someone else to speak for you. But you were either normal or born with a stronger sense of self than other people. So can you feel at ease with what the magazines and newspapers have written about you?

There must be some reason why you killed people. It's probably not a reason that most people would agree with, but at least I will try to understand, I promise. I can't promise that I'm capable of that, but I will try to understand, really.

At that point, Fujio noticed that Higaki was staring fixedly at him.

'It's a difficult letter,' Fujio said.

'Don't you understand it?'

'It's not that I don't understand it.'

'Then what's the trouble?'

'I...I wanted another kind of letter.'

'And what kind is that?'

'I don't know exactly. You know, something more romantic.'

'Do you have a romantic relationship?'

'Yeah. We're not children, after all.'

'Well, if you're not happy, stop reading,' Higaki said. He reached out to take the letter away, but Fujio held on to it tightly and continued to read.

I met the lawyer, Nagisa Kazami. I was afraid she might refuse to represent you if you wouldn't tell her the truth. She said quite clearly that it was up to you. It all depends on how you work to help yourself next time you meet with her. Anyone can offer help, but they can't pull you out of the hole you're in if you don't try to help yourself. Please give that careful thought and decide what you're going to do. At present, you're at the bottom of a pit.

The fact was that Fujio couldn't grasp the general idea of Yukiko's letter. He read it slowly and deliberately a second time. He was about to read it a third time when Higaki interrupted.

Later, when he tried to remember details of the letter, he couldn't. All he could recall was that it told him to tell the truth to the attorney. He muttered a curse. The letter was his property, and the police had not given him time to read it at leisure. He thought that was a violation of his rights.

Only the tone of the letter remained clear in Fujio's mind, that same kind, respectful and polite voice that Yukiko had used when they'd occasionally met in the past.

—*She's still using the same tone to me, even though I've killed people...*

Alone in his cell that night, an echo of those times came back to him. Fujio began to weep. He covered his head with his blanket to stifle the sound.

Fujio thought how Takarabe would like to learn that he'd been crying. A few days earlier, Takarabe had said something insulting about Yukiko—that even if she didn't have a man, she'd still be better off without a guy like him. To Fujio, that was despicable. Before Takarabe could move, Fujio upset the table in front of them, almost knocking Takarabe from his chair. After that, the Inspector pushed the table tight against Fujio, who began to feel a pain in his ribs as though they might break.

The struggle confirmed Fujio in his silence throughout the afternoon. In retaliation, the police withheld the bowl of rice with chicken, egg and vegetables that Yukiko had sent him until after 10 p.m., and by then it had turned completely cold.

No matter how much they pressured him, Fujio had resolved never to reveal where the corpses were buried. That was his only purpose in life. What hindered his determination was Higaki. When no one was around, Higaki sometimes said enigmatic things: 'Mr. Uno. Why don't you talk about the past?' or 'By the way, have the people you murdered come back to see you yet?'

Fujio sneered. 'What a childish kind of threat! People aren't fooled by childish things like hearing the sutras read on a tape and smelling incense.'

'No, there's no need for that,' Higaki said. 'I've tried it to see, but the people who were killed will certainly meet their killer sometime. The reason is that they don't know *why* they had to be killed. I think they come back to ask about that. The sooner they come, the less painful it is. The later it is, the heavier it gets on you.'

'Well, I'm not threatened by stuff like that,' Fujio said, but Higaki's quiet smile sent a shiver down Fujio's spine.

Now, in the patrol car, Higaki was sitting next to Fujio in silence, letting the sea air sweep over him. Inspector Takarabe yawned deeply.

After a while, Higaki said to Fujio in a low voice, 'Are we still on the right road?'

'Yeah, we are,' Fujio replied.

The jabbering noise of the police radio in the car spoiled the quiet mood.

'According to the map you made,' Takarabe said, 'this is close to the place where you threw out Tomoko Shimada. Right?'

Fujio seemed to be annoyed at this.

'Inspector, I didn't *throw* her out,' Fujio said. 'I just let her out here, naked.'

Following Takarabe's words, Fujio thought that he might stop talking.

The road they were on was basically following the Pacific Ocean, but at that point it headed slightly east, and Fujio glimpsed the first light of dawn breaking over the horizon.

Dark as it was, the sea had its own color of life and it was filled with a sense of movement. The darkness was alive. Through it, a smudge of gold was growing, announcing the arrival of the sun. Fujio's heart was pounding.

But the sea was indifferent to Fujio and returned no signal of approval.

Fujio's weakness had always been his explosive emotions. His mother had spoiled him. Friends and teachers despised him as a fool or disliked him, but most people just ignored him out of coldness. Now, the sea showed no sign of responding to him.

—*The ocean's indifferent; it ignores me whether I love or I kill. In a way, the sea has already enveloped all life and death, and so it can't be surprised, it can't withdraw, it doesn't even judge. I could cry out from cliffs at the edge of the ocean for a body to come forth; the sea simply wouldn't hear...*

Fujio smiled at his own thoughts of how the sea's serenity betrayed his attentions.

'What are you laughing about?' Takarabe demanded.

'I'm not laughing,' he replied.

—*Whenever I try to feel calm, this jerk gets in my way! He makes me feel sick inside. But how perfect it would be to fall to my knees in awe before the serenity of the boundless sea!*

'Around here?' Higaki asked as they approached the place Fujio had drawn. It was slightly off target, as he intended.

'No...I don't think this is the right place,' Fujio answered.

'I want you to think about it carefully. Real carefully,' Takarabe said in his ear, obviously wanting to lay hands on his prisoner. Fujio said nothing. He didn't wish to lessen the time he could hear the ocean by arguing with Takarabe.

'Go on, just a little more. Then turn left at the crossroads at the top of the hill.'

'If we go up there, that's where Tomoko Shimada was found,' Higaki said, as though he had a map of the district in his head.

'Look. I told you, I don't know about Tomoko Shimada,' Fujio told him. 'I said goodbye to her, and that was all. As I was turning the car around, she saw her chance and ran away.'

He directed the car about 15 meters down a side road lined with trees planted as a windbreak, and then told the driver to stop.

'OK. I think this is the place. But I'm like a dog—I have to put my feet on the ground to be sure.'

Higaki opened the car door.

At that moment, enveloped by the air, Fujio was dazzled. Up to then, he had been breathing the stale air of the jail, so the fresh air was like a rebirth for him. It was air that had never yet been sucked through human lungs, and Fujio was drunk on the taste of it.

Holding his cuffed hands out in front of him, he was aware of being held from behind by the rope around his waist. He took a few steps. The lack of exercise of the past weeks, or possibly some psychological effect, tangled his feet; he felt he couldn't move forward.

A moment later, Fujio squatted down on the ground. It wasn't enough to feel the ground only with the soles of his feet: he wanted to contact it using his whole body.

Inspector Takarabe was the first to notice this and he rushed over to Fujio, shouting for him to get up, shaking him by the shoulder. Fujio merely rounded his back and Takarabe kicked him with his knee.

'I don't know!' Fujio exclaimed. 'If I don't sit here and look, I can't remember the place.'

That was a lie, of course, but also, apart from that, it was a shout of truth straight from his heart.

'All right, let's go.'

Fujio heard this and felt the hand of Higaki on his left arm.

'Stand up and look around. You can see the whole area.'

It was more of suggestion than a logical statement, but a whisper in Fujio's mind acknowledged that it was natural. In order to see the morning sun, his eye level would have to be higher.

'Is this the place?' Higaki asked, pressing him for an answer. There was no sign at all of allowing him to stroll around.

'Where the jam company girl was?' Fujio inquired in a kind of imbecile tone.

'When you did it to Tomoko Shimada, where was the car stopped?'

'Just where your patrol car is stopped now,' Fujio answered. 'And the place where she died, where is that?'

'The cliff, about ten meters from that bench.'

'Eh? Is the cliff that steep there?'

'Just in one place, where it drops off straight to the sea. It drops straight down and there's a ledge. That's where she died.'

'That's terrible', said Fujio. 'I wonder why she didn't look for help from someone on the road?'

'Just try to think how you'd have treated her if she'd done that,' Higaki said in his precisely official voice.

'I came through here, to this tree. I remember I couldn't decide which way to go.' Fujio was muttering. He began to walk around aimlessly. But just then, Takarabe called out to the 20 or so men of his team in a commanding voice that shattered the stillness.

'This way?' Higaki, too, was tense.

'This is the way. I'm sure of it.'

Beneath his breath, Fujio muttered, 'Don't get excited!'

—I'm going to show you one place, but the other two are still sleeping in a place you don't know...

And unless Fujio gave instructions, no one was ever going to find them.

He looked again at the eastern sky. He was glad when he saw the color of dawn in the bits of sky visible through the scattered pine trees of the forest.

'Mr. Uno,' Higaki said. 'I think you'd like to return the girl to her parents, wouldn't you? I know it. Please be obedient.'

'I'm a murderous fiend, right?' Fujio said. He laughed, but there was no strength in his laughter. 'That's what those guys writing in the weekly magazines say. Don't expect to find any conscience in a murderous fiend.'

'No, from the first I didn't suppose you had any conscience,' replied Higaki. 'But you chose morning yourself. You wanted to resolve everything before the sun comes up. That's only natural for animals.'

'Look, Sergeant. I'll make one condition. Just let me have a little smell of the sea air. That's all I want,' Fujio said, whispering.

For just one instant, Higaki looked into Fujio's face. 'Think it over carefully. If you're telling me you don't know and you're trying to fool me, we'll both be unhappy about that later on. So just play it straight.'

Fujio wondered about Higaki's words. Both deliberately and unconsciously, Fujio had set conditions for the police any number of times. Every time, though, Higaki had stubbornly rejected him. Higaki's pose was that he would not make any kind of deal. But now, Fujio was at ease, forgetting everything, breathing in the sea wind for a few minutes. It was something Higaki was not denying him.

—He said that we would both be unhappy. It's not something I can be proud of, but ever since I can remember, I've been unhappy. So even if Higaki says I'll be unhappy from now on, that's nothing to flinch at, is it? But if I do as Higaki said, would that make me happy? That's unlikely...

Fujio stopped thinking about all of that and looked at the sea. It was Takarabe's style not to allow him even one minute of repose. But Higaki had the men from the other car gather together close by. It was just a trick, an indirect way to give Fujio a little time to taste the sea air.

Quietly, Fujio took in the smell of the ocean through his nostrils. He had shut his eyes and he was smiling. At that moment, he could forget where he was and the kind of life he had lived. Fujio imagined himself as a small bubble on the waves, dissolving into the sea. His self became infinitely small and he imagined that something was embracing him.

—When you get smaller, does the evil imbedded in you also get smaller? Some people would say that was impossible. But if we suppose there are people who are enthusiastic about becoming great, there are also people who find peace in becoming small. It's the common notion that becoming great is always a worthwhile goal, the only good thing there is. But the opposite of that idea can give pleasure as well. In the last moments of my life, I will recall the smell of the sea, no matter how remote and isolated the place of execution might be, or how cruelly dark the man-made place is. And when I think of the sea, I will become so very small...

Fujio turned to the ocean and bowed his head. He anticipated this might be the last time he would ever look out like this at the sea, and this was his farewell. Again he stared toward that color of pure joy.

Then he turned to Higaki.

'Yeah, I've got it now. I'll show you the place. Kayo Aoki is there. Definitely.'

Chapter 23

AN INTRUSION

THOUGH it was not yet time for the summer rainy season, the rain had been pouring down steadily all day. When Yukiko returned home around 4 p.m., there was a man standing at the front gate dressed in a sweater and no tie and holding an umbrella. For a moment, she imagined he was there by chance, perhaps waiting to meet someone. But as she came closer, he looked inquiringly at her and asked whether she was Yukiko Hata.

'Yes, that's right,' she replied.

'My name's Takato. I'm in the editorial department of *Now Weekly.*'

'Oh? What can I do for you?' Yukiko was cautious.

'I would like to ask you a little about the serial killer Fujio Uno. I've heard that you know him.'

'From whom did you hear that?' Yukiko asked.

'From an acquaintance of our Editor-in-Chief. I wasn't told the name of the person he talked with.'

He was not a complete novice, but neither did he seem to be a hardened newspaperman, and his tone was mild enough. He was in his early thirties.

Yukiko thought it would be prudent to send him away there and then, but the fierce rain changed her mind. The cuffs of his light brown trousers were already soaked through.

'It's pouring,' she said. 'Please come inside.'

'Thanks a lot,' he said. Takato seemed relieved. He removed his shoes and entered the house, but it seemed that he'd been standing in wet socks.

'I'll get your room dirty, so if you have a cloth to wipe...,' he said hesitantly.

'Oh, just take your socks off so they can dry a little,' Yukiko said.

'Umm, I couldn't take off my socks; it's the first time I've visited you.'

—Ah, I remember reading somewhere that in Europe and America people don't take their shoes off when visiting, because it implies going to the bedroom with someone! Well, if some people feel that way about shoes, then maybe it's only natural that this young man should hesitate to take off his socks. Still, it would be unkind to make him keep wet socks on...

'I really don't mind.' Yukiko said. 'I'll put them in the dryer and they'll be ready in a minute.'

'Really? But they're dirty and...'

'Don't worry about that,' Yukiko said, taking the socks from him. She led him to the guest room. She could have put the socks directly into the machine, but because they were indeed somewhat dirty, she quickly washed them in soap first.

'I really appreciate your concern,' the man said, presenting his business card when Yukiko returned. His name was Norio Takato. 'You may not have seen our magazine?'

'Oh, I have seen it at the dentist's and at the bank,' Yukiko replied. From time to time, in fact, Tomoko brought the magazine home, but Yukiko had no intention of mentioning her since she was in the same business.

'The reason I've called on you,' Takato began, 'is that my company is trying to keep up with the Uno case, but we can't really grasp the character of the man. I'm visiting his acquaintances, trying to learn more about the real person. It would be a shame not to at least make an effort to understand him. May I ask, when did you come to know Fujio Uno?'

'Well, I do know him, but not very well at all. Actually, I can't give you any reliable information about him.'

'Can you tell me where you first met him?'

'Right here at this house. He commented on how pretty my morning glories were.'

'Morning glories? So does he like plants?' Takato said as he took out his pen and notebook. 'That's the first thing I've heard of it.'

'No. In fact, I later understood that he was not fond of plants. It was probably just an excuse for him to speak.'

'And how many times did you see him?'

'Three or four times, perhaps,' Yukiko said.

'Was that here?'

'Yes, here, and he also invited me to go for a drive.'

'And you went with him?'

'Yes. He drove for a couple of hours along the coast, and then back.'

'Did you just take a drive? Did you stop anywhere? For tea?'

'It was mid-day, and so we had lunch.'

'What did you talk about then?'

'Not much at all. Just that he was divorced from his wife. Things like that. But he did tell me that he was a salesman for a fertilizer company. I didn't even know that his family was in business.'

'And besides that time, did he come around to invite you out?'

'No, not to invite me out. It seemed that he was just in the neighborhood and so he dropped by.'

'You said that he stopped by more than once. That would suggest that he was fond of you. Am I correct?'

'No, not quite. You see, I do Japanese sewing for a business, and so I can talk with people without interrupting my work. I don't suppose there's anyone in his neighborhood with the kind of leisure that I have.'

'When you were with him, what was your impression of his character?'

—*There's something not quite sincere about his words, but perhaps I should ignore that if possible. The words 'when you were with him' imply a more positive connection than we had, but it will be a nuisance to correct everything he says...*

'I really couldn't say,' she replied. 'He spoke well and seemed to enjoy talking, whether telling the truth or not.'

'I have the names of two or three women that Fujio Uno seems to have known fairly well. I was wondering whether you have any information about them?'

'No, I don't.' Yukiko said.

'Well, he seems to have had some romantic connection with them; several women seemed to have liked him. One of the women was on bad terms with her husband, and it seems that she had a deeper connection with Uno...I wonder whether you have any information about that?'

—*Of course, there's Hitomi, but I shan't mention her...*

'No, none at all.' She responded quietly. 'I heard nothing at all about that kind of thing.'

'Please forgive me for asking, but when you were with Uno, did you even once feel you were in danger of being killed?'

'No.'

'I wonder why that was? Uno used the same approach with every woman. He invited them for a drive. Then he forced himself on them and killed...'

'Well, he didn't with *me*,' Yukiko said.

'You must have been kind to him. After all, you were even considerate enough to dry my socks.'

'I don't choose to do things for just anybody. But if someone has wet socks, I don't mind drying them.'

'Have you any idea what made him commit such crimes?'

'Only that he seemed to have a tenuous connection to the world. He may not have had the experience of being responsible for something that only he could do,' Yukiko suggested. 'They say that his mother spoiled him terribly as he grew up, and that his father was extremely quiet and soft. He never taught him anything about a man's responsibilities. And then he turned over the shop to their son-in-law, and Mr. Uno didn't help at the store. Even so, he wasn't short of pocket money. Something like that was certainly not a respectable kind of life, was it?'

'You seem to know quite a bit,' Takato said.

'It's what I've seen in the weekly magazines—maybe in yours,' Yukiko said.

'So far, he's killed two people, the boy Ken and Kayo Aoki. He drew two more women—Tomoko Shimada and Reiko Suga—into dangerous situations and essentially caused their deaths. That's what they say. So on top of it all there may be still more crimes. The police think there are other killings, and so they're looking into missing persons to see if any fit this case. Don't you know anyone he was close to?'

—I don't completely trust anyone reporting for a weekly magazine, but I don't think this man Takato has particularly bad intentions...

'I'm sorry. I don't know anything about his circle of acquaintances.' she said.

'There's a rumor that you are paying the fees for Uno's lawyer. Is that true?'

'No, nothing is settled about that. If his family pays the fees, there's no need for me to do anything. But if they refuse, I found a lawyer at Mr. Uno's request, and so I shall pay.'

'But even if you don't pay,' Takato said, 'certainly the government will assign a lawyer. There's no chance of him winning in court is there?'

—That's just a nuisance kind of question...

'The lawyer is an acquaintance of mine, and so if the Uno family doesn't pay, I couldn't impose upon her.'

'How much have you paid for the lawyer?'

'I haven't received a bill. In the lawyer's judgment, it would be best for the Uno family to pay. However, if the Uno family does not pay off the bill completely, then I will have to do something about it,' Yukiko explained frankly.

'Have you had any communication from Fujio Uno about that? Some word that he's grateful, perhaps, that his case is going well—anything like that?'

'I've received a letter.'

'What kind of a letter?'

'I haven't opened it yet.'

Yukiko had notice Fujio's letter in her mail box as she was about to leave that morning. On the return address of the rough paper envelope were just the initials 'F.U.', so she supposed it was from Fujio. She had simply placed the letter on the cushion in her workroom and left the house.

On the one hand, she had thought she didn't want to lose the envelope while out on her errand, but at the same time she hadn't really wanted to read the letter. She was slightly curious about what he was thinking now in jail, but she also considered that the letter might contain another of Fujio's shrewd requests set out at tedious length, and the last thing she felt like doing was to read it on the way to do her shopping.

'I wonder if you would mind if I looked at the letter?' Takato said.

'No, I really don't think that would proper,' Yukiko replied.

'Is there something secret in it?'

'Not at all. But since it contains personal matters, I can't show it to someone without the writer's permission.'

'But you won't know until you read it. I don't mind waiting if you want to look at it,' Takato said.

Yukiko lit a flame under the kettle to prepare tea. Then returned to her guest, taking Fujio's letter with her from the work room. She was feeling somewhat uneasy about this magazine reporter.

—Even if I read the letter in private and tell him what's in it, there's no telling what he might write if he doesn't believe me. On the other hand, if I unhesitatingly read it in front of him and then tell him the contents, he'll probably be satisfied and leave...

Yukiko ran her eyes over the letter.

I suppose your well? I'm OK too. There's not much point to being well in a place like this.

Yukiko felt disappointed with this beginning. In her previous letter, she had written that there was no need to be in great shape while in prison. And in the same sentence Fujio wrote 'you and I;' but she didn't have such a close connection with him as all that.

I met the woman lawyer Mrs. Kazami and to tell you the truth I was surprised to see a woman. I understand her first name is Nagisa. Not a bad name but I don't like women with glasses. Shes blunt but she seems to get to whats necessary so that's OK with me.

The only pleasant thing in this place is to dream. I met a lot of women in my dreams. The police say I killed every woman I've met but thats not so. There was H who I went to Yokohama with. Then there was H.G. who translaited the book on Venice. There was also J.Y. who refused to go to school and wanted to have a hut in the mountains. And then there was the madonna at the apartment holding her new baby. They all sparkle like stars and when I think of it my life was not so bad. All of them come to meet me in my dreams.

But the last one was you. You are a woman I would not ordinarily be able to meet. I worshipped you and all because of those morning glories. I made a poem about those flowers.

My empty heart and my sorrow too is blue.
Morning glories die in daylight struggling
In the shadow outside and the brilliant daylight.

Probably my family will pay for the lawyer so just let them. I especially want to make my brother-in-law pay. I didn't kill any woman I'd want to let go on living. The ones I killed or abandoned were good for nothings. One was a fool who couldn't make a place for another person on a crowded train. Another was just too greedy. And the rest were just sluts. I hate that kind. I hate those who don't get punished for that. I don't hate those who suffer for sleeping around.

Please forgive me for not planting those morning glorie seeds. If I were outside I really would plant them. Believe me that's the truth.

Fujio's letter was hollow and filled with mistakes. Takato had been staring at Yukiko's face while she read.

She quickly finished and said, 'I'm sorry, but I can't let you read his letter. It's really a confession of his private life.'

'What does he say about the lawyer's fees?' Takato asked.

'He says that his family will pay the expenses.'

'Does he say anything else?'

'He wrote a poem. A poem about morning glories.'

'Could you let me see just that?'

'No. You would probably print it in your magazine. Do you intend to pay for the manuscript?' Yukiko said half in jest, but Takato took her seriously.

'Of course we will, and at a high price.'

'In that case, I shall consult with the lawyer next time I see her and tell her that you wish to buy the poem. I will let you know her reply about whether or not she will sell it,' Yukiko said quite formally.

'Did he write anything else?'

'He wrote a little about his reasons for killing and for not killing. Something to the effect that he didn't kill every woman he met. That's what he's been telling to the police.'

'My editor wanted to know about that, too. The story about him makes it sound as though he treated all women badly. I suppose there should be something in his defense.'

'One feels sorry for people killed in an accident. All traffic accidents are a pity. But Mr. Uno killed consciously and deliberately. It's difficult to defend that.'

'I suppose there are other women like you that he didn't murder— acquaintances, so to speak. I think we'd like to write about that, for his sake even.'

At that moment, the tea kettle began to whistle in the kitchen, signaling that the water was boiling. It was an English-style kettle that Tomoko had bought just the previous month. She was concerned that Yukiko would get involved in her work and forget the kettle on the gas flame.

'Just a moment,' Yukiko said to her visitor. 'I'll make the tea and be right back.'
'Oh, please don't bother,' Takato said.
Yukiko stood up, then hesitated.
—*I don't want to leave Fujio's letter there on the table, but taking it with me would be too obviously impolite, as if I was saying I can't trust Takato...*
Casually, she picked up the letter and placed it on a shelf with some knick-knacks at a distance from her visitor.
—*Well, that could be taken simply as clearing a space for the tea...*

The following day, Yukiko went to her bank and withdrew the entire amount of her time-deposit savings, a total of 300,000 yen, even though the deposit period had not expired. The assistant manager appeared and asked what she needed the money for, adding that it would be better for her to leave the money on deposit and take out a guaranteed loan. But Yukiko laughed off the suggestion, saying that she was not used to borrowing. At the same time, she was also aware of how little she understood economics. Rather than going through the red tape for the slight difference in interest, she told herself it was as though she was depositing the money in a savings account. In addition to the 300,000 yen, Yukiko withdrew 200,000 yen from her passbook account. She sealed the 500,000 yen total in cash in an envelope, and then went directly to the Kazami law offices.

At the office, the two young women secretaries apologized to Yukiko that Counselor Kazami was out just then, even though Yukiko had come without an appointment.
'That's all right. Please give this to her,' Yukiko said, presenting the envelope.
'Well, accepting money isn't...'
'It's all right,' Yukiko said. 'I'll telephone later.'
'Alright. When Mrs. Kazami returns, I'll have her call you immediately.'

Mrs. Kazami called Yukiko soon after 7 p.m.
'I'm sorry I missed you, but I went out to Chiba today,' she said. 'You didn't have to pay that much. Mr. Uno's family said that they would pay his legal fees.'
'But the problem is that they haven't actually paid, I suppose?'
'There has only been one week of investigation expenses since your first request,' Kazami said.
'But, presumably, you've not been paid for the week?' Yukiko replied.
'That's true. But the Uno family has been busy during that time, and they may not been be able to get down to things right away...'
'If it were my son, I would transfer money the next day for his legal expenses.

However, I'd like you to keep the money as a deposit. You should use it in case the Uno family does not pay. Is that all right? And if the Uno family finally pays, I'll accept the money back from you.'

'All right,' Kazami agreed, 'that's what we'll do. I'm not patient enough to go into repeated arguments and counter-arguments!'

'I received a letter from Mr. Uno,' Yukiko said.

'Oh? Last time I went to interview him, he said it took him three days to write a letter to you.'

'This letter's not so long that it would take three days to write.'

'In detention, even when you're writing a letter, there's a guard in the room with you. That must make it harder. He talked to me about the other two people he killed. He's aware that the police have quite a bit of evidence on that, but he thinks that if he tells them where the bodies are, he will go to trial and receive a death sentence all the sooner.'

Yukiko had a busy week ahead of her. It was her impression that with each passing year, fewer women were wearing kimono; but even though this was not her usual busy season, she had been steadily at her sewing all week. In the past few years, there had been an increase in the number of women choosing to wear traditional dress when they went abroad. For some time now, men had been leaving for new duties abroad with their families, and husbands and wives often had to appear together at academic and international meetings. Kimono seemed suitable for the many special programs and sightseeing trips organized for the women on those occasions.

Yukiko worked steadily, although from time to time she felt disturbed by various things that seemed to be rolling around inside her head like pebbles.

—*Why did that reporter from Now Weekly come to see me?*

There was no subsequent communication from him, of course. Yukiko looked for a newspaper advertisement for the magazine without finding any mention of it.

—*I wonder what day of the week it goes on sale? Perhaps I missed it...*

For human beings, not knowing about something means that it doesn't exist. But one day Yukiko was made to realize that those small pebbles in her mind were more than silent gall stones.

On various occasions, Yukiko had met and spoken with a woman by the name of Takako Kamioka at church. Takako was in her early fifties and rather plump; she gave the impression of being intelligent and capable. At the church bazaar, she was the kind of person who could plan things and take the initiative and work without too much discussion. One day, without calling first, Takako appeared at Yukiko's house.

'Excuse me for dropping in like this while you're working...,' she said.

'Not at all,' Yukiko said. 'Please come in.'

'Thank you. I'll only stay a few minutes.'

Whatever she wished to say, it seemed inappropriate for her to remain standing in the hallway.

'I hope you'll excuse this intrusion, but there is something I thought I ought to talk to you about. I wonder if you've seen this weekly magazine?' Takako removed a copy of *Now Weekly* from her leather-and-batik handbag and set it on the table in front of Yukiko. The headline in bold letters on the cover proclaimed '**The Women Around Fujio Uno**'. 'I was told that your name appears in this as one of "the women around Fujio Uno." I thought you should know about the article, if you haven't seen it already, and so I dropped by.'

'No, I don't know anything about it,' Yukiko said. She looked for the page with the article and ran her eyes over the text.

Yukiko remained composed, even though the article made her feel somewhat uneasy. The article described five women associated with Fujio. She was the final one.

The area where Miss Y. (38) lives is not far from the ocean and the scene of Uno's murders. Her house is close to the sea and surrounded by the smell of the ocean breeze. There, while she works alone at her Japanese sewing, her thoughts turn to Uno.

Miss Y. likes to raise flowers and plants morning glories each year. Uno and she became close friends when the flowers were in bloom and Uno had stopped to admire them. This is the person Uno calls his 'last woman.'

Miss Y. is a Christian and was therefore shocked to learn about Uno's other women.

"At first, I thought how pitiful a person he was. I would have paid his legal expenses, but I thought better of it when I came to know the circumstances. My sympathy is simply exhausted," she said, not concealing her despair.

No matter how fiendish a murderer a man might be, if he is completely honest a woman will cling to some hope to the last. But, having been betrayed, Miss Y. seems to be quite chagrined.

Uno has been abandoned by his last girlfriend.

One could hardly blame a reader for identifying Yukiko, for Takato had taken a photograph of the front of her house which, though not too clear, appeared in a small circle on the page.

Yukiko smiled and said, 'Yes, Mr. Uno did speak to me and came to look at the garden. I told the police about that, but I am *not* Uno's girlfriend.'

'Of course not,' Takako replied. 'I told everyone that I couldn't imagine you'd have any connection with him.' She seemed quite relieved, hearing Yukiko's explanation. 'But even father Izumi apparently said that you might know Fujio Uno. So some people seem to believe this article. And that's such a difficult thing.'

'Yes, I explained to Father Izumi about Mr. Uno speaking to me, and so he already knew we'd met.'

'Then do you think it was Father Izumi who gave this peculiar story to the magazine?'

'No, I don't think so. I think it was just the writer's speculation,' Yukiko said.

'It's certainly disagreeable.'

'When did the magazine come out?'

'Two days ago.'

Yukiko calculated the days. The article had appeared only three days after Takato had visited her. In her naive way, she had supposed that the story might appear a week or two later at least.

'May I borrow this magazine?' Yukiko asked Takako.

'Oh, yes, please do. I don't need it.'

When Takako departed, Yukiko immediately returned to the guest room where the magazine was placed.

—So it was a mistake to trust that reporter, after all. Very likely he secretly took a photograph of the letter while I was out of the room getting tea, and then he made his article by searching based on the initials and little hints in the letter…

Yukiko was shocked to find that the article quoted the morning glory poem precisely.

—Fujio may be a murderer, but that's still an infringement on his rights as the writer of the poem! People will think I sold it to the magazine…

She felt her fingertips chill at the thought.

Yukiko calmed herself and read in the article about the other four women described in the article as 'Fujio's women.' 'H' was presumably Hitomi. The person referred to as the 'apartment Madonna holding her new-born child' was surely Mitsuko Kanaya, the victim in the rape incident. Thankfully, not even the weekly magazine had been able to find out exactly who she was. In any case, it seemed that Fujio's attack upon her had been a matter of chance. Naturally, the article did not come out and say clearly that the writer had been unable to discover who she was. His posture was that they could not report the details of the incident in the mass media as a matter of principle. About the other women, it said that they were able to meet a certain 'J.Y.', who wanted to own a mountain hut, and also 'H.G', who had translated something about the city of Venice.

Yukiko kept herself in check and read the article for a second time. The reporter said that 'while she works alone at her Japanese sewing, her thoughts turn to Uno.'

—It could hardly be otherwise! Someone I happen to know turns out to be not only a murderer, but a serial murderer! Of course I was amazed to discover that. It's only natural that I can't get the matter out of my head…

The reporter had used the phrase 'her thoughts turn' which offered the clear connotation, if the reader wished to perceive it, that Yukiko had some romantic feelings for Fujio. On the other hand, the article said that it was because she was a Christian that she had been shocked to learn that he knew other women.

—I can only think that the reporter wrote that because he knows nothing about Christianity. If he understood what it means to be a real Christian, he would have no reason to write that, since my faith includes the realization of the depths of evil that humans are capable of…

On top of everything, the words attributed to Yukiko in the article were entirely fabricated. She had never said anything about Fujio having other women, about regarding that as betrayal, or about stopping payment of his legal expenses. Yukiko had taken the money for the lawyer's expenses only the day after the reporter had visited her.

—I don't mind paying money for Fujio simply because I felt there was something to love somewhere in a person who is now called 'a murderous fiend.' He came into my world one day amongst the bright morning glories, and he committed crimes that I would never otherwise encounter during my whole life. I intend to pay the price for that meeting, rather like a fee for watching a drama. Perhaps that's an indelicate way to put it? So I should say, as payment for the experience of being in the midst of this unimaginable situation.

If you happen to pass by the scene of an accident where someone has been injured and is lying trembling beside the road, you will take off your coat and cover the injured person even without having any connection to them. At the time, you don't stop to think about whether the coat was new or expensive, or that it will be stained with blood. That, at least, is my posture with regard to Fujio.

In Father Izumi's sermons, he has talked about the nature of love that Christ expects of human beings. It is quite different from the natural love we might have for another person. In the Greek manuscripts of the New Testament, the word 'love' is differentiated from 'natural affection' and 'brotherly love.' What the Bible says about loving one's enemy is based upon the tragedy of humans being unable to love an enemy. Though we may not naturally love a person, we can yet be without rancor; and, if we have the will, we can perform the same actions that we would through love. She understood that the Bible prescribes this kind of love for our divided hearts, commanding us to follow the more difficult

378

path wherein love can even be filled with contradiction and bitterness.
The reporter from Now Weekly was surely ignorant of the contradiction with
human nature and the consequent suffering involved in the Christian
commandment on love. He simply took the common idea that if there was
another woman involved, I would certainly think myself betrayed and stop
payments to the lawyer!

She read what Takato had written about the other women, but she was puzzled
as to how he had uncovered material about Hitomi. Yukiko wondered if Hitomi
had spoken to someone else other than her about that day. If not, it suggested
that it was Yukiko herself who must have revealed the identify of the woman
referred to as 'H' in *Now Weekly*.

Yukiko's fingertips felt chilled again as she read this treatment in the magazine
article. Through the lead the reporter had to Hitomi, he had also discovered
where her husband worked and had talked with him about everything. Yukiko
considered that to be extremely cruel. However, Hitomi's husband came through
splendidly. 'If I take what you say as the truth, then somehow we should be
grateful that she is alive,' he was quoted in the article. Of course there was no
photograph of the apartment where Hitomi lived, and there were no specifics
about her husband's work or other matters. So they might be saved from the
distressing trouble with the public that Yukiko was having to suffer. And yet, if
she was the source of the rumor, they might deeply resent her. She trembled as
she read it again.

Regarding the person indicated by the initials 'H.G.' who had translated a
book about Venice, Takato had written:

> She seemed to have some lingering attachment to this bold and free soul: 'We
> met in a bookstore. He was naive and didn't know a thing, so I taught him. I'd
> do the same for anyone. If I'd known he was going to be so famous, I would
> have examined more closely what kind of a person he was—in some safe sur-
> roundings, of course. Ha, ha, ha.'

The girl he had picked up referred to as 'J.Y.' disliked school and idly wandered
around town. The article quoted her as saying such things as:

> 'Being with him was more fun than going to school. He had lots to say. I didn't
> think he was so bad at all. He was real nice to me.'

The two of them had apparently gone for a drive, then stopped at a coffee shop
and gone to a hotel.

Yukiko didn't believe any of it. When she saw what was written about her, she could only wonder if anything written there was true about the other women. She truly wished to find out why the magazine had done this kind of thing; she felt it was close to thievery. As she looked at Takato's business card, Yukiko felt considerable misgivings. Presently, she took up the phone and dialed the company's number. She asked to be connected with Mr. Takato of *Now Weekly*.

'Takato has not come in today,' the man who had answered the phone said sullenly, but not impolitely.

'What time will he be in?' Yukiko asked.

'Well, I don't know what his schedule is today. May I ask who's calling?'

Yukiko said that she was one of the people from whom Takato had gotten information about the Fujio Uno case. The man, who was apparently in the editorial department of the magazine, asked her to wait a moment while he transferred the call. The voice of the next man to answer was as indifferent as the one before.

'What can I do for you?' he asked.

'After Takato-san came to get information from me,' Yukiko said, 'he wrote something quite different from what I told him, and so I'm calling to find out why he did that.'

'I see. The fact is, Takato is not a regular member of our staff. He's what we call a 'stringer,' a free agent who contracts to write on a topic of the week. At other times he works for other companies, so I wouldn't know where he is when he's out on other work. However, I'll let him know what points are mistaken if you wish to tell him.'

'Yes. He wrote things that I absolutely did not say. And then, about Fujio Uno's poem—that was in a letter that came to my house, and I did not have permission to show it to anyone. I believe that the man called Takato took a photograph of the letter while I was out of the room preparing tea.' Yukiko went on to explain the rest of the meeting.

'I won't know until I ask Takato,' the man said, 'but I wonder if the problem came up when you put the letter aside and left the room. I wonder if he interpreted that as a suggestion that he might look at it?'

'And I wonder if that could be the interpretation for a letter I put somewhere far away from where he was sitting and where he could not reach it?' Yukiko's voice showed disappointment rather than anger.

'Well, I wasn't present and so I can't tell you anything more,' the man said. 'But when Takato returns next week, I'll ask about that and have him reply to you.'

'Besides all that, do you intend to pay a fee for the use of Mr. Uno's poem?'

'Yes, of course we do. I can't give you an answer immediately, but it's likely that Takato may have spoken already with our accounting department. Actual payment is made two or three weeks after publication.'

'However, I believe that you should have had Mr. Uno's permission first before publication.'

'Takato will be in next Tuesday. I will have him call you then. Could you give me your telephone number?'

Yukiko thought that would be futile, and so she ended her call. There was nothing she could do. She felt depressed.

—The conversation I had with Takato that day was confidential, but there is no way to prove anything about the content of our conversation. I have no way to counter him if he claims to have heard one thing, no matter how I might try to deal with him. And how difficult all this must be for Hitomi; she must feel that suddenly her privacy has been completely destroyed...

Yukiko felt confused and finally decided that she would have to tell all of this to Nagisa Kazami. She telephoned to the lawyer's office and was told that she was away in Chiba working on another case and would not be returning until late.

'Is there any way to contact her at her destination?' Yukiko inquired. She heard only that Kazami would be moving from place to place so could not be contacted.

'Then I will call her early tomorrow,' Yukiko said and hung up the phone. Mrs. Kazami had told her that the best way to catch her was around 8:30 in the morning.

It was already late in the day, but Yukiko didn't feel like preparing dinner. For the first time she knew what it was like to have people pointing at you behind your back. When she went out shopping, she had the feeling that people were muttering, 'Well, look at that, will you!' Of course, she was probably being oversensitive. Her face hadn't appeared in the article, and so there was no way that anyone could distinguish her.

Inevitably, however, there were rumors among the people at her church, even among those who said she certainly did not seem to be the kind who would be so involved. Salacious stories that entertained the dull-minded spread with great speed.

Day turned into evening and darkness spread through the room where Yukiko was sitting. She didn't turn on a light; she was comfortable in the darkness, and she had no wish to meet anyone or to go outside. For the first time, Yukiko understood the meaning of the world growing narrow.

Then, at a little past eight o'clock, the ring of the telephone stabbed through the darkness. Yukiko thought for certain that it would be Nagisa Kazami, but it was Tomoko's voice.

'Oh, Tomo-chan, how are you?'

'How do you think I am?' said Tomoko, sounding angry. 'Don't sound so normal! Have you seen that magazine?'

NO REASON FOR MURDER

'Yes, I saw it today.'

'You did? How?'

'Someone from church saw the photograph of the house and recognized it.'

'Under the circumstances, that's about all it takes. Did you meet that reporter?'

'Yes. Because I had no idea what he was going to write if I tried to avoid him.'

'Yuki-chan, when are you going to grow up and stop being so stupid?' Tomoko sighed. 'You're really not so ignorant of the world, you know. You have no idea what they will write when you talk with them.'

'They said he was a stringer, not a regular member of the company.'

'Of course they did. Then they can get away without any responsibility. I was afraid it would come to this. The moment you felt there was something odd about Uno, I was sure this would happen unless you stopped seeing him.'

'Tomo-chan, what do you think I should do? Really, what *Now Weekly* published was hardly anything at all.'

Yukiko knew that she had to remain calm, and she wanted Tomoko's advice. No matter what kind of business came up, she thought she should always listen modestly to the opinion of someone who knew better than her about it.

'Just do whatever you wish. You've got yourself involved in this foolishness, and there's no easy way to get out of it.'

'Yes, that's true,' Yukiko replied softly.

'And Mitsuko Kanaya's situation has gone from bad to worse. Her home life is a real mess, and it's totally due to that man.'

'What's happened? What did she do after that?'

'Well, if you're interested, go and have a look for yourself.' With that, Tomoko abruptly hung up the phone.

To calm herself, Yukiko went to her sewing room and sat with her legs folded under her. Her cushion was old-style, stuffed with cotton and rather thin and hard, perhaps proof of the saying that the tailor is the last to be well outfitted. She could have bought a nice cushion with soft, artificial stuffing, but she had made this one from some old silk clothing that had been passed down to her from her grandmother's time. She had never got around to repairing it. She thought that this flattened thing stuffed with natural cotton might be best for doing her work.

Seated on her cushion at her familiar spot, she had often thought out things in the past. A brilliant person would have found an answer immediately, but Yukiko needed time to find her way. Sometimes she would think over the same problem for days, or even months. But she had come to believe that this uncertain process was necessary for her. In human life, everything except death was a process, and though it might seem foolish, repeated time and again, she felt we probably need that tempo itself.

Seen against all that had happened, Yukiko wondered if there was any purpose at all in a person like Fujio Uno being born.

What good was it to kill a healthy young boy and those young women? Yukiko didn't like living by calculation. There are many slips in human calculations, but there seem to have been an awful lot of miscalculations in Fujio's life especially.

Yukiko believed that once a stain was made it could not be removed. She had once heard it said that there was only one person in all Japan who could completely remove a stain from dyed cloth. And, in popular opinion, it was impossible even to try to remove the stain of disgrace. You could only live with it, Yukiko told herself, though she remained dissatisfied with that answer. For her, happily, there was God. She was not a good Christian, and while she had not been understood by the reporter from the weekly magazine, she hoped that she was understood by God.

But, for the moment, she was concerned with what Tomoko had said, and she decided to try calling Mitsuko on the phone. Yukiko's 'hasty actions' did not seem to have produced any direct injury to Mitsuko, and now that Yukiko was more controlled about her feelings, her emotions had cooled into consideration of her own safety. The feeling embarrassed her.

Yukiko waited nearly an hour, turning matters over in her mind. Then she stood up and went to the phone to call Mitsuko. The phone rang a dozen times with no response; Yukiko supposed that Mitsuko was away from her apartment. That did relieve her feelings slightly. It suggested she was really reluctant to call Mitsuko.

But just as she was about to give up, a voice came on the phone with so little life in it that it seemed more like an echo from the depths of hell than a human utterance.

'Mitsuko? This is Yukiko Hata, Tomoko's sister,'

'Oh, I haven't heard from you in a while.' Mitsuko's words were an automatic reaction.

'How are you doing? Tomoko and I have been concerned about you.'

As she said these words, Yukiko felt the pain of the situation with special sharpness.

'Thank you for calling,' Mitsuko said.

'How has your husband been doing?'

Yukiko didn't touch on the matter of Mitsuko's pregnancy.

'My husband...is in hospital,' she said.

'Oh? What's the matter with him?

'I don't know exactly. He's in the psychiatric ward.'

Yukiko hardly knew how to continue the conversation.

'So is there something specifically wrong?'

'I don't know, really. At first, it seemed to be something like withdrawal since he wasn't going to his office. He seemed to be suffering a little for a while, but now he seems to have no feeling at all. He's not suffering; he just watches television every day at the hospital.'

'I suppose it's good that he's enjoying television,' Yukiko said.

'Yes, he's watching, but when I ask him, he doesn't know what program he's watching.'

'What could it be?'

'It's like he's brain dead, or in a trance.'

'That's terrible!' Yukiko replied. 'He's only...how old?'

'He's just thirty-five.'

'Please excuse me for saying this, but nobody really knows the cause-and-effect relationship, so it may not be because of that. Perhaps the incident precipitated something that was hardly apparent in the past?'

'I don't know. I don't have any idea at all. He just went over to the other side.'

'What other side?'

'Who knows? Someplace not in this world.'

'But your husband's still alive.'

Mitsuko's voice seemed to be sinking into a dark void. Yukiko had the feeling she was watching her through a videophone. Mitsuko must have been bending down. Yukiko felt that she was standing in front of her and that her voice expressed her posture. A listener can tell when someone is bent over speaking, even though the person can't be seen; there is always a certain echo in the voice.

'You said your husband was in hospital and there's no special treatment, right?'

'That's right,' Mitsuko said.

Mitsuko spoke very few words. That often means that the telephone conversation is bothering the person at the other end, but in this case Yukiko didn't think that was the reason.

'Do you think it would be better for him to return home? It would be livelier for you,' Yukiko suggested.

'Yes, but even if he came home, he wouldn't say anything. It would be like living with someone who looks like him but isn't him, like being with a living corpse. That would be all the more bitter.'

'And how about you? Have you been well since then?'

It was the best question Yukiko could come up with in the situation. She hadn't asked Tomoko about how Mitsuko had resolved the pregnancy resulting from the rape.

'I've been well, thank you,' Mitsuko replied.

'And the baby has been doing well?'

'Yes.'

'I suppose it's grown quite big?' Yukiko said. 'Mitsuko, I was wondering if I could visit you? Would that be all right? Tomorrow perhaps?'

'Yes, please do,' Mitsuko said.

Yukiko thought that she would make no surmises from what she had heard. She said that she would visit about ten o'clock the following morning. Mitsuko said that would be fine.

—*Could this really be the lively editor who Tomoko thought so highly of?*

After hanging up the phone, Yukiko checked to see that the doors were locked. In the corridor, there was a window without shutters, and Yukiko went there to check on the weather. That evening the moon was nearly full. To Yukiko, it was as though, by some magic, time had come to a standstill. She was sometimes asked whether her life was lonely without children, but it seemed to her that God had given her the gift of delusion to take care of that. In a household where nothing is raised, humans don't grow old.

—*I wonder what Fujio's doing now? Is he already sleeping? He said that the interrogations are severe; perhaps even at this hour he's in the brightly-lit interrogation room of the Miura Police Station? On the other hand, if he has already returned to his cell, he should be feeling extreme horror on a quiet, moonlit night like this...*

Chapter 24

A BIRTHDAY GIFT

Dear Mr. Uno,

I have heard from the lawyer, Mrs. Kazami, that she visited you and that you are well. I'm glad about that. When people are well, they can think properly. Some popular opinion has it that precisely because someone is sick they can think deeply, and healthy people can't do that, no matter how they try. For people like that, illness is a wonderful thing. However, I am a weak-spirited person, and even if I'm pricked by a thorn, I can't do a thing, as happened the other day.

I raise cucumbers, eggplants and tomatoes in my little garden of barely ten square meters. While I was working there, a thorn stuck in my finger. I removed it with a needle, but it seems that part of it remained deeply embedded and I couldn't get it out. I didn't want to go to the doctor with such a trifling thing, and so I was resigned to the bit of thorn coming out by itself. For the whole day that thorn made me feel uneasy.

I know that time is more precious for you than it is for me, though you have to think about your miserable situation. But being in tolerably good health is at least a happy thing.

I learned from Counselor Kazami that you are going to reveal two more dead bodies. If I were to write and say 'Please tell them about it quickly', you would assume that I have been directed to write that by the police. You would become angry, and so I will say nothing. I am neither cooperating with the police nor going against them.

I am sure the police want to know about the 'apartment Madonna and child' you wrote about in your letter to me. I know you didn't kill her, but clearly she was your victim, so the police must think that if they hear about her from you, then it may lead to the discover of the bodies of the two young women. However, I won't say who she is or where she is.

Recently, I visited her at home. I found that her life and her family are effectively destroyed. Her husband is now in a psychiatric hospital. I couldn't find out from her the exact name of his illness. You may say that possibly his illness dates from before that incident, but that would only be the root of his illness, and you are the immediate cause for what has happened to him.

The 'apartment Madonna' is now nearly mute and can speak only a few words.

A Birthday Gift

Her apartment's in disarray. Garbage is piled up in the kitchen and a disagreeable odor floats through the rooms. The window curtains are torn in places. Nothing has been repaired.

That 'Madonna' was not a slovenly person in the past. She was pretty, and she was a hard worker—an acquaintance of mine knew her well from that time, and she says that she was a proper kind of person, demanding equal rights with men and advancing at her job the same as a man—the kind of active person who would have repaired damaged curtains immediately.

You should also know that the child you saw that day is doing well. He's a healthy child and laughs a lot. But I am concerned if the mother is giving the child balanced nourishment. According to you, the story of the 'apartment Madonna' was simply a rape that went well. It's only your lack of imagination that allows you to think that.

I'm afraid that your action destroyed not only the husband and wife but that it will probably make a mess of the child's life as well. When the child grows up, very likely he'll try to find out from people why the ordered lives of his mother and father were suddenly destroyed soon after he was born.

The child saw your actions perfectly that day. You may say that a child that age won't remember a thing. However, I'm certain that people do remember extraordinary events from their infancy. And you violated the mother right before the child's eyes.

I will now tell you the most saddening thing of all.

I learned from Counselor Kazami that you said you "were really in love with her then." Even though that is a totally selfish way of loving, I realize that you are probably not lying. As a consequence of your action, she became pregnant; the child is yours.

For a moment, I foolishly imagined that she might be able to continue the pregnancy. My sister laughed at that idea. Still, having heard the story of the child lost to your former wife when she was pregnant, I was constrained by the thought that the child was yours, even if by chance. If there is one child in the world that has your blood, I thought that you might be happy.

When I told that to my sister, she was amazed and said that kind of case was one of the specific reasons abortions were allowed. Even so, I had some small hope that the mother might perhaps reject the idea of an abortion. But I was just being foolish. No one will raise a child that is the seed of such misery, and I suppose the general public understands that as the wise thing to do.

In any case, it was natural that she had an abortion. After all, the child was created by the person who caused the destruction of her family. It is not just that you killed several young women and a child; you ended up by killing your own child.

That night, I thought about you being instrumental in killing your own child, and my heart truly ached. Perhaps I should say this revenge was imposed upon you—but it was the child who was killed, not you. And the woman cannot be blamed for that.

The idea that a child is born innocent is just a theory. Human beings are not so reasonable. If that child was alive, then every time the mother scolded it for some prank she would wonder whether she was scolding the child because of her grudge against you. Nobody could endure being burdened with that.

I also want to apologize for what has leaked out about the content of your letter. I believe that Counselor Kazami has already told you and explained the circumstances, and you magnanimously said that it was all right. And about the poem: I heard that you are satisfied with the ¥5,000 they paid for the manuscript.

Also, I have heard that since then you have published what seem to be your notes titled "Why I Killed the Women and the Child," and that you were very pleased for it to appear in the mass media. In fact, all the weekly magazines have published articles with such titles as "Conversation with Uno," and "Uno's Views on Life," which may or may not contain any truth. They've been swarming around you like ants.

However, most articles are jeering things with titles like "How Terrible to Be Killed Because You Didn't Sit Properly in the Train!" and "Department Store Clerks Who Don't Know Where Things Are Sold—Be Careful!!" And the other day in one newspaper, there was a letter from an elderly woman reader saying, "It's bad to kill, but I agree it's really terrible the way young people don't sit properly on the trains."

According to one magazine, Ken Okada said, "If you kill a child like me, it will be a loss to society and to the nation," and that you exploded because of that. But Ken's words are now becoming a popular saying. For example, if someone spills some coffee, other people describe it as 'a social loss.' It's even abbreviated to 'so-loss.' I'm sure that this will please you. You have probably never had so much attention.

Since it has some connection with you, I'll tell you a bit about my own life. I believe that you heard from Counselor Kazami that I'm generally believed to know you well? Although my face didn't appear, a photograph of my house was published, without my permission, in connection with the matter of that magazine getting hold of your poem. All of that apparently happened because I foolishly admitted to being an acquaintance of yours—but I could hardly do otherwise.

You said you were attracted by the 'Heavenly Blue' morning glories that day, and so you stopped at my front garden. After that you seemed to need someone like me—always busy with work but with an empty mind—to sooth your own overwrought head, since you didn't have any friends.

The first mistake I made was in trusting that reporter. Even though I complained to the editor, the reporter didn't return my phone call. I soon gave up. My sister told me that often people like novelists might seem at first glance to be intellectual, but they are all basically gangsters, and it's best not to associate with them. I suppose that journalists are the same.

About four days after the first article was published, my telephone rang. A completely different magazine was calling and wanted to meet and talk with me. I wondered how they found out my name and address. It was really something. I said that I wouldn't meet with anybody, but the phone continued to ring morning and night.

I heard that you said to Counselor Kazami that it is better the magazines write something bad about you than nothing at all. Of course you would think that, and that's your business. But still, if you really think that, then from the very beginning you have lacked the sensibility to feel people's contempt. Or perhaps it has just been worn down?

Whenever I heard the telephone ring, I was sure it was from one of the weekly magazines, and I wondered what I should do. It could be bad for my work if I didn't answer the phone, but I decided not to pick up the phone for about ten days. During that time I tried to think of what to do. I put a pillow under the phone and wrapped the whole thing in a blanket, but I could still hear it ringing and it got on my nerves. Generally people will give up after ten days if something's no good, I thought, and I usually give up after only about three days—or after calling just three times! And so I decided not to answer the phone for ten days.

But that afternoon the doorbell rang. I called out to ask who it was and found that it was the reporter who had reached me on the telephone. I didn't open the door, nor did I respond any further. The doorbell rang many times, but I just went on with my work inside. In such circumstances it's better to continue working and try to keep your composure instead of worrying about it and bearing it in silence. I suppose that even if I were suffering a fatal disease, I would still continue to water the flowers, sew and wash clothes as far as my strength would allow.

The reporter remained outside the gate for more than thirty minutes, then finally went away. I was relieved, and thought that would be the end of it.

However, the next morning, about 7:30, he arrived again.

"I'm sorry that you've come so early, but I've decided not to meet with anyone regarding the Uno matter," I said. Then he said, "I really want to talk with you, and I'll just wait until you change your mind."

I said nothing at all to that, and so from that time on he sat at my front gate. He didn't move from there at all. He disappeared at night, but he was there again by 8 in the morning. I didn't go out of the house for five full days, nor did I answer the telephone.

You might think I wouldn't go to that extreme, but he actually stayed at the gate in front of the house for four days! He probably thought that I would have to go outside sometime. And then—although I may have been imagining this—I had the feeling that he thought I would become afraid of what people would think and finally break down and allow him inside. But I resolved simply to remain quiet.

My food selection was limited. On the other hand, I found that it's just as well to eat up what's in the house. I suppose that every household has lots of canned or dried food leftovers that are a nuisance. I ate one such thing each day, seasoning it carefully, and I regarded that as a small test of my cooking skills! I also started to feel happy about the steadily diminishing materials on my kitchen shelf.

Besides those things, the few vegetables I raise in my garden kept me going—spinach, garland chrysanthemums, mustard spinach, and bok choy. Although I only planted them in my spare time, they have grown quite well, and while they'd hardly be enough for a household of adults, they're enough for one person.

As it happened, my sister returned home on the fifth day. She needed something from here, and she said she'd called numerous times, but since I didn't answer, she thought I might have died or something. So she came to find out what had happened. When she saw that I was alive and well, she seemed to be angry and immediately went back to Tokyo.

I still hesitate a bit about going out because I have the feeling that people might gossip about me if I go into town. But I want to say that I've had a good experience. The fact that I have been able to remain silent is because God is within me. It is a happiness to experience life alone with that. Being alone can be bitter, but I have the feeling it is something basic to the way human beings live. I don't mean it sarcastically when I say that is an experience I owe to you.

I learned from Counselor Kazami that you asked about my birthday. It's June 10th.

You once gave me a small blue porcelain dish. I wonder what I would have felt if I'd known then that you'd stolen it? Since I learned about that, I've kept it wrapped in paper, without using it, so that I might return it. On someone's birthday, you should really try to give them something that pleases them.

I pray for you every day,

Yukiko Hata

Yukiko received Fujio's next letter on June 20th. He mis-wrote the characters for 'soul searching,' and the lighthearted tone of the letter totally lacked sincerity.

June 18
Dear Yukiko Hata,

I got your letter. Sorry for all the troubles you had! It seems that this matter has

A Birthday Gift

been causing trouble everywhere. I'm deeply sorry. But I'll do some deep soulsearching.

Bet you like your birthday present this time. Because you said its what you wanted (I heard it from Counselor Kazami!) I took them to the bodies of the two women I killed. Believe me that was the last card I had to play.

I thought I'd show them one this year for your birthday and one next year for your birthday but the two were buried close together and there was a pretty good chance they would find them at the same time and so I thought you'd be twice as happy if they came up with two.

When they got Yoko Miki and Yoshiko Yamane out I was pretty disappointed. The place was really close to your house so I thought I could go near your place on the way, but the cops screwed that up.

The dawn was great at the place by the shore where I let the Shimada girl out of the car. I think my life has been quite good whatever others might think. But still I wanted to go near your house.

I wanted to see your house one more time. Just once would be fine. I know there's no chance of meeting you, but if those blue morning glories were in bloom it would be fantastic! I know it isn't the season yet for morning glories. I want to ask you to plant some morning glorie seeds for me, OK?

The blue I see is my youth
which I now regret.
And taking blue flowers with me
I'll return to the sky.

Life here isn't too bad. I'm writing some poems. Sometimes I feel really bad and there are days when I think I'll never be discouraged by the police. People are saying I'm a murdering fiend or that I'm not human but I'm the one who knows best whether I'm a murdering fiend or not human.

I'm really just an ordinary guy. I'm glad I didn't become like one of those people who easily criticises me. I wood rather be a criminal than a good man who blames other people for everything.

I heard my mom has broken down. My father was always sickly, but he's still obstinately hanging on. After all the people who put up a strong front are the ones who get hit worst.

When they caught me that brother-in-law of mine looked like a ghost and now he looks a lot better and seems happy my mother wrote to me the other day. He's been hoping I'd be put here so I bet he's relieved. Some nights I think that I'd like to live a long time just to harass him and then sometimes early in the morning I think I'll just give up and die.

I'm really angry about the guy from the weakly magazine whose keeping you locked in. If I was there I'd stop it.

Take care,

Fujio Uno

July 10

Dear Mr. Uno,

I received your last letter. Even though you made some mistakes in writing, there was nothing I didn't understand, and I liked your poem much more than the one before.

I'm sure that there are few women in the world who have received such a birthday present as I have. In material terms, your gifts were a stolen dish and two corpses. I felt as though a Greek myth or some story from the Old Testament had come to life.

Concerning all that, it was before dawn on June 10th. I was still asleep and was woken up by an unfamiliar sound. There were a number of vehicles heading in the same direction, toward the shoreline road. If they'd been going toward town, I thought, it would have been a fire. But it was odd to hear several cars going on the road to the shore where there is almost nothing.

I dozed off again, and then, I suppose, the sounds got louder. It was just a little after seven o'clock and the sound of the cars mixed with voices of people hurrying past my house. In a little while, I heard on the news that two bodies had been recovered. The newspapers wrote that you said you wouldn't tell them until the end where the bodies were, in order to delay the court and stretch out your life. But that's not what happened.

If that was your present to me, I thank you for it, no matter how hard it is to say that.

When I think of how the families of those two young women will receive the bodies of their daughters, I am so distressed that I can hardly read about it, even though I hear about it all the time. A woman from my church called Takako Kamioka came to visit and told me about the article in a magazine that seemed to be about me. Sometimes she comes to visit me and I more or less confide in her. She said that Yoko Miki's husband broke down and cried and said that he should have paid more attention before it all came to this. The husband himself runs a plumbing company and works even on Sundays. He said that his wife was cheerful and managed their home very well, and he could only think that she was tempted by evil for having being involved with such a man.

Yoshiko Yamane's case was even more pitiful. Her home life was pretty bad. It seems that her mother's second husband was a teacher, but he hardly ever spoke with his stepdaughter. Her mother probably thought that since she was marrying a teacher, he would be fond of children, but in fact he was completely indifferent to the girl. He was the kind of man who comes home and does nothing but read girls' comic books. Of course, there are all sorts of people in the teaching profession. But with Yoshiko Yamane's family, it seems that there were no emotional ties at all for her at home, not even hateful ones. He was probably a mild enough father since he just quietly read comic books. But isn't indifference the highest form of cruelty?

At Counselor Kazami's office, I confronted the two women you killed—only in photographs, of course. I needed time to prepare myself before I looked at the pictures, though it was only a few seconds. I've never seen pictures like them before.

First she brought out a few pictures of Yoshiko Yamane. The first was a full-length shot. It may have been taken towards dawn, or at least while it was still dark, since the grass and the trunks of the trees stood out as white. It looked like the setting for a ghost scene in a kabuki play.

In the next picture, there seemed to be two bent human figures lying on the ground. I thought they'd been left on the ground, but then I noticed they were in front of a hole that had been dug.

I want to tell you first of all that when they dug up those women you killed with your own hands, their bodies looked terribly aged, both of them. The surprise of seeing that simply paralyzed my mind. There were wounds and decomposition, but both of their bodies were halfway turned into dolls, and where you could see the skin of those terrible figures it was like that of very old women. Frankly, even though they had changed so much, something in those bodies remained from when they were alive. For those women, death appeared clearly as an extreme kind of aging. Because of the circumstances of their murder, there was a sudden, unnatural kind of aging that covered them like a mosaic. I was terribly shocked. The sight took my breath away; I felt that I had to tell you how they really were.

Yoshiko Yamane was no longer human. She was only a lump of mud. She gave the impression of being a rotting straw doll buried in the ground, and, without knowing the circumstances, someone as naive as myself might have thought that the body had been partially burned. Also, even though her body had been buried and was at least halfway decomposed, it was quite evident from the photograph that her tongue was sticking out of her mouth. Was she trying to the very last to cry out? I gasped when I saw that.

Yoko Miki's body was in the same condition. Her face looked more like that of E.T. than the face of a human being, even though I've never actually seen that popular movie. Her nose was sunken, her eyes were just two little balls about the size of olives, and her teeth were exposed.

Wasn't the fact she was once pretty the reason you wanted to speak with her?

Of course it was. But aside from the fact of your having tea or going for a drive with a married woman behind her husband's back, why didn't you feel some love for such a pretty and lively woman like that?

That day there were a number of helicopters flying around here creating a lot of commotion. I just tried to keep myself together by continuing with my work.

I think that you should have seen those two bodies.

Yukiko Hata

August 5

Dear Mr. Uno,

As you requested, I planted the morning glory seeds, and recently the flowers have come into bloom.

Until last year, my morning glories blossomed vigorously in the smoky, golden light of morning, but this year I felt there was a deeply sad color to the flowers. Some days I feel that the sadness is irremediable, that it's just something that has to be endured. There are so many things like that. I feel that I know how to bear it now.

I heard from Counselor Kazami about you making lying confessions again. She laughed and said that you were aiming to confuse the police. If she'd been talking about someone I'd never even seen, I might simply have been amazed or laughed along with her. Did you really say, "You're making a big mistake if you think those are all the bodies. I buried a Filipina near Moroiso, and there's another office girl at Araiso"?

Why are you saying that you killed people when you didn't? Do you want to be the object of attention that much? There's no glory or anything else in being noticed by people, you know. Human happiness is a matter of being understood by a few good friends and living under the sun and stars quietly and freely in some corner of town. But there is a great difference between what you and I like in life.

It seems that your trial will begin in the fall. Counselor Kazami and I rarely mention the probable outcome of your trial. It's too bad for her that there's no chance of winning, and it's too painful to speak about the consequences. However, Mrs. Kazami is not complaining about the case, and she hasn't given up all hope—although I don't wish to suggest that you will receive a lighter sentence. This has nothing to do with your sentence—to put it clearly, it has nothing to do with the judgment of human law. What remains is the question of how you will live during the time you have left.

I'm not saying "Please repent," or anything like that. I detest talk like that. Whatever you feel is up to you, and I don't want to interfere. Because you are the master of the time that you have—whether you throw it away in a ditch or use it well, depends upon you alone.

There is something else. Quite by accident the other day, I met Hitomi, the woman you took to Yokohama. There has been no solution to her problems with the people in her life. She has been dragged through the mud by the mass media, and while her husband continues to visit the other woman and his daughter, he cannot completely discard Hitomi. She has forgiven him that. Even though she is suffering greatly, she asked me to tell you that she is grateful to you for saving her life. You have killed people and you have also saved a life. God will remember both of those acts.

Yukiko Hata

Chapter 25

A Big Tree on a Hill

August 29

Dear Yukiko Hata,

How are you doing? I'm doing fine. You once wrote that I didn't need to take care of my health but I'm OK. I've got to be so that I can fight with the police.

That business about showing where the bodies were for your birthday present was sort of a figure of speech. I didn't mean exactly that.

How about I tell you the real reason. It was in May and I heard a bush warbler singing outside my cell. I hadn't heard one here till then because this building is made of concrete and the doors are thick iron. But for some reason that day I heard a warbler. It was the song of a bush warbler in flight. I listened to it singing for a while. When I was a child I went a lot to my grandmother's place in Atami. She was paralyzed then, but when she saw my face it always made her happy. At my grandmother's house there was always a bush warbler crying even when it wasn't spring. I really hated to go to my grandmother's house because there was always a funny smell in the old woman's room. It wasn't like urine or anything. It was like something terribly sweet, and my chest felt bad right away. My grandmother would tell me to come close to her. I'd get held by her because I had to then I'd go out to the verandah and not go near her again. The bush warbler here made the same sound. So I was just confessing as my duty to my grandmother.

It wasn't really a birthday present so I don't want you to thank me or anything. OK?

I'm working on my poetry and I think its getting better! I've even had orders from the weeklies. But before that I want you to look at it so I'll give you a sample of something I've improvised.

When I go into a lonely valley
I'm filled with sadness,
In the empty shadow of friendship
Drips the blood of battle.

If a weekly magazine says it wants this then you can sell it the same as before.

You can take a commission. Me creating poems is getting famous here. The night guard sometimes ask me to check his poems.

I suppose you heard that they set a date for my first court hearing? I thought I could invite you and I asked for a ticket, but they turned down any special treatment. Thats really bad. The court is made up of a defendent and a complainent appearing in court, but they say they can't get me even one lousy ticket! The only way to get a ticket into the court is by lotary. They let all the mass media into the courtroom, and since there are a lot of other people who want to get in the only way they can manage it is by lotary. Really something isn't it! I'm really sorry that I can't send you a ticket.

Did that guy from the media come around any more? I'm concerned. Its irritating I can't be there to protect you.

Fujio Uno

September 10

Dear Yukiko Hata,

I've been really worried since I last wrote. Counselor Kazami said that from the first you didn't feel like coming to the court. When I think about it, you're right. If you'd come you'd be exposed to all the mass media. Like being my woman who has come out of concern for me. You're not my woman. I don't know whose you are but anyway you're not mine. I wanted you to be but frankly I have the feeling you're God's woman and I can't compete with God.

I told you a lie the other day. I didn't have any malice. Staying in miserable place like this makes me put on a bold front. When I say that I want to meet you I seem to fall to pieces emotionally so I was sorry I couldn't invite you to the courtroom.

Actually, I just wanted to meet you. I was looking forward to the day of the trial. That was because I thought I might have a chance of meeting with you. That was the only pleasure in the trial. So long as the hearing was a long way off my life would be extended but thats as it may be. I would sell a day of my life to be able to meet you.

Whatever happens is all right with me. Nobody in the world knows what I think, and because I'm a murdering fiend theres nobody who understands whats on my mind.

Its bad for both you and Counselor Kazami. You said that you would pay for her services, but I just don't feel at all like fighting the court. Its really just as bad as fighting with the police.

These days I think a lot about the past. I suppose a normal guy talks to his kids about the past. The kids remember it and they tell it to there kids as well. Generally the kids fall asleep while they are listening but even so they remember it. It turns into a fairy tale. It's a fairy tale like a cristal.

I liked trees. Not tree climbing. I just liked trees for themselves. I like a big tree on top of a hill especially. In the summer when there are huge white clouds in the sky I like a big tree where there are some cows resting there in the shade under the tree. When I die I'm going to become a tree! And since I didn't produce any children I'll get kids and workers to take a nap in my shade.

I wanted you to listen to some things about my childhood. Once I made a bet with a friend about how far I could walk on a railway line. I was scared and I thought that my heart would leap out of my mouth.

I decided to own one of the trees in the grove of oleander trees in the cematery. When you look at the individual oleanders in the cematery all their colors are different. I secretly adopted a red oleander that bloomed with a special color.

I was surprised when I caught a baby badger. At first I didn't know what it was. It wasn't a dog or a cat or a rabbit.

When I was 12 I nearly drowned in the ocean. It would have been better if I'd died then. When I was 19 I ate entrails at a weird shop in front of the race track and came down with diarea. I should have died then too.

I received the dictionary you sent in. I assume its because the spelling in my letters was terrible, but if my writing here seems a little less bad please think its thanks to that.

Fujio Uno

October 3

Dear Miss Hata,

How are you? I went through my first trial hearing. I decided not to look toward the crowd, but I knew by the mood there were a lot of people there.

Those guys who have come to see my trial are the worst kind of fools. They think they are morally so much better than I am and they sit there with such total selfconfidence. I think those guys who have confidence about what is right are all fools. Especially one sneering old geezer over on the side. I have no idea who he is. He is probably a guy who has come to court thinking he is going to hear a sexy story! I can tell who those types are. And besides they come in and listen for free.

OK. I looked once at the crowd area. I thought you wouldn't come, but I looked all around the place. What I saw was all those foxfaced types who had come to condemn me. And then the guys from the media write things like "With a Sneeking Look He Survays the Spectaters."

I don't hear the words going around the courtroom too well. I told Counselor Kazami that my strength was gone. I'm down. I feel like I haven't had enough vitamins. When I said so the police told me that my nourishment had been calculated and that there was no shortage of vitamins. But somehow I really feel down. When I said that to Higaki one day he brought his own vitamins for me to take. The result was that I began to feel a bit better. Even so, I don't feel like my usual self. I'm wondering whats the matter with me?

I heard a story that the Shimada girl used to form a group of a few people to take turns helping a schoolmate in a wheelchair going and coming from school. They worked out a schedule so that someone did it on Monday another on Tuesday. Like that. Anyway because it was kids when she was playing dodge ball and she wanted to continue playing she had another kid who was going in that direction anyway help with the wheelchair. The kid in the wheelchair didn't mind and went home alright. But her father heard about it one night at dinner during some casual conversation and got real mad. He said she had to do her duty and he asked her "What is more important? Playing dodge ball or your responsibility?"

I heard the story from the police. So I told them "Look, officer, I don't like interpreting everything morally. And I think that Shimada giving his daughter a lesson like that is not necessarily for humanistic reasons. I think he taught his daughter that as a way to make money."

Please ask Counselor Kazami about the next court date. If you don't want to come into court then please stand on the street where I go by in a car. I'm asking you because I just want one glimpse of you.

Fujio Uno

The last couple of lines of the letter had been painted over with magic ink. Possibly the police judged them to be a ploy for escape. But since they had been written with a ballpoint pen, it was still possible to read them.

November 20
Dear Miss Hata,

It happened very suddenly. I will be transferred to Yokosuka Prison. They will put me in a holding cell inside the jail. When I am over there I am not intending to give them anything. Back here there are a lot of fools but also some geniuses. I can't give you their names. (And anyway this letter is going to be censered)

Sergeant Higaki said "You'll be near your home" but I wonder what that house was to me anyway? I know my father and mother were good to me. But it was like being there pet. I always thought they felt lucky when I was a nice sweet boy. That bunch never thought about me spending the life of a human being.

Didn't you once say theres a soul in being human? At the time I thought that was foolish talk. I thought sex was more important than that. Well I still think so.

I wanted to hold you. Just once would be OK. Thats my only deep deep deep regret.

But I'd go to your house and when we talked (I forget completely what we talked about) I was really surprised, realizing that there are those kinds of talk as well in the world. Until then everything my family had talked about was just skin deep. You know...What made someone rich. Who was with someone or who was splitting up. Who had sold a house or who had made money in stocks. How someone did in the election or someone getting ahead or getting into a school. That sort of stuff.

My father used to say "You've got to take responsibility when you do that kind of thing." He hardly said anything except at times like that. My mother was the same way. I don't know how many times I heard her say "You'll get involved. It's best to break off." The one thing that makes me really happy for once is that those two are completely involved with me. Even at this moment I'm sure those two are still wondering how they can avoid being involved with me!

If you and I were living together I could have sex with you and we could talk about the soul. Talking about the soul won't satisfy the stomach, but its good for kids. They can survive just on mist. There are a lot of things that I haven't experienced in this world, and one of those things is talking about the soul.

I don't regret that much. You once told me "Everyone dies with something on their mind" and I remember that every day now. I don't even remember why you said it or even the circamstances. But that was before I committed those crimes so you were probably just talking in general.

I remember how you looked when you said that. What surprised me was how refreshing it was. I thought you were really right. What you said is now a consolation to me. I think it would be OK if I forgot everything else you said and just remembered that. Thanks a lot. Really.

More later,

Fujio Uno

December 15
Dear Mr. Uno,
December has come around so fast. I decorated a small Christmas tree. During this season I've thought a lot about you. I shouldn't wonder that you dislike Christmas and all that goes with it. Well, that's all right, too. If it were not for you, I would probably feel the same way—say, if the person on my mind was a woman who was in hospital with some hopeless illness.

Your remarks about your parents were dismal. I've never been a parent, but I would have thought that a parent would be all the more supportive of a child in jail. People get together and speak ill of their child, and in your case their child is described as a "fiend." And on top of that, you are called a "brutal, murdering fiend."

But for your parents you will always be their beloved "Fu-chan." Even the police don't expect adverse testimony from parents about a child. A parent is always an ally of the child. If I were your parent, I would try to live a long time for the day when you would return home. No matter how many years or decades it would take, I would always be anticipating the day when you would return, and I would think of heating the bath, preparing some food you like and some cake, setting out soft underwear, and drying the futon on a warm day. That is far from avoiding involvement. Indeed, I think that would be my complete objective.

I learned about your transfer.

Isn't everywhere the same? You really are not free to walk about, and that is hard for anyone. They say that even when the body is held prisoner, the heart can still be free. Something that difficult, however, is almost impossible and so it's selfish of me to tell someone else to be that way.

I haven't attended church since those incidents, but that's not your responsibility. I've deliberately avoided it since I feel awkward about meeting people. Instead, I've been praying at home. However, I shall go this Christmas and pray for you. I imagine that you want to know exactly what I will pray for?

Well I'm offering up a clever prayer. I will ask God to do what is best for you. Humans lack the strength to see the best way for themselves, and so I am asking God for you. There may be many cases where the way God chooses is different from what a human wants. I feel that God will certainly know what any of us want. You may have a good laugh at this, but if you laugh you'll feel better! On Christmas night, I think I will put my little tree by the window and place a small candle at the top. I feel that the flame will guide the souls of those who have love for me and they will come to visit. I once told someone that and they laughed and said it was a completely Buddhist idea. But there's nothing at all bad about the Buddhist way.

Please write to your parents. Be good to them, please.

Yukiko Hata

December 24

Dear Yukiko Hata,

To tell you the truth, I'm sick of you pushing religion on me. I'm just not suited for God and all that. If there is a God then he is making the world go backward and its a mess. I have nothing to do with that.

My 'villa' here isn't too bad. Its just very businesslike. The food is a bit better than before. Sergeant Higaki didn't say farewell and I have the feeling that he avoided the last moment. Or maybe he was busy or just didn't know what to say. At times like that its better just to flee let me tell you.

There was an interesting thing at the final court session of this year. I'm a little more at ease in court these days. I'm getting used to it. Now I can ignore the audience. I can ignore those no good bums on the seats—sorry, not such a good play with words!

The prosecutor is a guy named Yamada or maybe its Yamaguchi. When he asks about the women I knew he always makes mistakes with their names. He said "Reiko" instead of "Yoko" at least a dozen times. He so rough and insensitive! Each time he does that I have to correct what hes said. I say "Do you mean Reiko instead of Yoko?" or "Are you really asking about Yoko? The one who worked at the department store was Reiko. Do you want to ask about Reiko?" Thats the way it goes. I am really disgusted with that guy. And there was some laughing in the crowd.

I've really had enough of this court. One of the bailiffs is reading a paperback book. Theres a sign that says no one in the audience may read newspapers or magazines. Even so this guy continues with his paperback. It must really be interesting. I wish him well though because I haven't seen any young people reading a book as eagerly as that for a long time.

I regret that I couldn't become a writer. A poet is all right, but I would have liked to become a writer who writes mystery novels that people couldn't stop reading. Do you think I could do it? I know a lot about crime.

In court one of the men who holds the rope thats around me sweats a lot from his head. During the court session, he repeatedly lifts his cap and wipes off the sweat. Its probably some kind of disease like an automatic nerve. He ought to have that treated because hes still young.

Not that it matters or maybe it does matter but pretty soon it will be New Year. Probably my last New Year.

I can't believe that I'm not going to meet you again in this world. Somehow I had the feeling that you would come to hear the trial. I guess I'm optimistic. I even dreamt that you'd come.

It seems to be cold outside. Don't catch cold.

Fujio Uno

January 23
Dear Y.H.,

I was really mad! The guy here was deliberately late in delivering your letter to me. They gave me some story about being shorthanded at New Year and said the censer was late or something. I mean its common sense to deliver a New Year card within the first two weeks of the year! Because of them my New Year was screwed up. I didn't feel like celebrating the New Year so I went on a hunger strike.

F.U.

January 30
Dear Mr. Uno,

What in the world can you be thinking about? During the New Year season, didn't you think of the families of the six people you directly or indirectly killed? Last New Year those young people enjoyed a feast. They chatted and enjoyed themselves, and wore nice clothes. Do you think their families will ever forget that? When they're walking along a street, the parents will suddenly see the back of a girl or a child about the same age as their own child, and unconsciously they will hasten to catch up and look into the child's face just to make sure it's not theirs. If they were to speak their minds, they would tell you they thought that just maybe the dead person might be alive and hidden somewhere.

I can't take that kind of vague attitude you seem to have, so I have to reply.

I've also been thinking that I'd like to meet with you. The reason is not that I trust you. Good or bad, I accept you as you are. I hope that you will improve, but that is a matter between you and God, who you despise. He taught us one thing: "Judge not." But make no mistake—that doesn't negate the court's decision. The court that you are now facing and the judgment of the depths of a person's soul are two different things. One is judgment by humans beings, the other is the judgment of God. Human courts are founded upon legalistic authority. Something that is accusable is brought to court; and we must assume that things that are not possible to complain about are not crimes, at least to the extent that there is no hanging.

However, the questions of morality and what a person is as a human being remain. The word of God about that is "Judge not," and "Leave judgment to God." Because we do not know the truth about what transpires in another person's heart, He told us not to become God and prosecute other people.

I realize now that I never have understood you and never will. You are you, in both your good and evil sides. And it's not out of fear of the mass media that I'm not attending your trial. The reason is that one day I realized I had nothing to lose—not dignity, nor a troublesome child. All I have is a certain amount of money. So what should I fear?

As for my becoming distant from you, that is simply because in my heart I do want to meet you. But out of regard for the six families who have lost something irreplaceable, I feel that we shouldn't meet. They can't meet the people they loved, so you and I shouldn't meet, either.

Yukiko Hata

February 3

Dear Y.H.,

The way they handle the mail here is a sloppy mess. If I write about the censer being late, your letters will come even later. That's their revenge. I can see their method.

I'm doing fine. I don't know whether I can win this or not, but I'm reading some law books. I know you blame me for murdering the girls and those kids but they were all worthless and deserved to die.

If you don't have anything to lose and you're not afraid you're just the same as me. But you're not free as long as you have God and morality. I don't have those things, so I'm absolutely free. Morality is completely old stuff. Even as a theme for literature its old stuff. Critics will just laugh at a novelist who writes about that.

Also it is a strong point with me that I'm not loved. If you think that you are loved you don't want to lose that love and you do something unreasonable. However I'm not bothered. Its true what you said, that love changes easily and hatred doesn't change. And so people are going to hate me forever and that won't change.

You're the only one in the world who seems to be suffering any feeling for me. You just don't have a righteous hatred for me. Its no good when things aren't stable, so please hate me more. You probably heard this from Counselor Kazami, but I lied to you again. It was a complete black lie that I went on a hunger strike and didn't eat any New Year treats. I ate up everything. I've got an appetite. I wonder why I like to tell lies? No deep reason, I guess. I always do things without any profound reason. There's no profound reason why I killed those people so we have to say there was some shallow reason.

Also I'm not the only one. There are a lot of guys who do bad things for not much reason. A shallow reason is like shallow love—it's very ordinary.

Compared to that I think my feeling for you is pretty deep. I'm really not sure. Sometimes its shallow, sometimes deep.

Theres not much to talk about here. The things I try to write about are not too pleasant. The only thing I can talk about is the soul. Theres nothing to say about any pretty girls passing by, or about some good place to go to eat. I'm all through. My soul didn't exist a long time ago so maybe my feelings were just empty and I put all my energie into sex. I haven't been aware of a "soul" even once in a year. They didn't teach me about that in school.

Do you remember you once told me it was good to be bored? At the time I thought it was foolish but anyway now what you said pops into my head a lot. Thats probably just because I'm bored.

Take care.

F.U.

February 15

Dear Mr. Uno

I'm both saddened and relieved that you are feeling better even for a day, without having the strength to confront reality.

What is sad has to do with you not being able to truly recognize reality. Perhaps that's because you are not in the state of being rational? But it is painful to be truly aware. When I don't understand a situation, I know it's best for me to be at ease with it. In that sense, when you are not struggling with anything, it will be good to feel happiness just for one day.

You seem to think that you could write a good mystery story because you know in detail about your own crimes. But you have only killed a handful of people—

isn't that right? A mystery writer who writes about murders all his life has to kill hundreds of people. So it's unreasonable to have such a high opinion of yourself. Further, if you don't have a profound reason, but can only think of shallow reasons, will you be able to continue killing people in your writings in an interesting way? I think you would soon run out of material.

I'm not a particularly moral person. To say, as they do these days, that morality is out of date, is to take a shallow attitude, I feel. Whatever people have handed down as thoughts, is old or new, interesting or not interesting—as far as I'm concerned. And out of that we just choose whatever we like, according to our own taste.

There are all kinds of elements in moral situations, but I just want to avoid things that are noisy, showy, or aggressive. If a situation is veiled, or quiet, or something like that, it puts my mind at ease. In morals, too, if something is what I think of as being subtle, it shouldn't put pressure on people. It's not something shared with society, but rather its a personal possession. I've never thought that I wanted to share morality with someone. I feel it's like a white canvas on which nothing is yet drawn, a silent room which accepts any sounds of music and nature, a litmus paper that has not yet been dipped into a solution. In future, it will be a white canvas on which anyone should be allowed to draw anything.

Please think about the future.

It's not just you. None of us have unlimited time. Perhaps you intend to pretend right up to the end, to continue bluffing through with your shallow way of thinking? If you say that you have chosen to do that, then I won't offer any objection. But I do think it's a waste. Please try to spend your time to the fullest.

I think we should always be in the mental state of old people even if you're a youth of 19. The present time is strange; everyone is making themselves up to be young. It's not at all becoming. True happiness belongs only to people who think of themselves as old and who expect they will die tomorrow.

I heard that your mother was released from the hospital. I think that is just fine. If people have enough strength to stand up, they are healthy.

I'll put a pressed daffodil in with this letter for the nice odor it has.

Yukiko Hata

March 19
Dear Miss Hata

Its raining today. I've always hated rain. You once said that you liked rain a lot. You said that you liked rain for raising flowers and trees. Thats the way it goes.

There wasn't a daffodil in your last letter. The only things in their heads around here are the rules. They allow letters but they think that a pressed flower isn't included in the rules. A book is all right and so is bread or a magazine. But a pressed flower is not on their list. These guys really like to give out punishment.

And besides they probably think the flower might be soaked in some poison!

However their plan was upset because there was just the slightest bit of odor left where the flower was pressed. It only lasted a moment. I just smelled it once and then it was gone. It really made me dizzy. It was like some narcotic smell that I'd never in the world had before.

Recently I've been thinking like "this is the last" something or other. Even when I look at the scenery from the car on the way to court I start thinking "this is the last."

I've never felt like this before and its really strange. Thinking that something is the last isn't a big thing, but its eating at my mind.

There was a pretty flower outside the other day.

In fact, I didn't know it was called a "magnolia" and at first I didn't pay any attention to it. I was a blank and so I asked the guard. He said it was called in Japanese by a name that sounds the same as the word for a 'fist'. I was so surprised. I thought it was bad for a flower as pretty as that to be named after something for bashing people. I think its more like a bird thats become a flower. Just like I'll become a tree on a hill. When a bird dies it becomes a magnolia flower.

I think its strange that even when I remember those people I killed I can't feel sorry for them. Thats the truth. What do I have to do to feel sorry? Please tell me what you think.

If you tell me to pray or recite the sutras for those women and kids I'll do it. But I didn't think of them as being human. It was too bad about Tomoko Shimada. I thought that she would search for help naked. I sure didn't think she would fall over a cliff.

And I didn't have in mind to kill Reiko Suga, either. I just got rid of her like a piece of scrap paper. She was complete junk.

The rest of them were bitches, nothing you could call a woman. No idea of chastity. Just greedy sluts. Thats like me, right? Please tell me how I ought to moan for them. The same with that schoolboy. Sure his parents probably loved him. But in fact he was a brat. I get a pain in the gut when I think of a kid like that becoming a government official.

I think at court next time I'll see my last cherry blossom. Though I could have gone flower viewing with you I didn't. I was really a fool.

Fujio Uno

April 26

Dear Yukiko Hata

Its driving me crazy that I haven't had a letter from you in such a long time. I know its only been two months, but you probably don't realize how long that is to me.

I couldn't catch even a glimpse of the cherry blossoms. They got scattered in the rain. The court was postponed from the 3rd to the 10th. I don't know the details but I heard it was for the convenience of the prosecutor. That made me mad. I'm beginning to get the idea the court runs on its own sweet time. The prosecutor will ask for sentencing pretty soon but I'm calm about that.

They don't understand me at all. So I'm not looking for understanding from anybody. For me its a relief. People make a mistake when they think that others think about them. When I heard some candidate bragging about himself at election time on TV to me it was the most disgraceful thing there is. He wants people to think well of him and then grovels with his nonsense talk. I may be garbage but so are they.

If I give up on people understanding me then I might get understanding from God. But unfortunately I'm not in Gods favor. What I'd like is that you understand me a little. But I don't suppose thats possible. Ever since I was a child I've had perverse habits. Being like that is kind of a pleasure like opium. I don't suppose you've ever had any experience like that?

I don't mean to be too rigid but thinking about "this is the last time" is not something I've experienced before. Everything seems to be sparkling. Really ordinary things impress me. When my mind is calm that is. Because I get mad at the guys here a lot.

You're a gentle person and so you will grow old amidst the sound of the wind and the leaves falling. Time and again moments will come to your mind as the last flower and the last rendezvous (I had to look that one up in my dictionary!) or the last doze before you die. Then I hope you'll pass away with your mind at peace and enter Nirvana!

My "last" somethings are pretty poor and thats a pain in the neck. What I'm seeing just isn't much. Don't tell anyone but I don't like to look weak. Thats all. Right. One thing that occupies a big place in my "lasts" is a cockroach. It's a lot of fun to look at that cockroach. I watch him and don't chase him away. It makes me feel tremendously free to think I'll become a cockroach.

I wonder how it is outside. Are the flowers blooming? Is it really spring? What does the wind smell like? Damn! And what kind of clothes are you wearing? I'd like to take them all off you!

I had a dream. I was going to meet you at a bus stop. I was late for the appointment, but my feet were all tangled and I couldn't walk. It's probably because I don't get enough exercise these days and I have a fear that I won't be able to walk. If I really could meet you I'd start waiting three hours early.

Fujio Uno

Chapter 26

STANDING AT THE CROSSROADS

May 6

Dear Mr. Uno,

Please pardon me for not writing. It's because I have been so busy with my work. There are many formal events in the spring, and since even lots of young women wear kimono, I can't be late with my deliveries. For young women it's an important opportunity to appear in public in kimono, and because I work on contract, I have to think of my work ahead of my own convenience and of yours. And so I've put off writing.

I understand that you are suffering where you are. At times people have to suffer with no let up. Perhaps it is at such times that people become truly human.

I'm completely alone now. Since your arrest, my sister doesn't come home at all and she hardly ever calls on the telephone. Even the people at church see me as 'the woman who has had some connection with a murderer.' People who would be glad to sit next to the Prime Minister have an air of not wishing to be next to me!

Thanks to your visits here, I now know the taste of complete loneliness. I'm immersed in it, sad and neglected. It's a bitter thing, yes, but I do not think it is a waste of my life.

At first, my feelings were shaken, but now I'm maintaining a clear view of things. I have gone beyond the values of the world of people and I have come to know the importance of not losing the warm reality I have at hand. I'm not being sarcastic when I say that because I made your acquaintance I've become a more complex person. I wish to thank you for giving me that opportunity. And I ask you to be grateful for the sadness, loneliness and suffering that have been given to you, because that is your chance to change yourself.

In my last letter, I complained about you not experiencing any fear in the way you cut off people's lives. Very likely I preached to you about that, but I decided I was not entitled to do that. If I suppose you feel nothing at all, then perhaps I should assume it is not your responsibility. If I say this kind of thing, people will be angry and exclaim, "How can a man who has killed six people not be held responsible?" Still, telling someone to feel who does not have that ability is next to impossible.

I once read somewhere about an unusual person who was not aware of pain or cold. Morally speaking, you're exactly that way. I think that such a limit to your ability is truly a pity. That is all that I have to say about you.

There is one business matter. Your family is paying for nearly all the court expenses. When I say 'nearly', I mean that Counselor Kazami has reduced her fee greatly and your family has paid that. However, in gratitude, I have also paid something to her.

There is still one problem that has arisen since your court appeal of the other day. Your family doesn't wish to involve themselves beyond this. They feel that from here on the government should pay your legal expenses.

If you want Counselor Kazami to continue with your case, then I shall provide for that. Please let her know how you feel.

Yukiko Hata

May 12

Dear Yukiko Hata,

They asked for the sentencing as I expected. I didn't shake and my heart was quiet. That was because I was thinking of you a lot. When I think of you my mind is strangely quiet. I feel that you are my support.

I really wanted to see you. Just one more time I wanted to see you.

Meeting with someone is such a strange and important thing. I understand how meeting with a person can be the greatest happiness, but I don't suppose that everyone has noticed this.

Counselor Kazami said "The court makes use of public money. If you want to live, that right remains for you." Its strange how she says that in the same tone as asking how the dog next door is doing or whats for dinner.

I told her "If thats how it is then in repayment for the world hating me lets use up the publics tax money right to the limit!" Only I felt like that was just some game with words.

But your money is what you earn in that quiet room, with the end of that tiny needle and your slender fingers, right? And you're going to use that for me? Thanks, but I'll go with a public defender instead. I don't care if the lawyer is that loser of a shabby, slobbering old man. It might just be fun to put that guy on a lot. I'd be interested in fighting with a doctor or a lawyer who took no interest in a penniless patient, a dependant.

Since the day the prosecutor asked for sentencing I've been cheerful. At the trial I was calm. One of the judges was a woman. She sat at the far right, and she was still inexperienced. She was thin and had a sallow complexion and her sharp but pretty face was absolutely without any expression. I felt like trying to count the number of pimples on her face. If she doesn't have any pimples then I'll know she's not human.

Is spring moving along?

I think nature is a pretty cruel thing. Even if people die flowers keep on blossoming. The wind keeps on blowing.

Fujio Uno

May 16

Dear Mr. Uno,

I don't think nature is cruel. It's aloof, but it's also especially gentle. Even though you say you are well, it struck me as unnatural, and so I'm writing to you hurriedly.

In your last letter you used the phrase 'a lot.' There is no need for anyone to do anything 'a lot.' It's enough for us to be sad and suffer quietly whatever we are given. I am not preventing you from using the public defender. As for the alternative of using my money, I don't feel that I have anything else to spend it on. I live in a house on a piece of land, which is a luxury in today's Japan, and I don't think that my sister would chase me away. I'm not in need of money or anything else.

Please don't tell lies. And please don't be impetuous.

Yukiko Hata

May 23

Dear Mr. Uno,

By chance last night, I came across some words that I want you to read, and so I will send only them this time. I suppose you think of yourself as being in a bad dream, all alone and standing at the crossroads of fate, but that would be a mistake.

Saint Paul, who was a founder of the early Church, wrote to the people of Corinth and said, "Brethren, the appointed time has grown very short; from now on, let those who have wives live as though they had none, and those who mourn as though they were not mourning, and those who rejoice as though they were not rejoicing, and those who buy as though they had no goods, and those who deal with the world as though they had no dealings with it. For the form of this world is passing away."

It's not only you. It is true that time is running out, because everyone is advancing toward death.

Yukiko Hata

June 17

Dear Mr. Uno,

I heard of your final sentencing on television just now. I think that the families of the six people you killed are pleased. When something cruel is done, people hope that the guilty person will die wretchedly. That is the usual sentiment. I wouldn't say this to anyone else, but because the sensibilities that might link you with other people are shattered in your case, I am telling you.

But please do try to go on living. When you are alive, there is a possibility that you will continue to change. Up to now, I think that you have changed a good deal.

I heard from Counselor Kazami that an appeal must be filed within two weeks.

The Heavenly Blue morning glories I planted last month have begun to sprout.

Yukiko Hata

June 22
Dear Yukiko Hata,

Thanks for your letter and everything.

I don't know how many times I've already read the Criminal Code, Section Two, Appeals Clause. I've read a hole through the pages! I don't want to play the fool. I thought I'd remain calm. According to you its normal not to be calm. So can I be trembling angry?

Aside from such thoughts, there's something else I feel. I mean, deep in my heart there's another current of feeling. And it disterbs me a little. The person called Miura, who is now Minister of Justice, seems to have signed for three executions to be carried out as soon as he was appointed. I suppose he's cleaning the slate. Counselor Kazami told me this.

Thanks for the Heavenly Blue morning glories. That's all I can say. So they will blossom a third time this year? I feel like I'm in a dream. The past two years have really gone fast. The time seems to have flown by. They've been good days. If they'd been bad days it would seem to have gone on longer.

Fujio Uno

June 23
Dear Miss Hata,

Just one thing. Please answer.

I will not appeal if you love me.

Fujio Uno

June 28
Dear Mr. Uno,

By being born in the same period, we met by chance.

While being saddened for you, I love you deeply.

To write only this has caused me pain for these past two days.

Yukiko Hata

August 27
To: Mrs. Kazami Nagisa
Dear Counselor,

I hope that you are well?

Even though the trial is over, I have by no means forgotten you. I called you on the phone yesterday at about four in the afternoon; however, the line was engaged. These days I feel reluctant about using the phone, and so I was truly relieved it was busy. However, after that I thought that I should write to you and tell you all that has happened. I thought that might burden you less. Please pardon me for taking up your time with this trivial thing when I am sure you are very busy.

I learned the other day that Mr. Uno has been transferred to Sendai. That will surely be his last journey. I wonder what kind of flowers he saw on that trip, "the very last" as he used to say?

Pleasant summery weather has returned to the peninsula here. Someone once wrote about it as a place where people from Tokyo come for "soft breezes, the sound of the sea, and the peaceful gold of the sun." It's terrible to have a "murderous fiend" on the loose here. It's too bad if people can't doze peacefully on the beaches.

The day before yesterday, I received a sudden visit from a person by the name of Taizen Kuriyama. He was dressed in a business suit but he is, in fact, a Buddhist priest who is the chaplain at the Sendai Prison. It seems that Rev. Kuriyama met with Mr. Uno there. I don't know all the details of the meeting, or whether Mr. Uno requested it or whether, as a kindness, the prison people asked the chaplain to visit him. Whatever the case, I am happy about it. It is just marvelous that someone can pay him a visit. I believe that visiting sick people is an important part of the work that the prison chaplains do. I am shy of meeting people and so I hardly visit at all. I suspect that I lack something of human warmth.

According to Rev. Kuriyama, Mr. Uno's attitude was unclear, neither irritated nor cursing people or the world. He just didn't know what to make of Mr. Uno. He said that he seemed more like a drunken person, but since that was not likely in jail, he gave up trying to draw any conclusions as to what kind of person he was. I felt that Rev. Kuriyama was a very good person. Certainly I couldn't think as deeply as he does.

Mr. Uno told him that he was a Christian, and Rev. Kuriyama apologized that he knew nothing about that. Something seemed strange, however, and he asked him what church he went to. He replied that he didn't go to any church in particular. "A friend of mine is a Christian," was all he said. When Rev. Kuriyama asked him which friend, Mr. Uno gave him my name and address. He asked him if he wished him to have a priest, a friend of his, come to visit, but all he got in reply was a grin.

I should tell you that I haven't written to Mr. Uno since he was transferred to Sendai. But it's not that I'm avoiding it, and I certainly haven't forgotten about him. I'm aware of his existence 24 hours a day, like a thorn in my consciousness.

Now, about Rev. Kuriyama coming to my house. Mr. Uno seemed to become agitated, although a bit more comprehensible, when he talked about seeing me standing on a certain corner on the day he was taken away to Sendai Prison. Rev. Kuriyama decided to pay me a visit after hearing about how important I was to Mr. Uno.

It seems that the vehicle that took Mr. Uno from Yokosuka Prison to Sendai left before dawn. He claims to have seen me standing on a corner of a certain business street, where there was no one else about. Whoever he saw, it wasn't me. I had not been informed about when he was to going to be taken to Sendai. According to Rev. Kuriyama, Mr. Uno sent me a letter when the time for his transfer was set, but that letter never reached me. That was to be expected, of course. If I had known the time of his transfer, I might have become an accomplice to an escape attempt, so I feel that he would not be allowed to send such a letter. And as I think about it now, it seems unlikely that he would have been told much before his time of transfer. For him there would be nothing to prepare, as there would be for most people, and very likely he would simply have been told that he would leave the next day. That being the case, I believe what he said about sending a letter to me was just one of his lies. It's his nature to tell lies quite calmly. But if not, I wonder who the woman was, standing there on a main street before dawn when the shops were still closed? Whoever she was, I would like to thank her, even if she was just an apparition.

The feelings that Mr. Uno had for me were probably a delusion, but all of us live with faith in such things. Don't you think that he was seen off by a phantom of myself that had become fixed in his mind? When Jesus was nailed to the cross he called out, "My God, why hast thou forsaken me?" And so perhaps Mr. Uno, in an explosion of rage, thought that I had abandoned him. Anyway, thanks to that unknown person, he might have settled his account with this world. He acknowledged his life as his own and then, for the first time, he acknowledged he was leaving this world forever.

Of course, no one will ever really know what is on that man's mind. I think the general public optimistically overrate their ability to understand what other people are thinking. They really lack a sense of modesty regarding people they don't understand.

I told Rev. Kuriyama everything about meeting Mr. Uno and afterward. And of course Mr. Uno is not particularly a Christian, but I think Rev. Kuriyama's visit must have brought him some comfort. I asked him to visit Mr. Uno again if the opportunity arose.

I also heard from Rev. Kuriyama that Mr. Uno was like an empty shell, and my heart ached when I heard that. I don't know why, but I had hoped he would somehow be his usual stubborn self to the very last. Still, today, I think that perhaps his present mental state might be for the better.

It's no more than a guess on my part why he has changed like this. Being sentenced to death is beyond the imagination of most people; perhaps some defensive instinct works to dispel harmful emotions that you find inconvenient. For the insane, it is the same as there being no reality. On the other hand, in so far as we are not insane, it helps if our awareness is dulled, no matter how. It might be that his 'attitude' is merely a pose. Is it possible to escape the death penalty due to sudden insanity?

My wishing to meet with you for a talk concerned the final letter I received from him on June 26. He presented me with a choice that I struggled with for days. He entrusted his fate to me for a while. I tremble even now at the thought of why he thought of putting it that way. When I, alone, said, "I love you" to him—a person who had been rejected by everyone else—I handed him over to die. In truth, even though I decided to do that by myself, I feel that in the present atmosphere it is something that would be approved by society. It would be shameful for the world to have tried to prolong his life. And it would be a waste to use more money after the court had given its decision. Did you read the letter to the editor in the newspaper that said the money used in his trial would be better used on welfare for the elderly?

In cases like this, you don't hear the slightest suggestion about abolishing the death penalty. I wonder about that. We only seem to talk about abolishing the death penalty when there are no hateful criminals around at the time. But when some terrible criminal appears, or when the victim's family say they hope the criminal will be executed, then the media put that out strong enough. But now, when there is a 'murderous fiend' gloating before a pitiful blood-smeared corpse, we may be truly sincere if we extol the abolition of the death penalty, for there is always some anguish accompanying forgiveness.

Even though I strove to bring the trial quickly to an end, and stop his appeal, my action probably differs little from the 'justice' and 'good sense' of society. And so I do not suffer from direct or indirect criticism. Rather, in a literal sense, I defended use of the nation's precious tax money in the unproductive trial of Fujio Uno. With forgiveness, there is suffering; death becomes the compensation for love.

Even at a time like this, there are still those who say, "A guy like that deserves to die." But in my life so far, there has been nothing that offers a direct motive for killing a person. Now, however, clearly by my choice, I have handed one person over to die. I had to make that decision within two days. Even now, I'm still torn in my dreams about the time during which I thought so much about how to answer his letter. In fact, I dream a lot these days. Until now I hardly dreamt at all.

There's no point in me smoothing over this matter for you. I shall speak frankly. I was in no way romantically involved with Fujio Uno. To be precise, only once did I show him a favor. On that day, both he and I were feeling sad. I wished to escape from reality and so I went along with his wish and so I ventured to be caught up in his life. Still, in such a mood he did not take a fancy to me.

What he asked of me in his letter was just that I answer one thing. The choice that he gave me was to take his life or to take his love. I don't think that he was quite so clear about the matter, but his letter was a cry of desperation and he placed love in the foremost position. At that time, if I had said "I don't love you, so please appeal," he might have clung to the idea that my love was contained in that.

However, I think that the love I sent to him was a merciless thing. I sent him love in exchange for his death; I didn't love him in exchange for his death. I was not pretending to console and love him because he was sentenced to death.

I think I've felt this way for a long while. I've always bowed my head in deep sadness before that person's strange existence. I wonder why a person like that is born on this earth at all. A person who seems to be born simply to murder people has no responsibility in this life—or so everyone thinks. However, I can only believe that because he is such a person, he will become the object of God's love. God has said thus and I have known those words for some time. If I had not known that, I would probably have felt better about it all.

"Those who need a physician are not the healthy but the infirm. I seek not sacrifice but compassion. I have come not for the just but for the sinner."

To put it directly, Counselor, I am both relieved and saddened to know of Fujio Uno as he is now. The reason is that if he was clearly awakened to the truth, I would probably feel something was quite unnatural about it. Of course, such splendid people probably exist. However, there is nothing more natural than him having grown senile by being exposed to the harsh realities of life and death. The moment he received my letter, he ceased to be a human being. And so he has not replied to my letter—he is just happy in his delusion about me.

At times, there is nothing I can do but weep as I remember these things. This world is cruel. I don't have to repeat this maybe, but please allow me to write to you if I suffer again,

Yukiko Hata

September 17
To: Mrs. Kazami Nagisa
Dear Counselor,

Thank you so much for the gift of the fish you brought yesterday. It was quite unexpected and delightful of you to be so considerate.

I wonder who gave you so many fish so that you could share them with me? Those were certainly the most delicious filefish and grunts that I've ever had—I couldn't stop eating them! You were concerned there were too many, but I greedily accepted them all so that I could pass some on to my neighbor. Also my sister returned home when I least expected it. She had been busy with her work during the summer and was rather tired, so she was glad to come home and be master of the house while I prepare the meals!

Of course, resolving matters concerning Fujio Uno was part of the reason for her return. I imagine that she was relieved when his death sentence was confirmed. She was worried that at sometime in the distant future he might be released from prison and come around here again. His death sentence has brought a feeling of relief to a lot of people. In a way, it's really astonishing that when someone dies the people around him should feel relieved, but perhaps in a way it's not so very strange after all. When a good person dies, the people around all grieve; but when an evil person dies, people are relieved. It's not difficult to imagine that a death like that will bring relief to some people. In fact, almost everyone will feel happier following the death of Fujio Uno. But I don't feel that way.

While we were having the delicious fish last night, I thought of how it would taste to him, too. Of course, he can't enjoy that kind of thing any more because he killed people. No matter what I'm doing these days, my thoughts turn toward him. I feel pity for him, and I'm in awe at how different human lives can be. I am not innocent of causing a death because I acceded to his death; but I couldn't kill anyone the way he did.

I didn't mention it to you when you were here yesterday, but it pleased me very much that you brought your family along with you. Your son has grown quite a lot since that time when I first saw him, hasn't he? I suppose that you haven't been able to go out as a family much since you took on the Uno case; yesterday must have been a rare moment to relax together. Your family seemed to be the very picture of happiness.

I hope this idea doesn't sound too strange, but for the sake of Fujio Uno, I now think that there should be some happy families. But even after a person like him dies, it won't help him rest in peace if all the remaining families are unhappy.

However, since his sentencing, I also have the feeling that today there is someone happily alive somewhere with a firm goal in life, and that is a kind of farewell to Mr. Uno. Yesterday, for the first time in quite a long while, I met the person that he wrote of as 'H'. She is the woman he picked up when she was about to kill herself, which resulted in saving her life. Her husband had a child by another woman and she noticed that he was drifting toward the other woman. She felt that she should die so that the mother and child could lead a happy life. She had had such thoughts until recently, but an odd kind of solution has developed in her life now.

Although it may seem a rather strange situation, her husband now spends three days of the week at the child's house, and then the last four days of the week he returns to his wife's house. The next week he reverses the pattern. At first, there were times when she was torn apart by the thought of the three of them eating together around the table when she was all alone. But then she realized that when her husband was with her, the mother and child were alone eating their meals at the other house. So the feeling of emptiness was mutual. Such a thought seems to have been the first step in her change.

The second step, she said, was that on the days when she was alone, she decided to think of herself as living alone. She started setting up appointments so that she was out all day. She would put on a new suit of clothes and something like a nice, large, gold brooch, and go to the theatre, or to a culture center. In that way, she came to think about enjoying herself and the freedom she had in being alone.

The third stage was just the other day. She wanted to visit Australia with a friend for a few days, and although her husband was scheduled to spend the weekend at her house, she told him she was sorry, but would he please stay at his other place that week. She had a wonderful time in Australia, and the trip gave her a taste for traveling abroad. She said that having once sent her husband to stay over with the other woman, it was so convenient that it could become habitual—so she has to be careful.

What is even more interesting is that her husband has taken quite an interest in her activities and he has asked her to remain at home as much as possible because there are lots of things to talk about. She laughed when she told me this and said, "Somehow I seem to be involved in a tragic love that doesn't allow us to be together."

So she has managed to get through it all. Little by little, that day of hell has receded. Were it not for Fujio Uno, she said, she would not be alive today. She told me that she prayed for his life when anyone spoke ill of him, and she believes, too, that there are other people besides herself to whom he brought happiness. I said to her, "But he just said whatever came into his head." She replied, "It doesn't matter if he lied. Weren't we saved by a lie? If you are deceived when you're really down, then you can perhaps find the strength to pull yourself up again." Her insight is remarkable. I really don't know if anyone was saved by Fujio Uno's lies, but it's quite probable that a lie has saved someone, sometime. Certainly, H was helped to recover.

However, the family that endured his rape has remained in a tragic state. The husband remains in bad condition. His psychological illness was obvious, but recently his physical condition has declined as well. I heard that it's his liver. It seems that he may not have long to live. The woman herself seems to have lost all will to live. According to my sister, who went to visit their home, there is an odor in the house when you enter. She glanced into the kitchen sink and used the toilet, and then smelled the child's clothing when she held it. But she couldn't discover the source of the odor. Very likely the whole house wasn't cleaned properly, and so there was a peculiar odor throughout. Her friend isn't a sloppy person by nature, but she is quite weak. She's not in any way responsible for what happened to her, and in my view it would be better if she just held her head up with pride. I think people need that kind of coolness. But it was all because of Mr. Uno; until that day she was lively and happy, she polished her house inside and out, and she was always cheerful with her healthy child.

The morning glories here are blooming very well; the vines growing up through the limbs of the dead tree dress it up and make it very attractive. I don't cut down dead trees but put them to work instead! I've strung out a trumpet vine on a dead lilac tree. The vine is only two years old and still small. My sister brought the lilac from Hokkaido and I was sure it wouldn't take hold. But since I like fragrant flowers so much, I tried to keep it. A few years later it blossomed a bit, and in its last year it blossomed a lot, so I thought it might be able to survive in this district. But the following year it was exhausted and finally died. Now, after a few years, that same lilac tree is blossoming with a trumpet vine. Even a tree can support a plant that has nothing to do with itself.

How pitiful it is for Mr. Uno. If I were condemned to death, I think I would bequeath my body for use in an organ transplant for someone. At least that would be a testament to life. If we get to a time when we don't need organ transplants, I will try to think of something else. However, I didn't say any such thing to him. We are not family, and he has to decide things related to life and death by himself.

Yesterday, quite by chance, I was talking with a gentleman at the flower shop. He said that he was not a specialist, but the Heavenly Blue contains something like an acid amide, and it can produce hallucinations in human beings—or so the American Indians believe. Its poisonous qualities are weak, but he said that it produced an effect rather like that of taking LSD—although I don't know anything about that. Could it be that Fujio Uno and all that happened were just dreams and fantasies?

Yukiko Hata

Since that spring, the Iwamura house next door to Yukiko had stood empty. Naoko, the old lady's daughter, who didn't visit her mother right away when she was in hospital, said that she was consulting with relatives to decide about the place. But in fact she seemed to have promptly looked for a buyer. People who had lived a long time in the neighborhood talked about the unbelievably high price being asked for the house, and there was gossip that only some real estate developer could afford to buy it to build apartments.

From the end of September, people occasionally visited the house and went inside, but they were always strangers and probably customers of the real estate agent. Then, one October day, when Yukiko was sweeping at her front gate, she caught sight of Naoko. Yukiko made a small sound in surprise and stood there with her broom in her hand. Naoko greeted her and came over through the short cut between the houses.

'I've been so busy that I've just neglected this house,' Naoko said. 'But we have found a buyer for it and so I've come to complete the moving.'

'That's good,' said Yukiko.

'An elderly couple is buying it. They're going to re-model it a bit, and this will be their retirement house. So I think it will remain quiet. Also, the atmosphere of the neighborhood won't be changed, and...'

'Oh, I see,' Yukiko said, relieved that an apartment block wouldn't be built there.

'I would have been around sooner to clear things out,' Naoko said, 'but I have neuralgia and the pain was so great that I could hardly breathe.'

'They say that it's very hard to cure neuralgia,' Yukiko said.

'Yes, I've taken some Chinese medicine. That helps a lot, but the pain comes back occasionally. It's too late for menopause, and it's really a nuisance being incapacitated.'

'Is someone coming to help you with the moving?'

'Well, my husband is ill, you know, and our son works. So there's no one to help. But there's not much to do, so I'll work by myself for a couple of days. Then the day after tomorrow a truck will come by to take away odds and ends, and I think that will finish it.'

—*They seem to be a cold sort of family. Of course, a sick person can't come to help with the moving. But what is the son doing that he can't come? If he's working far away in Hokkaido or Kyushu, not coming to help is understandable, but not coming to help for even one day seems very inconsiderate to his parents...*

'I have some work to do during the morning,' Yukiko said, 'but if it's all right with you, I could give you a hand this afternoon.'

'Really? I don't want to impose, but that would be a help,' Naoko replied.

'With a little assistance, you'll soon have things in order,' Yukiko said. Sewing was an odd kind of work. With other activities, the more you worked, the more exercise you had. But with Yukiko's tasks, the busier she was, the less she moved.

Yukiko thought she could keep fit even without exercise, but recently she'd had some frightening thoughts about her legs giving out sometime during her forties or fifties. It had occurred to her that doing something more physical for a day or two would be good for her, not to mention being helpful to Naoko.

It was just as Naoko had said. In a house without occupants, there were a lot of things that one could only think of as trash. Naoko was not particularly critical, and she often told Yukiko just to throw things out.

'But this is still useful...' Yukiko would say, 'and it's not damaged in the least.'

Then Naoko would change her mind, saying, 'Really? Then perhaps I'll keep it a for a while.'

Of course, Yukiko herself often threw things out just for the sake of keeping her house uncluttered and under control, but it was still an effort to throw things away. Most people hate to discard household things, and so their living space tends to disappear.

'I think it's really important to throw things away,' Naoko said. 'With the price of land so high these days, if you don't keep the inside of your house so that you can move about you, you soon get to the point where it's like losing a lot of money. That's what my husband says, anyway. And our house is just filled with too many things. It will be terrible when we take in all this from Mother's house. So I decided to get rid of as many things as possible.'

Yukiko's arms and legs hurt a little, proof that she was tired. Later, when she got into her bath, she was overcome with drowsiness. She knew she was going to enjoy a deep sleep, thanks to the exercise.

Yukiko had promised to help Naoko the next day at the same time. She did her own work during the morning and the more physical work in the afternoon. Her fingertips turned rough through handling dusty objects. With rest and application of enough cream that night, by the next day her skin would be healed, with no rough fingers to hinder her work.

It was easy to criticize the cool treatment of Naoko's mother. But to an outsider, there was always some aspect of another family that remained invisible. Hatsu Iwamura had appeared to be a pitiful old lady, but maybe there was something about her that made her daughter want to abandon her? But for Yukiko that was of little consequence. She thought only of improving whatever was before her eyes, one by one, little by little.

Working quickly to get things ready for moving, you soon get tired. Yukiko didn't look very far ahead, but just bustled about getting things together. She was thinking more of her own house than Naoko's moving. For a moment, she imagined she might be quite an expert at this. Yumiko amused herself by being self-conceited. In return for her help, Naoko gave her a brand-new, portable clay cooking stove and a bag of charcoal.

That second day, Yukiko was even more tired and she again slept soundly.

Normally she was awake between five and six o'clock, but the next morning she didn't open her eyes until she heard Tomoko was up and about.

Breakfast was not particularly elaborate. Tomoko often started the coffee herself, and Yukiko merely set out the bread and butter, and sliced a persimmon or a pear, or washed some grapes.

Noticing how her sister was moving, Tomoko said, 'You worked so hard yesterday, doesn't your body ache?' She was being sarcastic about Yukiko doing too much, but she was also amused by the way things were going.

'You're right, it does,' said Yukiko. 'As soon as I got up, my legs ached, but they're almost all right now.'

'Of course. It's only natural to feel a little tight the day after getting some exercise.'

The two sisters ate without having much conversation. Before going off to work, Tomoko looked carefully through the newspaper. Their conversation was just a brief link between pages. She left for work a little after ten o'clock.

The truck that had been parked in front of the house next door had left at nine o'clock; then the neighborhood had become quiet. It seemed as though a clear slice of autumn had slipped in from the ocean.

Yukiko looked outside and then returned to her sewing room. Tomoko had left the television blaring. As Yukiko was about to turn it off, Fujio's face appeared on the screen. For an instant, Yukiko wondered what he had done this time. But the news broadcast was announcing that Fujio Uno's sentence had been carried out that morning. A disinterested voice recited the main events of the case, and photographs of the six people he had killed directly or indirectly came on the screen.

Yukiko tightly clutched the back of a chair, supporting her body with both hands.

—*What time was it, when he…? While I was enjoying a superbly refreshing sleep, he was meeting his death, passing over that awful, heart-crushing line…*

As Yukiko thought about it, her heart was seized with an almost purely physical pain.

She had imagined that Fujio's silence since the end of June had been because of his growing awareness of being drawn into a narrowing, dark and hidden road that would subsequently broaden out to an immense space. And from there he would, at last, stagger out to an emptiness lit by a universe of stars. Then Fujio could only float along, a fool alone in the universe. Neither love nor hatred reached that realm. Only the sound of the motion of the stars broke the silence. It would be an emptiness disturbed only by the cold smile of faint light pouring from stars billions of light years away. In her mind, Fujio appeared as a cowering child.

Yukiko couldn't think what to do. She wasn't cold; yet, inside, she felt herself continuing to shiver.

—*Perhaps Fujio is not yet used to being dead? Where might he be? Perhaps he's out there, floating, facing eternity in silence, at the edge of a universe so distant he will never return…*

She understood now the meaning of loss. Loss was pure suffering. She turned off the television, determined to confront this quiet autumnal day as if she was having a bad dream.

—*Today will be as ordinary as yesterday. Fujio's death was not the punishment of a murderous fiend. The day should be quiet so that I can feel his passing as I would the death of anyone else. However many people have died each day since the beginning of earth, it has always been a succession of unmarked days. Today, as yesterday, the best thing will be for me to take up my needle and sew...*

And yet she couldn't calm her beating heart, and her fingertips continued to tremble. It was a new feeling for Yukiko. The pounding of her heart made it impossible to hold her needle. She gave up the idea of working and sat in a chair at the kitchen table.

Her mind was preoccupied, her gaze fixed on nothing in particular. From the kitchen she could look right across her sewing room to the outside. She had a vague sensation that there was something drawing her attention out beyond that. But for a while she didn't focus her consciousness on it. Then she raised her gaze to the limit of her field of vision...and her eyes fixed upon a brilliant cluster of Heavenly Blue flowers. Over the last couple of days, in all the commotion of moving, she had failed to notice how many flowers there were. And not only that. Earlier in the year, after she had carefully trimmed back the vines, there had been almost no blossoms at all. Only in some shaded spots did one or two blue flowers appear, but nothing to draw any attention.

Yukiko went slowly over to the glass door of the verandah and opened it. She slipped into her wooden garden sandals. She was trembling and her movements were unsteady. She started stepping along the stone pathway of the garden walk. She stumbled and nearly twisted her ankle just before reaching the clusters of flowers opened there in the bright autumn sunlight.

It was only by chance that these exotic flowers continued to blossom in late autumn, while the sun was yet high. People recalling how the transient morning glories usually wilt with the morning dew might dislike the strength of the Heavenly Blue, but Yukiko loved the brash vigor of those flowers that had waited even while she overslept without fading.

It was no illusion, the flowers trembling in the morning breeze.

—*It's a kind of sign...Fujio returning to earth, not floating out to some distant reach of the eternal universe...just as though he's come to see the morning glories again...and through them, he's sending me a wordless greeting...*